WARRIOR CLASS

Power-hungry oilman Pavel Kazakov has an audacious aim to restore Russia to glory by building a pipeline through the Balkans, backed by the Russian army, but Kazakov hasn't reckoned with Patrick McLanahan, the US Air Force general who is determined to stop him. When McLanahan is sent on a mission deep into Russia, events spiral out of control and soon he must decide whether to obey his isolationist new President – or to follow his instincts and create havoc...

WARRIOR CLASS

WARRIOR CLASS

by

Dale Brown

Magna Large Print Books
Long Preston, North Yorkshire,
BD23 4ND, England.

British Library Cataloguing in Publication Data

Brown, Dale
    Warrior class.

    A catalogue record of this book is
    available from the British Library

    ISBN   978-0-7505-2873-3

First published in Great Britain in 2001 by HarperCollins Publishers

Copyright © Target Direct Productions, Inc 2001

Cover illustration by Jacey © Harper Collins Ltd. 2003

The Author asserts the moral right to be identified as the author of
this work

Published in Large Print 2008 by arrangement with
HarperCollins Publishers

Magna Large Print is an imprint of Library Magna Books Ltd.

Printed and bound in Great Britain by
T.J. (International) Ltd., Cornwall, PL28 8RW

ACKNOWLEDGMENTS

Thanks to Colonel Richard Y. Newton, Fifth Bomb Wing commander, and Major Randy 'Max' Allen, B-1B Lancer instructor pilot, for their technical expertise and insights. Thanks also to Lieutenant General Donald O. Aldridge, USAF (ret.), for his assistance, encouragement, and friendship.

Thanks to Sara Toutin for all her hard work.

Thanks to my friends Les Busick, Duane and Debbie Deverill, and Bob and Donna Goff for their extraordinary generosity.

To Hunter and Diane, my joy and inspiration.
Thanks for flying along with me.

AUTHOR'S NOTE

This is a work of fiction. All persons, places, things, and events in this story are a product of the author's imagination, and any similarity to real-world people, places, events, and organizations is coincidental. Although some real-world events and organizations are mentioned in this story to enhance authenticity, they are not intended to describe or portray any real-world persons, tactics, beliefs, or policies.

This story makes reference to a joint American-Ukrainian military campaign against Russia, which is described in my novel *Chains of Command;* to aircraft, Lithuanian research centers, characters, and situations described in *Night of the Hawk;* and to the Tin Man technology I first described in *The Tin Man.*

Visit my website at *www.megafortress.com,* where you may leave your comments.

REAL-WORLD NEWS EXCERPTS

RUSSIANS OPERATE ALONE NOW

European Stars & Stripes, July 26, 1999 – Russian troops in Chechnya are free to operate in the US sector of Chechnya without an American presence. But NATO may never find a way to change the Russians' attitude about being Serb allies.

REPORT SAYS RUSSIA SUPPLIED SERBS WITH MISSILES, BREAKING EMBARGO

London, Aug. 3, 1999 – (Reuters) – *Jane's Defence Weekly* said in a report to be published on Tuesday that Russia was believed to have supplied Serbia with air defense missiles before NATO started its bombing campaign against Kosovo in March.

...The report quoted a high-ranking Serbian officer as saying the first shipment of between six and ten incomplete Russian S-300PM missile systems entered Serbia by land, hidden in railway wagons carrying scrap iron, in early 1999. It quoted sources as saying an unspecified quantity of the missile systems was smuggled into the country in a Russian humanitarian convoy, hidden in what appeared to be fuel tankers.

KOSOVO ALBANIANS PROTEST RUSSIANS

Philadelphia Inquirer – About 1,000 ethnic Albanian protesters marched toward a Russian base to show their opposition to Russian peacekeepers in the south-eastern Kosovo town of Kosovska Kamenica while two US Apache helicopters whirred overhead and American troops stood by. The march ended without incident.

RUSSIA'S STEALTH FIGHTER MAKES RARE APPEARANCE AT AIR SHOW

Los Angeles Times, August 18, 1999 – Russia's S-37 Berkut, or Golden Eagle, was the main performer at an international air show held near Moscow. The stealth jet, with its forward-swept wings, made only a brief appearance.

RUSSIA FUMES AT US OVER DISARMAMENT AND KFOR

Moscow, August 21, 1999 – (Agence France Presse) – Storm clouds gathered over US-Russian relations Friday after sharp differences emerged on nuclear disarmament and the Kosovo peacekeeping effort, two pillars of cooperation between Moscow and Washington.

'After the whole episode with Kosovo, the Russians feel that militarily they were disregarded and badly treated by NATO. The only way of making the NATO nations realize this is to remind them that Russia is a nuclear power,' Viktor Kremenyuk, deputy director of the US–Canada Institute, a Moscow think tank, said.

US DOWNPLAYS INCIDENT WITH JETS, RUSSIAN BOMBERS

Washington Times, September 19, 1999 – The National Security Council said an encounter Thursday between US jets and two Russian bombers flying near Alaska was 'militarily insignificant.' The Russian planes were in international airspace, taking part in a training exercise, and moved closer to the Alaskan coast than has happened during the past six years. Officials said the American jets scrambled routinely, as they always do when an unknown aircraft approaches US territory.

A GENOCIDE, A POLITICAL COUP. SOME DEMOCRACY

by Zbigniew Brzezinski – *Wall Street Journal, January 4, 2000* – Vladimir Putin's accession to the Russian presidency was the work of oligarchs and army-security chiefs who wanted to pre-empt any semblance of a democratic vote scheduled for June. The attitude of Putin, as shown in Russia's brutal treatment of Chechnya, should be taken as a warning of future problems.

NATO EXERCISE ENDS IN MORE CLASHES

European Stars & Stripes, April 13, 2000 – Marines from the 24th Marine Expeditionary Unit left Greece the same way they arrived for NATO's Dynamic Response 2000 exercise in nearby Kosovo: dodging rocks, red paint bombs and insults from anti-NATO demonstrators along the route. The 80-vehicle convoy made it to the embarkation point at Port Litohoro without injuries, but four vehicles had their windshields smashed.

Washington in Brief – Washington Post, April 14, 2000 – For The Record – NATO is asking member countries to provide 3,500 troops for the Kosovo peacekeeping operation to replace battalions that are leaving, but no additional US forces are likely to go, Pentagon spokesman Kenneth Bacon said.

PUTIN EYES DEFENSE OF RUSSIAN INTERESTS IN CASPIAN

Moscow, Apr 21, 2000 – (Reuters) President-elect Vladimir Putin expressed concern on Friday that foreign competitors were eyeing the oil-rich Caspian region, where Moscow has traditionally dominated, and called on Russian firms to get more involved.

'We must clearly understand that the interest of our partners, Turkey, the United States and Britain, in this region is not accidental,' Russian agencies quoted him as telling a meeting of his advisory Security Council.

...Russia wielded economic mastery over the Caspian basin throughout the Soviet era when the oil-rich republics were part of a single state. But the newly independent states, with diplomatic support from the United States and Turkey, want to build export routes bypassing Russia, which would sharply reduce its influence in the region...

RUSSIANS WOUNDED IN KOSOVO

International Herald Tribune, May 25, 2000 – Two Russian soldiers were wounded when two anti-tank rockets smashed into their base in western Kosovo. Russian soldiers also came under gunfire overnight on five occasions. The attacks followed a Tuesday afternoon altercation between Russian troops and a former commander of the ethnic Albanian Kosovo Liberation Army.

PUTIN, SCHROEDER HAIL 'NEW START' IN KEY ALLIANCE

by Martin Nesirky – *Berlin* (Reuters) – *June 10, 2000* – Russia and Germany declared a new and fruitful start to a vital European alliance Thursday when President Vladimir Putin, once a Communist spy in Dresden, met German Chancellor Gerhard Schroeder.

…'Germany is interested in a strategic partnership with Russia,' Schroeder said. 'Not just Germany but all Europe has an interest in maintaining close and friendly relations with Russia.'

Putin said: 'Germany is Russia's most important economic partner in Europe. We consider Germany to be at the core of European integration. As such, our conversation with the chancellor has a double significance for Russia.'

UKRAINE HOSTS BIG NATO EXERCISE, RUSSIA MISSING KIEV

(Reuters) – *6/19/00* – Ukraine begins unprecedented 10-day naval exercises with NATO and several former communist nations on Monday, but Russia, still deeply suspicious of the

Western defense alliance, plans to stay away.

...Russia, Ukraine's former imperial master, resents Kiev's warm ties with NATO and regular military exercise in the Black Sea region, where Moscow's might and influence have waned dramatically since the collapse of the Soviet Union in 1991.

This is no time to hear that we have violated human rights. This is not true. It is not good for my hearing. It is not good for my hair. I know the real situation and think that Russia needs to be more cruel... We will resist and use weapons, and not only nuclear ones. We will throw you into the English Channel. We will drive all the human rights advocates to the tunnel between London and Paris and brick them up in there.

– VLADIMIR ZHIRINOVSKY,
RUSSIAN ULTRANATIONALIST LEADER
REUTERS, APRIL 7, 2000)

Prologue

Blair House, Washington, DC
20 January 2001

'Well, what the hell are they *doing* in there?' the chief clerk of the United States Supreme Court whispered excitedly. He knocked again on the door of the Truman Quarters, the master guest suite of Blair House. Behind him waited the chief justice of the Supreme Court, along with several aides, Secret Service agents, and Blair House staff. Who the hell would keep the chief justice and most of the rest of the world waiting like this?

A few moments later, the President-elect himself opened the door. 'Come in, please, gentlemen,' he said, his ever-present half-smile on his face. 'Welcome. Hope we didn't keep you too long.'

'Of course not, Governor Thorn,' the chief justice responded, with a faint smile. 'Don't be silly – I'm the one disturbing *you*. This is your time. Probably the last real peace and quiet you'll have for a very long time.'

The president-elect shook his head and smiled as if he was completely oblivious to what was going to happen soon. 'Nonsense, Your Honor. Peace is a state of mind, not a function of time, place, or sound.'

'Of course.' The chief justice and the clerk looked at each other and exchanged a single silent comment as they entered: Yep, he's a strange one, all right.

25

The clerk looked at his watch, then at the chief justice with not a little concern as they were admitted inside. The president- and vice president-elect were supposed to be at the west portico of the Capitol in twenty minutes for the start of the inauguration-day ceremonies. The festivities had in fact already started: a military pass-in-review in honor of the outgoing president and vice president, a concert by the Marine Band, the invocation, and various poetry readings celebrating the first peaceful transition of power in the United States of the new millennium.

The vice president-elect would be sworn in first at ten minutes before noon, followed by a song or march of the vice president-elect's choice while the players on the dais repositioned themselves. The vice president-elect, who happened to be one-half Seminole Indian, had chosen the 'John Dunbar theme' by John Barry, from *Dances with Wolves*, with Michael Tilson Thomas conducting the New World Symphony. The president-elect's swearing-in was supposed to start at thirty seconds before noon, timed so that at precisely one second after noon, the president-elect should be uttering the words 'So help me God.' The swearing-in would be followed by the first playing of 'Hail to the Chief' by the Marine Band, then the President's inaugural address to the nation, followed by a reception with the congressional leadership, Supreme Court members, and other dignitaries and guests in the Presidential Room of the Capitol.

Then there would be the parade down Pennsylvania Avenue to the White House – the newly sworn President and Vice President and their wives were expected to continue the Jimmy and Rosalyn Carter tradition and walk a good portion of the twelve-block parade route. Later tonight, there were inaugural balls scheduled all across Washington – about fifteen in all – and the new President, Vice President, and their wives were expected at least to put in an appearance and take one turn around the dance floor at all of them. Everything was being coordinated down to the second, and there was intense pressure by organizers on everyone – even Supreme Court justices – to keep on schedule.

Thorn extended his hand to the chief justice of the Supreme Court as the latter entered the room. 'Chief Justice Thompson, good to see you again,' he said. 'Here to do the preliminaries, I presume?'

'Yes, Governor,' the chief justice said, a bit impatiently. 'We're a little pressed for time, so we'd better–'

'Yes, I know, I know. The precious schedule,' the president-elect said, his smile disarming. The room was packed, but everyone was on their absolute best behavior, sitting quietly without fussing or any sign of nervousness. The president-elect had five children, all less than eight years of age, but there was not a peep out of any one of them except for polite whispers – everyone thought they were the most well behaved children on the planet. 'We're ready for you now.'

The dark horse had a name, and it was Thomas Nathaniel Thorn, the former boy-governor of Vermont. Tall, boyishly handsome, his wavy hair thinning but still blond – Thorn was only in his mid-forties – with dancing blue eyes and an easy smile, he looked like anything but the fastest-rising star on the American political scene. As the founder and leader of the Jeffersonian Party, Thorn was the first alternative-party candidate since Abraham Lincoln and his fledgling Republican Party to be elected to the presidency.

The vice president-elect, Lester Rawlins Busick, the former six-term senator from Florida, and his wife, Martha, were inside as well, with their two grown children. Busick, a former southern 'Reagan' Democrat – fiscally conservative but socially liberal – was an old political pro and very well respected inside the Beltway. But he had parted ways with his party on several issues, and had soon come to realize that his message could better be heard from the forum of the hot new Jeffersonian Party rather than if he were just another veteran senator shouting against the political hurricane. Despite Busick's strong reputation and sheer physical presence, however, he was practically invisible in the crowded hotel room.

The door was secured, and the onlookers gathered around, with an aide discreetly snapping pictures. The chief justice shook hands with everyone, then said in a rather rushed tone of voice, 'As you know, Governor Thorn, the Twentieth Amendment to the Constitution of the United States prescribes the actual moment at which you take office, which is one second after twelve o'clock noon today. Article Two, Section One of the Constitution also mandates that you take the oath of office before assuming your responsibilities as president of the United States.

'Therefore, since there is a big ceremony with a

lot of people and a lot of things that can conceivably go wrong between here and the official swearing-in...' he paused slightly – they were very late already, so this was certainly a case of one of 'those things that can conceivably go wrong' – '...it is customary to administer the oath of office before the public ceremony, so that at the moment your term of office does officially commence, you will have already been sworn in and we avoid any constitutional questions. I'm confident you will have no objection to taking the oath twice.' Thorn just smiled that peaceful, confident half-smile, the one that helped power him past an incumbent Republican, President Kevin Martindale, and a nationally recognized Democratic front-runner and all the way into the White House. 'Very good. You have the Bible, I see, Mrs Thorn. Let's proceed.'

Amelia Thorn held out an antique Bible, one that could be traced back to President Thomas Jefferson's family, in the direction of the chief justice's voice. Amelia Thorn had been blind since an early age, the result of childhood diabetes, but hers was a true story of perseverance and strength: she was an experienced jurist, a mother of five, and had held a seat on the New Hampshire State Supreme Court before resigning to help in her husband's presidential campaign. 'Please place your left hand on the Bible, Governor Thorn, raise your right hand, and repeat after me: "I, Thomas Nathaniel Thorn, do solemnly swear..."' Thorn recited the oath of office flawlessly, passionately, with his eyes on his wife, and hers on him, lifted toward the sound of his voice. The task was repeated with Lester Busick, with his wife Martha holding the antique Bible open to a passage in the Book of Isaiah.

'Thank you, Governor Thorn, Senator Busick.' The chief justice could still not legally call them 'Mr President' or 'Mr Vice President' yet, but he shook their hands and congratulated them nonetheless. 'I wish you the best of luck and the prayers of a nation. Now, I think we should be on our way, or else the producers and directors choreographing the show today will all be very angry at us.'

'We're not ready yet,' Thorn said.

The chief justice looked aghast. 'Excuse me, Governor?'

'We're not ready.' Thorn motioned to the seats arranged in front of the huge fireplace in the hotel suite, and quickly but quietly, Busick and his family and Thorn's family sat down and joined hands. 'We have one task to perform before we leave. You are welcome to join us, or you can observe, or you can make your way to the Capitol.' He led his wife to the love seat facing the fireplace, the White House visible across the street through the windows flanking it, then sat down and nodded to those around him. 'Close the eyes, please.'

To Chief Justice Thompson's great surprise, they all closed their eyes and fell silent, hands joined, heads bowed. He looked at his clerk, then at his watch, then at the amazing spectacle before him. 'What ... what are they doing?' he whispered to a Secret Service agent assigned to the family. 'Are they praying?'

'I don't think so, sir,' the agent replied quietly. 'I think they're meditating.'

'Meditating? *Now?* The man's going to be sworn in as president of the United States in less than a half hour! How can he think about *meditating* at a time like this?'

'They do this twice a day, Your Honor, every day,' the agent said matter-of-factly. 'Twenty minutes. *Exactly* twenty minutes. All of them.'

It was then that the chief justice realized that all the stories he had heard about Thomas Nathaniel Thorn were probably true. This was impossible ... unacceptable! 'Governor Thorn, please, we should be going.' No response. Thompson raised his voice in his most commanding courtroom tone: *'Governor Thorn!'*

One of the children opened her eyes, looked at the chief justice, then looked at her mother quizzically, but closed her eyes again when Amelia didn't react. 'You may join us, you can observe, or you may leave,' Thorn said in a very quiet but perturbed voice, keeping his eyes closed, 'but you may not disturb us. Thank you.'

Chief Justice Thompson knew his presence was demanded at the Capitol, knew he had to be there – but he couldn't make himself leave. He stood, transfixed, and watched in amazement as the minutes ticked by and the hour of transition approached. There were several urgent radio and phone calls, all answered by the Secret Service, but the Thorns and the Busicks could not be disturbed.

Thompson considered saying something, perhaps even ordering them to get their asses in gear and get going because the *nation* was waiting for them, for God's sake, but some unexplained force kept him from saying another word. He couldn't believe the children – even the infant seemed to be resting, and the toddlers didn't move a muscle. He had never before in his life seen toddlers sit still for so long – his own grandchildren, although very well behaved, seemed to have nanosecond attention spans.

Precisely twenty minutes later, the Thorns opened their eyes – it was as if a silent command had passed between them, because they all did it together. The Busicks opened their eyes when they detected the Thorns stirring. None of them looked sleepy in the least – in fact, they looked energized, refreshed, ready to power ahead. The older children quickly leapt into action without being told to do so, checking the younger children's diapers and helping Amelia Thorn pack up. Within moments, they were ready to leave.

'Governor, Senator, we ... we'd better hurry,' Chief Justice Thompson stammered, still not believing what he had seen with his own eyes.

'No hurry, Mr Chief Justice,' Thorn said. 'We have lots of time.'

'But it'll take at least ten minutes to get to the Capitol, even with an escort, and at least ten more minutes to get up to the–'

'We're not going to the Capitol,' Thorn said. The Busicks and the Thorns were out the door, led by Secret Service agents scrambling to clear the way. They bypassed the elevator and headed right to the ancient stairway.

'You're ... you're *not* going to the Capitol?' Thompson asked in shock. But he, too, had to hurry to keep up with the family.

'The ceremony there is to honor President Martindale and Vice President Whiting, Your Honor,' Thorn said. 'The people elected me to work for them, not to give speeches or put myself on parade.'

'But ... but the Congress, the other dignitaries, the invited guests, hundreds of thousands of citizens from all over the country – they're all waiting for you at the Capitol. What are they going to say when you don't show up?'

'Same thing as they would if I did show – maybe kindlier, since they won't have an inaugural speech to pick apart,' Thorn said. 'No matter, Your Honor.'

'You're not giving an inaugural speech?' Thompson cried in stunned amazement. 'You're joking, of course.' He knew he wasn't.

'I've got work to do. I've got a cabinet to get confirmed, several dozen federal judges to appoint, and a government to run. I promised the voters I'd get right to work, and so I shall.'

The Thorns and Busicks marched downstairs, across the ornate lobby of Blair House, and right across Pennsylvania Avenue past the barricades and the District of Columbia Police to the security gate at the White House. The crowds were thin, more than the usual number of tourists and passersby on the pedestrians-only street, but most of them were still along the parade route. In a few moments, however, a small crowd was gathered around them. Thomas Thorn shook a few hands, but he remained purposeful as he and his vice president-elect marched their families up to the security gate.

The Secret Service agents radioed ahead as fast as they could, but the group was still stopped by angry and confused Park Police. 'What the hell is going on here?' the guard asked.

'I'm reporting for duty,' Thorn said confidently. 'Open up.'

'*What?*' the guard shouted. 'Who the hell are you, bub? Back the–' and his jaw dropped as recognition began to dawn.

The chief justice stepped up.

'I am Joseph Thompson, chief justice of the Supreme Court of the United States. I have just administered the oath of office to these two gentlemen. Governor Thorn and Senator Busick...' The chief justice looked at his watch – it was now twelve-oh-two. '...I mean, *the President and Vice President of the United States* wish to enter the White House and begin their work.'

By that time, the Secret Service Presidential Protection Detail had responded, moving the crowd back, clearing the way, and providing the proper authentication to the startled and shocked Park Police and uniformed Secret Service officers. The security guard couldn't believe it was happening, but he buzzed open the gate and admitted the new President and Vice President of the United States and their families onto the grounds of their new home.

'Mr President, are you sure you want to do this?' Chief Justice Thompson asked again, as urgently as he possibly could. 'This is ... certainly unprecedented.'

'There is nothing in the Constitution that directs me to have an inauguration ceremony, give a speech, parade through the streets of Washington, or put ourselves or our families on display,' Thorn said. Thompson quickly scanned two decades' worth of studying and teaching the US Constitution, and he realized Thorn was right: there was no Constitutional mandate or public law that said there had to be any sort of ceremony.

'Our inauguration is not a victory celebration, Mr Chief Justice,' Thorn went on. 'We've just been given an important job to do – nothing more, nothing less. There's nothing to celebrate. I'm disrupting my family life, putting my dreams and aspirations on hold, and opening myself to all sorts of public scrutiny, doubt, and danger – all to do the people's business. I see no reason to celebrate anything but the peaceful transition of power in the world's greatest democracy. If anyone should celebrate, it's the voters who chose to exercise their right to choose their form of government and to choose who should lead it. As for me, I'll get right to work.'

Chief Justice Thompson could say nothing else. He held out his hand, and Thorn shook it warmly. Thorn and Busick shook a few more hands, and to cheers and chants of *'Thorn, Busick! Thorn, Busick!'* led their families forward to the White House and marched into history.

Prizren, Kosovo, Federal Republic of Yugoslavia that same time

'Usratta mozhna! That cowardly bastard did not

even have the guts to attend his own swearing-in!' Chief Captain Ljubisa Susic, chief of the Prizren Federal Police Force, Kosovo, Federal Republic of Yugoslavia, laughed at the television with glee. He prided himself on his excellent knowledge of Russian, especially obscenities. 'At a time when the eyes of the whole world are upon him, he decides to hide in the White House and play with his vice president's meat pole, *on igrayit z dun'kay kulakovay!*'

Susic was in his office, staying late so he could watch the satellite TV broadcast available only in the headquarters building. Here in his office he had peace and quiet, the television picture was reliable and relatively clear, he had maraschino – strong, expensive Serbian cherry brandy – and he had his pistol, which he was required to carry while on the base but forbidden to carry outside. That was another example of the idiotic rules he had to follow because of the NATO occupation of Kosovo: he could carry a weapon when he was surrounded by a hundred heavily armed guards, but when he was on his own outside the headquarters compound, he had to be unarmed for fear of inciting unrest and fear in the civilian population – most of whom would gladly put a bullet in his head or a knife in his back.

Prizren, in the southern section of the southern Yugoslavian province of Kosovo, was the head-quarters of KFOR MNB (S), or Kosovo Force, Multi-National Brigade – South, the NATO-sponsored, United Nations-sanctioned peace-keeping force composed of fifty thousand troops from twenty-eight nations around the world, including the United States, Great Britain, Germany, and Russia. KFOR was set up to patrol Kosovo and attempt to minimize any more ethnic confrontations while the world community tried to find a solution for the problems associated with the disintegration of the Federal Republic of Yugoslavia.

And there were plenty of problems. There was a Republic of Kosovo provisional government, sanctioned and even funded by the United Nations, which was scheduled to become the de facto government of the semi-autonomous republic in less than four years. No longer illegal, the Kosovo Liberation Army was more active than ever, with a force now estimated at more than fifty thousand men, equaling the size of the NATO, United Nations, and Russian peacekeeping forces combined. The KLA was supposed to have disarmed years ago, but that had never taken place – in fact, they were now reported to have heavy weapons such as antitank rockets and man-portable antiaircraft missiles, supplied by Iran, Saudi Arabia, and other Muslim nations.

The KLA advertised itself as the heart of the soon-to-be independent nation of Kosovo's self-defense force. It wasn't true in the least. The KLA was composed mainly of ethnic Albanians, mostly Muslim, and clearly did not treat all Kosovo residents alike. They hated ethnic Serbs and Orthodox Christians, but also discriminated against any foreigner and most other ethnic minorities inside Kosovo, such as gypsies, Romanians, Italians, Jews, and Greeks. Although not sanctioned by the United Nations or NATO, KLA soldiers had

37

begun wearing uniforms and carrying weapons, touting itself as the one and only authentic native Kosovar police force.

In the meantime, Kosovo was still a province of Serbia, supposedly subject to Serbian and Yugoslavian federal law. Susic had the unfortunate task of trying to enforce the laws in a region where lawlessness was the rule rather than the exception. Prizren Airport was still operated by the Federal Republic of Yugoslavia as a national and international airport, and it had to be secured and operated in accordance with Yugoslavian and International Civil Aeronautics Organization law. Its radar installations, power generators, communications links, satellite earth stations, warehouses, and fuel storage depots were also essential to Yugoslavian sovereignty and commerce. No one in NATO or the United Nations had offered to do any of these tasks for Yugoslavia. But the KLA was making that mission almost impossible.

The NATO peacekeeping mission in Kosovo was in complete shambles. NATO allies Italy and Germany still had peacekeepers in-country, but were constantly squabbling over their role: Italy, with its eastern bases overloaded and closer to the fighting, wanted a much lower-profile presence; Germany, fearful of losing dominance over European affairs, wanted a much more active role, including stationing troops in Serbia itself. Greece and Turkey, NATO allies but longtime Mediterranean rivals, had virtually no role in peacekeeping operations, and it was thought that was the best option. Russia also wanted to reassert its presence and authority in eastern

European affairs by supporting its Slavic cousins, counterbalancing Germany's threat.

And then there was the United States of America, the biggest question mark of all. What would the new president do? He was such an enigma that few analysts, American or foreign, could hazard a guess. The United States had twice as many peacekeepers stationed in or around Kosovo as all the other participants combined, easily outgunning both Germany and Russia. But this relegated them to the role of babysitter or referee. The Americans seemed less concerned with keeping peace in Kosovo than with reducing hostilities between European powers.

'This new president is either a nut or a coward,' Susic added. The television on the all-news channel showed thousands of people outside the American Capitol milling around, as if undecided about what they should do. 'Look at them – standing around with their thumbs up their asses, because their New Age retro-hippie president is back hiding in the safety of the White House.' Other remote camera shots showed presidential advisors – not yet Cabinet members, because the United States Senate had not confirmed them – arriving at the White House to confer with the President. 'How embarrassing. Do you not think so, Comrade Colonel?'

'Do not underestimate this man, Captain,' Colonel Gregor Kazakov said, draining his cup of brandy, which Susic immediately refilled. 'He has the strength of his convictions – he is not a political animal like the others. Never confuse a soft-spoken nature with weakness.'

Susic nodded thoughtfully. If Kazakov thought so... Kazakov was a great soldier, an extraordinarily brave and resourceful warrior. Gregor Kazakov was the commander of the Russian Federation's four-thousand-man Kosovo peacekeeping mission, charged with trying to maintain order in the Russian sector of this explosive Yugoslavian republic.

He was a hero to Susic because he had exhibited something relatively rare and unusual in a Russian military officer – initiative. It was Gregor Kazakov, then just a major, who, in June of 1999, upon secret orders from Moscow, had taken elements of his famed 331 Airborne battalion in two Antonov-12 transports low-level at night through the dark, forbidding Bosnian highlands, and then parachuted 120 elite Russian commandos, two armored personnel carriers, man-portable antiaircraft weapons, and a few days' worth of ammunition and supplies onto Pristina Airport, thus yanking away the key position in Kosovo right out from under NATO's confused, uncoordinated noses. The Russian paratroopers had captured the airport with complete surprise and no resistance. The entire operation, from tasking order to last man on the drop zone, had taken less than twelve hours – again, amazingly fast and efficient for any Russian military maneuver. A small company of British paratroopers, sent in as an advance team to set up for incoming NATO supply flights, had been politely but firmly rolled out of bed by their Russian counterparts and ordered to evacuate the airport.

NATO had E-3 Airborne Warning and Control

radar planes above Bosnia, Albania, and Macedonia monitoring air traffic over the entire region, and at one point two US Navy F-14 Tomcats from an aircraft carrier in the Adriatic Sea had been vectored in on them, intercepting them shortly after they'd lifted off from the Russian air base in Bosnia. The F-14s had warned the planes to turn back, and even locked onto them with their missile-guidance radars, threatening to fire if they didn't reverse course. But Kazakov had ordered the An-12 pilots to continue, and the Americans had eventually backed off without even firing a warning shot. The move had surprised the entire world and briefly touched off fears of NATO retaliation. Instead, Russia had gained in hours what weeks of negotiation had failed to achieve – a role in the peacekeeping efforts inside Kosovo. NATO had not only blinked at Kazakov's audacity – they'd stepped aside.

Of course, if NATO had wanted to take Pristina Airfield back, they could have done so with ease – Kazakov himself would have readily admitted that. Kazakov's troops, although elite soldiers and highly motivated, were very poorly equipped, and training was substandard at best. Peacekeeping duty in Bosnia had the lowest funding priority, but the government wanted mobile, elite commandos in place to assure dominance, so Kazakov's men were woefully unprepared. The assault on Pristina Airport had been the first jump most of the men had made in several weeks, because there was very little jet fuel available for training flights; everything from bullets to bombs to boots was in short supply. But the surprise factor had left the Americans, British, French, and German peacekeepers frozen in shock. One hour, the place was nearly deserted; the next hour, a couple hundred Russian paratroopers were setting up shop.

The mission's success had sent a surge of patriotic, nationalistic joy throughout Russia. Kazakov had received a promotion to full colonel and the People's Meritorious Service medal for his audacity and warrior spirit. In the end, the event had marked the beginning of the end of the Yelstin administration, since it was obvious Yeltsin either had not sanctioned the plan, fearing reprisals from the West, or, more likely, had known nothing about it in the first place. Less than a year later, Yeltsin had resigned, his Social Democratic Party was out, and Valentin Sen'kov and the new Russia-All Fatherland Party, not communist but decidedly nationalistic and anti-West, had surged into the Kremlin and Duma in large numbers.

Kazakov could have been elected premier of Russia if he'd wanted to get into Russian politics – no doubt a much tougher assignment than any other he had ever held. But he was a soldier and commander, and wanted nothing more than to lead Russian soldiers. He'd requested and been authorized to command the Russian presence in all of Yugoslavia, and had chosen to set up his headquarters right in NATO's face, squarely in the middle of the hornet's nest that was Kosovo – Prizren, in southern Kosovo, the largest and most dangerous multinational brigade sector. Kazakov commanded two full mechanized infantry battalions, four thousand soldiers, there. He also commanded an eight-hundred-man

Tactical Group, composed of a fast helicopter assault force, in the Kosovo Multi-National Brigade – East headquarters at Gnjilane, and was an advisor to the Ukrainian Army's three-hundred-man contingent there as well.

Now the troops had been in place for almost two years, with only minimal-duty out-rotations, so the men were slack, poorly trained, and poorly motivated. All they received here in Kosovo were constant threats from ethnic Albanian civilians and Kosovo Liberation Army forces – most of whom roamed the streets almost at will, with very little interference from NATO – and increasing cutbacks and inattention from home. The new president of Russia, ex-Communist, ex-KGB officer, and ex-prime president Valentin Sen'kov, promised more money and more prestige for the Russian military, and he was beginning to deliver. But no one, not even President Sen'kov, could squeeze blood from a turnip. There was simply no additional money to invest for the Russian Federation's huge military.

'The question is,' Susic said, gulping down more brandy, 'will Thorn continue the American buildup in Kosovo and continue to support revolutionaries, saboteurs, and terrorists in Albania, Montenegro, and Macedonia, like his predecessor? Or will he stop this maddening scheme to break up Yugoslavia and let us fight our own battles?'

'It is hard to tell with this president,' Kazakov said. 'He is a military man, that much I know – an army lieutenant in Desert Storm, I believe. He is credited with leading a team of commandos hundreds of miles into Iraq, even into Baghdad itself, and lazing targets for precision-guided bombers.'

'That mealymouthed worm was a *commando?*' Susic asked incredulously. He hadn't paid much attention to the American political campaign. 'He would not be qualified to shine your boots, let alone be called a commando, like yourself.'

'If it was a lie, I believe the American press would have exposed him in very short order – instead, they verified it,' Kazakov said. 'I told you, Captain, do not underestimate him. He knows what it's like to be a warrior, with a rifle in your hands sneaking into position, with your enemies all around you in the darkness. His outward demeanor may be different from other American presidents', but they are all pushed and pulled by so many political forces. They can be quite unpredictable.'

'Yes, especially that last one, Martindale,' Susic said. 'A real backstabbing snake.' Kazakov nodded, and Susic felt pleased with himself that he had made an observation that this great warrior agreed with. 'The master of glad-handed robbery – shake hands with the right hand, club you over the head with the left.' He started to pour Kazakov more brandy.

But Kazakov held out a hand over the glass and rose to his feet. 'I've got sentry posts to check,' he said.

'That's what junior officers are for,' Susic said, filling his glass again. Kazakov glared at him disapprovingly. Susic noticed the stare, ignored the brandy, and got to his feet as well. 'Excellent idea, Colonel. I think I'll join you. Always good to show some brass to the troops.'

The early-evening air was crisp and very cold, but the skies were clear and the moon, nearly full, was out. It was easy to see the perimeter of the headquarters compound and its five-meter-high barbed-wire-topped fence. Crews were busy keeping snow from piling up on the fence, which was wired with motion detectors – they would certainly be deactivated now while they worked. That meant that the guard towers and roving patrols were more important than ever, so Kazakov decided to check those first. Kazakov got clearance from Central Security Control on his portable radio. 'Follow me, Chief Captain.'

'Of course, sir,' Susic said, then caught his tongue. To his great surprise, Colonel Kazakov began removing his greatcoat as he headed for the steps to the first security tower. 'Where are you going, Colonel?' he asked.

'We are going to climb up and check on our guard towers,' Kazakov said. 'We need to get a report from the duty sergeant in charge.'

'Would it not be easier for him to report to us?'

'Let's go, Captain. A little exercise won't hurt us.'

'We're ... we're climbing up *there?*' Susic asked. He pointed up to the top of the six-story tower. 'Without your coat, sir?'

'Your uniform would be soaked clear through with sweat by the time you got up there,' Kazakov pointed out, 'and then you'd freeze to death. Take off your coat and let's go. Leave your hat and gloves on. Let's not take all day, Captain.' The commando leader began trudging up the

45

steps. Susic had no choice but to follow. Kazakov was already to the second floor by the time Susic even mounted the steps.

The tower cab was not very large or very warm – heaters would fog the windows – but they had good, strong Nicaraguan coffee and German cigarettes, which Kazakov gratefully accepted from the surprised and impressed security force sergeant. Kazakov was careful to hide the glow from the cigarette, cupping it inside his hands – a glowing cigarette inside the dark cab could be seen for miles by a sniper. 'Everything all right tonight, Sergeant?' he asked.

The sergeant handed Kazakov his logbook. 'Slightly higher passerby count than last night, sir,' he replied. The guards kept a count and a general description of everyone who passed within sight of the towers – since the headquarters was located on one of the main roads to and from the airport, it was generally busy, even at night in bad weather. 'Mostly gawkers coming to look at the big bad Russians.'

It was busy because the Russian compound was the scene of almost daily demonstrations by Albanian Kosovars, protesting the Russian presence in their province. Most times, the demonstrations were noisy but small, a few dozen old men and women with whistles and bullhorns chanting 'Russians Go Home.' Lately, however, the protests had gotten larger, more hostile, closer to the fence line, and now there were more young men in the crowds – probably Kosovo Liberation Army intelligence-gatherers, probing the Russian perimeter. Kazakov took these new demonstrations very seriously and ordered doubled patrols during them, which further strained his force. But the Kosovars needed to see a large, imposing Russian presence. The moment they detected any weakness, Kazakov was sure they would pounce.

'Your response?'

'Increased patrols – on foot, unfortunately, no more vehicles available from the motor pool – and a request in to the captain of police in Prizren and NATO security office to step up patrols in and out of the city as well.'

'Very well,' Kazakov said. He shot a murderous glance at Susic, still trying to struggle up the steps. He then went over, exchanged places with the sergeant in the cab, and leaned forward to look through the low-light and infrared sentry scope. 'Where are the additional foot patrols, Sergeant?' he asked, after scanning for a moment.

The sergeant looked a bit embarrassed. 'I ... I asked for volunteers first, about thirty minutes ago, from the oncoming shift,' he replied hesitantly. 'My men have been pulling overlapping fourteen-hour shifts for the past three weeks, sir. They're exhausted–'

'I understand, Mikhail, I understand,' Kazakov said, only slightly perturbed. 'If you want, I'll be the bad-ass: I order an extra platoon on foot patrol, beginning immediately. Relay the order. Then get me the commander of the NATO security unit. I don't want to talk with the duty sergeant or the officer of the day – I want the commander himself, that German major with the Scandinavian name.'

'Johansson. Yes, sir,' the sergeant said, reaching

for the field telephone. 'What about the chief captain of the police?'

'I will deal with him myself.' Kazakov continued to scan as Susic, huffing and puffing as if he were about to have a heart attack, entered the cab. Despite the cold temperatures, he was still bathed in sweat. 'Captain, my sergeant tells me he requested additional police patrols outside the perimeter. He has received no response. What is the delay?'

'I ... I will see to it immediately, sir,' Susic panted. 'Just ... just let me catch my breath.'

'Are you ready to continue our rounds, Captain? Let's go. I want to inspect every inch of the fence line tonight. You can issue the order from the portable radio.' Kazakov was out the door and heading down the stairs before Susic could say another word.

'Yes ... yes, sir,' Susic panted as they headed down the staircase. He was struggling with his coat, not sure whether he should keep it off or put it on. 'I'll be right behind you, Colonel!'

'Let's go, Captain, let's go.' Kazakov was trying not to appear hurried, but something, some unknown fear, was driving him forward, faster and faster. Susic could no longer keep up. 'As fast as you can.' He hit the bottom and started striding toward the main entrance guard post, about three blocks away.

In the glare of a few streetlights, he could see soldiers running toward the same building, and seconds later the sound of gunfire was heard. What in hell was happening? He pulled out his portable command radio and keyed the mike:

48

'Security One, this is Alpha. Report on disturbance at the front gate.'

'Open channel, Alpha,' the duty sergeant said. 'Can you go secure?'

'Negative.' They were lucky if they had any secure communications capability at all, let alone on their portables. 'Blue Security, report.'

'Fireworks! More fireworks,' the guard at the front gate reported. 'All stations, all stations, noisemakers over the fence only. Blue is secure.'

Kazakov slowed his pace a bit. This was almost a nightly occurrence, and one of the most maddening ploys by the ethnic Albanians to stir up the Russians: throwing small strings of firecrackers across the gate, usually propelled several dozen meters through the air by slings made of sliced-up inner tubes. It was just enough harassment to jangle the nerves of the most experienced, steady veteran fighter, but not enough to warrant a stricter crackdown on fireworks or noisemakers in Prizren.

There was a lot of pent-up frustration venting on the security net by angry guards. Kazakov jabbed his portable's mike button: 'Break, break, *break!*' he shouted. 'Essential communication only!'

'Alpha, this is Hotel.' That was the duty sergeant. 'Do you want a security sweep? Over.'

Kazakov considered that for a moment. That was part of the dance they did out here almost every night: the Albanian Kosovars did their demonstrations and popped a few noisemakers off in the compound, the Russians spent most of the night doing a security sweep, finding nothing, and they were exhausted by end of watch. This irritating cycle had to be broken, *now!* 'Negative. I want a full all-stations check and verification.

'Break. Delta, meet me at Blue right away. Out.' Delta was the call sign of his tactical operations chief. If, instead of a security sweep, the Russians did nothing – except secretly send out a few two-man patrols a few hundred meters past the fence – then if the hooligans were bold enough to try launching another volley, maybe they had a chance of nabbing a few of them. It was very illegal to send Russians outside the compound at night, but that was only a KFOR and NATO regulation, and Kazakov didn't feel too obligated to follow their rules. It was also supposedly illegal for anyone to launch noisemakers into the Russian compound, but NATO obviously wasn't doing anything about *that*.

Kazakov turned to Susic, who was trying to appear as if he were tying his boots, when in fact he was breathing heavily and looked like he might pass out. 'While you're resting there, Captain, listen: I have a plan. I'm going to send a few roving patrols out to see if we can catch some of whoever's launching those noisemakers. I want some of your men to accompany my commandos. Meet me at the security building right away, and be careful.'

'Don't worry about me, Colonel,' Susic shouted. 'I'll meet up with you right away.' Even though he had been going downstairs, Susic was exhausted – too much deskwork, too little exercise, too much maraschino, Kazakov decided. If they made it through this night, he'd have to–

Kazakov's attention was diverted to the sound of another string of noisemakers going off – close enough this time to smell the acidy gunpowder. 'My God, not again.' He removed his radio from his belt to ask for a report...

...when suddenly he saw a bright yellow flash of light from *inside* the section of fence just east of the security building. He knew instinctively what it was. 'Captain!' he shouted, turning toward Susic, then dodging away. 'Move! *Move!*' But he knew it would be too late – the bullets were probably already in flight.

They were. The entry wound was less than the size of his little finger, but the exit wound tore the back of Susic's head off.

Kazakov threw his legs out from under himself just as a bullet plowed into the pavement behind him. He rolled and rolled until he landed in the street, then leapt to his feet and dove behind a dark lightpost. A sniper! Probably KLA, but close enough to the fence to get a good shot off at lone figures at night. This was the first time something like this had happened in the Russian compound.

As his mind raced to assemble a plan of action, he found himself thinking the weirdest thoughts, such as: Damn, this sniper is good. The time delay between the bullet hitting Susic in the head and the gunshot sound was considerable, meaning that the shot had been done over a very long distance, at night. Remarkable men, those snipers. Training one took years and perhaps millions of rubles for a really good rifle and...

More fireworks, just a few dozen meters away – he heard them slap the pavement in front of him

51

just before they popped off. Kazakov wished he had his armored staff car just then – that sniper was still out there, using the noisemakers as cover for his attacks. He pulled his radio from his web belt: '*Apasna, apasna,* this is Alpha, snipers along the fence line east of Blue, all personnel man your duty posts and prepare to repel attackers! Repeat, snipers on the fence line, Charlie is down. Full nighttime challenge. All stations, report status to security control!'

'Alpha, *gdye vi?* Say position!' It was the duty sergeant. 'Take cover! Units will respond to your location. Say position from Blue.'

A tremendous explosion made Kazakov duck. It was a direct antitank rocket hit on the security building near the main gate. He had obviously underestimated these Kosovo Liberation Army thugs – they must have very good weaponry to strike that building from far away.

'Blue has been hit! Blue is hit!' Kazakov shouted into the radio. He swept his AKM-74 assault rifle across the slowly clearing billowing smoke around the security building. There were armed men jumping across the damaged walls and structures, silhouetted against the fog of blasted concrete and dirt, but from fifty meters away Kazakov couldn't tell if they were Russians or KLA. But they were jumping from the outside in, so Kazakov assumed they were enemy KLA rebels. He fired at a couple of them who were clustered close together, then immediately rolled left several times, got to his feet, and scampered in a low crouch behind a concrete street signpost. It was a good thing he'd moved – seconds later, the spot from where he had fired was cratered with bullets.

There was nothing he could do here, Kazakov thought grimly. He hated the idea of turning his back on any surviving perimeter guards, but the invaders had the upper hand, and he was alone. Better to retreat, find help, and organize a counterassault in force.

Kazakov had just started running back toward the headquarters building when he saw his command car speeding around the corner, a gunner manning the gun turret, its headlight slits in place to mask its approach. He waved, and the vehicle veered toward him. The command car held four armed infantrymen along with a radio operator, aide, driver, gunner, and security man. If it was fully manned, it might be enough to mount a good counterassault until more troops moved into—

Kazakov was so busy planning his next move that he failed to notice that the command car was heading right at him. By the time he realized something was wrong, it was too late. The armored car plowed into the colonel at over thirty kilometers an hour.

His thick winter battle dress uniform and helmet saved his life, but Kazakov was knocked near unconscious by the force of the impact. All he could register were excited, now jubilant Albanian-speaking voices, and flashlight beams sweeping across his face.

'*Dobriy vyechyeer*, Colonel Kazakov,' one of the Albanian voices said in very good Russian. 'Good we should bump into you like this. We were on our way to visit you when your men informed us you were inspecting the security posts.'

'*S kyem vi?* Who are you with?' Kazakov muttered. 'What unit?'

'You know who, Colonel,' the man replied. 'We are your sworn enemies. We have vowed to do everything in our power to force you to leave our homeland. You are invaders, trespassers, and murderers. The penalty for murder in Kosovo is death. Your sentence will be carried out immediately.'

'You have already murdered many Russian soldiers,' Kazakov said. 'Reinforcements are on the way. Leave me and save yourselves or you will all be slaughtered.'

'I would have preferred it if you simply begged for your life, Colonel,' the man said. 'But you do bring up a good suggestion. We should withdraw from here immediately. *Das svedanya*, Colonel Kazakov. *Spasiba va vychyeer.* Thanks for the wonderful evening.'

'*Idi v zhopu, pizda,*' Kazakov cursed.

The flashlight beam shined directly into Kazakov's eyes, and the man's face moved close enough that he could smell the alcohol, cordite, and blood on the man's uniform. 'You want to inspect the security posts, Colonel dirt-mouth? *Kharasho.* Allow me to take you there.'

Kazakov's legs were chained to the back of the command car, and the rebels dragged the colonel's body through the streets of Prizren, firing into the sky in jubilation. Kazakov remained conscious for several blocks until his head hit the debris of a destroyed truck and he was mercifully knocked unconscious. His last thought was of his wife and his three sons. He had not seen them in so many months, and now he knew they would never see him again: they would never permit the family to see a corpse as bad as he knew his was going to look.

At the front gate to the Russian security zone, the colonel was hung upside down over the entry control point road, stripped naked, then riddled with machine-gun fire until his body could no longer be recognized as human. The rebels were long gone before United Nations reinforcements arrived.

Chapter One

Zhukovsky Flight Research Center, near Bykovo, Russian Federation the next evening

Even with many high-intensity lights ringing the area, it was almost impossible to see the big transport plane through the darkness and driving snowstorm as it taxied over to its parking spot. Its port-side turboprop engines, the ones facing the terminal building, the honor guard, a small band, and a group of waiting people, had already been shut down, and as soon as the plane was stopped by ground crews with lighted wands, the other two engines were also shut down. The ramp suddenly became eerily quiet, the only sound that of a long line of hearses' wheels crunching on snow. On one side of the transport plane's tail, seventeen hearses waited; on the other side were seventeen limousines for the family members, plus several official-looking government vehicles. From the official vehicles, two men surrounded by security guards alighted and took places beside the honor guard.

The transport's cargo ramp under the tall tail motored down, and the receiving detail marched over and stepped up the ramp, as the first limousine pulled out of line and maneuvered over to receive its passenger. The band began to play a solemn funeral march. A few moments later, the receiving detail slowly wheeled out the first casket, draped with the flag of the Russian Federation. As the honor guard and officials saluted and lowered flags in respect, a woman clothed all in black, wearing a black veil under her black beaver pelt hat, stepped forward from the line of limousines and reached out with both hands to gently touch the casket in silent greeting, as if wishing to not disturb its occupant but to welcome him home.

Then, suddenly, her grief turned to anger. She cried aloud in anguish, piercing the frigid, snowy evening like a gunshot. She pushed the attendants aside, then grasped the Russian Federation flag in her gloved hands, pulled it off the casket, flung it to the ground, and rested her right cheek on the smooth gray surface of the casket's lid, sobbing loudly. A young man, tall and clothed in black as well, held her shaking shoulders, eventually pulling her away from the casket as it was escorted to the waiting hearse. The young man tried to comfort and support the woman as he led her to her own waiting limousine, where other family members were waiting, but she pushed him away. The limousine drove off, leaving the young man behind. The commander of the escort detail picked the flag up off the snow-covered ramp, quickly folded it, and gave it to one of the limousine attendants, as if unsure of what to do with it now.

The young man remained behind. He watched silently as the remaining sixteen caskets were escorted out of the big transport plane and placed into their hearses, and he remained, ignoring the snow falling heavier and heavier, after all the limousines, the escort detail, and the color guard had departed. None of the other family members spoke to the officials, and they did not attempt to speak with the family members. The officials returned to their limousines as soon as the last hearse drove away.

The young man saw he was not alone. A tall, distinguished-looking older gentleman, also in a black fur beaver-pelt hat and rich-looking sealskin coat, stood nearby, tears running unabashedly down his cheeks. They looked at each other across the snow-obscured ramp. The older man approached the younger and nodded politely. *'Spakoyniy nochyee, bratam,'* he said in greeting. *'K sazhalyeneeyoo. Kak deela?'*

'I've been better,' the younger man replied. He did not offer his hand in greeting.

'I'm sorry for your loss,' the older man said. 'I am Dr Pyotr Viktorievich Fursenko. I lost my son, Gennadi Piotrievich, in Kosovo.'

'I am sorry,' the young man murmured. There was a glimmer of recognition in his eyes.

'Thank you. He was a lieutenant, one of the security officers. He had been in the army only eight months, and in Kosovo only two weeks.' No other comment from the young man, so Fursenko went on: 'I assume the unit commander, Colonel Kazakov, was your father?' The young man nodded. Dr Fursenko paused, looked at the younger man, waiting for an introduction, but none was forthcoming. 'And that was your mother, I assume?' Again, nothing. 'I am sorry for her as well. I must tell you, I can't help but agree with her sentiments.'

'Her sentiments?'

'Her anger at Russia, at the Central Military Committee, at the general state of our country in general,' Fursenko said. 'We can't seem to do anything right, even help our comrades hold on to a tiny republic in the backwaters of the Balkans.'

The younger man glanced over at Fursenko. 'How do you know I'm not an internal security officer or MVD, Doctor?' he asked. The MVD, or Ministry of Internal Affairs, conducted most government intelligence, counterintelligence, and national police activities inside the Russian Federation. 'You could be investigated for what you just said.'

'I don't care – let them investigate me, imprison me, kill me,' Fursenko said, his voice filled with despair. 'They are undoubtedly better at killing their own people than protecting their soldiers in Kosovo or Chechnya.' The young man smiled at that comment. 'My research center was torn down, my industry that I have worked in for twenty-five years has all but closed down, my parents are gone, my wife died a few years ago, and my two daughters are somewhere in North America. My son was all I had left.' He paused, looking the younger man up and down. 'I would say that you could be MVD or SVR as well.' The SVR was the new name for the KGB, which conducted most foreign intelligence activities for Russia but was free to act inside the country as well. 'Except I think you are dressed a little too well.'

'You are a very observant man,' the young man said. He regarded Fursenko for a moment, then extended a hand, and Fursenko accepted it. 'Pavel Gregorievich Kazakov.'

'Pleased to meet–' Fursenko stopped suddenly, then squinted his eyes. 'Pavel Kazakov? *The* Pavel Kazakov?'

'I am very impressed by what you are doing at Metyor, Doctor Fursenko,' Kazakov remarked, his voice deep and insistent, as if silently urging Fursenko not to dwell on what he had just figured out.

'I ... I...' Fursenko took a moment to regain his composure, then went on 'Thank you, sir. It is all due to you, of course.'

'Not at all, Doctor,' Kazakov said. 'Metyor is a fine group.' Most large privatized companies in the Commonwealth of Independent States belonged to organizations called IIGs, or Industrial Investment Groups, similar to corporations in the United States. IIG members were usually banks, other IIGs, some foreign investors, and a few wealthy individuals, but the primary member of any IIG was the Russian government, which controlled at least twenty percent but sometimes as much as ninety percent of any venture, and therefore had ultimate control. Metyor was one of the lucky ones: only thirty percent of the IIG was owned by the government. 'And I am familiar with your old venture, the Soviet aircraft design bureau in Lithuania called Fisikous.'

It was Fursenko's turn to look uncomfortable, which pleased and intrigued Kazakov. In conducting his due-diligence before investing in any new company, especially a troubled but high-tech concern like Metyor, Kazakov always put his extensive private intelligence operatives, most of them former KGB, to work learning all there was to learn about the previous holdings of the IIG, which in this case was a research and development institute called Fisikous. What he had found out was nothing short of astounding.

The Fisikous Institute of Technology had been an advanced aircraft and technology research facility in Vilnius, in what was then the Lithuanian Soviet Socialist Republic, now the independent Republic of Lithuania on the eastern end of the Baltic Sea. Fisikous had been on the cutting edge of Soviet aircraft design, attracting the brightest engineers from all over the Soviet Union and the non-aligned nations. The big name at Fisikous had been a young scientist named Ivan Ozerov, who'd been the resident low observable technology – stealth – expert. No one knew anything about Ozerov, except that in a short time at Fisikous, under the direct supervision of the chief of the facility, Pyotr Fursenko, and another man who most suspected was KGB, he'd become the number-one design expert in all of the Soviet Union. Ozerov was brilliant, but weird and unpredictable, occasionally launching into wild tirades in English at the slightest provocation or agitation. Scientists there had long suspected Ozerov of being either on LSD or simply psychotic – he was far more than just eccentric. But there was no question that his work, especially on the incredible Fi-170 stealth bomber, had been nothing short of genius.

But there had been problems at Fisikous. The Baltic republic of Lithuania was driving toward independence from the Soviet Union, and Fisikous represented all that was bad about life under Soviet rule. Ivan Ozerov had disappeared during some kind of military action. Some said the American CIA or Special Forces had kidnapped Ozerov. Others said Ozerov had not been Russian but a captured American scientist, codenamed 'Redtail Hawk,' brainwashed right there at Fisikous by the KGB, and that the military action had really been a rescue mission. Even the Fisikous-170 stealth bomber, a one-hundred-and-twenty-thousand kilo warplane, had been stolen.

'When the Union collapsed, I went back to Russia to head up some other aerospace design bureaus,' Fursenko went on. 'I was going to retire or emigrate to the West, because the industry had all but disappeared in the Commonwealth. But when my wife died, I ... I stayed on ... well, mostly just to have something to do.'

'I understand,' Kazakov said sincerely. 'I think that's important.'

'They had better *kofye* and *romavaya babas* in the labs than I could afford as a pensioner anyway,' Fursenko admitted with a faint smile. 'There's not much money in Metyor, but we're doing important work, incredible things. I didn't mind not getting paid as long as I could keep on working and get real coffee. No offense, sir. It is rewarding work, but the pay is terrible.'

'No offense taken. My mother made the best *romavaya babas* when I was a kid,' Kazakov said. He sighed. 'Now I think she would use a handful of them to choke me if she had the chance.'

Fursenko didn't know what to say or do – he was afraid to smile, nod, or even move. He was very surprised and a bit wary after hearing the apparent warmth in Kazakov's voice – not something he had ever expected to hear at all. 'I couldn't help but notice, your mother ... seemed rather upset at ... well...'

'At me, yes,' Kazakov admitted. 'She does not approve of what I do.'

'And at Russia also.'

'She blames the Russian government for the sloppy way it supports our troops overseas,' Kazakov said. 'She blames me for everything else.'

Fursenko definitely did not feel comfortable discussing *this* man's personal life – that was an area he had no desire whatsoever to explore. He extended his hand, and Kazakov took it warmly. 'It was a pleasure to meet you, *Gaspadeen*–' Fursenko had used the more modern post-Union breakup, more 'politically correct' term for 'mister,' but he automatically stopped himself, then said, '*Tovarisch* Kazakov.' That was what most Russians had called each other back when there was a strong, fearsome, proud empire: Comrade.

Kazakov smiled and nodded approvingly. 'My condolences for your loss, *Tovarisch* Fursenko.'

'And to you, sir.' Fursenko turned and quickly strode away, feeling very uncomfortable with that man knowing his name or even standing behind him.

Kazakov stood by himself on the ramp, reflecting on this very strange evening. First the death and return of his father in shame, without any honors; his mother's outburst and her rejection; and then this chance meeting with one of the Cold War's most famous and brilliant weapons designers. Pavel Gregorievich Kazakov didn't believe in fate – he wielded too much power to believe that anyone else decided your future – but there had to be a reason, some definite path, that this chain of events signaled.

At one time, Doctor Pyotr Viktorievich Fursenko had been considered the finest and most imaginative aerospace and electromagnetodynamics engineer in all of Europe. Since the age of thirty, he had been the director of several Soviet aircraft and weapon design bureaus, building the most advanced military aircraft, missiles, bombs, avionics, and components imaginable...

At least, they had *thought* it was the best. Fursenko's word had been considered physics law until Ivan Ozerov had shown up at Fisikous. When Ozerov had started working at Fisikous, completely shattering the old beliefs and understandings, the Soviet scientists had realized exactly how far behind the United States they were on advanced warplane technology, especially low observable airframe, devices, systems, and counter-stealth technology.

This had only spurred Fursenko to even greater heights of genius. Even though the collapse of the Soviet Union meant the collapse of big, super-secret, well-funded agencies like Fisikous, it had also meant that Fursenko could travel and attend classes and seminars all over the world to learn more about modern warplane technology. When Ozerov had disappeared, probably back to whatever planetoid or genetic-engineering incubation tank had spawned him, Fursenko had again taken the lead in Russian aircraft and weapons design.

And now Kazakov knew where he was, had met

him, and could even be called his boss – because Kazakov owned over sixty percent of Metyor Industrial Investment Group. The genius Fursenko had been at his disposal all this time, and he hadn't even known it! But how to take advantage of this development? His mind began racing...

Only when the cargo ramp was finally raised and the transport plane made ready to be towed back to its hangar did Kazakov finally turn toward the three government vehicles behind him, which had also remained.

The middle and left side cars suddenly started up and drove off, leaving one car behind. A guard in a dark suit, wearing a machine pistol on a strap, emerged from the remaining vehicle, a stretch limousine, and opened a door for the young man. Kazakov brushed snow off his shoulders, then removed and brushed snow off his hat, revealing a shaved head, and stepped inside. The door closed behind the young man with a heavy *CHUNK!* that revealed its heavily armored doors and windows. The limousine drove off.

Inside was one man, a military officer in his early sixties, seated on a side-facing seat. Before him was a communications console, complete with satellite transceivers and television and computer monitors. A very pretty uniformed female aide sat in the forward aft-facing seat, with a similar console before her. She glanced at the young man, gave him an approving half-smile, and returned to her work.

'You did not even try to pay your respects to my mother, General,' the young man said acidly, without any sort of formal greeting.

'I did not think it would have been wise to try to console her in her obvious hysterical grief.'

'So, who were in the other cars?' the young man asked. 'The president? The defense minister?'

'The national security advisor, representing President Sen'kov, and the assistant minister of defense for European affairs, representing the government. I represent the military.'

'I had hoped the president would be courageous enough to attend,' the young man said bitterly. 'Not only does the commander-in-chief not attend, but he schedules the return flight for the dead of night in the middle of a snowstorm! What happened to your compassion, your responsibility to thank the families for their sacrifice?'

'We may have extended that courtesy, if your mother did not desecrate the flag so,' the old officer said. 'That was a most disappointing display. Most regrettable.'

'She is the widow of a man who died in the line of duty, doing a job few officers wanted,' the younger man said. 'She has given her life for the army. She is entitled to her grief – however she wishes to express it.' The young man looked over, but the officer did not respond. He took a breath, then reached behind the seat, lifted a crystal glass, and sniffed it, while at the same time checking out the aide over the rim of the glass. 'I see you still prefer American whiskey and attractive aides, Colonel-General,' the young man said.

'Observant as always, Pavel Gregorievich,' Colonel-General Valeriy Zhurbenko replied, with a smile. He reached into a compartment under the desk and withdrew a bottle of Jim Beam and two shot glasses. He poured, gave a glass to the young man, raised his own glass, then said, 'To Gregor Mikhailevich, the bravest and finest officer – no, the finest *man* – I have ever known. My best friend, my confidant, a soldier's soldier, and a hero to mother Russia.'

'To my father,' Pavel Gregorievich Kazakov said, raising his glass. As the general raised his glass, he quickly added, 'Who was killed because of the gutless, cowardly, inept members of the Army of the Russian Federation and the Central Military Committee.'

Colonel-General Zhurbenko, deputy minister of defense and chief of staff of the Armed Forces of the Russian Federation, paused with his glass a centimeter from his lips. He considered Kazakov's words, shrugged, and downed his whiskey.

'At least you have the guts not to argue with me,' Kazakov said bitterly.

'Your words hurt and offend me, Pavel,' Zhurbenko said resignedly, as his aide refilled their glasses. 'If they were said by anyone else, regardless of their rank or title, I would have him imprisoned, or executed.'

'My mother as well, General?' Kazakov asked.

Zhurbenko gave no response. He was accustomed to threatening political and military rivals – but Kazakov wasn't a rival, he was a superior. Even if he didn't carry the name of Russia's most famous and beloved soldier, he would quite possibly be the most powerful man in Russia.

Pavel Gregorievich Kazakov had started out wanting nothing more than to be the privileged son of a dedicated, fast-rising officer of the Red

Army. Thanks to his parents, he had enrolled in the Russian Military Academy in St Petersburg, known then as Leningrad, but found he had no love of the military – only for partying, smoking, drinking, and hell-raising, the wilder the better. To avoid embarrassment, his father had had him quietly transferred to Odessa Polytechnic University in the Ukraine Soviet Socialist Republic, near their winter home. In a place where he was just another one of many spoiled sons of high-ranking Communist Party members attending school in the 'Russian Riviera,' he had had to transform himself in order to stand out and start to build a future for himself.

Pavel couldn't do it. Being comfortable and taking it easy was his style, not doing what others thought he should be doing. Free from the confines of Leningrad and his father's watchful eye, he'd partied harder than ever. He'd experimented with every imaginable adventure: ice sailing on the Black Sea, parachuting, rock climbing, extreme sports like road luge and boulder biking, and pursuing the most beautiful women, single or married, on the Crimean Peninsula.

Drugs were everywhere, and Pavel tried them all. It was whispered that Pavel had burned all of the hair off his head and face while freebasing cocaine, which was why he kept his head shaved now, to remind him of how low he had once sunk. But before that time, nothing had been out of bounds. He'd quickly gained a reputation as a man's man, and his fame and notoriety had grown in inverse exponential proportion to his grade point average. One day, Pavel had disappeared

71

from the nightclub scene in Odessa. Most everyone had assumed he was dead, from either an accident during one of his daredevil extreme sports, an overdose, or a shootout with rival drug dealers.

When Pavel Kazakov had returned to Odessa years later, he had been a changed man. The head was still bald – he no longer needed to shave it – but everything else was different. He was off drugs, wealthy, and sophisticated. He'd bought one of the nicest homes on the Black Sea, began contributing to many cultural events, and become a respected financier, internationally known market-maker, and venture capitalist long before industrial investment groups and conglomerates were common in Russia. Of course, the rumors surfaced – he had KGB agents in his pocket, he transported thousands of kilos of drugs in diplomatic pouches, and he killed his competitors and adversaries with cold, ruthless detachment.

His biggest and most dramatic acquisition had been a nearly bankrupt oil and gas company in Odessa. The company had gone into a steep tailspin after the breakup of the Soviet Union and the drop in world oil prices, as had many oil companies, and Kazakov had acquired the company weeks before it folded completely. Many had speculated that Pavel Kazakov's drug connections had led him to develop a legitimate, Soviet-sponsored and Soviet-secured company; some said that it was an attempt by Pavel's father to use his status and influence to try to get his son cleaned up and into a legitimate line of work, but far enough in the hinterlands of the Soviet empire so that even if he did screw up, he wouldn't be an embarrassment. In any case, Pavel had dropped out of school in Odessa and become the president and largest individual shareholder, owning just slightly less stock than the company's largest shareholder, the Russian government itself.

Pavel's strategy to make the company, which he called Metyorgaz, profitable, despite the downturn in the oil industry had been simple: find oil where no one else would even think or dare to go, and pump and transport it as cheaply as possible. His first choice had been to go to Kazakhstan, the second-largest of the former Soviet republics but one of the most sparsely populated and capitalized. The reason: the former Kazakh Soviet Socialist Republic had been and still was the dumping ground of the Soviet Union.

The Communists had begun denuding the republic with the forced collectivization and relocation of millions of Kazakhs in the 1930s. They'd wasted billions of dollars and many years trying to grow wheat, cotton, and rice in one of the harshest climates in the world. Nuclear waste dumped throughout the republic, along with thousands of above-ground nuclear tests and accidents, had killed millions of persons over thirty years. Leaking radiation, pesticides, herbicides, raw sewage, and livestock waste had contaminated well water, livestock, and food, killing or injuring millions more. Spent ballistic missile and orbital rocket stages crashing downrange from the Baikonur Cosmodrome, Russia's main space launch facility, had poisoned and killed thousands more. Local communist authorities, without consulting one expert, had built or enlarged several irrigation

73

canals to plant cotton, completely draining the already heavily polluted Aral Sea, and creating one of the worst ecological disasters of the 1980s. The forty thousand square mile inland sea, the fourth largest in the world, had shrunk to more than sixty percent of its size, scattering contaminated and polluted salt across the once-fertile Kazakh plains.

Pavel Kazakov had continued with the Russian tradition of raping Kazakhstan. He'd chosen the easiest, cheapest, and highest-producing ways to pump oil, no matter how it hurt the land or how badly it polluted the Caspian Sea. Even after the required bribes to Kazak and Russian government officials to bypass what few environmental regulations were enforced, Kazakov had made immense profits. The gamble had paid off big, and Metyorgaz soon became the third-largest oil and gas producer in the Soviet Union, behind government-run Gazprom and the richest semi-independent Russian oil producer, LUKoil. Metyorgaz became the largest Russian Caspian Sea oil producer by far.

He increased his wealth and prestige by taking another gamble. The Russian government had mandated that Caspian Sea oil flowing into Russia be transported to the huge oil distribution terminal in Samara, about seven hundred miles north along the Ural River near Kujbysev, through which all of the oil flowing from western Siberia passed. The existing pipeline had a capacity of only three hundred thousand barrels per day, and Kazakov envisioned pumping six to seven times that volume in just a few short years. He had to find a better way.

The answer was clear: build his own pipeline. Neither the Russian Federation nor the newly independent Republic of Kazakhstan had money for this, so Kazakov took it upon himself to beg, borrow, and enlist the help of dozens of financiers around the world. He raised more than two and a half billion dollars and started the largest oil and gas pipeline project in the world, a nine-hundred-and-thirty-mile behemoth line from Tengiz, Kazakhstan, to Novorossiysk, Russia, on the Black Sea. Capable of transporting almost a million and a half barrels of oil a day, with expansion possibilities to almost two million barrels per day, the pipeline had opened up previously abandoned terminals and pipelines on the Black Sea in Ukraine, Moldova, Bulgaria, and Turkey. Although Kazakov had to pay huge sums in fees, taxes, leases, and bribes to the Russian and Kazakh governments, he still became one of the wealthiest individuals in Europe.

He used his newfound wealth and started investing in supertankers and refineries, shifting from the oil-producing and -pumping business to the shipment and refining business. The refineries in Ukraine, Bulgaria, and Turkey were happy to have him oversee operations, and they made Kazakov even wealthier. He modernized a half-dozen facilities in those three countries, making them far more efficient and cleaner than any yet developed in Eastern Europe.

But his core problem still remained: his main customer was still Russia or Russian client-states of the Commonwealth of Independent States, and their oil refining industry was one of the worst in the world, hopelessly outdated and inefficient. Kazakov could pump it profitably, but he lost money every time he sold product to the CIS, because they could not afford to pay very much for it and payments sometimes took a long time. The real money lay in shipping oil to Western European refineries, and that meant shipping oil through the Bosporus Straits into the Mediterranean. The problem was, the number of tankers transiting the Straits was already huge – an average of ten supertankers a day, added to all the other traffic in the Strait, meant wasted time and money, not to mention the tariffs Turkey extracted for each barrel of oil passing through its country. Despite his enormous wealth, Kazakov was a runt among giants when it came to competing with multinational Western oil producers.

Naturally, as Pavel Gregorievich Kazakov's wealth and prestige grew, so did the rumors. Most claimed he was a Russian Mafia boss, with an organization more influential and powerful than the Russian government; others said he was a drug dealer, tapping into Kazakhstan's other major export – heroin – and using his contacts in both the East and West to transport thousands of pounds of heroin per month throughout Europe; others said he was a spy for the Americans, or the Chinese, or the Japanese, or whoever happened to be the scapegoat of the month.

The bottom line for Colonel-General Zhurbenko was this: no one, not even he, with all his access to military and civilian intelligence resources, knew for sure. That made Pavel Kazakov a very, very dangerous man, and an even more dangerous adversary. Zhurbenko had too many children, grandchildren, dachas, mistresses, and foreign bank accounts to risk stirring up the mud trying to find out – he was sure Kazakov could take all of them for himself if he chose.

Which is why when Kazakov asked that question about his mother, Zhurbenko replied nervously, 'Of course not, Pavel,' taking a deep sip of whiskey to calm his nerves. When he looked over at Kazakov again, he saw the young entrepreneur's eyes shaded in the interior lights of the back of the limo, hooded – like a snake's, he thought. 'You know as well as I, Pavel: the Army hasn't been the same since our humiliation in Afghanistan. We could not even bring a bunch of ragtag goat herders to heel there. Afterward, we couldn't defeat one rebel army in our own backyard, even if they were just some unemployed factory workers with a few black market guns. Vilnius, Tbilisi, Baku, Dushanbe, Tiraspol, Kiev, Lvov, Grozny twice – the once feared Red Army has become little more than a bump in the road for any two-bit revolutionary.'

'You let those Albanian peasants chop up my father like a suckling *pig!*' Kazakov said hotly. 'What are you going to do about it? Nothing! What did I read in Interfax this morning? The Russian government is considering *removing its peacekeeping forces from Kosovo?* Seventeen soldiers are slaughtered by KLA marauders, and now the government wants to turn tail and *run?* I thought surely we would send a battalion of shock troops or a helicopter assault brigade into Albania and mow down every last one of the rebel bases!'

77

'We have only four thousand troops in Kosovo now, Pavel,' Zhurbenko argued. 'We barely have enough operating funds to keep them minimally operational–'

'"Minimally operational"? For God's sake, General, our troops are having to *forage for food!* If I were in charge, I'd take one evening, send in an entire brigade to the last man, and blow every known or suspected KLA base to hell, capture their supplies, interrogate the prisoners, burn their homes, and to hell with world opinion! At the very least, it would give our soldiers something to do. At best, it would allow them to avenge the deaths of their brothers in arms.'

'I agree fully with your passion and your anger, young Pavel, but how little you know of politics or how to prosecute a war,' Zhurbenko said, trying to keep the tone of his voice lighthearted. Kazakov took an angry gulp of whiskey. Zhurbenko certainly did not want to get on this man's evil side, he thought as he tried to appear as understanding and sympathetic as he could. 'It takes time, planning, and most important, money, to execute an operation such as that.'

'My father invaded Pristina with less than twelve hours' notice, with troops that were barely qualified to do the job.'

'Yes, he did,' Zhurbenko had to admit, although it was not the city of Pristina, just the little regional airport. 'Your father was a true leader of men, a risk taker, a born warrior in the tradition of the Slavic kings.' That seemed to placate Kazakov.

But in the intervening silence, Zhurbenko

78

turned over the question in his mind. Go into Kosovo with a brigade? It would take months, perhaps half a year, to mobilize twenty thousand troops to do *anything*, and the entire world would know about it long before the first regiment was loaded up. No. It was silly. Kosovo was a lose-lose situation. The murder of Colonel Kazakov and sixteen other soldiers in Kosovo only reinforced what Zhurbenko already knew – Russia needed to get out of Kosovo. Kazakov was certainly a brilliant businessman and engineer, but he knew nothing of the simplest mechanisms of modern warfare.

But perhaps a smaller force, one or two light armored battalions, even a Spetsnaz airborne regiment. Pavel Kazakov's father had parachuted in an infantry company right onto Pristina Airport, right under NATO's nose, and caught the world off guard. It hadn't been a shock force, just a regular infantry unit – Zhurbenko was sure all its members hadn't even been jump-qualified at the time. A well-trained Spetsnaz unit of similar size, perhaps reinforced by air, would be ten times more effective. Why couldn't they do it again? NATO's presence in Kosovo was only a bit smaller than it was in 1999, but now they were deeply entrenched in their own little sectors, in secure little compounds, not daring to roam around too much. The Kosovo Liberation Army had free rein. But they weren't regulars – they were guerrilla fighters. Dangerous, even deadly in the right situation, but no match for a Russian special forces team on a search-and-destroy mission.

The general noticed something that he had

almost missed in his effort not to anger this young industrialist: Pavel Kazakov was passionate about something – the welfare of Russian soldiers in Kosovo, the ones his murdered father had commanded. He spoke about 'our' soldiers, as if he really cared about them. Was it just because his father had been one? Did he now feel some sort of kinship with the soldiers killed in Kosovo? Whatever it was, it was a sudden glimpse behind the eyes of one of the most inscrutable personalities in the world.

'This is very interesting, Pavel, very interesting,' Zhurbenko said. 'You would advocate a much stronger, more forceful role in Kosovo?'

'Kosovo is just the beginning, General,' Kazakov replied acidly. 'Chechnya was a good example of a conflict well fought – bomb the rebels into submission. Destroy their homes, their places of business, their mosques, their meeting places. Since when does the Russian government condone independence movements within the Federation? Never.

'Russia has interests outside our borders that need protecting as well,' Kazakov went on. Zhurbenko was fully attentive now – because he had been thinking along the very same lines. 'The Americans are investing billions of dollars into developing pipelines to ship *our* oil, oil discovered and developed by Russian engineers, to the West. What do we get out of it? Nothing. A few rubles in transshipment fees, a fraction of what we're entitled to. Why is this allowed to happen? Because we allowed Azerbaijan and Georgia to become independent. The same would have happened in

Chechnya if we allowed it to happen.'

'But what about the West? Don't we need their investment capital, their coordination, the cooperation of their oil industry?'

'Ridiculous. The Western world condemned our actions against Chechnya because it is politically popular to oppose Russia. The Americans are as two-faced as they can be. They condemned our antiterrorist security actions against one of our own republics, but NATO, a military alliance, attacks Serbia, a sovereign country and close ally, *without a declaration of war*, and ignores the indignation from the entire world!'

'But we did nothing because we needed Western financial aid, Western investments—'

'Rubbish,' Kazakov said, taking an angry gulp of whiskey. 'We went along with NATO's aggression against Serbia, remaining silent while our Slav brothers were being bombed, all to try to show support for the West. We were buffaloed into espousing the same rhetoric they were feeding the rest of the world – that opposing Slobodan Milosevic and so-called Serb ethnic cleansing would be more in line with the sentiment of the world community. So we remained silent and then joined the United Nations 'peacekeeping' efforts.

'So what has the West done for us in return? Nothing! They think of different reasons not to provide us assistance or restructure government loans to suit their own political agenda. First they blamed our actions in Chechnya, then they blamed the election of President Sen'kov and the formation of a coalition government with a few Communists in it, then they blamed so-called human rights abuses, then weapons sales to countries unfriendly to America, then drug dealers and organized crime. The fact is, they just want us to *heel*. They want us pliable, soft, and nonthreatening. They don't want to invest in us.'

'You sound very much like your father, do you know that?' Zhurbenko said, nodding to his aide to refill the young man's glass. Pavel Kazakov nodded and smiled slightly, the whiskey starting to warm his granite-hard features a bit. He still looked evil and dangerous, but now more like a satisfied crocodile with a fat duck in his mouth than a cobra ready to strike.

In fact, General Zhurbenko knew, Colonel Gregor Kazakov had never made a political comment in his entire life. He'd been a soldier, first, foremost, and ever. No one – very definitely including Zhurbenko – knew what the elder Kazakov's opinions of his government or their policies had been, because he'd never volunteered his thoughts, no matter how casual the surroundings. But the fiction seemed to work, and the younger Kazakov seemed more animated than ever.

'So what do we do, Pavel?' Zhurbenko asked. 'Attack? Resist? Ally with Germany? What can we do?'

Zhurbenko could see Kazakov's mind racing furiously, lubricated and uninhibited by the alcohol. He even smiled a mischievous, somewhat malevolent grin. But then he shook his head. 'No ... no, General. I am not a military man. I have no idea what can be done. I cannot speak for the government or the president.'

'You're speaking to me, Pavel,' Zhurbenko

urged him. 'No one else around to listen. What you say is not treasonous – in fact, it might be considered patriotic. And you may not be a military man, but your background in international finance and commerce combined with your brilliance and intelligence – not to mention your commendable upbringing as the son of a national military hero – certainly qualifies you to express an educated opinion. What would you do, Pavel Gregorievich? Bomb Kosovo? Bomb Albania? Invade the Balkans?'

'I am not a politician, General,' Kazakov repeated. 'I'm just a businessman. But as a businessman, I believe this: a leader, whether a military commander, president, or company chairman, is supposed to take charge and be a leader, not a follower. Our government, our military commanders, must *lead*. Never let anyone dictate terms. Not the West, not rebels, *no one*.'

'No one can argue with that, Pavel,' Zhurbenko said. 'But what would you have us do? Avenge your father's death? Tear Kosovo, possibly Albania, apart looking for his murderers? Or don't you care who the murderers are? Just avenge yourself on any available Muslims?'

'Damn you, General, why are you taunting me like this?' Kazakov asked. 'Are you enjoying this?'

'I am trying to get through to you, young Gregorievich, that it is easy to point fingers and be the angry young man – what is hard is to come up with solutions, with answers,' Zhurbenko said. 'Do you think it was easy for Secretary Yejsk and Deputy Minister Lianov to have to retreat to their cars without grieving with the families?

83

Those men, the entire Kremlin, the entire high command, are suffering just as badly as you, as badly as your mother. Except the anguish you feel now is the anguish that we have been feeling for years, as we watch our great nation slip into disarray, powerless to do anything about it.'

'What would you have me say, General?' Kazakov asked. 'Start a nuclear war? Go back to a communist empire? Engage the West in another Cold War? No. The world is much different now. Russia is different.'

'Different. How?'

'We have allowed our friends, our former client states, our former protectorates, to break away from us. We built those little republics into nations. We didn't have to let them go. Now they turn on us and turn toward the West.' Kazakov sat silently for a moment, sipping whiskey, then said, 'They voted for independence – let us compel them to join the Commonwealth again.'

'Now we are getting somewhere, Pavel Gregorievich,' Zhurbenko said. 'Compel them – how?'

'Carrot and the stick – then *plomo o plata,* lead or gold,' Kazakov said.

'Explain yourself.'

'Oil,' Kazakov said. 'Look at all we have built over the years, all the places the Soviet Union invested to try to gain a foothold in Western commerce, only to lose it all. Oil terminals and refineries in Ukraine, Moldova, Bulgaria, Georgia. We gave billions to Yugoslavia to help build terminals and refineries and pipelines in Macedonia, Montenegro, Kosovo, and Serbia. They are all going to waste, or they are going to bloodsucking

Western conglomerates.'

'What are you talking about, Pavel?'

'General, I agreed with our participation, my father's participation, in Kosovo, because I believe Russia has a vested interest in the Balkans – namely, to help bring Russian oil west.'

'What oil?'

'Caspian Sea oil,' Kazakov said.

'How much oil?'

'In ten years, with the proper infrastructure in place and under firm political and military control – five million barrels,' Kazakov said proudly. 'Two and a half billion rubles – about one hundred and fifty million dollars' worth.' Zhurbenko didn't seem too impressed. He took another sip of whiskey – looking bored, until Kazakov added, 'A *day*, General. One hundred and fifty million dollars a day, every day, *for the next fifty years*. And we pay not one ruble to anyone in duties, taxes, fees, or tariffs. The money is all ours.'

Zhurbenko nearly choked on the Jim Beam. He looked at Kazakov in complete shock, a dribble of whiskey running down his cheek. 'Wha ... how is that possible?' he gasped. 'I didn't know we had that kind of oil reserves anywhere, not even in the Persian Gulf.'

'General, there is oil in the Caspian Sea that hasn't even been *discovered* yet – perhaps a hundred times more than we have discovered in the past twenty years,' Kazakov said. 'It could be equivalent to the oil reserves in Siberia or the South China Sea. The problem is, it doesn't all belong to Russia. Russia owns only one-fifth of the known reserves. Azerbaijan, Kazakhstan, Turkmenistan, and Iran own the rest. But Russian workers and Russian capital built most of those other nations' petroleum industries, General. Now, we pay outlandish prices for limited leases from those same countries – so they can use *our* equipment and *our* know-how to pump oil that Russia discovered. We must pay millions in bribes and fees, plus a duty for every barrel we ship out of the country. We pay huge salaries for unskilled foreign laborers while Russian men, educated oilmen, and their families starve right here at home. We do this because Russia didn't have the balls to hold on to what was rightfully theirs all along – the Soviet republics.'

'One hundred fifty *million dollars* ... per *day*,' was all Zhurbenko could murmur.

'Instead of pumping oil, refining it, shipping it to the greedy West, and taking our rightful place as the world's greatest nation,' Kazakov said, draining his glass, 'we are welcoming our heroes home in caskets draped with the flag of a dying, gutless government. No wonder my mother wanted that flag off her husband's casket. It is a disgrace. Tell that to the president when you see him.'

They fell silent for several minutes after that, with Zhurbenko exchanging only a few whispered words with his aide and Kazakov sipping on a couple more shots of whiskey until the bottle was empty. The limousine soon pulled up before an apartment building about ten blocks from the Kremlin, with unmarked security cars parked at each corner and across from the entrance. A security guard and a receptionist could be seen through the thick front windows.

Zhurbenko easily maneuvered around Kazakov and exited the limousine. 'My driver will take you wherever you would like to go, Pavel,' the commander of the Russian Federation's ground forces said. He extended a hand, and Kazakov took it. 'Again, my deepest condolences for your loss. I will visit your mother in the morning, if she will see me.'

'I will see to it that she receives you, Colonel-General.'

'Good.' He placed his left hand over Pavel's right, pulling the young man closer as if speaking in confidence. 'And we must keep in touch, Pavel. Your ideas have much merit. I would like to hear more.'

'Perhaps, General.'

The limousine drove off and had gone for a couple blocks before Pavel realized the general's aide was still in the car. 'So,' Kazakov said, 'what is your name ... Colonel?'

'Major,' the woman replied. 'Major Ivana Vasilyev, deputy chief of the general's staff.' She shifted over to the general's seat, then produced another bottle of Jim Beam and a glass. 'May I pour you something more to drink?'

'No. But you may help yourself. I assume you are officially off duty now.'

'I am never really off-duty, but the colonel-general has dismissed me for the night.' Instead, she put the bottle and the glass away, then turned to face him. 'Is there anything else I can offer you, Mr Kazakov?' Pavel let his eyes roam across her body, and she reciprocated. Vasilyev smiled invitingly. 'Anything at all?'

Kazakov chuckled, shaking his head. 'The old bastard wants something from me, doesn't he, Major?'

Vasilyev unbuttoned her tunic, revealing the swell of round, firm breasts beneath her white uniform blouse. 'My orders were to escort you home and see to it that any wishes you have are taken care of immediately, Mr Kazakov,' she said. She removed her neck tab and unbuttoned her blouse, and Kazakov noticed she wore a very unmilitary sheer black lace brassiere. 'The general is interested in your ideas and suggestions, and he has ordered me to act as his liaison. I have been ordered to provide you with anything you wish – data, information, resources, assistance – anything.' She knelt before him on the rich blue carpeting, reached out to him, and began to stroke him through his pants. 'If he wants something specific from you, he has not told me what it is.'

'So he orders you to undress before a strange man in his car, and you do it without question?'

'This was my idea, Mr Kazakov,' she said, with a mischievous smile. 'The general gives me a great deal of latitude in how I might carry out his orders.'

Kazakov smiled, reached to her, and expertly removed the front clasp from her brassiere with one hand. 'I see,' he said.

She smiled in return, closed her eyes as his hands explored her breasts, and then said as she reached for his zipper, 'I consider this one of the perquisites of my duties.'

The White House Oval Office, Washington, DC
the next morning

'Mr President, I know you meant to shake things up in Washington – but I'm afraid this bombshell is surely going to explode in your face when it gets out.'

President Thomas Thorn stopped typing into his computer and swiveled around to face his newly ratified Secretary of Defense, Robert G. Goff, who had marched into the Oval Office almost at a trot. Along with Goff was the Secretary of State, Edward F. Kercheval; the Vice President, Lester R. Busick, and Douglas R. Morgan, the Director of Central Intelligence. 'Read the final draft of the executive order, did you, Bob?'

Goff held up his copy of the document in question as if it were covered in blood. 'Read it? I've done nothing else but go over it for the past eighteen hours. I've been up all night, and I've kept most of my staff up all night, too, trying to find out if this is legal, feasible, or even *right*. This is completely astounding, Thomas.'

Robert Goff was known throughout Washington as a straight-talking, no-nonsense man. A retired US Army veteran, three-term congressman from Arizona, and acknowledged military expert, at age fifty-one Goff was one of the new lions in Washington, not afraid to stir things up. But the President's plan made even him gape in astonishment. Next to Goff was the head of the Joint Chiefs of Staff, Air Force General Richard W. Venti. Tall, thin, and young-looking for a four-star general, Venti was a veteran fighter pilot and the former commander of US Air Forces in Europe before being appointed to the Joint Chiefs of Staff. Unlike Goff, Venti preferred to keep his emotions and his thoughts to himself.

Noticeably absent from the meeting was the President's Special Advisor on National Security Affairs, known as the National Security Advisor – because President Thomas N. Thorn hadn't appointed one. It was part of a major shakeup in the Executive Branch, a drastic downsizing that was designed to make Cabinet officials more responsive and responsible, both to the public and to the President. So far in the new Thorn administration, over three hundred White House and executive branch personnel slots had been eliminated simply because the President and his staff had refused to fill them. The functions of several White House offices, such as Drug Control Policy, Management and Budget, and several political liaison offices, would be reassigned to other departments or simply eliminated.

'I know we talked about what we might do to change things in the Department of Defense and in the entire government,' Goff went on excitedly, 'but ... *this?* You can't possibly seriously intend to actually implement any of this.'

'I am going to do all of it, and I'm going to finish it by the end of this year,' the President said with a confident smile.

'Changing priorities as far as peacekeeping deployments – I don't think you'll get too much opposition,' Goff said. 'Another few rounds of base realignments, with no closures – I think that

90

will sell, too.' He motioned to the draft speech and the President's staff's attached comments. 'But this...'

'Bob, remember when we first talked about the possibility of doing this?' Thorn asked, his ever-present smile warm with the memories. Robert Goff had been one of Jeffersonian Party candidate Thomas Thorn's earliest and strongest supporters, giving up his seat in Congress during the campaign to help Thorn. They had been close friends ever since.

'Of course I remember,' Goff said, smiling in spite of himself. Thomas Thorn had this irritating way of disarming almost any agitated situation or person. 'But we were young and stupid and naive as hell back then.'

'It was less than a year ago, funny man,' Thorn said with a smile. 'We were in Abilene, Texas, at one of the first Jeffersonian Party rallies. It was cold, and I think it had snowed the night before. You and three of your volunteers had to stay in the same room at the Holiday Inn because we barely had enough money to keep going for another month; Amelia and I had three of the kids licking stamps for the mailers while they were watching cartoons. We didn't even place in the Iowa caucuses, and we barely qualified for the ballot in the New Hampshire primary, so we decided to work on the Super Tuesday states. You hoped that a hundred folks would show. Our podium at the open house at the Army post was a real honest-to-goodness soapbox–'

'A bunch of cases of laundry detergent from the mess hall, covered over with a tablecloth.'

Thorn nodded. 'But two thousand folks showed up, and we had to stand on top of a bus and use one of those big loudspeakers they use on firing ranges to make ourselves heard.'

'I remember, Thomas,' Goff said. 'That was the beginning. The turning point. What a day. We ended up winning New Hampshire without hardly setting foot in the state.'

'But remember when we took that tour of the base, and we saw all those hundreds of M1 Abrams tanks lined up in the marshaling area?' Thorn went on. 'Rows and rows and rows of them, as far as you could see, like furrows in a freshly plowed field. And they told us that *none* of those tanks had ever fired a shot in anger. They had second- and third-generation tanks there that had *never even left the base* except for training exercises. We saw artillery pieces, armored personnel carriers, mobile bridges, tents, vans, support vehicles, Humvees, rocket launchers, even radar systems and air defense missile batteries – all had not been used since Desert Storm, if they had ever been used at all.'

'I know, Thomas,' Goff said. 'But we've been at peace since Desert Storm. It doesn't mean they won't *ever* be used...'

'We talked about what an incredible waste of resources it all represented,' Thorn went on. 'Unemployment in the United States is at an all-time low and has been for years. Companies are begging for qualified, trainable workers. Yet we are spending billions of dollars on weapon systems that may never be used in combat, weapons that were designed to fight *yesterday's* wars. Someone has to operate that equipment, train others to use it, maintain it, train the maintainers, and someone has to keep track of all the stuff they need to operate and maintain it. It was a huge infrastructure, a massive investment in manpower and resources, and for what? What purpose did it serve? We said it was senseless, and we wondered what we could do about it. Well, this is what we're going to do about it.' The President looked at General Venti. 'What are your final thoughts, General?'

Venti thought about his response for a moment, then: 'We can argue the merits of the numbers, sir,' he replied. 'The Army spends five point three billion dollars a year on readiness and training for weapon systems that have never been used in war. The Navy spends ten billion dollars a year manning, equipping, and maintaining a fleet of nuclear attack submarines that have never fired a shot in combat. We spend another twenty billion dollars maintaining a nuclear deterrence force, and we hope to God we never have to use *it*, despite the threat from China and possibly Russia.'

'It's the emotional factor that'll be hard to counter, Mr President,' Goff interjected. 'There are still lots of World War Two, Korea, and Vietnam vets out there who will see this plan as a betrayal of trust. Your political opponents will use that. Several previous administrations made such drastic budget cuts that what you are about to do is inevitable, but you will still be blamed for it.

'There is still a great threat out there, Mr President,' Goff went on. 'China has already attacked American territory with nuclear weapons, and we think they will again. Although every prediction model and every analyst thinks it's unlikely, former empires such as Japan, Germany, and Russia could rise up and threaten American interests. Nonaligned, theocratic, and rogue nations could threaten American interests at any time with attacks ranging from simple kidnappings to cyberforce to nuclear weapons. The proliferation of weapons of mass destruction has increased tenfold since the breakup of the Soviet Union.'

'I want to hear from the general, Bob,' the President said. He nodded, urging him to speak. Goff looked frustrated and a bit angry, but held his comments.

'Frankly, sir, I think it's about time we start thinking about fighting future wars on *our* terms,' the Air Force general said. 'In a time of relative peace, this is the time to prepare for twenty-first- and even twenty-second century wars. We must do away with the old equipment, the old tactics, and the old fears and prejudices.

'This nation also somehow got sidetracked in its thinking about the role of the military,' Venti concluded. 'The military has always been a place to send kids that lacked discipline, but in more recent years the military has become a sort of extension of the welfare state. Fighting and possibly dying for your country took a back seat to learning a trade, getting an education, and providing someplace cool to go after high school. We are spending millions of dollars a year to recruit kids to join, but they're joining for all the wrong reasons. The problem is not that we lack well-qualified recruits – the problem is, the military became too big, too bloated. We had a military looking for a reason for existence. We were dreaming up missions for the military that had little to do with national security and everything to do with political posturing. I think it's time we stop that.'

'Spoken like a true Air Force officer, one whose career and retirement are secure,' the President said, with an inquisitive smile.

'And the Air Force makes out pretty well in the new plan, I've noticed,' Goff added. 'The Air Force and Navy should be thrilled about their new status.'

'I'm speaking as the chairman of the Joint Chiefs, not just as an Air Force officer, sir,' Venti said to Goff. 'I think the plan is a good beginning. It signals a positive change in military strategy for the twenty-first century. It's a change that I feel is badly needed. I'm completely behind the President.'

'But what will your men say when the changes happen? What will your sister services say?'

'The true soldiers will do what they're told,' Venti said honestly. 'The rest will squawk. They'll call you a traitor. They'll call for your resignation, perhaps try to impeach you. That's when you need to show them the strength of your convictions. Will the public outcry be louder than what your heart is telling your head? If you can listen to your heart while the storm of public and world opinion is beating down on you, everything will turn out okay. That's your dilemma, sir, not mine.' Venti sighed, looked away for a moment, then added, 'And as for my career and retirement: they may be secure, but I'll still be forever known as the man who presided over the biggest shakeup in US military history since the draft.'

'At least you're okay with this,' Thorn said. Venti looked sternly at his commander-in-chief, even after the President gave him a wink. To the Secretary of State, Edward Kercheval, the President went on, 'Okay, Ed, I know you've been waiting for a crack at me. Fire away.'

'You know how I feel about this plan, sir,' Kercheval said ominously. Unlike Goff and most others in Thorn's administration, Edward Kercheval, former ambassador to Russia in the Martindale administration and a career State Department employee, was not a close friend of the President's. But the President insisted on open dialogue and direct communication between the Cabinet officers and the Oval Office, and Kercheval had made it clear early on that he would take every opportunity to do so. 'I'm afraid this plan will undermine our entire foreign policy structure. Hundreds, if not thousands, of programs, agreements, letters of understandings, and memoranda on hundreds of issues and topics, from diplomatic agreements to aviation to intelligence listening posts to food shipments, rely in part on security guarantees put in place decades ago. Your plan threatens to destroy all of those protocols.'

'And we're bound to abide by these agreements,' the President asked, 'even if I feel they're harmful to the nation?'

'Those agreements are *contracts*, Mr President,' Kercheval said. 'Unilaterally breaching a contract carries consequences – legal action, loss of prestige, loss of credit, loss of mutual cooperation, loss of trust. Maybe even more dire consequences.'

'So I'm stuck with agreements and commitments I never negotiated, I don't understand, and no one in Washington can explain.'

'With all due respect, Mr President, your job, and ours, is to make yourself familiar with all those treaties and agreements,' Kercheval insisted. 'That's why we have a government and a bureaucracy – to help keep track of all there is to know about government. Simply implementing your program isn't the proper way to do it. The best way is to renegotiate the treaties and agreements you find objectionable. You don't just knock over the first domino in the row, because then they'll all fall over, one by one, and you may not be able to stop it once it starts. You take your time and remove one domino at a time, or you stack them differently, or you reinforce them so when another hits it, from any direction, it will still stand.'

'You forgot the other way, Ed: you get up off your chair, away from the table, and stay home,' the President said.

'Then none of the other kids of the block will want to come over to your house and play,' Kercheval suggested, reluctantly playing along with the awkward simile.

'I think they will,' the President said. 'Because when some other bully comes along and knocks down those dominos, and they're not strong enough to stop it from happening, they'll come back to us.'

'So you want to play foreign policy blackmail with the rest of the world, sir?' Kercheval asked. 'My way or the highway? That doesn't sound like responsible government to me, sir. With all due respect.' It was obvious Kercheval accorded very little respect at all when he said 'With all due respect.'

'Responsible government starts with someone taking the responsibility, and that's what I'm going to do,' the President said. 'I made a promise to the American people to protect and defend the Constitution. I know exactly what that means.'

'Mr President, I don't question your motives or your sincerity, or else I never would have agreed to serve on your Cabinet,' Kercheval said. 'I'm just trying to advise you on what's in store for you and this government if you go ahead with this plan. A lot of nations, institutions, and individuals around the world owe their way of life – perhaps even their very *life* – to the perception of the peace, strength, and security of the United States of America. What you are proposing might erase a lot of that. That could cause a ripple effect that will wash over the entire world.'

'I'm well aware of that, Ed–'

'I don't think you are, Mr President,' Kercheval interjected.

The others in the Oval Office turned and looked at Kercheval with shock, then at the President. Even Kercheval expected an explosion. Although Thomas N. Thorn's public persona was one of quiet, peaceful, dignified ease with the world, they all knew that the President had once been a trained professional killer – some powerful emotions bubbled just below the surface.

'Edward, the United States has been obsessed with dealing with these little rogue nation brushfires ever since the Persian Gulf War,' the President said. 'Somalia, Haiti, Iraq twice, Bosnia, Kosovo, North Korea – we seem to have peace-keeping forces in every corner of the planet. Then, when a major confrontation such as China flares up, we don't have the resources to pull together to counter them. We have to rely on unconventional forces to do something that our regular forces should do, and I'm not comfortable with that.

'The way I see it, the problem is twofold: our forces are too big and unwieldy to respond quickly enough, and we're spending too much time, resources, and attention on these little regional brushfires. Not one peace-keeping operation we've undertaken, with the possible exception of Haiti, has been successful. We've wasted billions of dollars and a lot of international prestige on operations that have not advanced American peace and security one bit. I'm tired of it, I think our military is tired of it, and the American people are tired of it.'

'These "brushfires," as you call them, could cause a much wider conflict, sir,' Kercheval maintained. 'There was never any doubt about Iraq – they threatened the West's primary oil supply. Other regions, such as the Balkans, are not as clear, but just as important. Ethnic violence in the Balkans has directly caused one world war and indirectly caused another. By intervening in these small conflicts, we've prevented them from escalating into much more serious, continentwide wars.'

'I wasn't convinced during the campaign, and I'm not convinced now,' the President said. 'We were assured by the previous administration that intervening in Bosnia and Kosovo was in our national interest. Now I've received all the data that the previous commanders-in-chief received, and I don't see it. Either I'm not as smart as they were and I'm missing something, or there is nothing there that threatens our peace and security. Which is it, Edward?'

'I think it's important to look beyond the present and look to the geopolitics of the region, sir,' Kercheval said by way of response. 'Russia is cracking down on dissenters within its own borders. It wants to reestablish ties with Serbia and is threatening any Eastern European nation that wants to join the European Union or NATO. That's enough provocation for me, Mr President. That is *very* evident to me. Can I explain it any better?'

The last sentence caught everyone's attention in the room, including the President's. Instead of taking a return shot, however, the President nodded, politely terminating the discussion. 'I appreciate your candor, Ed,' the President said, without a trace of malice – it sounded as if he really meant it, the Secretary of State thought. He turned to Douglas Morgan, the Director of Central Intelligence. 'Doug? Comments?'

'How will this affect ongoing intelligence operations?' Morgan asked. 'We have several dozen fully authorized and active field operations in progress, especially in the Balkans, Middle East, and Asia. You're not going just to pull the plug on them, are you, sir?'

'Of course not,' the President replied. 'In fact, I

see no reason to change any aspect of intelligence operations. I think it's just as important to maintain a strong and active intelligence and counter-intelligence operation, perhaps even more so if my plan is fully implemented.'

'Perhaps because the world will see this plan as something like cowardice and think that every American governmental function will implode as well?' Kercheval interjected.

If the Secretary of State meant to stir up another argument with the President, it didn't work. Thorn simply looked at Kercheval, nodded, and said with a smile, 'Something like that, Ed, something like that.' To the others in the room, he offered, 'Anything else?' When no one said anything, Thorn turned directly to Kercheval, hands outspread, eyes riveted on him as if saying, 'C'mon, Ed, if you want another shot at me, go ahead and take it.'

Kercheval shook his head. That was all he could do. He had voiced his objections for weeks, had had all the input he was allowed and more, and now even challenged the President's veracity. The man was obviously determined to do it.

'We're going to implement the plan immediately, then,' the President said resolutely. Goff and Venti's faces looked grim. Thorn added, 'Let's get it started, Bob.' He reached over, opened the folder before him, and signed the cover sheet of the executive order. 'There you go, gentlemen. Let's do it.'

Goff picked up the document and looked at it as if it was a copy of a death certificate. 'I'm sure this is the most historic document I'll ever hold in my hand.' He looked at Thorn with a mixture of awe and shock. 'We'll put it in motion right away, Mr President. I have my first closed-door congressional hearing scheduled for next week, but when word leaks out about this, I'm sure that'll be pushed up, more hearings will undoubtedly be scheduled, and some may even want to go unclassified. I'll be sure to have the White House and Pentagon counsels set up the ground rules.'

'Good luck, Bob. I'll be watching.'

'Are you going to mention it in the State of the Union address?'

'I do not intend to make a State of the Union address,' Thorn said.

'*What?*' the others exclaimed, almost in unison.

'Mr President, you can't be serious,' Kercheval said, his voice almost agitated. 'Skipping the inaugural was bad enough–'

'I did not "skip" the inaugural, Ed. I just chose not to attend.'

'It was political suicide, Mr President,' Kercheval insisted. 'It made you look like a laughingstock in front of the entire world!'

'I got my entire Cabinet confirmed in two weeks, and by the end of this month I'll have every federal judge position filled,' the President said. 'I don't care if the world thought it was crazy, and I don't care about political suicide, because there is virtually no political party behind me.'

'But not giving a speech before Congress–'

'Nothing mandates either an inaugural at the Capitol or a speech before Congress,' the President reminded him. 'The Constitution mandates a swearing-in and an oath of office, which I did. The

Constitution mandates an annual report to Congress on the state of the union and my legislative agenda, and that's what I intend to do. I will deliver my budget to Congress at the same time.

'You think it's political suicide – I say that it tells Congress and tells the American people I mean business. Congress knew I was serious about forming and running my government, and they helped me get my Cabinet confirmed in record time. My judges will be sworn in in months, and in some cases years, before the previous administration's were.'

Kercheval still looked worried. Thorn stood, clasped him on the shoulder, and said seriously, 'It looks suicidal to you, Ed, because you've been stained by Washington politics, which most times bears little resemblance to either the law or the Constitution.'

'*Sir?*' Kercheval asked, letting a bit more anger seep into his voice. 'Surely you're *not* implying...?'

'I don't know Washington politics,' the President went on, ignoring Kercheval's rising anger. 'All I know is the Constitution and a little bit of the law. But you know something? That's all I need to know. That's why I know I can choose not to show up for an inaugural or a State of the Union speech, and have complete confidence that I'm doing the right thing. That kind of confidence rubs off on others. I hope it'll rub off on you.' He went back to his desk, sat down, and began to type again on the computer keyboard at his desk. 'We meet with the congressional leadership this morning,' he said aloud, without looking again at Kercheval. 'First conference call is scheduled for later this afternoon, isn't it, Ed?'

'Yes, sir. The prime ministers of the NATO countries,' Kercheval replied, completely taken aback by the President's words. 'It'll be a video teleconference from the Cabinet Room at three P.M. Tonight's video teleconference is with the Asian allies, scheduled for eight P.M. Tomorrow will be the second round at ten A.M. with the nonaligned countries of Europe and Central and South America.'

'Any advance word?'

'The general assumption is that you're going to announce the removal of peacekeeping forces from Bosnia, Macedonia, and Kosovo,' Kercheval replied. 'That rumor started last week. Already, France and Great Britain have announced their intention to pull out if we pull out. Russia has already hinted they will pull out of Kosovo, but our formal announcement might make them change their mind. Germany will likely stay in both Kosovo and Bosnia.'

'Why is that?'

'It's right on Germany's doorstep, and the Balkans have been of great German interest for centuries,' Kercheval said. 'Unfortunately, most of the historical connections are negative ones, especially the more recent ones. The Third Reich received a lot of support from sympathizers in the Balkans in their quest to wipe out "unclean" races like Jews and Gypsies. Germany has continued to be a close supporter of Croatia – they fully sponsored Croatia's admittance into the United Nations, long before their break from Yugoslavia, and they have supported Croatia's attempts to get land and citizen's rights from Bosnia. Besides, Germany sees itself as the one and only counter-balance to Russian encroachments in the Balkans. They'll stay.'

'I need to know for certain,' President Thorn said. 'Let's get Minister Schramm on the line before the teleconference. I'm committed to our plan, but I don't want to leave our allies flat-footed.'

'Mr President, this will simply not be taken any other way except as the United States with-drawing from an unwinnable situation in the Balkans,' Kercheval said. 'It will absolutely throw US foreign policy into chaos!'

'I disagree, Ed—'

'Our allies will see it as nothing but the United States turning tail and running away,' Kercheval went on angrily. 'We have risked too many lives over there to just turn our backs now!'

'*Enough,* Mr Kercheval,' the President said. The room was instantly quiet. Everyone in the Oval Office noticed it – that little bit of an edge to the President's voice, the one many people knew was under the surface but had just not been seen before.

The President was an ex-Army Special Forces officer, well-trained in commando tactics and experienced in various methods of killing an enemy, and a man doesn't live that kind of life without certain traits being indelibly engrained into the psyche. Thorn's political opponents saw this as an opportunity to try to portray the upstart as a potential mad dog and had exposed his military background in grisly, bloodcurdling

105

detail. They had maintained, and the Pentagon finally confirmed, that as an Army Special Forces platoon leader, Thorn led over two dozen search-and-destroy missions in Kuwait, Iraq, and – secretly – into Iran, during Operation Desert Storm. Needless to say, the fact that US forces had been secretly in Iran during the war, with America promising not to threaten Iran as long as it stayed neutral, did not sit well with Iran or with many nations in the Persian Gulf region.

As a first lieutenant, Thomas N. 'TNT' Thorn had commanded a Special Forces platoon tasked with sneaking deep into various enemy-held territories and lazing targets for precision-guided bombing missions. He and his men were authorized to use any and all means necessary to get close enough to a target to shine it with a laser or mark it with a laser frequency generator so that the target could be hit by laser-guided bombs dropped from Army, Air Force, and Navy attack planes or helicopters.

His own accounts and those of his men told the story: he had pulled the trigger of a weapon or withdrawn a blade in combat over a hundred times, and had confirmed kills on over a hundred men. Most were from relatively short distances, less than fifteen yards, using a silenced pistol. Some were from almost a mile away, where the bullet reaches its target before the sound. A few had been from knife-fighting distance, close enough so Thorn could feel his victim's final gush of breath on his hand as he drove a knife into an unprotected neck or brain stem. This didn't include the countless number of enemy forces killed by the laser-guided bombs he and his team had sent to their targets – the estimated final 'head count' was well into triple digits.

But rather than horrifying the voters, as the opposition candidates had hoped, it had drawn attention to him. At first, of course, it had been the spectacle – everyone wanted to see what a real-life assassin looked like. But if they had come to see the monster, they had stayed to hear the message. The message had soon become a campaign, which had become a race, which had become a president. But though most had never seen the monster, they assumed it still existed.

They had caught a glimpse of it just now.

'I'd like to speak with Minister Schramm after the meeting with the congressional leadership, but before the videoconference,' the President said, and this time it was an order, not a request or suggestion. 'Set it up. Please.' At that, the meeting came to an abrupt and very uncomfortable end.

Office of the President, The Kremlin, Russian Federation
the next morning

'It cannot be true,' the president said. He took a sip of coffee, then set the cup back on its delicate china saucer and stared off through the window of his office into the cold rain outside. 'It is amazing what a few weeks can do.'

'The report has not yet been confirmed, Mr President,' Army General Nikolai Stepashin replied, refilling his coffee cup. 'It may not be true. It may be an elaborate hoax, or a security test, or a joke.' The general, wearing a civilian suit too big for him and a tie too small, still looked very much like the grizzled field commander that he was. He downed the coffee, his third that morning, but craved more. 'But the information in the intercept was so crazy, and the Chancellor's reaction so strong, that I thought it best to pass it along.'

'Tell me what this means,' Valentin Gennadievich Sen'kov, president of the Russian Federation, said. 'Someone please tell me what in *hell* this means.' Sometimes, Sen'kov thought, the more he learned, the less he knew, and he understood even less.

Fifty-two-year-old Valentin Gennadievich Sen'kov was the leader of the Russia All-Fatherland Party, formerly the Liberal Democratic Party under Sen'kov's mentor and friend, President Vitaly Velichko. But when Velichko was killed in the joint American-Ukrainian attack on Moscow following Russia's attempt to reunite its former empire by force, Sen'kov, a former KGB agent and former prime minister, had been named acting president. He had been quickly voted out of office in the national elections that soon followed; his name and that of his party had been so tainted by Velichko's failure that he'd had the name of his political party changed so the Russian people might not recognize it and associate it with past failures. He'd held on to his seat in the Federation Council, the Russian Parliament's upper house, by his very fingernails.

When the reformist government of Boris Yeltsin

had failed to lift Russia out of its economic, political, and morale doldrums, Sen'kov and his new Russia All-Fatherland Party had been called upon to support the government and help restore the citizens' confidence in it. Yeltsin had been able to hold on to power only by bringing back Sen'kov, and with him a few vestiges of the old Soviet-style authoritarian government. Sen'kov had finally been back in the Kremlin, no longer an outcast, first as foreign minister and then as prime minister. When Yeltsin, helpless in his alcoholic haze, had been forced to resign in disgrace, Valentin Sen'kov had been chosen by a unanimous vote of Parliament as acting president. His election, just four months before the US elections, had been a landslide victory for the conservative Neo-Communist Party.

Sen'kov seemed to take over where Velichko had left off, but this time the Russian people had responded positively to his political views and actions. Sen'kov immediately crushed the rebellion in Chechnya; he pledged to modernize Russia's nuclear arsenal; and he resigned his nation from membership in the Council of Europe, the judicial body formed to resolve conflicts between European nations, because the Council had denounced Russia's actions in Chechnya but refused to speak out against the NATO bombing of Bosnia or Serbia. His brand of quiet toughness and conservative, nationalistic ideals resonated well with the Russian people, who were growing tired of seeing their country become nothing more than a very large third-world nation. In the national elections that soon followed, the Russian

All-Fatherland Party under Valentin Sen'kov had captured a huge majority in both the Federation Council and the Duma, and he had been elected the new president.

'What is happening? What are they trying to do?' Sen'kov asked himself. 'The Americans are actually going to leave Kosovo, leave Bosnia, leave the Balkans, leave NATO, *leave Europe?*'

'Sir, what it means, if true, is that the United States is imploding – literally as well as figuratively,' Stepashin said. Stepashin was the director of the Foreign Intelligence Service. He looked at the other members of the president's Cabinet there for the impromptu meeting: retired Rocket Forces General Viktor Trubnikov, minister of defense; Ivan Filippov, the foreign minister; Sergey Yejsk, aide to the president on national security affairs and secretary of the Security Council; and Colonel-General Valeriy Zhurbenko, the first deputy minister of defense and chief of the general staff. 'For years, ever since their president's foreign policy debacles, domestic stagnation – and personal indiscretions – the Americans have been like frightened children.'

'Is the tap in the German chancellor's office reliable?' President Sen'kov asked.

'As reliable as any microwave tap set up over a week ago,' Stepashin replied noncommittally. 'The Germans will undoubtedly find it and shut our tap down. They may already have discovered it and are feeding us crap, just so they can watch us have these early-morning meetings and chase our tails around for a day or two. We may spend a few weeks having to sift through mountains of data and thousands of pages of transcribed phone conversations and find out it is all garbage.' He thought for a moment, then added, 'But usually when a tap is discovered, the chancellor and most of the members of Cabinet retreat to alternate locations or go on a foreign trip until their offices can be swept. No one has left Bonn, except for the vice chancellor, and he had a meeting scheduled in Brazil for weeks. In fact, the Cabinet has had two unscheduled meetings since President Thorn's call last night. I believe the information to be factual.'

'What are you talking about, General?' National Security Advisor Yejsk asked. 'The United States is the most powerful nation on Earth. Their economy is strong, their people are happy, it's a good place to live and invest and emulate. Like Disneyland.' He chuckled, then added, 'Apparently not like EuroDisney, though.'

'Nikki is right,' foreign minister Ivan Filippov said. 'Besides, it's a societal and anthropological fact: the wealthier the nation, the more they tend to withdraw.'

'The United States is *not* going to withdraw from anything,' Minister of Defense Trubnikov said. 'Withdrawing from peacekeeping duties in Kosovo and Bosnia – what the hell, we were all considering it, even before the death of Gregor Kazakov. Great Britain and Italy were looking for a graceful way out; the rest of NATO, the French, and the nonaligned nations will not remain behind if the others pull out.'

'That leaves Russia and Germany,' President Sen'kov said. 'The question is, do *we* want to be in the Balkans? Sergey? What do you think?'

'We have discussed this many times, sir,' National Security Advisor Sergey Yejsk replied. 'Despite your predecessor's talk of unity between Slavic peoples, we have virtually nothing in common with the Serbs or any interest in the civil wars or the breakup of Yugoslavia. The Yugoslavs are nothing but murderous animals – they invented the word "vendetta," not the Sicilians. The Red Army proportionally lost more soldiers to Yugoslav guerrillas than we did to the Nazis. Marshal Tito was the biggest thorn in Stalin's side since that smug pig Churchill. We stood behind the Serbs because that stupid bigoted shit Milosevic opposed the Americans and NATO.' He paused, then said, 'We should get out of the Balkans, too, Mr President.'

'We should stay,' Trubnikov said immediately. 'The Americans will not leave the Balkans. Macedonia, Slovenia, Bulgaria – they want to make them members of NATO. If we leave, NATO will swarm into Eastern Europe. They'll be knocking on the Kremlin doors before we know it.'

'Always the alarmist, eh, Viktor?' Foreign Minister Filippov said with a smile. 'We should stay in the Balkans simply because the Americans are leaving. We milk the public relations value for all it's worth, then depart when we can sell that to the world, too. We are staying to keep the warring factions apart; now we're leaving because we have restored peace and stability to the Balkans.'

'The problem is, getting out before our forces lose any more soldiers like Gregor Kazakov,' Yejsk added. 'If we sustain heavy guerrilla losses and then depart, we look like cowards.'

'Russia will not flee either Chechnya or the Balkans,' Sen'kov said resolutely. 'I like the public relations idea best of all. If it is true, and the Americans leave the Balkans, it will be seen as a sign of weakness. We can exploit that. But remaining in the Balkans might be a waste of resources at best and dangerous at worst. After a few months, maybe a year, we depart.' He turned to General Zhurbenko. 'What about you, Colonel-General? You have been rather quiet. These are your men we are talking about.'

'I met with Pavel Gregorievich Kazakov, the night the caskets returned to Moscow,' he said solemnly. 'He was angry because you did not attend the return.'

'Pavel Gregorievich,' Sen'kov muttered bitterly. 'A chip off the old block, except his piece flew in an entirely different direction. We did a profile of the families of the dead soldiers that could attend the service, General. I was advised that it would be politically unpopular for me to attend. The analysis proved correct: Gregor's wife virtually spat on the flag, in front of the other families. It was a very ugly scene. It only heightened whatever power Pavel Gregorievich has in this country.'

'I spoke with him at length, and so did my aide,' Zhurbenko said. A few of the president's advisors smiled at that – they were well familiar with some of Major Ivana Vasilev's unique talents and appetites. 'Pavel Gregorievich doesn't want power, he wants wealth.'

'And he is getting it, I suppose – a hundred drug overdoses a day in Moscow, because of uncon-

113

trollable heroin imports by scum like Kazakov,' Stepashin said acidly. 'A mother will sell her baby for a gram of heroin and a hypodermic syringe. Yet Kazakov jets around the world, to his homes in Kazakhstan, Vietnam, and Venezuela, raking in money as fast as he can. He does not deserve to bear Gregor Mikhailievich's name.'

'Did he threaten you? Did he threaten the president?' National Security Advisor Yejsk asked.

'No. He made us an offer,' Zhurbenko replied in a quiet voice. 'A truly remarkable, unbelievable offer.' He had agonized over the decision to tell the president and the Security Council about Kazakov's incredible proposals. He had harbored ideas about trying to manipulate events himself, but decided that was impossible. But if he had the full support of the government as well as the military, it might actually work.

'He says he can sell two and a half billion rubles' worth of oil *per day* with a pipeline from the Black Sea to Albania.' He looked around at the stunned faces in the president's office. 'The plans for the pipeline exist, but it has not yet started because of all the political and domestic unrest in southern Europe, primarily Macedonia and Albania. But if the unrest ceased, or if the various governments turned in Russia's favor, the pipeline project might be accelerated.'

'What was he offering, General?' Sen'kov asked in a low voice.

'More money than any of us have ever imagined,' Zhurbenko replied. 'He wants to invest a quarter billion dollars to build the pipeline, plus another quarter billion in what he calls "divi-

114

dends" to investors. Hard currency, in foreign numbered accounts, untraceable. The pipeline can start flowing oil in about a year. And he offered more – he offered a way for Russia to once again become a great superpower, to regain its lost empire. He devised a way for Russia to earn untold millions of dollars a day in oil income, like a Middle East sheikhdom.'

'How can you believe anything that degenerate shit says?' Yejsk asked angrily. 'He is a spoiled drug dealer who happened to get rich by stinking up half the Caspian Sea with his wildcat rigs. Where is Russia's share of the wealth he has created? He shifts his money around in Kazakh, Asian, and Caribbean banks so fast no one can keep up with it, and yet he argues loud and long that his fees and tariffs from Moscow are too high. He should be reimbursing Russia for destroying the Caspian caviar trade, not to mention the thousands of lives he's destroyed with his heroin imports.'

'Sir, I knew Gregor Mikhailievich Kazakov for thirty years, since before we graduated from the Academy together,' Zhurbenko said. 'I've known Pavel Gregorievich since the day he was born. I was his best man at his wedding when his father could not attend because he was fighting in Afghanistan. He is genuinely angry because he feels the Russian government has let him down, broken the trust with him and the military. Russia and her military forces are dying, sir. Not just because of hard economic times, but from a lack of respect, of prestige around the world. Pavel knew this. And he offered a possible way to fix the problem.'

'It is doubtful to me that Kazakov cares one way or another about Russia or the army, Colonel-General, as long as he gets whatever he wants,' Foreign Intelligence Service director Nikolai Stepashin said to Zhurbenko. 'I knew and respected Colonel Kazakov as well, but I never knew his son to be anything but a wild drug addict who could kill without hesitation if it meant more money or power for himself. The people like him because he is a colorful character, like Al Capone or Robin Hood – both criminals in their own countries. This "dividend," Colonel-General, was a polite term for a bribe. He wants you to use the army for his own purposes, and he is willing to pay you handsomely for it.'

Zhurbenko looked at the other men in the office sternly. 'I know full well Kazakov was offering me a bribe. I'm not interested in Kazakov's bribes – to him, it's a normal way of doing business. I do not work that way,' he said. 'And when it comes to killing, Nikolai, you and I are both trained to do it without hesitation or moral question. He does it for the money – we do it for the honor of serving Russia. He may be a gangster, but he also gets results.

'But forget about the bribe. Think about the opportunity to bring some nations back into our sphere of influence. We use the army or we use Kazakov's money – it's just a different form of power, a different tool of government and foreign relations. The outcome is the same – the enhancement of the power and security of mother Russia. I think it is worth a look.'

The Cabinet officials looked at the floor,

quietly, for several very long moments; there were no outbursts of outrage or indignation, no protests, no denials. Finally, one by one, they looked at President Sen'kov.

'I am *not* going to soil my first elected term in office by getting involved with bloodthirsty gangsters like Kazakov,' President Sen'kov said. 'He will not dictate foreign policy. Colonel-General Zhurbenko, stay away from that hoodlum.'

'But sir...'

'I understand his father was your friend, but it is obvious to me that even Colonel Kazakov wanted to stay as far away from his son as possible,' Sen'kov said. 'He is a murderous animal, and we have our hands too full as it is with antigovernment terrorists to worry about dealing with underworld drug lords. That is *all*.'

The High Technology Aerospace Weapons Center, Elliott AFB, Groom Lake, Nevada that evening

As she expected, there he was, and her heart sank. Better try one more time, she thought, although she already knew how the conversation would go.

'Hey, Dave,' Captain Annie Dewey said, as she activated the retina scan lock and entered the engineering lab. 'The shuttle leaves in ten minutes. Are you ready?'

Colonel David Luger looked up from his computer terminal, looked at the clock, then looked at his watch and shook his head in surprise. 'Oh, no. Man, is it that late already?' he asked. 'I'm sorry. I lost track of time.'

'No problem,' Annie said, trying to sound cheerful. 'But we'd better hurry.'

'Okay. This'll work.' He furiously typed in more instructions, waited for a response, then waited some more. He glanced at Annie and gave her a sheepish smile, glanced at his watch again, and then at the screen. A few moments later, he shook his head. 'Man, the mainframe is slow tonight.'

'Dave, we have to leave. It takes ten minutes just to get to the shuttle terminal.'

'I know, I know, but I can't back out until this subroutine is finished. It'll only take a second.' She walked over to him and massaged one of his shoulders. She took a peek at the screen. Just by reading the heading, she knew what project he was working on, and knew he'd never be able to leave it at this point. As if confirming what she already guessed, Dave shook his head, muttered an 'Oh, no, don't do this to me,' and punched in more instructions.

'Problem?'

'I hate to do this to you, Annie,' Luger said, 'but I need to finish debugging this routine and upload it to the firmware lab tonight so they can get the processor ready to install on an LRU motherboard for its test flight. This is a new error code, and I have to track it down. I'm sorry, but I don't think I can go with you tonight.'

'C'mon, Dave,' Annie protested. 'This is the third weekend in a row you'll be stuck out here. We've had to excuse ourselves out of four events at the last minute. On Monday I head off to Ukraine to help bring in the bombers for the joint NATO exercises – I'll be gone for a week.'

'I'm sorry, Annie, but this can't be helped.'

'The test flight isn't until Monday morning,' Annie reminded him. 'This is Friday night. I know you'll be back out here tomorrow and Sunday working. Why not take a break for just one night?'

'I would, Annie. You know that.' She knew of no such thing, but she let that one slip by. 'But I'm right in the middle of this debug routine. If I finish this in the next half hour, I can knock off early and we can spend some time together at home.'

'But the next shuttle doesn't leave here for two hours. We'll miss the party.'

He raised his hands in surrender, but put them back down quickly to enter more instructions. 'I can't leave this routine now, Annie – I'll lose all my work if I exit now, and I'll have to start over. I'll be on the next shuttle home, I promise.'

'That's what you said when we missed the six o'clock shuttle.'

'I can't help it,' he said. 'Why don't you go without me this time? You can spend some time at the party. I'll get a car to take me home, and I'll meet up with you there. Deal?'

Her pent-up anger and frustration let go at that moment. 'David, this is silly. You have six programmers and technicians on your staff that can debug that routine for you in half the time Monday morning in plenty of time to load on the chip.' He turned toward the computer, his head bowed, his hands flat on the table beside the keyboard. 'You have got to think about yourself once in a while. You need a break. You're working yourself to exhaustion. You don't eat, you don't sleep, you don't socialize.' He seemed frozen, staring blankly into the desk. 'Don't you want to be with me tonight, Dave?' No reply. 'David? Are you listening to me?'

Still no reply – at least, no reply to *her*. When the computer beeped to let him know that it had found another problem, he responded instantly, punching in more code. One moment, he was seemingly immobile, staring into nothingness; the next, he was as animated and alert as ever. Weird.

'All right.' There was no use arguing or ranting at him. They weren't married – they weren't even an official 'couple,' at least not in his eyes. If he wanted to stay, there was nothing she could do to change his mind. 'I'm off. I'll see you at home.'

'Okay, Annie,' David said cheerfully. He was typing away on the computer, his head bouncing up and down to some internal song or rhythm, blissfully going on as if she had not said a word. 'Have fun. I'll be on that next shuttle. Bye.'

Annie Dewey never felt as alone as she did when she stepped aboard the almost full Boeing 727 shuttle plane that would take her from Dreamland to Nellis Air Force Base. Another typical night – alone.

The trick had worked like an absolute charm since his days in high school back in Billings, Montana: the best way to meet women is to help your buddy's girlfriend throw a party. Naturally, she wants to invite all of her girlfriends to the party, so she gives their names, addresses, and phone numbers to you. *Voilà!* Instant black-book update. During the party, he and his friends would find out more about the girls, then update the black book even more. Did they have a car? Their own place? Did they like the outdoors? Movies? Quiet dinners? Wild parties? Did they have money? Were they looking for a commitment, companionship, or just a good time? Then, whatever was planned for the weekend, they would invite the appropriate women to join them. Most important, they were sure to stay away from the ones that wanted a commitment.

Duane U. 'Dev' Deverill, had certainly aged since high school, but in mind, body, and spirit he was still eighteen years old, and loving every minute of it. His entire life had been a study in taking advantage of opportunities as they presented themselves. He had never thought of himself as college material, but seven years after the end of the Vietnam War, the Air Force had been tempting young men and women with full four-year college scholarships to boost enrollment, so Dev had signed up. He'd never thought of himself as a flyer, but he'd accepted a navigator slot. He'd been the top graduate in his class and had had his choice of the best assignments right out of navigator training. He'd chosen the best assignment available: weapons systems officer aboard the then brand-new F-15E Strike Eagle fighter-bomber. As a young captain, he'd been a flight commander during Operation Desert Storm in his F-15E squadron and racked up an impressive mission effectiveness rating and an Air Medal for his outstanding performance in combat.

Despite a meteoric career progression, he'd left the active-duty Air Force and joined the Kansas Air National Guard, flying the B-1B Lancer bomber. When the One-Eleventh Bomb Squadron of the Nevada Air National Guard had started recruiting for experienced crew members to form their new B-1B squadron in Reno, Deverill had joined immediately. He'd become one of the unit's full-time Guardsmen, helping to turn the fledgling unit into one of the best combat units in the United States Air Force. Dev had remained the same ever since he'd left Montana: supremely confident without being too arrogant, knowledgeable without being tiresome, aggressive without being annoying. He knew he was good, and everyone else knew he was good. If they forgot that fact, he was right there to remind them, but otherwise he was content to stay just a head above everyone else around him without stepping on anyone on his way to the top.

While the One-Eleventh 'Aces High' was on temporary duty at the Tonopah Test Range, and a few of their bombers were undergoing modification at Dreamland, Dev shared a two-bedroom apartment with another Air Force officer, a public affairs officer at the Fifty-seventh Wing at Nellis Air Force Base, outside of North Las Vegas. It was a classic 'bachelor pad,' and they took full advantage of it every chance they had. The apartment complex had a nice clubhouse available for the tenants to use for parties, along with the required pool, spa, and fitness center.

Right now, Dev was in 'intelligence collection' mode at a party he was throwing for his roommate's girlfriend's birthday. Along with steering guests toward the drinks and food and making introductions, Dev was also gathering information on the women he didn't recognize. He was a master at making each and every bachelorette feel special and welcome without alienating or favoring any of them.

He was in the middle of yet another introduction when a newcomer caught his eye – and he found his legendary cool suddenly fizzle.

What was it about Annie Dewey that excited him? he wondered. There were plenty of great looking women here, most of them not in the Air Force; many of them had successful entry-level or mid-level managerial careers, and a couple of them were better-looking than Annie. He couldn't quite identify what it was that attracted him to her.

Annie was trim and athletic, bordering on thin – typical Air Force. Concerned that she would be discriminated against by other Air Force pilots because women did not have as much upper-body strength as men, Annie had changed her exercise regime to include more upper-body strength sports such as rock climbing and volleyball. The difference showed: Dev noticed well-defined shoulders, back, and arms, tapering down to a thin waist, tight butt, and shapely legs. She did not have very big breasts, but the rest of the package more than made up for that.

It was his opinion that other men saw her physique, her many female friends and far fewer male friends, and her profession, and assumed

Annie was gay. Truthfully, Dev had thought so, too – or else he had never really thought too much about her at all. But then he'd started noticing her and the HAWC chief of aerospace engineering, Colonel David Luger, together all the time, and he'd noticed that little whatever-it-was about her come alive. That's what had made whatever attracted him to her ignite.

And, he noticed, Luger wasn't with her tonight. She was dressed nicely, in a silky form-fitting dress with thin spaghetti straps, sandals, and a little gold ankle bracelet on her right ankle. Her light brown hair was up, as usual, but in a flight suit it made her look a little butch – in that dress, it exposed her thin neck and well-defined shoulders, making her look even more attractive. He looked hard without trying to stare to see if she was wearing a brassiere, and realized with a faint shock that she wasn't. She was so buff that very little beneath that silky dress jiggled at all.

What was it about her? It wasn't pure sexuality, although she certainly was sexy. Allure, Dev thought, that's what it was. Allure. She was alluring. She was obviously looking for something or someone in her life, but she was willing to stay out of the spotlight and wait until she found it. Dev definitely sensed a deep, smoldering passion inside her. Even if she had been gay, she still would've had that animal allure about her – now that he realized she probably wasn't, it made him think even more about the possibilities of unleashing some of that passion in his direction.

He hoped to hell Luger wasn't her type. To be honest, Dev had no idea whose type Luger could be. He seemed a nice enough guy, just a little detached, distracted, out of place. Annie had some kind of connection with him. Either she saw something in that weird engineer from Texas, or she was throwing a pity party for him. A romantic connection? Luger didn't seem the type. Maybe he was the gay one.

'Heels!' Dev said, as their eyes met. Most everyone at the squadron knew everyone else by their call sign – it was unusual for someone to use their Christian names in casual conversation. He came over and gave her a quick peck on the cheek, then reached up and squeezed her shoulders in his hands. Good God, he thought, I wish I had shoulders that tight. 'Thanks for coming.'

'Thanks for inviting us.'

She used the word 'us,' Dev noticed, but she was alone. Her voice told him that she was disappointed at not being an 'us' at the party. 'Where's Colonel Luger?'

'Still out at the lake,' Annie said. They called Elliott Air Force Base, near dry Groom Lake, the 'lake' when away from there. 'Sorry he can't make it.'

'I know he has a pretty important test coming up,' Dev said. 'Those HAWC guys get obsessed when a big test is happening. They all seem to disappear in their little rabbit holes, afraid to do anything that might screw things up. Problem is, they're *always* like that, even when they've done good.'

'They're not exactly party animals,' Annie agreed. She looked around the room, then at him, then around to the pool area.

'I hope you brought your suit,' Dev said. 'The pool is nice and cool, and the hot tub will be perfect once it starts to cool down outside.'

'I should have brought a suit, but I didn't.'

Dev was going to give her his standard line, 'Well, you know, around here, bathing suits are optional,' but for some reason he didn't use it on Annie. Was he afraid of offending her, chasing her away? He was amazed at his own odd feelings. Since when did he care so much about what others, especially women, thought of him?

'We can get you a suit if you'd like to go swimming later,' Dev offered, 'or just take a rain check.' She smiled at him – he was pleased to think he had said the right thing, caring and helpful without being too pushy. 'Can I get you something to drink? I make a pretty good margarita. I'm doing mango and strawberry tonight.'

'I'm not into that stuff,' she said. That was the first hint of resistance from her, and his hopes sank. But then she suddenly stopped looking past him, took a deep breath as if she had just decided something, and said, 'But if you're making margaritas, I know you have tequila, and I see some Coronas around, so I'll start with a shot and a Corona.' She looked directly at him with incredible liquid blue eyes that looked like they could stop a freight train in its tracks, and asked, 'Care to join me?'

Dev smiled and nodded. 'Best offer I've had all day,' he said.

The party had ended just before midnight, but for Dev and Annie it was only getting started.

They stayed and talked well after everyone else had gone. They both quit drinking shots before too long, but had nursed their Coronas and then white wine and San Pellegrino. After one A.M. the apartment complex residents stopped coming down to the pool and hot tub, so they decided to give the hot tub a try.

The pool deck was dark, illuminated only by a few sidewalk edge lights, step lights, and the parking lot lights several dozen yards away. Both Dev and Annie wore bathrobes, and carried plastic cups of Chardonnay to the spa. The hot, dry desert air cooled quickly after sunset, and there was a breeze blowing, so it felt much cooler now. 'Man, I've been in the hot sun all day, but I'm ready for the hot tub,' Dev was saying. He turned on the bubble pumps, set his wine down on the concrete deck, shed the robe, revealing his black Nike bathing suit underneath, then sat on the edge of the spa and let his feet dangle in to test the water. 'Perfect,' he said. He took a sip of wine. 'I'm glad you could–'

He stopped and gulped. Annie took off her borrowed bathrobe – revealing only her birthday suit. Her breasts were indeed small, but larger than they appeared beneath her dress, and incredibly firm. Her shoulders and arms were not just well-toned – they were ripped, as were her stomach and thigh muscles, lean, taunt, and striated. She watched him closely as she eased into the warm bubbly water with a confident, satisfied smile on her face.

'I – I hung a bathing suit on the doorknob for you,' he reminded her.

'I know. I saw it. Thank you,' she said. 'That was a very considerate thing to do. You don't mind I didn't use it, do you, Dev?'

'Are you kid... I mean, no, not at all, Heels.' She leaned back, her elbows back on the edge of the spa with her breasts tantalizingly obscured within the bubbles on the water's surface, and sipped her wine. He felt like a dork now, with a bathing suit on, so after he got into the hot tub, he slipped it off and placed it on the edge of the tub.

After several long moments, he stopped trying to get a look at her breasts and relaxed. As always, his attention drifted up to the sky. The nearby buildings and the lights from the parking lot washed out most of the sky, but he could still see a few stars shimmering overhead. 'Finally starting to see the summertime constellations,' he said. 'That's Vega, in the constellation Lyra. You can just start to see the head of Scorpio down over the building.'

'Must be a navigator thing, having to learn all the stars and constellations,' Annie said.

'They still taught celestial navigation in nav school when I went through,' Dev said, 'although they phased it out shortly after I left. They taught us how to use a sextant, do a precomp – figure out what the star positions are *supposed* to be – shoot the stars, sun, and moon, and plot a celestial, pressure, and speed line of position. Get two good star shots with a small bubble and a steady autopilot, add in a good pressure LOP and a true airspeed line from a good air data system, and a good nav could plot your position within five to ten miles.'

'Five to ten *miles?*' Annie exclaimed.

'I know – ridiculous, huh?' Deverill agreed. 'The absolute worst inertial nav system back then could keep you within a mile or two with an update every thirty minutes. Nowadays, the worst INS gets you within a quarter-mile with one update, and GPS can get us within six feet. But it was pretty amazing to think that navs throughout history fought wars across the oceans with little more than a star to guide them. It's a lost art.'

'Show me what you're looking at,' Annie said. She picked up her cup of wine and waded over to him, turned around, and sat beside him, then leaned back against his chest. It both shocked and pleased him at the same time. The damned bubbles still obscured her breasts. He put his left arm around her shoulder and across her neck, clasping her right shoulder, and he could feel her nipples against his arm. Stars, Dev, he shouted at himself, think of *stars* now, celestial navigation, precomps, star tables, air almanacs

'Now, what were you looking at?' she murmured. Her head was tilted back against him, the back of her head in the water, but she wasn't looking at the stars.

'I was trying to look at you,' he said softly, and he bent down to kiss her lips. A bolt of electricity shot through his body, the physiological responder he was trying hard to distract sprang to life, and he kissed her deeper, harder. She returned the kiss, then took his hand from her shoulder and placed it on her breast. 'God, Annie, you are so sexy.' She said nothing, but her right hand drifted down to his stomach, then his thigh, and then to his fully attentive and waiting member. She stroked him a couple times. He moaned with pleasure ... and then realized she had stopped. 'Annie, *please*...'

'I can't, Dev,' she whispered. She reluctantly twisted away from him, moved away from him – not to the other side of spa out of reach, but definitely apart from him – and laid her head back on the edge of the spa and covered her face. 'I'm sorry, Dev. It is not you, believe me ... *believe* me.'

'Then what is it?' But he knew the answer the second he asked the question: 'Luger. You're in love with him or something.'

'Or something,' she said. 'I wanted to, but ... I don't want this to turn into a retribution thing.'

'You mean, sleeping with me just to get back at Luger.'

Annie nodded. 'I'm sorry, Dev. I mean, you're great-looking, and you got a great bod, and you got the eyes, and the butt...'

'Wow. Women really talk like that about guys?'

'Only certain guys,' she said, with a smile. He liked her warm, honest smile. He'd never thought of her as a friend before, only as a colleague and maybe a future conquest, but now he was talking to her like a friend, and he enjoyed it. He still wanted to see her underneath him or on top of him, but it wasn't an urgent need anymore.

'So what's the story with you two?'

'What's to tell?' she replied. 'I fell for him, I thought he fell for me. But he's got his work, and that's pretty much his whole life right now.'

'You said "right now" like you don't really believe it.' She looked at Dev, angry that he'd said it – and angry that he was right. 'Listen, Annie, if you say women talk about men like I know men talk about women, then men and women are more alike than they are different, right?' Annie said nothing. 'So the only thing you can be certain about is that you can't change a guy. Dave Luger will be the same as long as he wants to be, as long as whatever he gets out of work is more important or more pleasurable than what he gets from other people. It sucks, but that's the way it is.'

'So what do I do about it?'

'Annie, everybody does the same thing,' Deverill said earnestly. 'You're here in this hot tub for the same reason that Colonel Luger is there in the lab – because whatever you're looking for here, whatever you hoped to find here, is better than waiting alone in your apartment for a man that will probably never come.'

'If I want to be here, then why do I feel so bad about it?'

'Because you have feelings,' he replied. 'You care about him. You care about what he might think. But you have to trust yourself. Trust your feelings.' He paused, regarding her thoughtfully, then asked softly, 'You love him, don't you?'

'Yes.'

'You probably haven't slept with him, but you love him anyway.' She was going to say something angry at him, but she couldn't – because, dammit, he was right. 'Maybe it's the real thing, then,' he went on. 'Maybe you feel guilty because you don't *really* want to be here.'

'I should follow my feelings, then.'

'Absolutely.' She rubbed her eyes, then hid them. It seemed as if she was embarrassed to be

131

sitting there with him, afraid she was showing how stupid and naive she was. He drained his wine, then reached for his bathrobe, preparing to leave. 'Shall we?'

'Yes.' But instead of leaving, Annie put her hand on his arm, firmly, forbidding him to move. She moved close to him, her face a little fearful but excited at the same time, and she reached under the surface of the bubbling water and found him. Despite their very serious, very non-sexual discussion, it sprang instantly back to life like the trouper it was.

'Annie?'

'You said follow my instincts,' she said. She crouched above him, still holding him, then kissed him warmly, deeply, as she maneuvered herself onto him. 'I'm following my instincts. This ... is ... where I want to be, right ... now.'

Chapter Two

Nellis Air Force Base,
north of Las Vegas, Nevada
several days later

'Jee-*sus*, look at those suckers *haul ass!*'

It seemed as if the entire crowd of about two thousand onlookers said the very same thing as two sleek aircraft came into view on final approach to Nellis Air Force Base's main runway. Even from ten miles out, they were clearly visible. Yet unlike most large aircraft, such as airliners or military jet transports, this aircraft didn't seem to be flying slower than normal – in fact, like the fighter jets that escorted it, it seemed to be going very fast indeed.

It used the NATO nickname 'Backfire.' But in the Republic of Ukraine it was known as 'Speka,' meaning 'heat,' and that described the Tupolev-22M perfectly. It looked like a very large jet fighter or a small, compact bomber, with a long pointed nose, sleek lines, variable-geometry 'swing' wings, and two very big, very noisy afterburning engines. It carried a wide range of weapons, including all of the Commonwealth of Independent States' air-launched weapons. It had half the payload of the B-1 bomber, but much greater speed and range; and it was air-refuelable, which meant it could attack targets anywhere on the planet on short notice with minimal support. It was sleek, fast, powerful, and even sexy-looking. All of these

135

factors made the Backfire bomber arguably one of the world's most devastating attack planes.

There were many reasons for Ukraine not to have anything to do with the Backfires, or any expensive offensive weapon system, for that matter. Ukraine, the largest and most populous ex-Soviet republic besides Russia, had one of the smallest gross national products in industrialized Europe – every bit of its industrial output was needed to maintain its fragile existing infrastructure and maintain a modicum of a decent life for its citizens, with hardly anything left over for exports, long-term capital improvement, or warfighting. Despite its geographical and strategic importance, Ukraine spent a fraction of what other countries its size spent on defense, and it would be difficult to maintain the fleet of relatively high-tech planes.

Upon splitting off from the Commonwealth, Ukraine's entire strategic attitude had changed as well. Ukraine declared itself a 'nuclear-free' country, isolated itself from the ethnic and economic turmoil engulfing most of eastern Europe and the Russian enclaves, and resisted joining any outside military alliance. Ukraine had few outside enemies except for its tenuous relationship with its former parent, Russia, so the long-range supersonic Backfires had been considered nothing more than a useless, dangerous money pit. In fact, plenty of countries, including several Middle East countries, had offered as much as one billion dollars each in hard currency for the planes. So they had been too expensive to fly, not apparently vital to the security of Ukraine, and worth billions in badly needed cash.

But times quickly changed, and Ukraine had found it could no longer afford to live in splendid isolation. Russia became more and more reactionary and more aggressive against its former Soviet republics, increasing the pressure on its neighbors to join the new Commonwealth – what many saw as the rebirth of the Soviet empire – or suffer its wrath. When Ukraine had refused to renew its membership in the Commonwealth and at the same time applied for membership in the North Atlantic Treaty Organization, Russia had exploded.

In 1995, Russia had staged a series of deadly attacks against military bases in several of its former republics, including Moldova, Lithuania, and Ukraine. Russia had called these bases 'suspected terrorist training facilities' and threats against Russia and the Commonwealth of Independent States, and had accused their former republics of persecuting ethnic Russians. The Russian attacks had been swift and devastating. Only when Russia had attacked NATO warships on the Black Sea had anyone tried to oppose the Russian war machine. Rebecca Furness, at the time the first female combat pilot in the United States Air Force, and her tiny Air Force Reserve unit from Plattsburgh, New York, had flown a series of precision strike raids deep into Russia that had helped stop the conflict before it flared into a general east European thermonuclear war. Patrick McLanahan, flying the original EB-52 Megafortress, had done the same in defending Lithuania against attacks by neighboring Belarus and Russia.

Already devastated by a slow economy, no

foreign investment, and a general lack of confidence in its reformist government, Russia had finally refrained from any more military forays for several years. It was completely unable to influence events concerning former close friends Iraq, Serbia, and North Korea. Russia, whose landmass spanned almost half the globe's time zones and whose natural resources were unmatched by any country in the world, was quickly becoming a third-rate power.

The rise of nationalist, neo-Communist leaders like Valentin Sen'kov had changed all that. Russia had reasserted its influence in deciding the fate of Bosnia, Serbia, and Kosovo, and it had used considerable military force to subdue the breakaway republic of Chechnya. Ukraine, because of its domineering location on the Black Sea, its large Russian population, and because it hadn't been properly brought into line during the 1995 conflict, clearly saw itself as next in line if it refused to toe the Russian line.

Ukraine's answer: stop acting like a target, and start being a true European power and member of the world community. It started a conscription program – every high school student received ten weeks of military basic training as a condition of graduation, and every able-bodied person had to belong to a reserve unit until age forty – and increased defense spending tenfold. Ukraine had beefed up its Black Sea fleet, started training its ground forces using German, Turkish, and American doctrine instead of Russian, and rebuilt its air forces – including reactivating the Tupolev-22M fleet. Since the 1995 conflict with Russia, twelve of the surviving twenty-one Backfire bombers had been returned to service.

The most important change: increased integration with NATO military command structure and doctrine. Full integration would take many years, but the beginning of this important step in NATO's push toward Asia was taking place now. Two of the supersonic swing-wing bombers were at Nellis Air Force Base in southern Nevada, participating in US Air Force-sponsored joint NATO air combat exercises. They were the most powerful, most anticipated, ex-Soviet warplanes ever to come to America.

'How about we have a little fun, guys?' Captain Annie Dewey asked. The thirty-five-year-old brunette B-1B aircraft commander from the One-Eleventh Bomb Squadron, Nevada Air National Guard, was sitting in the right seat of the Tupolev-22M supersonic bomber. Per United States regulations, a US military pilot had to be on board every multi-crew-member combat aircraft landing on an active military airbase. The nonstop flight from Ukraine to Las Vegas had taken only nine hours, including two aerial refuelings.

'What do you have in mind?' Colonel-General Roman Smoliy, the crew commander, asked. With his square jaw, gray flattop, piercing blue eyes, square nose, and broad shoulders tapering to thin ankles, Roman Smoliy looked like he had been cast for a Hollywood movie. Smoliy was the chief of staff of the Ukrainian Air Force. Before the conflict with Russia, Ukraine had had a force of two hundred intercontinental bombers, equal to that of the United States, a mix of Tu-95 Bear turbo-prop bombers, Tu-22 Blinders, and Tu-160 Blackjack supersonic bombers, along with the Tu-22M Backfires. After the war, only fifty had remained. It was General Smoliy's job to decide if Ukraine should have any long-range bombers at all, and that meant learning how to employ them in battle. 'Nothing boring, I take it?'

'How well you know me already, General,' Annie said. She spoke briefly on the radio, got the clearance she was looking for, then said, 'Escorts, you're clear to depart. See ya on the ground.' The two F-16C Falcon air defense fighters, who had been escorting the big Russian bombers on their flight across the United States, wagged their wings and split off. 'Okay, General, one-time good deal – all the airspace within thirty miles of Nellis, including over Las Vegas, is yours. Show us what these babies can do.'

General Smoliy broke into a wide grin, then reached across the center console, took Annie's hand, and kissed it. 'Thank you, Captain.' He secured his oxygen mask with an excited *SNAP!* and took a firm grip on the control stick. '*Doozhe priyemno*, Las Vegas,' he said. 'Pleased to meet you.' He then jammed the throttles all the way to full military power and swept the wings back as far as they could go. He started a tight left turn back toward Las Vegas, his wingman in tight fingertip formation. It did not take long for the formation to overfly the Strip. They had descended to just a thousand feet above ground level. They did two three-sixties over the downtown, using the Stratosphere tower as their orbit point.

After the second orbit, just to make sure as many

folks as possible were watching, Smoliy called out, *'Dvee, drova, tup!'* and he plugged in full after-burners. The two Tu-22Ms easily slid through the sound barrier, booming all of downtown Las Vegas. He then aimed directly for Nellis Air Force Base. Still traveling well past the speed of sound, both heavy bombers flew down the runway only two hundred feet above ground, creating a double rooster-tail from the supersonic shock wave that could be seen twenty miles away.

At the north end of the runway, Smoliy pulled his throttles back to military power, yanked his bomber into a hard ninety-degree right-bank turn, and swept the wings forward, quickly slowing the big bomber down below the sound barrier. By the time they rolled out on the downwind side, they were at the perfect altitude and airspeed for the approach, and Smoliy and Dewey began con-figuring the bomber for their overhead approach. The second Tu-22M was precisely thirty seconds behind him.

'That was *awesome*, General!' Annie shouted, after she double-checked that the landing gear was down and locked. 'Totally awesome!'

'Thank you, young lady,' Smoliy said. 'I do en-joy watching young excited women.' He nodded to her, then said, 'The aircraft is yours, Captain.' Surprised but excited, she put her hands on the controls, and Smoliy patted her on the shoulder to tell her she had the aircraft. 'Make us proud.'

She did. Annie Dewey made a perfect touch-down on Nellis's main runway and taxied to their parking spot, the applause of the huge crowd aud-ible even over the roar of the idling engines. When both aircraft swept their wings partially back and shut down their engines simultaneously, the applause replaced and then easily surpassed the noise of the engines. After the crew stepped out of their aircraft, General Smoliy drove the cheers and applause to even greater heights when he stepped out to the end of the red carpet laid out for him on the tarmac and kissed the ground. The greetings, hugs, handshakes, and shoulder-slapping went on for a long time. General Smoliy greeted the Air Warfare Center commander, Major-General Lance 'Laser' Peterson, and most of the others in the reception party like long-lost brothers.

The Ukrainian bomber crew members also met other foreign aviators, including the commander of the Turkish Air Force, Major-General Erdal Sivarek, who had arrived with several of his air-craft and two jet transports carrying equipment and spare parts earlier in the day. The big Backfire bombers were parked directly across from the Tur-kish F-16s, and the size difference was astounding. The size difference carried over to the two commanders – the Ukrainian general was almost a foot and a half taller than the Turk. The meeting between the two commanders was cordial but icy; General Smoliy did not reserve the same jovial friendliness for the Turkish officer as he did his American hosts.

'General Sivarek, *merhaba,*' a voice behind Sivarek said after the encounter ended. '*Gunaydin. Nasilsiniz?*' It was Rebecca Furness, recently promoted to full colonel, the commander of the One-Eleventh Bombardment Squadron of the Nevada Air National Guard, based at Tonopah

Test Range northwest of Las Vegas. 'Do you remember me, General?'

It took only a moment for the Turkish officer to recognize her, and his face, which had been dark with moodiness, brightened considerably. 'Major ... no, *Colonel* Rebecca!' Sivarek exclaimed. *'Siz nasilsiniz?* I am glad you are well.'

'It's been a long time,' Rebecca said. 'It's nice to see you, but it's a time I'd sooner forget.'

Rebecca was the commander of the 111th Bombardment Squadron of the Nevada Air National Guard, the only unit in the United States flying the EB-1C aerial battleship. Until their new base was built in Battle Mountain, Nevada, her little unit of six EB-1C bombers was temporarily located at Tonopah Test Range, or TFR, in western Nevada inside the Nellis range complex.

She had first met Sivarek just a few years earlier, during the Russian-Ukrainian conflict, when a power-mad Russian president had tried to reunite parts of the old Soviet Union by force. The Russians had used the pretext of Russian citizens being abused by governments in former republics to send the Russian Army in to reoccupy the republic. When Ukraine had put up a fiercer than expected resistance, Russia had retaliated with tactical nuclear weapons. The United States, fearful of allowing the conflict to escalate to an all-out nuclear war, had sent in only a few tactical air units to Turkey, including an Air Force Reserve unit from Plattsburgh, New York – Rebecca Furness's old unit, flying the RF-111G Vampire bomber, the first iteration of Rebecca's EB-1C Megafortress flying battleship.

Although Rebecca's unit had acquitted itself well in several skirmishes against the Russians, the general feeling was that NATO and the United States had let their Turkish allies down. Several bases in Turkey and several warships had been destroyed by Russian attacks, yet the United States had refused to commit sizable forces against Russia. Only the heroism of Rebecca's tiny unit, and the desperate bravery of what was left of the Ukrainian Air Force, had prevented an all-out war – and saved Turkey.

'It is indeed a small world. I am glad you kept up with your Turkish. *Agzina siglik!* Health to your mouth.'

'*Tesekkur ederim, efendim,*' Rebecca replied, giving him a slight bow. '*Biraz konusuyorum.* And that's about all I remember.'

Sivarek clapped his hands in approval. 'So, what unit are you with?'

'I'm with the Nevada Air National Guard,' Rebecca replied. Sivarek noted with considerable interest that Rebecca did not go into any details. 'We're participating in some of the exercises with your squadron and the Ukrainians.'

'Very good. I noticed your air force does not fly the RF-111s anymore. I would have welcomed the chance to try our hands at them.' He nodded toward the Tupolev-22M Backfire bomber. 'Those whales will be no trouble for us.'

'They might have some surprises for you.'

'We have encountered them before, over the Black Sea on training flights and patrols,' Sivarek said. 'The Ukrainians seem unsure about pushing them to their full capability. It is understandable,

144

I suppose. But I hope NATO is not counting on them for much.'

'Maybe we can help them improve their tactics.'

Sivarek nodded, his face darkening again, his lips thinning in frustration. 'Your new friends in eastern Europe, I suppose,' he said. 'Turkey has been coming here to Red Flag and other exercises for over twenty years, but it seems as if we get little respect from the United States regarding affairs in our region. But when Ukraine wants to play NATO warriors, the world comes running.'

'I think that's not quite accurate,' Rebecca said. But she knew he was at least partially correct. During the Russia-Ukraine conflict, Turkey had suffered tremendous loss of life and property, but afterward relations between Turkey and the West had mostly gone back to the way they were, as if the conflict had never happened at all. Instead of rushing in to help Turkey modernize its military, NATO's easternmost ally had been left to rebuild and rearm by itself, with no more than ordinary levels of support and cooperation from the United States or NATO.

'You are a loyal American officer,' Sivarek said with a smile. 'I would have liked very much for you to have stayed in my country with your incredible RF-111 fighter-bombers after the conflict.'

'I didn't know that.'

'The RF-111, the Vampire I believe you called it, would have been ideal for Turkey's defense,' Sivarek explained. 'A single aircraft with reconnaissance, counterair, close air support, heavy bombing, antiship, and electronic-warfare capabilities? We would have liked very much to have two squadrons. Unfortunately, you sold them all to Australia. That was a dark day for Turkey.'

'Some would have said it was a bright day for the Kurds and the Greeks.'

'We are not at war with Greece, nor will we ever be,' Sivarek said. 'All parties realize we must find a peaceful settlement to the Cyprus question. But the Kurds – they're a different song. They are butchers, terrorists, anarchists, and spawns of Satan.'

'The sight of F-111s bombing Kurdish villages would have sickened most Americans,' Rebecca pointed out. 'I understand the media paints a different picture than you'd like – they are portrayed as oppressed persons, persecuted by fundamentalist Muslim governments, denied a homeland by both Iraq and Turkey. The government will always be seen as the oppressor, and the Kurds as heroic refugees, like the Jews. Their hardships will be seen as the faithful struggling against tyranny.'

'*Aci patlicani kiragi calmaz* – the worthless don't suffer hardships,' Sivarek said. 'So Turkey, a NATO ally, is scorned by the West. Ukraine once aimed nuclear weapons at your country. Iran once tried to sink an American aircraft carrier and has engineered countless terrorist attacks against American interests, but you court their favor now so you can import their oil and counterbalance a resurging Russian hegemony. Turkey has cooperated with America for thirty years, standing on the front line of defense against Russia, yet we are virtually ignored. What is Turkey supposed to say about this American foreign policy?'

'The old saying goes, if you don't like American foreign policy, wait a few days – it'll change,'

Rebecca said.

'Ah yes – your new American president, the Jeffersonian hippie president,' Sivarek said, with an amused, slightly mocking smile. 'I think he will break up NATO. This will leave Turkey all alone to face the Russians. Very unfortunate. What will you do then? Will you come back then and help defend my country, Colonel Rebecca? Or will you come to the aid of your new Ukrainian friends instead?'

'I don't think the President will ever actually leave or break up NATO,' Rebecca said. 'It would not be in our best interests. But I would very much like to speak with you about your country and your defense needs.'

'Oh?' Sivarek smiled that swarthy, cocky smile. 'You never did mention what unit you are with, Colonel Rebecca.'

'No, I didn't,' Furness said with a sly smile. She extended her hand, and he shook it warmly. *'Gidelim*, General.'

At that same time, when Annie Dewey emerged from the lead bomber's crew compartment, she was met by Colonel David Luger, and she ran happily into his arms. 'Oh, God, David,' she breathed, 'it's so good to see you.'

Luger murmured a 'Welcome back' to her, but she could tell immediately that his attention was elsewhere. When she looked at him after their embrace, she saw him staring with an almost blank expression at the Tupolev-22M Backfire bomber. 'Hey, David,' she said, studying his face with growing concern. 'Everything okay?'

'Sure ... sure...' But everything was not all right. She thought she began to feel his hands grow cold, and she swore that his face was looking paler.

'You've seen one of these things before, haven't you?' she asked. 'I thought you knew all there was to know about every warplane in the known galaxy.'

'Yes ... yes, I know all about "Speka."'

'Speka? What's that?'

'Hey! My copilot! Annie!' they heard behind them. It was General Roman Smoliy. 'Hey you, I did not know you had eyes for any other man but me! Who is this usurper daring to compete with me for your affections?'

David Luger turned – and looked into the face of Hell.

'General, this is my good friend, Colonel...' But Annie's introduction was cut short when Luger suddenly turned and strode quickly away. 'David!' she called after him. But he was quickly lost in the crowd that had come to see the big Ukrainian bombers up close.

Annie turned back to Smoliy. 'I am so sorry, General. I don't know what...' But when she looked at the big Ukrainian pilot, he was staring at the spot where Luger had been standing, with an odd expression on his face. 'General Smoliy? What's wrong?'

'Nothing, *Harniy*,' he replied absently, using his pet name for her, 'Beautiful.' 'It is nothing. I thought I saw ... but it is impossible.' He shook off the image, took Annie's hand, and kissed it. 'He is special to you, no?'

'He is special to me, yes.'

'Good for you,' Smoliy said. 'Very good. Take care of him.' Annie tried but couldn't read any-

148

thing else in the big general's eyes to give her a clue about what was going on.

A few hours later, after the welcoming celebrations and brief meetings with the commander of the Air Warfare Center and the wing commander, the Ukrainian and Turkish commanders were escorted to their quarters, and General Peterson walked over to his secure battle staff room inside the base command post. Two officers were there waiting for them. 'Well, well, so they do let you out of the sandbox once in a while, eh, Earthmover?' he said to one of the men waiting for him.

'Only on special occasions, Laser,' Lieutenant-General Terrill Samson, commander of the High Technology Aerospace Weapons Center, responded with a smile. The big three-star black general extended a huge hand to Peterson. 'You remember my deputy, Patrick McLanahan?'

'Sure do,' Peterson said, shaking hands with McLanahan. 'That job at the Fifty-seventh Wing is still yours for the asking, Muck. Even though you're a bomber puke, you're still the best man for the job. Put your name in the bucket, and you're in the pipeline. I'll pick up that phone and set aside an Air War College slot for you right now. Just say the word.'

'Thanks, General,' Patrick said, 'but I'm very good right now.' In his mid-forties, solidly built and unassuming, his blond hair slowly but surely turning gray, McLanahan looked more at home as a policeman or a high school wrestling coach, but in fact he had spent most of his professional life designing and testing exotic high-tech war-

149

planes for the US Air Force. He had never really aspired to be a wing commander. What he'd really wanted was what he'd just received – recognition of his talents from his superiors. More than anything else, that made his career complete.

'I'll bet you are,' Peterson said, smiling and giving Samson a wink. He invited the two to sit down, then offered them cigars. 'Heck, we don't use the battle staff room for anything these days except when you jokers from Dreamland come wandering back to the real world,' he said, 'so I turned it back into a smoking-okay room. I know it doesn't jibe with the smoke-free Air Force, but what the hell.' At that, both Samson and McLanahan lit up. 'So you want to take a look at the Backfire, huh? You guys going to start flying them up there in Dreamland now?'

'Maybe,' Samson replied. 'They might be the only long-range intercontinental bombers in NATO pretty soon.'

'What are you talking about, Earth–?' Peterson stopped, his jaw dropping open and a curl of smoke escaping. 'Holy shit. The rumors are *true?* The United States will leave NATO? Leave Europe?' Samson nodded. 'Do you have details?'

'Not many I can share with you right now,' Samson replied. 'American units will leave European bases by attrition, which means that units will slowly draw down over time until they become non-mission effective, at which time they'll close down. A few units, especially those involved in treaty obligation duties, will be replaced with Reserve and National Guard units until the treaties can be renegotiated.'

'This is incredible!' General Peterson shouted. 'The United States will simply *leave Europe?* Ignore sixty years of partnership in maintaining the peace and simply *go home?*'

'Afraid so,' Samson said. 'There are already bills before Congress authorizing our withdrawal from NATO, but the President has said he will cut off nonessential funding for overseas units. When they run out of money and can't fulfill their missions, they'll go back to the States. Funding for NATO itself will draw down over five years.'

'Wow' was all Peterson could say. He shook his head. 'What about the other rumors? The Army...?'

'Slash and burn,' Samson said.

'No troops stationed overseas?'

'How about no active duty Army combat troops ... *anywhere,*' Samson said. '*None.* The only active duty Army will be administrative, support, research, training, and special operations. The rest will be Army Reserve and National Guard only, with no overseas bases on non-US-owned territory. If the country needs an army, the President will have to go before Congress and ask for it, and Congress will have to come up with the money. The only forward-deployed infantry troops will be Marine Corps expeditionary forces serving afloat, and Guard and Reserve forces on training days.'

'My God. What is Thorn smoking? Is he crazy? The American people will revolt against him. Europe will be ripe for the picking.'

'That remains to be seen,' Samson said. 'Anyway, we start gearing up for more long-range missions. We're going to start seeing a lot more foreign air forces here at Nellis training with our guys, because now they have to be responsible for defending their own territories as not only the frontline force, but the sustaining force until the US gears up and deploys the Reserves. HAWC is interested in the tactical and strategic bombers, and right now, that's the Backfires and any other forces that can carry standoff weapons. We want to see how the Ukraine stacks up against the Turkish Air Force.'

'Judging by Smoliy's and Sivarek's personal relationship, I'd say we're going to have a wild time in the ranges in the next few weeks,' Peterson said. He studied Samson for a moment over his cigar, then turned to Patrick and asked, 'You going to be playing along with them? Get some of your supersecret toys up there? Mix it up a little with them?'

'What supersecret toys are you referring to, sir?' Patrick asked, then masked his smile with a cloud of aromatic cigar smoke.

'Ah, don't give me that brainwashed bullshit, Muck,' Peterson said, with a laugh. 'All I ask is that if you want to play on my ranges, brief the crews as much as possible on the performance parameters of whatever you'll put up against them. You don't have to give away any secrets – just a heads-up so no one gets hurt. This is still a training environment. I don't want these guys thinking we're chasing them across the sky with UFOs or something.'

'Deal,' Patrick said.

Peterson shook his head again, then took a deep drag from his cigar. 'No Army. The cockroaches are going to be taking over the kitchen now for *sure.*'

Later that evening, several Nellis Security Force officers escorted two US Air Force officers into the isolated revetment area on the east side of Nellis Air Force Base, away from the main parking ramp, where the two Ukrainian Tu-22M Backfire bombers were parked. Already there beside one of the bombers was General Roman Smoliy. He was puffing away on a cigar impatiently as the two officers approached.

'Hey, *Harniy!* Pretty lady captain!' Smoliy greeted Annie Dewey. 'I did not expect you tonight – I expect you to be dancing all night with my men. I told them all about you and those gentle, talented hands of yours.'

Annie Dewey approached Smoliy, and she and the officer with her saluted. Smoliy returned the salute with the butt end of his cigar. 'It is too late, and I am too relaxed, for protocols,' he said. He turned his attention to the other officer and said, 'If you don't mind, Colonel, I want to be with my men tonight. It has been a long day.'

Colonel David Luger said nothing, but stared back at Smoliy, then up at the big Tupolev-22M Backfire bomber behind him. 'This won't take long, General. I promise.'

'Good, good,' Smoliy said. He studied Luger carefully for a moment, his eyes narrowing, then looking askance as if trying to dredge up some long-forgotten images in his mind. He looked again at Luger, opened his mouth, closed it. Luger looked back at him, then removed his garrison

153

cap. Smoliy gulped, his mouth and eyes opening wide in surprise, and he gasped, *'Idi k yobanay matiri...'*

'Da, General,' Luger replied in casual, remarkably fluent Russian. *'Dobriy vyechyeer. On zassal yimu mazgi.'*

Annie Dewey turned to David in surprise. 'I didn't know you spoke Russian–'

'Ozerov,' Smoliy gasped. 'Ivan Ozerov. You're *here?* Here in America? *In an American military uniform?'* David Luger swallowed hard. He hadn't heard that name in years – but it was his, all right.

Luger was a fifteen-year Air Force veteran from Amarillo, Texas. His aeronautical engineering background and expertise in computers, systems design, and advanced systems design, along with his years as a B-52 bomber navigator bombardier, had made him one of the most sought-after aviation project leaders in the world. If Dave Luger were a civilian, he would certainly be a vice president of Boeing or Raytheon, or an undersecretary of defense at the Pentagon ... and if it hadn't been for the Redtail Hawk incident, he might be head of an Air Force laboratory.

But in 1988, following a secret B-52 bombing raid engineered by the High Technology Aerospace Weapons Center against a ground-based laser site in the Soviet Union, Luger had been left for dead on a snow-covered runway in Siberia, then captured and brainwashed while being nursed back to health by the KGB. For five years, he had been forced to use his engineering brilliance to build the next generation of Soviet long-range bombers.

To the US military and intelligence community, David Luger had been a traitor. The CIA had thought he was nothing more than an AWOL US Air Force B-52 bombardier that had deserted and joined the other side. The security level at the High Technology Aerospace Center was so high that no one, even the CIA, knew Luger had been on the EB-52 Old Dog bombing raid against the Kavaznya laser site or that he had been left behind at the Siberian air base at Anadyr and presumed dead; the cover story, devised by the previous director of HAWC, General Brad Elliott, had stated that Luger had died in a crash of a top-secret experimental aircraft. The CIA knew that Luger was in the Soviet Union, and assumed he had defected. All they really knew was that a highly intelligent Air Force Academy grad, American citizen, B-52 crew member, and member of a top-secret weapons research group with an advanced degree and a top-secret security clearance, had been advancing the state of the art in Russian long-range bombing technology by an entire generation.

He had been discovered and rescued by Patrick McLanahan and a special combined Air Force-Marine Corps Intelligence Support Agency operations team called Madcap Magician just before the CIA had been going to carry out plans to terminate him, at the same time averting a certain all-out war between the newly independent Baltic states and a resurgent Soviet-style military government in Russia. It had taken another five years to deprogram, rehabilitate, and return Luger to his life as an American aviator and expert aerospace engineer.

He'd made it back, fully reintegrated into the supersecret world at Elliott Air Force Base, Groom Lake, Nevada, home of the High Technology Aerospace Weapons Center. He'd won his promotion to full colonel after years of dedicated work, both in his personal and professional life, and had successfully managed to drive the years of torture out of his consciousness. But now, with the arrival of the Tupolev-22M Backfire bomber and its commander, Roman Smoliy, the awful horrors were back...

...because Roman Smoliy, then a young bomber pilot with the Soviet Air Force assigned to the Fisikous Research and Technology Institute in Vilnius, Lithuania, had been one of Luger's chief tormentors.

'Ozerov? Who's Ozerov?' Annie asked. 'Dave, what's going on?'

'It's not Ivan Ozerov, General, it's David Luger,' he said, ignoring Annie, letting his eyes bore angrily into Smoliy's. 'I was never Ivan Ozerov. Ozerov was an invention by a sadistic KGB officer at Fisikous who tortured me for *five fucking years*.'

'I – I didn't know!' Smoliy stammered. 'I did not know you were an American.'

'You thought I was some kind of egghead goofball genius, sent to Fisikous to try to tell you how to fly a Soviet warplane,' David said. 'You took every opportunity to make my life miserable, just so you could be the strutting hotshot pilot.'

'Dave, let's get out of here,' Annie said, a thrill of fear shooting up and down her spine. 'You're really scaring me.'

'Why are you doing this, Colonel?' Smoliy asked, pleading now. 'Why are you haunting me now? Everything is different. Fisikous no longer exists. The Soviet Air Force no longer exists. You are here in your own country–'

'I just wanted you to know that it was me, General,' Luger said acidly. 'I wanted you to know that I'll never forget what you and the other bastards at Fisikous did to me.'

'But I did not know–'

'As far as you knew, I was a Russian aerospace engineer,' David said. 'But I was weaker than you, weak from the drugs and the torture and the mind-control crap they subjected me to for so long. I was *one of you*, for all you knew, and you still shit all over me!' He stepped toward the big Ukrainian officer and said, 'I will never forgive, and I will never forget, Smoliy, you sadistic bastard. You're in *my* homeland now.'

He turned on a heel and walked away. Annie looked at Smoliy in complete and utter confusion, then ran after Luger. 'David, wait.'

'I'm outta here, Annie.'

'What is going on? Where do you know him from? Fisikous? Lithuania? How could you know him from an old Soviet research center?'

They went back to the staff car. Luger said nothing for a long while, until they were outside the front gate at Nellis. 'Annie... Annie, I was at Fisikous. Years ago. I... Christ, I can't tell you.'

'*Can't tell me?* You were at a top-secret Soviet research center, and you can't tell me how or why?' Annie asked incredulously. 'David, you can't keep a secret like this between us. It's obviously some-

157

thing deeply personal, hurtful, even ... even...'

'Psychological? Emotional?' David said. 'Annie, it goes far deeper than that, way deeper. But I can't tell you yet. I'm sorry I brought you along.'

'You brought me along because we share, Dave,' she said. 'We're together. It's not you and me anymore, it's *us*. You asked me along because you thought you needed my support. I'm here for you. Tell me what I can do for you. Let me in.' She paused, then asked, 'Does it have to do with that Megafortress memorial in the classified aircraft hangar? The Kavaznya mission? Those charts, your flight jacket with the blood on it, the story General McLanahan told us?'

'I can't, Annie' was all Luger could say. 'I ... I'm sorry, but I can't.'

'Can't ... or won't?'

He had no answer, no more words for her the rest of the evening. He was silent as he walked her to her apartment door, then as she kissed his cheek and squeezed his hand good-bye.

**Metyor Aerospace Center
IIG headquarters,
Zhukovsky Air Base, Moscow,
Russian Federation
the next morning**

'Thank you for coming, Comrade Kazakov,' Pyotr Fursenko said, extending a hand in greeting. 'Welcome to your facility.'

Pavel Kazakov had arrived at the Metyor Aerospace Center facility very late in the evening, after

158

the swing shift had gone home and the factory and administration building maintenance workers had finished. He was accompanied by two aides and three bodyguards, all with long seal-skin coats. When they set off the metal detectors built into the doorway in the rear of the administration facility, but kept right on walking alongside Kazakov, Fursenko knew they were heavily armed. Kazakov himself was dressed casually, as if he had left his home for a walk around his estate – he resembled many of the swing-shift engineers or middle managers at the plant, working late in the office.

'So, what is so important that you needed me to come at this hour, *eenzhenyer?*' Kazakov asked. His voice was stern, but in fact he was nervous with anticipation.

'I thought very long and hard about the things we spoke about when we met, Comrade,' Fursenko said. 'Someone needs to punish the butchers who killed your father and my son in Prizren.'

Kazakov looked around the first hangar they entered. The huge forty-thousand-square-foot hangar, its ceiling over fifty feet high, was in immaculate condition, clean, well-lit, and freshly painted – and completely empty. The young financier was visibly disappointed, growing angry. 'You, Doctor?' Kazakov asked. 'With this? What do you intend to do? Invite them all here for a game of volleyball?'

'Crush them,' Fursenko said. 'Destroy them, exactly the same way they destroyed our family members – swiftly, silently, in one night.'

'With what, Doctor? I see a bucket and a mop

159

in that corner and a lamp on that security desk. Or do those things transform themselves into weapons at your command?'

'With this, Comrade,' Fursenko said proudly. He walked to the back of the hangar. The back wall was actually a separate hangar door, dividing the massive building into a semi-secure and secure area. He swiped a security card, entered a code into a keypad, and pressed a button to open the second set of hangar doors.

What was inside made Pavel Kazakov gasp in surprise.

In truth, it was actually hard to see, because the aircraft was so thin. Its wing span was over one hundred and forty feet, but its fuselage and wings were so thin that it appeared to be floating in midair. The wings actually swept *forward* – the wingtips were in line with the very nose of the aircraft. The wings swept back gracefully to a broad, flat tail, where the engine exhausts for the four afterburning jet engines were flat and razor-thin, like the rest of the aircraft. The aircraft stood tall on long, seemingly fragile tricycle landing gear. There were no vertical control surfaces – the tail area swept to a point and simply ended, with no visible flight control surfaces whatsoever.

'What ... *is* ... this thing?' Kazakov breathed.

'We call it *Tyenee* – "Shadow,"' Fursenko said proudly. 'It was officially the Fisikous-179 stealth bomber that we built here at Metyor from plans, jigs, and molds we recovered before Fisikous was closed. Over the years we added many different enhancements to it to try to modernize it.'

'"Modernize it"?' Kazakov asked incredulously.

'You don't call this "modern"?'

'This aircraft is almost twenty years old, Comrade,' Fursenko said. 'It was one of my first designs. But back then, I simply did not have enough technical knowledge about stealth design versus aerodynamic requirements – I couldn't make it fly *and* be stealthy at the same time. I worked on it for almost ten years. Then Ivan Ozerov came along and made it fly in six months.'

Kazakov stepped closer to the aircraft and examined it closely. 'Where are the flight control surfaces?' he asked. 'Don't airplanes need things on the wings to make them turn?'

'Not this aircraft,' Fursenko explained. 'It uses micro-hydraulic actuators all over its surface to make tiny, imperceptible changes to the airflow across the fuselage, which create or reduce lift and drag wherever it's needed for whatever maneuver it is commanded to perform. We found we didn't need to hang spoilers or flaps or rudders into the slipstream to make it turn, climb, or fly in coordinated flight – all we needed to do was slightly alter the shape of a portion of the fuselage. The result: no need for any flight control surfaces in normal flight. That increases its stealthiness a hundredfold.'

Pavel continued his walkaround of the incredible aircraft, eventually coming to the bomb bay. There were two very small bomb bays – they looked big enough for only a few large weapons. 'These seem very small.'

'Tyenee was just a technology demonstrator aircraft, so it was never really designed to have weapons bays at all – the bays were used for instrumentation, cameras, and telemetry equipment,' Fursenko said. 'But we eventually turned them back into weapons bays. They are large enough for just four two-thousand-pound-class weapons on each side, about sixteen thousand pounds total. There are external hardpoints under the wings for standoff weapons as well, which would be used before the aircraft got within enemy radar range. Tyenee also carries defensive weapons, built into the wing leading edges itself to reduce radar cross-section: four R-60MK heat-seeking air-to-air missiles, specifically designed for this aircraft.' Kazakov looked, but he could not see the missile muzzles – they were that well-concealed.

They climbed a ladder up the side of the nose to the crew compartment. Despite the size of the aircraft, there were only two tandem ejection seats inside, and it was extremely cramped. Power had already been applied, and the thick bubble canopy had been slid back to its retracted position. The main flight, navigation, and aircraft systems readouts were on three large flat-panel monitors on the forward instrument panel, with a few tape-style analog gauges on each side. Kazakov immediately sat in the pilot's seat in front.

Fursenko knelt beside him on the canopy sill, explaining the various displays and controls. 'The aircraft is electronically controlled by a side-stick controller on the right, with a single throttle control on the left instrument panel,' Fursenko said. 'Those four switches below it act as emergency backup throttles.'

'It seems as if there are no controls to this plane,' Kazakov commented. 'No switches, no buttons?'

'Most all commands are entered either by voice, by eye-pointing devices in the flight helmets where you choose items on the monitors, or by touching the monitors,' Fursenko explained. 'Most normal flight conditions are preprogrammed into the computer – the initial flight plan, all the targets, all the weapon ballistics. The pilot just has to follow the computer's directions, or simply let the autopilot fly the flight plan.

'The defensive and offensive systems are mostly automatic,' he went on. 'The aircraft will fly itself to the target, open the bomb doors, and release the correct weapon automatically. The bombardier in back normally uses satellite navigation, with inertial navigation as a backup, all controlled by computer. In the target area, he can use laser designators or imaging infrared sensors to locate the target and guide his weapons. The defensive weapons can be manually or computer-controlled. The bombardier also has electronic flight controls in the rear, although the aircraft does not require two pilots to operate successfully.'

'This aircraft is amazing!' Kazakov exclaimed. 'Simply amazing! I have never seen anything like it before in my life!'

'The technology we use is at least ten years behind the West,' Fursenko said. 'But it has been well tested and is solid, robust equipment, easy to maintain and very reliable. We are developing standoff attack and cruise missile technology that we hope someday will make Tyenee a most deadly weapon system.'

'When can I fly it?' Kazakov asked. 'Tomorrow. First thing tomorrow. Get me your best test pilot and a flight suit. I want to fly it as soon as possible. When can that be?'

'Never,' Fursenko said in a grave voice.

'*Never?* What in hell do you mean?'

'This aircraft has never and will never be cleared for flight,' Fursenko explained solemnly. 'First, it is banned by international treaty. The Strategic Arms Reduction Treaty limits the number and specifications of nuclear weapon delivery systems that can be flown, and Tyenee is not on the list. Second, it was never intended to be flown – it was a test article only, to be used for electromagnetic lobal propagation studies, stress and fatigue testing, weapon mating, wind tunnel testing, and computer-aided manufacturing techniques.'

'But it *can* fly? You have flown it before?'

'We have made a few flight tests...' Fursenko said.

'Make it flyable,' Kazakov said. 'Do whatever you need to do, but make it flyable.'

'We don't have the funding to–'

'You do now,' Kazakov interjected. 'Whatever you need, you'll have. And the government need not know where you got the money.'

Fursenko smiled – it was precisely what he'd hoped Kazakov would do. 'Very well, sir,' he said. 'With funding for my engineers and builders, I can have Tyenee flying in six months. We can–'

'What about weapons?' Kazakov asked. 'Do you have weapons we can try on it?'

'We only have test shapes, weighted and with the exact ballistics of live weapons, but with–'

'I want real weapons on board this aircraft when it flies,' Pavel ordered, as excited as a kid with a new model plane. 'Offensive and defensive weapons, both fully functional. It can be Western or Russian weapons, I don't care. You'll get the money for whatever you can procure. Cash. I want trained crews, support crews, maintenance personnel, planners, intelligence officers – I want this aircraft operational. The sooner, the better.'

'I was praying you'd want that, too,' Fursenko exclaimed proudly. He turned to the mafioso in the left seat of his creation and put a hand on his shoulder. 'Comrade Kazakov, I've hoped this day would come. I have seen this aircraft stolen, nearly destroyed, nearly scrapped, and all but forgotten in the collapse of our country. I knew we had one of the world's ultimate weapons here. But all it has done in the past eight years is gather dust.'

'No longer,' Kazakov said. 'I have plans for this monster. I have plans to make most of eastern Europe bow to the power of the Russian empire once again.'

With myself at its head, he thought to himself. With no one but *myself* at the top.

Kazakov spent several hours at the facility with Fursenko. While they spoke, Kazakov was on the phone to his headquarters, requesting background information on key personnel involved in the Tyenee project. If they passed a cursory background examination – bank accounts, address, family, time of employment, criminal record, and Party affiliations – Kazakov arranged to speak with them personally. He was impressed with the level of excitement and energy in each member of the project. It all made sense to Kazakov: the only persons who would still be working at Metyor would be persons committed to the company, like Pyotr Fursenko, since other firms in Europe were certainly busier and the future looked brighter than here.

The most impressive man in the entire facility beside Fursenko himself was the chief pilot – currently the *only* full-time pilot at Metyor – Ion Stoica. Born and raised in Bucharest, Romania, Stoica had trained as a pilot at the Soviet Naval Academy in St. Petersburg and served as a naval aviation bomber pilot, flying the Tupolev-95 Bear and Tupolev-16 Badger bombers in minelaying, antiship, missile attack, and maritime reconnaissance missions. He'd served briefly in the Romanian Air Force as an air defense wing commander and instructor pilot in the MiG-21 fighter, before returning to the Soviet Union as a test pilot flying for Pyotr Fursenko at the Fisikous Institute. When Fisikous had closed and the Soviet Union imploded, Stoica had gone back to his native Romania, flying and instructing in MiG-21 and MiG-29 air defense fighters, before accepting a position again with his old friend Pyotr Fursenko at Metyor Aerospace in 1993.

Stoica thoroughly thought of himself as Russian, and was grateful to Russia for his training, education, and outlook on world and national affairs. He thanked the KGB's role in eliminating the dictator Nicolae Ceausescu from power in Romania and restoring a more traditional, pro-Soviet communist regime, rather than the brutal Stalinist one that had ruled Romania for most of his life.

Pavel Kazakov found Stoica to be a hardworking, single-minded, almost fanatical Russian patriot who thought of his efforts to design a high-tech aerospace weapon system to be an honor rather than just a job. When Romania had been admitted to the Partnership For Peace, NATO's group of ex-Warsaw Pact nations being considered for NATO membership, Ion Stoica had emigrated to Russia and become a citizen a year later. Like most of the principals at Metyor, Stoica had been happily subsisting mostly on cafeteria food and sleeping in the Metyor factory in between irregular and sparse paychecks.

By the time Pavel Kazakov was finished with his inspections, interviews, and planning sessions, the day shift had already arrived and the workday was in full swing – which for Metyor Aerospace was not very busy at all. Kazakov was escorted out the back to his waiting sedan by Fursenko. 'Doctor, I am most impressed with the aircraft and your people,' he said, shaking the director's hand. 'I want you to use every effort to get Tyenee ready to fly as soon as you can, but you must maintain absolute secrecy – even from the government. If any authorities come by or anyone asks any suspicious questions, refer them to my headquarters immediately. Tyenee is to remain under wraps from anyone except those whom I have spoken to and cleared directly. Do you understand?'

'Perfectly, *tovarisch*,' Fursenko replied. 'It is indeed an honor to be working with you.'

'Decide that later, after we have begun our work,' Kazakov said ominously. 'You may well rue the day you ever spoke to me out on that tarmac.'

Office of the Minister of Economic Cooperation and Trade, Government House, Tirane, Albania the next morning

The aide was already pouring strong black coffee and setting out a tray of caviar and toast when the minister walked into his office. 'Good morning, sir,' the aide said. 'How are you today?'

'Fine, fine,' Maqo Solis, the Minister of Economic Cooperation and Trade of the government of the Republic of Albania, replied. It was a rare sunny and warm spring day, and it seemed as if the entire capital was in excellent spirits. 'What do we have this morning? I was hoping to get a massage and steam bath in before lunch.'

'Quite possible, sir,' Solis's aide said cheerfully. 'Staff conference meeting at eight A.M., scheduled for one hour, and then a status briefing on Turkish port construction projects afterward, scheduled for no more than an hour. The usual interruptions – trade delegate drop-bys, phone calls from People's Assembly legislators, and of course your paperwork for the morning, all organized in order of precedence. I'll schedule the massage for eleven.'

'Make the interruptions brief and the high-priority pile small, Thimio, and you can schedule a session for yourself after work – on me,' Minister Solis said. He started to flip through the messages that needed answers before the eight o'clock meeting. 'Anything in here that I need to look at right away?'

'Yes, sir – the call from Pavel Kazakov, Metyor

168

IIG.' Minister Solis rolled his eyes and snorted in exasperation, his mood already darkening. 'He wants to schedule a meeting with the Office of Petroleum Resource Development, and he wants you to set it up. He says they will not cooperate without your help.'

'They will not cooperate because Pavel Kazakov is a lying, cheating, thieving, murderous back-stabbing pimp,' Solis retorted. 'He thought he could bribe his way through the government to get approval to build his pipeline to Vlore? I threw him out of my office once, and I will do it again if need be.'

'He says he expects to start construction of the Burgas to Samokov section of the line through Bulgaria within three months, and win approval of Samokov, Bulgaria, to Debar, Macedonia, within two months,' the aide said, reading the lengthy message from the communications center. 'He says he feels your office's lack of cooperation is unfair and biased, and will negatively impact the perception of the project to his investors.'

'Thimio, you can stop reading his ranting – I'm not interested,' Solis said. 'Who in God's name has ever heard of a drug dealer building an oil pipeline? It must be a scam. Contact the Bulgarian and Macedonian development ministries, and see if what Kazakov says is true.'

'Yes, sir.' The aide produced an ornate leather-wrapped box. 'The message came with this.'

'Was it scanned by security?'

'Yes, sir, and examined personally.' Solis opened it. It was a gold, pearl, and platinum watch with ruby numerals, a Rolex knockoff, but a very expensive one.

'God, will he never stop? Get rid of it,' Solis said disgustedly. 'I won't accept it. Turn it in to whatever agency is supposed to regulate foreign gifts, or keep it yourself.'

'Yes, *sir*,' the aide said enthusiastically. He knew the minister could get in trouble for accepting foreign gifts – but rarely did – but aides could not. 'Sir, the message goes on.'

'Go on to the next item, Thimio.'

'I think you should hear this, sir,' the aide said. 'Mr Kazakov says that he will look most harshly on any refusal to facilitate negotiations with the government on completing the pipeline. He emphasizes "most harshly." He further says–'

'He has the *balls* to threaten *me?*' Solis shot up from his seat and snatched the message out of his aide's hand. 'Why, that motherless bastard ... he is! He's *threatening* me with retaliation if I do not expedite the approval process for his pipeline. He is actually saying *'You will live to regret any inaction, but the government may not.'* How dare he? How dare he threaten a minister of the Albanian government! I want the National Intelligence Service on his ass immediately! I want the Foreign Ministry and State Security to contact the Russian government to arrest and extradite Kazakov for openly threatening a foreign minister and a foreign government in an attempt to force us to cooperate with him!'

'Sir, he may be a criminal, but he is reputedly a powerful Russian and international Mafia boss,' the aide warned. 'All of the actions you mentioned are legal and proper responses. Kazakov will follow no such legalistic protocols. If we lash out, he may just follow through on his threats. Someone will get hurt, and Kazakov will probably remain on the loose, protected by the government officials that he bribes for protection. Don't fight this weasel. Stall him, pretend to cooperate, and let the bureaucratic wheels grind away on him. Once he finds Albania uncooperative, maybe he'll reroute to Thessaloniki, as he's threatened to do before, or up through Kosovo and Montenegro to Dubrovnik or Bar.'

'A Russian oil pipeline through Greece? That'll be the day,' Solis said, then grimaced. 'Well, stranger things have happened. Besides, who would want to build a pipeline through Kosovo or even Montenegro? They would have to spend billions to try to guard it, or billions in rebuilding it every year. Those provinces will never be stable enough to make that kind of investment as long as the Serbs are in charge. Even Pavel Kazakov can't bribe all the warring factions.

'No, he wants his pipeline to go through Albania, and Vlore is the logical spot – a sheltered harbor, easy access to the Adriatic and Italy, good transport infrastructure, docks, storage, and refineries already in place,' Solis went on. 'But the last thing we want is a monster like Kazakov to establish a foothold in Albania. If we stall him, express our anger, and throw up enough road-blocks, maybe he'll take his drug money and sell his pipeline interests to some American or British oil conglomerates. That would be ideal.'

'So I should have the staff draft a letter in response–'

171

'Politely acknowledge receipt of his message, but wait until he's complained at least three times before sending the response,' Solis said, with a smile. 'Then have it sent to Kazakov by ground post – in due time.'

'Very good, sir,' the aide said. 'And should I initiate a hostile foreign contact report with NIS and Minister Siradova of State Security?'

'Don't bother,' Solis replied casually, as he began flipping through the morning messages once again. 'Kazakov is a murderous punk, but he's only dangerous in Russia. If he even dares try to step foot inside our borders or tries any strong-arm tactics with us, we'll nail his rotting hide to the wall.' He looked at his aide and winked. 'Enjoy the watch, Thimio.'

Zhukovsky Air Base, Moscow, Russian Federation
several weeks later

Pavel Kazakov had never really known his father. Gregor had spent far more time with his soldiers and his duties, first in the Red Army, then the Russian Army, than he had at home. He had been little more than a distant memory, a stranger to his family as much as he had been a hero in Russia.

At first Pavel had known him only through the letters he would write to his mother. They would sit around the dinner table mesmerized as their father related stirring stories of military life, adventures overseas or on some deployment or exercise. He'd then issued disembodied orders to

172

his three children from the field – study harder, work harder, volunteer for that project or this work-study program. His orders had never failed to have the same dire level of consequences if not followed, even though he was hardly around to enforce them. Later, Pavel had known his father mostly through word of mouth on post or in newspaper accounts of his adventures across Europe and southwestern Asia. He'd certainly been larger than life, and men at every post and every city had had enormous respect for him.

But even as his legend had grown, Pavel's respect for him had dwindled. It was more than just being away from home all the time: Pavel began to believe that his father never really cared for his family as much as he did his uniform. It became much more important for Pavel to see how far he could go to twist the old man's ass than to try to earn the respect and love from a man who was never around to give it. Pavel found out too quickly that he could buy – or force others to give – love and respect cheaply on the street. Why pursue it from a living legend who was never around when it was so easy to get everywhere else?

But after his father's death, Pavel had realized several things. First, their government had let them all down. That was intolerable. But most important, Pavel had let his father down. Gregor Kazakov had had national respect because he had earned it – even from his son?

Nah, that was all bullshit, Pavel Kazakov reassured himself. The government had liked Colonel Kazakov because he was a damned mindless military automaton who accepted every chickenshit job and every useless and mostly suicidal mission without a word of complaint. Why? Because he hadn't known any better. He'd been a brainwashed military monkey who had had precisely one original thought in his whole military career – the invasion of Pristina Airport in 1999. The Russian people had liked him because they had damn few heroes these days and he'd been the handy one. He'd represented not one true inspirational virtue. Gregor Kazakov had been a uniformed buffoon who had died serving a brainlessly bankrupt and inept government doing a thankless, objectiveless, useless peacekeeping mission in a crappy part of the world. He'd deserved to die a horrible, bloody death.

Yet Pavel Kazakov found it useful to invoke the old man's name as he addressed a small group of technicians and support workers in the now closed-off main hangar complex, standing before the amazing Metyor-179 stealth aircraft:

'My friends, the work you have done in the past several weeks has been extraordinary. I know my father, Colonel Gregor Kazakov, would have been proud to know each and every last one of you. You are true Russian patriots, true heroes to our fatherland.

'We have meticulously planned this mission, gathered the best intelligence, prepared and tested the best equipment, and trained many long hours for this moment. The result of your hard work is right here before you. You are the champions. It has been a privilege for me to work beside you to make this mission a reality. I have one final word to all of you: thank you, and good hunting. For Gregor Kazakov and for Russia, *attack!*' The group of about one hundred engineers, technicians, support crews, and administrators broke out into furious applause and cheers.

Maybe the old fart did have some purpose in his life, Pavel thought.

Ion Stoica, the chief test pilot at Metyor Aerospace, and his systems officer, a Russian ex-fighter pilot named Gennadi Yegorov, quickly boarded the Metyor-179 stealth fighter-bomber and performed their power-off, power-on, and before-engine start checklists. The interior of the aircraft hangar was then darkened, the doors rolled open, the aircraft was towed outside, and the engines started. All of the checklists took just a few minutes, because they were all computerized – the crew members had only a few checklists that they themselves had to perform to verify the computer's integrity.

Now they sat to wait for the signal to depart.

Zhukovsky Air Base east of Moscow was an active Russian Air Force military airfield, with several squadrons of Tu-95 Bear and Tu-22M Backfire heavy bombers located there, along with several types of trainers, transports, and other support aircraft. Maintaining secrecy at such a base was not difficult, although it was by far a top-secret facility. The air-field lights were always extinguished before any aircraft launch at night to hide the type and number of aircraft departing – a standard Soviet-era tactic, even in peacetime. Although the main base complex was close by on the north side of the runway, and a small housing area a few kilometers to the southeast, the runway itself was fairly isolated. No one could see the runway complex at night except the control tower personnel and security patrols that ringed the runways during every launch to keep away prying eyes.

About three hours before sunset, two Tu-22 Backfire bombers began to taxi toward the active runway on a scheduled training mission from the main secure parking ramp, east of the Metyor facility. Backfire bombers always did all missions in pairs, from takeoff to touchdown, and so both bombers taxied into position at the end of the runway, staggered so their wingtips were less than fifty feet from one another. Behind them on the hold line was an old Ilyushin-14 twin-piston transport plane, nicknamed *Veedyorka*, 'The Bucket.' Even though the plane was almost fifty years old, it was a rather common sight on most Russian airfields, shuttling parts and mail on short hops from base to base throughout the Commonwealth. It seemed quite comical to see one of Russia's most advanced aircraft, the Backfire, sharing a runway with one of Russia's most low-tech birds.

After extending their variable-geometry wings to full takeoff extension, the Backfire bombers began their takeoff roll. The leader plugged in full afterburner and released brakes, shooting a plume of fire and clouds of thick black smoke behind him. Exactly six seconds later, the wingman plugged in his afterburners, and ten seconds after his leader, released brakes and shot down the runway after his leader. The clouds of black smoke in their wakes seemed to make the night even darker, despite the bright afterburner plume they trailed. When they reached midfield, not yet airborne but close to rotate speed, the Il-14 Bucket taxied forward to the end of the runway. It was required to wait two minutes after the Backfires departed because the wingtip vortices of the two departing supersonic Backfires could easily flip the old transport over.

It never made it to takeoff position. Something happened. The tower controllers noticed a bright spark on the right engine, followed by a flash of fire on the ground, followed a few seconds later by a tremendous explosion as the right engine exploded. The right-wing fuel tank ruptured, sending hundreds of gallons of avgas pouring onto the ramp. The transport was ablaze in less than twenty seconds. The tower controllers immediately hit the emergency alarm, which activated the lights at that spot on the runway and called out the base fire department. Security and rescue crews began to respond immediately.

In the confusion, no one on base noticed when a thin, black, almost invisible aircraft taxied along a midfield taxiway near the Metyor Aerospace facility, pulled onto the active runway, and began its takeoff roll. The smoke from the departing Backfire bombers partially obscured it, but anyone else who might've noticed it depart in the confusion of the fire at the other end of the runway would've thought it was a third Backfire bomber. They may or may not have noticed that the third aircraft used only minimum afterburner power, no taxi lights, no anticollision lights, and no position lights during its takeoff run. Since it started its rolling takeoff run near midfield, it needed every remaining foot of Zhukovsky's fifteen-thousand-foot-long runway before it left the ground, but once airborne, it climbed faster than the Backfires and quickly disappeared into the dark.

Unlike other aircraft flying so close to Moscow's airspace, the Metyor-179 stealth bomber did not use its transponder, the transmitter that alerted air traffic control of its position, altitude, and airspeed; neither did Stoica and Yegorov contact anyone on their radios, or check in with air traffic control or air defense command headquarters. Once its long, spindly landing gear was up, the Mt-179 virtually disappeared.

The Mt-179 Tyenee's flight control computer, coupled with air data and fuel sensors, leveled the stealth bomber at twenty-eight thousand feet – from now on, the computer would automatically adjust altitude based on best range fuel burn and aircraft gross weight, step-climbing as the aircraft got lighter, achieving the perfect balance between the power needed to climb and the faster airspeeds and lower fuel burn at higher altitude. It didn't have to worry about deconflicting itself with other aircraft, staying out of restricted airspace, or getting permission to cross national boundaries: its collision-avoidance system detected and displayed the location of any other transponder-equipped aircraft so it could avoid them in time; and because no radars on the ground could detect the aircraft, it was free to fly any course and any altitude the crew chose. Stoica had to make a couple of precautionary turns in Moscow's airspace to remain clear of some commercial air traffic that might get too close, and a few times they did get a solid 'chirp' on their radar detectors, strong enough to know they might have been detected – no stealth system was 100 percent effective – but otherwise they proceeded on a direct 'great circle' course to their initial point. There was not enough air traffic around Kiev, Bucharest, or Sofia, the three largest cities on their flight path, to worry about deviations.

During the two-hour flight to their initial point, Stoica and Yegorov busied themselves with checklists and updating their intelligence information. The Mt-179 did not have a datalink system that automatically updated their attack computers, as many American and some Western attack aircraft did. Instead, ground technicians sent simple coded messages on a discreet, scrambled satellite communications channel. The ground controllers received information from commercial photoreconnaissance satellites, military communications taps from Zhukovsky and other military sources that they could access, and even news reports on television and on the Internet, then encoded the information and transmitted it to the crew. The two crew members decoded the messages, then made notes and symbols on their strip charts.

Near Cluj, Romania, the flight control computer commanded Stoica to pull the throttles nearly all the way back to flight idle to save fuel, and the Mt-179 Shadow started a shallow descent from about thirty-six thousand feet. In idle power, the cockpit was very quiet. The two crew members finished their checklists, took one last nervous pee into piddle packs, tightened their restraining harnesses and lap belts, and refastened oxygen masks and donned fireproof gloves. The action was about to begin.

The last item on the checklist: Stoica reached back over his right shoulder as far as he could, and Yegorov reached forward and clasped his hand. No words were necessary. That was a tradition they'd started from the first day working together on the Metyor-179 stealth aircraft.

But then, they'd done it before every test flight; now, it was to say 'good luck' on their first strike mission.

As they crossed western Bulgaria and into Macedonia, the radar warning receiver in the cockpit of the Metyor-179 bleeped – but instead of the usual ground-radar S symbol, they saw a 'bat-wing' symbol with a circle inside it. 'NATO AWACS radar plane, eleven o'clock, range forty miles,' Yegorov reported. 'We're coming into extreme detection range now.'

'Here we go,' Stoica said. 'Prepare for attack.' From its vantage point thirty miles east of Skopje, Macedonia, at thirty thousand feet, the NATO E-3A Airborne Warning and Control System (AWACS) radar aircraft, using its powerful AN/APY-2 radar mounted within the thirty-foot rotodome atop its fuselage, could see any normal aircraft flying inside Yugoslavia at any altitude and airspeed, as well as monitor aircraft flying in most of western Bulgaria, Bosnia, parts of Croatia, most of northern Greece, and parts of northern Italy.

Although the Mt-179 was not a normal aircraft, Russian stealth technology such as was employed on the Metyor-179 Shadow was not perfect, and the closer they got to central Macedonia, the closer they got to the E-3 AWACS radar plane.

180

Soon, the radar warning receiver was bleeping almost continuously. They did not want to waste fuel trying to circumnavigate the radar craft, and they would waste even more fuel trying to duck down to low altitude too soon.

But they were carrying the solution – the R-60 defensive heat-seeking air-to-air missiles.

'Acknowledged. R-60s ready for launch,' Yegorov reported. Stoica pushed the power up until the Mt-179 had broken the sound barrier. Two minutes later, Yegorov said, 'Coming in to extreme launch range. Ready to uncage.'

'Uncage missiles,' Stoica ordered. Yegorov hit a switch, which opened up a tiny titanium shutter in the wing leading edge, uncovering the R-60's heat-seeking sensor. His mouth and throat were dry and his forehead damp from the anticipation. In all his years flying for the Russian and Romanian Air Forces, he had never fired an air-to-air missile in anger – now, as a civilian, he was about to shoot down one of the biggest, most important support aircraft in the NATO arsenal. A few moments later, they received a SHOOT warning light. 'Clear for launch,' Stoica said.

'Ready, ready, *now.*' Yegorov hit the launch command button, and an R-60 missile leaped out of the left-wing launch chamber. Seconds later, Yegorov fired a second missile from the right. 'Two missiles away. Bye-bye, Mr AWACS plane.'

'O-1, this is C-1,' the senior controller called on the ship's intercom. 'We've got an intermittent unknown target bearing zero-two-zero, range twenty miles, no altitude. Request permission for

181

beam-sharpening mode.'

The operations crew commander of the sixteen-person NATO AWACS crew, a British Royal Air Force colonel, called up the senior controller's display on his own station. The radar sometimes couldn't see small or weak targets very well until they switched from long-range scan to short-range but high-intensity beam-sharpening mode, which concentrated more energy on weaker targets. 'Clear,' the commander radioed back. 'Crew, radar in narrow BIM, reconfigure.' The rest of the crew needed to know when the radar was going to be switching modes because they could be flooded with targets in seconds – everything from birds to clouds to balloons could show on radar now, until the computer 'squelched' out slow-moving targets.

The unknown target immediately popped into clear view. 'Contact, bearing zero-one-five, range nineteen miles, descending through angels twenty, airspeed six-five-zero knots, negative IFF, designate as Hostile One. Hostile contact, crew.'

'Can we get some patrol aircraft up here to take a look?' the deputy commander, seated beside the commander on the first console, asked.

'Patrol aircraft? What patrol aircraft?' the commander said. 'Our patrols packed up their kits and departed. Thanks to the Americans, we have no air patrols over KFOR anymore.'

It was true. A month earlier, President Thorn of the United States had announced that the United States was pulling its ground and air forces out of KFOR and sending them home. The only American forces in southern Europe right now were Air Force E-3C AWACS radar planes, E-8A Joint

STARS (Joint Surveillance, Targeting, and Reconnaissance System) radar planes, and a Navy-Marine Corps task force off the coast of Croatia in the Adriatic Ocean, plus the Sixth Fleet still operating in the Mediterranean Sea. All other air and ground forces, including almost ten thousand troops in Kosovo, Macedonia, and Montenegro, along with five thousand troops in Bosnia, were gone...

...and not just out of the Balkans, and not just back in the United States, but *gone:* the units had been disbanded, and the soldiers reassigned, offered early retirements, or involuntarily separated from military service.

The United States was in the midst of a massive demilitarization never seen before. Troops were being pulled out of Europe and Asia in staggering numbers. Billions of dollars in military equipment was being sold, given to allied forces, or simply left in place. Virtually overnight, American military bases in Germany, Belgium, the Netherlands, and Norway were empty. Military and civilian cargo vessels were lined up in harbors all throughout Europe, ready to transport thousands of troops and millions of tons of supplies and belongings back to North America.

The European members of NATO and the non-NATO members of KFOR vowed to continue the United Nations peacekeeping efforts in Kosovo and the Balkans, but without the United States, it seemed almost pointless. But the European nations had been demanding a greater role in security missions in Europe, so few could really complain when the United States

unceremoniously left the field and went home –
no one really expected it to happen so suddenly.

'Who's the closest air defense assets we can call
on?' the commander asked.

'The Three-thirty-fourth Fighter Squadron out
of Thessaloniki,' his deputy said, punching up the
unit's satellite and airborne telephone channels to
its command post. 'They have cross-border air
defense arrangements with Macedonia – they can
scramble fighters and have them up here in ten
minutes.'

'Get them up here straightaway,' the commander ordered. 'Comm, C-1, broadcast warning
messages on all frequencies, get that hostile
turned around. Notify Skopje and American
Navy air traffic control about an unknown target
we have marked as "Hostile."'

'And if he doesn't turn around?'

'There's not a bloody thing we can do about it,'
the commander said. 'We might be able to convince Italy or Turkey to send a couple fighters up
to take a look, but even they don't want to waste
any fuel or airframe time on anyone who's not a
threat to their country. We just watch and–'

'*Snap target! Snap target!*' one of the radar technicians shouted. He immediately marked the new
high-speed target with a blinking circle symbol,
then sent an alert to every crew station. 'Designate
Highspeed One ... snap target, snap target, second
high-speed target, designate Highspeed Two.'

'O-1, this is C-1,' the senior controller on board
the AWACS radar plane radioed on intercom to
the operations crew commander. 'We've got target
Highspeed One, climbing through angels forty,

184

range three miles and closing *fast*, speed eight hundred and increasing. Highspeed Two is following the same track, two seconds behind Highspeed One.'

'*Missile attack!*' the commander shouted. 'Missile evasion tactics, now! Shut down the radar! Countermeasures ready!' He punched the HOT button on his intercom panel so he could talk to both the ops crew and flight crew. 'Missile attack, missile attack, pilot, turn ninety left and descend to angles one-zero *now.*' At the same time, the crew defensive systems officer began sending out radar and infrared jamming signals and ejecting chaff and flare bundles, trying to spoof and decoy the incoming missiles.

But it was far too late – once the R-60 missile locked on, there was little a big aircraft like an E-3 AWACS could do to evade it. The missiles plowed into the aircraft with a direct hit, the first missile into the rotodome and the second missile into the forward fuselage section.

He could see it all clearly right in front of him, even though it was over three miles away: the decoys flying out of the AWACS plane, the flares a hundred times brighter and hotter than the aircraft; the AWACS plane trying a steep turning descent, one that the crew had obviously practiced before but still looked so steep and fast that it was doubtful if the crew could have pulled out of it even if they survived the missile attack; then the twin streaks of light, the huge blossoms of flames, the pieces of the jet flying apart, and the rolling, tumbling mass of burning metal and jet fuel on its final flight, straight down.

'Target destroyed,' Yegorov reported.

'I see it,' Stoica gasped. 'My God. How many?'

'Twenty crew members. Sixteen operations, four flight.'

Stoica switched the multifunction display to another mode so he wouldn't have to watch the plane burn on the ground. 'They should have gone home when the Americans did,' he murmured. 'Leaving an AWACS radar plane up here, all alone, with no air cover? It was suicidal.'

'It was homicidal – and we did it,' Yegorov said. 'But we've got a job to do, just like they did. Business is business.'

The Mt-179 Shadow headed southwest, still in a shallow, high-speed descent. As they approached the Yugoslavian republic of Kosovo, Stoica increased his descent rate until they were at five hundred feet above the ground at six hundred knots airspeed. Ground radar coverage was much better in United Nations-patrolled Kosovo, and they had to be at terrain-masking altitude long before they reached the radar pickets. Using the infrared scanner, Stoica could easily see all the terrain even in pitch darkness. Ten minutes later, they crossed the Albanian border and swept down the gently rolling hills across the Drin River valley to the town of Kikesi I Ri, or New Kukes, in northeastern Albania.

New Kukes was a relocated town, built by the Albanian government only thirty years earlier with Soviet assistance; the old town had been deliberately flooded after construction of a hydroelectric power-generating dam on the Drin River. The valley is narrow and hilly, with what seems like a perpetual foggy haze obscuring the ridges and mountain tops nearby. The native population of twelve thousand had swelled to over one hundred thousand with Kosovo refugees, although that number had decreased to just a few thousand refugees since KFOR had established its peacekeeping force in 1999 and allowed the refugees safe passage across the border. The huge Kukes carpet factory employed nearly a thousand workers, and the copper and chromium mines in the region employed another few thousand. But by far the biggest employers in the region were the black-market weapons salesmen, the Albanian Mafia, the drug lords, and the prostitutes, preying on the refugees and supporting ethnic Albanian Kosovar freedom fighters in their continuing struggle to form an independent Muslim nation in Kosovo.

The center of both legitimate and illegitimate commerce in north-eastern Albania was the Kukes carpet factory, several kilometers from the center of town; it was by far the biggest industrial facility in the entire valley. The refugee camps that had been set up near the factory were smaller than before, but the remaining parts of the camp had evolved into a semipermanent series of shacks, tents, and wooden buildings, reminiscent of an Old West mining camp evolving into a real town, with ankle-deep mud streets, wooden sidewalks, almost no running water, and just as many animals wandering the street as vehicles. Several of the larger wooden buildings, two or three stories high, were saloons, restaurants, or shops on the ground floor, with offices on the middle floors and apartments on the upper floors for the wealthier merchants, government officials and bureaucrats, and underworld bosses and lieutenants.

Behind the wooden buildings were the shacks for the workers, and beyond those was the tent city, built by NATO military engineers and international relief organizations, for Kukes' other group of residents – the Kosovo Liberation Army training center. At any given time, over five hundred men, women, and children as young as fourteen and as old as sixty were in training at the Kukes camp by Kosovar instructors, overseen and administered by the Albanian Army. They trained in hand-to-hand combat, mountaineering, land navigation, basic maneuvers, and small-arms tactics, along with political and religious indoctrination courses. The top twenty percent of each class were sent to Albanian regular army bases at Shkoder, Gjader, and Tirana for advanced military training; the top five percent of those, who showed especial aptitude in military arts as well as hotter than usual hatred for non-Muslims, were sent to training centers in Libya, Sudan, Egypt, and Algeria for advanced combat and terrorist training.

Under the NATO peacekeeping umbrella, safe from hit-and-run raids by Serb paramilitaries and border police, the Kukes training camp was allowed to grow and flourish. In exchange for food, housing, and training, the recruits worked the carpet factory and mines, provided security for the smugglers and drug dealers, and did odd jobs around the tent city. An hour before sunrise, with the first hints of the morning light filtering through the low overcast, the day shift workers were having breakfast and getting ready to head to work, and the graveyard shift for both the mines and the carpet factory were just getting ready to leave – when the Metyor-179 Shadow stealth bomber began its bomb run.

The first targets to hit were the antiaircraft defensive emplacements. Like most Soviet-era client-state factories, the Kukes carpet factory had several antiaircraft gun emplacements mounted on the rooftops, mostly twin-barreled 37-millimeter optically guided units with a few single 57-millimeter heavy-caliber guns. Kukes had six 37–2 emplacements and two 57–1 emplacements, scattered throughout the compound, with the 37s at the corners and on the east and west sides of the compound along the river and the 57s in the center of the compound; two additional 37–2 units and two 57–1 units were situated near the hydroelectric power plant east of the town.

But most of these weapon systems had been decimated by the Albanian civil war of 1997 and had been only partially refurbished in response to the Serbian aggression in neighboring Kosovo. The radars and electro-optical sensors had long ago been stolen and sold for food or drugs, leaving the guns with only iron sights with uncalibrated and grossly inaccurate lead-computing mechanisms. The gun emplacements on the dam were not a threat – it was easy to maneuver around them, and the gunners never reacted to the jet's presence anyway. The smaller-caliber guns were probably not a threat, especially if they were only optically or manually guided. But the big 57-millimeter guns could be trouble. They had to be neutralized.

Using the infrared sensor, Yegorov targeted the two gun emplacements from ten miles away, well outside the antiaircraft gun's maximum range. The Mt-179's laser rangefinder/designator clicked down the range. Inside seven miles, the Mt-179 Shadow started a steep climb to three thousand feet above ground. Inside five miles to the target, well outside the antiaircraft artillery's maximum range, Yegorov opened its right bomb bay doors and released a Kh-29L *Ookoos*, or 'Sting,' missile.

The Kh-29L Sting missile dropped free of the right bomb bay, fell for about a hundred feet as it stabilized in the slipstream, then ignited its solid-rocket motor. The missile's semi-active laser guidance seeker homed in on the reflected energy of the Shadow's laser designator. Yegorov had only to keep the crosshairs on the target, carefully magnifying and refining his aimpoint. He steered the missile in for a direct hit on the base of the 57-millimeter gun emplacement, blowing a hole in the roof and sending the gun crashing through to the dozens of workers below. Yegorov immediately switched to the second 57-1 emplacement and sent it crashing through the roof just like the first.

Yegorov then switched his infrared sensors to the front of the carpet factory, targeting another Sting missile at the main administrative entrance to the plant and the last missile at the main worker's entrance, where hundreds of workers were leaving or entering. Each Sting missile had a six-hundred-pound high-explosive warhead, and the devastation was enormous. Secondary explosions from each of the Sting missiles fired on the factory blew out windows with tongues of fire, finally collapsing part of the administrative section. Rolling waves of fire belched from the workers' entrance as the Sting missile broke open gas and fuel lines inside the plant.

Stoica started a steep climb, then rolled left to survey the damage. '*Ahuyivayush'iy*, Gennadi,' he said. 'Right where we planned it.'

'*Shyri zhopy ni p'ornish,*' Yegorov replied. 'Couldn't have missed that if I tried.'

Stoica flew outbound about three minutes – long enough for folks to think the attack was over and start coming out of hiding – then executed an easy turn back toward the plant at five thousand feet above ground. Yegorov immediately locked his infrared sensor on the last four remaining targets: the refugee center, which according to Kazakov's intelligence acted as the terrorist training center; the Red Cross/Red Crescent Aid Center, suspected of being a terrorist headquarters because supposedly it would never be targeted in an attack; the distribution center, where food and supplies were unloaded from trucks or rails, warehoused, inventoried, and disbursed to the camp residents; and finally the building with the largest restaurant and shops, suspected of being owned and filled with Muslim terrorists.

The Mt-179 made only one pass, dropping just two weapons – two PLAB-500 laser-guided fuel-air explosive canisters. Each FAE canister created a cloud of highly flammable gas several hundred feet in diameter. The gas mixed with oxygen in the air, and was then detonated by releasing explosive charges into the cloud. The resultant explosion, resembling a miniature nuclear mushroom cloud, was a hundred times greater than the equivalent weight of TNT.

Over two hundred men, women, and children died instantly in the two huge fireballs; another one thousand persons died or were injured and thousands more were left homeless in the ensuing firestorm as the entire town was consumed in the galloping wildfires caused by the fuel-air explosives. The fires would last for days, spreading to char hundreds of thousands of acres of surrounding forests. Investigators would later find nothing but devastation.

Ministry of Foreign Affairs, the Kremlin, Moscow, Russian Federation less than an hour later

'Minister Schramm. What a pleasant surprise. Good morning to you.'

'Let us dispense with the pleasantries, Mr Filippov,' Republic of Germany Foreign Minister Rolf Schramm snapped. He was in the living room of his residence in Bonn, with only a jogging suit on, surrounded by his senior advisors. 'I am watching the news of your little attack on Kukes, Albania. My God, man, has Sen'kov lost his senses? Or is he not in charge of the government anymore? Has the military finally taken charge?'

'Calm yourself, Mr Minister,' Russian Federation Foreign Minister Ivan Ivanovich Filippov said in stiff but passable German. 'Albania? What–?' He was at home, not even dressed yet. He im-

192

mediately ran out of the bathroom and flipped on the television. Nothing on Russian TV on anything happening in Albania. What in hell was going on? 'I ... I cannot comment on what has happened, Minister,' Filippov said. He couldn't confirm nor deny anything – nor would he, even if he could.

'I want you to pledge to me, Mr Minister, that these attacks have *ended*,' Schramm said. 'No more attacks in the Balkans. You must promise me this is not the prelude to an offensive in the Balkans.'

Filippov was excitedly pressing his radio button that rang his aide's radio – there was no answer. 'I will not promise anything, Minister,' Filippov replied, winging it as best he could. He did not want to say he didn't know what was going on, but he didn't want to admit culpability, either. 'Russia will act in its best interests. We will never negotiate or deal that away. Never.' At that moment, his housekeeper opened the door, and Filippov's aide came rushing in with a thin file. He saw that the TV was on and switched it over to CNN International. Sure enough, there was a remote broadcast from somewhere in Macedonia – it looked like a plane crash.

'What I cannot understand is the attack on the NATO E-3 radar plane,' Schramm went on. 'Why did you attack the radar plane? Are you mad? NATO will certainly find out it was Russia, and they will certainly retaliate!'

'We categorically deny any such involvement!' Filippov retorted – it was an almost automatic response to any such allegation, no matter how truthful it really was. But he still gulped in surprise. *Someone shot down a NATO radar plane?*

This was tantamount to an act of war! 'What will Germany do, Minister?' Filippov asked cautiously. 'You will participate in the investigation, of course. Has Germany already decided to punish Russia?'

'If this is a prelude to an attack by Russia, Minister Filippov,' Schramm fumed, 'Germany and NATO will stand firmly against you.'

Russian Federation Foreign Minister Ivan Filippov suppressed a chuckle – he dared not make fun of NATO or Germany's part in it, no matter how ridiculous or unrealistic it was. Schramm was in no position to threaten Russia with anything, let alone a unified NATO response.

'Mr Foreign Minister, again, I assure you, Russia is committed to the peace and security of the entire Balkan region,' Filippov said, still not confirming or denying any involvement in whatever was going on. 'Russia has been the target of many anti-NATO and anti-peacekeeper attacks in recent weeks. We know for certain that the Multinational Security Brigade – South, under German control, was their target again. We will act whenever we see the threat is genuine.'

'Really?' Minister Schramm remarked. 'Why did you not share this information with us? A combined Russian–German strike force would have been very effective and would have undoubtedly waylaid the criticism you most certainly will have to endure once word of this attack spreads.'

Filippov's head was still scrambling to catch up with the events swirling around him, but he noted a very different note in Schramm's voice – he wasn't talking about the incident anymore. His entire train of thought was moving in a completely different direction, and it had nothing to do with confrontation. 'I do like the idea of Russia and Germany joining forces in the future,' Filippov said, 'and I am glad you have the courage and insightfulness to see the benefit of such a union.'

There was a slight but noticeable pause on the line; then: 'I have long thought that the entire Balkan conflict has been a great economic and political drain on all concerned,' Schramm said. 'The atrocities committed by both sides in this conflict have been brutal and violent, and had to be stopped. But NATO and the nonaligned nations have spent hundreds of millions of dollars trying to devise a peaceful solution, and the violence seems worse than ever.'

'I could not agree more, Minister.'

'But what is the endgame here?' Schramm asked, the frustration evident in his voice. 'The factions in the Balkans have been fighting for centuries. There are acts of total barbarism on both sides, but it seems that only the Christian acts of violence against the poor Muslims are publicized in the world press. For some reason, the Muslims became the underdogs, and the Americans seemed to come to their rescue.'

'We have long spoken about the possibility of why the Americans supported the Muslims,' Filippov offered, 'namely, to garner support and friendship from the oil-rich Arab countries, in hopes the Americans would be allowed to build land bases in Persian Gulf nations so they could move their expensive, vulnerable aircraft carriers out of the Gulf. They were so afraid of Iran or Iraq sinking one of their carriers in the Gulf that they made a deal with the devils in the deserts of Arabia to support their Muslim brothers in the Balkans.'

'I do not know the reason for why the Americans chose one side over the other,' Schramm said. 'But when America speaks, the rest of the world, especially Europe and NATO, must listen.'

'Nonsense,' Filippov interjected. 'Germany is not compelled to follow any nation, even the United States. You have the fastest-growing and most powerful economy in Europe, and your growth far exceeds any other country in the world, even America.'

'In any case, Germany has been forced to support a foreign policy that is not always in our best interests,' Schramm went on cautiously. 'We have been forced to stand back and watch as our own peacekeepers harbor Muslim terrorists that attack fellow Christians. Muslim bandits are now free to roam the Balkans, killing innocent Christians, selling drugs under NATO protection, and are still receiving and trading millions of marks in weapons from Iran and Saudi Arabia each year. It makes absolutely no sense at all to me.'

'To me as well, Minister,' Filippov said. 'I agree with you completely. But we must be careful. Russia's action against Kukes was an emotional strike against terrorists. I abhor violence, but I was glad to offer my support for the plan. We cannot let the situation spin out of our control, however. The Muslims will undoubtedly retaliate against KFOR peacekeepers. We must be careful that we do not set southern Europe ablaze simply because we wanted to avenge our soldiers' deaths.'

'The danger is real, Mr Filippov,' Schramm

said. 'Especially now, since the United States pulled out of KFOR.'

'I agree, Minister,' Filippov said. 'The only clear way of reducing tension in the Balkans and salvaging our own national pride is to disengage from the brutal but pointless course we have set for ourselves. The bloodlust between the rival factions in the Balkans is not worth the life of one German or one Russian.'

'I have long advocated constructive disengagement in the Balkans,' Rolf Schramm said. 'I never recommended anyone simply depart, like the Americans did – that only creates a power vacuum that aggressors on all sides will seek to exploit for themselves. The American president was exceedingly irresponsible in his decision just to pull out of Europe as he has done. But I have long pushed to find a way to develop a plan where our forces can leave the battlefield but still remain involved and active in steering the region to some sort of peaceful structure.'

'I know you have, Minister – as leader of the opposition, I remember you were an outspoken critic of the previous government always seeming to knuckle under to the twisted politics and logic of the United States,' Filippov said. That was not entirely true – there was no doubt Schramm was far to the right politically of his predecessors, and he had made a few speeches in favor of getting out of the Kosovo Force, but he was certainly no Willy Brandt or Helmut Kohl – his European vision was limited to whatever it took for him to rise to his current office. 'What did Clinton or Martindale know of European geopolitics? All they cared about was their legacy and their domestic political power base. They used the crisis in the Balkans for their own gain. Now that the Americans are gone, it is up to Germany and Russia to take a leadership position in Europe.'

'Very well said, Mr Filippov: disengage from the fighting but still maintain a presence in the region,' Schramm summarized. 'The Americans tried and failed to force a peace not just in the Balkans, but in the Middle East, the Indian subcontinent, even Ireland. Now that the Americans have turned tail and run, we must take up the cause of peace and justice in our own land.'

'Very well put, Minister,' Filippov said. 'Russia is only concerned about one thing: supporting our Slavic brothers against the growing wave of violence and anarchy by Muslim separatists who seek to establish fundamentalist Islamic regimes in majority Christian nations. We care nothing if Kosovo becomes an independent republic or a Muslim enclave. But if they seek to trample the rights of Christians to their historical landmarks and their ancestral lands, we have an obligation to help. And if radical Islamic countries like Albania try to export their brand of murder, terrorism, and intimidation on the smaller, weaker oblasts in the Balkans, it is in our interests to resist those attempts by any means necessary.'

'And Germany wants only peace, security, stabilization, and freedom of commerce and communications in the Balkans,' Schramm said. 'We want our friends in Croatia and Bosnia to be safe from harassment and civil rights violations by the Muslims and Serb extremists. We wish no ill will toward the Serb people – we only want all to coexist in peace. We must forget the historical animosities that have ruined the peace in the Balkans for far too long.'

'I heartily agree,' Filippov said warmly. 'Russia pledges its support to assist in these efforts. We want peace as much as Germany, and we have the political and cultural ability to influence Serbian actions that are not in keeping with peaceful resolution of conflicts. We can certainly help keep any radical Serb elements from disturbing free trade and communications in the region.'

'That'd be a generous and valuable contribution to peace,' Schramm said. 'Sir, I feel there must be a quid pro quo. What can you suggest?'

'Germany is nothing but a stabilizing, independent-minded, powerful force in Europe,' Filippov said as sincerely as he could, his mind fairly whistling with the effort to think of the right amount of sugar and bullshit to feed Schramm. Filippov's aide was staring, dumbfounded, as his superior was virtually *inventing* a Russo-German alliance of some sort while standing wet in his bathrobe in his bedroom! 'It is the largest and most powerful nation in Western Europe, and it deserves a leadership position far greater than the scraps left to you by the United States and NATO. But now with the United States turning its back on the Western alliance, it is clear to me that Germany must take its rightful place as the leader of the European Union. Let the North Atlantic Treaty Organization dissolve. It has served its purpose and has become an outdated, unwieldy, even dangerous anachronism.'

'So if Germany reins in the Western European nations, Russia will contain and control the Eastern European nations?' Schramm asked. 'Germany and Russia work together to create a lasting peace in Europe?'

'Exactly. Well put, Minister,' Filippov said. 'There is no reason we should work at cross purposes when we are being pulled together by common goals and common enemies.'

'Some will say this is too similar to the Axis alliance before the Great Patriotic War.'

'Our countries are radically different now – the *world* is different,' Filippov responded. 'There are no Third Reich, fascist, or communist regimes in place in our countries. We are all stable, democratic, open societies ruled by law and by the people, not by megalomaniac dictators. And I do not propose an alliance for now, although one can certainly be contemplated in the near future. All I suggest is that we use our individual influences to work together to bring peace and stability to eastern and southern Europe.'

Schramm nodded in agreement. 'I like the sound of this, Mr Filippov,' he said. 'We work together to bring peace to the Balkans, not apart. We throw off the old ties and forge newer, stronger ones together.'

'Exactly,' Filippov said. His aide had been furiously writing on a pad of paper, and he finally showed his superior his notes, trying to toss out any other ideas as long as he had the German foreign minister's ear. 'And there are many other areas of cooperation we can explore, as well,' Filippov said, his mind racing again, trying to think of more avenues of cooperation that could keep this sudden foreign affairs windfall on firm ground.

'Such as?'

Filippov read the third or fourth line of his aide's notes, then looked up in a wide-eyed expression.

The note said simply, *Kazakov's oil?*

He paused, again writing and rewriting the script in his head a dozen times, before saying, 'Such as Europe's reliance on so much Middle Eastern oil. Russia is a major world oil exporter, yet Europe buys less than ten percent of its oil from us. Germany gets less than twenty percent of its oil from Russia, and we are your neighbors! Correcting that situation would offer enormous advantages to both our economies.'

'I think this is a matter to be discussed in a meeting of our commerce and energy ministers, Mr Filippov–'

'It is a foreign relations matter as well, Minister Schramm,' Filippov interjected. 'We know why Europe imports little oil from Russia – recent history will certainly not convince some persons in our respective countries to become too closely linked. That is understandable. But look at current events. Europe cast its lot with the United States for its long-term military and economic security, and it now appears that gamble has lost. The United States no longer needs Germany.

'Russia knows better, sir. Russia has natural resources, raw materials, more than any nation on Earth – including petroleum, massive reserves that cannot even be fully explored for two generations, let alone tapped. The known Caspian Sea oil reserves are five times greater than those in the Persian Gulf, and only a fourth of the oil fields have even been fully explored.'

'Yet Russia exploits these reserves only for itself,' Schramm pointed out. 'It is fine for you to speak of tapping these fields – but then all pipelines lead only to Russia, to Samara or Novorossiysk.'

'Exactly so, Minister,' Filippov said. 'But we have a plan to invest over a billion dollars in the next year to build a pipeline linking the Black Sea with the Adriatic Sea. We have some influence in Bulgaria; Germany has considerable influence with Albania. If the United States leaves NATO and leaves Europe, as our information suggests, they will abandon any plans to build a base in Vlore, and Greece and Turkey will lose their great benefactor and will have to fend for themselves. Turkey will certainly leave Albania and Macedonia to their own fates.'

'You are proposing a Russian oil company build a pipeline from the Black Sea to the Adriatic?' Schramm asked incredulously. 'A private company, I assume? Gazprom only builds pipelines in Russia. LUKoil wanted to build a pipeline through Ukraine and Poland to the Baltic Sea, but its investors scattered after the Russian invasion of Ukraine, and the company is teetering on the edge of bankruptcy. That leaves...' There was a pause, and Filippov heard a muted gasp. 'You're not suggesting *Metyorgaz*? Pavel the Playboy?'

'I'd prefer not to reveal too many details about the proposal for now, Minister,' Filippov interjected. He was surprised when Schramm mentioned Metyorgaz, Kazakov's oil company cum

202

drug distribution front company. But then again, Germany was very closely linked with Albania, and it certainly had a major presence in the Balkans. They'd certainly be aware of any large-scale development projects proposed for the region. And Kazakov was an international crime and business figure – they *certainly* would be on the alert for anything he might be involved in. 'I will say that Russia is committed to developing the Caspian Sea petroleum resources and serving all of Europe with inexpensive oil. That is of great benefit to us all. Russia is securing commitments from many different sources to do just this, and we look to the leaders in the European Union to help us.'

'You sound like a sales brochure now, Herr Filippov,' Schramm said, with a nervous chuckle. 'Germany is indeed looking for safe, secure, reliable sources of energy. Our dependence on Middle East oil is not desirable, yet it is a relatively cheap and reliable source–'

'As long as the United States secures peace in the Middle East,' Filippov interjected. 'What if the United States withdraws from the Middle East as we see they have done in Europe? The price of oil will skyrocket, and supply will be in greater jeopardy. Germany needs to secure its own source of oil, right here in Europe, not the Middle East. The Caspian Sea oil reserves are the answer. The problem is, what will Turkey do with oil transiting the Bosporus Straits if instability sets in? Where will you go to get oil from Asia? To Syria? Israel – if it even exists in five years? Will you need to invade Turkey in order to get oil shipments through the Bosporus?'

There was a lengthy pause from Bonn. Filippov was going to ask Schramm if he was still on the line when the German foreign minister finally asked, 'So the attack against Albania was not a retaliatory strike, but only the beginning of a campaign to secure land and rights to build this pipeline to Europe?'

'I cannot comment further on this morning's events,' Filippov repeated. He certainly could not – he had no idea what had happened except that a NATO radar plane was a burning hunk of metal in Macedonia. But his word rang true, loud and clear. A secret attack on Albania to secure pipeline rights? Kazakov was just crazy enough to do something like that... 'As for the rights to build a pipeline – we do not want bloodshed. We hope to *convince* the respective governments in southern Europe to participate in this lucrative and important expansion.'

'I see,' Schramm said woodenly. Any person could hear the words between the words, the thinly veiled threat. 'We will talk more of this, Minister Filippov.'

Filippov hung up the phone, feeling as drained and shaky as if he had just run a two-kilometer sprint. 'What ... in ... *hell* is going on?' he shouted to his aide. 'What in hell just happened?'

'It sounded to me,' his aide replied with a smile, 'that you have just negotiated an alliance with Germany to divide the Balkans between you, sir.'

'But what about Albania?' Filippov asked. 'What happened in Albania?'

The aide shrugged and replied, 'Does it matter now, sir?'

Chapter Three

Zhukovsky Flight Research Center, Bykovo (Moscow), Russia
several days later

'Everyone freeze! This is a raid! No one move!'

The uniformed Spetsnaz shock troops burst into the Metyor Aerospace building without warning, automatic weapons drawn, thirty minutes past midnight. They quickly fanned out through the first floor of the building. They were followed by plainclothes Glavnoe Razvedivatel'noe Upravlenie (GRU), General Staff Intelligence Directorate, agents, with bulletproof vests under their long coats, carrying small automatic pistols.

Pyotr Fursenko and Pavel Kazakov were sitting in Fursenko's office when the agents burst in without any further warning, guns leveled. Kazakov was casually sipping a glass of fine French sherry and enjoying a Cuban cigar; Fursenko was nervously guzzling coffee and chain-smoking bitter Egyptian cigarettes. 'How much longer were you going to make us wait?' Kazakov asked, with a smile. They did not answer, but roughly hauled both of them to their feet, out of the office, and out to the main hangar floor.

There, surrounded by plainclothed agents and uniformed Spetsnaz special forces commandos, was Sergey Yejsk, President Sen'kov's national security advisor, and Colonel-General Valeriy Zhurbenko, chief of the general staff. Fursenko looked at both men in wide-eyed shock. Pavel Kazakov merely smiled and looked directly at Yejsk and Zhurbenko in turn.

Yejsk nodded to the officer in charge of his detail, and he had his men roughly search both civilians. Fursenko looked horrified, his body jerking away at every soldier's touch; Kazakov merely allowed the search without resisting, smiling confidently at Yejsk. The soldiers put the two men's hands up to the backs of their heads, then slapped the hands with the barrels of their rifles to warn them to keep them there. When the soldiers were finished, Yejsk stepped over first to Kazakov, who looked directly back at him, and then over to Fursenko, who looked very much like a doe caught in headlights.

Yejsk stepped closer to Fursenko until he was almost nose to nose with him and asked, 'Do you know who I am?' The scientist nodded. 'Do you know who these men are?' This time a shake of his head. 'They are the men that will tear this building apart piece by piece, take you to prison, and throw you naked into a cold four-by-four-foot cell if I do not like the answers you give to my questions. Do you understand?'

Fursenko nodded so hard, every soldier in the hangar could see it. Kazakov merely smiled. 'That's an easy one,' he said. 'Are you done? Can we go now?' His guard whacked him on the side of his head with the barrel of his rifle.

'I will give *you* an easy one, Doctor – where is the bomber?'

'Which bomber?' Now it was Fursenko's turn to get a shot to the head.

A soldier ran up to Zhurbenko and whispered in his ear. 'What is the combination to that door lock, Doctor?' Zhurbenko asked. Fursenko gave it to him instantly, and moments later they had the secure hangar door open and the lights on. Inside they found nothing but an aircraft skeleton, roughly resembling the Metyor-179 bomber, with several large pieces of composite material, wiring, and engine parts scattered around the polished floor. 'What is *that?*' Yejsk shouted.

'Our latest project, the Metyor-179. It didn't work,' Fursenko replied uneasily.

'The *real* Metyor-179. Where is it?'

'It's right there, sir,' Fursenko replied. 'That's all there's left of it.'

'*Ni kruti mn'e yaytsa!* Don't twist my balls!' Yejsk stepped up close to Fursenko and slapped him backhandedly across the face. 'One more time, Doctor – where is the -179?'

'Stop hitting the poor doctor on the head, Yejsk,' Kazakov said. 'You don't want to ruin that fine brain of his.'

'*Zakroy yibala!* Shut your fucking mouth!' Yejsk shouted. 'I should do the world a favor and put a bullet in your brain right now!'

'That's not why you came here, Yejsk, or we'd be dead already,' Kazakov said. 'But of course, then you would be, as well.' His eyes fell, and he motioned down, inviting Yejsk to look. Yejsk and Zhurbenko glanced down at their crotches and saw tiny red dots of light dancing on their clothing right near their genitals. They looked at all the soldiers in the hangar and saw red laser dots on their heads, their shoulders, and their crotches –

every man had at least three dots on him, all centered on areas not protected by bulletproof vests.

'You dare threaten me?' Yejsk cried out, beads of sweat popping out on his forehead. 'I will tear down everything you own and dump it into the Black Sea, and then I will have your broken corpses tossed on top of it all.'

'Well, well, General Yejsk, you are beginning to sound just like a gangster,' Kazakov said. His eyes narrowed, and the casual, relaxed, amused smile disappeared. 'We stop the bullshit now, Yejsk. You came here on the orders of the president to find out what we're doing and to get in on the action.' Yejsk glared at Kazakov, but Kazakov knew that he had guessed correctly. 'Now, I suggest we send all of these security men home for the evening, and let's talk business.'

'You had better cooperate with us, or you'll wish you were back humping goats in Kazakhstan,' Yejsk said angrily. With a wave of his hand, Yejsk dismissed the Spetsnaz troops, leaving only two personal bodyguards. He could see none of Kazakov's men in the rafters anymore – but they hadn't seen them up there the first time, either. The rumors were obviously true – Kazakov had an army of former Spetsnaz commandos, well-trained and now well-paid and loyal, working for him.

'Where is the bomber, Pavel?' Zhurbenko asked. 'We know it departed here two hours before the attack against Kukes, Albania, and now it's missing.'

Kazakov lit up a cigar, then offered one to

Zhurbenko and Yejsk – Zhurbenko accepted. 'It's safe, being hidden in several different secret locations in three or four different countries.'

'What in *hell* do you think you're doing?' Yejsk thundered. 'Conducting your own little foreign policy campaign, your own little imperialistic war? Don't tell me you actually loved your father so much that you stole a stealth bomber and killed hundreds of men, women, and children to *avenge* him?'

'I wouldn't bother to pick up the phone to save my father,' Kazakov said, a malevolent grin on his face. 'Besides, he died precisely the way he wanted to die – maybe not with his boots on, but at least within spitting distance of his enemy. He probably called them names just before they put a rope around his neck – that would appeal to his sense of defiance. I've got better things to do with my time and money than launch off on some romantic quest to avenge a man who didn't care one shit about me.'

'Then what *are* you doing?'

'I am creating a favorable economic and political climate for myself – and if you and that patsy Sen'kov were smart, a favorable economic climate for Russia, too,' Kazakov said.

'How? Are you going to bomb every national capital in the Balkans and the Transcaucasus, just to lay down some pipe?'

'I won't have to,' Kazakov said. 'The raid on Kukes was a warning. Unless you blabbermouths leak the information sooner and reveal me, I will go to the Albanian and Macedonian governments and make the same offer to them. If they refuse my generous offer, they will suffer the same fate.'

'You're insane!' Yejsk retorted. 'You expect one aircraft to bomb two sovereign governments into submission so you can build a pipeline through their countries?'

'I am hoping Russia will intervene,' Kazakov said. 'Russia should come to those countries' assistance and guarantee their security. With Russian troops firmly but discreetly in place, the security of both those republics and my pipeline will be assured. In a year, the pipeline will be in place and we can all start making money.'

'This is the most asinine idea I have ever heard!' Yejsk said. 'Do you just expect these governments to roll over and play dead? What about–?'

'NATO?' Kazakov interjected. 'You tell me, Comrade National Security Advisor – will NATO be a factor?' He smiled when he saw Yejsk look away, lost in thought – his intelligence information was accurate. The United States was indeed pulling out of NATO and leaving Europe. This was truly the opportunity of a lifetime, and finally some high-ranking members of the Russian government were beginning to notice it, too. 'Who else? Germany? I have information that says that there is an extraordinary level of co-operation growing between Russia and Germany, now that the United States is removing itself from Europe and NATO.'

'So why do we need you, Kazakov?' Yejsk asked angrily. How in *hell* did this punk gangster know so much? 'You're nothing but a drug dealer. Why does Russia need any cooperation from you and

Fursenko's pretty toy?'

'Go ahead and try,' Kazakov said. 'Try to march Russian Army troops into Macedonia now, without an invitation – Greece and Turkey will declare war, and it might drag the United States back into Europe and the alliance. As I understand it, the United States hasn't left NATO yet – you will certainly give them a reason to stay. Invade Albania, and Germany will feel threatened and may break off your new little détente. You *need* me, Yejsk. You need the Metyor-179 to perform precision, devastating, and most important, *deniable* destruction in the Balkans and the Transcaucasus. If the republics believe you are at all behind this, the game is up. But if you make them believe that they need Russia's help, you assert control over your former sphere of influence again, and I get the economic, military, and political stability I need to invest two billion dollars into the region.'

'This sounds like some kind of protection racket, Pavel,' Zhurbenko said. 'Why should we be a part of it? Why can't Russia pledge to invest in a pipeline? Have GAZPROM or LUKoil build the pipeline and we pay for the project with revenues from the oil purchases?'

'If you could do it, you would have done it already,' Kazakov argued. 'Both those companies are wallowing in corruption and debt, mostly because of the bungling and interference from their biggest shareholder, the Russian government, and its inept bureaucracy. With my plan, neither Russia nor the republics lay out any money at all – I pay for the pipeline. It belongs to me. I pay a prenegotiated flowage fee to the republics, which is pure profit for them, in addition to the profits they make if they decide to buy and refine some of the crude in their own refineries. I will make them a good deal for the crude.'

'And so what does Russia get?' Yejsk asked. 'What do *we* get?'

Kazakov smiled broadly – he knew he had them now. Once they start thinking about *themselves* and their cut of the action, Pavel knew they were hooked. 'Overtly, Russia gets a flowage fee from the oil that I transport across Russia and ship out of Novorossiysk,' Kazakov replied. 'Covertly, I will pay a percentage of the profits for protection of my pipeline. Russia maintains a presence in the Balkans again, plus you earn whatever you can squeeze out of the republics. I know Russia is very good at milking the republics it has sworn to protect – Macedonia, Bulgaria, and Albania should be no different. I will offer the same ... incentives, shall we say, to Macedonia and Albania.'

'*Plomo o plata?*' Zhurbenko asked. 'If they accept they get rich, and if they refuse they get dead?'

'It is a win-win situation for all of us,' Kazakov said. 'It is an offer no one can refuse.'

'An offer you can't refuse, all right,' Linda Mae Valentrovna Maslyukov muttered to herself, as she finished her stretching exercises and then began a simple black-belt karate *kata* routine while standing on a narrow gravel turnout on the side of the road near the end of the runway.

Linda Mae was an electronics expert from St

Petersburg, the daughter of a Russian father – a former Russian consul and trade negotiator based in New Orleans and Los Angeles – and an Irish-American mother from Monroe, Louisiana. Although she'd been born in New Orleans and had spent most of her life in the United States, when her father had been reassigned back to Moscow, she had eagerly gone along. Her long, flaming red hair and sparkling green eyes made quite an impression on the boys and professors at Ioffe-Physico-Technical Institute in St Petersburg, but she didn't allow her popularity to interfere with getting first a bachelor's, then a master's degree in science in semiconductor heterostructures.

Linda had renounced her American citizenship in 1995 after receiving her master's degree, which completely opened up her career paths in Russia. With a citizen's fluency in both English and Russian and advanced degrees in sophisticated electronics technology, she had her choice of jobs and salaries. She rejected a few more lucrative job offers in Moscow and professorships in St Petersburg to go to Zhukovsky and work in a communications design laboratory. Because of her prior US citizenship, she could hold no higher than a Secret security clearance, but she still enjoyed a good lifestyle and a high level of prestige from her colleagues and fellow workers. She often spoke about moving to Moscow or St Petersburg, but the talk always faded – mostly after meeting a new pilot or senior officer from one of the bomber squadrons at Zhukovsky.

No one knew the real reason why she stayed at

Zhukovsky, why she broke off torrid affairs with high-ranking officers, why she was satisfied with a relatively low salary at Zhukovsky when she could command much higher wages in the city. The reason: Linda Mae was a paid spy for the United States of America. Whatever she might have made elsewhere was more than compensated for by numbered Cayman Island bank accounts, where she hoped to retire the second it looked like her cover was going to blow.

She had just downloaded the latest tap from a passive listening device she'd installed in the Metyor Aerospace hangar several weeks before. Metyor had never had very much activity until recently, right around the time that the father of Metyor IIG's largest shareholder, Pavel Kazakov, had been brutally killed in Kosovo. Suddenly, Metyor Aerospace was buzzing with activity. Before it got too hairy over there, she had managed to plant listening devices inside the main hangar and in the administrative offices. No matter how old, young, married, busy, or noninterested they were, her red hair, green eyes, luscious Louisiana breasts, and sassy attitude attracted men like nothing else, and she practically had free access to Metyor. But no matter how hard she tried, it was impossible to get inside the secure hangar or get close to the facility director, Pyotr Fursenko. The old fart had to be gay – she'd tried all of her feminine charms on him, to no avail.

Linda had not seen it depart, but she knew the Metyor-179 was gone the day after the raid on Kukes, Albania. There was no doubt in her mind that it had done the raid. She'd pieced together snippets of other conversations and could draw a fairly detailed timeline of the entire mission, all the way back to when live weapons were uploaded, what kind they used, where they got them, the strike routing – even details on what they would do if they encountered an AWACS radar plane, which obviously they had. The listening devices were very, very effective.

Unfortunately, in order to prevent detection, they were extremely low-power devices, which meant she had to get very close to the facility in order to download the stored recordings; they also had to be very-low-frequency transmissions in order to penetrate the radio-resistant steel hangar, so each packet of data, although compressed, took a long time to download. She had to bring the downloading device somewhere where it would be within the two hundred meters' range of the pickup/transmitters. She needed at least one minute to download five minutes' worth of conversations, so the recorder had to be within range for at least thirty minutes.

Linda could never get permission to live at base housing, and at the current time she didn't have a boyfriend who lived there, so she had to disguise these download sessions by taking up jogging. The main road around the airfield at Zhukovsky led from the main base area around the long northeast-southwest runway and all the way to the housing area on the south side of the base. Every day, after working late in her office or in the design labs, Linda would go to the base gymnasium, stretch or lift weights for an hour or so to let the traffic die down, then change into a jogging suit, put on her Austrian-made portable tape recorder, and jog the main road all the way to the housing area, rest or visit friends who lived there, and then jog back. As long as she was within two hundred meters of the Metyor hangar, the transmitter would feed digital packets of data into the CompactFlash memory card inside the tape recorder. She made sure she stopped many times along the way – although she was fit enough to run a marathon if she wanted to, she would stop every kilometer or so to check her pulse, make like she had to get her breath back, watch airplanes land, or just do some karate *kata* or stretch. The entrance to the Metyor Aerospace facility sometimes had a friendly guard on duty, so she stopped there often to chat, flirt, or do whatever was necessary to hang out long enough to collect data.

She could also listen to the data as it was downloading – dangerous, but it helped to remind her of the importance of what she was doing, why she was risking her life to get this information to the United States. Ever since things started buzzing inside Metyor, she started listening to the downloads – and it scared the hell out of her. This development was even scarier. They were actually going to use the Metyor-179 to…

She heard the rustle of tires on gravel coming up behind her. She had the headphones on, so she pretended not to notice. She switched the data downloader off, switched the Russian rock music back on, tried some jumping jacks, unzipped her jogging suit jacket about halfway down her chest, then took the headphones off.

'*Prasteetye, gaspazha,*' a man said behind her.

218

She pretended to be startled and turned around. It was a base security police vehicle, with two officers. They didn't have their flashing lights on, so maybe this wasn't an enforcement stop, just a friendly...

At that instant, the officer behind the wheel turned on the flashing red and blue lights. Oh, shit, what was this about?

'*Da?*' Linda asked in her most seductive, disarming voice, adding just a hint of her Louisiana accent to try to put them off guard. 'What's going on, fellas?'

'Miss Maslyukov, we would like to ask you some questions,' the officer outside the vehicle said. 'Would you mind coming with us, please?'

'May I ask what this is about, officer?'

'We will explain everything at base security headquarters, Miss Maslyukov,' the officer said. It was then that Linda noticed it – a strange antenna bolted to the hood of the trunk. A scanner, probably to detect eavesdroppers. That was new to the base. It must've come from outside the base, because if the base commander wanted any sort of electronic gear, he came to Linda's shop to get it.

'*Kharasho,*' Linda acknowledged. She stepped toward the officer outside the car. Once out of the glare of the headlights, she looked inside the vehicle. No dog. The other officer was still in the driver's seat, still seat belted in, the radio microphone in his hand casually watching her approach, a cigarette in his left hand. Obviously, he expected this to be a very routine pickup.

She knew, whatever happened, she must not get

219

inside that car.

The second officer had a large metal flashlight in his left hand, his right hand behind his back, unsnapping a pair of handcuffs from his utility belt pouch. As she approached the officer outside the car, she noticed he was doing exactly what she expected him to be doing – staring at her chest, the flashlight beam focused right on her cleavage. 'Please put your hands behind your back, miss,' the officer ordered, in a not-too-forceful, almost anticipatory voice.

'Like this?' Linda put her hands behind her back without turning around, which served to push out her breasts even farther. The second officer's attention was fully riveted on her tits.

She didn't know where the strength came from. Maybe it was from worrying about this very moment for so long. Maybe it was some sort of heroic, defiant gesture. Maybe she had just watched too many episodes of *Charlie's Angels*. Whatever it was, wherever it came from, it was happening whether she thought it was safe or sane or whatever. Prison, interrogation center, Hell, or the Cayman Islands. One way or the other, she was on her way.

Just as the second officer took a step toward her, still paying attention to nothing else but her white billowy breasts, Linda executed a perfect snap kick, just like her black-belt-qualifying *kata* move. It missed by a mile, nailing the officer in the shins. But the officer seemed frozen, as if he couldn't believe what she had done, which gave her the opportunity to line up an even better kick. Her second attack was right on target, her right foot burying itself deeply into the officer's groin. He made a loud, long grunt and bent over nearly double. She quickly stepped beside him and jammed her left foot into the side of his left knee. The joint buckled, and he went down on his left side – exposing the side arm on the right, its safety strap unfastened. She snatched it out of the holster. He reached out, grabbing for her, but she twisted out of reach.

'Astanavleevat'sya! Stop!' The first officer, much younger than the second, seemed confused about what to do – get out of the car, call for help, or pull out his weapon – so he tried everything at once. He seemed to be moving in slow motion, while at the same time Linda's head was spinning as if everything was happening in triple speed.

The pistol she had taken from the second officer was much heavier than she thought – and it fired much easier than she thought, too, two rounds going off at the slightest finger pressure. The first round went through the passenger's side window into the car, spraying the first officer with glass and shattering the instrument panel. The second went somewhere off into space over the car. 'Get out of the car!' Linda yelled. 'Get out!'

'Freeze! Don't move!' the officer shouted. His hand squeezed the microphone transmit button. 'Emergency! Officer down! I need assis–'

Linda only wanted to put a bullet through the car radio – at least that's what she told herself. But when she stopped squeezing the trigger, the driver's side window was shattered and the officer's head was blasted apart like a hammered coconut, with strings of blood-soaked hair sur-

221

rounding a gory hole.

It took all of her physical and emotional strength to go around to that car door, reach across the pool of brains, blood, and bones on the dead officer's lap to unfasten his seat belt, and drag the corpse out onto the ground. Somewhere in the background noise of the blood roaring in her ears, she could hear the second officer shouting, probably into a portable radio, but she didn't care. She jumped into the police car, shifted it into drive, and sped away. The first left turn took her to the road to the back gate of the base. She saw emergency lights and, not realizing they belonged to her car, she sped up. The guard shack to the back gate was coming up fast. She saw the automatic assault rifle in a holder next to her and for an instant thought about grabbing it and trying to shoot her way off the base, but she sped by the guardhouse before she could act on the idea. Linda heard several sharp raps on the outside of the car – bullets fired from the security officers on duty at the guardhouse – but it kept running.

At the end of the access road, she took a left turn, which took her toward the nearest city, Itslav. She finally found the switch for the emergency lights and shut them off.

Now that she was on the move, things actually began to get clearer for her, because Linda rehearsed her escape procedures several times a year, and she knew exactly what to do. The one thing the American Central Intelligence Agency did well for its agents was plan an escape system.

There were four contact points around

Zhukovsky Air Base. On a signal from Linda sent via a secret satellite signal beacon in the recorder, or after some trigger event – and a murder at Zhukovsky certainly qualified as a trigger event – a person would begin to visit the contact points on a regular basis. Linda had no idea who it was, when he or she would show, or what he or she would do – it was up to her to identify the person and make contact. If it were her contact person, she would be taken to a secret location, identified, and then inserted into a preestablished exfiltration network set up inside Russia for exactly this purpose. All Linda had to do was to activate the satellite signal beacon in the recorder and...

...But when she reached down to her side, she realized she didn't have the recorder. The second guard must've torn it off her when they struggled.

After swearing hotly in English, Creole, and Russian for several moments, Linda collected her thoughts and calmed herself. The signal beacon wasn't important. Certainly all the excitement at the base would activate the escape network. All she had to do was make her way to one of the contact points, properly meet up with the contact, and then do exactly what she was told to do until she was safe.

Her first task was to ditch the police car. She selected a utility company parking lot, about ten miles away from the base, hiding it between two large trucks that looked as if they hadn't been moved in a while. She kept the handgun, after counting and finding three rounds still in the magazine – the assault rifle was much heavier than she thought, so she left it in the car – then walked all the way back out of the lot and onto the highway. Linda was tempted to try hitch-hiking east on the highway toward the nearest contact point, but her handlers advised against that. Too many escapees got caught that way. The south side of the highway had numerous businesses and lighted parking lots along it, but the north side was mostly open fields of winter wheat turned mushy from melting snows, with a small river farther north beyond the trees. She crossed the highway at a dark place, as far as possible from streetlights, walked away from the highway to the tree line about a kilometer from the highway, then began to parallel it, heading eastbound. Linda passed a few businesses and parking lots between her and the highway, but none of the lights or fences extended to the tree line, so it was a fairly straight shot. Her handler was very explicit – stay away from roads, rivers, railroads, transmission lines, any sort of travel path.

Several hours later, she arrived at an intersection where a bridge took traffic north across the river, and where there was a tavern that she sometimes visited, still open and still inviting. Linda even thought she saw cars belonging to friends of hers, good friends that had known her for years. She was tired, aching, hungry, freezing cold, cut, bruised, and bleeding from crossing fences and snagged by branches and sticker bushes. She could stay hidden in the parking lot, wait for her friends to show, ask for help, maybe get a ride to someplace close to the contact point...

No, no, *no*, she admonished herself. Again, her

handlers were very specific – stay away from everyone, no matter how close or trusted they were. Reluctantly, almost whimpering in pain and fear and weakness, she trudged through the ankle-deep, half-frozen mud behind the tavern, keeping to the shadows. She followed a dirt path toward the river and found another path that led under the bridge abutment. Under the bridge, she found some homeless persons huddled under blankets with tiny fires in buckets, drinking vodka and eating discarded food from the tavern, and again she considered asking for something, anything, to help ease the cold and hunger. She could either use the gun to buy food or threaten to kill someone if they didn't help her. But she kept away, staying away from the hoboes and staying away from the narrow access road along the river's edge without their detecting her presence. Leaving even that tiny bit of civilization was the hardest thing she ever had to do.

But as she disappeared back into the shadows once again, she heard sirens behind her. Two police cars had pulled up to the tavern, lights flashing. If she had stopped, even for five minutes, she would've been trapped. If she had talked to the hoboes, and they were later questioned by police, they would surely have betrayed her. How about that? she thought – maybe her handlers really knew what they were talking about!

By the time the dawn started to peek above the horizon, Linda had reached the contact spot. There was a small dirt parking lot next to the river beside another north-south bridge, where during the summer vacationers could launch

225

rafts and float down the river toward the city. There used to be a small campground there, where rafters from farther upstream could spend the night, but a lack of funds and abuse by drug dealers and hoboes had caused the campground to fall into disuse and disrepair. Of the dozen campsites, only one still had a rickety picnic table on it. That was her contact point.

The ground was rocky and felt frozen, but there were plenty of trees and vegetation. Her job was to find a good hiding spot and wait. Sometime during daylight hours, her contact person would arrive at the contact point and somehow make himself known to her. She had to stay hidden the rest of the day and night. Surely, she thought, the hue and cry for her was out. Surely, she prayed, the network had heard of the murder on base and activated itself. Surely, she pleaded, her contact would realize she was on the move and show this morning.

But the time came and went, and no one showed. Tears flowed down her cheeks, and her lips trembled in fear and loneliness. Nothing. She had never felt so alone, so helpless.

Since it was now daytime and she was less than a kilometer from both the highway and the bridge – and if she could see cars, they might be able to see her – Linda had no choice but to crawl away to the densest part of the little patch of trees near the park, crawl into the deepest and darkest dirt gully she could find, and wait. The river was just a few meters away across the parking lot, but she didn't dare try to get water in daytime; there was even a coffee and doughnut vendor in the parking lot across the highway to the south, selling his goods to workers arriving at the steel scrapyard and woodworking factory on the south side of the highway, and even in her hole she could smell the boiled dough and strong black coffee. She always had rolled-up pancake crepes with jam, fruit, or cream cheese inside and coffee every morning, and now the emptiness in her belly was beginning to turn into a dull ache.

This was going to be impossible, she thought grimly. She had practiced her procedures, memorized her directives, and thought through her moves for years, and all the time thought she could do it, if she ever had to. But it was just barely twelve hours since going on the run, and she doubted whether she could make it even another twelve hours. Her handler said it could take days to activate the network, and then it was up to the contact person to decide if it was safe enough to try to make contact. Even then, the actual procedure took days – Linda wasn't supposed to contact the first person she saw, but had to verify simply by waiting and watching if he or she was the right one. Sleep was impossible – every sound, every car noise, every voice she heard was a potential captor.

From her hole, she could see the parking lot and campground. A few hoboes came around, searching the garbage cans. To Linda's immense shock, moments after the hoboes arrived, they were jacked up by local police and taken away. The police were everywhere, but they were out of sight, immediately pouncing on anyone who looked suspicious. After the arrest, the police would do a short search of the area, checking nearby bushes and trees for any sign of anyone else's presence. They would sweep denser bushes aside roughly with nightsticks, beating them and looking for evidence of anyone's presence, checking behind and around any shrubs that might be large enough to conceal a person, then disappear as quickly as they appeared.

It was hopeless, Linda thought. The contact person would never dare come anywhere near here, ever. Her handler had warned her exactly what would happen. Eventually, her hunger, loneliness, hopelessness, weariness, and fear would cause her to do something stupid, and she would be nabbed, and just like that, the game would be over.

She burrowed down as deep as she could into the dirt, sobbing softly to herself, afraid to show even the tiniest bit of skin outside her hole. It began to rain, big fat cold sleety drops, then soon started to snow. She had never been so cold in her life, and she knew she would probably die of hypothermia before long. When darkness fell, she felt brave enough to eat some dirty wet snow for water and carefully pile leaves and branches around herself, and with a sort of crude nest made for herself, she at least felt strong enough to make it through the night. But it was hopeless, useless. The police were everywhere, and the killing of a fellow cop only made them more determined to get the killer.

She expected, then soon hoped, that the police would swoop down on her and take her away any moment. Even being gang-raped and sodomized by vengeful police officers in an MSB prison cell would be far better than freezing to death.

High-Technology Aerospace Weapons Center, Elliott Air Force Base, Groom Lake, Nevada early the next morning

'Good morning, General Sivarek, General Smoliy, ladies and gentlemen,' Brigadier-General Patrick McLanahan said, as his image appeared on the secure videoteleconference screen. 'I am General Patrick McLanahan, here to brief the special mission portion of this morning's exercise. This briefing is classified Secret. Our rooms are secure, and this video-conference is being conducted on a secure closed circuit.' In the room with McLanahan were the pilots from the United States; in the conference room at Nellis Air Force Base were the crew members from Ukraine and Turkey involved in today's exercise.

Patrick hit the button on his wireless remote computer controller, and the first PowerPoint slide popped onto a separate frame on the Nellis videoconference screen. 'As you all know, the unclassified reason you're here is that you're on a goodwill tour of the United States and as part of NATO exercises here in Nevada. The classified reason is to test your aerial warfighting capabilities and to try to integrate your flight operations with some of the technologies we're developing for NATO. This is the first in a series of six missions we'll fly together to see how well we can coordinate both defensive and offensive operations from an aerial platform.'

'We have worked with AWACS controllers many times, General,' Sivarek pointed out.

'As have we,' Smoliy added. 'Both Russian and NATO versions.' The attempt at one-upmanship had been going on ever since the two had met. So far, it was still on a friendly, although sometimes childish, level.

'You won't be working with AWACS aircraft,' Patrick said. 'At this point, we cannot reveal what kind of aircraft will be involved.'

'I should think we will find out soon,' Sivarek said. 'If it is on the range and interfering with our pilots, we will shoot it down.'

'It is fair game on the range – if you can find it and take a shot, it's yours,' Patrick said. 'However, we ask you both to follow the range controller's directions. If you are vectored away or are issued a "knock it off" call, obey it immediately. We will attempt to keep you outside visual range of our aircraft, but we don't want to interfere with training, either.'

'This sounds very interesting,' General Smoliy remarked. 'It is an allied plane, but you do not wish us to see it. It will be controlling us, but you cannot tell us who or what it is. Very mysterious.'

'The entire concept is experimental at this point,' Patrick said. 'Although we have received clearance to perform these exercises, the actual program itself has not yet been approved. If the program is canceled in midstream, the less you know about it, the better.'

'You are not placing a lot of trust in us, Patrick,' Sivarek said acidly. 'We are allies – at least, I think we are still so.' Sivarek had made it very plain that he didn't care for President Thomas Thorn and his attitude toward supporting his Eurasian allies.

'There is no offense intended, sir,' Patrick said. 'You will be briefed on the entire program and the results of this exercise before you depart Nellis. Whether or not the program is implemented will be decided by others later.'

'*Bes para etmez*,' Sivarek remarked grumpily. Literally it meant, 'Does my head have a bald spot?' but in actuality it meant, 'What's the problem here?' But he nodded, indicating that he was through asking questions and was ready to continue. Smoliy, far more animated and affable, took another sip of tea and waited patiently.

Patrick gave a time hack, a weather report, and then briefed the mission lineup. For this first mission, both of the foreign general officers were 'playing.' Normally, Patrick discouraged this, but he could not talk them out of it – it was part of their 'prerogative,' and of course it was fun to be out on the Nellis ranges playing war. And because both foreign general officers were going to fly, naturally Patrick had to bump one of his flyers off one of the American planes so he could fly too. Yes, rank did have its privileges.

'Ornx 101 flight of two will defend inside the range,' Patrick went on. 'You pick your own patrol altitude. You will have your own controllers manning Tatil Control during the exercise.' The Dreamland ranges had a simple ground-controlled intercept radar facility set up for allied nations that still relied heavily on ground controllers, although most NATO nations now used airborne radar controllers. 'Sila Zero One flight of two will approach the range complex from the east – that's as specific as I get. Vampire will also enter from the east, plus or minus five minutes from Sila flight. You are cleared to Level Two maneuvers – no maximum altitude, minimum altitude of five hundred feet above ground level, maximum airspeed six hundred, maximum closure speed twelve hundred miles per hour, minimum vertical and lateral separation one nautical mile. We want you to be aggressive, but not dangerous.

'We will adjust separation from Vampire as necessary for operational security. Please be aware, Vampire may be employing a towed electronic countermeasures array, so be careful approaching from the rear quadrant. Again, if the range controllers give you a vector away from Vampire, follow their instructions exactly. You'll have plenty of opportunities to attack. Questions?' Patrick waited for the translators to finish and the two generals shake their heads, then concluded with: 'I must remind you, this briefing is classified Secret. Good luck, good hunting. This concludes my briefing. End of transmission.'

Patrick headed back to his office to pick up his flight gear and head over to the mission planning room for his crew briefing when the secure phone rang. He considered letting voice mail pick it up, but he knew that only a handful of persons had that number, so he answered it. 'McLanahan.'

232

'Ever wonder what we do when we retire, Patrick?'

Patrick recognized the voice instantly, although they had only spoken to each other a handful of times in the past twelve years. 'How are you, sir?'

'Sharp as ever,' the caller said, pleased that McLanahan had recognized his voice. 'I'm fine, General. You?'

'Fine, sir. How can I help you?'

'I have a project for you and your team.'

'I'm sorry, sir, but this is not a topic for discussion, even on a secure line.'

'Don't worry – I'll do all the talking,' the caller said. 'Been reading the intelligence files on the Balkans lately?'

'Other than what happened a few days ago with the AWACS plane – no, sir.'

'Something happened a few hours ago that could tear the whole place wide open,' the caller said. 'You'll be getting a call in the next few hours from the Pentagon, inquiring as to the possibility of your team participating in a high-risk, high-value cover mission. I need you to build a flight plan for a mission into Russia for one, possibly two, Megafortress bombers, and be ready to present it to the National Command Authority as soon as possible.'

'But I–'

'Just do it, Patrick,' the caller said – urgently, almost but not quite an order. Patrick knew he had no authority to order anyone to do anything. 'Have it ready to go ASAP, as complete as you can make it without having access to the details. When the warning order is issued, I want you ready to present the plan to the NCA.' And the line went dead.

Patrick had absolutely zero time to spend on this – the crew bus was going to depart for the flight line in ten minutes – so he furiously typed out an e-mail message to David Luger, relaying the strange request and asking him to work something up. He had no way of knowing if the voice on the other end of the line was really who he thought it was, but whatever was really going on, it would be a good exercise for David and the Operational Support Group.

A few minutes later, the phone rang again. 'Hey, Muck, what's this about?' It was David Luger, and he had already received the e-mail.

'A project I'm working on.'

'Did we receive a warning order?'

'No. But the requester said we will. I'd like to brief a mission package within three hours.'

'Piece of cake – seeing we have no concrete information such as a target time, weapon load, threat assessment, or mission objectives,' Luger said. 'But it would be more valuable to you if I had a few more details.'

'As soon as I get more information, I'll pass it along,' Patrick said. 'Meanwhile, have OSG put a package together.'

'Should I ask General Samson to review it if you're still up flying?'

Patrick immediately recognized what Luger was really asking: Is this job authorized? Does Samson know anything about it? Does Samson *need* to know anything about it? 'I'll brief him personally if and when we get a warning order,'

Patrick replied. 'Until then, no need to notify the boss.'

'Okay, Muck, you got it,' Luger said. 'You know the boss will get a flag in his security file the minute we open a new intelligence file and start pulling overhead imagery and data on the Russian Federation?'

'I know. If he asks, I'll brief him. But he'll be busy at Nellis with the Ukrainians and Turks. This thing may go away – or it may start to spin up, before he has a chance to notice the security flag and call a stop. Get your guys to work.'

'You got it. Have a good flight.'

Oh yeah, Patrick thought as he hung up the phone – he had a mission to fly. Enough intrigue for now – it was time to earn his living.

Aboard an F-16 fighter of the Republic of Turkey Air Force a short time later

'*Yyuz iki, nah sihl sih nihz?*' the lead pilot of the American-made Turkish F-16 Fighting Falcon fighter asked, glancing out his right cockpit canopy at the fighter jet flying loose formation on his right wingtip. 'Status check, 102.'

'*Cok iyiyim, shef,*' his wingman responded. Then, in English, he added: 'Full of joy, boss.'

The flight leader, Major-General Erdal Sivarek, smiled at his wingman's casual use of American fighter pilot's slang. All the years they had spent studying Western fighter tactics, military procedures, and even Western life and society, were obvious. Although using American slang was not officially approved in the cockpit, it helped to get everyone involved geared up and ready to fight.

Sivarek settled into his seat, quickly scanned his instruments, engaged the autopilot, and loosened his straps a bit, cursing his family's bad genetic luck as he did. Unlike the average Turk, Sivarek was just over five feet tall – he needed a specially designed ejection-seat-pan cushion to get the proper cockpit sill clearance, then had to extend the rudder pedals to their full extension so he could reach them. He was built like a fireplug, with a thick chest, thick waist, square head and jaw, and lots of hair – lots of hair on his knuckles, hair on his ankles, and a perpetual 'five o'clock shadow.' Sivarek, call sign *'Magara oglan,'* or 'Cave Boy,' was quick to tell everyone that being short and a little heavy helped him to fight off g-forces encountered in high-speed jet fighter maneuvering, which partially explained why he always pushed himself and his machine beyond the limits – and may have explained why he was the best of the best. Even though he was the commander of the Republic of Turkey's air defense fighters, he was also that country's best fighter pilot and one of the best F-16 Fighting Falcon pilots in the world.

With the MASTER ARM switch off, Sivarek selected each of his weapons to check connectivity. He carried a very light combat load on this patrol mission, just two AIM-7 Sparrow radar-guided missiles and two AIM-9 Sidewinder heat-seeking missiles, a 30-millimeter cannon with 150 rounds of ammunition, plus a centerline fuel tank. Sivarek then activated each of his radar's functions one by one to check them out. His improved F-16C Block 50 fighter, nicknamed *Ornx II* in Turkey, had most of the latest radar, computer, and weapons technology, and was one of the most advanced light combat fighters around, but he was already bored with it. It was agile, sophisticated, and simple to fly and maintain, but it lacked power, speed, and real load-carrying capability. Sivarek had seen the F-15 Eagle fighters and had lusted after one for years, but now the new F-22 Raptor fighters were ready for delivery, and he lusted after one of those now.

'*Yyuz iki hazirim,*' Sivarek's wingman, flying in an identical F-16C, responded on the interplane frequency.

'*Yyuz beer hazirim,*' Sivarek responded. '101's in the green.' He expected nothing else but one-hundred-percent combat-ready aircraft. His squadron was small, just six aircraft, but he firmly believed they were the best-maintained F16s in the world. 'Take spacing. Weapons check.'

'*Tamam,*' replied the wingman. Sivarek's wingman was one of his squadron's more junior officers, but an excellent pilot and inspired instructor. Normally, Sivarek liked to have his junior officers assume flight lead duties, but this mission was more important than most. They were up against an unknown number of strategic bombers attacking targets in the Tolicha Airfield. It was Sivarek's job to find it and stop it. They might have some fighter protection, type and number unknown.

At that very moment, Sivarek picked up a single, quick flash on his radar-warning receiver, ahead and to the left. He immediately turned toward the signal's bearing and, using hand signals, ordered his wingman to assume a combat spread formation, slightly high, slightly behind, and to the leader's right. Definitely an enemy radar signal. It was only there for two seconds, but it was long enough. Sivarek had to chuckle to himself. No matter how high-tech or stealthy a machine is, he thought, the slightest operator error meant the difference between evasion and detection, escape or capture, life or death. The bomber crew had obviously violated procedures by transmitting with their radar – that mistake would cost them dearly.

'Control, 101 has music, India-band search radar,' Sivarek reported.

'Acknowledged, 101,' the ground radar controller responded. 'Radar contact, unidentified aircraft, northeast of your position, low, seventeen miles. Weak radar returns. Stand by.' Sivarek knew the ground radar controller would be frantically switching radar modes, trying to refine the intruder's radar information. 'Still weak radar returns, 101. Fly heading zero-four-five, fly flight level two-zero-zero, stand by for further data. Clear to intercept.'

'Roger, Control.' It must be the stealth bomber, Sivarek thought – the ground radar should be able to see a normal aircraft by now. He turned right a little, offsetting the target slightly so he could use his radar to scan behind the enemy aircraft for other attackers, then switched on his attack radar. Two targets appeared: the closest was at his ten o'clock position, fifteen miles, large, low, and fast;

the other was about fifty miles behind the first, high, and outside the range they were using. Being outside the range didn't automatically exclude it from being a player, but because it was so far away, it wasn't in an effective cover position – it was still close enough to possibly launch missiles from long range or join in the fight after a high-speed dash, but the two F-16s had plenty of time to engage it after taking out the first. Sivarek highlighted each target and briefly activated his IFF (Identification Friend or Foe) interrogator, which scanned for friendly radio codes coming from the targets. No response. They were enemy aircraft, all right.

'Control, 101 flight has target lock, negative IFF. Bandit one is currently at my ten o'clock position, low. Bandit two is at twelve o'clock, fifty miles. We will take bandit one first. Requesting permission to engage bandit one, requesting clearance and advisories on bandit two.'

'Acknowledged, 101,' the ground controller reported. 'Copy negative IFF. You are clear to engage. Radar contact on bandit two, weak return, range fifty-three miles northeast. Will advise on his position. Clear to engage all bandits.'

'Acknowledged, Control, we are proceeding with the attack on bandit one,' Sivarek responded. Calmly and coolly, he selected the AIM-7 radar-guided missile and squeezed the arming button on his inner throttle. *'Radar launch ready,'* the sensuous female computerized voice responded. Sivarek called out *'Oldurmek!'* on the command radio to the ground controller and his wingman and squeezed the trigger, commanding a missile launch. Sivarek started a stopwatch on his knee-board to time the missile's flight time, then checked to be sure his wingman was still with him.

The bandit made a few high-bank but not very aggressive turns – it was easy to keep the radar beam on him. When the missile flight timer ran out, Sivarek radioed, 'Target down radar, target down radar.'

'Acknowledged, 101,' the ground controller replied. 'Good shooting. Range is clear, players are ready. Clear to engage at pilot's discretion.'

For at least the hundredth time this flight, Sivarek checked to be sure the MASTER ARM switch was still OFF, then replied, 'Acknowledged, Control. 102, you have me in sight?'

'Roger, lead.'

'One-oh-two, maintain visual spacing and take the lead. Check nose is cold.' That was a command to check that his weapons were safed as well.

'Acknowledged, 101, I have you in sight, at your four o'clock, high. My nose is cold. Leaving high patrol.'

'Roger.' Erdal looked up and to the right and saw his wingman, right where he said he'd be. 'I have you in sight, 102. Do you have the bandit on radar?'

'Affirmative, 102,' the wingman said.

'You are clear to engage bandit one, 102. You are clear to close in for a gun kill. I will take high patrol and keep an eye on bandit two. Good hunting.' Sivarek removed his oxygen mask as he started a quick climb to get a radar fix on bandit two. A quick kill, nice and neat. A very impressive showing so far for the visiting team.

General Erdal Sivarek was the fifty-two year-old commander of the Republic of Turkey Air Force, and was one of the true fast-rising stars in the Turk Hava Kuvvetleri, the Republic of Turkey Air Force. Sivarek had been an instructor pilot in several different foreign-made combat-coded tactical fighters, including the T-33 jet trainer, F-104 fighter interceptors, F-5E Tiger day interceptor, F-4E Phantom fighter-bomber, and the F-16 fighter-bomber. He'd won the coveted 'Sniper Pilot' wings of a senior experienced attack pilot a full year before most other pilots his age, and he'd made flight leader, operations officer, deputy commander, and commander of his *filo* far ahead of his contemporaries. Three of his five children, including one daughter, were following in his proud footsteps and joining the Turkish Air Force, a fact that made him far prouder than all his other achievements.

Sivarek's 'visiting team' consisted of the very best pilots of the Second Tactical Air Force Command, Turkish Air Force, temporarily assigned to the Nineteenth Aggressor Squadron at Nellis Air Force Base. The Turkish fighter pilots got a chance to train against advanced Western warplanes, and the American and NATO participants benefited by getting realistic adversary training against some of eastern Europe's best fighter pilots and the world's most advanced warplanes. Tolicha Airfield was not in Turkey, but was a large simulated airbase complex built in the high desert wastelands of south central Nevada, in the Air Force bombing ranges about two hundred miles northwest of Las Vegas. The 'airfield' had three long dirt runways, several plywood structures vaguely resembling military-looking buildings, a 'fuel depot' built of hundreds of steel fifty-five-gallon drums welded together, antiaircraft missile and artillery radar emitters to simulate actual airfield defenses, and even plywood or inflatable aircraft shapes set up here and there to make it look like a real operating airfield. And although the 'enemy' target was real and the F-16s did indeed carry live weapons, Sivarek never fired any missiles at it, only electronic signals to the range controllers – he, like his wingman, checked that the MASTER ARM switch was off about every twenty seconds. The range controllers would plot aircraft position and flight parameters at the time the attack signal was received and compute whether or not Sivarek had actually 'killed' his target.

'He killed the leader, Vampire,' Colonel David Luger, the senior mission control officer on this test flight, reported over the secure satellite commlink. Luger was in a special classified section of the Nellis range control complex, watching the exercise unfold before him on several multicolor electronic wall-size monitors. The Nellis range complex was in use twenty-four hours a day, seven days a week, by military units from all over the world, so special facilities were set up to monitor and control classified military weapons tests.

'Sila Zero One didn't make very many hard evasive maneuvers, about half the normal chaff drops, and didn't bother going lower than two thousand AGL,' David added, his Texas drawl coming through the scrambled satellite transmission. 'Just not very aggressive threat reaction.' He had seen every iteration of hotshot fighter and bomber pilots – and the 'target' in this exercise didn't measure up one bit.

'Copy, Dave,' Brigadier-General Patrick McLanahan radioed back. He was flying the right seat on the flight deck of an EB-1C Megafortress-2 strategic 'flying battleship,' an experimental B-1B Lancer supersonic bomber modified as a multipurpose attack and defensive weapons platform. 'We'll put all that on the debriefing tape. Where are they now?'

'Now, now – if I told you, we'd spoil the exercise,' Luger responded with a smile. David Luger had spent most of his Air Force career designing and flying experimental aircraft and was normally a quiet, reserved, almost nerdy guy. But once one of his warplanes was up in action, he took complete control, no matter how badly things appeared to be spinning out of control. 'You said you wanted max realism in this test, so you gotta find them yourself. No fair using other sensor links either – remember, we're simulating you're deep over enemy territory, with no overhead sensor support.'

'All right, all right, no harm in asking,' Patrick said. He signed off with a curt 'Later.'

Sometimes, McLanahan thought, it was as if David was working extra hard just to prove to everyone that he was okay, that the Russian brainwashing or his subsequent CIA deprogramming/reprogramming hadn't affected his mental powers. He had no hobbies, took no vacations, and had few relationships outside of the High-Technology Aerospace Weapons Center. Patrick was pleased to see a budding intimate friendship – hardly a romance yet, but promising – between Dave and Annie Dewey, one of the Air National Guard EB-1 pilots. If only Dave took enough time to get to know her better, David Luger might actually develop a personal life.

To his aircraft commander sitting beside him in the cockpit of the EB-1C Megafortress-2 bomber, nicknamed 'Vampire,' Patrick said, 'Luger's not going to let us sneak a peek, so I better get a fix on all our players. LADAR coming on.'

'Go ahead,' the pilot, Colonel Rebecca Furness, responded curtly. 'Make it quick, General.'

'Rog,' McLanahan said as he activated the LADAR, or Laser Radar. Using tiny laser emitters, the LADAR scanned the sky for fifty miles in all directions, including near-space, and 'drew' a three-dimensional image of all terrain, surface, and airborne objects. In five seconds, LADAR had scanned one hundred and twenty-five thousand cubic miles of earth and sky around the bomber, correlated the scan with known terrain features and current intelligence information, and stored the image in computer memory. Patrick deactivated the system and reported, 'LADAR down, Rebecca.'

Furness glanced over at the large multifunction display mounted on the mission commander's instrument panel, which showed a 'God's-eye' view of the battlefield. 'What do we got, MC?' Furness asked impatiently. Rebecca Furness was a twenty-plus year veteran of the Air Force, serving mostly in the Reserves and Air National Guard. She also had the distinction of being one of the first female combat pilots in the Air Force and one of the first to command a combat unit, the 111th Bomb Squadron of the Nevada Air National Guard – twice. Furness made it clear to everyone who would listen that Patrick McLanahan had been mostly responsible for her losing her command – and she grudgingly admitted that he had been mostly responsible for getting it back for her.

She could think of a hundred things she'd rather be doing than playing chauffeur for the boy general on yet another of his endless test flights. Rebecca had a squadron to assemble, and she knew that a lot of heavy hitters in the Pentagon, in Washington, and all over the world were watching her.

'The Falcons split up,' Patrick replied. 'Number two is chasing the leader while number one is sweeping to his six to check on the number two Sila. Looks like the number two Falcon's going to take his turn and get the lead Sila with a Sidewinder.'

'Well, let's not wait for them to kill both of our attackers,' Furness said. 'Let's bust a move.'

'Hold your horses, pilot,' Patrick said. 'We briefed this engagement a half-dozen times – you know the plan as well as I do. We want to see what they can do on their own first.'

'Why are we doing this support stuff anyway, sir?' Rebecca asked. 'You picked my unit because we're good at tactical bombing. The Bone was built to penetrate heavily defended airspace and attack high-value targets. Your Megafortress contraption can do that job better than even I ever thought possible. Why not let us do our job?'

'This *is* our job right now, Rebecca,' Patrick said testily. 'We are here to deploy a tactical strike support system. The EB-1C Megafortress aircraft are designed to be strategic airborne battleships – that means strike support, surveillance, and reconnaissance as well as attack. Our turn to have fun comes later.'

Rebecca Furness fell silent, disappointed but not surprised over the young general's lack of corporate knowledge. Her first combat unit, the 394th Air Battle Wing of the Air Force Reserve, had flown a modified F-111 G Aardvark supersonic bomber nicknamed the RF-111G Vampire bomber, which had been primarily designed for armed reconnaissance. Rebecca herself had dubbed the EB-1C bomber the Vampire in her old jet's honor. She had enjoyed the armed reconnaissance role back then. Each mission had been a combination of many different responsibilities – standoff attack, antiship, antiradar, antiairfield, minelaying, and antireconnaissance, along with photo-reconnaissance and data relay – and she'd enjoyed the challenge. Rebecca had been positive that, as the nation's first woman to fly in a combat unit, she had been assigned to the 394th because the Vampire was supposed to be a safe, standoff weapon system, not really designed to be a frontline attack unit. The possibility of her being shot down and captured was supposed to be low. But she'd commanded her flight and flown her missions with aggressiveness and courage that won her a lot of attention and praise, and eventually her own command of a combat unit.

But truth to tell, the RF-111 was not a huge success. It was fast, stealthy, capable, and carried a large variety of payloads, like the EB-1, but it was maintenance-intensive, needed a lot of aerial refueling and ground support, and was considered old technology and not a good buy for the military – again, like the B-1. Despite their success in Operation Desert Storm, all of the F-111 models were soon retired from service – and the first to go was the RF-111. Having one aircraft do a variety of missions looked good on paper, but if the sortie didn't launch or couldn't continue the mission, the entire strike package suffered greatly. In effect, the weapon system was *too* capable – instead of considering all the incredible things the plane could do, all the planners could think of was what would happen if the plane broke down and didn't make it to the target area. That was enough to kill the program.

The B-1 fleet came within a few votes of being moth-balled as well. Sixty of ninety planes were placed in 'flyable storage,' which meant they could be flown only after a few months of intensive resuscitation. The rest were transferred to the Air National Guard and Reserves as a cost-cutting measure. Patrick McLanahan and his research group at Dreamland had had other ideas for the fleet. He'd received enough funding to turn eight B-1B Lancers into EB-1C Vampire 'flying battleships,' operated by the Nevada Air National Guard in peacetime and federalized into the Air Force's Air Combat Command in wartime.

The Vampire could drop or launch every weapon in the US arsenal, including antisatellite and anti-ballistic missile weapons and every kind of cruise missile imaginable. Its three bomb bays could hold over sixty thousand pounds of ordnance, and external hardpoints on the fuselage gave it the ability to carry even more weapons. Rebecca was proud to command the nation's one and only Vampire unit. But the EB-1 was very much like a very big RF-111, and in this age of budget cuts and changing priorities, the second coming of the Vampire was very likely to suffer the same fate as the first.

Whether or not the EB-1C actually made it, Rebecca reminded herself that all these tests were helping to make Patrick McLanahan look pretty good, too. His use of the 'we' word, she thought, was being a little disingenuous. Patrick McLanahan seemed like a good guy, but all one-star generals were alike – they just wanted to be two-star generals, and all two-stars wanted was three stars, and so on. When it came right down to it, Rebecca was sure McLanahan would grab the next rung of the ladder and use her and everyone else around him as a step to help himself up.

He was certainly, as the old saying went, 'making hay while the sun shines.' Following his successful efforts both in protecting the United Republic of Korea from attack by China and at the same time protecting China from rogue retaliatory attacks by a power-mad Korean general with control of several dozen nuclear weapons, Patrick McLanahan had become an overnight hero, almost on a par with Norman Schwarzkopf and Colin Powell.

Many comparisons had been instantly made between him and his mentor, friend, former commander, and perennial thorn in the Pentagon's ass, Brad Elliott, the former commander of HAWC, although McLanahan was definitely perceived as more of a team player than Elliott. Patrick's promotion to major-general, his second star in three years, and eventual command of the High-Technology Aerospace Weapons Center – or possibly an operational command – were almost assured.

Now, Rebecca thought, he was going full speed ahead on every possible weapons program that popped into his head – or, more likely, every one that popped into his buddy Dr Jon Masters's head – and he was getting lots of funding and high-powered attention for almost every one of them. Jon Masters was the head of a small high-tech military contractor, Sky Masters Inc. that designed and built various pieces of hardware, including satellites, 'brilliant' cruise missiles, and satellite communications and reconnaissance systems. When most of the officers in charge of HAWC had been dismissed a few years ago because of the Kenneth Frands James spy scandal, McLanahan and his wife Wendy, an electronics engineer, had gone to work for Jon Masters – and Dr Wendy Tork still worked for him today. There was obviously a financial motive for Patrick to develop Sky Masters Inc's systems. It all looked a bit improper for such a direct pipeline between the military and civilian world to exist, but Rebecca was sure that relationship had been scrutinized by the Pentagon seven ways to Sunday by now.

Even though Rebecca questioned and maybe even resented McLanahan's business dealings, to tell the truth, she liked McLanahan's enthusiasm and drive. But she believed sometimes it was all being done at someone else's expense. Namely, hers.

'Vampire, this is Control,' Luger radioed to Furness and McLanahan on the secure Blue Force channel, 'Muck, the Ukrainians look like they're asleep or something. You're going to have to kick the Ukrainians in the butt a little. They seem to be taking this exercise a little too lightly.'

'Roger,' Patrick responded. He took another laser radar 'snapshot' of the area, studied it for a moment, then radioed on the tactical interplane frequency: 'Sila Zero-One, this is Vampire. You've got a bandit on your tail, seven o'clock, less than four miles! I have you at two thousand feet AGL. Recommend you descend, accelerate, begin evasive maneuvers, begin terrain masking, and prepare to respond to a heat-seeking missile threat.'

'Acknowledged,' the pilot responded simply.

Patrick waited – and nothing happened. 'Sila Zero-One, the bandit will be within missile range in five seconds. Get out of there! Now!'

'Give us a heading, Vampire,' the Ukrainian pilot said.

'A heading? *Any* heading! You need to get away from him *now!*'

'Our Sirena tail-warning system is inoperative,' the pilot reported. 'We do not have contact. We need a heading, please.'

'Oh, for Pete's sake...' Patrick was ready to

explode in frustration. He had just given them all the information they needed. Besides, they were two minutes from the target – they should be going balls-to-the-wall anyway! 'Sila Zero-One, do a hard break to the right toward that ridgeline, descend at least fifteen hundred feet, then reverse about two miles from the ridge and accelerate. Make him start thinking about hitting the mountains instead of lining up a shot on you!'

'Acknowledged,' the Backfire pilot said. He started a relatively slow turn toward the north, then reversed his turn almost immediately. 'Maneuver completed,' he reported. 'Returning to target heading. One hundred seventeen seconds to target.'

'I think he's more scared of the mountains than that F-16 pilot will be,' Rebecca said.

'Well, scratch one Backfire,' Patrick said disgustedly.

'Might as well let the Turks get some air-to-air work in and let the Ukrainians practice some bombing.'

'He's not doing anything – just heading direct to the target,' the second Turkish F-16 pilot reported. 'Apparently his tail-warning system is not functioning.'

'Your tail is clear, so he's not playing possum so a fighter can sneak up behind you,' Sivarek said. 'Give him a wake-up call with the radar and see what he does.'

'Roger,' the wingman said. He briefly activated his attack radar. Sure enough, the big Ukrainian bomber sped up slightly and made a steep banked turn to the south, pumping out chaff cartridges from its dorsal ejectors as he detected the F-16's radar sweep. The F-16's radar was effectively decoyed away from the bomber with the combination of chaff and electronic jammers, so the F-16 pilot merely shut off the radar. The Ukrainian bomber rolled right and headed back to his original course, speed, and altitude, as if the threat had suddenly disappeared. 'Level-one evasive maneuvers. Good jamming and chaff, but small altitude and airspeed deviations. He's back on original course and speed. No problem reacquiring.'

'Then take the kill and come join on me and we'll get the second bandit,' Sivarek said.

'Roger,' the wingman said. He immediately switched to Sidewinder missiles, got a locked-on tone seconds later – the Backfire's two big Kuznetov turbofans, developing almost fifty-six thousand pounds of thrust each in afterburner, were pumping out plenty of heat – and 'fired.' 'Missile away, two miles,' the wingman said. No need to start a stopwatch – missile flight time would be mere seconds at this range. 'Good kill.'

'Give him a flyby, then come join on me, zero-four-five at sixty-two bull's-eye, angels minus ten.'

'My pleasure, boss,' the wingman said. He cobbed the throttle to zone three afterburner, flew less than two hundred feet above the Tupolev-22M bomber, waited until he was clear, did two barrel rolls right in front of the Backfire's cockpit windscreen, then started a fast climb. Easy kill against what was once the most feared air-breathing weapon in the Soviet arsenal.

The wingman let his speed build until he went

supersonic, sending a crashing sonic shock wave washing over the bomber. That should wake him up. He then did a victory roll right in front of him, then pitched up and climbed out back to patrol altitude.

One down, one to go.

The threat warning receiver bleeped, displaying a batwing enemy-aircraft symbol on the God's-eye display with range, heading, altitude, and air-speed information. 'We got company,' Patrick announced to Rebecca. He reactivated the laser radar and took another 'snapshot' of the skies around them. 'They're both after the second Sila.'

'We gonna let him get shot down, too?' Rebecca asked sarcastically.

'Let's stick with the plan and see what happens,' Patrick said ruefully.

But with a few more flashes of the laser radar, it was obvious the Ukrainian bomber wasn't quite up to the challenge. When the F-16s hit the Backfire with its radar, the second big Ukrainian bomber started a rapid yet normal descent – wings level, lots of negative g's to blur the pilot's vision, and no steep-bank or inverted maneuvers to increase the descent rate. Patrick even suspected the Backfire bomber's pilot of pulling back on the throttles instead of pegging airspeed right at the max, as if he was afraid of overstressing his plane. The F-16 pilots had an easy attack run, and seconds later recorded a successful AIM-7 radar-guided missile kill.

'I've seen airline captains make more aggressive maneuvers with three hundred paying passengers on their plane,' Rebecca observed. 'Sheesh, does he *want* to get shot down? He have an urge to see an F-16 up close?' It certainly did look as if this new set of attacks on the Backfire bomber were going to be a walk in the park for the skilled Turkish pilots. 'What more do you need to see, General?' Rebecca added. 'The Turks are going to die of boredom if we don't do something.'

'Okay, okay, let's do it,' Patrick said finally. On the interplane frequency, he called out, 'Sila Zero-Two, bandits are at your twelve to one o'clock, thirty miles and closing at five hundred eighty knots.'

'Acknowledged, Vampire. We have them on threat receiver. Commencing attack.'

'Show me something, boys,' Patrick radioed. To the attack computer, he ordered, 'Ready Wolverine, attack route Alpha, sensor response, datalink active.'

'*Ready Wolverine, safe all,*' the computer responded, adding the recommended stop-attack order; then: '*Attack route Alpha confirmed, all sensors active, sensor response active, datalink active. Launch one Wolverine.*'

'Launch one Wolverine,' Patrick ordered.

'*Warning, launch order received, stop launch... Launch sequence commencing, midbay doors opening partial ... missile away ... launcher ready ... doors closed.*'

Patrick waited fifteen seconds until after the last Wolverine cruise missile had launched and the bomb doors closed, then keyed the secure primary UHF radio mike switch and said, 'Sila Zero-Two, this is Vampire Zero-One, you are clear to the target. Good hunting.'

'Acknowledged, Vampire,' a thickly accented Slavic voice responded. '*Prosteesiya haryachiy*. We are target inbound and weapons are hot.'

Both Rebecca and Patrick watched as their wingman took spacing and prepared for its descent. 'What a monster that sucker is,' Patrick breathed.

'It's a piece of shit,' Rebecca murmured.

'Maybe not,' Patrick added proudly. 'Give me a budget and a couple months, and I think I can make that big mother sing.'

'The million-dollar question is: *why?*' Rebecca asked. 'Ukraine can't afford to outfit their Backfire bombers like a Megafortress – that's at least thirty million dollars a copy, and those planes don't look like they're worth it. The crews will take years to train in advanced bomber strike tactics. Who's going to pay for all this? Hell, our new president is downsizing our military like crazy, and he doesn't believe in helping foreign countries – he's not going to pay it.'

'That's not my concern, Rebecca,' Patrick said. 'If they give me a budget to convert Backfires to Megafortresses, and train their crews on how to use them, I'll do it. I'll have the baddest-ass group of flyers in the neighborhood. I guarantee it.'

Well, well, Erdal Sivarek thought, finally these Ukrainian pilots are showing him something. He had locked up the second Ukrainian bomber on radar with ease, and immediately the second target started a rapid descent, over ten thousand feet per minute and steadily increasing. Very

255

impressive. Maybe the Ukrainians knew how to fly evasive maneuvers after all.

The radar box quickly danced to the right side of Sivarek's HUD, and he had to turn hard right to keep the target within the radar cone so the AIM-7 Sparrow missile could home in on it. That was odd – aircraft at this range normally did not move that quickly across the radarscope. The enemy aircraft was sending out jamming signals, but Sivarek's F-16's anti-jamming electronics were successful at hopping to another clear frequency and maintaining a lock...

...right up to the moment when the target suddenly junked left and skittered across the HUD in the other direction. Sivarek reversed his turn again, but it was too late – the target had jinked right off the scope. Somehow it had maneuvered hard enough to beat an F-16, probably the most maneuverable aircraft in the world, and completely disappear from sight!

'*Yyuz bir kor!*' Sivarek called out. 'One-oh-one has lost contact!'

'Lead, I've lost visual with you!' Sivarek's wingman called out. It was understandable – it was bound to happen after all that hard maneuvering. 'I'm at five thousand meters, climbing to high patrol altitude.'

'*Tabii,*' Sivarek replied, consciously forcing himself to slow his breathing to keep from hyperventilating. They had at least five hundred meters' altitude separation – they weren't going to collide. 'I'm trying to reacquire the target now.' He turned immediately to the target's initial heading and swept the skies with his radar, trying to spot the target again. Obviously, the AIM-7 missile wouldn't track without a radar lock, so he had wasted his last Sparrow missile. He felt foolish losing the target. But he quickly choked that thought away. No time to punish himself. Reacquire and kill the bastard, he ordered himself, then figure out why he lost him in the first place when he was back on the ground.

Thankfully, it didn't take long. The target had indeed returned to its original inbound track – predictable, but necessary for most bombers. Few bomber units taught their crews to plan multiple ingress tracks, in case the first one was compromised. If there was only one planned bomb run, the aircrew that survived an attack had no choice but to return to that very same track, and that made it easier for defenders to find them again. 'One-oh-one has reacquired bandit one,' Sivarek reported. 'Tied on and engaged.'

'Don't let him get away this time, Caveboy,' Sivarek's wingman admonished him, with a touch of humor in his voice.

'You will have your chance, Badger,' Erdal radioed back irritably. 'Now stay off the radio and join on me.'

'I have contact on *you*, lead,' the wingman reported, obviously still enjoying twisting his squadron commander's tail a little. 'Your six is clear.'

It was a tail chase this time, a piece of cake compared to the first head-to-head engagement. Sivarek locked up the target right away, maneuvered behind him, selected heat-seeking missiles, and fired another AIM-9 missile as soon as he got within range. Again, the bandit jinked right – same direction as last time. Sivarek took a chance and started a left turn, and sure enough the bandit jinked hard left. It was much easier to keep the bandit in radar lock once he anticipated the turn, and even though the target tried another hard turn, this time it was too late. He scored a direct hit.

'Splash two heater,' Sivarek announced. 'Do you have a visual on me?'

'Affirmative, lead,' Sivarek's wingman said. 'Clear to the south. I'm above and north of you. I'm in hot.'

Sivarek turned hard left, staying at his same altitude. Once his wingman announced he was clear, he started a climb back up to a cover position.

He would have to be sure to quietly accept a good amount of ribbing once the mass and unit debriefs began, Erdal reminded himself. 'Criticize in private, praise in public' was a good rule of thumb for the men, but the men always wanted to see if their commanding officer could take it as well as dish it out. He had to...

'Bombok!' Sivarek's wingman shouted over the interplane frequency. 'I have a visual on bandit two! It's a decoy! An unmanned aircraft!'

A decoy aircraft that moved as fast as a jet fighter, that was even more maneuverable than an F-16? Well, Sivarek thought, this was Nellis. They were playing in the ranges near Dreamland, the top-secret American weapons research facility. The Americans probably flew such exotic, high-tech aircraft every day, just for fun. He just didn't

258

expect to be up against one, that's all.

'Disengage, 102,' Sivarek ordered. He quickly scanned the sky, silently cursing himself. The other bandit must be the carrier aircraft – the real target. He had assumed because the second target was smaller and up high that it was not a threat. He should've had his wingman go after the second bandit. Sivarek immediately shoved in afterburner power and began a steep climbing turn, heading back to where he guessed the second bandit would be. 'One-oh-two, I'm reversing course, heading back to where I first detected bandit two,' Sivarek said. 'Join on me.'

'Two.'

Sivarek immediately got a radar lock on the second aircraft. It was in a steep descent at about eight hundred knots, just over the speed of sound. The radar immediately broke lock, jammed with much heavier jamming signals than before. 'Badger, I've got heavy music...' Just then, the F-16 radar indicated a sweep processor lock fault – the jamming was so intensive and the anti-jamming frequency hopping so rapid and intense that the radar finally gave up. 'Gadget bent. I've got a visual on bandit two at my twelve o'clock, five miles. He's started a rapid descent, heading your way. I'm engaged. I think this is another bomber. Reverse course and cover me. Acknowledge!'

'I copy, 101.'

The Turkish F-16's Sidewinder missile was fully capable of a nose-to-nose missile kill, especially with a target glowing nice and hot from a super-sonic descent. Their closure rate put him in firing position in seconds. He double-checked that the

259

MASTER ARM switch was OFF, selected AIM-9 on the weapons panel, got a flashing SHOOT indication in his heads-up display, then called out on interplane, 'Badger, target in range, I am–'

Suddenly his threat-warning receiver blared to life – an enemy fighter had him locked on radar, well within lethal range! He had gone right to missile guidance without using search radars.

'One-oh-one, Control, pop-up target at your three o'clock, ten miles, low,' the ground radar controller reported. 'Range telemetry flash records a missile kill. You have him in sight?'

At first he was going to say that it was unlikely he'd see any fighter ten miles away, but sure enough he saw him – it looked like another Tupolev-22M, only smaller. A B-1 bomber? 'I see another sweep-wing bomber, Control,' Sivarek said, 'but no fighter.'

'That's who recorded the kill, 101,' the ground radar controller said. 'He has just now recorded a kill on your wingman.'

'Kill? Kill with *what?* Sticks and stones?'

'Range control referee confirms that aircraft has air-to-air capability,' the controller replied. 'Report ready for counterair engagement.'

Sivarek whipped off his oxygen mask in exasperation, but he choked back his anger with a loud laugh. 'You bet we are ready for counterair engagement, Control!' Sivarek shouted. 'Let that pig just try to come at us again.'

'Roger, 101,' the controller said. 'Proceed to waypoint Tango at patrol altitude and hold for range clearance. Advise when established in patrol orbit.'

'Acknowledged,' Sivarek responded. 'Badger, join on me.'

'What happened, Caveboy?'

'We got shot down.'

'By who? I didn't see anyone! I got one squeak on my warning receiver!'

'They claim we got shot down by a B-1 bomber,' Sivarek said. 'Don't worry, it's our turn now. Join on me.'

'Hey, Muck, the Turks say they're pissed and they want a shot at you,' David Luger radioed, the humor obvious in his voice. 'Let's racetrack the Backfires back to destination D-3 and fly the ingress route again with two-minute spacing. Report reaching.'

Like knights on their chargers galloping back to the start of the lists for another pass at their opponents, the two Tupolev-22M bombers and the single EB-1 C Vampire escort traveled back to the northeast corner of the range. McLanahan reported their position just before reaching the point, and moments later they were cleared inbound.

'Looks like the Turks aren't going to mess with the Backfires this time,' Patrick reported, as he studied the first laser radar image. The Turkish F-16s were both staying high, practically ignoring the two Backfire bombers trying to fly in low under them. He touched the super-cockpit display on the right side of the Vampire's big instrument panel, then said to the attack computer, 'Weapons safe, simulated, attack targets.'

'Warning, weapons safe, attack command simulated

261

received, stop attack,' the computer responded. 'Scorpion missiles ready, launch two simulated.'

'Simulated launch two against each target at maximum range,' Patrick said. 'Got you now, boys...'

'Warning, launch command received...'

'Patrick, this is Control, emergency! Knock it off, knock it off, knock it off!' Luger suddenly radioed with the emergency 'stop attack' call. 'Abort the run. Abort the run. Return to base ASAP.'

'Knock it off, knock it off, knock it off!' Rebecca called out on the exercise channel. 'Stop launch!' The warning was echoed by the range controllers to the Turkish Air Force and their air combat controllers, and the computer canceled the launch command just as the forward bomb bay doors were opening. 'What the hell is going on, Luger?'

'We're going operational – right now,' David said breathlessly. 'Get on the ground ASAP.'

'Seats,' Lieutenant-General Terrill Samson said in a booming voice as he trotted into the High-Technology Aerospace Weapons Center's battle staff room, ordering everyone back into their seats from attention. McLanahan and Hal Briggs were already there, along with Colonel Furness and other members of the One-Eleventh Bomb Squadron and a few senior staff officers from HAWC. 'All right, all right, someone tell me what in hell's going on.'

'We just received a warning order ten minutes ago, sir,' Patrick responded. 'There's an incident occurring in Russia, and we've been asked to get ready to provide support.'

'That's not *entirely* true, sir,' Rebecca interjected. '*We* don't have a warning order. We haven't been authorized to do anything yet.'

'There exists an opportunity for the One-Eleventh to provide air support,' Patrick said. 'I think we should get moving on this immediately. The warning order will be coming through at any moment.'

Terrill Samson hadn't felt this kind of excitement since accepting this position at HAWC two years earlier. Although working at HAWC was certainly challenging and exciting, it never had the immediacy and vitality of a combat unit. They tested the world's most advanced weapon systems, true, but in the end mostly what Samson did was write a report, submit engineering data, and give the hardware back to whoever had built it.

Samson glanced at the raw eagerness on the face of Patrick McLanahan, HAWC's deputy commander. He was a natural-born leader, certainly deserving of his own command. But he had been with HAWC too long, seen too much, and did so much weird – and probably illegal – stuff with the high-tech gadgets that filled this place that there was no place for him in the real-world Air Force. How could he be asked to command a wing of B-2A Spirit stealth bombers, the most advanced warplanes known, when he *knew* that there existed in Dreamland planes and weapons that were a hundred times more advanced, a thousand times deadlier?

Samson was concerned. Patrick McLanahan's career had developed under the tutelage – most would use the term 'curse' – of Lieutenant-General Brad Elliott, Samson's predecessor and the man for whom their base had been named. To put it as politely as possible, Elliott had been a rogue officer, a completely loose cannon. He'd been killed on one of his infamous 'operational test flights,' where he had flown an experimental B-52 bomber – stolen right out from under federal agents – over China during the recent China-Taiwan conflict. Although his efforts had helped avert a global thermonuclear exchange, perhaps for the sixth or seventh time in his career at HAWC, one couldn't help but notice that most officials in the White House and the Pentagon had breathed a sigh of relief after hearing that Elliott was dead. The only thing that still kept them up at night was the fact that Elliott's body had never been recovered, so there was still a possibility that the bastard was still alive.

Patrick McLanahan had learned from Brad Elliott that, when the shooting starts and it seems like the world is on the brink of destruction, sometimes in order to get results it was necessary to color outside the lines. Patrick was much more of a 'team player' than Brad Elliott ever was – but he was no longer young, he had rank and certainly much higher status, and he was entering his second decade at the isolated supersecret desert research base. Like McLanahan, Terrill Samson was a protégé of Brad Elliott – he knew him, knew what a little power and a 'damn the torpedoes, full speed ahead' attitude could do to a man. Samson had chosen to follow his own path, and he'd earned his stars by playing by the rules. He was certainly worried that Patrick Mc-Lanahan was following the ghost of Brad Elliott down the wrong path.

'Time out, children, time out,' Samson said pointedly. 'I got a call saying that we received a warning order. Whatever we received, who's got it?'

'Actually, sir, I do,' Lieutenant Colonel Hal Briggs said.

'You do?' Samson knew that Hal Briggs was a highly trained and experienced commando and infantryman – serving as HAWC's chief of security was only one of his areas of expertise. He also knew that Briggs had been an operative in some highly classified intelligence operations unit that he had not been privileged enough to have a need to know. Briggs handed him a telefax from the command post, sent from the Director of Central Intelligence, authorizing Hal Briggs as the point of contact for this operation. 'Okay, I'm impressed,' Samson said truthfully. 'Well, Colonel, we're waiting. If you're permitted to tell us, let's hear it.'

'Yes, sir,' Briggs said. The tall, thin, black officer, who had been assigned to Dreamland longer than anyone else in the room, looked as excited as a kid who'd just been told he'd be going to Disneyland for his birthday. 'Since Patrick has been involved in operations of this sort before, I briefed him on the warning order. He gave me some suggestions, and then recommended I call you and the One-Eleventh in on it. Since I'm the man in charge of the team, I authorized it.'

'Proceed, then.'

Briggs motioned to Patrick, who punched instructions into his computer terminal, and a map of western Russia appeared on the large electronic computer monitor at the foot of the conference table. 'My team has been tasked to support a hostile rescue mission inside Russia. Apparently the CIA has a deep cover agent on the run outside Zhukovsky Air Base east of Moscow. The normal procedure was to activate an underground railroad-type network inside Russia to get her out, but the network was shut down.'

'Obviously, CIA neglected to tell the agent about this tiny detail,' Terrill Samson surmised.

'You got it, sir,' Briggs said.

'What team are you talking about, Colonel?' Furness asked, glancing warily at both McLanahan and Briggs. She was a full member of HAWC as well as the One-Eleventh Bomb Squadron and had complete access to the facility, but she also reminded herself that what she knew was probably only the tip of the iceberg – this place was so compartmentalized and so deep undercover that she'd probably be stupefied by everything that went on here.

'Unfortunately, I can't go into details, ma'am,' Briggs replied. 'I'll reveal as much as I can to give as much planning data to your guys, but you'll have to follow my lead on a lot of it. Anyway, CIA wants this agent out immediately. I fly out immediately. I'm going to pick up some gear at a friend of ours place in Arkansas, and then deploy with my team to Turkey to stage out of there.'

'Well, good luck,' Samson said. 'But I'm still confused. What's our involvement?'

'Hal was tasked to perform a hostile exfiltration deep in Russian airspace,' Patrick explained. 'I recommended that we provide air cover for his team.'

'*Air cover?*' Samson asked. 'What do you mean, "air cover"?'

'Here's the target area,' Patrick replied, motioning to the computerized map. 'In about forty-two hours, Hal's team will land somewhere near Zhukovsky, here, to attempt to extract the CIA operative. Hal expects heavy resistance – apparently they've been looking for the agent for about twelve hours already, and the search is intensifying. I suggested stealth airborne cover for the infiltration and exfiltration.'

'You mean, send Vampires into Russia to cover a CIA rescue operation?' Samson asked incredulously. 'C'mon, Patrick, you've got to be joking! We aren't in a position to provide any sort of air cover!'

'I disagree, sir,' Patrick said. He punched up the operational status readout for the 111th Bomb Squadron and displayed it on the screen. 'Out of six operational EB-1C Vampire bombers,' he summarized, as the readout popped up on the large electronic briefing board, 'two are available right now, one is airborne and can be ready to go a few hours after the first two are loaded, one is in post-maintenance and can be ready if necessary in about eight hours, and one is undergoing major modifications and is unavailable.'

Samson checked the data block for this set of information – and saw that Patrick had had this data pulled a few hours earlier. So this wasn't exactly the no-notice action meeting it looked like: McLanahan, most likely Luger, and maybe even Briggs had already gotten word about this operation and hadn't told him about it.

'But the One-Eleventh isn't operational yet,' Samson argued, deciding to hold off confronting McLanahan with his thoughts for now. 'We're still deep into the demonstration–evaluation stage. They won't be operational for at least another year.'

Patrick called up the roster of all the flight crews qualified to fly the Vampire strategic flying battleship. 'We've got the crews available, sir,' Patrick went on hurriedly. 'I'll take the lead plane. Major Cheshire can fly as my aircraft commander.' Major Nancy Cheshire was HAWC's chief flight test pilot. If Terrill Samson knew her better, he would be far more afraid of *her* transforming into an ideological clone of Brad Elliott than Patrick McLanahan or anyone else at HAWC. 'Colonel Furness and Colonel Luger can fly as the backup crew, followed by Dewey and Deverill. They're the most advanced of the One-Eleventh's initial cadre. Then–'

'Pardon me, sir,' Rebecca interjected, her eyes narrowing in exasperation, 'but you aren't in our squadron.'

'This will be an important mission for all of us. Major Cheshire and I have the most experience–'

'Excuse me, sir,' Rebecca said, more insistently this time, 'but with all due respect – you got us into this, and you have to let us finish it.'

'What the hell are you talking about, Rebecca?'

'Sir, you created this unit specifically for

268

missions like this,' Rebecca said. 'You gave us the tools, you trained us, and you prepared us. Now you've got to let us do our job.'

'This unit has been together for less than a year,' McLanahan said. 'It's not an operational unit, not by a long shot. Those planes still belong to us. If there's a mission to do–'

'Everyone, *stop!*' Samson cut in hotly. 'Listen to me, Patrick. We will never be approved for a mission like this. We *barely* got approval to form the One-Eleventh, and that was just a few months ago. We may have two birds ready to fly, but that's ready to fly test and evaluation missions on the ranges, not fly into combat – and sure as hell not over *Russia!*'

'Actually, sir – I went ahead and got approval,' Patrick said.

'*Say again?*' Samson boomed, his eyes blazing in fury.

'That was my call, sir,' Briggs said. 'Patrick ran the idea down to me, I called the DCI, Director Morgan; he happened to be meeting with Secretary of Defense Goff in the White House, he pitched the idea to him, spoke with Patrick for a while–'

'You spoke with the Secretary of Defense?' Samson asked. Left unsaid was 'Without notifying me first?'

But Patrick knew what Samson was angry about. 'I called you as soon as I was put through to the Secretary, sir,' Patrick said. 'He gave a provisional "go-ahead" a few moments later, pending clearance from the President. He should be talking to the President right about now. It happened pretty fast.' Patrick handed him a printout with a signed authorization from the SecDef. Samson stared in disbelief at his deputy commander, his lips taut, but said nothing else. 'I've already built the generation schedule, put the crews on crew rest – except myself, of course – and I'll have my first status briefing in–'

'Excuse me, sir,' Long interjected again, 'but that's *my* job. I'd appreciate it if you'd step aside and let me do it.'

'Major, I appreciate your enthusiasm, and this is not a criticism of you or your unit's skill or readiness,' Patrick said, typing more instructions into the computer as he spoke, 'but I'm in charge of this mission, and I'll take care of the planning this time around. I'd appreciate it if you'd stand by and help me get the maintenance and combat support staffs briefed and organized, and then we'll–'

'Hold it right there, Patrick,' General Samson interjected. 'I've heard enough. Patrick, this time you're wrong, and the major is correct, on all counts. You've done a good job training the One-Eleventh. They've done well, better than anyone's expected, given their recent history and repu-tation. Colonel Furness is also correct in pointing out that you are *not* a member of that squadron. And another thing: technically, the Vampires belong to the taxpayers, not to me, not to you. They are not *your* personal property.'

'I'm well aware of that, sir,' McLanahan said. 'I wasn't implying–'

'Frankly, General, I expected a little more sup-port for one of the teams you yourself created,'

Samson said. 'I know you want to get in on the action, but try not to slam one of your own to do it. I only need one word from you, Patrick: is the One-Eleventh ready to fight?'

Patrick looked at Furness and Long, who glared back at him, and then at the other representatives of the 111th Bombardment Wing 'Aces High.' Patrick found it was one of the hardest questions he'd ever had to answer: if he said 'no,' he'd be a liar, and if he said 'yes,' he'd be effectively cutting himself out of the unit and the mission he'd worked so hard to build. But there really wasn't any conflict over the question at all – and he knew it:

'The answer is, yes, sir, they are,' Patrick replied resolutely. 'They've flown every training sortie and every research mission we've asked them to fly; they've prepared well. The initial cadre is some of the best flyers I've ever worked with – they're aggressive, knowledgeable, and dedicated. They're ready to go kick some butt.' He turned to Rebecca. 'My apologies. I was out of line. Of course, it's your squadron.' His eyes were no longer ordering or demanding, but not quite pleading, either – not yet. 'But I do know more about the Vampires than anyone else on this base, and I've worked with ISA before many times. Put me on the inflight backup bird, along with Nancy Cheshire. She's the most experienced aircraft commander.'

'We can use your expertise in the virtual cockpit, sir,' Long said. It was too obvious that Long enjoyed watching McLanahan get a good hand-slapping by Samson and was only too anxious to give him one last jab in the ribs.

'No, I think having him in the backup bird is a good idea,' Samson interjected. 'But I'm going to exercise a little commander's prerogative and order Colonel Furness to fly as Patrick's AC. Nancy Cheshire and Dave Luger will command the virtual cockpit for the mission.' To Long, he said, 'Major, you're taking over planning for this operation. I'd like a mass briefing in twenty-four hours. According to the warning order, your planes are supposed to be over the patrol area in about forty hours.'

'Yes, sir. We'll be ready.'

'Colonel Briggs, I imagine you'll be on your way too,' Samson said with a smile. 'Stopping off for some wonder toys, I suppose?'

'Yes, sir,' Briggs said happily. 'I can think of one or two things we might need for a mission like this.'

'I'm sure you can,' Samson said. He extended his big hand, and Briggs shook it warmly. 'Good luck, good hunting. Tell me all about it when you get back.'

'You got it, General.'

General Samson dismissed his staff and the One-Eleventh squadron officers, but not before giving Patrick a warning glare. For the first time since they had been working together, Patrick McLanahan had come very, very close to stepping over the line. He had a much better reputation than that. Hopefully, it did not portend a sign of bad things to come. He made a mental note to sit down with Patrick after this was over with and have a talk – not a 'heart-to-heart,' but a real 'get the shit out of your ears' talk.

Most of the senior officers and NCOs headed right for the combat support staff mission planning room, which held a series of computers that would assist them in mission planning. As usual Patrick headed for the seat behind the master terminal – but he realized he had virtually pushed John Long out of the way. Patrick waited a few heartbeats to see if Long would let 'rank have its privileges,' but no chance of that. This was Long's chance to show what he and the One-Eleventh Strategic Squadron could do, and he was anxious to go. 'Sorry about that, John,' Patrick said. He yielded the seat to the One-Eleventh's operations officer.

'No problem, sir,' Long said, not bothering to disguise a smirk. Following McLanahan's lead, the HAWC staff officers gave up their seats to the One-Eleventh's staff members. Long handed him a printout. 'Here are the things I'll need you to work up for us, sir. We'll have a "how d'ya do" brief in two hours. Let me know if you need any help with that.'

'I can work better at the master console, Major,' Patrick said. But Long had already turned back and logged into the master terminal, ready to start building his flight plan, scheduling refueling and forward basing support, and downloading intelligence data. His flight commanders and support staff logged on as well, and in moments they were all busy entering data and running mission planning checklists.

If the little prick asks me to get coffee for him, Patrick thought as he left to head back to his office, I'm going to have to deck him.

The White House President's Study
that same time

The one good thing about this president, Secretary of Defense Robert Goff remarked to himself, is that he was totally accessible – because he never went anywhere. He was always working in the office, usually in the study adjacent to the Oval Office, except if conducting a small meeting with his staff or greeting visitors. Because he had a very small political machine behind him, he rarely did public appearances or Party fundraisers. If he had any free moments, they were spent with his wife and children upstairs in the residence. Robert knew enough not to disturb the President when he was meditating, usually at ten A.M. and three P.M., but otherwise President Thorn was working the phones or on his computer, being the chief executive.

Goff sometimes worried about his old friend. He didn't play golf, didn't jog, didn't sail, rarely visited Camp David, didn't do many of the things other chief executives were noted for doing to relax. His only relief from life in Washington was the occasional weekend visit to his parents' home in Vermont or his wife's mother's home in New Hampshire to see the grandkids. Other presidents were criticized for being 'trapped' in the White House by their duties and responsibilities, but Thorn seemed to get his drive and energy from the deluge of meetings, reports, briefings, and decisions he had to deal with every day.

Goff knew he was intruding on the President's meditation time, but he entered the study anyway and quietly took a seat on his favorite chair in a corner of the room, watching his friend, the most powerful man on planet Earth, in silence. The President sat quietly, hands folded serenely in his lap, his eyes closed, his breathing shallow and even. Goff had gone through the meditation lessons years ago, given by Thomas's wife, and he had tried to do it twice a day, but that practice had stopped long ago. If he tried very hard, he could remember his mantra. He told Thomas he still kept up with his meditation, and Thomas just smiled and nodded.

Well, Goff thought, maybe Thomas didn't need to take up golf or jogging or sailing. The President was in extraordinary physical condition, even though as far as Goff knew, he didn't exercise regularly. Seated there in a white shirt, his tie loosened and his sleeves rolled up above his wrists, he looked fit and trim. Bob had once asked Thorn about his lack of exercise, and he had responded by dropping down on the floor in his business suit and doing a handstand, holding his legs out completely horizontal with the floor for fifteen full seconds – first with two hands, then one hand, then *three fingers*. It was a most impressive display of strength and balance. Thorn claimed that it was part of the Vedic sciences, a harmony of spirit, mind, and body that allowed his body to do anything his mind commanded. He said the possibilities were endless – that was only a small sample of what he could do.

Of course, as a former Special Forces commando, Thorn had already done enough exercise to last twenty men a lifetime – to him, supporting his body with one finger might be child's play. Goff had a hard time believing any of that New Age yogi crap.

'You ever regret we did this, Bob?' he heard Thorn ask. He hadn't heard or even noticed the President conclude his meditation.

'Every day,' Goff responded. The President smiled. 'You?'

'No,' the President replied gently, and Goff knew that was the truth. The relaxed smile dimmed, replaced by a grim, no-nonsense visage. 'Something's happened? My first sensitive international intelligence crisis?'

Goff had no idea how the President could have guessed this – he had just gotten wind of it himself. 'Yes, sir,' Goff said. 'Doug Morgan and the Vice President are on their way. It has to do with Project Siren.' Goff knew he never had to back-brief the President on anything they had talked about within the past six to nine months – Thorn had a remarkable ability to recall the details of any discussion or briefing, no matter how informal or routine. He had been briefed on roughly three dozen on-going intelligence operations inside Russia alone, but he could recall major details about each and every one of them. 'She was flushed out of hiding, and the network set up to retrieve her broke down. CIA wants to pull her out immediately. They believe she might have information relating to the recent attack in Albania.'

'Deep inside Russia, near Moscow – Zhukov-sky, I believe?' Goff nodded. 'Has to be by air, then. They have someone in mind? Delta Force? Air Force Special Ops?'

'Intelligence Support Agency.'

'Which cell?' He then held up a hand. 'Madcap Magician, launching out of Turkey.'

'The very one, sir.'

'They need air support?'

Goff was flabbergasted – it was as if the President had already planned this operation in his head, considered all the possible hazards, and had come up with a full set of contingency plans. 'They're requesting specialized stealth air cover.'

'That deep into the heart of Russia, they want counterair, SEAD, antitank, antipersonnel, the works – they want someone from HAWC, right?'

'Yes, sir.'

'Sit down with Doug, Lester, and General Venti, give them the go-ahead,' the President said. 'Advise me when the operation is under way.'

'Don't you want to discuss this with the rest of the Cabinet, the Joint Chiefs, with the congressional leadership?'

'Bob, unless the Constitution's been rescinded in the past twenty minutes, I am the commander-in-chief,' the President said. 'You are my secretary of defense and national security advisor, and the Vice President is my chief of staff. I'm familiar with Project Siren, and I think I have an idea about the difficulties of doing a covert extraction so far inside enemy territory. I am therefore authorizing you to plan the mission with the help of your intelligence and military advisors and get it under way immediately.'

'But ... but what about the possibility of something going wrong?' Goff asked. 'Are you going to just authorize such a dangerous mission without considering all the dangers and ramifications first?'

'If we had the time, I would. But I presume we don't have the time to waste. ISA and HAWC are good choices. Get them moving.'

Goff, still stunned, could do nothing else but nod. The President nodded and got back to work on his computer. Goff headed for the door; then he stopped and said, 'This could be a very big disaster, Mr President. Are you sure you don't want to think about it some more?'

Without looking up from his work, the President asked, 'You haven't been keeping up with your meditation, have you, Bob?'

Goff shook his head and chuckled. It was Thorn's ass on the line, he knew it, and he didn't seem too perturbed by it. 'I'll get the mission moving immediately, sir.'

Chapter Four

Near Zhukovsky Air Base,
Russian Federation
two evenings later

'*Nasrat f karman!*' one of the hoboes exclaimed as the stranger emerged from the shadows. 'Well, well, what do we have here?'

The five hoboes under the bridge slowly rose to their feet as the woman in the jogging suit approached their tiny campfire. Outside, the freezing rain had started again, driven by gradually increasing winds; it would begin snowing soon, and this time they were in for measurable accumulations.

Even in the dim light, the hoboes could tell she was shivering uncontrollably. She may have once looked pretty, but her features were now pale and haggard. Her jogging suit, an expensive imported one, was filthy and encrusted with frozen mud and leaves. 'Who might you be, *sika?*'

'*Pamageetye ... pamageetye mnye pazahaista.* I ... I need help, please,' the woman stammered through chattering, blistered lips. 'Please ... please help me.'

'A pretty young thing like you?' the biggest hobo, obviously the leader of the group, responded. 'Of course, of course. Anything you want.' He stroked a thick, scraggly beard and licked his lips. 'But it'll cost you. Don't worry, though. It'll help you warm up.'

Linda Mae Valentrovna Maslyukov brought her

right hand up, the one holding the police pistol. 'Don't move, asshole,' she said weakly. The hoboes tensed, staring at the gun in total surprise. 'All I want is a blanket and some food. We don't want any police attention.' Two days in the freezing cold, with no shelter and no warm clothing, had finally taken its toll. She reasoned – probably correctly – that she was better off trying to get help from these hoboes under the bridge than risk being seen at the tavern. It was either die of hypothermia or risk being caught. 'Just give me some food and I'll–'

The piece of driftwood came out of nowhere, landing squarely on the back of her head. Already half-conscious from exposure, Maslyukov collapsed in a heap.

'You *huyisos!*' the big hobo shouted angrily at the hobo who had been hiding in the shadows and had clubbed Linda from behind. 'What did you knock her out for? I'm not going to fuck an unconscious bitch!'

'Well, then I will!' one of the other hoboes chimed in eagerly.

'*Uyobyvat!* Get the fuck out! I get first taste!' the big one said. 'You, get over to the highway and flag down a cop. This has got to be the bitch the police have been looking for. Maybe we'll get a reward for finding her. Take your time.' He bent down, pocketed the pistol, then unzipped the woman's jogging suit jacket and fondled her breasts. 'And someone get me some water and some vodka. Let's see if we can wake sleeping beauty up and have ourselves a party before the police get here.'

'It's her, all right,' the police officer said, holding the photograph up to the face. Even though her face was white with cold, streaked with frozen dirt, blood, and mucus, and the hair tangled and twisted, she was recognizable. The officer unzipped the top of her jogging suit, checked her carotid for signs of a pulse. 'She's still alive. Barely.' He then roughly fondled her breasts. 'Wow. Nice big American breasts.'

'Knock it off, *pizdasos*,' the first officer's partner said. 'Is the only way you can cop a feel with a woman is to find one half frozen to death?' He shined his flashlight over her body, noting the torn pants pulled halfway down her buttocks and the palm prints across her breasts. 'Besides, you want any of that after these *gavnos* pawed her? If she doesn't die of the cold or of any diseases from these animals, she'll die of shame once she finds out who touched her.'

They were at the edge of the river, several meters upstream from the bridge abutment where the hoboes lived. They had found the woman facedown in three inches of snow. The first officer shined his flashlight under the river overpass and saw a few faces. 'Disgusting pigs. How in hell could you give those animals any money?'

'*Shto ty priyibalsa ka mn'e?* We've been working double shifts for two days trying to find this *kurva*,' the second officer said. 'If they hadn't come forward, we'd still be working to find her, and you know we're not going to get paid any overtime. A few rubles is cheap goodwill for handing her over to us alive. If they killed her, I'd make sure they all got their balls handed to them.

Now stop copping a feel and call it in. The faster you leave her tits alone and have the MSB collect her, the faster we can go get a drink.' While the first officer pulled out his portable radio to call in their discovery, the second officer searched the woman, then covered her with his coat to keep her from dying of exposure.

'Ambulance and an Interior Ministry unit are on the way,' the first officer reported. 'ETA twenty minutes.'

'Christ, she might be dead by then,' the second officer said. 'We better take her to the hospital at Zhukovsky.' The two police officers picked her up and had carried her several dozen meters through the brush and rocky riverbank toward their car parked just off the bridge, when they heard the heavy rotor sounds of an approaching helicopter. 'Well, they got here fast. We'll stay put.'

'Sounds like a heavy chopper – must be army,' the first officer said. The helicopter flew out of sight, but they could hear it hover, then land nearby. It did not use any lights for landing – a very remarkable feat, considering the poor weather. A few minutes later, they heard a rustling of branches, but could see no one. 'Where in hell are they? What's taking them so long?'

'I'll go and–' But just then, their flashlights spotted a figure dressed in what looked like a bulky flight suit or battle-dress uniform, wearing what looked like a flying helmet. 'That looks like the pilot. Where's his crew? Or is he by himself?' He raised his voice and shouted, '*Vi zhdyotye kavoneebood?* Are you waiting for someone? Get over here!'

Suddenly, they heard a voice say directly behind them in terrible, electronically synthesized Russian, '*Ya plokha gavaryoo parooskee, tovarisch.* I don't speak much Russian, comrade. Neither does my friend over there.' They turned and saw a figure dressed in a dull-gray bodysuit wearing some sort of space-age full-face helmet with bug-eyed electronic sensors.

'*Who in hell are you?*' the first police officer shouted in Russian.

As if in reply, there was a flash of blue-white light, and bolts of lightning shot out from small electrodes on the figure's shoulders. The first police officer screamed, stiffened as if he had touched a high-tension wire, and fell flat on his face in the snow, twitching as if every nerve ending in his body was firing uncontrollably.

'*Yop tvayu mat!*' The second police officer swung his body, flinging his submachine gun hanging on its shoulder strap from behind his back around into his hands, and he fired a three-round burst from his hip from a distance of no more than fifteen feet. At that range, he couldn't miss ... but to his amazement, the stranger didn't go down, only staggered back a few steps. '*Ya nee paneemayoo...?*'

'*Spakoyniy nochyee*, dude,' the stranger said, and he hit the second officer with another bolt of energy. Sparks of electricity leapt from the officer's body to the gun until the officer finally fell unconscious to the ground.

The stranger quickly bent down to examine Linda Maslyukov. 'It's her, Chris,' he told his partner via short-range datalink. He hefted the woman over his shoulders in a fireman's carry.

'I'll take her. You cover us. Make sure our grimy friends behind us don't try to get too brave.'

'Roger. Follow me,' the second stranger responded, and he headed out back toward where the helicopter had landed.

But they had not gone too far when they heard the sound of several sirens approaching fast. 'Well, this is another fine mess you've gotten us into this time, Ollie,' the strangely costumed figure carrying Maslyukov said in an electronically synthesized voice. His helmet-mounted electronic displays showed a two-dimensional depiction of the vehicles, including their speed, direction of travel, and an electronic guess of the vehicle type, based on the strength of the millimeter-wave radar return. 'Aces, I've got a couple visitors at my three o'clock, three hundred and twenty yards, two inbounds. One armored vehicle, maybe a BTR.'

'Copy, Tin Man,' a voice belonging to Duane Deverill, mission commander of an EB-1C Vampire bomber flying nearby, responded. Seconds later, there was a tremendous explosion, and the armored personnel carrier disappeared in a ball of fire.

'Good shooting, Aces,' Briggs said. 'C'mon, Sarge, let's move.'

'For Pete's sake, sir,' the strange figure's partner responded in his microphone with an exasperated voice. The big commando, his face a death's mask in black and green camouflage makeup beneath his multifunction combat helmet, turned toward his partner, his mouth curled in a sneer. The US Marine Corps veteran looked like some sort of monster beetle – along with the oddly shaped helmet with large electronic 'eyes,' the commando wore a battle-dress uniform composed of thin ceramic armor plates, a web harness with several devices and pouches attached to it, and a utility belt with as many computer modules and sensors attached to it as weapons. 'It's *Stan,* not Ollie. Oliver Hardy would say that to Stan Laurel. And it's not *fine* mess, it's *nice* mess. "Here is another *nice* mess you've gotten me into, *Stan.*" You keep on mixing them up like that, sir, and I'll have to waste you.'

US Air Force Lieutenant Colonel Hal Briggs, the man carrying Linda Mae Maslyukov, shrugged his shoulders, which only accentuated his very unsoldierlike appearance. While his partner, Marine Corps Master Sergeant Chris Wohl, looked unusual in his insectlike exoskeleton, his commanding officer looked even stranger. Hal Briggs wore a sleek, dark gray body suit resembling a scuba diver's wet suit, with only a thin back-back, bullet-shaped shoulder-mounted devices, and a utility belt with several small modules attached. His helmet, too, had large bug-eyed electronic sensors, but it was a full-face helmet that completely sealed the outfit. He wore all-terrain boots with thick soles and strange extensions on the backs of his calves.

'Stan. Ollie, Sergeant Chris Wohl – they're all just a bunch of old farts to me,' Briggs quipped. He ignored Wohl's dark scowl. Through his electronic visor, he could see the exfiltration helicopter in the distance. 'Follow me.' Staying close to whatever cover he could find, but not really bothering to use proper cover techniques, Hal

Briggs dashed off in the direction indicated on his visor's navigation display. Wohl followed closely behind, taking a bit more care to keep himself concealed but not wanting to lag behind.

Air Force Major John 'Trash Man' Weston swore he could feel the heat from the exploding Russian armored personnel carrier through the cockpit of his MV-22 Pave Hammer special operations transport, even though he was a couple miles away from where the vehicle suddenly exploded, at night, in the dead of an eastern European winter. 'Check in, Tin Man,' Weston radioed. 'Was that explosion yours?'

'We're on our way, Hammer,' Briggs radioed back. 'That was our guardian angel helping out. Our ETA two minutes.'

Weston and his six-man crew were part of a team called 'Madcap Magician,' a secret cell of Intelligence Support Agency. The ISA was composed of a series of such cells, unknown to each other, deployed all over the world to assist the CIA in high-value rescues, high-risk attacks, reconnaissance, intelligence-gathering, or other missions considered too 'hot' for field operatives and too politically sensitive for the military.

This was by far the riskiest operation Weston's crew had ever flown as special ops crews: deploy from the US Special Operations Command detachment based at Batman Air Base in eastern Turkey across the Black Sea and the Republic of Ukraine, refuel at low level with an MC-130P aerial refueling tanker over eastern Ukraine near Char'kov, then fly another five hundred miles across southwestern Russia to the outskirts of

Moscow itself.

But that twelve-hundred-mile trip was only the beginning of Weston's extraordinary mission. Dodging civilian and military air defense radar coverage around Moscow and Zhukovsky Air Base, Weston and his crew had to search four different contact points around Zhukovsky Air Base, looking for a single agent who was probably in hiding. The MV-22's infrared scanner was the primary search sensor; if the sensor showed any individuals in the area, Weston would drop off Briggs and Wohl, who would search the area near each contact point for the agent. They had less than an hour loiter time to find her before fuel would run low and they'd be forced to return to the MC-130P Hercules tanker flying in northeastern Ukraine to refuel. They had enough daylight for only two such searches before they'd have to return to Batman Air Base before sunrise.

Their only advantage: they knew that the agent would be at one of those four contact points.

The thirty-two year-old aircraft commander, married and father of two, had been briefed on the importance and dangers of this mission, but he had volunteered anyway. As shitty as he felt his job was sometimes, being a spy for the United States government had to be an even shittier job. If he had the skills to attempt to save this spy's life, he had an obligation to use them. And with the MV-22E Pave Hammer I special operations transport, he definitely had the gear to do the job. The MV-22E was modified with more powerful engines and stronger wings for low-level flying; an air refueling probe for extended range; rugged landing gear for landing on unimproved surfaces; ultraprecise satellite and inertial navigation systems, night vision, forward-looking infrared scanners, and terrain- and obstacle-avoidance radar for treetop-level flying in any weather, day or night; and threat countermeasures equipment such as radar jammers, radar warning receivers, and decoys to protect the crew from hostile antiaircraft fire.

Of course, Weston would never ask his family the question about whether or not he should go. His wife was especially accustomed to the bliss of ignorance that surrounded her husband's job. The ISA deployed year-round to every corner of the globe. The wives and families never knew any details. The cell's rotation came up, they were gone, and sometime later – days, weeks, months later – they would return. The families watched the news and speculated about whether their husbands or wives were involved in that particular crisis, but they never knew for sure. The only indications that they might have been involved in something horrible were the faraway stares and wandering attention at the dinner table.

Sometimes, they didn't come back. Instead of reunions with loved ones, there were condolences, tears, and a flag folded up into a triangle. If they were lucky, they got the body back. Even then, no explanations. Never any explanations.

Quite unabashedly, Weston believed one other thing: the ISA picked the right guy for the job. John Weston, an ROTC cadet and high school chess champion from Springfield, Illinois, was pretty much a book-loving stay-at-home-with-the-kids ex-farm boy nerd most of the time, but he did have one quality absolutely no one disputed: he could make an MV-22 Pave Hammer transport plane dance.

Right now, however, he wasn't sure if all the dancing in the world could get them out of this mess. 'How's it look, Flex?' Weston asked.

'Like shit, boss,' Master Sergeant Ed 'Flex' Fratierie, the senior loadmaster, responded. The big amateur bodybuilder and Air Force special ops veteran was standing in the port-side doorway of the MV-22, strapped to the interior of the fuselage with a safety harness and wearing night-vision goggles. 'I don't see Tin Man. But I do see more heavy military vehicles coming down the road. ETA about five minutes.'

'Tin Man, Hammer, we've got company,' Weston radioed. 'Four minutes out. Better hustle.'

'Exfils inbound from the southeast and east, crew,' Fratierie radioed on the secure intercom channel, watching Briggs and Wohl through his NVGs. 'Identity confirmed.'

'Security out!' Weston ordered. Fratierie directed his three commandos to deploy around the MV-22 Pave Hammer tilt-rotor as guards during the evacuation. 'Get ready to–'

'Heavy weapons fire west!' one loadmaster shouted. 'Coming from one of the inbound vehicles. Range four klicks!'

'Aces will be coming in hot in twenty seconds,' Deverill reported. 'Can you catch him, Tin Man?'

'Roger,' Chris Wohl responded. 'I need a range and bearing to the inbound, sir.'

Hal Briggs stopped, then turned to the west and scanned the area with his helmet-mounted

291

sensors. He pointed away down the highway. 'Three point five K meters, Stan,' he radioed. 'Fast-moving, big – might be a wheeled APC.'

'Finally got it right, sir,' Wohl said. He raised a large weapon that resembled a cross between an M60 machine gun and a ray gun, sighted through a large electronic multispectral scope, aimed, and fired toward the highway. A hypervelocity projectile about the size of a cigar, but traveling five times faster than a bullet, hissed out of the weapon's muzzle with a sound resembling a loud buzzing cough. There was no recoil – the same electromagnetic impulses that sent the projectile on its way also dampened out the tremendous recoil.

Exactly three thousand and seventeen yards away, the depleted uranium hypervelocity railgun projectile shot through a half-inch of steel plating on a Russian BTR-27 wheeled armored command post vehicle racing down the highway, proceeded unimpeded through the six-hundred-horsepower diesel engine, through the fuel tank, out the back end, and into the engine compartment of a police car traveling fifty yards behind the BTR, before it finally stopped. The BTR's engine exploded, then the diesel fuel exploded. The police car was knocked sideways into the ditch as if it were a toy.

Wohl continued to scan the area with his electronic scope. 'I've got infantry moving in,' he reported. 'Three klicks out. They might be setting up a mortar or getting ready to shoot in grenades. We better move.'

'Pop smoke, pop smoke!' Weston ordered. Soon, thick clouds of gray infrared-blocking smoke wafted across the windscreen, covering every direction except the one in which they intended to takeoff. Hopefully the smoke would make it a bit more difficult for the mortar crews to range in on them. C'mon, Weston breathed, c'mon, *hurry!*

'More mortar fire! *Incoming!*' That time, Weston felt the explosion rattle his plane's fuselage, clumps of dirt, snow, and tarmac pinging off his props and fuselage. Despite the clouds of smoke swirling around the plane, the rounds were being quickly, expertly walked in. Another one or two rounds, and they'd have their range. Weston could almost feel the bad guys loading that deadly round into the tube, letting it slide down, hearing its ballistic charges light off with a loud *KA-BLAM!* The MV-22 rocked on its wheels, and two engines coughed and rattled as the overpressure from a large explosion forced air backward through the turbine engines.

But as he watched, one by one, Fratierie saw the oncoming Russian military vehicles blasted apart by some unseen force. The last to die caused a tremendous explosion as its magazine of antivehicle mortars was hit and detonated. But the nonmilitary vehicles – a police car and a second ambulance – were untouched.

'*What was that?*' Weston shouted on the secure intercom. 'Sing out!'

'Looks like our guardian angel took care of our newcomers,' one of his loadmasters responded. 'Lots of secondaries. Road's clear right now except for a police cruiser and an ambulance.'

Good shooting by someone out there, Weston thought. The driving rain and winds were dissipating the cover smoke quickly – there was no time to waste. 'How long until our exfils get on board?'

'All exfils under the tail. Wounded coming aboard.'

'Roger.' Weston revved the throttle, starting to feed in takeoff torque. 'Security, pull in. Let's get the hell out of here!'

The loadmasters acting as security forces started pulling back toward the plane – when suddenly they stopped, then dove for the ground. Weston couldn't hear anything over the roar of the engines until the last moment. It was the scream of an inbound mortar round. And as he looked on helplessly, one of his loadmasters disappeared in a blinding flash of light and an earsplitting explosion, just thirty yards from the plane.

'*Jesus!*' the copilot shouted. 'Candy got hit! Triggerman, Flex, check east, see if you can help Candy!'

'Negative,' Weston interjected, his words acidity in his throat. It was the hardest decision he had ever had to make, but one he made without any hesitation. 'Candy took a direct hit. Get in the plane. Let's go.'

'Cap, we can't leave our men behind–'

'We don't have any choice,' Weston said. 'Security, pull in, *now*. Flex, where did that mortar come from?'

'More inbound from the north on the other side of the river,' Fratierie responded. 'Can't pinpoint their location, but the round came from the north, probably the other side of the bridge. Aces, Aces, can you see the newcomers north of our position?'

'Flex, give me a countdown for when everyone's on board.'

'Twenty seconds, Cap ... fifteen ... ten seconds ... cargo ramp's moving, everyone on board! *Go! Go!*'

Weston poured in power right to the redline, and the MV-22 lifted off. He thumbed the nacelle control knob, which rotated the engine nacelles downward a few degrees, increasing their forward speed. As their forward speed increased, the MV-22's wings produced more lift, but because Weston held the nose down and kept the tilt-rotor aircraft at tree-top level, speed increased dramatically. As speed increased more, Weston eventually rotated the nacelles to full horizontal position, changing the Pave Hammer from helicopter to airplane mode. He activated the terrain-following radar and low-light TV sensors so he could see and avoid all terrain and obstacles outside in the darkness.

'Holy shit, we made it,' the copilot breathed. 'I thought we'd never–'

At that instant, the threat-warning receiver in the cockpit emitted a shrill *DEEDLEDEEDLE-DEEDLE!* tone, an A symbol appeared near the top of the display, and an instant later the electronic warfare officer shouted, 'Radar-guided triple A, four o'clock, break left *now!'* A ripple of antiaircraft fire erupted just to the right of the nose, tracers sweeping in their direction. Weston banked hard left, but not quickly enough. The twenty-three-millimeter shells of a mobile ZSU-23-2 antiaircraft artillery unit belonging to the Russian Federation Air Force's Troops of Air Defense detachment based at Zhukovsky Air Base ripped into the MV-22's forward fuselage. The force of the big shells piercing the plane's belly and hitting the copilot's body nearly pushed him right out of his seat and made him look as if he was trying to stand up and turn around to escape his bloody fate. Weston heard sounds of explosions, popping, and snapping of electrical circuits behind him; most of the electronic readouts and multifunction displays on the forward instrument panel extinguished, and a thin layer of blue electrical smoke filled the cabin. There was a loud squeal in the intercom, and Weston had to rip his helmet off because he couldn't shut it off. The cabin instantly got fifty degrees colder, with swirls of icy, rainy air penetrating the cabin. Ice immediately began to form on the windshield on the inside – soon it would ice over completely.

Weston pulled his copilot's shredded body off the center throttle quadrant, his shaking right hand and arm instantly covered in blood up to his shoulder. 'Oh shit,' he exclaimed. 'Flex! Give me a hand! Help me!' The senior jumpmaster rushed forward, unstrapped the copilot from his seat, and laid him on the deck. It seemed as if blood covered every square inch of the cockpit. 'Flex, get in the right seat, help me keep this thing level. We're all blasted to hell.' He kept the nose down, but the airspeed was steadily decreasing, and the vibration coming from the right wing was getting worse. 'Check the gauges, Flex. What else did I lose?'

'Fluctuating prop RPMs on the right,' the jumpmaster said. Weston pulled some power back to try to dampen the vibrations, but it had no effect. 'Looks like a bunch of gauges for the right engine are oscillating. Vibration is getting worse too.'

'Shit. I'm going to shut down number two.' Weston switched the MV-22's transmission system so that both rotors were being powered by the left engine, isolated the right engine's electrical, pneumatic, and hydraulic systems, then quickly shut off fuel to the right engine to shut it down. 'Airspeed's dropped off about forty knots,' he said, 'but I've got control. Vibration has decreased a bit.' He knew that was being very, very optimistic. 'Any more damage?'

'We got a bunch of c/b's that won't reset, and a blown fuse light on the number three inverter and current limiter,' the jumpmaster reported. 'Where's the current limiter fuse?'

'Not accessible inflight,' Weston replied. 'Let's start shedding electrical loads and setting up the electrical panel for single-inverter operation. Crap, what else could go wr–?'

Suddenly, it was as if the entire horizon ahead of them erupted into sheets of blazing gunfire. The plane had inadvertently drifted right over toward Zhukovsky Air Base, and almost every antiaircraft artillery piece on the base opened fire on them. Weston immediately banked hard left to try to get away, but there was gunfire in every direction. The arcs of glowing tracer rounds got closer and closer every second. Then, a searchlight popped on, and in a few seconds it had locked directly on them.

Time to die, Weston thought. No ejection seats, and not enough parachutes for everyone. His only chance was to try a forced landing, but if those triple-A units got a clean shot at them, there wouldn't be enough of the plane left to land.

Weston thought of his family, thought about the service his kids would have to attend, thought about...

Just then there were several sharp flashes of light, one after another, illuminating the cockpit like dozens of flashbulbs popping one after another. So this was what it was like, Weston thought, to take a direct triple-A hit? This was what it was like to die...

'God almighty,' the crew mission commander, Nevada Air National Guard Major Duane 'Dev' Deverill muttered. 'That was the *definition* of a wrong turn. Either Trash Man is lost, or he's just plain stupid.'

From twenty miles east of Zhukovsky, Deverill and his aircraft commander, Nevada Air National Guard Captain Annie Dewey, orbited above the hellish nightmare aboard a EB-1C Megafortress II bomber. They had watched the entire episode from high above, well above anti-aircraft artillery range, using the Megafortress's LADAR, or Laser Radar, to paint a three-dimensional image of the MV-22's entire approach and escape. The LADAR also imaged and targeted the positions of some of the advancing Russian forces.

'Is the MV-22 still airborne?' Annie asked.

'Yep,' Duane responded. 'The Longhorn got to him just in time. Bombers save the day again.' Deverill had released an AGM-89D Longhorn Maverick precision-guided missile when they saw the MV-22 drifting over toward Zhukovsky, and it had scored a direct hit on the antiaircraft artillery site that was about to open fire on them. The

Longhorn missile, an upgrade of the venerable AGM-89 Maverick missile, was fitted with an imaging-infrared seeker and a millimeter-wave radar that could detect and home in on vehicles as small as an automobile. It had a range of over thirty miles and was big enough to destroy a main battle tank or penetrate five feet of reinforced concrete. Along with a rotary launcher of eight Longhorn missiles in the center bomb bay and an extended fuel tank in the aft bomb bay, the Vampire also carried a rotary launcher with eight special air-to-air missiles in the forward bomb bay.

'Give 'em a break, Dev,' Annie said. 'It looked like they caught some triple-A back there after they lifted off. Maybe they're badly damaged.'

Duane snorted, politely conceding the point. 'You're right, Heels. I'd hate to think they just plain screwed up.'

Annie looked over at Deverill and studied him for a moment. How, she thought, could a guy so damned cute be so damned insensitive?

Annie couldn't help being drawn to him, despite his cocky, confident, self-indulgent attitude. If he wasn't so popular and highly qualified, he would be the biggest asshole on base. But he really knew his shit and he contributed a lot to the 111th Bomb Wing 'Aces High' and to his fellow crewdogs.

'I think he's in trouble,' Annie said after studying Dev's large multifunction display as it plotted the MV-22's position. 'We need to help him.'

'You know we're not allowed to do that,' Deverill said. 'We're not supposed to be here, remember? We're ghosts.'

'Ghosts who launched cruise missiles against a country that we're not at war with,' Annie pointed out.

'Hey, Heels, you're preaching to the choir,' Duane said. 'I'd be just as happy planting a few sticks of cluster bombs on the Russians any day. But the plan was not to descend below fifteen thousand feet or risk revealing our position in any way. If the world found out the US had sent us to fly air cover for an extraction of an American spy inside Russia, it could ruin relations with everybody. Longhorns from high altitude, yes. But if we get ourselves shot down by a lucky Russian gunner with itchy trigger fingers, we violate orders and the US of A gets egg all over its face.'

'Ask me if I care,' Annie said. She switched to a prebriefed tactical channel and keyed her mike switch: 'Hammer, Hammer, this is Terminator on red four. How copy?' No response. She tried several times and thought she heard a scratchy carrier tone, as if someone was keying a mike switch in response but no voice was going out. 'I think that's him, but there's something wrong. He might have serious battle damage. We've got to do a rejoin on him, get a look at him, and if necessary lead him home.'

'A B-1 bomber flying formation with a MV-22 tilt-rotor? It's kinda like the Great Dane wanting to screw the Chihuahua, isn't it?'

'Dev, I'm not going to sit up here and watch that Pave Hammer flight get chewed up by triple-A with guys I know on board,' Annie said resolutely. She paddled off the autopilot that was holding them in their cover orbit. 'Get ready to do a rejoin on that MV-22.'

'Heels, think about that first for a sec, dammit,' Deverill said earnestly. Annie glared angrily at her mission commander, but when she did, she realized that he wasn't giving her an order, just a suggestion. Annie sensed no fear in his voice, only concern that her brave efforts weren't going to do any good. He nodded toward the God's-eye display. 'He's at six hundred feet going only two hundred knots. To match him we'll have to sweep the wings forward and deploy flaps and slats, and we won't be stealthy anymore. That also means we can't release weapons and won't be able to use the electronic countermeasures stuff, except maybe for the towed decoy, which we might as well not use at that point, because our radar cross-section will obliterate the decoy. We'll be just as vulnerable as the MV-22, maybe even more so. At that speed and altitude, we'll be burning fuel like crazy, and we don't have a tanker scheduled to come in over the Black Sea. We may not make it out of the region. We'd have to abort to a base in Turkey.'

Annie looked at her mission commander, anger burning in her eyes – but not anger toward him. He was right. She hadn't considered any of those facts, and that made her angrier still – with herself. Annie Dewey prided herself on developing all the skills and knowledge necessary as an aircraft commander, and first on the list of skills had to be analyzing facts and proper decision-making. She wasn't demonstrating much of that right now.

'I hear what you're saying, Dev,' Annie said, 'and I agree with all your concerns. Every one of them. But it doesn't matter. I want to go down there anyway.'

Deverill's face looked grim, but he nodded, slowly. She felt that he would go along, but she didn't know if he was one hundred percent behind her, and that was important to her. Annie was quiet for a moment; then, without keying a microphone button, she spoke: 'Genesis, this is Terminator... Terminator to Genesis.'

A moment later, they heard, 'Go ahead, Annie. We're secure.'

'General, you been watching our situation?'

'Affirmative,' Lieutenant-General Terrill Samson replied. He was talking to Annie via the satellite-based micro-transceiver 'installed' into every member of the High-Technology Aerospace Weapons Center. With the tiny beneath-the-skin transceiver, they could speak with each other anytime, anywhere. 'Stand by one.' They heard Samon say, 'Genesis to Tin Man. How do you hear, Hal?'

'I hear you now, sir,' Hal Briggs responded. Hal Briggs and Chris Wohl had the same kind of subcutaneous microtransceivers as everyone else at HAWC. 'We're in deep shit here. The plane's pretty shot up and the copilot is dead. Looks like Trash Man lost all his cockpit displays. We need help right now or Trash Man's liable to fly us over another ack-ack site.'

'Stand by, Hal, I'll patch in Annie and Duane. Patch in Dewey and Deverill ... Annie, Duane, this is Samson. How copy?'

'Loud and clear, General,' Deverill said, his eyes wide with wonder. Deverill had been one of the first members of the Nevada Air National Guard's 111th Bomb Squadron to get the subcutaneous transceiver, a tribute to his skills as a bombardier and instructor. But the technology astounded him. It was as if Samson was talking to him over the ship's intercom. Deverill knew that they could patch a hundred others into their conversation; they could track their location, monitor their physiological status, and exchange data via small handheld computers.

'Hammer has taken casualties and severe battle damage. What do you have in mind?'

'A rejoin, using LADAR, and hope we can get within visual range.'

There was a long pause, then: 'The latest satellite weather observation shows very poor weather. Definitely not ideal conditions. What's your visibility? Any chance you'll get a visual within a half-mile?'

'Pretty unlikely.'

'Then a rejoin is not authorized.'

'Boss, if we don't help that flight, they're liable to get shot down right over the rebel position,' Annie said. 'The Russians might not enjoy the idea of an American special operations plane crash-landing over them – unless they shoot them down, of course.'

'And they'd be even angrier if they found out the United States was flying a stealth warplane over them,' Samson said. 'Operation not approved. Maintain altitude, continue to attempt to establish radio contact, and interdict any enemy opposition to the maximum extent possible. Do not attempt a rejoin.'

'Sir, with the laser radar, we can close to within a quarter-mile easily – we've done it before,'

Deverill said. 'At least let us give it a try. If we don't have contact within a half-mile, we'll abort.'

'And I should be able to help with my sensors,' Briggs said. The electronic suit of armor he wore also included sophisticated infrared and radar sensors, good to ranges as far as three miles.

There was another lengthy pause, then: 'Very well. Operation approved,' Samson said. 'If no contact within a half-mile, abort and return to patrol altitude.'

'Thanks, boss,' Annie said. She turned to Duane and said, 'Thanks for the support, Dev. I'll only do it if you're with me.'

Duane looked at Annie with a touch of concern – then that ever-present, cocky, Cheshire-cat smile crossed his face. 'I'm with you, Heels,' he said. 'I will always be with you.' Annie felt her face flush with embarrassment, and she thanked the stars he couldn't see her pleased smile behind her oxygen mask. 'Let's go and show those Madcap Magician pukes the way home.'

'I heard that,' Briggs interjected.

'Then let's do it, Dev,' she said.

'I'm right here with you, Heels,' Deverill said, with a smile, as he fastened his oxygen mask in place and lowered his clear visor. 'Show me some of your bad-ass pilot moves.'

Annie was happy to comply. She swept the wings full aft, rolled inverted, and dove for the ground, losing fourteen thousand feet in the blink of an eye. When they rolled wings-level, they were only five miles in trail from the MV-22 and closing quickly. Meanwhile, Deverill had punched up the laser radar and had the MV-22 Pave

Hammer aircraft locked on with ease. All the Vampire crew had to do was lower their electronic helmet visors, and they saw a virtual three-dimensional image of the MV-22 and showed its location when they looked in its direction, with tiny arrows showing which way to look for the target. Annie flew the rejoin as if she could see the aircraft through the clouds and darkness.

'Stand by, Hammer,' Annie Dewey said. 'We're moving in.'

'Rog,' Briggs replied. He had changed seats with Fratierie and was now in the copilot's seat, scanning the sky out the right-side cockpit windows with his suit's sensors. 'Come on down.'

'Stand by on towed arrays and counter-measures, Dev.' He swallowed hard, watching the laser radar display intently. Inside three miles, Annie announced, 'Okay, Dev, let's dirty her up.'

'Go for it,' her mission commander said. 'Towed decoy retracted, transmitters and counter-measures in standby. Ready.' Their threat warning receivers still showed antiaircraft artillery sites and search radars in the vicinity, but none aimed in their direction. 'I gotta tell you, Heels, I feel naked up here.'

'Me, too,' Annie admitted.

'Nah. That's only me undressing you with my eyes.'

'Har har,' Annie shot back – but he sounded truthful about that, and it made her smile again.

Annie slowed the plane to two hundred and fifty knots, swept the wings full forward, lowered flaps and slats to the approach setting. One hundred and sixty knots. It was still too fast, so Annie lowered the flaps to the next notch. The Vampire automatically settled into its before-landing nose-high attitude. It was a little weird flying with the deck angled up so sharply, flying next to another aircraft that was flying straight and level.

The LADAR showed the MV-22 in startling detail – including the shut-down engine, which showed blue-cold in their sensors, and the anti-aircraft artillery damage it sustained. 'Holy crap,' she exclaimed. 'They got blasted all to hell. They got the right engine shut down, but the prop's not feathered. The right side got all shot up.'

'Visibility looks like it's less than a half-mile up here,' Deverill said. 'If we got any chance of doing this, we gotta get within visual range.' Just then, the threat warning receiver emitted a slow *DEEDLE … DEEDLE … DEEDLE* tone. 'Soviet-made triple-A, probably a ZSU-23A, ten o'clock, range about ten miles. We're flying right into its lethal range. You gotta get him turned around in the next two minutes or we'll both be Swiss cheese.'

'Oh, hell,' Annie murmured. She dipped the nose and quickly scooted under the MV-22 to put herself between it and the triple-A site, and to put Deverill on the same side as the MV-22 so he could try to communicate with them while she flew the plane. She pulled off another notch of power and eased the big EB-1C flying battle-ship closer to the stricken turboprop. She had to fly formation cross-cockpit, looking through Dev's windows, but with the orange and yellow virtual 3-D image hovering in front of her eyes, it was as if she could look right through Dev's body and through the clouds and darkness and watch the big MV-22 transport move closer and closer.

'Where'd you guys go?' Briggs asked.

'I moved over to your left side, Hammer,' Annie said. 'We've got a triple-A site ahead. John, you're going to have to get a good visual on us real quick.'

'Copy, Heels,' Weston replied. Unlike the others, he couldn't see a thing outside the windows except darkness, interrupted occasionally by flashes of antiaircraft artillery fire.

Duane fished through his pubs bag stuffed into the cubby beside his seat and produced a three-cell flashlight. 'My K-mart special,' he quipped. 'I hope I remembered to change the damn batteries.' They worked the first time, and he shone the thin beam out the cockpit window.

Normally the beam was bright enough to inspect the deepest, darkest, tallest wheel wells of the EB-1C bomber even during the darkest pre-flight, but now it barely seemed to reach out to the Vampire's wingtips. 'Looks like we got some ice forming on the wings,' Deverill said. 'About a half-inch right now.' He looked over to be sure the bleed air anti-ice system was activated. Normally they wouldn't fly in conditions like this for very long – the B-1 bomber was very susceptible to ice accumulation and had terrible flight conditions with even a small load.

'Any sign of the MV-22?'

'Nope,' Deverill said. He could 'see' it through the electronic visor, but if he couldn't see it visually, the MV-22 crew couldn't see *them*. 'I've got you at half a mile, Heels.'

'I'm not stopping, Dev.'

'You don't hear me arguing, do you? Keep it coming.'

'Terminator, this is Genesis,' Samson's ethereal voice emerged from thin air. 'Genesis to Terminator. Status check.'

'We're at one-half mile, General,' Deverill reported. 'No contact.'

'We have you and the MV-22 on JTIDS,' Samson reminded them. JTIDS, or Joint Tactical Information Distribution System, allowed many different users to share information with each other. When the Vampire's laser radar locked on to the MV-22 transport, its position was instantly relayed via JTIDS to all authorized users, including General Samson. He could clearly see that they had moved closer than one-half mile. 'If you don't have a visual, cancel the rejoin and move back up to patrol altitude.'

'General, you saw the Zeus-23-4 site up ahead,' Deverill said. 'The MV's headed right for it. We've got a chance to get him turned around – we're going for it.'

'All the more reason to get the hell out of there,' Samson said. 'Climb out, nail that Zeus site, and try a rejoin again when the visibility improves. Do it.'

'We're only going to get one shot at this, sir,' Annie said hesitantly.

'I copy that, Annie, but I can't risk both of you,' Samson said. 'Abort and climb out. That's an order.'

Annie swore under her breath, then suddenly cobbed the throttles to full afterburner. As soon as she reached two hundred knots, she started raising flaps and slats and swept the wings to the climb setting. 'Dev, nail that Zeus-23!' she shouted.

'Crap, we're losing our ticket home,' Weston swore. The roar of the EB-1's afterburners rattled the cockpit windows, and the long tongue of flame from the four afterburners lit up the cockpit as if they overflew a searchlight. They could see nothing else except the four bright shafts of fire; then, seconds later, darkness again. They could smell the jet fuel and feel the heat of that very close encounter. 'We're deaf, dumb, and blind up here,' Weston said, hoping that stating the obvious could help them plan a way out. If they couldn't rejoin, Weston, his crew, his passenger, and his aircraft would probably never make it home.

'I got it, Heels,' Deverill said. With the plane no longer in automatic takeoff-and-land mode, he was able to program the attack computer again. He selected another Longhorn missile, slaved its autopilot to the coordinates of the antiaircraft artillery site, and programmed a launch. Deverill watched as the radar-enhanced infrared image of the tanklike mobile antiaircraft gun unit got bigger and bigger on his large multifunction display. From only five miles away, the kill came fast. The Longhorn's millimeter-wave radar locked on to the center of mass of the ZSU-23/4 and killed it in seconds.

But they weren't out of the woods yet. 'Another triple-A just popped up,' Duane said. 'Eleven o'clock, ten miles. Must be part of the same regiment. We should ... wait, another pop-up

309

threat. SA-6, twelve o'clock, twelve miles. They must've seen their buddy go up in smoke, and now they're hunting for us. We're bracketed. I think we just highlighted the MV-22. They can't see us, but they can see *him*.'

'Great. We just signed his death warrant,' Annie said. She cut the afterburners and started an orbit around the MV-22. 'The only chance we got is to get him to do a one-eighty, and then tag all those antiaircraft sites.'

'I'm on it,' Duane said. His fingers flew over the attack computer controls, trackball, and touch-screens, designating targets and programming the missiles for launch. As they completed their orbit, the attack computers opened the middle bomb bay doors and spit a Longhorn missile into space. 'Stand by for multiple missile launches.'

But their luck began to run out. The Longhorn missiles did have one major flaw: their big rocket engines, which ignited seconds after release, highlighted the launch aircraft like a bright neon sign. The other antiaircraft sites wised up and started moving to another firing location. Every time they launched another Longhorn missile, several ripples of 23-millimeter cannon fire streamed in their direction, and Annie was forced to dodge and jink away.

It was a valiant effort, but it didn't work. The AGM-89 Longhorn missile was able to lock onto a target once in flight, but without guidance corrections from the bombardier, its hit percentage decreased markedly. Deverill simply could not juggle six Longhorn missiles in the air at one time. After one orbit, there was still a ZSU-23/4 unit operational. 'All missiles expended,' Deverill said breathlessly. 'Triple-A still active, eleven o'clock, range indefinite. Sorry, Annie.'

'I'm not going to let that MV-22 get shot down,' Annie said.

'Terminator, this is Genesis,' Samson tried. 'We show all air-to-ground weapons expended. You're done for the night. Return to the refueling anchor.'

'Deactivate voice link,' Annie ordered to the satellite voice server.

'He can override,' Deverill reminded her. 'You can't shut off the general.'

'Just give me a heading and altitude on Hammer,' Annie said. 'I'll give it one more shot.'

'You're going to ignore Samson? He'll eat you for breakfast.'

'Do I gotta do it myself, Dev? Give me a damned vector to the MV-22.' Deverill shook his head, gave Annie a heading, altitude, airspeed, and range to the MV-22 Pave Hammer, then fell silent.

If it was possible, the weather had gotten worse – now, along with the structural ice, darkness, and poor visibility, they encountered strong, choppy turbulence. A few times, the turbulence was so bad they thought they had been hit by antiaircraft fire. In addition, the MV-22 was in a slight turn. At first it was in a good direction – northwest, away from the advancing Russian army – but the turn kept on coming, and now they were headed back the way they came, toward the oncoming forces.

Again, Annie began her rejoin on the MV-22. She lowered flaps right to the landing position to slow down and stabilize faster. But it was obvious after only a few moments that it was not going to be any easier – the pounding caused by the turbulence was getting worse by the minute. 'Damn it, I can't do it,' Annie said. 'The turbulence is too strong. I'm getting a cramp in my hand.'

'You've come this far, Annie. Keep it coming. Relax your grip on the stick.'

'I can't do this, Dev–'

'Heels, just shut up and move it in,' Deverill said. 'Nice and easy, but keep it coming. We've got about ninety seconds before we get within lethal range of that Zeus-23.'

Annie nudged the EB-1 closer, closer... 'Three thousand feet ... twenty-five hundred ... good closure, two thousand ... fifteen hundred...' But suddenly the MV-22 hit some turbulence and yawed hard left. Annie yanked the control stick left, avoiding a collision by just a few dozen yards. Annie had no choice but to bank away hard, back out to three-quarters of a mile.

'Why are they turning left?' Annie exclaimed, her voice strained and hoarse. 'Don't they realize they're about to get their butts shot off?'

'Never mind, Annie,' Deverill coached. 'Ease it back over. You can do it. Four thousand feet ... c'mon, Annie, time's a-wastin', get it over there ... whoa, *whoa*, a little too fast, two thousand ... good correction, fifteen hundred ... one thousand ... good, five hundred feet ... slide 'er over a hair more...' He scanned the sky with the flashlight aiming it where the electronic image said the cockpit was. 'Trash Man's probably got all his attention on his gauges, trying to keep himself upright. C'mon, you guys, look up, look *up!*'

'Crap, crap, *crap*,' Weston swore to himself. The primary electronic artificial horizon had gone out when the triple-A guns got them, and now the backup gyroscopic artificial horizon was starting to look wobbly. He glanced over at the pneumatic pressure gauge and saw it was two dots below the green arc – the backup gyro instruments would probably go out very soon. When that happened, he'd have to rely on the electric turn and bank indicator, the pitot-static altimeter and vertical velocity indicator, and the backup 'whiskey' compass – instrument flying at its most basic.

He knew he was in serious trouble. It would take all his skills to keep the big plane upright now. Any distraction, any emergency, any attack now that diverted his attention away from flying the aircraft, might send them into an unrecoverable death-spiral right into the ground. Weston tried to relax his grip on the controls, tried to loosen up.

'Where are you guys?' Briggs asked, frantically searching out the cockpit windows. 'My pilot's getting pretty antsy, and so's his gauges.'

'At your nine o'clock, less than a half-mile,' Deverill replied. 'Coming in fast.'

At that instant, Weston saw it – it looked like a flashlight beam, as if shining through a thick fog. Weston's eyes darted back and forth, from window to instruments. He then had to scramble to stop a steeper-than-anticipated left bank. Shit, that came out of nowhere! An instantaneous distraction was all it took to start a violent maneuver. Weston quickly realized he couldn't keep that up any longer – the plane was drifting farther and farther off course every time he looked out the window.

Suddenly he saw it, flying just below and to their left, less than a football field's distance away. How in the world they'd avoided a collision, Weston couldn't figure. 'Tally-ho! Tally-ho!' Weston crowed. 'Got you in sight!'

'*There it is!*' Deverill crowed. 'You see it, Heels?'

'Tally-ho!' Annie responded happily. Sure in hell, it'd worked. Her attitude changed instantly. Before she'd had visual contact, all she could think about was how to stay away from the MV-22. Now that she had visual contact, she wasn't going to lose sight of him again, even if Deverill had to open the window so they could hold hands together. 'I got you now, sucker.'

Her flying instincts and skills kicked in immediately. Seconds earlier, five hundred feet apart in the soup was too close – now fifty feet didn't seem unreasonable at all. She smoothly, expertly tucked herself right underneath the pilot's window – fortunately, the EB-1's high angle of attack, with its nose sticking high above the horizon, helped Annie to get closer than she ever thought she could do.

Just then, a shrill warbling *DEEDLEDEEDLE-DEEDLE!* warning tone sounded, followed by a AAA THREAT light on the threat warning display. 'Triple-A, ten o'clock, inside lethal range!' Deverill shouted. And then the shells came, bright yellow pops of light slicing upward through the darkness. Duane knew that for every flash of light he saw, there were ten others zipping around with it. The snake of shells swung hard in their direction. They were too close to turn in either direction – there was no way out.

Deverill shouted, 'Vertical jinks!' But it was too late. Dewey and Deverill heard what sounded like a rapid, heavy drumming on the left wing, followed by a heavy vibration emanating from the left wing and tail. The MASTER CAUTION light and several yellow warning lights illuminated on both sides. 'Fuel malfunction ... configuration warning ... flight control warning,' Deverill said. 'Looks like they shot the hell out of our left wing and tail section–' At that moment, the first red light on the warning panel illuminated. 'Oh, crap, number-one hydraulic hot warning light.'

'Annie, this is Dave,' a disembodied voice announced. It was Colonel David Luger, seated in the 'virtual cockpit' of the EB-1C Vampire bomber back at Elliott Air Force Base, which allowed several crew members and support personnel to remotely monitor the aircraft during its mission. 'Annie, I'm going to shut down your number-one primary and secondary hydraulic systems before it seizes and puts the entire system into isolate mode. I've also sent a test signal to your left flap and slat actuators, spoiler group, and adaptive wing actuators, and there's no response, so it looks like you lost all your left-side-wing flight controls. The rudder actuators seems okay, so you still have limited turn control via the rudder. Copy all?'

'We copy,' Annie said. 'We've got a pretty good vibration coming from the left side.'

'Could be a shot-up wingtip, spoiler, flap, or malfunctioning adaptive wing actuators,' Luger said. 'In any case, don't touch the flap or wing sweep controls or you'll put your hydraulic system into isolate mode and end up wrapping yourself up in a ball.'

'Roger.'

'Captain Dewey,' General Samson cut in, 'I want you out of there right now. That's an order. Return to the due regard point. We'll coordinate a tanker rendezvous.'

'I'm not leaving the MV-22 now that I'm in contact,' Annie said. 'He's on my wing, and he's going to stay there. If you want me to leave, get another plane up here to lead this guy. Otherwise he won't be able to keep himself upright.'

There was a long pause, then: 'Help is on the way right now,' Samson said in a tunnel-deep monotone that signaled how angry he was. 'An MC-130P is en route to top off the MV-22 and lead him home. Stay with him until the P arrives.'

'Thanks, boss,' Annie said. There was no reply. She knew she was going to catch hell for disregarding his orders. 'He sounded pissed,' she said to Duane.

'You did real good, Heels,' Deverill said. He reached over and patted her shoulder, then gave it a friendly rub. 'Let the big guy be pissed – that's his job. I'm your MC, and I think you did all right.' His touch was electric – it sent a current of warmth through her body. She dared take an eye off the MV-22 to glance at him, and he smiled at her across the dark cockpit.

An hour later, over the Sredneruskaja plains of southwestern Russia near the Ukraine border, the MC-130P special operations aerial refueling aircraft finally rendezvoused with the pair. Visibility had increased to just under a mile as the storm front began to move through the region, so there was little trouble during the rejoin. Just before the MC-130P got into visual range, Annie backed the EB-1C Vampire bomber away, out of visual range, while keeping a close watch on the damaged Pave Hammer aircraft. The stricken MV-22 made visual contact with the MC-130P less than a minute after the Vampire bomber moved away, and another minute later it was happily sipping fuel from the MC-130P's hose and drogue refueling system, using position lights on the MC-130P's wings and fuselage to stay straight and level.

'Thanks, you guys,' Hal Briggs radioed. 'A big thank-you from Trash Man and his guys too. You saved the day. You guys going to be okay?'

'We'll find out right now, Hal.' Annie started to push the throttles forward to get some better controllability, but the faster she flew, the worse the vibrations got. She could manage only another fifty knots without threatening to tear the EB-1C apart. 'Crap. We'll be up here all night,' she cursed.

'If we're lucky,' Duane said.

For the third time, Annie had to reapply the autopilot after it kicked itself off-line. 'Autopilot can't hold it anymore.'

'I think the vibration is getting worse. I've noticed you keep on pulling back on the power. We're down to two hundred and twenty knots now. I think we got major structural problems happening.'

'I know, I know,' Annie said. She paused, trying to think of options, but she was fast running out of them. Annie felt a loud, swift roaring in her ears as she realized she might have only one option left. 'I want you in your cold-weather survival gear. Now.'

'You go first,' Deverill said, his voice remarkably calm. 'I can hold it.'

'I said, get in your cold-weather gear and check your survival kit is secure. *Now.*' She watched with half-angry, half-sorrowful eyes as Deverill nodded, then safetied his ejection seat and began to unstrap. Annie spoke: 'Genesis, this is Terminator.'

'Go ahead, Annie,' General Samson responded.

'The vibration is getting worse,' she reported. 'I think we might be getting ready to lose part of our left wing. I've ordered Dev into his cold-weather survival gear.'

'It's that bad?'

'Affirmative. Sorry, sir. I think I'm about to break one of your planes.'

'Hey, it's *your* plane, Captain – you signed for it,' Samson quipped, his voice still eerily deep and dark. 'The Ukrainian border is just sixty miles ahead. Jump out as close to the border as you can. See any populated areas at all?'

'I can't see squat outside,' Annie said. 'I've been in the soup since forever. Visual display to cultural.' The voice command switched her electronic visor to display cultural features such as cities, towns, roads, and bridges. Just a handful of small cities were close by; the largest, Kursk, a town of fifteen thousand citizens, was right off their right wing. The eastern Ukrainian provincial capital of Char'kov was seventy miles straight ahead.

'We've alerted the Ukrainian Army and Border Patrols in eastern Ukraine, and they're mobilizing search-and-rescue forces,' Samson said. 'The

Ukrainian Third Army headquarters is in Char'kov, and they have a regional airport that we can secure if you can make it there. But the Russians have a major Troops of Air Defense base at Belgorod at your eleven o'clock, forty miles. The US Special Operations Command detachment at Batman Air Base has been alerted, and they'll forward-deploy to Ukraine to help out in case you drop into Russia.'

Annie could see the computerized depiction of the Russia-Ukraine border region. The Ukrainian city of Char'kov was beyond the horizon with an electronic arrow pointing to it, and she aimed right for it. 'I'm going direct to Char'kov at this time,' she said. 'If things get too rough, or if we get any company, I'll deviate further east around Belgorod.' She paused, then added, 'Sorry I screwed things up, General.'

'Well, you'll be happy to hear that the MV-22 and the MC-130P are doing okay,' Samson said. 'The MV-22 is still upright. They've refueled and they're on their way through Ukrainian airspace. They're reporting breaks in the weather farther west, so they're going to divert to Kiev. The crew sends their thanks. You saved all of them. Feel any better?'

'I'll let you know when I'm back home sipping a cold one, sir,' Annie said.

Suddenly, an electronic warning tone went off. Annie looked up. In her electronic visor, she saw a bat-wing symbol of an enemy aircraft. 'Enemy aircraft, five o'clock, thirty miles, heading south,' she announced.

'Sukhoi-27 Flanker,' another voice cut in. That

was Major Nancy Cheshire, also manning the 'virtual cockpit' back at Elliott Air Force Base, helping advise Annie as her 'virtual pilot.' 'Looks like single ship so far ... no, wait.' At that instant, a second enemy aircraft appeared, several thousand feet higher and slightly behind the first. 'He's got a wingman in high combat air patrol. Another Flanker. We got any help on the way, General?'

'The Ukrainian Air Force has scrambled some fighters from Kiev,' Samson replied. 'ETA sixteen minutes. Hang tight.'

By then, Duane Deverill was climbing back into his seat. He now wore a pair of insulated mukluks with leg gaiters reaching all the way to his knees instead of flying boots; a short winter-weight flight jacket; a pair of thick insulated mittens over glove inserts with a finger opening so he could work the controls; a watch cap under his flying helmet; and his survival vest and parachute harness over his parka. It took him an extra minute to readjust all his straps for the added bulk.

As soon as he was all strapped and plugged in, he announced the threat also. 'Go get in your survival gear, Annie,' he said urgently. 'I'll keep an eye on this bastard.'

'No. He's flying away from us.'

'Even better reason to clear off and get in your cold-weather gear,' he said. 'I've got the aircraft. Get going.'

Annie nodded and began to safe her ejection seat when suddenly they heard a fast-pitched *DEEDLEDEEDLEDEEDLE!* tone in their headsets. Annie looked up. A yellow triangle was now emanating from the pointed top of the bat-wing

320

enemy aircraft signal, the computer's estimate of the enemy aircraft's radar range and sweep – and it was completely surrounding the aircraft symbols of the MC-130P tanker and the MV-22 Pave Hammer transport. The yellow color meant that the radar had locked onto them.

'That Flanker just locked up the -130s!' Deverill shouted.

'We gotta do something!' Annie shouted. 'We're well within Anaconda range. Let's get 'em warmed up!' The AIM-152 Anaconda missile was the Air Force's newest air-to-air missile – so new that it was still several years from deployment. The AIM-152s, carried in a rotary launcher in the forward bomb bay, was unique because it was the first air-to-air missile that did not need to be guided by its launch aircraft – it could be launched against a target designated by another aircraft or ground radar station. It used a scramjet propulsion system that gave it extremely long range, in excess of eighty miles, and a top speed of over five times the speed of sound, making it capable even against incoming ballistic missiles or reentry ballistic missile warheads. Once in the predetermined vicinity of the enemy aircraft, the Anaconda activated its onboard radar and infrared sensors to locate its target, or it could continue to home in on sensor signals passed from other aircraft.

'We can't launch missiles – the bomb bay doors are inhibited from opening when we're in takeoff or land mode,' Deverill reminded her.

'Then override it!' Annie shouted.

'We still can't do it,' Nancy Cheshire radioed to the crew from the 'virtual cockpit.' 'We never tested a missile launch from this high angle of attack or this configuration. We don't know how the missile will fly if we launch it in your present configuration or airspeed. It could fail to stabilize, the wingtip vortices or uneven flow patterns from the flaps and slats could disrupt it during the rocket pulse, the missile could accidentally arm – dozens of things. It just hasn't been tested!'

'Dammit, I don't care! Override the lockouts and launch those suckers!'

'Stand by,' Cheshire finally said, after a momentary pause. A few moments later: 'Try to prearm the weapons, Dev.'

Deverill spoke 'Ready Anaconda missiles' into the voice-command computer.

'AIM152 ready,' the computer responded, and it presented a target reticle in his electronic visor. Deverill looked at the attacking enemy aircraft, centering the bat-wing symbol in the center-aiming reticle, and spoke: 'Attack.'

'Warning, aircraft configuration error,' the attack computer responded, then added the computer's next recommended command: *'No attack. Ready.'*

'Override configuration error and attack,' Duane said.

'Warning, configuration error override, aircraft still out of launch parameters,' the computer responded. *'AIM152 in range. Recommend launch two. Ready.'*

'Launch two,' Deverill ordered.

'Warning, launch command received, stop launch ... bay doors opening partial ... missile one away, seven remaining ... launcher rotating ... missile two away, six remaining ... bay doors closed,' the computer responded. When the bomb bay doors opened, it

322

felt as if the entire bottom of the EB-1C Vampire was ready to shake off. But seconds later, both AIM-152 Anaconda missiles could be seen for a brief instant flying off into the murky sky, trailing a wobbly line of fire through the storm-filled sky. Moments later, as the missiles accelerated through Mach 2, they heard two distinct *BOOMs* as the missiles' scramjet motors ignited.

Just then, the triangle from the bat-wing symbol turned from yellow to red. 'Oh, shit, missile launch!' Annie exclaimed. 'You bastards ... c'mon, Anaconda baby, nail that sucker!' A few seconds later, the triangle changed from red to yellow, then to green again. 'What happened?'

'Jammers,' Deverill said. 'The MC-130P has almost as many electronic jammers as a bomber. They might have just saved their lives.'

It did. Exactly thirty-seven seconds after launch, the computer reported, *'Splash one target,'* along with the next recommended command: *'Attack target two.'*

The second Su-27 Flanker made several heading and altitude changes, as if uncertain what had happened or what to do. He made a complete one-eighty, scanning the skies around him – and then the triangle disappeared and a green, then yellow, circle appeared around the bat wing. 'He's got *us* locked up!' Annie shouted. 'Get that SOB!'

Deverill centered the target reticle on the second Flanker. 'Attack,' he ordered. The computer gave him the same warnings as before, and as before, Deverill overrode them and ordered, 'Launch two.'

'Warning, launch command received, stop launch

323

... *bay doors opening ... missile three away, five remaining ... launcher rotating...'*

But the first missile did not appear from under the belly. The EB-1C hit a patch of turbulence right at the instant the missile was ejected from its rotary launcher. The ejector's push was canceled out, so the missile failed to push free of the bomb bay doors. Instead of a smooth *SWOOOSH!* of a successful launch, they felt a tremendous *BANG!* as the missile struck one of the bomb bay doors. Instead of falling free, the missile clattered underneath the partially open bomb doors, caught in the disturbed air swirling under the bomber caused by the deployed flaps and slats and the bomber's high nose-up flight attitude.

'Missile four...'

'Stop launch!' Deverill screamed into the voice-command system.

But it was too late. '*...away, four remaining,*' the computer spoke. The second missile shot off the launcher – smack into the first missile, still caught under the bomb bay. The first missile went spinning out of control, thumping hard against the bottom of the Vampire's fuselage until it reached the number-two engine's intake. It bounced hard off the mouth of the intake, nearly cracking the entire nacelle off the wing. The disruption of airflow caused the number-one and -two engine to do a double compressor stall – the fire was still on inside the engines, but now there was no smooth airflow directing air and hot gases out through them. The overtemp automatically caused the power-plant control computer to shut both engines down.

The sudden yaw created by the loss of both engines momentarily sent the EB-1C bomber into a wild left skid. This sent the second Anaconda missile back bumping across the belly until it reached the hot exhaust of the number-two engine – where it exploded. Luckily, the computer had already shut the engines down, or else the explosion of the Anaconda missile's sixty-pound fragmentation warhead, added to the white-hot jet fuel from the engines, would have destroyed the aircraft instantly.

Even with full right stick and full right rudder, Annie Dewey could not keep the plane flying straight – it was in a severe left yaw no matter how hard she struggled and trimmed. Duane grabbed his control stick to help, and he couldn't believe what he felt – a deep, heavy, relentless vibration. 'Annie...?'

'I've got it, Dev, I've got it,' she responded. The strain and the vibration rattling in her throat disguised her voice so much that she seemed like a completely different person sitting across from him. 'Check the warnings and cautions and let me know what we got left.'

'Computer has shut down number one and two,' Deverill said. 'Fire extinguishers popped on both of them, so they're done for the day. Hydraulic system is in isolate. Three generators are off-line – wait, we got two, so we got the emergency and primary bus energized. Forward bomb bay doors are still partially open – it feels like they're dragging in the slipstream and might be leaking hydraulic fluid. The navigation, weapons, and ECM systems are in reset. Heading system is spinning up again. Navigation is by satellite only until our ring-laser gyros come back up. We're a mess, Heels, but we still got two good blowers.'

'Except we're going nowhere fast,' Annie said. 'I'm going to pull a little power off number four and see if we can straighten out.' She pulled a notch of power off on number four, then made a tiny forward adjustment when the Vampire felt sloppy and uneasy. But she was able to regain some directional control. Their airspeed was down to one-fifty – just thirty knots above landing speed, right at the edge of a stall in straight-and-level flight – but they were still flying. 'All right, all I need now is a heading out of no-man's-land and a runway big enough to set this mother down.'

'Annie, the Ukrainian fighters are five minutes out, crossing the border and heading right for you,' Nancy Cheshire radioed. 'Hold present heading, squawk modes one, two, and four. The cavalry's coming. Hold on.'

'Your heading is one-seven-zero, Annie, direct Char'kov,' Duane said. 'We lost about a thousand feet – let's try to gain a little altitude.'

Annie started a very slow climb. Normally the EB-1C Vampire could climb at over ten thousand feet per minute at gross weight – now she was lucky to get five hundred feet per minute without feeling the sloshing, muddy, unsteady wobbliness of an impending stall. A stall with two engines on one side out meant a spin, and the B-1 bomber did not tolerate spins well. Annie had done them only in the simulator, and she liked at least twenty thousand feet above ground level before attempting spin recovery.

'Looks like I really screwed up, didn't I?' she asked.

'Don't see how,' Duane said. 'Our mission was to make sure ISA got the spy out of Russia safely. You saved their asses three times today. That's a pretty good night's work.'

'I think I'm going to be screwed, blued, and tattooed when I get home.'

'You're a hero, Annie,' Deverill said. 'You should be proud of what you've done. You should... *Oh, shit.*'

Duane stopped, and Annie glanced over to him to see what was the matter. She saw him staring out his right cockpit window. She looked – and saw why. The second Sukhoi-27 Flanker fighter was perched right beside them, less than a hundred feet away. Without the threat detection gear, the Flanker had been able to sneak right in and get a good look at them.

'Oh, hell,' Annie murmured. 'Busted.'

'You gotta admit, that's some pretty good flying,' Deverill said.

'Pretty good for a bastard who tried to blow two unarmed cargo planes out of the sky,' Annie added. Now that the fighter pilot saw that the crew members of the bomber had him in sight, he turned on all of his exterior lights. The brightest light lit up his twin vertical stabilizers, which featured the red star of the Russian Air Force. 'A Russian air defense interceptor,' she breathed. 'Perfect.'

'I'll bet he's not too pleased we blew away his leader.'

'How far are we from the Ukrainian border?'

'Thirty-nine miles.'

'My God,' Annie said, 'where the hell are those Ukrainian fighters? They should've rendezvoused by now.'

'Sixty seconds out,' Cheshire replied. 'They've got you and the Flanker in radar contact.'

'This bastard's right next to us, on our right side,' Annie said excitedly. 'If anyone farts, we're going to trade paint. Get 'em down here and help us!'

At that moment, the Su-27 moved in closer, less than fifty feet away, and a burst of cannon fire erupted from the right-wing leading-edge muzzle. Annie screamed into her oxygen mask. The Russian fighter pilot seemed to be sitting right next to her mission commander. They could both clearly see him making an up-and-down motion with a flashlight – the international signal for 'turn and follow me, you have been intercepted.'

'Kiss my ass, Boris,' Annie said. 'I'm not turning.'

As if the Russian heard her, he maneuvered in front of them, then stroked his engines into zone one afterburner. The white-hot afterburner flame threatened to blow out their windscreen. The Russian fighter then smoothly, expertly slid back into impossibly tight formation, crowding them even more, and the Russian again made a 'follow me' light signal.

'Genesis, this is Terminator,' Annie radioed, the fear plainly obvious in her voice. 'Where the hell are those Ukrainian fighters?'

'We see him,' General Samson responded immediately. 'You've got three more inbound from Kiev, about one hundred miles southeast. ETA, five minutes.'

'How about some help up here?'

'Stand by,' Samson replied.

'"Stand by"?' Deverill shouted. 'Boss, we need some help right *now* or we're going to get hosed.'

'We're having some ... diplomatic problems,' Samson said.

'Say again, Genesis?'

'Just hold your heading and keep coming for the border,' Samson said. There was an unusual sense of urgency in his voice. Terrill Samson never got grim-sounding about *anything*.

'Talk to us, General,' Annie said, almost pleading.

'The ... the Ukrainian government is inquiring about the nature of your mission and the events leading up to this intercept,' Samson said. 'The Ukrainians won't engage Russian fighters unless they cross the border. I doubt if they'd try to take on a Russian Flanker even if they *did* cross the border. Ukrainian pilots are good, but they're not stupid.'

'You mean, *they won't help us?*'

'You just hold tight. I'm going to brief the Pentagon and the White House by teleconference any minute now.'

'Any suggestions?'

'Sure. But you don't want to hear them.'

'Oh, shit,' Annie breathed. 'I'm not letting them have this plane.'

'Try to make it to the border,' Samson said. 'Do whatever you need to do to keep those fighters off your back. Make up a plausible story. Use your feminine wiles on them, sweet-talk them, promise them a night they'll never forget, anything you can think of. They might be surprised enough to hear a woman on the radio that they'll leave you alone. They might be waiting for orders, too.'

'And what if that doesn't work?'

'Just hope it does work. Stay calm. We're right here with you.'

Annie ordered the computer to set the number-two radio to 243.0, the universal UHF emergency channel, and keyed the mike button: 'Russian fighter off my right wingtip, this is Annie. How are you tonight?'

'Unidentified American bomber aircraft, this is Unit Two-Zero, Fifty-fourth Air Defense Fighter Regiment, Voyska Protivovozdushnoy Oborony, Zhukovsky,' the Flanker pilot responded. 'You are in violation of the sovereign airspace of the Russian Federation. You are ordered to follow me for landing at Zhukovsky. Do you copy? Over.'

'Am I over Russia right now?' Annie asked, with all the feminine innocence she could muster. 'My navigation system must be *all* screwed up. I thought I was over the Black Sea. Oh dear, this is pretty embarrassing. Why don't you just point me toward the Black Sea and I'll get out of your hair. Pretty please, commander?'

'I have observed your aircraft launch weapons at V-PVO aircraft, and I observe one of your weapons bays is partially open,' the Flanker pilot replied angrily. 'I suspect you of attacking and destroying a Russian air defense aircraft, and attacking Russian military forces. That is an act of war, and I am authorized to divert you to a suitable airfield for detention and interrogation of you, your aircraft, and your crew. You will be given all rights under the Warsaw Convention regarding treatment of airspace violators. I am authorized to take any actions I feel I must take to ensure your compliance. I order you to turn to a heading of one-five-zero immediately or you will be shot down.'

'Hey, honey, you've got it all wrong,' Annie said sweetly. 'I didn't attack anyone. I've got two engines shut down and major damage to my aircraft. I don't have any weapons on board – this is an unarmed training flight. Do I look like a fighter plane? I was on my way to land and have apparently gone off course. If you can offer any assistance, I'm sure my company will reward you handsomely. I'll *personally* see to that. Just let me turn back toward the northwest, and I'll see to it that you're compensated in full. You have my promise, commander.'

There was no response. The Sukhoi-27 Flanker merely pulled up and out of sight.

'Hey, Nancy,' Annie said, 'you see where this guy went?'

'He's at your four o'clock, slightly high,' Nancy Cheshire replied. 'Moving to six o'clock, one mile.'

'We got any weapons yet, Dev?'

'Weapons just came on-line,' Deverill replied. To the weapons computer, he spoke, 'Ready Ana-condas. Target aircraft at six o'clock, one mile. Attack.'

'*Warning, configuration error,*' the computer responded. '*Warning, bay doors not ready. Warning, airspeed too low for safe weapon release. Stop attack.*'

331

'Override configuration error,' Deverill ordered. 'Override airspeed inhibits. Emergency open forward bay doors. Launch two.'

'Warning, configuration error override … warning, weapon airspeed limit override, no safe separation … warning, bomb bay doors not latched.' They received bomb door open indications as the computer merely unlatched the forward bomb bay doors and allowed them to gravity-fall fully open. *'Warning, launch command received, stop launch…'*

'Annie! Dev!' Cheshire shouted over the satellite transceiver. *'Get out! Get…!'*

It felt as if they had crashed headlong into a brick wall. The Flanker pilot had fired two R-60 heat-seeking missiles at the EB- 1C Vampire, and both missiles had hit the only operable engines on the right wing. The engines exploded, igniting jet fuel in the right-wing and aft body tanks.

Both Annie Dewey and Duane Deverill knew the time had come. When Nancy Cheshire issued her warning, their hands were already reaching for the ejection handles, and by the time the fireball engulfed the Vampire bomber, the ejection seats had already cleared the plane and they were blasted free.

Chapter Five

High-Technology Aerospace
Weapons Center (HAWC)
a short time later

'I've alerted the weapons teams, sir,' David Luger shouted as he dashed into the battle staff area. General Samson and John Long were already there, checking computerized charts and satellite imagery of the shoot-down area, along with several other staff and operational members from both HAWC and the 111th Bombardment Wing. 'They're ready to upload a full hard target penetration load on every Vampire we got. I've got the combat support team putting together an intel package and attack routing scenario to the shoot-down area immediately – they can have DTECs and flight plans ready to brief in three hours. I've also called a secure dataconference meeting with ISA to put together a plan of action.'

'Wait a minute, Colonel, just wait one god-damned minute,' Long interjected angrily. 'You HAWC guys are forgetting – again – that you don't command the 111th. We don't just go launching off into space with bombs and missiles and start shooting everybody up, especially the Russians. We need authorization, and we need a warning order and frag order. We need to coordinate our efforts. I'm not going to start launching Vampires without a plan of action.'

'There's no time for that,' Luger shot back. He

went to a nearby computer terminal, calling up the maintenance status of their aircraft. 'We can launch three birds in about six hours. In the meantime, we can divert Rebecca and Patrick to a refueling anchor over the Baltic Sea. We can also–'

'Hey, Luger, that's my job,' Long interjected. 'You don't work for Aces High.'

'Get off your ass, Major!' Luger retorted angrily. 'Annie is out there on the ground in goddamned Russia! We need to get her out of there *now!*'

'Colonel, Major, knock it off, *now*,' General Terrill Samson cut in. 'Everyone relax–'

'*Relax?* We can't relax!' Luger exploded. 'Do you realize the danger if Annie or Dev gets captured by the Russians? Do you realize what the Russians do to captured fliers? Huh? *Do you?*'

'Dave, ease off–'

'They'll twist their minds, empty their brains, use drugs or chemicals or physical or mental torture to make you reject or deny everything you've ever believed.'

'What in hell are you blabbering about, Luger?' Long asked. 'You been watching too many spy movies.'

Terrill Samson knew what John Long did not – that when David Luger spoke about being tortured by the Russians, he spoke from personal experience. He put a hand out toward his chief engineer. 'Easy, David, take it easy–'

'I will *not* take it easy, sir!' Luger shouted. 'You have *got* to put out an alert to every intelligence and special operations team within a thousand miles of that shootdown point – tell them to mount up and get a search-and-rescue operation started *immediately.*'

Long shook his head in exasperation. Look at this hotshot HAWC smart-ass going to pieces, he thought. They're all a bunch of blubbering candy-asses. 'Take a pill, Colonel–'

'*Shut up,* Long,' Samson said. 'David–'

'If you won't do something now, General, *I will!*'

'*Colonel!*' Samson shouted. He finally stopped, but his chest was heaving as if he had just gone three rounds in a boxing ring.

Samson looked at his chief engineer with serious concern. Luger had reported his two contacts with the Ukrainian bomber forces commander, who happened to have been one of the test pilots at the same facility where Luger had been held captive years ago. He'd considered sending him off on leave while the Ukrainians were at Nellis, to avoid any further complications, but he'd let Luger override him. He'd seemed just fine. Obviously, those two brief encounters had dredged up a lot of very bad memories. 'Stand at ease! That's an order!' Samson's booming voice finally seemed to shake Luger out of his near-panicked anguish. 'We're going to help them, Colonel, I promise you. But we need to devise a plan of action and get approval from Washington. Prepare your planes and get weapons uploaded right away, but I don't want anyone launching. Is that clear?'

'Yes, sir,' Luger said. He took a deep breath and wiped cold sweat from his forehead. Quickly, his tortured mind began to think rationally. 'But if the decision is made to do a rescue, we should brief up the teams and launch as many Vampires as we can to forward strike locations. If Annie and Dev can evade capture long enough, we might be able to rescue them, but we need to get ISA units moving *now*. If the Russians capture and then release Annie and Dev right away, we'll just come home. But if they don't, we want to be in a position to nab them before they get moved all the way back to Moscow.'

'I said, no one launches without my go-ahead. End of discussion.' To Long, he said, 'I'm preparing for a briefing to the National Security Council staff right now. I'll get you clearance as quickly as I can.'

'Yes, sir,' Long said.

'We are still receiving life signs,' Luger said, checking the satellite communications server's readouts on Deverill and Dewey. 'Still no voice contact. The longer they're on the ground, the better the chances of them getting caught. General, at least give us clearance to refuel and divert Furness and McLanahan in the mission backup plane. We can schedule a tanker and get it turned around in minutes.'

'Request denied,' Samson said. 'Furness and McLanahan follow their original recovery routing back here – no alterations unless I get approval from the White House. That is all. Major, you're with me. We should be getting a videoconference call from the White House any minute.' Luger was left with nothing to do, so he got ready to depart.

'Colonel, are you going to be okay?' Samson asked just before Luger reached the door.

'I'll be all right, sir,' he responded evenly.

'I would like you to assist in preparing available

Vampire aircraft for weapons upload and launch in case we're given the go-ahead,' Samson said. 'John will be working with me here to get ready for the NSC brief. I'm sure it would be a big help to have you and Major Cheshire in the maintenance area supervising things.' John Long said nothing, but nodded.

'I'll be over there if you need me, sir,' Luger said.

'And David? Advise General McLanahan and Colonel Furness on what's happened.' He paused, staring at Luger as if punctuating his next order: 'I want them to continue on their recovery track. Under no circumstances are they permitted to try a rescue mission without prior authorization. Is that understood?'

'Yes, sir. I'll advise them.'

'They can contact me directly via satellite if they have any other information, or if they have recommendations, but I want them to head on back otherwise,' Samson said again. For some reason, he felt a strong need to repeat his orders to Luger. 'No heroics. I don't want to lose any more aircraft over Russia.'

'Understood, sir.'

David Luger went over to the maintenance hangar complex and briefed the chief maintenance officer, the chief civilian engineer, and the NCO in charge, on what was happening, but he was wise enough to let them do their thing without hovering around them. Besides, he was too angry and frustrated – at Samson, at Long, at himself – to think and organize effectively.

His mind drifted away to his friend and lover,

on the ground in Russia. He activated his sub-cutaneous satellite transceiver and spoke: 'Dewey, this is Luger... Heels, this is David – can you hear me? Please answer, Annie. Can you hear me?' His voice choked as he thought of her lying on the ground half a world away, and he too far away to help her. 'Annie, answer me, please ... answer me, goddammit...'

No reply.

He understood General Samson's order. Samson wanted to be sure Patrick returned – meaning, he fully expected Patrick to turn around and fly cover for Annie and Dev. Luger knew what could happen if he disobeyed him – but also knew that Patrick McLanahan was Annie's best hope to avoid capture. Samson could have contacted McLanahan himself via the satellite transceiver and directly issued the order to him. He was purposely vague about it. Did he want Patrick to fly cover – or was he passing the responsibility to his second-in-command?

Again, Luger activated the worldwide satellite transceiver: 'Luger to McLanahan.'

'Go ahead, Dave.'

'We've got a situation, Muck,' Luger said, and he ran it down for him.

'Come to a heading of one-two-five, *right now*,' Patrick said urgently. His mouth was dry, and his fingers shook as they flew across the large super-cockpit touchscreen display. 'Heading back to our due-regard point. Steering is good. Take it.' The due-regard point was a special point in a flight plan where flights were 'dropped' or 'accepted,' without any air traffic control agencies knowing or responsible for where the flight went – they were used primarily by classified military flights. They were currently over southern Norway, well out of range of any ground radar sites, but they still used satellite communications and GPS to call in their position to transoceanic air traffic controllers. 'I'll call Oslo Transoceanic and get a clearance.'

'Clearance? What in hell are you talking about?' Rebecca Furness asked. She had to paddle off the autopilot to prevent the EB-1C Vampire bomber from automatically following the new steering command Patrick had given. 'We're not turning around and flying hundreds of miles back through Russian airspace. Are you nuts?'

'Rebecca, one of our planes just got shot down – one of *your* planes, a point you made very clear to me the other day,' Patrick said. 'Two of your crew members are *on the ground in Russia*. If they get captured, it'll be an enormous security breach for the United States. It'll be the military classi-fied information discovery coup of the decade!' He scanned his flight information. 'I can have us over the shootdown point in less than two hours. I'll download Annie and Dev's position from the satellite server, and Dave will upload the updated tactical order of battle to us, so we can–'

'Hold on, General,' Rebecca said. 'Why didn't General Samson or someone from the Pentagon call us?'

'They're probably deciding exactly what to do,' Patrick replied. 'Terrill won't be in charge – it'll be someone at USAFE, or it might be turned over to the Director of Central Intelligence or Defense

Intelligence Agency. It might take them hours just to decide who the hell is in charge. By that time, we can be over the shootdown point and helping Annie and Dev. If the Intelligence Support Agency or US Special Operations Command launches a rescue sortie out of Turkey, they can be over the shootdown spot at the same time we arrive, and we can cover them. Let's *go*, Rebecca!'

'I don't know—'

'Rebecca, don't hesitate now,' Patrick urged her. 'Those are *your* people on the ground. We can help them. We just got a refueling, so we don't need gas—'

'We've been talking with Oslo Transoceanic for the past fifteen minutes,' Rebecca argued. 'We've broadcast our aircraft type on open channels. If we turn around, they'll be able to track us.'

'Not if we go in hard,' Patrick said. 'We've got enough fuel to go in low right now. But we need to get turned around *now*, Rebecca. Every pound of fuel we waste going westbound is one pound less we'll have over the shootdown point.' When Furness still hesitated, Patrick added, 'I know I can't tell an aircraft commander to do anything he or she doesn't think is safe—'

'Damn straight.'

'—but I'm ordering you right now, Colonel, as your superior officer: turn right to a heading of one-two-five, center up the steering bug, and prepare to commence hostile airspace penetration operations at the original route entry point. Do it *now*, or by God, I'll prosecute you to the fullest extent of the law when we get back to base.'

'You're crazy, McLanahan,' Rebecca exploded.

'You'll never be able to convict me of disobeying an order like that. You'll be laughed out of court – probably court-martialed yourself.'

'Are you going to refuse my order?'

'It'll be daylight by the time we reach the shoot-down point,' Furness argued. 'We'll be sitting ducks–'

'You don't know that,' Patrick said. 'All we do know is that Dev and Annie *are* sitting ducks right now. We are the only chance they have of escaping or getting rescued. Now I'm ordering you once more – center up the steering bug *now*.'

Rebecca Furness looked into Patrick McLanahan's eyes and saw nothing but red-hot fury in them, unlike anything she had seen in the short but intense time they had worked together. She knew that, although it was probably unauthorized, his was not an unlawful order. The Rules of Conduct under the Uniform Code of Military Justice stated that she was not obligated to obey unlawful orders or orders that violated her own morality. This did neither. If she obeyed his order, she felt certain she could not be prosecuted for doing so.

Damn it, Rebecca, she admonished herself, stop thinking about the legalities and start thinking about what could happen if you *don't* do it! Dev and Annie could be captured. They were only a few miles from the Ukrainian border – if they were unhurt from the ejection, they still had a chance to make it across the border. The Russians might still go after them, but that's why they needed to be there for them.

Rebecca released the paddle switch on her control stick, which allowed the Vampire bomber's

343

autopilot to follow the computer's steering signals. They were on their way back to Russia.

In the Sredneruskaja Plains, near Obojan, Russian Federation
that same time

There was only one way to describe what ejecting out of an exploding aircraft was like: pure, unadulterated violence.

Annie Dewey's only warning of what was about to occur was when the overhead hatch blew free, her shoulder and lap belt straps tightened, the leg restraints snapped her ankles back so they wouldn't flail around during the shot, and the ejection seat slid backward against the launch rail. Then her body was racked by immense pain as the main rocket motor fired her clear of the aircraft. The force exerted on the human body during the ejection sequence had been compared to hitting a brick wall in an automobile traveling twenty miles an hour – headfirst – and Annie probably would've doubled that number.

The sky, which had been cold, dark, and stormy all night, was a blaze of hot yellow and red flames. Annie lost her oxygen mask right away – that'll teach you always to lock it in tight, she somehow managed to admonish herself throughout the chaos – and the helmet almost came flying off with it. The only thing that helped catch her helmet was the chin strap digging into her nose. She was sure her nose was broken. Time for that nose job she always wanted – maybe she would finally get Nicole Kidman's nose at last.

Because the Vampire was flying at such a slow speed – almost approach speed – and they were relatively low to the ground, the ejection sequence happened fast and violent. She got both rocket motors on full ignition right away, which tripled the force exerted on her body. Thankfully, that ride was over in less than two seconds. She then got the mule-kick in the back from the man-seat separator, a thick nylon strap along the back of the seat that tightened and propelled her away from the ejection seat pan like a slingshot. Next the drogue chute deployed, which whipped her body upside down, followed almost immediately by the shoulder-cracking snap of the big main chute. Fortunately, the Vampire bomber was still accelerating away, and her chute did not open inside the rapidly growing fireball that used to be her warplane. Annie got half a dozen good swings in her chute, but all she remembered was crashing into the frozen rocky earth in typical Air Force crew member fashion: feet, butt, back of head.

The wind tugged at her half-inflated parachute, as if insisting that she get up, but Annie wasn't going to move one inch, even though she was almost facedown in the snow. She could smell and taste blood, so she knew that at least two senses were working. A few moments later, her hearing kicked in as she caught the sound of her beloved B-1 bomber crashing into the low hills, not far away. The ground heaved and rumbled like an earthquake – touch was okay, too. She tried the last sense, sight, but that didn't seem to want to work quite yet. Four out of five – not bad

345

for just hitting the ground under a parachute after ejecting from a shot-up bomber.

Her plane was gone, history. An incredible, almost overwhelming, sense of fear, dread, and guilt washed through her brain. What have I done? she asked herself. If I had followed orders, I'd still be flying far overhead, out of range of anti-aircraft guns and safe from Russian fighters. I'd still be able to protect the special operations guys with her weapons, or vector in fighter support, or jam Russian radars, or a whole number of other things. The MV-22 Pave Hammer crew might have been able to fly the plane out themselves. Or what if a trigger-happy Russian fighter jock got both them and the MC-130P tanker as well? Her rescue attempt would have been a waste. What if everything she did was all for nothing?

The fear and the cold caused her to shiver. It was hypothermia setting in. Annie didn't care. She had failed. She had probably killed Dev, and she had certainly caused the loss of a multimillion dollar warplane. The Russians were obviously going to find the wreckage and discover who and what they were. Their secret would be out. She would be captured, Dev's body taken to some grimy little prison morgue, maybe broadcast around the world so Dev's poor parents could see his mutilated body. The United States would suffer one of its greatest foreign policy and military embarrassments since Iran-Contra. The United States government might disavow any knowledge of their mission. Lives and careers would be ruined. Everything the United States said or did for the next decade would have the stink of this failure tainting it.

I might as well die, Annie thought. Death would certainly be preferable to living with the shame of what her decisions had caused tonight. She was probably already blind, certainly shattered from the ejection and the hard landing. So not only would she be a national disgrace, but if she lived, someone would have to take care of her. She'd have to be fed through a tube, shit in a pair of diapers like an infant, be set out on a patio like a potted plant so she could get some sun so she wouldn't shrivel up and die, and the attendant would know who she was and would be embarrassed and probably disgusted to have to take care of such a loser oh God why did I do it why didn't I listen to orders oh Jesus I want to die let me die don't let me live like a paraplegic vegetable being hated by my mother and father oh mom oh dad I'm sorry I apologize I only wanted to help I thought I was doing the right thing I...

It was a clump of snow falling off a branch and landing a few inches from her face that finally snapped her out of her despair. It sounded like a footstep, and a thrill of panic – a new panic – shot through her head. I'm not dead. I'm going to be captured. Should I pretend to be dead or unconscious? What if they just shoot me to make sure I'm dead? What if I...?

NO! she screamed at herself. Stop it! Stop talking yourself into dying or screwing things up even worse than you already have! She had a crew member out there somewhere who probably needed her help. She had a duty to herself and to her country to get out and make it back into friendly territory. Stop feeling sorry for yourself, Annie Dewey, and get on your damn feet and *move!* If Dev Deverill dies because you were too busy feeling sorry for yourself, then you *do* deserve to die! *Get up, you bitch,* and act like a real American airman instead of a whiny overprotected coed!

She heard no voices and no more footsteps. Good time to get the hell away from here. Hands and arms, working. Good. Try to roll over ... no, bad, *very bad,* excruciatingly painful back pain, like ice picks were being driven up her spine. She tried to return to her original spot to try to relieve the pain, but her body was telling her, too late, Annie, there's no pain-free way to move now. She cried out as she rolled over on her back. The pain seemed to constrict her throat, cutting off her airway, strangling her. Now panic was setting in again. She couldn't breathe, couldn't see, and the pain in her back was mind-numbing. Stars swam in her field of vision, and she prayed she would pass out to save her from the pain.

She wasn't that lucky. The only soothing thing she felt was the cold and wet snow against her back. The pain was still there, still as sharp as ever, but at least she felt it, and at least she could move. She wasn't paralyzed. Even through the shattering pain, she felt a twinge of hope. Maybe she would be all right.

Annie reached up to her eyes and immediately found one source of her vision and breathing problems – her helmet had shoved itself down over her face. Making the slightest movement only increased the pain even more, but she was able to unsnap the helmet and pull it off her head. Her fingertips found a deep crack in the helmet – it had saved her life. A gash like that on her skull would've easily killed her.

The snow on the back of her head felt good, and several moments later she started to see and sense more things – flickers of fires in the distance against the stormy skies, the acid smell of burning jet fuel, and the creaks, shrieks, and groans as the Vampire bomber continued its death-rattles; wet icy snow falling on her face, cold moisture seeping through her flight suit and cold-weather gear against her butt. She wasn't wearing ultra-cold-weather stuff, but she was wearing insulated long-underwear, thick wool socks, a turtleneck long underwear shirt, and cold-weather Thinsulate flying gloves. The pain felt like it was subsiding. Now she started to be afraid of going into shock if she got too cold, so it was important that she get moving. Get up, Annie, she told herself. Find Dev. Find the survival gear. Find shelter. Get away from the crash site and hide.

The pain came back full force as soon as she tried to get up, but she knew she had no choice – either get up and have a chance of surviving, or stay on the ground and freeze to death or get captured. With the helmet no longer muffling her, she was able to cry out as loud as she dared, but she knew searchers would be on their way and she didn't want to risk being captured. Crawling to her hands and knees seemed to take a half hour, but she did it. Reaching up to unfasten her parachute risers and unbuckle her parachute harness seemed to drain every erg of strength from her body, but she did it. Pulling on the nylon strap that connected her harness to the survival pack seemed an impossibility, like trying to pull a cruise ship into its dock after someone on deck threw her a line, but she did it. Now, with the survival pack clutched safely in her arms, she felt better. I may be hurting, she thought, and I may be down hard, but I'm not out of the game yet.

Walking was out of the question, so she crawled. She didn't know which way to go, so she decided just to go away from the glow of the fires from the crash scene. That seemed a good choice, because the direction she chose was downhill. After a few dozen yards, she found a big pine tree. Feeling around its base with her hands, she noticed the ground underneath the thick bottom branches was dry, so she crawled underneath. Hey, she thought, those survival instructors were right: it's surprisingly comfortable in here. It smelled good, and after a few moments, it even started to feel warm. Man oh man, what a break. She heard a scampering sound and figured she had probably disturbed some ground squirrel's rest, but she didn't much care who or what she was sharing that warm, soft, pine-needle-cushioned ground with right now.

She knew she had to keep going. She had only moved a very short distance away from her landing spot, and they could find her easily by her drag marks. But she had to take time to check herself out, get her thoughts together, decide on a plan of action, then do it.

The first thing she had to do was take care of herself. Annie opened the survival pack, a square green nylon case about eighteen inches square, three inches thick, and weighing about twenty pounds. A tiny red-lensed flashlight was right on top, which helped her inventory the rest of the kit – even that tiny bit of artificial American-made light helped to lift her spirits. She was finally back in control of her environment, at least a little bit.

Four pint-sized cans of water – she drank one can immediately and put the others inside the leg pockets of her flight suit. Waterproof matches – inside her flight suit, between her T-shirt and long-underwear shirt. Survival rations: dried beef bars, granola bars, fruit bars, chocolate bars. One dried beef bar and one fruit bar in her flight suit, the rest back in the survival pack. Folding knife, in her flight suit. A space blanket, silver on one side, black on the other, in her flight suit. Vacuum-packed sleeping bag, compressed and squished into a nine-inch-long, three-inch-diameter tube, in the survival kit. Pretty amazing shit. Signal mirror, around her neck, along with a magnetic compass. Wool cap, on her head. Aha, the good gadget: combination satellite survival radio and GPS satellite navigation receiver – in her flight suit pocket, along with two spare batteries, which went inside her T-shirt next to her skin to keep them warm.

Signal flares, smoke signaling devices, flare gun with forest-penetrator cartridges, back in the survival pack. Booklets, fishing kit, first-aid kit, mittens, compression bandages, snare wire, a wire saw, aspirin tablets, water-purification tablets, a small tarp to make a tent, nylon twine, a radiation tester, two pairs of socks sealed in plastic, a canteen – all stayed in the survival kit for now, except she popped two aspirins and washed them down with water to help take the edge off the pain in her back and shoulders. Everything but nylon stockings, chewing gum, gold pieces, Russian rubles, and condoms ... oops, a moment later she found the condoms. They stayed in the survival kit.

Annie felt immensely better after she closed up the survival kit. She had read that the vast majority of crash victims who died while in a survival situation never even bothered to do the simplest things, like seek shelter or open their survival kits. They were either in a daze, in shock, or simply couldn't believe the situation they were in. Most of the time they ended up dropping all their gear and walking off in circles until they died of exhaustion, hypothermia, or shock. The old saying was that crash victims who died in survival situations died of embarrassment. Annie understood that feeling very, very well right now.

Checking herself out didn't take long. The pain in her back was immense, now spreading from her spine and radiating out to her legs, arms, and neck. Her nose creaked and snapped like cellophane, and in the survival mirror she could see blood covering her cheeks and chin and thickly caked in her nose, but if there was any pain from the broken nose it was being overshadowed by the pain in her back. Her whole body was sore, and she knew she was going to find some humongous bruises. Her butt hurt badly, and she thought she might have a broken tailbone. No other obvious injuries. Annie counted herself very, very fortunate. She knew that she could have easily...

'Annie, this is McLanahan. Do you hear me? Annie?'

'General!' Annie exclaimed aloud. The global satellite transceiver they'd planted under her skin, powered by the thick rubber-coated bracelet on her ankle, sort of like a futuristic miniature OnStar assistance device – my God, it was working, even way out here in the middle of nowhere. 'I hear you! I hear you!'

'I read you loud and clear, too, Annie,' Patrick McLanahan said. 'Lower your voice. I assume you're safe for now. What's your situation?'

'I'm under a tree,' Annie said. 'I was just resting, checking my survival gear out. I'm okay. My back hurts, I got a broken nose and maybe a broken butt bone, but otherwise I'm okay.'

'Good. You did the right thing,' Patrick said. 'You can divvy up the survival gear later.'

'Already did it. I even had some water and a couple aspirins.'

'Good job. Okay. We're with you now, we have your location, and help's on the way. You're going to have to find Dev, then find as safe a place as you can to hide until we can send in the rescue teams.'

Annie almost burst into tears when McLanahan mentioned the 'rescue teams' – she finally felt she might make it out of this alive. 'What about Dev?' she asked. 'Are you talking to him? Can you find him too?'

'We're still picking up life signs from Dev, but there's no answer from him,' McLanahan said. 'He's about two hundred yards east of you, but we can't be too precise. If you feel up to it, I'd like you to try to join up with him, check him out, hide him if you can, and help him. Are you able to move?'

'I think so,' Annie replied.

'We know the weather's bad, but that will help you stay concealed,' Patrick said. 'It'll be tough going, but give it a try. I'll direct you as best I can, but you have to move several yards before your position will update, so it's imprecise. I don't want you falling into a ravine trying to find him in the dark, and I don't want you to get captured. If you can't do it safely, go back to your nest there, or find another hiding spot, and stay hidden.'

'I'll find him. Don't worry.'

'Good. We're putting together a rescue package for you as we speak. The entire Intelligence Support Agency is gearing up to launch a rescue. You're heroes for what you did for Weston and his crew, Heels. They'll move heaven and earth to get to you.'

'Thank you, sir,' Annie said, not embarrassed by the gush of joy and relief in her voice. 'Thank you so much. I – I'm sorry for what I did. I disobeyed orders, and I got us shot down. I take full responsibility for whatever happens.'

'The cost of the Vampire is already being deducted from your paycheck, Annie,' McLanahan quipped. 'You have about three hours until local sunrise, so you'd better get moving. Take it nice and slow and easy. Good luck. We'll let you know if we hear from Dev.'

Annie looped the survival kit across her body under her right arm, pulled the watch cap down over her head and ears, then crawled out from under the pine tree. The pain in her back was still there, but thanks to the aspirin and her improved attitude, the pain was only talking, not screaming, to her now. Sure enough, the snow and wind had increased in intensity. Visibility was almost zero. Fortunately, the snow was less than a foot deep, which made moving relatively easy.

'General, I'm heading east,' she spoke into the frigid air. 'A Pave Hammer tilt-rotor hovering overhead would sure be welcome right about now.'

'We're right here with you, Annie,' came the reply. 'The PJs are on the way.' Annie didn't ask how far out they were or how long it would take for them to arrive – she didn't need to ask any questions when she potentially wouldn't like the answer.

It was slow going. Using the compass from around her neck, Annie simply went from tree to tree, about ten yards at a time. She used the flashlight sparingly, shining the beam just two or three yards ahead at a time to avoid detection. She tried to count paces but gave up after tripping a few times on rocks, relying on the subcutaneous transceiver and Patrick McLanahan's deep, solid, reassuring voice to guide her.

She had gone perhaps fifty yards when she heard a noise. She turned and saw a pair of headlight beams slicing through the freezing rain. As the headlights got closer, she realized she was only about a dozen yards above a dirt road. The truck using the headlights shifted into a lower gear and slowed. 'Oh, shit,' Annie said softly, 'a truck just came out of nowhere. I think they saw me.'

'Can you hide?' Patrick asked.

'I'll try,' Annie said. The truck was heading toward her, up a slight grade. Annie immediately ran forward in the opposite direction, not daring to use the flashlight. She extended her arms out in front of her, but still couldn't help colliding with trees, crashing into boulders, and tripping on rocks. The pain was back full force. But she ignored all of that and kept on running. She didn't care what direction, only that it was away from the truck. 'I ... don't hear the ... engine revving anymore,' Annie panted. 'It must have stopped.'

'Keep going as long as you can, then find cover,' Patrick said.

'I'll try,' Annie said, breathing hard. 'I'll...' She tripped once again and fell, sprawled out facefirst in the snow. She was about to leap to her feet and keep running when she realized that she hadn't just tripped on something – she had hooked her foot on something ... something like string ... like...

...parachute risers.

Annie wheeled around and dropped to the snow. She caught the risers again and pulled. More nylon cords came out of the snow. My God, they *were* parachute risers! 'I found a parachute! I found a parachute!' she cried out.

'Lower your voice, Annie. I can hear you fine,' McLanahan said. 'Is it Dev?'

'Stand by.' She frantically pulled on the risers she could find, the snow flying in all directions. No, wrong direction – she found the white parachute canopy. She whirled around and began pulling and digging in the other direction. Please, God, oh please, let it be him. Let him still be alive

She found the body under four inches of fresh snow, lying faceup. He still had his helmet on, his clear visor down and his oxygen mask connected.

His parachute risers were wrapped around a nearby tree, meaning he had either landed in the tree and then fallen, or was dragged and crashed into it. Using the red-lensed flashlight, she whipped off the oxygen mask's bayonet clips on the side of his helmet. A gentle cloud of steam escaped. 'General, I found him!' Annie said. 'I found him! I think he's still alive!'

'Thank God,' Patrick said. 'Check him over as best you can before you move him.'

'He looks like he's okay, just unconscious,' Annie said as she began to examine him. He was securely bundled up in the cold-weather gear she'd seen him put on. She saw a big scrape against the left front side of his helmet and guessed he must have hit a tree face-first. 'I don't see any broken bones. He's just unconscious,' Annie repeated.

'If he's still in his parachute, unfasten his risers and drag him as far as you can away from there,' Patrick said.

Annie unclipped the parachute risers from Dev's harness, then retrieved his survival pack, laid it on his chest, then grabbed his parachute harness near his shoulders and pulled. Although Deverill was tall, he wasn't very big, but he wouldn't budge. She pulled harder, throwing her weight into it, and finally broke him out of the crust of snow so he would move. But she could only move him a few inches at a time, and soon found that she couldn't keep him from sliding down the embankment toward the road. This was not going to work. If she kept on moving him, he'd eventually slide all the way down, and then whoever was in the truck, or whoever might follow them toward the Vampire's crash site, would...

A flashlight beam swept across her. They were coming! They were a couple dozen yards away, but they were getting closer by the second. She heard voices, angry men's voices. They were tracking her.

There was nowhere else to go but down the embankment. Annie turned Dev's body so his head was facing downhill. He moved much easier now, so she pulled faster. The flashlight beam swung in her direction again, much closer now. She crashed against a tree, swore gently, maneuvered Dev's body around the tree, and continued to pull.

Excited, frantic voices now. Annie guessed they had found the parachute. It was only a matter of time now...

Unexpectedly, Annie reached the bottom of the embankment, fell, and landed hard on the frozen dirt road. She twisted an ankle trying to land on her feet and couldn't help but cry out in pain. The flashlights again swung right in her direction.

They had them now...

Borispol Air Base, Kiev, Republic of Ukraine that same time

The landing was anything but pretty – in fact, it was more of a controlled crash than anything else. With most of his hydraulic system gone, Major John Weston had no control of most of the flight surface, engine nacelle control, or landing gear systems. He was able to use the emergency blow-down system and got one good main landing gear and the nose gear out of the sponsons. But it didn't matter – since he had no control of the engine rotating system, he couldn't switch to helicopter mode. They were going to hit hard no matter how good the Trash Man was.

Borispol Air Base was a large combined Ukrainian air force and army aviation base. Weston got a general layout of the base from his flight information publications. The northeast side of the base housed the army aviation *eskadriyls*, with Mil-8 and Mil-6 heavy transport helicopter squadrons and one Mil-24 attack helicopter squadron; the south side had a mixture of fixed-wing air defense, attack, bomber, and transport planes. Weston used the large runway to get oriented, then slowly, carefully, diverted over to the taxiway opposite the blast deflectors beside the mass helicopter parking ramp. If he lost any pieces of his Pave Hammer aircraft, at least they probably wouldn't hit any Ukrainian aircraft, and he wouldn't close the runway by crash-landing on the main runway.

'Hang on!' Weston shouted behind him over the roar of the windblast and engine noises. 'Prepare for a hard landing!' Normally he would've said, 'Prepare for a copilot landing,' but he didn't think the shades of his dead copilot would appreciate the humor. As he touched down, traveling at least thirty knots beyond normal approach speed to maintain controllability, the first to arrive were the tips of his rotors, chewing huge double gouges into the taxiway. As soon as the rotors stopped, all lift ceased, and the MV-22 slammed into the pavement. The landing gear collapsed instantly, and the Pave Hammer aircraft began a long, ugly belly-slide, stopping four hundred feet later in the dirt between the taxiway and runway.

Weston had all of the major systems shut off several seconds before they landed. Ignoring the emergency escape system in the cockpit, he leapt out of his seat, stepping carefully over the body of his copilot in the aisle, and went to assist his surviving crew members in the evacuation. But Wohl, Briggs, Fratiene, and the surviving PJs had quickly evacuated Linda Mae Maslyukov out of the already-extended aft cargo ramp the moment the aircraft stopped, and had moved her several hundred feet upwind from the crash-landing site.

The aircraft was not on fire, just smoke belching from each seized engine, so Weston accepted the grisly but important task of carrying his copilot's body out of the aircraft. He half dragged, half carried him as far upwind as he could, then laid him on the grass as carefully as possible. Exhausted, shaking from the buckets of adrenaline coursing through his bloodstream, very glad to be alive, Weston collapsed on the grass upwind of the aircraft. His job was over for now. All he needed was a beer and his wife and kids by his side.

Ukrainian soldiers and airmen were running over to them, jabbering excitedly. Several of them spoke English, and they hurried to help the PJs attend to Siren. They started an intravenous drip to try to rehydrate and nourish her, and a Ukrainian medic began dressing her wounds. Ukrainian firefighters knocked down the smoldering engine fires quickly. Weston was introduced first to the security forces first sergeant, and then to a progressive string of higher-ranking officers, until the base commander himself finally appeared.

Hal Briggs and Chris Wohl, looking like some sort of sci-fi Starship Troopers, walked up to them. Since they had just landed on a Commonwealth air base and might still be pursued by the Russian Air Force, both of them were on guard: Briggs had his helmet on, scanning the sky and the base for any sign of a threat; Wohl had his huge electromagnetic antitank rail gun out and ready. 'Guys, this is the base commander, Brigadier-General Mykhaylo Sakhan, commander of the Second Aviation Division here at Borispol.' Briggs saluted; Wohl stood silently, his rail gun at port arms.

'And who are you, sir?' Sakhan asked, after he returned his salute, staring in amazement at both their strange outfits and their weapons.

'Our code name is Tin Man, sir,' Briggs replied in his electronically synthesized voice. 'We are American military personnel. That's all I am authorized to reveal to you.'

'*Neechoho,*' Sakhan said. 'We were warned by your American state department that you would be arriving, although they said nothing about arriving spacemen.'

'We need one of your helicopters to return to Russia, sir,' Briggs said simply.

'What happened?' Weston asked.

'Our guardian angel took a hit. Terminator is down. We're going in after them.'

'Damn. I wish I had my ride.' And he meant it – all thoughts of relaxing with his family and a

361

cold one were gone. Dewey and Deverill had risked their lives to save his. 'You guys get out of here. We'll be okay.'

'Unfortunately, I cannot help you,' Sakhan said. 'I have not received authorization from my superiors to assist you in violating Russian territory. I understand lives are at stake, but your government has not made the reason for all this activity clear to us. Perhaps you can explain who you are and what you were doing in Russia, and I can pass this information along to my superiors.'

'Unfortunately, that's not possible, sir,' Briggs said. 'But I assure you, my government will take full responsibility for our actions and reimburse you in full.'

'Would you sell me your strange outfit, or allow me to rent it for a while, or accept my assurance that whatever I might do with it would not be your responsibility?' Sakhan asked with a smile.

'No, sir.'

Sakhan raised his hands. 'So there we have it. You can expect a representative from your embassy to arrive shortly, and we will secure the wreckage of your aircraft and assist your injured in any way we can.'

'I'm sorry we couldn't get any authorized assistance, sir,' Briggs said.

Sakhan narrowed his eyes. 'This means what, soldier?'

Briggs and Wohl walked down the taxiway and made their way over to the mass helicopter parking ramp. Sakhan and several of his officers and personnel followed. They walked down the middle of the ramp until they saw a Mil-8MTV twin-turboprop helicopter gunship readying for takeoff, with a machine gun mounted on the nose but its weapon outriggers empty. 'We'll take this one,' he said.

'*Pereproshooyoo?*' Sakhan exclaimed, the rising anger apparent in his voice. 'You will "take" this helicopter? What do you mean?'

'I mean, sir, that I will take this helicopter to Russia on a rescue mission, or my associate will destroy it.'

'Destroy it? How dare you?'

Briggs turned to Wohl. 'Demonstrate,' he ordered.

Wohl turned and, shooting from the hip, fired a depleted uranium projectile into another parked helicopter about a hundred yards away. The projectile created a bright one-inch contrail through the moist predawn sky that was very visible under the ballpark lights illuminating the ramp. Several large pieces of the helicopter's engine compartment flew off, and the rotor mast listed sideways so far that one rotor blade tip sagged all the way to the ramp.

'*Gavnuk!* That little display of false bravado just cost your government five million dollars, and cost you a year in prison!' Sakhan shouted. He turned to two of his security men standing behind him and issued an order in Ukrainian.

But when the guards leveled their assault rifles on Briggs and Wohl, Briggs immediately sent both of them to the tarmac with one quick electric blast each from his electrodes. Wohl covered Briggs with the big rail gun but did not aim it at anyone. The other officers around Sakhan were stunned, not daring to make a move. Briggs nodded toward another helicopter. 'Now that one.'

'*Nee! Zhoda! Zhoda!* Very well, very well,' Sakhan said angrily, holding up his hands. 'If you wish to kill or maim dozens of my men just so you may sacrifice your lives and the life of one of my helicopter crews over Russia, I cannot stop you. But I wish you to know that you are in violation of Ukrainian law and I will see to it that you are punished.'

'Thank you, sir,' Briggs said. He and Wohl trotted over to the helicopter that had just started engines; meanwhile, Sakhan had issued orders over a portable radio to the crew. As the two Americans approached, several crew members departed the helicopter. When Briggs and Wohl climbed aboard, only the pilot and copilot remained.

Briggs strapped into the flight engineer's seat behind the copilot, then swiveled the seat so he sat between the two pilots. He saw their shocked reactions as they stared at the weirdly outfitted man. 'Stand by for instructions,' he told the pilot. He nodded in return – obviously he understood English and could hear Briggs's synthesized voice. Briggs activated his satellite transceiver: 'Briggs to Luger secure.'

'Go ahead, Hal.'

'Me and the master sergeant just got a ride,' Briggs said. 'We might need to smooth things over with the Ukrainian army, but we'll deal with that problem later. I need a heading and as much intel as you can give me to the shootdown point.'

'Roger. Be advised, Dewey and Deverill have

been captured.'

'Oh, shit.'

'Annie is still in contact with us,' Luger went on. 'They were captured by locals and turned over to Border Police. They're not on the move right now – we think they're in a vehicle, but stationary right now. Deverill is unconscious. Stand by ... your magnetic course is one-one-seven degrees, range two-two-three nautical miles. One thousand feet AGL should be a good emergency safe altitude for you.'

'I've got a good visual on the terrain,' Briggs said. 'We're on our way. ETA, seventy minutes.' The Ukrainian pilots did not have night-vision goggles, but Briggs could see everything with perfect clarity with his electronic visor sensors. 'One-one-seven degree heading, boys,' Briggs shouted to the pilots. 'And step on it.'

'Step on it. *Bistra. Ochen bistra.* Haul ass, right, Mr Robot?' the pilot echoed, laughing. Obviously, the pilots were much more excited about this mission than the base commander was. They lifted off the ground and headed off, staying just above the treetops.

Codlea, Romania
that same time

About a hundred miles north-northwest of the Romanian capital of Bucharest, nestled within the foothills of the Transylvanian Alps, Codlea was the site of a former Warsaw Pact bombing range and dispersal airfield, long ago sold to Pavel Kazakov –

he never said why a Russian 'businessman' needed an entire military base in the Carpathian Mountains, and the Romanian government, after seeing how much Kazakov was willing to pay for the abandoned ghost town of a base, didn't ask.

Romania was a rich source of weapons, fuel, maintenance personnel, intelligence officers, and fighters – all it took was money, and the supplies seemed unlimited. Romania, once only a junior member of the Warsaw Pact, had developed a substantial weapons-manufacturing industry during the Nicolae Ceausescu regime, manufacturing license-built and copies of Soviet and Chinese weapons of all kinds, from small-arms ammunition to jet fighters. With the fall of the Soviet Union, Russia and China flooding the markets with weapons, and hard economic times in most of Eastern Europe, those weapons factories turned to the underground weapons dealers to stay alive. Kazakov was a regular and welcome customer in Romania.

From the outside, the big hangar looked as decrepit and as much in danger of collapse as all the buildings out there. But on closer inspection, one would first notice that the tall five meter-high barbed-wire fence surrounding the hangar was new. As one got closer, it'd be apparent that the peeling paint, loose siding, and rusty bolts on the outside of the hangar actually hid a sound-proof steel lining, and that the old hangar door actually sat squarely on well-lubricated rollers. Although grass still popped up through cracks all over the runway and taxiways, some of the grass was clearly mashed down in places, denoting very recent activity by heavy vehicles.

Inside the fifty year-old hangar was one of the world's most modern aircraft – the Metyor-179 'Tyenee' stealth fighter-bomber. After its raid on Kukes, Pavel Kazakov had had Stoica and Yegorov fly the plane to this isolated, virtually unknown destination, where fuel, maintenance, and weapons were waiting. A crew of thirty technicians and workers were standing by, ready to check out the plane, download postmission data from its computers, and get it ready for its next mission.

After its first taste of action, the Mt-179 was in almost perfect condition. The pilot, Ion Stoica, was examining the aircraft with the maintenance chief during an early-morning status briefing. 'That's the worst of it, Mr Stoica,' the maintenance supervisor said. He pointed to the leading edge of the wing near the muzzles where the air-to-air missiles were fired. 'The missiles are ejected from the launch tubes by a slug of compressed nitrogen gas. The gas slug is supposed to push the missile thirty to forty meters from the wing before the missile's motor fires, to avoid any exhaust damage to the wing. For some reason, the missiles are only being pushed ten to fifteen meters away before the motor ignites. The tube's shutter, which is titanium, protects the inside of the wing from exhaust damage, but the exhaust is badly corroding the surface of the leading edge, and it appears that the shutter is partially open when the motor fires, because we are seeing some heat damage inside the launch tube itself.'

'What do you recommend?' Stoica asked.

'Several things: a larger and higher-pressure nitrogen bottle, bigger feed lines to the launch tube, redesigned replacement seals inside the launch tube, perhaps a faster-acting shutter to protect the tube, and perhaps some extra titanium sheathing around the muzzles to protect the wing,' the maintenance chief said.

'How soon can we get these things?'

'Not long at all – if we were at Zhukovsky,' the maintenance chief said. 'Out here in the middle of Transylvania, there's probably not a piece of titanium anywhere for three hundred kilometers. It will take time to obtain and fabricate these parts. And if Mr Kazakov moves us again, it will only delay repairs even longer.'

'Can we still use the interior launchers?' Gennadi Yegorov, the Mt-179's weapons officer, asked.

'You see how much damage was done after one launch, Mr Yegorov,' the maintenance chief said. 'One more launch could severely damage the composite wing, and then we're looking at a long and complicated repair job. If it damages the structure around the launch tube, we could be looking at replacing the entire inboard wing section – that could take weeks, even months.'

Yegorov looked at Stoica, then shrugged. 'We can keep the tubes loaded in case of emergencies,' he suggested, 'and depending on our mission, we can load missiles on wing pylons.'

'How much do loaded wing pylons increase our radar cross-section?'

'*Ya nee znayoo*,' Yegorov replied. 'I would guess about ten to fifteen percent – more if we had air-to-ground missiles. But if we needed the stealth capability more than the missiles, we could always jettison the pylons and we would regain our stealth cross-section, and we'd still have air-to-air weapons on board in case of emergency.'

'The internal launch tubes that you did not use on your last flight are loaded with R-60s and they're ready to go,' the maintenance chief said. 'We need to clear the damage from the other launch tubes before we can load missiles in there. We can get the shutters to retract, but we need to find out if there's any internal damage.'

'You'd better get started, then,' Stoica said. 'I don't know what the boss has in store for us, but I'd like to be ready to fly as soon as–'

Just then, one of the planning officers ran up to them. 'Did you guys hear? There's some kind of air defense emergency declared on the Russia-Ukraine border. The Russian Air Force is scrambling dozens of jets. Sounds like a war going on!'

They all hurried over to the operations office, where they monitored several UHF, HF, and satellite channels belonging to the Russian Air Force and other Russian military agencies, courtesy of Colonel-General Zhurbenko. It did indeed sound as if a full-scale air war was in progress. Several Russian aircraft and air defense sites had already been destroyed. The entire southeast military district was under an air defense emergency.

'*Vi shooteetye!*' Yegorov exclaimed. 'I wish we were up there! We could show them all what a *real* fighter jet can do!'

Stoica shrugged, then looked at the maintenance chief. 'Well, let's go. Load those missile pylons on board, give us a full load of missiles, and let's see what happens.'

'You're crazy!'

'We need to test what our detection threshold is for pylon-mounted weapons,' Stoica said. 'We still have some darkness left – we'll be back over the Carpathians well before daylight. Let's do it.'

Everyone had the same thought – what will Pavel Kazakov do when he finds out we launched his stealth fighter without permission? – but everyone was game if Ion Stoica was willing to okay the flight. If he was going to take the heat, that left everyone else off the hook.

The maintenance crews already had pylons ready to upload – they just had to transfer weapons from the weapon storage area: several steel and concrete containers flown in by transport plane – to the maintenance hangar. Stoica selected two R-60 heat-seeking air-to-air missiles on each pylon, plus one R-27 radar-homing missile mounted on the bottom of the pylon. The R-27 missile, developed at Metyor Aerospace, was designed to attack airborne radar aircraft and electronic warfare aircraft from long range – the missile could home in on enemy radio, radar, or jamming transmissions, as well as be guided by the Mt-179's fire control radar.

Although the Tyenee with its long forward-swept wings, seemed to completely engulf the mounted weapon pylons, the externally mounted weapons also obviously spoiled the stealth fighter's smooth, sleek lines. 'It's certain our stealth characteristics are going to suffer,' Stoica said. 'But we need to find out by how much. If we can penetrate

Belgorod airspace and cruise around undetected, we know we have a good system.'

'And maybe we'll bag ourselves a Ukrainian or Turkish fighter,' Yegorov said happily. He waved a sheet of paper. 'I've got the latest radar plots and fixes on the unidentified aircraft – we can be there in twenty minutes.'

Aboard the Ukrainian Mi-8 helicopter

Just as the first rays of light were peeping over the horizon, the Ukrainian helicopter crossed the Russian border. 'Dave, how are we doing?' Briggs asked via the satellite transceiver.

'Five degrees right, then straight ahead, thirty-one miles,' Luger replied. 'Belgorod early-warning radar is forty miles south, but I think you're below their coverage. Continue terrain masking. Dewey and Deverill are on the move. Looks like they're in a vehicle, heading southeast toward Belgorod. They might be on the highway, judging by how fast they're moving. They're about twenty miles north of the town of Jakovlevo. We're trying to get a good satellite image of the area to see if we can identify the vehicle, but I don't think there's time. I'll vector you in as close as I can, and then you'll have to take it from there.'

The chase took only a few more minutes. The highway they were following was growing quickly – it was the main highway between Moscow and Sevastopol, running almost the entire width of western Russia. Traffic was increasing rapidly as the workday began. 'This is going to be like finding a needle in a haystack,' Briggs said grimly. 'We can see several dozen vehicles out here.'

'Twelve o'clock, five miles,' Luger said. 'Speed forty-eight knots ... four miles, straight ahead ... three miles ... speed forty-five knots...'

Briggs used his electronic visor to scan every vehicle. Traffic was starting to get busy as they got closer to town, so everyone was slowing down together. There were no military-looking vehicles apparent.

'Annie, this is Hal secure,' Briggs radioed. 'Don't answer. I can't see your vehicle. I need you to do something to distract the driver and make him swerve or slow down or pull off the road. Scream, throw a tantrum, swear, anything. We're just a few seconds out.'

'Two miles. You got them yet, Hal?'

'Nothing. Every vehicle was in line. No one pulled off the road, no one swerved, no one sped up or slowed down.'

'One mile,' Luger reported. 'Distance and speed are getting more unreliable, guys. The system just isn't precise enough to give you an exact bead on them. See anything?'

'Nothing. Nothing that looks like a prisoner transport, or a military vehicle, or anything unusual at all. A few buses, a bunch of station wagons, a bunch of minivans.'

'Then we'll have to do it the hard way,' Chris Wohl said. 'Rotate left, translate sideways.' As the pilot turned the big chopper so it was flying sideways down the highway, Wohl leaned out the starboard side cargo door, raised his rail gun, aimed, and fired. Both dual left rear tires of a large passenger bus exploded. The bus swerved left, blocking the highway and stopping traffic. 'Make a low pass over the stopped cars, and keep an eye out for a response.'

It did not take long at all. From a large but otherwise plain black sedan, very much like dozens of others on the highway, Briggs saw a soldier in camouflaged battle-dress uniform emerge with an AK-74 assault rifle in his hands, staring at the low-flying helicopter. 'Tally-ho!' Briggs shouted. 'There's suspect number one! You got him covered, Sarge? Don't let him get a shot off at our ride.'

'Roger,' Wohl responded. He already had the gunman in his sights, and Briggs hoped he wouldn't pull the trigger – a human body shot with a blunt one-pound projectile traveling over three thousand feet per second would burst apart like an overripe melon.

Briggs didn't wait for the helicopter to hover or position itself near the suspect vehicle – he simply ran to the open port-side cargo door and leaped out, with the helicopter still over a hundred feet in the air and flying about thirty miles an hour. A fraction of a second before his feet hit the pavement, a burst of jet propellant from his boots softened his fall. Another blast of propellant flung Briggs through the air, and he landed right beside the flabbergasted gunman. A lightning burst of electrical energy from an electrode dropped the startled gunman before he could even think about leveling his rifle.

The windows in the sedan were inch-thick bulletproof glass, but they were no match for the electronically controlled armor that turned Briggs's fists into battering rams. He cracked open the left rear window first and peered inside. The moment he saw two passengers wearing HAWC black flight suits inside, he raced into action. He shot another burst of high-voltage disabling energy into the second armed guard sitting in the aft-facing passenger seat. At the same moment, another shot from Wohl's rail gun disabled the sedan's engine with a tremendous *KA-BANG!* and flying pieces of engine block before the driver could speed away through traffic. One pull through the broken window, and the thick bullet-proof door popped free of its frame.

Briggs immediately found out why Annie couldn't respond – she and Deverill were hand-cuffed to the floor, their mouths taped shut, and a hood pulled over their eyes. One quick yank, and the handcuffs popped off their floor bolts, and he hustled the two fliers out of the disabled sedan.

'Stand by, sir, we're coming down,' Wohl radioed.

'Hurry it up,' Briggs radioed back. But as he watched the sky while the Ukrainian chopper came in for a landing, he saw something else that made his blood turn to slush: four Russian Mi-24 gunships, armed to the teeth. At the same instant, two Russian fighter planes screamed overhead, providing air cover for the gunships.

The game was up. The rescue mission was over. The gunships were bearing down on them quickly, two staying high opposing the Ukrainian chopper, the other two swinging wide apart, swooping in low to cover Briggs and the others on the ground. The only thing they could do now was surrender. There was no way they could–

Suddenly, the two high Mi-24 gunships lining up on the Ukrainian helicopter swerved, ratcheted back and forth across the sky unsteadily, then dove for the earth, trailing a thick cloud of smoke. The two low Mi-24s swerved left and right, popping bright decoy flares and ejecting bundles of chaff. The two heavily armored Mi-24s were able to autorotate to hard but survivable landings several hundred yards away. They heard loud *BOOOMs* across the sky as the MiG fighters sped away, either running from or looking for a fight.

'Tin Man, this is Terminator Two,' Briggs heard General Patrick McLanahan announce on his personal satellite transceiver. 'Splash two Hinds. We're defensive with two MiGs coming around after us. Get off the ground as fast as you can. We'll try to put these MiGs down and keep the other Hinds off your six.'

'Sweet lord, someone's looking out for us!' Briggs crowed. 'C'mon, Sarge, get that beast on the ground and pick us up now before our luck runs out.'

The White House Situation Room, Washington, DC that same time

'I'm afraid, Mr President,' Robert G. Goff, the US secretary of defense, said solemnly, 'that this might be the worst peacetime military incident since the Francis Gary Powers U-2 spy plane affair.'

Secretary of Defense Goff was giving a late-night report to President Thomas Thorn in the White House Situation Room, which was very much like most conference rooms anywhere except for the sophisticated communications capabilities – the President could pick up the phone in front of him and talk to virtually anyone on the planet, even those aloft or afloat. Arrayed around Thorn were Edward Kercheval, the Secretary of State; Air Force General Richard W. Venti, the Chairman of the Joint Chiefs of Staff; and Robert R. Morgan, Director of Central Intelligence. Vice President Lester R. Busick was seated beside the President.

'I'm sure it's not that bad, Robert,' the President said in a soft voice. 'As far as we can detect, the world has not stopped spinning on its axis. Run it down for us.'

For most folks, the President's quiet tone and demeanor, his soft-spoken attitude, and his almost constant level of energy were a calming influence. But with these men, in this situation, it was beginning to get annoying. For Robert Goff, his friend the President's constant lack of ... alacrity, for lack of a better term, was beginning to get infuriating.

'Yes, sir,' Goff began, after taking a deep breath. 'The rescue mission for Siren was a success. Unfortunately, just before exiting Russian airspace, the EB- 1C Vampire bomber used for air cover, was shot down by Russian air defense forces.'

'Maybe this Vampire wasn't as survivable as we were led to believe,' the Vice President scoffed.

'The best-laid plans, Les, the best-laid plans,' the President said, gently admonishing his vice pre-

376

sident. 'The only real failure is the failure to try.'

Busick hid a scowl and fell silent. It was obvious to most of the nation that Thomas Thorn and Lester Busick were definitely two different men; if given a choice, most folks in the know would never pick these two men to work together in the White House. Thorn was a complete Washington novice; Busick was the archetypical Washington insider. Busick worked best when operating in crisis mode; Thorn treated every incident, from the lowliest political flap to the most serious world crisis, with the same quiet, understated coolness. He had a sort of Jimmy Carter innocence about him and a seemingly Ronald Reagan-type detachment from the seriousness of a particular incident, but at the same time his finely tuned mind kept his staff and advisors well coordinated and moving generally in unison.

For many years, Lester Busick had seen himself as the ultimate Washington puppetmaster, the man in the wings pulling the strings of power – but with the advent of Thomas Nathaniel Thorn on the political scene, he could tell right away that he was being outclassed. The difference was that Thorn pulled the strings without seemingly lifting a hand.

'What about the Vampire's crew?' the President asked.

'Sir, Air Force Lieutenant-General Terrill Samson was in charge of the cover mission – he's with us on a secure videophone link. I'd like to bring him in on our discussion.' Thorn nodded, and an aide activated the link. Samson was seated in his battle staff area at Dreamland, along with Major John Long. 'General Samson, this is Secretary Goff. I'm here with the President and the National Security Council in the Situation Room. Who's with you, General?'

'This is Major John Long, operations officer of the 111th Bombardment Squadron, the unit that the aircrew and aircraft were assigned; he is the acting commander. The unit commander, Colonel Furness, is the aircraft commander of the backup aircraft and is en route back here.'

'Very well, General. What's the latest on the crew?'

'Both crew members are alive,' Samson said. 'One crew member is still unconscious. The crew was captured by local Russian militiamen and transferred to the Border Police, who are taking them to an unknown location, presumably a Border Police regional headquarters, possibly Belgorod.'

'The plane was destroyed in the crash, General Samson?' the President asked.

'Our telemetry indicates that the plane was completely destroyed, sir,' Samson replied.

'Telemetry?'

'We monitor hundreds of different parameters of every weapon system involved in our missions by satellite, sir.'

'Too bad you can't monitor your human "weapon systems" the same way, General,' Busick quipped.

'In fact, sir, we can,' Samson said. 'We're in constant voice contact with all of our personnel, and we monitor a range of readings on each one, constantly by satellite.'

'You do?' the President asked incredulously. 'You know where they are, what they say, whether their hearts are beating or not?'

'Exactly, Mr President,' Samson said. 'My staff has been monitoring them continuously during this mission. We are not currently in voice contact, but we are monitoring life signs and they are alive. We can also plot their positions with some degree of accuracy, and we've determined that they are indeed on the move.' Thorn's eyebrows arched in amazement. 'Their situation appears to be quite desperate. I'm afraid they've been captured and will be in the Russian military prisoner system shortly.'

'Amazing,' Busick gasped. 'So you know exactly where they are right now? Why don't we just go in and get them, then?'

'My thoughts exactly,' Defense Secretary Goff said enthusiastically. He turned to the Chairman of the Joint Chiefs of Staff. 'General Venti?'

'General Samson's cover mission included a number of contingency operations, including an armed rescue mission,' Venti said. 'If I know General Samson and his staff, he's got his folks moving already.'

'We do, sir,' Samson said. 'We're hoping that the forces controlling Dewey and Deverill are not regular military or paramilitaries, but reserves or local police. There are few regular army forces stationed on the Ukrainian border. If we launch a rescue mission before they are transferred to regular military control or taken out of the frontier region, we might be able to rescue them successfully.

'The Intelligence Support Agency cell that was successfully rescued by the Vampire bomber crew is safe on the ground in Ukraine at an airfield outside Kiev,' Samson went on. 'They want permission to procure a helicopter and return to the shootdown area. They are the closest special-ops capable forces in the area – they can be on scene in about two hours, depending on what kind of transportation they procure. The next-nearest forces would be in Turkey, at least three hours away plus generation and briefing time.'

'We seem to have decided on an armed hostile infiltration action,' the President observed. No one replied. 'I may sound incredibly naive here, gentlemen, but why don't we just ask the Russians to give our people back to us?'

'I'm afraid we couldn't expect too much help from the Russians once they found out who they had in their possession, sir,' Robert Goff said, trying hard not to look too shocked at the President's seemingly childish question. 'I mean, in a very real sense, our crews are hostiles, enemy attackers, just as if we were at war. They flew a strategic bomber inside Russia, shot down Russian aircraft, destroyed Russian military property. They don't have any reason to be nice to us. I expect them to delay returning the crew until they have had ample time to interrogate them thoroughly. Then they'll examine the wreckage and interrogate them some more about the technology they'll undoubtedly find. They could be prisoners for a very, very long time.'

'The best opportunity to get them out is *now*, sir,' Venti stressed. 'Although they appear to be taken by paramilitary forces, they're still not in the hands of trained prison guards or professional soldiers. If we can get to them right now, we have the best chance of rescuing them.'

'And then once the crew is out of the Russians' hands, we can do our own stalling technique,' Goff went on. 'The Russians will have what's left of the bomber, but they won't have the crew. That's far more important. They'll ask a ton of questions, accuse us of everything under the sun, and condemn us for our warlike actions. But they won't have anything.'

The President nodded, seemingly unconvinced. He looked up and saw General Samson deep in a discussion with a new officer that had entered the videoconference picture. The discussion they were having out of mike range appeared to be getting rather heated. 'Problem, General Samson?' he asked. Samson looked at the camera, then jabbed his finger at the newcomer beside him. 'General?'

'Maybe a potential problem,' Terrill Samson said. 'Stand by one.' The President and his staff allowed Samson to confer with his staff for a couple of minutes. Samson was obviously struggling to retain control of his anger. Finally, he faced the camera once again and explained, 'Sir, it seems that a rescue mission is already under way – in fact, the Vampire crew has already been recovered, alive.'

'*What?*' almost everyone in the Situation Room exclaimed.

'We didn't authorize any rescue mission,' Vice President Busick said. 'General Samson, I've had to put up with shenanigans from you boys in Dreamland for years. Is it happening again, even with Brad Elliott gone? Was this one of your patented stealth sneak attacks?'

'God, I hope not,' Venti murmured in exasperation. 'What's going on, Earthmover?'

'Easy, folks, easy,' the President said, keeping his hands folded before him, seemingly unflustered by this news. 'A few minutes ago, you were going to recommend such a mission – now you're upset because you all didn't get to push the "go" button. Continue, General Samson.'

General Samson took a deep breath and ran it down for the National Security Council staff. 'Exactly as we were planning, the Intelligence Support Agency members who'd been taken to a base outside Kiev obtained use of a Ukrainian helicopter, penetrated Russian airspace, and located Dewey and Deverill using their personal microtransceivers,' Samson said.

'My God, that's incredible,' Robert Goff exclaimed. 'Amazing. Who organized this, General? You?'

'No, sir – my staff officers and the commanders on-scene,' Samson replied. 'There is a complication, however. The Russian Federation Air Force is bearing down on them. They...' He paused, then said under his breath, 'Genesis to Briggs ... conference in McLanahan ... conference in Luger ... everyone, stand by.'

'General, am I to understand that you are actually talking to your men in the middle of some sort of combat rescue mission over Russia that is happening right now?' the President asked incredulously. 'You are making some sort of global conference call and listening to what's going on without a radio in your hand, a microphone to your lips, or a speaker?'

Samson had to pull himself away from eavesdropping on the fire-fight half a world away to respond to his commander-in-chief: 'Yes ... yes, sir. Part of my unit's security infrastructure is a satellite tracking and communications system that is ... is implanted into every member of my organization.'

'*Implanted?*'

'A subcutaneous satellite transceiver,' Samson explained. 'We monitor all personnel constantly, year-round, worldwide. We can listen in on their conversations, talk to them, locate them, even record vital signs.'

'Extraordinary,' Secretary of Defense Goff breathed. 'I've heard of such devices, but I never believed they would ever be used in my lifetime.'

'Never mind the gee-whiz stuff – what in hell's happening out there?' Busick interjected hotly. 'And I still want to know why the National Security Council wasn't apprised of this operation? Who the hell has the balls to put a mission like this in motion without getting permission first?'

'Sir, firstly, I take full responsibility for whatever's happening out there,' Samson said. 'Those are my people and my aircraft. No one else is responsible.'

'I see plenty of heads rolling here – but the first one *will* be yours, General Samson. Count on it. Now what in hell is happening?'

Not since he had been a seventeen-year-old

enlistee doing ditch-digging jobs in a Civil Engineering unit in Thailand during the Vietnam War – literally digging ditches, trenches, latrines, and garbage pits – had Terrill Samson ever felt so helpless and clueless. Back then, it had been because he was a know-nothing airman. This time, it was because of Patrick McLanahan and David Luger. McLanahan and Luger had gone behind his back and executed this goat-fuck mission without one word to their superior officer. It was betrayal of the worse kind. Samson felt humiliated, castrated by his own people.

McLanahan wasn't a genius, a legend, a hero – he was a back-stabbing traitor.

'We ... we have another aircraft flying as air support for the Intelligence Support Agency operatives,' Samson said, putting as much strength and authority in his voice as he could, even though he realized it had all but completely drained away. 'The support aircraft is one of mine, too. Colonel Furness of the One-Eleventh Bomb Squadron and General Patrick McLanahan, my deputy, are flying the backup EB-1C Vampire bomber. They apparently heard about the shootdown, reversed course, returned to Russian airspace, and are now engaging the Russian attackers...'

'My *God!*' someone gasped – Samson couldn't tell who it was.

'Two Russian helicopter gunships have already been shot down ... no, wait, now one Russian jet fighter has been shot down,' Samson reported, still listening to the action being played literally in his head through the subcutaneous satellite transceiver. 'The Ukrainian helicopter with the other

384

two Vampire crew members on board is airborne and almost back into Ukrainian airspace. Two more gunships are in the area, and one or more fighters. The Vampire is reengaging all of them.'

'A bomber ... hunting down *fighters?*' Secretary of State Kercheval exclaimed. 'How can they do that?'

'I still want to know, who in *hell* gave the order for them to be shooting down Russians?' Busick thundered. It was a rhetorical statement – aimed not at General Samson, not at Secretary of Defense Goff, but right at the President of the United States.

But President Thorn wasn't going to be drawn into a conflict with anyone, not even his friend and closest advisor – and perhaps also his biggest critic. He rested his head in his left hand, tapping on the corner of his mouth with his index finger, studying the videoteleconference screen with Terrill Samson's anxious, animated face looking back at him. It was as if he was watching someone watch a video replay of a bad car accident, or a bullfight, something potentially violent – you felt like asking, 'What's going on?' every five seconds.

Finally, the President picked up the phone beside him and said to the White House communications officer: 'Get me President Sen'kov of the Russian Federation on the line.' It took only a few moments until someone in the Russian president's office answered. 'This is President Thorn. I am in the White House with members of my national security staff.'

'This is President Sen'kov,' the voice of the Russian translator said. 'I am in my residence surrounded by generals and defense ministers who believe we are under attack by the United States. You are calling about the illegal violation of Russian sovereign airspace near the Russia-Ukraine border, I assume? Is this some sort of prelude to war, Mr President? What is the meaning of this?'

'I'd be happy to explain,' Thorn said. 'The United States was conducting an intelligence operation inside Russia, near Moscow.'

The men in the Situation Room looked stunned. Sen'kov must've been equally stunned at that revelation, because it took him several long moments to respond: 'Please repeat, Mr President.'

'I said, the United States was conducting an intelligence mission near Moscow,' Thorn repeated, as calmly as if he were describing a rare painting or a Mozart opera. 'We were trying to rescue an agent that was spying on one of your military installations. We inserted a special operations team inside your country, and we used a long-range stealth aircraft to cover the team in case it was discovered.'

'Mr President!' Lester Busick retorted. '*What are you doing?* You can't reveal that information to the Russians?'

Thorn hit the microphone kill-switch on the telephone. 'Les, don't you think the Russians already know all this?' he asked. He released the switch: 'As you know, President Sen'kov, the special ops team made it out, but your military forces shot down the stealth bomber. Some of our special operations forces and another stealth aircraft went in to try to rescue the crew of the first stealth aircraft before your forces could imprison them.'

'One moment, please, Mr President,' the translator said. The men in the Situation Room could only imagine what was going on in the minds of the Russian president and military advisors. The translator finally said, 'President Sen'kov thanks you for your candor, Mr President, but he still demands that the United States take full responsibility for what your forces have done.'

'I fully intend to,' Thorn said. 'Allow me to continue: At the present moment, our respective forces are engaging one another in an air battle. Three of your helicopters and one fighter have already been shot down. But I do not wish for the battle to go on. I am hereby ordering the crew of the stealth aircraft to disengage if you order your defensive forces to let them go.'

'With all due respect, Mr President,' Sen'kov said through the translator, 'the Russian people would not care to see its forces merely surrender with a hostile enemy force flying overhead. They are and always will be determined to fight to the last man to defend their homeland.'

'Mr President, I will order my forces to disengage, but I will also tell them that they are free to defend themselves if they are attacked,' Thorn said. 'I feel quite certain my aircrews can survive and make it out of your country, but I don't wish for them to hurt any more Russians. I strongly urge you to accept my suggestion and order your forces to disengage.' Thorn kept the line open and said to the videoteleconference screen, 'General Samson, order the Vampire to disengage immediately. It may open fire only if fired upon first.'

A moment later: 'Order received and acknowledged, sir,' Samson responded. 'Vampire is proceeding direct to the Ukrainian border at maximum speed and at low altitude.'

'I've issued my orders, and they have been acknowledged, Mr Sen'kov,' President Thorn said. 'Let's stop this right now, shall we?'

'This is an insult. This is unacceptable.' The translator's voice was monotoned and even, although they could very clearly hear the Russian president shouting at the top of his lungs in the background. 'You commit an act of war upon the Russian people, and you expect us to just turn our backs and walk away?'

'I am prepared to offer you one hundred million dollars in reparations for the damage and expense my forces have caused,' Thorn went on. The mouths of every man in the Situation Room dropped open in surprise. 'In addition, I offer five million dollars for every Russian killed by my forces during the operation, plus a public admission of guilt and a public apology, broadcast on international television.'

'Mr President, what in the *world*...?' Busick sputtered. '*You can't do that!*'

'I'm going to do it,' Thorn said. 'I promise, upon my mother's name, I'll do it this afternoon, in Russian prime time.'

'A public apology? A public admission of guilt? No conditions?'

'No conditions,' Thorn said. 'I have authorized my forces to stop all hostile actions – they are authorized only to defend themselves now. In any case, I will make my apology and explanation this morning, ten A.M. Washington time, and I will announce the reparation payment. If the Russians will tell me how many of their men were killed by my forces, I'll announce that payment as well. My only wish right now is that no more lives are put in jeopardy.'

'You ... you will admit all, Mr President?' Sen'kov asked.

'Everything.'

'Such as what kind of aircraft were involved in this intelligence operation?'

'Certainly,' Thorn replied. 'The rescue from near Moscow was accomplished by an MV-22 tilt-rotor special operations aircraft called a Pave Hammer. It carries a crew of six, several machine guns and air-to-air missiles on a retractable launcher, and defensive transmitters and expendables. The crew belong to a unit of the Intelligence Support Agency, a directorate of the Central Intelligence Agency set up to perform missions such as this.

'The cover aircraft were EB-1C stealth bombers called Vampires, which are highly modified B-1 bombers designed to penetrate heavily defended airspace and attack a wide variety of–'

'You dared to send nuclear-capable B-1 bombers over the Russian Federation? How dare you? This is tantamount to war!'

'They were simply the best aircraft available to protect our rescue aircraft,' Thorn said matter-of-factly. 'You are not foolish enough really to believe our aircraft would be carrying nuclear weapons, are you?'

'I do not know what to believe!' Sen'kov's translator said over the obviously agitated voice of the Russian president. 'You announce this as casually as if you had sent me a birthday present! Are you mad? Are you insane?'

'Think what you like, Mr President,' Thorn said. 'Allow me to continue. The Vampires belong to the One-Eleventh Bomb Squadron, a unit of the Nevada Air National Guard, currently based at the Tonopah Test Range in Nevada. The Vampires were carrying a mixture of air-to-air, air-to-ground, and antiradar weapons – I don't know the exact combination, but I'll get that information for you if you wish. Their primary mission is the suppression of enemy air defenses and antiballistic missile defense. Their mission was to recover an agent who was spying on Russian military bases near Moscow. The personnel that were rescued by the MV-22 commandeered a Ukrainian helicopter at a base near Kiev, which is what they used to travel back into Russia to extract the downed air-crewmen.'

'Very interesting, Mr President,' Sen'kov said. Robert Goff could easily envision Sen'kov's advisors hurriedly writing all this information down. It was an intelligence bonanza, and it was being supplied direct from the horse's mouth – the President of the United States! 'And the purpose of this spying?'

'To determine the extent of Russian involvement in the recent attack in Kukes, Albania, where several hundred men, women, and children were ruthlessly murdered in an air raid,' Thorn replied hotly.

'*Russian* involvement?' Sen'kov retorted. 'That's ridiculous, Mr Thorn. Investigators from NATO and the United Nations, including members of your own FBI, have no evidence of who might have caused that devastation. Rival drug lords, Macedonian mercenaries punishing Albanian gunrunners for cross-border raids, even rival Muslim sects have been blamed. But Russia had absolutely nothing to do with it.'

'The United States has information that a Russian stealth bomber launched from Zhukovsky Flight Test Center committed those attacks. I'll be sure to tell the world *that*, Mr President.'

There was silence at the other end for a very, very long time. Finally, the translator said, 'You will be spreading lies to cover up your culpability in this entire affair.'

'I will tell the truth, President Sen'kov – the *entire* truth,' Thorn said pointedly. 'I'll admit we were spying on you, and I'll admit we flew aircraft into Russian airspace illegally. I will publicly offer the reparation payment, and I will also offer compensation to the families of any Russians that were killed during the operation, once you verify what that number is.' It was a clever tactic: in order to increase the award, the Russians would have to admit that many Russians had been killed – which wouldn't look too good for Russia's military. 'I'll then present the information recovered by the agent, which I am told not only proves that the attack originated in Russia, but was sanctioned by the Russian government.'

'Lies! All lies!'

'Mr President, I am prepared to admit to

everything,' Thorn shot back. 'I will tell the world the honest truth. I'll present photographs, details of the aircraft, where they came from, and exactly what they did. I will plead guilty to ordering an illegal overflight and undeclared hostile military action against the Russian Federation. I will then play the recordings the agent obtained during the surveillance. The world will believe *me*, President Sen'kov. I guarantee it.'

It was an unbelievable, stunning tactic. The others in the Situation Room were shocked into silence, afraid to move or even breathe. Could this work...?

'Mr Thorn,' the translator said in his usual toneless voice, after another lengthy pause, 'we feel a public statement is unnecessarily belligerent and inflammatory to the Russian people, and we demand you refrain from such a propagandist spectacle. We accept your offer of reparation payment of one hundred million dollars. The Russian government expects it to be paid forthwith. Your admission of guilt is sufficient and a matter of record.

'President Sen'kov has ordered all defensive forces to cease their attacks but to closely monitor all foreign aircraft for any sign of hostilities, and they have been ordered to respond immediately with overwhelming force should any foreign aircraft initiate hostile actions,' the translator went on. 'The Russian government considers this matter closed, with a final admonition: if the United States spreads any information about this incident or any related incidents whatsoever, Russia will use any and all measures to force the

United States to deal with the consequences.'

And the connection was terminated.

The members of the National Security Council looked at each other in stunned silence. Finally, Secretary of Defense Goff said under his breath, 'Did ... did what I think just happen really happen? Did the president of Russia just let an armed American stealth warplane fly through his country?'

'Sure – for one hundred million dollars,' Vice President Busick retorted. 'Pretty sweet deal for him.' He turned to the President, who was sitting quietly, even serenely, at the conference table. 'The money wasn't necessary, Mr President. The Vampire was almost out of Russia anyway. The first Vampire crew was safe–'

'The money was nothing but a token of good faith – or call it a bribe,' the President said. 'Sen'kov knew we had won anyway – he had to save face in front of his generals, and a hundred million bucks goes a long way toward doing just that. Plus, he realizes now we had the goods on him. The incident is over, and everyone wants it that way. Let's all go home.' He stood and headed for the door. But before he departed, he turned back toward the videoteleconference screen and said, 'General Samson?'

'Yes, sir?'

'I want a full report on this incident from you and from General McLanahan as soon as he returns from his trip through Russia. I assume he *will* actually come back this time?'

'I'll see to it, sir.'

'The only matter we still need to discuss is what

to do about my military officers who plan and execute military operations in foreign countries without permission,' the President said grimly. 'That kind of insubordinate, illegal *bullshit* needs to be dealt with right away, once and for all. I hope I'm making myself clear to everyone.'

Over southern Russia
that same moment

The threat warning receiver was a wild, confusing mixture of signals, and Gennadi Yegorov was having a tough time sorting them out. 'I can't quite make out what all the fuss is about,' he said to Ion Stoica. They were both listening intently to Belgorod Radar Center, trying to co-ordinate the flight paths and defensive alignment of at least six Russian jet fighters and one SA-10 surface-to-air missile site. 'I can't tell if they haven't found the intruder, or if they've found him but can't lock onto him, or found him but aren't authorized to attack.'

Stoica, piloting the Metyor-179 Tyenee stealth fighter-bomber, readjusted his grip on the control stick and worriedly shifted in his ejection seat. 'I think we're too late,' he said. 'Whatever it was got away.'

'I'm not so sure,' Yegorov said. 'I just heard another message about unidentified aircraft heading southwest.'

'Well, that's right toward us,' Stoica said. 'Let's hope we get lucky. How's the infrared sensor this morning?'

'*Atleechna*,' Yegorov said. 'Better than usual – must not be very much humidity in the air. Range is about sixteen kilometers.' He paused, listening to the busy, often confusing cacophony of radio transmissions, then said excitedly, 'There! A traffic warning to another aircraft, unidentified intermittent radar target, ten kilometers south of Boriskova, heading westbound, altitude unknown.' Stoica banked hard left and headed for that spot. 'Very indistinct radar fixes – he's less than thirty miles from the air defense radar site at Belgorod, but they can't lock him up.'

'It must be a stealth aircraft,' Stoica said. 'Could it be an American stealth aircraft?'

'They can't get a good fix on him – but the detection threshold is getting closer for us the farther we head northeast,' Yegorov warned his aircraft commander. 'Thirty kilometers more and they'll be able to see us.'

'Those weapon pylons are as bad as radar reflectors,' Stoica said.

'That answers our question – we wear pylons, and our stealthiness goes away,' Yegorov summarized. 'I suggest we go home and bring Comrade Kazakov's plane back to him before we dent a fender.'

'You say we have thirty kilometers before we need to turn south again – let's take it,' Stoica said. 'My dogfight antennae are going nuts. Whoever's out there, he's close.'

'Did I ever tell you what I think of your so-called dogfight antenn–' But Yegorov stopped before finishing – because a target had just appeared on the infrared search-and-track sensor. 'Wait a minute ... contact!' he crowed. 'Eleven o'clock low, range unknown. Weak infrared return, but it does not correlate to any other radar targets.' He reached up and patted Stoica's shoulder. 'I'll never bad-mouth your antennae again.'

'Congratulate me later – let's first see if we can eyeball this guy,' Stoica said. He offset himself slightly south of the target.

'If we can see him on the IRSTS, he's well within R-60 range,' Yegorov said. 'I'm ready.'

'I'd like to get a visual on him first,' Stoica said. 'I don't want to waste any missiles on just a cargo plane.'

'We're not on a mission, Ion – we're joyriding over Ukraine and Russia aboard a five-hundred-million-ruble stealth fighter,' Yegorov told him. 'We came here to see how close we can touch air defense radars with loaded pylons aboard. We know now – not very close at all. Let's go home before we break something major.'

'We finally get a fix on this guy, something it looks like the rest of the Russian Air Force could not do, and you want to let him go and go back home?' Stoica said, with not a little humor in his voice. 'What happened to the bloodthirsty aerial assassin I met dropping bombs on Afghan villages a few years back?'

'He makes too much money and is too afraid of having his nuts cut off by his gangster boss,' Yegorov said.

'This guy shot down some fighters and helicopters,' Stoica reminded his backseater. 'If you tell me you're not the least bit curious about who he is, we'll go home.' There was no reply. 'Ha! I thought so. Hang on!' Stoica began a gentle left turn as the target began passing off their left side, beginning a tail chase to better line up on the target's hot engine exhausts.

'*Sleeshkam pabol'she,*' Yegorov said, as he studied the infrared image. 'He's a big one. Four engines? I think he has four engines!'

'Four engines – he's got to be a stealth bomber!' Stoica said. 'It doesn't explain who shot down the Russian aircraft, but this is a pretty big catch. We'll deal with his escort after we take this big bastard down. What do you say, partner?'

'I'm with you,' Yegorov said excitedly. He entered commands into the weapon computers and immediately received a TARGET LOCK indication. 'Two external R-60s ready and in range. Your trigger is hot.'

'Missiles away!' Stoica lifted the trigger guard off the control stick and squeezed the trigger. Two R-60 air-to-air missiles, one from each wing pylon, screamed off into space after their quarry less than five kilometers away...

As soon as the two R-60 missile motors ignited, a super-cooled electronic eye in the tail of the EB-1C Vampire bomber detected them and issued a MISSILE LAUNCH warning, and at the same time automatically ejected decoys and activated the bomber's electronic countermeasures system. '*Missile launch! Break left! Now!*' Patrick shouted.

The Vampire's attack countermeasures systems were the most advanced in the world. Instead of simple chaff and flare decoy bundles, the Vampire ejected small cylindrical gliders that carried wide-spectrum electromagnetic transmitters that simulated the heat and radar signatures of a real plane. It also carried a towed transmitter array from which all the radar jamming signals were sent – in case the enemy launched home-on-jam weapons, the array would be destroyed, not the Vampire.

But the Metyor-179 was too close, and the decoys didn't have time to power up to full illumination. While the first R-60 missile missed by a few dozen yards, the second R-60 did not. It briefly veered right after one of the decoys, then turned back left toward the Vampire. As it passed over the tail, its proximity fuze detected a near miss and detonated the seven-pound fragmentation warhead. The high-energy burst of shrapnel blew the upper half of the EB-1C's vertical stabilizer completely away just above the horizontal stabilizer.

The explosion twisted the bomber around like a corkscrew, nearly flipping it completely inverted. Without a rudder, Rebecca had no roll or yaw stability. They were at the mercy of fate. If the plane recovered, they were saved – if not, their only chance would be to eject.

Somehow, it corkscrewed back to level flight. They had lost two thousand feet of altitude – Patrick found themselves just a thousand feet above ground. 'Get the nose up, Rebecca,' he warned. 'One thousand AGL.'

'I got it,' Furness said. She had almost no roll control at all, and she found herself muscling in more and more left stick. 'Elevons feel like they're stuck in a right turn. I think it'll trim out … no, I can only trim part of it out. I've got limited pitch control too. Dammit, check my instruments.'

'Rudder servo, elevon servo A, autopilot roll channels A and B, pitch servo A, secondary hydraulics, tail radar, tail warning receiver, and towed countermeasures arrays out,' Patrick said. 'Looks like we got hit in the tail. Engines, electrical, primary hydraulics, and computers are okay. Can you hold it?'

'I think so,' Rebecca cried. 'Where in hell did he come from?'

'First priority – get him off our tail,' Patrick shouted. 'LADAR on!' The laser radar immediately located the enemy aircraft less than three miles away. He touched the enemy aircraft symbol on his supercockpit display. 'Attack target.'

'*Warning, attack command received, stop attack ... doors coming open...*' The forward bomb bay doors opened, and a single AIM-120 Scorpion AMRAAM missile was ejected into the slipstream. After stabilizing for a few seconds, its first-stage rocket motor ignited. It shot ahead of the Vampire bomber, then executed a wide, looping 'over-the-shoulder' flight path toward the Metyor-179 stealth fighter.

Normally the missile relied on the Vampire's tail radar for initial guidance to its quarry. But with the aft-facing radar gone, the AIM-120 missile had only the last known position, heading, altitude, and speed of the target for guidance. As it approached the spot in space where the enemy aircraft should be, it activated its own onboard radar and started to search.

'We got him!' Stoica shouted. The sudden *POP!* of the R-60's warhead exploding and the brief trail of fire and burning metal were unmistakable. 'Stand by, I'm going to let him have a couple more. Here goes...' Just then, he saw a brief flash of light in the distance, like a fireworks rocket flying sideways. 'What the hell was that?'

'It's a missile!' Yegorov shouted. *'Break right! Get out of here!'*

Stoica did not hesitate. He threw the Mt-179 stealth fighter into a hard-right ninety-degree bank turn, shoved in full afterburner power, and pulled the control stick back to his belly. At the same instant, Yegorov ejected decoy chaff and flare bundles. The emergency maneuver worked. Without a reliable target position, the Scorpion's onboard radar locked onto the largest target it could find on its way down – the cloud of fine tinsel-like chaff – and blew up harmlessly several hundred yards from the stealth fighter.

'He launched a missile at us!' Stoica shouted in utter shock. 'That bastard *launched a missile at us!*'

'That's either the biggest fighter I've ever seen,' Yegorov said, 'or American stealth bombers now carry air-to-air missiles.'

'That bastard is *dead!*' Stoica shouted. He rolled left and activated the attack radar. This time, the enemy aircraft appeared on the screen immediately. 'Not so stealthy anymore, are we? We *did* hurt you. Missiles aw–' But before he could squeeze the trigger to launch two more R-60s, another missile flew into the sky and arced back toward them. Stoica swore and executed a hard-left break as Yegorov ejected chaff and flares from the right-side ejectors. The second missile missed, but not by as much this time.

'Ion, let's get the hell out of here!' Yegorov shouted. 'This son of a bitch can shoot back at us!'

'I'm not letting him go!'

'Ion, stop it! You already nailed the guy. He's bugging out. Let him go before he gets off a lucky shot and nails *us*.'

'*Pizda tib a radila!*' Stoica swore in Russian. But he knew Yegorov was right. This guy, whoever it was, definitely had some teeth. Besides, one glance at his fuel gauges told him the other story: going into afterburner twice, plus carrying two external wing pylons, really sucked away the gas. He had enough fuel for one more shot – but he elected not to take it. Reluctantly, angrily, he turned left and headed south toward Romania.

'He's bugging out,' Patrick said, as he studied the God's-eye view on his supercockpit display. 'He's heading south ... into Ukraine.'

'Dammit, General, this is the *last* thing we need,' Furness swore. 'We're on an unauthorized and probably illegal mission – and now we have battle damage, *serious* battle damage! I'm not even sure if we'll be able to air-refuel this thing without a rudder and with only partial elevon control.'

'Wonder where he's going?' Patrick mused. 'If he was a Russian fighter, shouldn't he be headed the other way?'

'Are you listening to me, McLanahan? We almost got shot down. *You* almost got us shot down.'

'We were told by General Samson that the Russians agreed to let us go,' Patrick told Furness. 'All the other Russian aircraft returned to base – all except one, a fighter with very low radar cross-section. Now he's heading south into Ukraine. What's up with that?'

'You're lucky to be alive, our tail is shot to hell, and all you can think of is where the guy that almost killed us is headed?'

'LADAR coming on,' Patrick said. He tracked the unknown aircraft for just a few minutes longer until it disappeared from his screen, just fifteen miles away. Definitely a stealth fighter, Patrick thought – the laser radar had a range of over fifty miles. 'He's still heading south. No change in heading. Maybe we should follow him, try to reacquire.'

'Why the hell not?' Rebecca asked sarcastically, the anger thick in her voice. 'Our ass is grass if we go home now anyway.' Rebecca continued on course back home, and Patrick did not argue any further.

Chapter Six

Over the Baltic Sea
days later

From the outside, it resembled a normal Boeing DC-10 Model 30F, with no windows and with big cargo doors instead of passenger doors. Customs inspectors in Aberdeen, Scotland, two days earlier had found only a cavernous empty cargo hold, with a few dozen passenger seats on rolling pallets bolted to the forward part of the compartment, along with portable lavatories. This particular DC-10 had some unusual cargo-handling equipment installed inside – some sort of outsized equipment in the back of the cargo compartment, along with large doors underneath – but its American FAA Form 337 airframe modification sheets and logbook entries were in perfect order.

After stopping in Scotland for two days, during which time workers began loading the plane with cargo, the crew had filed a flight plan direct to Al-Manamah, Bahrain, with sixty thousand four hundred and fifty pounds of oil drilling parts and equipment. Again, the forms were all in order, and the cargo carefully inspected by both United Kingdom Inland Revenue officials, as well as shipment supervisors representing the Bahraini company receiving the parts, and the German insurance company that had written the shipment insurance policy for the four thousand mile flight. It was now obvious why they needed this particular plane and its unusual gear – some of the parts, including oil well pipe, manifolds, and valves, were massive, far too large to fit through the side cargo door. The parts had simply been hoisted aboard the plane through the cargo doors on the bottom. After a three-hour weather delay and another hour coordinating a new international flight plan across the ten countries they would overfly on their nine-hour flight, they finally got under way shortly before sunset.

But as soon as the flight was airborne, the twenty technicians and engineers aboard the aircraft got to work. The oil-drilling equipment that resembled massive cast-iron pieces were easily and quickly disassembled – they were actually composed of lightweight steel sheeting over polystyrene foam. Pump manifolds became control consoles; oil-drilling valves became test equipment and toolboxes; and oil-drilling pipe became pieces of two unusually shaped missiles.

The missiles had a curly-sided triangular cross-section, rather than a conventional round torpedo shape, with the bottom side slightly broader in an aerodynamic 'lifting body' fuselage design. They had no conventional wings or control surfaces such as tail feathers or fins. When the missiles' flight control system were tested after assembly, the missiles' skin actually seemed to undulate and ripple, like the scales of a swimming fish. The missiles' engine inlets and exhausts were narrow slits both atop and at the weapon's tail. Tiny sensor arrays covered the outside, looking in all directions. Each missile weighed about three thousand five hundred pounds. They were slid inside a pressure-sealed chamber over the curious cargo doors on the bottom of the aircraft fuselage.

By the time the missiles were in place, the DC-10 was over northern Belarus, fifty miles west of the city of Vitebsk. The technicians still inside the aft part of the cargo compartment donned helmets, parkas, gloves, and oxygen masks, and signaled on intercom that they were ready for the next step. The mission commander nodded, took a sip of Pepsi from a large squeeze bottle, keyed a microphone button, waited for the secure satellite transceiver link to lock in, then: 'Hey, Archangel, this is Mad Dog.'

'Go ahead, Mad Dog.'

'We're all ready to go. Say the word.'

'Do it.'

'Got it. Buzz me if you change your mind.'

'Very well. Good luck.'

'Don't need it, but thanks. Later.' He turned to the aircraft intercom: 'Okay, guys, countdown is under way, T minus two minutes and counting,' Doctor Jon Masters reported. 'Final prelaunch checks complete, running pregyro spin-up checks, awaiting RLG alignment in forty-two seconds. Stand by for launch chamber depressurization.'

Jon Masters was happiest in his lab or on a computer design system, but he enjoyed actually going out and firing a few of his babies off every now and then. In his early thirties, with boyish good looks bordering on impish, Jon Masters was the Bill Gates of the military hardware and weapon contractors. He had earned his Ph.D about the same time most kids were learning to drive a car, and he had helped NASA build a worldwide tracking and data system and had been made chairman of a small high-tech weapons firm in California by the time most young men were getting their first real job. A few years later, he was firmly in control of his company and known the world over as an innovative inventor and designer. Sky Masters Inc. developed hundreds of different strategic and tactical military systems – everything from miniature satellite reconnaissance and communications systems, to high-tech aircraft, sensors, and air-launched weapons.

His most lucrative contracts had always been the top-secret stuff – satellites launched specifically for a classified mission, stealth warplanes, and Buck Rogers-like high-tech weapons. His company actually manufactured few of his designs – he found it much more profitable to license the designs to other high-tech firms. But this project was different. He'd personally supervised every aspect of this mission. This was the ultimate request, and the ultimate challenge – he wasn't going to let anyone down. Jon Masters had a long enough string of successes working for classified top-secret projects that he could afford to be cocky, but he knew that if it could go wrong, it might go wrong, and he could never be positively sure until the mission was over.

The countdown went smoothly and swiftly. It took less than thirty seconds to spin up and align the RLG, or ring laser gyro, which provided super-accurate attitude and heading information to both missiles' autopilots and navigation computers. Once the RLG was aligned, the chamber in which the missiles sat was depressurized, and the final data download began. Launch aircraft position, airspeed, altitude, and heading, along with target coordinates and last-second enemy antiaircraft intelligence information, was dumped to the missiles' onboard computers, checked, then rechecked by computer in a matter of seconds. One more self-test was accomplished, the launch aircraft began a shallow climb, the cargo doors on the bottom of the fuselage were opened, and both missiles were ejected one by one into the slipstream.

The missiles were only in the air for a few minutes when an alert sounded. 'Grant Two reporting a flight-control malfunction,' one of the technicians reported. 'Looks like the entire left-side adaptive wing actuators are out.'

'Did you try a recall order?'

'It responded in the affirmative, then started reporting off-track,' the tech replied. 'It's trying to make its way back to us, but it can't steer.'

'Cripes,' Masters exclaimed under his breath. 'And that was the best one in the fleet. Did we get a data dump yet?'

'Yes, sir. Grant Two sent a complete data dump as soon as the malfunction occurred, and I requested and received another one. Blytheville acknowledged the fault and data dump, too.' The missiles always collected engine, systems, environmental, attitude, and computer data for the last thirty minutes of flight, like a flight data recorder did on an airliner, and it uploaded that information via satellite back to the launch aircraft and to Sky Masters Inc.'s headquarters in Blytheville, Arkansas. The upload came regularly throughout the flight, just before reaching their target, and whenever there was a glitch.

Jon Masters reached over to a red switch cover, opened it, inserted a key into a lock, turned it, and then pressed a button. Ten miles away, the second missile exploded. 'Eighteen million down the tubes,' he muttered. There was no such thing as insurance for an experimental missile – especially one being used illegally. 'How's Grant One?'

'Straight and true, on course, all systems in the green.'

Jon nodded. Well, he thought ruefully, that's why we launch two at a time, even with the best systems – and he had the best systems around. Just ask him.

Grant One (Jon Masters always named his devices after US presidents) continued its flight, descending smoothly from thirty-nine thousand feet under battery power only, heading east. Several minutes after launch, with its battery power halfway depleted, it automatically started its turbojet engine, but kept the power-off glide going until reaching five thousand feet above the western Russian lowlands. The engine throttled up as it began to level off, then reported one last status check to its mothership. Jon responded with a final 'go-ahead' order.

The missile accelerated to four hundred and eighty knots airspeed and descended to one thousand feet above ground level as it cruised north of Moscow, skirting the long-range air defense and air traffic control radars ringing the city. Every twelve seconds, it updated its inertial guidance system with a fix from the Global Positioning

System navigational satellites, but after only a forty-five-minute low-level flight, its navigational error was less than sixteen feet.

Twenty-five miles northeast of Moscow, it turned south, descended to five hundred feet above the earth, and accelerated to five hundred and forty nautical miles per hour as it approached the air defenses ringing Zhukovsky Flight Test Center near Bykovo. It had already been programmed with a course that would take it around major known cultural features such as tall transmission towers or buildings, but the missile also used a comb-size millimeter-wave radar to alert it of any unknown obstacles in its path. The radar was sensitive enough to detect the high lead and sulfur content of the smoke coming out of some factory chimneys in its path and easily circumnavigated them as if they were obstructions.

The missile turned on its imaging infrared sensors seventy seconds prior to target, then uplinked the images via satellite to Jon Masters aboard the DC-10 launch aircraft. The image showed the base in fine detail, with reds, pinks, purples, and oranges forming enough contrast to see buildings. A white box surrounded the computer's best guess as the intended target. From ten miles away, it was hard to tell if the box was on the right building, but in less than a minute, he'd find out.

It was off, but not by too much. The navigation system had drifted off a few dozen yards, and the white box was centered on an adjacent hangar. Jon entered commands into the computer, froze the image in computer memory, then used a trackball

411

and rolled a crosshair cursor over the proper target impact point – a spot three-quarters of the way across the roofline – and commanded the missile to hit that exact spot. He then made sure the terminal maneuver was programmed as a PUP – Pull Up, Push Over, in which a few seconds before impact the missile would climb a few hundred feet and then plunge itself down onto the target point. Several air defense radars in the area had detected the missile – rather, they had detected *something* out there – but the missile's stealth characteristics made it impossible to get a solid lock on it.

The last few seconds of the missile's three hundred mile flight were the most spectacular. Eight seconds before impact, Grant Two made its steep climb. The imaging infrared picture stayed locked on target. Then, just before the missile reached a thousand feet above ground, it did an even steeper dive. Jon caught a glimpse of the roof of the Metyor Aerospace building for just a few seconds before the missile hit.

The radar in the missile's nose gave the exact distance to impact, and at the proper moment, the computer ignited a small armored rocket device in the missile's nose that shot a five-hundred-and-fifty-pound high-explosive shaped-charge warhead through the thick concrete and steel-sheathed roof, allowing most of the rest of the missile to pass through. Once inside, the main charge detonated: a two-thousand-pound high-explosive incendiary warhead, which created a massive three-thousand-degree fireball inside the secure section of the Metyor IIG research hangar. The force of the blast, combined with exploding fuel and natural gas lines, added enough energy to the blast to rip the entire hangar open like a popped balloon. Everything inside the hangar and within five hundred yards of the blast was instantly roasted to ash.

Jon Masters whooped and cheered like a kid at a rodeo when his screen went blank – he knew his missile had scored a direct hit. 'Hey, Archangel,' he said to nobody, still reveling in his long-distance victory, 'come take a look at this mess. Man, what a day.' He clicked on his intercom. 'Good kill, guys,' he announced. 'Grant Two bit the dust, but Grant One made us proud. Come on up and take a look at the video if you'd like, then let's put our little models back together – we've got three hours to make this plane look like just another trash-hauler carrying oil-drilling parts again before we land.'

Radohir, Bulgaria
later that morning

'*Halt!* Stop! *Astanavleevat'sya!*' yelled the Bulgarian military officer in as many foreign languages as he could think of, running at top speed toward the engineer's trailer, the AK-74 assault rifle held high over his head. 'Stop, in the name of the law!'

Pavel Gregorievich Kazakov, wearing a long black leather coat – which discreetly covered a Kevlar bulletproof vest underneath – and black fur cap, looked up from the rolls of blueprints and engineering specs, saw the angry officer running toward them waving the rifle, and rolled his eyes

413

in exasperation. He was standing with a group of aides and engineers on the back porch of the mobile engineer's headquarters trailer, which had been transported to southwestern Bulgaria, just thirty-five miles west of the Bulgarian capital of Sofia and less than fifty miles from the Macedonian border. 'Now what?' he shouted angrily.

'He's got a gun, sir,' one of the engineers said nervously.

'What is with these Interior Ministry assholes?' Kazakov muttered. He nodded to one of his bodyguards standing a few feet away. 'Doesn't he realize how dangerous it is to be carrying a weapon like that? Someone could get hurt. Or he could be mistaken for a terrorist and shot by mistake.'

The bodyguard smiled, pulled out a German MP5K submachine gun with an eight-inch Sionics suppressor fitted, and leveled it at the approaching officer, keeping it low and out of sight. '*Gatoviy, rookavadetel,*' he said in a low voice as he clicked the selector switch from the S setting to the three-shot setting. The eyes of some of the engineers and assistants standing nearby widened in fear– Is he really going to shoot that soldier? they thought. He looked agitated, and he was carrying a gun, but he certainly wasn't threatening.

Kazakov thought about giving the order, then shook his head. '*Nyet. Zhdat,*' he said, with an exasperated voice. His bodyguard took his finger off the trigger but kept the muzzle leveled at the officer. As long as the Bulgarian officer had the rifle in his hand he was a potential threat, so the bodyguard did not lower his own weapon, but kept careful watch as the officer approached the group. 'He has made so much noise, half of Bulgaria has already heard him. Plenty of time to take care of him later, if the need arises.' The officer shouted several angry words in Bulgarian at the group, jabbing toward the mountains and the nearby dam with the rifle. 'Don't these Interior Ministry officers speak Russian anymore? What in hell is he saying?'

'He is Captain Todor Metodiev. He is not from the Interior Ministry, but from the Labor Corps of the Bulgarian Army, sir,' a translator said.

'The Labor Corps? What's that?'

'A sort of engineer branch of the army, but also used in civil work projects,' one of his aides replied.

'Another damned bureaucrat with a uniform and a gun,' Kazakov said disgustedly. 'What does he want ... as if I don't already know?'

'He wants us to stop work immediately, dismantle all of the equipment, remove all construction materials from the mountainside, and move our operation back to Sofia,' the translator said. 'He says we do not have the proper documentation for this operation.'

'Remove everything from the mountain!' Kazakov exclaimed. 'We have *over three thousand kilos of dynamite* and at least a kilometer of Primacord up there! Can't he see I have loaders, tractors, earthmovers, and dump trucks lined up five kilometers down the road – the road *I* had to build, to comply with yet more Bulgarian laws – ready to move earth? Is he crazy? We have all the proper documentation already! We are *drowning* in documentation!'

Metodiev kept on talking all through Kazakov's retort and the translation. 'He says we do not have a required permit from the Labor Corps. They are in charge of the reconstruction project on the dam. He says the demolition can create serious damage to the dam and the river itself if there are mudslides or shifting earth. In the interest of safety, he demands we remove all materials from the mountain immediately or he will send in Labor Corps troops to do it for us and then bill us for the labor.'

'Bill us, eh?' Kazakov sneered. 'Wonder how much his bill is to leave us alone right now?'

This was a common occurrence throughout the business world, but especially so here in Bulgaria – the official shakedown. Graft and corruption were commonplace in business all over the world, but Bulgarians seemed to be the master at it; every two-bit bureaucrat, military, or paramilitary officer had stopped by his many constructions sites in the past few months, carrying yet another official-looking edict or notice, then unabashedly putting his hand out – some of them *actually doing just that*, putting their hand out – expecting payola right on the spot.

To Pavel Kazakov, payola was a normal, routine part of doing business – he even included it in his budgets. Generally, the closer he was to Russia, the less developed the region, or the more Russian the influences in the region, the lower the payola. Ten to twenty percent was a good figure to use in Russia, the Transcaucasus, most of South and Central America, the Middle East, and Africa; twenty to thirty percent in eastern and southern Europe, the Indian subcontinent, and Asia; forty percent in western Europe; and forty to fifty percent in North America. That was one reason he didn't do much business in the West – payoff expenses were always high, and the local Mafia organizations were generally better organized, better protected, and deadlier if crossed. His reputation was also better – meaning, more feared – in eastern Europe and western Asia.

But there was a protocol to follow, too. In most of the rest of the world, payments were made only to the head of the labor union, or to the city or county engineer, police chief, inspectors, compliance officers, tax assessors, or the local army barracks commander. In Bulgaria, everyone had their hand out. The main guy was supposed to keep only a cut of the payoff, maybe twenty or thirty percent, and use the rest to grease the palms of his chief subordinates, immediate bosses, and anyone with whom he wanted to curry favor. Payola was meant to be shared – that's how the institutions of graft and corruption survived and flourished. Many times, the bosses neglected to do that, thinking that because they were the boss, they were too powerful for anyone to retaliate against.

Pavel was all too happy to give payoffs in order to get a project done, as long as everyone else understood and played by the rules. He also enjoyed giving lessons on proper payola management.

'Tell him to leave the paperwork for us, and we will complete it and turn it in to his superior officer,' Kazakov said, mentally dismissing the officer.

'He says he has been ordered to collect the

paperwork now, or he will order his men onto the mountain to arrest us and dismantle and confiscate all of our equipment.'

Kazakov closed his eyes against a growing headache. 'For the love of God...' He paused for several long moments, his eyes closed tightly, resting against the chart table; then: 'How many men does he have with him?'

'About fifty, sir. All heavily armed.'

Too many for his security staff, Kazakov thought – next time, he vowed to bring more men. He sighed, then said, 'Very well. Have him and his men report to the senior site foreman at Trailer Seventeen. I will radio ahead and authorize Mr Lechenov to give Captain Metodiev his "paperwork." Get out of here.'

As the Bulgarian army officer departed, Kazakov's aide stepped up to him and asked quietly, 'Trailer Seventeen is–'

'I know.' He watched as the Bulgarian officer gathered his men together and started marching them up the dirt access road into the forest. About a dozen Bulgarian soldiers armed with automatic weapons stayed behind – it appeared that they were guarding the trailer until their commander returned. 'Peasants,' Kazakov spat. 'Let's get back to work.' But their work was interrupted by a satellite phone call. Kazakov picked it up himself – only a handful of persons had access to the number. '*Shto?*'

'They know,' a voice said. 'The Americans, the president, everyone knows.'

'Stop talking in riddles,' Kazakov said. He recognized the person talking as Colonel-General

Valeriy Zhurbenko, the chief of staff of the Russian Federation's armed forces and Kazakov's unofficial liaison to the Kremlin. He motioned for his aides to dismiss the engineers from the trailer. Once they were hustled out, Kazakov said, 'This is a secure line, General. Speak so I can understand you.'

'Metyor was bugged,' Zhurbenko said. 'The Americans rescued a spy last night that was taping conversations inside the facility.'

Kazakov got to his feet, stunned. 'How do you know this?'

'Because the American president *said so* to Sen'kov,' Zhurbenko replied incredulously. 'The American president admitted to him that they were operating a spy at Metyor, admitted sending in an exfiltration team, and – you will not believe it – sending in a stealth aircraft, *a stealth supersonic bomber*, to cover the operation!'

'What?' Kazakov exploded. 'The Americans flew a stealth bomber over Russia? *Last night?*'

'Not just one – *two* stealth bombers!' Zhurbenko said. 'One aircraft was shot down near the Ukraine border. The Americans apparently flew a second one through Russia to protect the forces that went in to rescue the first bomber's crew members. And the American president mentioned to Sen'kov that they had heard information on the bugs that an aircraft from Metyor was involved in the attack at Kukes.'

'Unbelievable,' Kazakov said. 'Well, this means our operation may need to be stepped up a bit more.'

'Stepped up? You mean canceled, don't you?'

'Canceled? There is no way in hell I'm going to cancel this operation now!' Kazakov retorted. 'I've already laid one hundred and sixty-three miles of support and utility structures through some of the shittiest countryside in all of the Balkans. I'll be ready to start laying pipe in another two months in Bulgaria, and I can start in Macedonia soon as well. I've got foundries in seven countries ready to ship five hundred and fifty *miles* of pipe starting next month and extending over the next seven to nine months! I'm right on schedule, Colonel-General. There is no way I can survive if the schedule is delayed even one month, let alone canceled! I've written a quarter of a billion dollars in checks already, and I haven't laid one centimeter of pipe or shipped one liter of crude yet! I cannot afford to waste one dollar or one hour.'

'We are not just under suspicion or surveillance, Kazakov – we are under attack!' Zhurbenko said. 'Do you understand? The Americans flew into Russia and were virtually unopposed! We cannot stop them.'

'Stop them? From doing what?' Kazakov asked. 'They sloppily executed a routine rescue mission. They lost a stealth warplane – that cost them dearly, believe me. Nothing that was done affects our plans. The only thing I'm waiting for, Colonel-General, is a commitment from the Russian Army to move when it must.'

'It takes time to move the numbers necessary,' Zhurbenko said. 'Colonel-General Toporov said he has mobilized the first three brigades and can insert the first airborne battalion at any time–'

'One battalion? That's not enough. That's not *nearly* enough!' Kazakov said. 'When the time comes, I need an entire airborne brigade off the ground and on its way. When the invitation comes to allow Russian troops into place, I don't want a lousy battalion – I want at least a brigade of men on the ground, followed quickly by armor and air defenses, and set up within three days. Anything else would be a waste of our time.'

'That is impossible.'

'You have no idea about the opportunity that has presented itself here, Colonel-General,' Kazakov snapped. 'The American fiasco has only bolstered our plan. Why hasn't news of this been broadcast around the world? Why haven't we exposed the Americans' hostile mission?'

'President Sen'kov thought that if the American president went on international television and told the world why he launched the operation,' Zhurbenko explained, 'that it would embarrass Moscow even more than Washington.'

'And well it should,' Kazakov said. 'But the American president didn't go on television, did he? He made a deal with Sen'kov to help him, to keep him from losing face. That was his fatal mistake. Roust all of your contacts in the media and give them all the details of the operation. Everything. When it is exposed and the American president tries to deny what happened, world support of the United States will crumble.

'And then,' Kazakov went on happily, motioning to his chief engineer and his assistant, 'when the stealth warplane strikes again in another part of eastern Europe, the world condemnation of the United States will continue to strengthen. Get on it right now, Zhurbenko. And tell that idiot Toporov to get off his fat ass and kick his senior officers into mobilizing those occupying forces, or he will suddenly find himself taking a little nap – on the bottom of the Caspian Sea.'

Kazakov terminated the call to Zhurbenko with an angry push of a button. Damn cowards, he thought. The country is collapsing all around them, and all they can think of is playing it safe. Are the Americans playing it safe? Just when they thought the new president, Thorn, was going to be a baby in a carriage, he orders two stealth bombers to overfly Russia. Very gutsy move.

He dialed his secure phone once again, calling his airfield in Romania. 'Doctor, I want the cover taken off our roadster. Get it ready to cruise.' There was a noticeable pause, and Kazakov thought he detected a sharp intake of breath. 'Pyotr, is something wrong?'

'The ... er, the boys already had the roadster out, sir.'

Kazakov nearly dropped the phone in surprise. *'Shto?'* he asked breathlessly. *'Nu ni mudi*, Doctor.'

'No, I'm not kidding,' Fursenko said. 'Some damage from the last ... er, drive was repaired. They planned a local test drive to check the repairs–'

'You can talk plainly, Doctor. I cannot. Tell me what in hell happened.'

'Stoica and Yegorov heard about an air defense emergency on the Russia-Ukraine border. They launched and secretly followed the Russian air defense radar controllers' vectors. They said they were checking the stealth characteristics while carrying weapon pylons. That's what they told me...'

'What happened, Doctor?'

'They got into a dogfight,' Fursenko said. 'A dogfight with what they think was an American stealth bomber – a stealth bomber that *fired two missiles at them.*'

'*What?* You're kidding! You are *fucking* kidding!' No reply, just labored, excited breathing. 'Are, they all right? Did they make it back?'

'They are fine. The plane is fine. They came out of it well. They hit it. They said they hit it. It got away, but they were victorious!'

'How dare they ... how ... why in hell did they...?' The engineers and aides in the trailer couldn't help but stare at Kazakov now – their boss was bug-eyed and his voice had risen two octaves with excitement. 'I will be back there as quickly as I can. I want to see our two boys when I get there. If they move, if they are even in the damned bathroom when I get back, they are dead. Was there any damage to the roadster?'

'Minor damage, but from a previous flight,' Fursenko explained. 'We need to make some design changes to the missile launch tubes in the wings – the wings are being damaged by missile exhaust. Some more titanium for strengthening, perhaps some more powerful gas generators...'

'Fine. Get what you need at "home" and see to it immediately.'

'"Home?"' Fursenko paused again, confusion and panic in his voice. 'You mean, Metyor? Back at Zhukovsky?'

'Of course that's what I...' Kazakov stopped, his throat turning dry once again. 'What is it *now*, Doctor?'

'You haven't heard about Zhukovsky?'

'I am in the middle of nowhere in fucking Bulgaria, Doctor. Spit it out.'

'My – I mean, our – I mean, *your* facility was destroyed last night,' Fursenko said in a voice so shaky he could hardly make himself understood.

'*What?*'

'The military says it was a natural gas leak,' Fursenko explained. 'The natural gas explosion apparently mixed with some jet fuel or other petroleum products and incinerated the entire building. Nothing is left. *Nothing.* Nothing within seven hundred *meters* of the building is left.'

'Natural ... gas ... explosion ... *ni pizdi!*' Kazakov shouted. 'Don't bullshit me! There has to be an explanation, a *real* explanation!'

'Sir, six men were killed inside the facility. Dmitri Rochardov, Andrei–'

'I don't give a shit about a couple janitors and night watchmen!' Kazakov shouted. 'I want you back there immediately. Find the best forensics experts you can. I want that blast site sealed off and covered, I want every living being that sets foot inside that facility screened and approved by me personally, and I want every piece of debris and ash examined with a microscope. Natural gas explosion, my ass – that was the work of a saboteur, or a military strike. I want to know what kind of explosion it was, and I want to see evidence – no speculation, no guesses, no hypothesis. I don't care if the investigators are out there until winter –

I want to know exactly what happened, and I want to know *immediately!*' And he disconnected the call with an angry stab.

For a brief instant, he felt things were beginning to spin out of control. He had these feelings often, and his instincts always served him well – he knew when to get in, when to push, when to back off, and when to get the hell out. The voice told him to get the hell out. The American air force and military spy agencies had stumbled across his operation. It was simply too incredible to believe the absolute bad luck. The voice said, *'Get out. Run. Run before it's too late.'*

Pavel looked around himself. The problem was, he was moving too fast to just stop abruptly. He had already spent a quarter of a billion dollars to get the project started. He was going to pony up another quarter of a billion out of his own personal fortune. Investors and lenders in two dozen countries around the world were lining up ready to help him raise another one and three quarter billion dollars to build the entire line. Word travels fast.

Problem was, he was going to pay another quarter of a billion dollars in loan interest, bribes, and dividends to all these investors in the next year or so before any oil revenues started to come in. He was deep into it. Some of these investors were the world's biggest arms dealers, drug dealers, industrialists, generalissimos, and government finance ministers. They had been promised a hefty return on their investment, and they would not be happy at all to hear that the project was off, even if they got their principal back.

But the more recent development, his ace in the hole – this encounter with the American aircraft. The Americans had at first torn up the Russian air defenses as if they never existed. But then his stealth fighter happened on it, and was victorious. Stoica and Yegorov were typical fighter pilots, cocky and arrogant – everything was a victory for them – but Fursenko would never lie to him. If he said his boys were victorious, they were.

That meant the Metyor-179 had gone up against the West's most fearsome weapons – first the NATO AWACS radar plane, and now an American stealth bomber with air-to-air weapons – and had prevailed. It was undefeated in battle. It had flown right into the midst of NATO, American, and Russian air defense weapon systems, and was untouched.

That was the reason why he decided to continue. For the first time in his life, he ignored the little voice in his head. It was still telling him to get out, cut your losses and run, but he tuned it out. The Tyenee stealth fighter-bomber was the key. That was his ticket to victory. He had to keep the business side tight, and hope Stoica and Yegorov could handle NATO and the incompetent Americans.

Keep it tight. Deal with the business end like always.

'Sir?' one of Kazakov's aides interrupted hesitantly. 'Those Bulgarian soldiers are waiting at Trailer Seventeen. They are complaining there's no foreman there.'

Kazakov shook his head. Damned cowards. Sometimes it took a little courage to get something done.

He walked over to a metal case sitting on the desk, unlocked it, and opened the lid. Inside was a series of switches and a large red guarded switch. He flicked three of the switches, then turned a key, which illuminated red lights on the panel.

'Uh ... sir? You've armed the explosives panel.'

'I know that.'

'Those Bulgarian soldiers. They are up there. They–'

'Shut up,' Kazakov spat. He opened the red safety switch guard and pressed a button. It suddenly seemed as if the ground was a carpet being shaken from two kilometers away – the earth rolled and shook like an earthquake, with its epicenter right under their feet.

High up on the mountains above them, thousands of acres of forests suddenly disappeared in a cloud of flying dirt and debris. Nine square kilometers of the mountain was instantly leveled in a huge notch cut out of the mountains, as if a huge ice cream scoop had swooped in and taken a huge chunk out of the earth in one quick motion.

Kazakov nodded to his bodyguard, then pointed out the window at the dozen Bulgarian soldiers who had stayed behind to watch over Kazakov. The bodyguard smiled, then walked out of the trailer. The soldiers were looking up at the tremendous explosion that had engulfed their comrades, frozen in shock and fear, wondering what to do. The bodyguard simply lined up behind them, set his MP5 submachine gun to full auto, and mowed them down. He waved, and a huge front-loader moved in, scooped up the bodies, then trundled down the access road to carry them up the mountain and dump them within the carnage.

Kazakov gave his aide a warning glance as he calmly shut off the arming panel and closed and locked the lid. 'Clumsy Bulgarians,' he said, as his other engineers and technicians rushed into the trailer. 'Those idiots must have set off some of the charges and brought half the mountain down upon themselves. How unfortunate.' The engineers stared openmouthed at their superior and wisely kept silent. A moment later, as Kazakov was about to leave, his walkie-talkie beeped. 'What is it now?'

'This is Milos up on the north ridge,' one of the project engineers radioed. 'There's a problem. That explosion appears to have caused a large fracture in the dam. It might give way completely. I sent a man down to the village below the dam and to Sofia to warn them.'

'Fine, fine,' Kazakov said. 'Another example of fine Bulgarian workmanship.' He threw the walkie-talkie on the desk in the engineer's office and headed out to board his private helicopter. How about that? he thought – maybe that Bulgarian Labor Corps officer *did* know what he was talking about after all.

High-Technology Aerospace Weapons Center, Elliott AFB, Nevada two days later

The C-141 Starlifter transport plane arrived from

428

Ankara, Turkey, shortly after sunset. Like most inbound flights, it was told to taxi directly inside a hangar to unload its cargo and passengers under cover. But there was a very different reason for this plane to do so – it would have seemed strange for spy satellites to take pictures of a welcome-home party.

Every assigned person and employee of Elliott Air Force Base, almost two thousand in all, were on hand, and they gave Captain Annie Dewey, Major Duane Deverill, Lieutenant-Colonel Hal Briggs, and Master Sergeant Chris Wohl a thunderous round of applause and cheers as they emerged from the crew door of the Starlifter. First to greet them was Lieutenant-General Terrill Samson, along with Brigadier-General Patrick McLanahan and Colonel Rebecca Furness. Furness and McLanahan had arrived the night before to a more muted but equally happy reception by the base personnel.

The jubilant crowd surged forward, all wanting to reach out, touch, and congratulate the victorious airmen who had successfully completed their first assigned covert combat mission. Even though they had lost a plane and the Intelligence Support Agency team had lost two men, the agent they'd been sent in to get had been recovered safely, and most important, their fellow Dreamlanders were all safe. That was cause for celebration.

'Welcome back, everyone, welcome back,' General Samson said. 'Thank God you're all right.' He shook hands with each one of them, then turned to the crowd and raised his hands to silence them. 'Folks, listen up,' he said. 'Before we

429

congratulate these men and women from Aces High and from Dreamland on a job well done, let's first bow our heads and ask the Lord to welcome the two ISA commandos into his home. We thank them for their supreme sacrifice.'

After a short pause with bowed heads, during which the hangar was as silent as a church, Samson said to the newcomers, 'I'm sorry to have to do this, but you're going to have to do your celebrating as you make your way to another intelligence, operational, and maintenance debrief.'

'Can't we even take a couple hours to relax, maybe take a shower, sir?' Annie Dewey asked. She kept on scanning the crowd, looking for someone. 'I don't think anyone could stand to be in the same room with me for more than sixty seconds.'

'I know you've already had nonstop debriefs in two continents already,' Rebecca said. 'But we need to get the information down so we can formulate even more questions to ask you in the future. You guys know the drill. Every flight is a research test flight. Welcome back. Good work.'

'You may spend the rest of your careers debriefing,' Patrick said, as he shook hands with every one of them. 'We'll have food and drinks for you inside, and I promise we'll make it as brief as any military debriefing can be.'

Annie Dewey wasn't satisfied with just a handshake – when she got to Patrick and Rebecca, she gave each one of them an unabashed kiss on the lips. 'You guys saved our butts,' she said. 'I'll never be able to thank you enough.'

'Thank Hal and Chris – they're the ones who really deserve it.'

'Keep those two away from us, sir,' Master Sergeant Wohl said in his typical gruff voice. 'I can't be in the same building with them anymore without one of them thanking me, touching me, admiring me, or offering to do something for me. It's making me ill.' He endured another kiss from Annie to punctuate his complaint.

'Spoken like a true American hero, Sarge,' Briggs quipped.

Annie scanned the crowd again. 'Where's David?' she asked in a low voice.

'Getting ready for the operational debrief, I imagine,' Patrick said. 'You'll see him inside.'

'C'mon, pilot, let's *go*,' Duane Deverill said, clasping Annie by the waist and arm from behind as if leading her in a tango through the crowded hangar. 'Let's get the bleep-bleep debriefs over with so we can celebrate keeping our asses for a few days longer!' Annie could do nothing else but let Deverill carry her along through the throng of well-wishers.

The debriefings went smoothly and quickly. Annie and Dev knew the real work was ahead of them, so they tried to relax, be as helpful as possible, and as clear and concise as their patience and level of weariness would possibly allow. Each aircraft continuously burst-transmitted encoded data via satellite back to Dreamland during every sortie, so there was no lack of hard information; but the aircrews' testimony was necessary to match the raw numbers with the operator's input and perspective. It would be even more valuable when it came time to begin designing new and better systems to avoid any deficiencies encoun-

431

tered during the mission. As long as humans flew war machines, they would always need as much, perhaps more, data from the humans as they did from the machines themselves.

After many hours of wave after wave of engineers coming into the conference room to ask questions, Annie realized that it was over – and that David Luger had never shown up. She collected her notes and checklists and took a last sip of water, crestfallen.

'What's up, AC?' Dev asked. He was still as pumped up and animated as he had been when he got off the C-141 – he had the strength and stamina of a cheetah. 'You look down. Tired?'

'A little,' she said evasively.

'What can I do to cheer you up?' Dev asked. He began to gently massage her, starting from behind her ears and moving down her neck to her shoulders. 'I must warn you, my hands are licensed.'

'Yeah, right.'

'It's true – I'm a licensed doctor of chiropractic and a licensed massage therapist,' Dev said. 'You think there's any money in being an Air National Guard B-1 radar navigator? I work singles' resorts six months out of the year, make ten times what I do in the Guard, and I get to put my hands on beautiful women all day long. It's a great racket.'

Annie felt her body tense up when Dev first touched her, but after only a few seconds, it was obvious that he did indeed have very skilled hands. He seemed to know precisely where to rub hard and where and when to do it softly. In moments, her body was relaxing in the grasp of Deverill's warm, powerful hands. 'That feels so good, Dev.'

'Thank you,' he said softly. He continued to caress her, now expertly working the myriad of knots out of her spine and back muscles. The tension was rinsing away under his fingers like a torch to ice. 'I know I've said it already, but I want to say it again: thank you for digging me out of the snow and rescuing me.'

'You would've done the same for me – only better, I hope,' Annie said. 'Thank you for supporting my decisions, as half-assed as they were. I know you didn't agree with all of them, but you backed me up anyway. It meant a lot.'

'You're the aircraft commander – it's my responsibility to back you up and offer my opinion, and your responsibility to make the decisions,' Dev said. 'You did everything you were supposed to do, and more. You saved my life and the lives of many others. You should be proud of yourself. I am very proud of you.' She felt his lips on the back of her neck, and the touch sent high-voltage electric currents throughout her body.

'Did you know,' he said, suddenly breaking the mood change between them, 'that the muscles of the body build up huge quantities of lactic acid during periods of stress and fatigue – a by-product of anaerobic respiration, where the muscles burn glucose in the absence of oxygen? Lactic acid causes fatigue and can even cause cramps and muscle deterioration. The acids will eventually work their way out over time, but a properly done massage helps the lactic acid move out quicker.'

'Is that why it feels sooo damn good?' Annie cooed.

'Exactly.'

'Mmm. Well, it does,' she said. She let him continue his work. Normally she was extraordinarily ticklish, but he was even able to massage her sides and ribs without her reacting at all. His hands moved down to the base of her spine, almost to her buttocks, but there was no way she was going to let him stop. 'So tell me, Dev – why did you feel the need to tell me the technical reasons for a massage? Do you think I'll respond better if it's done in a more scientific atmosphere? Once a test pilot, always a test pilot?'

'It's working, isn't it?' he responded. When he felt her body stiffen in protest, he added quickly, 'No, no, that's not why. Only kidding.' She gave him a humorous sneer, but relaxed and let him continue. 'Maybe I told you the technical theory behind massages to distract you from the fact that I'm touching you – and loving every last second of it.'

Annie turned away from him, ending the massage therapy, and gave him a weak smile. 'Thanks, partner,' she said. 'I appreciate the massage – and the thought.'

'I hear a "but" coming,' he said. He took her hands in his and looked deeply into her eyes. 'Annie, wait a minute. I gotta get this out before I explode.'

'Dev, now's not the time–'

'Yes, it is. I'm crazy about you. I have been for a long time, ever since you joined the unit. We've gone out a few times, but you've always treated it as either a casual meeting with a superior officer talking business, or palling around with your older brother. Beyond that, you've been too busy to notice me. You're acting like our one-and-only night together was wrong, that I should be ashamed of what we did.

'I'm putting you on notice, Annie, that I'm not going to do that anymore. One thing I learned from this ordeal that I didn't tell the debriefers tonight is that life is too short. If you want something, you'd better go for it now, because tomorrow you might find yourself facedown in snow unconscious after ejecting from a supersonic bomber over hostile territory.' Annie laughed in spite of herself – if it hadn't actually happened to them, she would really think it was funny.

'Dev–'

'It's Colonel Luger, isn't it?' Deverill asked. Annie looked into his eyes and nodded. 'Pardon me, Annie, but that guy is a little weird, don't you think? I mean, I've known workaholics before in my time, but he's got them all beat. It's like he's possessed or something.' He could tell she was rejecting his observations – but he could also tell that she knew his observations were correct. 'Where is he tonight, Annie? If he's your man, why isn't he here with you? Everyone else turned out for our arrival – where was Luger?' She couldn't answer him, because she didn't know, and didn't understand.

'I'm not going to bad-mouth the guy, and I'm not going to say anything else, except this: I want you, Annie,' Deverill said. 'I think we have something together. I want to find out. I think you do, too. And if Colonel Luger wants you, he has a funny way of showing it. You deserve a lot more

435

than that. I can give it to you. Can he?' He gave her a kiss on the forehead, a soft, lingering kiss, as warm as his hands. 'I'm not going to make you decide now, Annie,' he added sincerely. 'But I also have to remind you: I get what I want. I think you want something more too.' He then departed, leaving her a smile and a light touch on her cheek. 'I'll call you.'

Annie stood by herself for several long moments without moving, trying but failing to sort out all of the conflicting emotions racing through her head and her heart. There was a decision to be made, questions to be answered. She apparently wasn't going to get any answers tonight, because the man she loved wasn't with her to offer them. Annie considered using the subcutaneous transceiver to call him, and then decided against it. She picked up her helmet bag and headed for the dormitories and some well-deserved and much-needed rest.

A pair of sad, tortured eyes from across the hallway watched as they both departed.

In an adjacent debriefing room, Major-General Roman Smoliy, the commander of the aviation forces of the Republic of Ukraine, had finished all of his debriefing notes and was leaving, when he noticed the lights on in the debriefing room across the hallway, across from the one where Dewey and Deverill had debriefed their sortie. He peeked inside and, to his surprise, saw Colonel David Luger sitting by himself. His arms were straight down at their sides, his head was bowed, his feet were flat on the floor.

Smoliy recognized that posture – it was the posture demanded of prisoners when allowed to sit and rest in their seats.

'Colonel Luger?'

David snapped his head upright, then placed his arms on the table, palms flat and facing down. Another prisoner posture, called seated attention. Luger quickly snapped out of it, turning to look to see who it was. When he recognized Smoliy, his eyes grew dark, and he got to his feet, his body language challenging and defensive at the same time. 'What are you doing here, General?'

'I was allowed to conduct a debriefing of Colonel Briggs, Master Sergeant Wohl, Major Weston, and the others involved in the mission who landed at Borispol,' Smoliy replied. 'I will conduct an analysis of Russian air defenses and the effectiveness of your stealth technology on the different weapon and sensor systems.' He nodded quizzically at Luger. 'May I ask what you are doing here?'

'No, you may not.'

'Why were you not at the reception, or why did you not participate in the operational debriefing?' Smoliy asked.

'None of your business.'

Smoliy nodded. 'Very well. I am not your commanding officer – I cannot compel you to answer.'

'Damn straight.'

'It is your choice.' Smoliy looked carefully at Luger, then added, *Zdyes ooyeezhzhayoo seechyas.* You may leave now.'

Luger's eyes did an extraordinary transformation – instantly turning meek and passive, then moments later blazing with white-hot anger, then instantly passive again. It was as if Luger had momentarily gone back to the hellhole in which he had been imprisoned in Lithuania years before, responding robotlike to commands from his brutal, sadistic overseers; then wanting momentarily to fight back; and then almost at the same moment slipping into a passive, protective, detached fog; then angry, almost homicidal. All in the blink of an eye. *'Idi k yobanay matiri,'* he spat.

Luger tried to walk past Smoliy on his way out, but the big Ukrainian general put his hand out to stop him. 'You are no longer a prisoner, Colonel,' he said. 'You are a free man, an American. You are a colonel and an engineer in the United States Air Force.' Luger's eyes blazed into his. 'And I am no longer your enemy. I am no longer your tormentor. I do not deserve for you to make remarks about my mother like that.'

'You will always be the sick motherfucker that took advantage of a helpless, tortured human being at Fisikous,' Luger shot back. 'I'd kill you if I could.'

'I know what you are feeling, Colonel–'

'Like hell you do!'

'I know,' Smoliy said. 'Seeing you again all these years after Fisikous reminded me of the heartless, cruel shit I was back then. I have thought of nothing else since the moment we met, Colonel, *nothing!* Thinking of the way I twisted your life in that place tortures my sleep every night.' He studied Luger for a moment, then added, 'As it has done for you, too, I see. And because of it, you could not bear even to speak with Captain Dewey and Major Deverill, because the thought of *you*

438

interrogating a fellow prisoner of the Russians was abhorrent to you. No matter that it would be in a different time, a different place, and a completely different manner – it would be an interrogation, and that you could never do.'

'Idi v zhopu, Smoliy! Kiss my ass!' Luger cried in both Russian and English, and he pushed the big Ukrainian out of his way and stormed off.

Headquarters, High-Technology Aerospace Weapons Center, Elliott AFB, Nevada the next morning

'Come in, guys,' Lieutenant General Terrill Samson said, as Patrick McLanahan and David Luger appeared at his doorway. It was early the next morning. All three senior officers were in the office earlier than usual; Patrick and David had found the e-mail note on his computer to come see Samson as soon as they got in that morning. The mood was rather somber – Terrill Samson definitely had something on his mind.

Then the two junior officers got the line they had been dreading: 'Shut the door.' It was a closed-door meeting. Oh, shit.

After Patrick did so, he and Luger were motioned to chairs, and Samson took his seat behind his desk. The seat of power, the position of authority, Patrick thought. Samson had other, more casual chairs in the office – he could have sat next to his officers, signaling a friendlier discussion on more equal levels. The signs were not looking good at all.

Patrick did not have to wait long for the hammer to fall, either: 'General McLanahan, Colonel Luger, I want your requests for retirement on my desk by close of business today,' Samson said simply.

'*What?*' Luger exclaimed.

'May I ask why, sir?' Patrick asked immediately.

'Because otherwise I'll be forced to bring you up on charges of insubordination, issuing an illegal order, unauthorized use of government property, unauthorized release of lethal weapons, unauthorized overflight of foreign airspace, and conduct unbecoming an officer. I'll also charge Colonel Furness with the same charges, so you'll take her down with you. Colonel Luger will be charged with disobeying a direct lawful order, insubordination, dereliction of duty, and conduct unbecoming an officer. All offenses, if found guilty, carry a maximum sentence of fifteen years' confinement, forfeit of all pay and benefits, demotion, loss of retirement benefits, and dishonorable discharge. I'd like to avoid all that, so I'm asking for your resignations.'

'Are you notifying us of this action, or are we permitted to discuss this with you first?' Luger asked.

'You got something to say, Colonel, say it. But it won't change my mind. I thought about this ever since that Russian sortie. This is the best option for you, this organization, and me. To spare HAWC from any more adverse attention, I want you two to take it. Billions of dollars and hundreds of important programs are in jeopardy. But go ahead. Speak freely.'

'I gave the orders to turn around and fly that cover sortie, sir,' Patrick said. 'And David's job was to keep me informed and feed me information on the tactical situation. Colonels Luger or Furness don't deserve to be charged with any violations. You can't convict them of anything if they obeyed a lawful order.'

'I specifically ordered Colonel Luger to tell you to make sure you came back on your return routing unless ordered to go somewhere else,' Samson said. 'Luger not only did not relay that order, but he assisted you in providing data for your illegal strike. I won't tolerate that kind of insubordination.

'As for Colonel Furness – it doesn't matter if she obeyed your orders, and you know it,' Samson went on angrily. 'She was the *aircraft commander*. The decision was hers to comply with your orders or not. She could have legally refused and faced her own court-martial – and I predict she would have been found not guilty of any charges. But you gave an unauthorized order, she knew it was unauthorized, and she followed it. She'll face the same charges.'

'But if I resign, she won't face any charges?'

'That's my prerogative,' Samson said. 'I can give her an administrative reprimand. It'll stay in her personnel records for a year. If she keeps her nose clean, her record automatically gets expunged. She can also request retirement, and I'll see she gets it. After all she's done for you, General, she doesn't deserve a dishonorable discharge.'

'Sir, General McLanahan and Colonel Furness

441

were on a fully authorized mission,' Luger pointed out.

'That's right – I was the backup plane on the mission, sir,' Patrick said. 'I already had full authority to proceed.'

'Negative,' Samson said. 'The idea of a backup ship is to pick the best *one* aircraft to fly the mission, not to send *two* aircraft into hostile airspace.'

'I'll argue that it's exactly what I did,' Patrick said. 'Annie and Dev had been shot down. I'll argue that it was my responsibility to continue the mission for which I was briefed–'

'Your mission was to assist Madcap Magician in extracting Siren,' Samson said, his voice showing the irritation of having to argue with his normally respectful, introspective deputy. 'That mission was accomplished by Vampire One, before they were shot down. You weren't authorized to conduct any other operations over Russia.'

'The "other operation over Russia" was to help *save Annie and Dev,*' Patrick said, his voice showing a slightly incredulous edge. 'I was notified of the incident, and I immediately responded to render any assistance necessary.'

'And what about the attack at Zhukovsky? Are you going to tell me that was part of the operation?'

Patrick's face went blank. 'What attack on Zhukovsky?'

'There was a huge explosion at Zhukovsky Flight Test Center right around the time you re-entered Russian airspace,' Samson said. 'One target was singled out – Metyor Aerospace's research-and-development facility. The authorities said it was a natural gas explosion. CIA obtained some information from the Russians investigating the incident. The building was hit with a high-explosive incendiary device, at least a two-thousand-pounder – about what you'd use in an air-launched cruise missile. Even more – the roof was punched in with a shaped-charge penetrator explosion before the main explosion. Sounds like a cruise missile attack to me. Care to tell me about that?'

'I don't know anything about it, sir.'

'I'll inventory the weapons storage area, Patrick,' Samson warned him. 'I'll check every logbook entry, every millimeter of security tape, until I find out the truth.'

'I'm telling you the truth, sir – I have no idea what happened at Zhukovsky,' Patrick said. 'It wasn't me. But I strongly resent your tone. It appears to me you've already decided I did it.'

'General, I don't give a shit if you resent my tone or anything else,' Samson snapped. 'You had the incredible, unmitigated gall to fly a warplane over Russia without authorization and clearance, kill Russian soldiers, and destroy Russian property. You almost got shot down. I could have lost two valuable crew members and another top-secret warplane over Russia. It was bad enough you went over my head and got the National Security Council to buy off on this mission–'

'Sir, I did not get anyone to "buy off" on this mission,' Patrick said. 'Yes, I transmitted my plan directly to SecDef without clearing it through you first, but you know I was going to consult with you on my first opportunity–'

'No, I don't know that – and that's the problem,' Samson interjected. 'I absolutely *do not* believe you would have consulted with me if you thought you could get away with it otherwise. The proof of this was you returning to Russian airspace without clearance. You could have called and made your case at any time. But you flew for an hour in the wrong direction and never called. Neither did Colonel Furness. You didn't call because you thought you might not get the answer you wanted. You didn't pitch the mission to me because you thought I would have refused to allow it.'

'Would you?'

'It doesn't matter now, does it, General?' Samson exploded. 'You went ahead with it anyway. You conducted your own private little war.'

'Why are you doing this, sir?' Patrick asked. He was not pleading – it was a true query, asked honestly and sincerely. 'We brought Dewey and Deverill home safely–'

'No, the *President* brought them home safely,' Samson argued. 'The President was on the phone with Russian president Sen'kov for less than ten minutes and had him agreeing to allow the exfiltration to go ahead without interference. In fact, the President had gotten Sen'kov to agree not to shoot *your* asses down – he not only saved Dewey and Deverill, but he saved yours, Briggs's, and Wohl's butts as well. Pretty extraordinary, since you had already illegally shot down three Russian aircraft by then.'

'So you've already decided we're guilty of court-martialable offenses?' Luger asked. 'You've decided that we're guilty, so you're asking us to resign rather than face charges?'

'It doesn't matter at this point, Colonel – I believe you're guilty of breaking faith with me, the men and women you serve with, the Air Force, and your country,' Samson said. 'I *have* judged you guilty of that. I'm advising you of all this because I thought you both deserve an opportunity to accept retirement and avoid any blemishes on your records. I advise you to take the offer. Even if you win in a court-martial, you'll never work here·again, and I seriously doubt if there's any command in the Air Force that will accept either one of you.'

Patrick got to his feet and took a step toward Samson's desk. 'Permission to speak freely, General?'

'This will be your last opportunity to do so.'

'What are you really afraid of, sir?' Patrick asked. 'What did I do that is forcing you to give me a summary dismissal? Are you afraid I made you look bad in front of the President?'

'You definitely did that, General,' Samson said. 'I was for damned sure the dumb-shit nigger general who can't keep his hotshot troops in line. But you already cemented that thought into Washington's head earlier with your one-man operation over China and with stealing the One-Eleventh's bombers to work for your project here at Dreamland. It's Brad Elliott's wild-card reputation, shifted over to you by default. You're Patrick McLanahan. You're the technical wizard, the lone wolf. Everyone else around you are bit players in your one-man play to keep the world safe for democracy. My career was over the

445

minute I was assigned here with you.

'Most of all, McLanahan, I'm afraid of what you're becoming,' Samson went on. 'I knew Brad Elliott. He was a friend, my teacher, and my mentor. But he changed into something to be feared in my Air Force – the rogue, the loose cannon. His way or no way. I got away from him as soon as I could, and I knew I made the right decision.'

'I was proud to work with him,' McLanahan said.

'I was, too,' said Luger. 'He saved my life. Twice.'

'But you both stayed too long, and you got corrupted by his twisted visions of good and evil, right and wrong, duty and vanity, responsibility and bigotry,' Samson said. 'Sure, Brad got things done. Yes, he was a hero, to me and to a lot of folks. But he did it all *wrong*. He did it *ir*responsibly. He did it illegally. Your hero, Patrick, David, and mine, was wrong. Either you couldn't see it, or you ignored it. Or maybe you liked it. You enjoyed the power and freedom this job gave you. "Absolute power corrupts absolutely," and there's nothing like the power of a two-hundred-and-fifty-ton B-52 on an attack run. Is there?'

Samson stood up, leaned forward on his desk, and let his eyes bore into McLanahan's. 'The only way he could be stopped, Patrick, was to *die*. If you were allowed to keep on doing what you did over Russia, and you got to pin on three or four stars, or were selected to run the Department of Defense, or advise the President on national security policy, or even become president yourself – you'd be just as dangerous to

446

world peace as Brad was.

'The only way to stop you, Patrick, is either for someone in authority to slap you down, hard, or die yourself. That's the final outcome I'm trying to save you from: dying as an imperfect, desperate, schizophrenic man, like Brad Elliott. I have the authority as your commanding officer to do something before you corrupt the world with your brand of ambush-style warfighting. The buck is stopping here. I only wish someone had stopped Brad before he went over to the dark side.'

'Brad ... Brad was none of those things, General Samson,' David Luger said, in a small, quivering voice. They did not hear him mutter something else beneath his breath, something in Russian.

'You say you knew him so well – I say that's bullshit,' Patrick snapped. 'You only *think* you knew him. I think all you really wanted was a nice, comfortable command, to wear your stars but not shake up the system too much. Brad Elliott did just the opposite. They gave him three stars and a command like no one else's, even though he pissed off half of Washington on a regular basis. He created machines and aviators that had real courage and real determination. Even after they fired him, he still came back a hero. He's saved the world a dozen times, sir. Is it my insubordination that makes you angry – or is it your own frustration at never having taken your bombers into battle?'

'I'm not frustrated about never being in battle, General,' Samson retorted, perhaps a little too vehemently. 'No real soldier ever wants war, and they sure as hell don't regret never going. It is enough for me to serve my country in whatever way I'm asked, whether it's slopping tar on runways in Thailand in one-hundred-degree weather or leading the world's greatest military research facility. I don't go around *creating* wars to fight in.' That comment hit home with Patrick. He lowered his eyes and stepped back away from Samson's desk.

'End of discussion,' Samson said. 'The charges stand, General, Colonel. Submit your retirement requests by seventeen hundred hours or I prefer the charges to the judge advocate general.'

'Don't wait until then, sir,' David Luger said. 'I can give you my answer now: I'm not voluntarily resigning or retiring. I've been through too much in the past few years just to give it all away. If you want to penalize me, just do it.'

'I recommend you think about it some more,' Samson said sternly. 'You have too much at stake to risk your retirement and honorable discharge. Your background and ... other factors might not make you a popular or extremely sought-after candidate for a corporate or other government position.'

'*Excuse me*, General?' Luger asked, far more politely than Patrick would have. '*Ty shto, ahuyel?*'

'What was that? What did you just say, Luger?' Samson exploded. David did not reply, but seemed to wither under Samson's booming voice and averted his eyes to the floor, his arms straight down at his sides. 'I've been watching you for the past several weeks, Colonel Luger, and especially since that Ukrainian general showed up. You reported your former contact with that man and detailed some of your experiences with him in

Lithuania, but then refused to take leave while the Ukrainian contingent was here. That was a big mistake in judgment that I believe has emotionally and psychologically unbalanced you.'

'*What?*' McLanahan retorted.

'You could be a danger to yourself and to HAWC,' Samson went on. 'You're obviously failing to recognize this, both of you. If you don't retire, I'll be forced to have you confined as a matter of national security as well as the safety of this facility.'

David Luger didn't look stunned, or surprised, or angry, or even disappointed – he looked completely hollow. He stood motionless; his head bowed, his arms hanging limply at his sides, as if in complete surrender or emotional shutdown.

Patrick McLanahan exploded. 'Hey, Dave, forget about all that! He's full of shit,' he shouted. No reaction. He took David by the shoulders and shook him, gently at first, and then harder. 'Dave. You okay, Texas?'

At that moment, Hal Briggs and two of his security officers entered the office. Every room at Dreamland was continually monitored with video and audio, and security units were trained to respond to even a hint of violence or a breach in security. One of the Security Force officers had his MP5K submachine gun drawn and at port arms; the other had his hand on the handgrip of his weapon but did not draw it. Briggs had his hand on his pearl-handled .45-caliber automatic pistol – the one that had once belonged to Lieutenant General Brad Elliott, his mentor – but had not drawn it either.

'Dave! Dave, are you all right?' McLanahan cried to his friend and partner. It appeared as if Luger was in a semicatatonic state, unable to move or respond. 'Jesus, Hal, it's like his entire voluntary nervous system has shut down. Call the chopper and let's get him airlifted to Las Vegas *now*.' Briggs and the second security officer safetied their weapons and quickly, firmly, took McLanahan and Luger out of Samson's office, while the third man continued to cover the action with his drawn weapon.

As he was being hustled out, McLanahan turned to Samson and said, 'We're not finished here, Samson.'

'Seventeen hundred hours, General,' Samson responded. 'On my desk. Or else.'

On the Albania–Macedonia border that evening

Once one of the world's greatest empires under Alexander the Great, the Republic of Macedonia had been in an almost constant state of occupation and combat for over two thousand years, brutally repressed and colonized by Rome, Byzantium, the Huns, the Visigoths, Turkey, Bulgaria, Greece, Nazi Germany, and Serbia. It was not until the 1980 death of Yugoslavian strongman Josip Broz, known as Marshal Tito, and the collapse of the Soviet Union in 1992, that Macedonia was able to slip out of the grasp of regional overseers and declare itself an independent democratic republic.

But independence was not without conflict.

Macedonia had been a 'melting pot' of many different ethnic and religious peoples for thousands of years, and now they all wanted a say in the direction and future of their newly independent republic. Those forces – Albanians, Greeks, Serbs, Slavs, Turks, and Bulgars – all sought to drive the new nation apart and carve it up for themselves.

As a result, most of Macedonia's borders were heavily armed and fortified, and the nation invested heavily in counterinsurgency and border patrol forces. Border skirmishes, especially between Muslim Albania and Orthodox Christian Macedonia, were so common and so brutal that almost since its first day of membership, United Nations peacekeepers had been sent to Macedonia to try to keep the peace and settle border claims between it and its neighbors. Macedonia had become a favorite route for Albanian gun-runners to ship weapons to Kosovo Liberation Army rebels, and there had been many border skirmishes between Macedonian Army forces and well-equipped smugglers.

The government of Macedonia vowed to vigorously defend its borders against any nation that tried to violate its sovereignty and neutrality, but it was a poor nation, with only a small conscript army, so it was forced to ask for outside help. The US-led North Atlantic Treaty Organization was allowed to stage security, surveillance, and supply missions out of bases in Macedonia during the Kosovo conflict. In return, Macedonia was made a member of the 'Partnership For Peace,' the group of prospective NATO members, was offered millions of dollars in military and economic aid by the West, and was being considered for full membership in the European Union and the World Trade Organization.

Some of the bloodiest battles between Albanian gunrunners and Macedonian police and border guards were near the town of Struga, on the northern shore of Lake Ohrid in the Vardar Valley of southwestern Macedonia. It was an easy, straight shot northward up the valley to the Yugoslavian province of Kosovo and the heart of central Europe, and southbound to Lake Ohrid and eventually to the Aegean Sea. The city of Ohrid, a few miles away, was known as the 'Jerusalem of the Balkans' because of its combination of Christian – Catholic, Episcopal, Orthodox – and Muslim holy sites, churches, mosques, monasteries, cathedrals, along with several castles and fortifications dating back to the rule of Alexander the Great.

After the attack on Kukes, tensions on the Macedonia-Albania border were at a fever level. Army of the Republic of Macedonia troops, in retaliation for Albanian cross-border raids and skirmishes, were suspected of setting off the two massive explosions at the carpet factory in Kukes, Albania, killing hundreds. The Albanian Army was looking for revenge. Sniper, guerrilla, and sabotage attacks along the border rose in frequency and intensity, threatening to set off a large-scale war. The tiny Army of the Republic of Macedonia boasted more modern weapons than its adversary to the west, supplied mostly by the United States in years past, but Albania had the tactical and numerical advantage. Albania enjoyed a three-to-one manpower advantage, a

452

four-to-one artillery advantage, and a six-to-one armored personnel carrier advantage, and those forces overlooked the Macedonian forces from the mountains along the border.

That's why it was hard for anyone to understand the reason why the Macedonian Army suddenly commenced an artillery barrage against several security outposts west of Struga. Just before midnight, eyewitnesses claimed that two self-propelled 70-millimeter artillery units opened fire on two Albanian observation posts – little more than wood and rock shacks – that overlooked Lake Ohrid.

The Albanian Army immediately returned fire. The border defense positions were not equipped with any modern sensors or special equipment for artillery duels at night – no night vision, no counterfire radar – so it was rather amazing that the self-propelled artillery units that were suspected of opening fire first were hit and completely destroyed by the first volley of return fire. But the Albanians didn't stop there. Once the SPAs were destroyed, the nearest Macedonian firebase was next, then the nearest main base, and finally the city of Struga itself. For the next three hours, the Albanian Army pounded the city with artillery and rocket fire from eleven positions overlooking the city, some as far as eight miles away.

'Perfect,' Gennadi Yegorov, the weapons officer aboard the Metyor-179 stealth fighter-bomber, said. 'The Albanians are reacting better than we anticipated.'

The plan was simple. Some of Pavel Kazakov's

men in Macedonia had stolen and driven the two artillery pieces – both mobile but not capable of firing a round – from an armory in Bitola. The self-propelled artillery pieces were undergoing maintenance and had had their gun barrels removed, so they looked like just another military vehicle as they rumbled down the highway. In only three hours, they made the drive west to Struga and waited.

Meanwhile, the Mt-179 launched from its secret base near Codlea. With the NATO AWACS aircraft out of the action – it had not yet been replaced until whoever had shot the first one down had been discovered – it was child's play to make the flight from Codlea across Romania, Bulgaria, Kosovo, and Macedonia to Ohrid. The Mt-179 was loaded with four heat-seeking air-to-air missiles in its wing root launchers, along with four laser-guided missiles in its weapons bay. The Metyor-179 had a powerful imaging infrared and low-light TV sensor in a retractable pod in the nose, along with a laser target illuminator.

Once the dummy self-propelled artillery units were rolled into place and Kazakov's men hightailed it for safety, the charade began. One quick twin launch on the observation posts from fifteen miles away, a two-minute three-sixty turn, and a second twin ripple launch on the SPAs to erase the evidence, and the stunt was complete. Kazakov's operatives had placed infrared emitters on the artillery units and near the border observation posts to make it easier for Yegorov to find and attack the targets from maximum range.

'Eta l'ehchi chim dva pal'tsa abassat. It was easier

than pissing on two fingers,' Ion Stoica remarked, as they started to receive radio messages about the rapidly intensifying fighting between Albania and Macedonia. 'That attack had no business working, you realize that? The same with our departure from Zhukovsky and the success of our attack on Kukes.'

'We were lucky,' Yegorov said. 'It's sheer paranoia. Besides, those two were ready to fight anyway – they have been for almost ten years. We just provided a little push to get them going.'

'So we're contributing to the natural order and progression of political and cultural exchanges between fellow Balkan nations, eh?' Stoica asked, laughing. 'I like that. We're humanitarians, working to make the world a better place by allowing the natural harmony and rhythms of the region to develop.' Their second combat flight was even more successful than the first – and it provided the spark Kazakov needed to set the Balkans ablaze.

Instead of returning to Romania, Stoica and Yegorov flew across Bulgaria and the Black Sea, on their way to a Metyor-owned industrial facility and airstrip near Borapani, Republic of Georgia, the site of another Metyor pipeline. The return flight was smooth and uneventful. The Mt-179 was enjoying a brisk tailwind over the Black Sea that was pushing their ground speed to well over nine hundred kilometers an hour, even with the throttles pulled back to best-range economy power. At forty-one thousand feet, the sky was clear and the visibility unrestricted, with the stars shining so brightly that they appeared close enough to touch. There was a half moon on the rise, but it would be no factor – they would be on the ground long before anyone on the ground could see the aircraft with moonlight. Because of fuel considerations, they had already planned a steep, rapid descent at idle power through Georgian airspace instead of flying through Turkish coastal radar at low altitude, relying on the Tyenee's stealth characteristics to keep it invisible.

Yegorov offered to watch the aircraft, and Stoica gratefully took a catnap while his weapons officer filled out his poststrike reports and recorded computer logs, with the autopilot handling the aircraft. The autopilot was set for constant-Mach hold, which adjusted aircraft altitude automatically as gross weight decreased so they could maintain the most fuel-efficient airspeed – the Mt-179 very gradually climbed as gross weight decreased, up to forty-five thousand feet, the aircraft's maximum operating altitude, or a lower altitude set by the pilot.

But Stoica didn't set the proper maximum altitude. If he had bothered to double-check his weather forecasts from his preflight briefing, he would have read that the forecast contrail level over the Black Sea for their return flight was just over forty-one thousand feet. Yegorov had no autopilot controls in the aft cockpit except for disconnect, and in any case he was too distracted to pay any attention. Visibility directly behind the Metyor-179 was poor from the cockpit anyway, so even if he had looked outside, he would not have noticed anyway...

...that the Mt-179 was drawing a long, thick white contrail across the night sky over the Black

456

Sea. Illuminated by the moon, the condensation trail was bright enough to be seen for fifty miles across the clear, cold sky – bright enough to be spotted by a flight of two Republic of Turkey F-16s on a late-night air intercept training mission in the Samsun Military Operating Area off the northern coast of Turkey over the Black Sea.

The two Turkish fighters, both single-seat F-16C Block 50 models, were from the Fifth Main Jet Base, 151 Jet *Filo*, based at Merzifon about two hundred miles, to the south. Because of weather, their training flight had been delayed several hours. For flight currency, both pilots had to complete a high-level- and low-altitude radar intercept, including flight time to and from the Military Operating Area and reserve fuel; they had to carry almost four hours' worth of fuel, which meant they had to lug around two huge external fuel tanks, which really decreased the F-16s' maneuverability and fun. One plane would fly out to the edge of the MOA at a particular altitude and then head inbound, and the other aircraft would try to find it and complete an intercept. The radar controllers at Merzifon monitored the intercepts and could provide some assistance, but since the purpose of the exercise was for the pilot to find the 'enemy' himself, the pilots rarely asked for a vector from the ground radar controllers.

It was the last intercept of the night coming up, and after several hours of delays and nearly three hours of yanking and banking, all participants were ready to finish up and go home – their normal duty day was going to start just a few hours after landing, so the faster they finished, the more sleep time they'd get. Zodyak One, the flight leader, was the hunter, and his wingman, Zodyak Two, was the quarry. Zodyak Two was at thirty-nine thousand feet, preparing to simulate a high-speed penetration from high to low altitude, while Zodyak One was at normal patrol altitude of twenty-nine thousand feet. Their external lights were off; Zodyak One had his radar searching the sky below, while Zodyak Two as the attacker had his radar off.

The leader knew that the last intercept had to be a low-altitude one, so he was concentrating his search below him for his wingman. But it took just a few minutes for him to realize that his young wingman had snookered him, and he began to concentrate his search up high. It took him several radar sweeps to make contact before he finally locked the second F-16 up. '*Orospu cocugu,*' he swore to himself. 'Trying to screw me up, eh?' He raised the nose of his F-16 and pushed the throttles to full military power, preparing himself to begin the chase. 'Control, Zodyak One, radar contact, bogey bearing zero-two-zero bull's-eye, range eight miles, descending from angels three-nine. I am...'

Then he saw it – a bright, fast-moving contrail, streaking eastward. It looked close enough to cause a midair collision with Zodyak Two – the guy was certainly well inside the MOA. '*Knock it off! Knock it off!*' the leader shouted. 'Unknown aircraft in the MOA! One is level at base plus twelve.'

'Acknowledged,' Zodyak Two responded. 'Level at base plus ten.'

'Control copies your knock-it-off call, Zodyak One,' the ground radar control responded. 'We show no aircraft on radar, One. Say bogey airspeed and altitude.'

'Acknowledged.' The leader tried to lock his radar on the newcomer, but he could not get a radar lock-on. 'Negative radar, I must have a bent radar,' he reported. 'But I have a visual on his contrail. I estimate his altitude as angles four-two, heading eastbound.'

'Zodyak One, stand by.' The leader knew the controller would be on the phone to Air Force air defense headquarters. Moments later: 'Zodyak flight, Control, if you can maintain visual contact, we'd like to get a look at him. Warning, we have no radar contact and cannot provide intercept vectors or safe separation. Say state.'

'Zodyak One has zero point seven hours fuel until bingo,' the flight leader said. *'Dogru.'*

'Zodyak Two has zero point six until bingo. *Dogru* too.'

'Roger. Zodyak Two, your leader is at your one o'clock, seven miles, base plus twelve. Turn right heading zero-four-five to join, maintain base plus ten. Negative radar contact on any other traffic. Zodyak flight of two is cleared MARSA tactical with unknown aircraft. Zodyak One, squawk normal. Zodyak Two, squawk normal and ident ... radar contact, Zodyak Two, report when tied on and joined up with your leader, then squawk standby when within three miles.'

'Zodyak flight copies all,' the leader said. 'Let's push it up, Zodyak flight.'

'Two tied on radar. I'm in.'

Ion Stoica was jarred awake by the blare of the radar warning receiver and Gennadi Yegorov frantically shouting, 'Bandit! Bandit! Twelve o'clock, range ten miles!'

'Bandit? What in hell...?' Stoica berated himself for falling asleep so deeply – he should have taken the speed pills to keep him alert. He first checked his engine, systems, and flight instruments – and noticed right away that their altitude was way too high. 'Gennadi, dammit, we're above forty-three thousand! We were briefed not to go above forty-one!'

'All I have is autopilot annunciators back here, Ion,' Yegorov retorted. 'As far as I can tell, everything was fine. You set the autopilot, not me!'

Stoica knew he was right – Yegorov's instruments would show only status and malfunctions, not settings. That was *his* job. They had obviously picked up another nearby aircraft who had seen them by an infrared scanner or by their contrails. He had to get away from him *fast*.

'X-band pulse-Doppler fire-control radar, twelve o'clock, six miles – shit, I think we picked up a Turkish F-16,' Yegorov said. He searched his rear-view mirror. 'Contrails! We're making contrails!'

'Hang on!' Stoica pulled the throttles to idle, rolled the Mt-179 almost inverted, and started a steep left turning descent. He turned exactly ninety degrees to his original heading, which should blind a pulse-Doppler radar system. If the tailpipes could cool down and if they could spoof the radar, they could make a descending dash across the Black Sea and get away. It was their only chance. They could not outrun an F-16; and this close to Turkey, the other aircraft probably had more fuel.

This was not good at all.

'He maneuvered as soon as we locked him up on radar,' the flight leader said on the command channel. 'He must have a radar warning receiver. He's trying to notch left, fly away from the Turkish coast and blank himself out.' He had already anticipated a left turn, and he simply turned with him. The F-16's radar never broke lock.

'Zodyak Two has music,' the second F-16 reported. Jamming signals. Definitely a hostile aircraft.

'Control, Zodyak flight, our bandit has notched in response to our radar lock, and it now appears he's attempting to jam our radars,' the flight leader reported. 'We're both *dogru* at this time.' The word meant 'correct,' but in reality it meant, 'We have no weapons at all. How about getting some help up here?'

'Roger, Zodyak flight, an air defense emergency has been declared,' the ground radar controller reported. 'Cekic One-Zero-One flight of two is airborne, ETA ten minutes.'

'Roger,' the flight leader responded. The air defense strip alert birds got off the ground fast, but ten minutes was far too long. In ten minutes, this guy could be in Georgia or Russia. But they had him for now – there was no way they'd let him go without getting a look at him. 'Zodyak flight will be bingo fuel in fifteen minutes, so we'll stick with him until Cekic gets here.' He switched his

461

radio to the number-two radio and set the UHF GUARD channel. 'Let's give him a call and see if he's in a cooperative mood tonight.'

'Bandit at our four o'clock, five miles ... four miles,' Yegorov said. 'I think he locked on. He's pursuing. He's ... shit, he's got a trailer. Bandit Two, three o'clock, twelve miles and closing. I think he–'

'Attention, attention, unknown rider, unknown rider,' they heard on the UHF GUARD channel, the international emergency frequency, 'flying north off the Samsun three-five-zero degree radial, one hundred ten miles, this is the Republic of Turkey Air Force, please respond with your call sign, type, and destination, squawk normal and ident.'

'We're outside his airspace!' Yegorov said. 'He can't bother us, can he? He can't shoot us down out here! We're in international airspace!'

'No, but if he gets a look at us and reports us, our cover will be blown,' Stoica replied grimly. Well, if he wants to get a look at us, by all means, let's oblige him, he thought. 'Get the R-60s powered up and ready for launch.'

'Wait a minute, Ion,' Yegorov said. 'All we have are internal missiles. We shouldn't launch them unless it's an absolute emergency.'

'You want this Turkish prick to get a look at us?' Stoica asked angrily. 'Give me the R-60s right now!'

Yegorov reluctantly powered up the weapon systems. They still had all four of their wingroot-launched R-60 heat-seeking missiles ready to go.

'Missiles ready ... muzzle shutter open. Bandit one is six o'clock, nine miles, bandit two four o'clock, seventeen miles. Give me a target.'

'Here we go.' Stoica pulled the Metyor-179 into a steep climb, went inverted, then rolled out aiming right for the lead F-16. In seconds, they had closed the distance between them.

'Locked on!' Yegorov shouted. 'Shoot!' He fired two R-60 missiles as soon as they were within range.

It all unfolded in the blink of an eye, so fast that the Turkish flight leader did not notice – the rapid change in altitude, the rapid decrease in relative speed and distance, followed suddenly by an even faster decrease in relative distance and two bright flashes of light. 'Missile attack!' he shouted. 'Evasive action! We're under attack!' The flight leader immediately popped decoy chaff and flares – before realizing he didn't *have* any chaff or flares – then shoved in full afterburner power, went to ninety degrees left bank, pulled on the control stick until he heard the stall-warning horn, then rolled out and yanked the throttle to idle.

It was a last-ditch defensive effort, hoping against hope that the missile would lock onto the afterburner plume and then lose track completely when he shut off the burner, and the Turkish F-16 flight leader knew it. He knew he was toast long before the R-60 missiles plowed into his tailpipe and exploded, blowing his fighter into a huge cloud of flying metal and flaming jet fuel.

'Control, Control, *aman allahim, bombok,*

Zodyak One has been hit! Zodyak One has been hit by two missiles!' the young pilot aboard Zodyak Two screamed on the command channel. 'I do not have a radar lock! I am completely defensive! Do you have radar contact on the bandit?'

'Negative, Zodyak Two, negative!' the ground radar controller responded. 'Negative radar contact! Recommend vector heading one-niner-zero, descend to base plus zero, maximum speed. Get out of there now! Cekic flight is inbound, ETA eight minutes, base plus twenty.'

The wingman thought momentarily about avenging his leader: searching the skies with radar and eyeballs and with sheer luck, then finding the *pic* that had shot his friend and teacher down. But what he did was turn around back toward land and plug in full afterburner power. As much as he wanted to fight, he knew he had nothing but anger with which to do it, and that would do him no good at all. 'He's turning! He's bugging out!' Yegorov crowed. 'Full afterburner power – running scared at Mach One. So long, great Turkish warrior.' But his celebration was short-lived, because he had fault indicator lights on both missile launch tubes, and they would not clear. The missiles' rocket motors had obviously damaged the titanium launch tube shutters, leaving them partly open or jammed inside the tubes.

Stoica immediately turned eastbound once again, descending at idle power to keep his heat signature as low as possible and to try to hide in the radar clutter of the Black Sea until they were out of maximum radar detection range. 'Don't laugh too hard, Gennadi,' Stoica said. 'That was very nearly us crashing to the Black Sea. Now we have to pray we have enough fuel to make it to base – we could end up at the bottom of the Black Sea if we're not careful.'

They were very lucky – one engine flamed out shortly after landing, and they barely had enough fuel to taxi off the runway and to the parking ramp before the second engine flamed out. The ground support crews had to frantically get a towbar and tug and pull the Metyor-179 into its hangar before anyone spotted the plane. The fuel tanks were literally bone-dry.

The attack was a complete success – but neither Stoica nor Yegorov felt like celebrating anything except their own survival.

Chapter Seven

KFOR Headquarters, Camp Bondsteel, Pristina, Kosovo
later that morning

'The situation is unraveling before our eyes, gentlemen,' General Sir Edmund Willoughby, commander of the North Atlantic Treaty Organization's Kosovo Force (NATO KFOR), exclaimed. 'I have the unfortunate task of advising everyone here this morning that the Former Yugoslavian Republic of Macedonia has just declared war on the Republic of Albania, and vice versa.'

The conference theater, once a motion picture screening theater, erupted into a hubbub of shock and anguish. Willoughby was presiding over an early-morning strategy session of all of the KFOR commanders at Camp Bondsteel, the headquarters for all NATO and United Nations peacekeeping forces in Kosovo, set up at a motion picture production studio near Pristina Airport in Kosovo. Also in attendance at Camp Bondsteel was the United Nations Special Envoy of the United Nations Preventative Diplomacy Mission, or UN-PREDEP, Ambassador Sune Joelson of Sweden. UNPREDEP was the military-civilian command that had taken over for the United Nations Protection Force in Macedonia in 1995 to try to restore law and order between Albania and Macedonia when border clashes had threatened to escalate to all-out war.

469

'Have we any information on what touched off this incident?' *Oberst* (Colonel) Rudolph Messier, the German KFOR commander, asked.

'Nothing,' Willoughby responded. 'Eyewitnesses claim that Macedonian artillery units opened fire and destroyed several Albanian observation posts. Macedonia denies this, but claimed that those observation posts were really target spotting units, and they say they intercepted several coded messages broadcast from those posts that they believed were target grid reports.'

'That does not sound like sufficient provocation to open fire,' Colonel Misha Simorov, the Russian KFOR commander who had taken over Colonel Kazakov's post, said.

'Exactly – and that goes double for Albania,' Air Force Lieutenant-Colonel Timothy Greer, the American KFOR commander, interjected. 'Over one hundred and sixty confirmed deaths in Struga so far. Albania hit several historical locations, too.'

'I am sure this was a knee-jerk response to the Macedonian attack against Kukes,' Simorov said. 'Two to three times as many died there.'

'I'm not disputing the seriousness of either attack, sir,' Greer said to Simorov. 'But why bombard a town with sustained artillery and rocket attacks for almost four hours over some hothead artillery officer lobbing a few across the border?'

'You seem so eager to minimize the danger in this, Colonel,' Simorov said. 'Macedonia committed an act of war – a preemptive strike against an observation post along a critical communications and transportation route. It certainly could have been interpreted as a prelude to an invasion.'

'*Invasion?*' Greer retorted. 'Macedonia invading Albania? With what? The Albanian army outnumbers Macedonia's by two to one; Macedonia has virtually no armor or artillery. That's a ridiculous notion.'

'Absurd or not, Colonel, an artillery assault–'

'*Suspected* artillery assault,' General Messier said. 'There is no hard evidence yet that Macedonia had any artillery of any kind near Struga.'

'–An artillery assault in that area could easily be construed as the prelude to an invasion,' Simorov went on, despite the interruption. 'That highway where the fighting broke out is the main transportation route between the Aegean and Adriatic Sea, between Greece and Albania. If Macedonia takes control of it, tanks can be roaring into Tirane within hours. They can encircle Tirane with ease.'

'*Encircle Tirane?*' Greer again asked incredulously. 'Colonel Simorov, this is nonsense. Albania is not being threatened by anyone, especially Macedonia.'

'Then whom, Colonel?' Simorov asked angrily. 'Who else would want to slap Albania down?'

'No one is trying to–'

'Macedonia is supported and is being armed by NATO,' Simorov said. 'Only NATO benefits by destabilizing Albania and strengthening Macedonia. Perhaps I should inquire to the NATO secretary-general what he has in store for Albania?'

'Colonel Simorov, as the KFOR commander and a deputy chief of staff of the NATO High Command, I assure you NATO has no designs on Albania,' Willoughby said. 'Quite the contrary, NATO and all of Europe would benefit greatly

471

by forging closer ties with Albania. Macedonia is a friend and prospective member of the Alliance, but they are not being armed by NATO, nor are they acting as a NATO military surrogate.'

'Sir, only NATO and Macedonia stand to gain if an invasion of Albania is successful,' Simorov said. 'Macedonia wants to cut off all arms and drug smuggling across its borders, and it wants to be able to eject ethnic Albanians from its territory at will. What better way to topple the Albanian government and create a safe, secure outlet to the Adriatic Sea than by committing mysterious hit-and-run attacks in Albania, along the main corridor linking two seas, and then letting NATO make excuses and apologies for its actions?'

'I don't know what you're talking about, Colonel,' General Sir Willoughby said seriously, 'but if you please, let us hear some constructive suggestions rather than wild speculation. What should we do now? Both the United Nations and the European Union are waiting for recommendations.'

'Obviously it is in all of our best interests to keep the fighting from escalating, *ja?*' Colonel Messier said. He turned to Ambassador Joelson and went on, 'With all due respect, sir, UN-PREDEP has been a dismal failure. I almost wish we had kept the Protection Force in place. Even Swedish peacekeepers are ineffective in this situation. We need an armed military force in place in both Albania and Macedonia to prevent this conflict from reigniting a general Balkan and possibly even a European war.'

'I agree: The United Nations Protection Force

was, with all due respect, a failure,' Colonel Simorov said, nodding toward the Italian force commander. Italy had supplied most of the peacekeeping force in UNPROFOR-Albania about eight years earlier. 'Besides, Italy has all but withdrawn from NATO peacekeeping efforts in the Balkans anyway.'

'Italy finds it is safer and better for ourselves to patrol and police our own borders,' the Italian colonel said. 'Perhaps it might be better if Macedonia did the same.' He turned to look at Lieutenant-Colonel Greer and said with a sneer, 'Of course, the Americans would certainly provide a credible force – if the American president would ever agree to provide more than a token air base and logistics force to assist. Just when Europe seems to be on the brink of all-out war, the Americans decide to become conscientious objectors.'

'The United States is willing to do its part to provide protection forces for NATO member nations,' Colonel Greer said. 'The United States is not divorcing itself from any potential crisis situations–'

'Certainly not divorce – it is more like *frigidity!*' the Italian commander shouted. That got a chuckle from most of the KFOR commanders – all except Greer, of course.

'Very funny, sir,' Greer said, with a smile that he hoped would disarm the growing tension in the room. 'I disagree with Colonel Simorov – the Italian peacekeepers were most effective in Albania, as has been UNPREDEP in Macedonia. I can't explain this sudden outbreak of hostilities. Macedonia and KFOR have been relatively successful in reducing arms smuggling into Kosovo through Macedonia. Weapons are still getting through Albania. But we trace much of the instability in the region to the Kosovo Liberation Army's activities. KFOR needs time to work to be effective until we find a political solution.'

'Easy for you to say, Colonel – your commander was not skinned and burned alive in the streets of Prizren,' Simorov said acidly. 'The Russians have suffered half of all KFOR casualties in Kosovo at the hands of Muslim rebels. The incidents of violence increase every day. Obviously, our presence in Kosovo is not enough – we must cut off and flush out the source of weapons and guerrillas. That means stationing peacekeepers in Albania. And since Macedonia appears unwilling or unable to stop this flow of Muslim freedom-fighters and weapons into Kosovo, someone must set up border security forces in Macedonia.'

'And the United States disagrees,' Greer said. 'I don't understand this sudden need to expand the peacekeeping operation's scope of involvement. Two small-scale border skirmishes don't signal a complete deterioration in the political situation. Let's not act too hastily.'

'Pardon me, Colonel,' Simorov said, 'but I think the United States has forfeited its right to comment on how KFOR deploys its forces or accomplishes its mission. Contributing a few cargo planes and reconnaissance satellites doesn't add up to a peacekeeping force with equal responsibility.'

'Let us stop wasting time with squabbling,' Colonel Messier said. 'If the Americans and

Italians refuse to participate, others must step in to help quickly stabilize the situation. Pending approval from my government, I can deploy my forces south from Pec, Kosovo, into Albania. We've received a certain amount of relative good-will from the Albanian government in the past – I think the United Nations and NATO can convince the Albanian government to allow German peacekeeping forces into the region. We can limit our movements, say, from the Bigorski Monastery southward to the Lake Ohrid area, restricted to north of the Elbasan-Thessaloniki Highway. Naturally, if the Albanian government allows us to do so, we can cover and patrol more extensively throughout Albania.' He stood up and pointed to a large map against a wall. 'With permission, we can even perhaps cover both sides of the border.'

'German troops moving into both Albania and Macedonia?' Colonel Simorov retorted. 'Pardon me, *Oberst*, but I would very much like to see a more balanced force in place. The Russian contingent is by far the largest force still remaining in the region, except for Germany and perhaps Britain. I will propose to my government that Russia move a portion of its peacekeeping forces south from Prizren to the Lake Ohrid area, perhaps headquartering in Bitola. That way we're close enough to assist if there's an outbreak of hostilities, but we're not breathing down anyone's neck either.' He nodded to Messier and added, 'Next to the Germans perhaps, the Russians enjoy the worst reputation in this part of the world.'

'I think that honor is now reserved for the Americans,' the Italian commander said. Many of the commanders laughed – but the Italian colonel was serious.

'The English and French can maintain their positions in Kosovo,' the German commander summarized. 'With assistance from the other nations involved, I believe Germany can maintain a sufficient presence in Albania to quell any violence, and certainly with the Russians across the border in Macedonia, we can calm the situation dramatically. We stay out of sight unless there's fighting or unless we see signs of illegal activity, such as arms smuggling. It is a workable interim solution until the diplomats can find a more lasting mechanism for keeping the peace.'

There were no other nations willing or able to offer a better solution, so the resolution passed unanimously. At that, with a simple voice vote, the Balkans were carved up once again.

Government House, Skopje, Republic of Macedonia that same time

'Tell that rat bastard Kazakov to get the hell out of Skopje – his visa is to be revoked immediately!' Branco Nikolov, the prime minister of the Republic of Macedonia, shouted. 'I am canceling my appointments with him now and to eternity!'

Nikolov hated gangsters like Kazakov, and the reason was simple: Macedonia was one of seven nations in the world legally authorized to cultivate, store, sell, and ship pharmaceutical opium. While it was a very lucrative enterprise, perfectly suited for a mostly agricultural country like Macedonia, the nation had to endure constant scrutiny and immense challenges to make sure the opium was not getting into the hands of illegal-drug makers. Macedonia expended quite a bit of its gross national product on internal and border security to combat the evil influences of men like Kazakov.

It didn't make any difference that Kazakov wanted to talk about something else entirely – getting licenses and leases to build a huge pipeline across Macedonia from Bulgaria to Albania. It didn't matter. Kazakov was scum.

Just then, the phone rang. Nikolov picked it up and listened. His assistant saw his shoulders droop and his jaw drop open. 'Sir?'

Nikolov looked up at his assistant, surprise and disbelief etched across his face. His eyes again fell to the desk. 'Get Kazakov ... no, *ask* Comrade Kazakov to come in.'

'*Sir?*' the assistant gasped. 'I thought you said...?'

'Just do it,' Nikolov said in a low, panicked voice. 'That was the President. The United Nations Security Council is voting later this morning on a resolution to send Russian peacekeepers into Macedonia from Kosovo.'

'*What?* Russian troops in Macedonia? It cannot be!'

'They are on the move right now,' Nikolov said. 'The resolution is expected to pass by the end of the day. Three thousand Russian troops from Prizren, another five thousand troops expected to fly into the capital by next week and move to Bitola to set up observation posts along the

Albanian border. The *Germans* will be patrolling the Albanian side. The goddamned Germans–'

'But ... but what about Kazakov? What does he have to do about this?'

'I don't know, but I feel his fingers pulling some strings in all this,' Nikolov said ominously.

'How so, sir?'

'Don't you see? The Russian troops from Prizren will be following a route exactly identical to the routing Kazakov's proposed pipeline will take. Kazakov will practically have Russian troops guarding every centimeter of his proposed pipeline.'

'But that's got to be a coincidence, sir,' the assistant said. 'The duplicity falls apart at the Albanian border. Kazakov will never get approval from Albania to extend his pipeline project into Albania.'

Nikolov looked worried enough to chew a fingernail, something his assistant had never before seen him do. 'But if he *does* do it, if he *does* get permission, there's nothing we could do about it with Russian troops occupying half our country,' he said. 'Better to make a deal with Kazakov now – the fewer enemies we have, the better.'

Near Resen, Republic of Macedonia
the next day

'C'mon, kids, let's get going!' Chief Master Sergeant Ed Lewis, NCOIC of the 158th Fighter Wing, Vermont Air National Guard, shouted through the mess tent door. 'It's a beautiful day outside, we're having a great time, and breakfast was exceptionally good today! Let's move it!' The Chief greeted his troops like this every day at 0645. He was usually the first one in line when the chow hall opened up at 0600, but he had already led PT at 0530 and had conducted an informal first sergeant's meeting at the breakfast table.

Inside the tent, his troops made a few raucous comments as they got up from the picnic bench-style tables, policed up their trays and areas, and headed outside. Lewis spoke a little Macedonian and greeted every Macedonian soldier in his own language, which he knew sounded funny as hell in his thick New England accent. The weather was miserable, the conditions were poor most times, the workdays were long and hard, the food was plentiful but bland, and they were six thousand miles from home – but Ed Lewis and his Green Mountain Boys loved every minute of it.

For the second year in a row, members of the Vermont Air National Guard were participating in a Partnership For Peace program called Cornerstone, where NATO and Macedonian military units worked side by side, shared equipment, learned about each other's capabilities, trained together, and did some good work for the locals at the same time. For Cornerstone 2001–3, the encampment was in a rural area fifteen miles north of Resen in south-central Macedonia. Spring flooding had decimated a number of villages in the area, so construction units of the US Navy Seabees and US Marine Corps, led by units of the 158th Fighter Wing 'Green Mountain Boys' of the Vermont Air National Guard, had been sent in to rebuild roads, schools, bridges, and other buildings, help the local utilities restore and restart service, and supply drinking water to the citizens.

This was the second time that Chief Master Sergeant Ed Lewis, first sergeant of the 158th Fighter Wing of the Vermont Air National Guard, had been in Macedonia during his training rotation. To tell the absolute truth, he enjoyed the hell out of it. Southern Macedonia was very much like his native Milton, Vermont – rural, rugged, isolated, lush, a little backward, wet, sometimes cold and gray, other times sunny and spectacularly beautiful. The people were friendly and very hospitable. Most everyone spoke English, at least much better than Lewis spoke Macedonian or Greek, which was a real benefit to Lewis and his contingent of one hundred Guardsmen and the other American service members here.

The troops were treated like neighbors here. If a soldier paused longer than normal on the street, a woman would come out of a nearby house and invite him inside to rest, or offer him or her coffee, cakes, or delicacies such as lamb's head soup. They never gave directions to anyone – the locals would always escort a lost soldier to his destination, no matter how far out of their way it was. If an American did the simplest courtesy for a Macedonian, even as trivial as stepping aside to let him or her pass, or holding a door open, the next time you'd meet that civilian, he or she would offer to launder your uniform, take you for a drive around town to see the sights, or have you meet every one of his relatives. Although living in the field was tough on all of them, the locals did everything they could to make the foreigners seem welcome.

The latest and biggest project by Cornerstone 2001 was restoring a flooded school campus. The combined elementary, middle, and high school complex, which also served as a local medical clinic, day-care center, farmer's market, veterinary clinic, and vocational-technical school, had been badly damaged when the nearby Czur River had spilled over its banks in the springtime rains and runoff, and nearby damage and contamination to wells and water-treatment facilities had left the area without any sanitary facilities or healthy water supplies. It was Lewis's job to coordinate the activities of the Green Mountain Boys, along with a few soldiers from other NATO countries, Macedonian Army conscripts, and local paramilitaries and townspeople into an effective construction unit.

The first task was organizing this mishmash of foreigners, soldiers of different branches, and locals, but that's where Lewis really shone. He had been organizing things all his life, starting with his baseball card collection, his Little League team, his senior class in high school as class president, and yard stock in the lumber yard where he had worked as the day-shift foreman for the past ten years. He used an effective combination of communication skills, cajoling, horse trading, force, and his keen powers of observation to identify leaders, followers, or slackers, and put them in the right place. After fifteen years in the Air Guard, including two months in Saudi Arabia during Desert Storm, he also knew a lot about taking a bunch of kids – the conscripts in the Macedonian Army were all between eighteen and twenty years old – matching them up with the veterans, and letting the old farts lead.

Once the job for today was outlined for the groups, they launched off on their own. The job was to pump out standing water from the campus, strip out water-damaged walls and floors, inspect the structure for signs of weakness or damage, repair or replace the foundations and structures, rehabilitate the grounds, and then get them ready to refurnish. About half of the campus was still under water, some of it as much as two feet high, so they had big trailer-mounted pumps ready to go. But before anyone stepped into even a quarter-inch of water, Lewis had the 158th Medical Services Squadron and the 158th Civil Engineering Squadron, Environmental Control come in and test the soil and water for signs of contamination. This part of Macedonia was fairly pristine, and there were few villages upstream, but Macedonia did quite a bit of cattle farming in the highlands, and cattle waste and disease caused all sorts of problems, not to mention the real hazards if they found any dead cattle carcasses or corpses. So nobody touched anything unless it was signed off on by the medical and environmental guys.

Lewis's troops were just fanning out to begin work when he heard choppers in the distance. It was not unusual at all – the international airport at Ohrid just a few miles to the west had a military facility where most of the United Nations troops were stationed; and being fairly close to the border and to the two-millennium-old historical sites of southern Macedonia, the area was very heavily patrolled – but Lewis stopped to search

482

for them and watch them approach. Macedonia had a few American surplus UH-1 Hueys and a few old ex-Soviet Mil-17 transport helicopters, but these choppers sounded even bigger – and it sounded like a lot of them inbound.

There were. Popping up from a low-level high-speed inbound approach to the schoolyard was a formation of three Mil Mi-24V 'Hind-E' helicopter gunships in a wide V formation. The big armored choppers zoomed in at treetop level, and as soon as they cleared the tree line, their noses lowered again, rapidly picking up speed. He could even see the big gun turret in the front under the nose sweeping back and forth, looking for targets, locking on and tracking any large vehicle or military-looking building – he swore the lead chopper's gunner locked on to *him* and had him dead in his sights. Lewis had seen plenty of Russian helicopters throughout the Balkans in his years here, but all of them had been unarmed. These were armed to the teeth with rocket pods, anti-armor missiles, bombs, mines, even air-to-air missiles filling every attach point on their weapon pylons. That was a major violation of NATO and United Nations directives – but even more than that, they were scary as hell.

Lewis had never seen a Russian helicopter on an attack run before, but he imagined this was exactly what it looked like. He withdrew his walkie-talkie from its belt holster and keyed the mike button: 'Cornerstone Alpha, this is Cornerstone One.' Alpha was the unit's commanding officer, Colonel Andrew Toutin, the commander of the 158th Fighter Wing, currently located at the Corner-

483

stone operation headquarters in Skopje.

'Go ahead, Chief.'

'Sir, I've got an eyeball on three big Russian helicopter gunships ready to overfly the Resen school grounds, and they are armed. Repeat, they are armed to the teeth.'

'*What?*' Toutin shouted. 'What in hell was that? *Armed?* Are you saying you clearly observe weapons on board these helicopters?'

'Affirmative, sir. Many weapons. Many weapons.'

He could imagine his boss swearing long and loud off-air – the boss, a salty old veteran fighter pilot with over twenty years' active duty service and over ten years in the Vermont Air Guard, usually used expletives frequently and often creatively in everyday conversation. 'I'll call it in to NATO headquarters here, Chief,' Toutin said. 'Contact the Macedonian security NCO and make sure they keep their weapons out of sight. If the choppers try to land, keep the civilians away from them.'

'Roger all, sir,' Lewis responded. 'Break, break, Seven, this is One.'

'This is Seven,' the Macedonian noncommissioned officer in charge of the security forces for Cornerstone responded in broken but passable English. 'I see the Russians too, Chief. I copy Alpha, we keep our weapons out of sight, and I will order the police chief to get the civilians indoors. I will initiate a security checkpoint report and verify orders. Stand by.'

The Russian gunships completed their low pass over the campus, then split up and disappeared over the horizon, flying so low they were hidden by trees almost immediately. The thunderous roar of the Hinds masked the sound of more helicopters coming in. These were Mil Mi-8T troop transport helicopters, huge twin-turboshaft monsters carrying fuel in external pylons instead of weapons. Lewis saw six of them dart in toward the school from three different directions, all from treetop level and at maximum forward speed. Spreading out across the campus, the helicopters suddenly pitched up to quickly slow their forward speed, then settled rapidly to the ground in three pairs spread out about three hundred yards apart. Seconds after the transports hit the ground, heavily armed Russian soldiers in dark green camouflage BDUs and with camouflaged faces and weapons spread out to guard the helicopters and took cover positions behind nearby buildings. As the transport helicopters departed, the Hind-E gunships cruised nearby, ready to pounce if any enemy activity popped up.

Pretty damned efficient, Lewis thought grimly. Everywhere he looked on the campus, there was a Russian infantryman. They were probably not outnumbered, but they were clearly outgunned.

One of the Russian soldiers set up a smoke-wind direction torch on the parking lot, and moments later a lone Mi-8 transport arrived. This one was a little different: it off-loaded only eight security troops, and it was festooned with antennae all over its fuselage. Along with the security forces, an officer with full battle gear stepped off the helicopter, flanked by a few aides, staff officers, and a civilian. Aha, Lewis guessed, the boss has just arrived.

Somehow, for some reason, Lewis had a bad feeling about this. He knew about the border skirmish between Albania and Macedonia, the declaration of war between them, and the decision by NATO to allow Russian peacekeepers into Macedonia, but he'd never expected this. The Russians were supposed to be arriving at Ohrid International Airport, about forty miles west, and setting up patrol lines north and south along the Albanian-Macedonian border. What were they doing here? And why the airborne assault – why not just drive in?

He knew the proper procedure would be to let Toutin handle this – but instead, Lewis holstered his walkie-talkie and headed out to where the Russian officer had just alighted. 'Chief, where are you going?' one of his clerks asked.

'To talk.'

'But shouldn't we go get the colonel?'

'It'll take him an hour to get here.'

'What about the major?' The on-site commander of the Cornerstone detachment in Resen was the wing intel officer, Major Bruce Kramer. To put it mildly, Kramer hated Macedonia. As far as anyone knew, Kramer spent all his time in his tent, writing letters to his congressman asking to get him the hell out of the Balkans.

'Forget about him,' Lewis said. 'I'm going out to talk with them. If the colonel calls, tell him the Russians have landed and it looks like they're taking over the joint.' Lewis wished he had his Kevlar and his web gear. Although the Green Mountain Boys were indeed a combat unit and had seen plenty of action over the years, here in Macedonia they had no capability to fight anyone, especially Russians. At least he hoped to act the part of a field combat noncom, even if he couldn't look like one.

The Russian security guards let him approach, keeping one eye on him and another on their field of fire. All weapons were at port arms or raised upward – none were aimed at NATO or Macedonian troops. Encouraging sign, at least. When he was about five paces from the commanding officer, a stern look and a half-turn to the left by one of the officer's security guards, which would have allowed him just to lower his rifle to shoot, stopped Lewis cold. No question of his desires or intentions if he did not comply.

Lewis saluted, but did not wait for a return salute before lowering his. The Russian did not return the salute. He had to shout over the roar of the Mi-8, which was idling but had not shut down. 'Who are you and what do you want?'

One of the aides shouted a translation into his commander's ear, received the reply, then passed the word to the other soldiers nearby. 'Captain Rokov is in charge,' the aide said. 'He has ordered that all NATO and Macedonian forces stationed here are to be gathered here immediately.'

Lewis noted that the colonel never wanted to know who Lewis was or desire to see the commanding officer – obviously he didn't care who he or anyone else was. 'Why, sir?' Lewis asked.

'You will do as you are ordered, Sergeant,' the aide repeated.

'I have not been instructed to follow your

487

orders, sir,' Lewis replied. 'If you don't mind, I'll wait until I receive orders from my commanding officer.'

'Where is your commanding officer, Sergeant?'

'I am the commander of this detail,' replied Lewis. Not technically correct, but he was in charge at this moment. 'I am in direct communication with KFOR and NATO commanders in Skopje. If I am instructed to do so, I will carry out your orders, but until then, I am respectfully asking you to withdraw your men from my AOR. We have our orders, and I intend to see they are carried out.'

'What are your orders, Sergeant?' the aide asked. 'What is your currently assigned area of responsibility?'

'That's "Chief Master Sergeant" or "Chief" to you, sir,' Lewis admonished him. 'I am not at liberty to discuss my orders with you. My AOR extends throughout Bitola province, but you may ask NATO headquarters in Skopje for the exact boundaries. You may contact NATO headquarters in Skopje and inquire there. Now please move your troops off the school campus. They're interfering with our work and scaring the locals. I suggest bringing your choppers back here and helocasting your troops to Ohrid International Airport. You'll find much better accommodations there anyway.'

'Perhaps you will accept some help from our men?' the aide asked, after making the translation and listening to the colonel's reply. 'Tell us what you would like to do, and Captain Rokov will assign some of his men to assist, in the spirit of cooperation.'

'Tell the captain no thanks, but we have things well under control.'

At that moment, there was a shout behind him. Two Russian soldiers were dragging Major Kramer out of one of the school buildings. He had been badly beaten up, and a line of blood was coming out one of the soldier's nostrils.

'*Shto teebye?*' The civilian that had exited the Mi-8 helicopter with Rokov stepped forward toward the captured officer.

'Hey! Leave him alone!' Lewis shouted. Two soldiers stepped in front of Lewis, rifles raised.

The civilian grabbed Kramer by the hair and lifted his face up, screaming something at him. The soldiers that were carrying Kramer shouted something to Rokov. The aide translating for the Russian commander said, 'They say he was hiding in one of the condemned buildings with a radio, calling in an air strike against our position.'

'That's bullshit!' Lewis shouted. 'We are a construction unit, helping the Macedonians rebuild this school campus.'

The civilian continued to yell at Kramer, but the American looked like he was only half conscious. The civilian then pulled a pistol out of his coat and aimed it at Kramer.

'No!' Lewis shouted. He managed to knock over the soldiers blocking his path and started to run toward Kramer. Captain Rokov pulled his side arm from its holster, jacked a round into the chamber, and put two bullets into Chief Master Sergeant Lewis's back from less than fifteen feet away. He was dead before he hit the ground. The civilian holding Kramer smiled, turned to the dazed American, and put two bullets into his head from point-blank range.

'Hold your fire! All units, *hold your fire!*' Rokov screamed. The civilian let go of Kramer, wiping blood and bits of brains off his coat and pants. The soldiers let him drop, unsure of what to do. 'Order the troops to spread out, find the rest of the NATO and Macedonian soldiers. Capture them if possible, kill them if necessary,' Rokov ordered, holstering his pistol. 'As soon as this site is secure, bring in the second and third waves of troops and start moving south toward the main highway. I want the highway in both directions secure before noon.' Aides hurried off to relay his orders.

The captain turned, stooped down, and looked at the man he had killed. It was his first kill. The last way he ever wanted to do it was to shoot a man in the back. Worse, the man was unarmed. He had shot an unarmed soldier in the back. He would never live that truth down.

Rokov tore a patch off Lewis's BDU jacket and handed it to another of his officers, his intelligence officer. 'What is it?'

'It's ... it is the One-fifty-eighth Fighter Wing, as expected, sir,' the aide said nervously, obviously frightened by the double murders. 'An F-16A Air Defense Fighter unit based in the province of Vermont, north-eastern United States, part of the American Air National Guard reserve forces. Responsible for continental air defense. Sometimes deploys to Iceland or Canada.'

Rokov had to struggle to drag his consciousness to the present. Two unarmed American soldiers were dead. What in hell had they done? But it was too late to fret over it. 'An American air defense fighter unit deployed out here? Why?'

'I do not believe they are a real fighter unit, sir,' the intel officer said. 'I believe they were sent out here as an advance unit, setting up air defense and surveillance operations in southern Macedonia.'

'But why down here in this river valley?' Rokov asked. 'Why not in the highlands themselves, or a few kilometers farther east where they have a clear unobstructed view of the frontier? This is the worst place they could have picked if they were going to set up any kind of radar or line-of-sight communications system.'

'I still believe this is an intelligence-gathering unit, sir,' the Russian intel officer said resolutely, although the confusion and uncertainty was evident in his eyes. 'They have set up this site as a listening post, disguised as some sort of humanitarian aid project.'

'Well, dammit, find the officers, find the equipment, and find the crypto gear, and do it quickly!' Rokov ordered, snatching the dead NCO's patch away from the confused intel officer. 'The main body of the Fifty-first Airborne Regiment will be moving through here tonight, and I don't want any sort of recon groups or intelligence-gathering devices to be operating when they do. Now get going.' The aide hurried off, glad to be out of range of the captain's rising anger.

Rokov stuffed the patch in his BDU jacket pocket. Gunfire started to erupt nearby, along with shouts in Russian to stop, more shooting, the sounds of terrified men and women screaming. More shooting, more screaming – this time, the sounds of screaming children, lots of them.

This just didn't make sense, he thought. His observer had said the Americans had set up a special forces recon base here in the Czur Valley to monitor Russian troop activities, and his intel staff had confirmed the report. Then some reports had come in saying the group was not a special forces or recon team, but a civil aid project team called Cornerstone. The intel staff maintains they are a recon group, merely disguised as a civil aid project. Then he receives a report saying the Americans were part of an F-16 Fighting Falcon fighter unit, which raises all sorts of new suspicions.

Rokov turned to the civilian passenger beside him and asked, 'Well, Comrade Kazakov? I see no signs of American special forces or recon teams here. This place has no helicopters, no communications outlets, and is located in the worst possible location.'

'Did you expect the Americans to be standing out here in the open waving in welcome as you flew in?' Pavel Kazakov asked derisively. He was taking some rough survey shots with a portable laser/GPS transit, measuring elevations and distances from the school to the river, making mental calculations on exactly where he was going to lay his pipeline. It was never a good idea to build a big pipeline too close to the main highway, but it still had to be accessible. This was a perfect spot for a pumping and metering station. The flooding concerned him, so he had to find where the mean water level had been, so he could update the flood charts and make calculations on the water table. 'It sounds like your men are digging the real enemy troops out right now.'

'I see no evidence a battalion-size force ever has been here,' Rokov observed. 'I see no evidence of armor, weapons concentrations, antiaircraft weaponry, fuel storage, or marshaling yards. Where is all this heavy military equipment you reported?'

'You have been on the ground five minutes, Rokov – did you expect all the answers to just pop out at you so quickly?'

Rokov looked at Kazakov suspiciously. 'I find it interesting, Comrade,' he said warily, 'that with all the resistance we were told to expect here, with all the danger requiring a heliborne assault by an entire airborne infantry company, that you decided to come along. It was a very large risk. It makes me wonder if there were any heavy forces here at all.'

'Were you hoping for a firefight, Captain? Anxious to win some more medals?'

'All I'm looking for are some straight answers–'

'I'm not here to answer questions for you, Captain,' Kazakov snapped. 'I've been authorized to accompany you on this operation, and that's all you need to know. It is your job to secure this location and then move south to secure the stretch of highway near Resen to prepare for the Fifty-first Airborne Regiment to move up from their positions near Bitola.'

Captain Rokov turned to Kazakov in some surprise. 'And how did you know about the Fifty-first's jumping-off point near Bitola?' he asked. 'I learned about it in a top-secret briefing just before we mounted up for this assault.'

493

'More stupid questions,' Kazakov scoffed, ignoring the question. He anchored a measuring tape to a stake and started to walk. 'I've got my work, Captain, and you have yours.'

'Wait one minute, Kazakov–'

'That's *Mr* Kazakov to you, Captain!' Pavel snapped. 'I warn you – do not try me. Go about your business, *now*.'

'Or what, *Mr* Kazakov?'

'You suddenly think you're so tough, Captain Rokov?' Kazakov spat. 'You're the one who shot an unarmed American noncommissioned officer in the back. Your career is over.'

'That is a failure of discipline and a personal shame that I will live with for the rest of my life,' Rokov said. 'But what of you? What is your interest in all of this?'

'None of your business.'

'Perhaps the rumors are true, Comrade – you are letting the army obtain and secure land for your oil pipeline through the Balkans,' Rokov said. 'You make up a fantasy story about American spies and Macedonian saboteurs in order to get a recon company to land you on this site, then you busy yourself surveying it. What's next? Will you order a Mi-28 to carry in your bulldozers and cranes?'

'What I would concern myself about, Captain,' Kazakov hissed in a low voice, stepping nose to nose with the Russian infantry officer, 'is your fiancée and her four-year-old daughter in Rostov at her new job at the Zil plant. She just got moved to the graveyard shift so she can work while her daughter is in bed, I understand. It would be a shame to hear that she was hurt coming home after a long night at work.'

'How in hell could you possibly know...?' And then Rokov stopped short. Kazakov knew about his fiancée and her daughter the same way he knew about the Fifty-first doing an airborne assault tonight – he had either powerful connections or well-informed spies, and either way he could not hope to fight him.

'I see we now understand each other,' Kazakov said, nodding and putting on a sly, knowing grin. 'You did a fine job this morning, Captain. The assault was swift, accurate, precise, and well-executed. My suggestion to you: report that these filthy American spies attacked you after your men discovered their spy network, and you had no choice but to defend yourselves. You may even take credit for killing both spies. I'm sure your men can devise a way to make it appear as if the shootings were in self-defense – maybe take these corpses out to the forest and put some bullet holes in their bodies that are going in and out in the proper direction. Let's not have any more cross words between us. I will stay out of your way–'

'And you had better stay out of mine, Kazakov,' Rokov said.

'*Zamyechateel'niy*,' Kazakov said. 'Very good. I see we understand each other perfectly.'

Rokov maintained eye contact with Kazakov for a long moment, but eventually stepped away to supervise the mopping-up operation. Minutes later, more troops started to arrive; already, the first few American soldiers were being herded into the parking lot, hands on top of their heads like captured prisoners of war.

Yes, the operation was indeed going quite well. Kazakov could easily envision the pumping and transfer station right here. The terrain climbed rather steeply just west of here on its way into the Lake Ohrid area, and a pumping station was necessary to get it up and over. Knock a few of these rotting flooded-out buildings down, use the rubble to raise and grade the elevation, and it would work out perfectly. What did these peasants need with a school here? Resen was only fifteen miles away – they had plenty of schools there they could attend.

With luck, he was back on schedule and marching forward nicely to completion. No use in letting a few Americans get in the way.

Coronado, California
the next evening

His son's eyes lit up like on Christmas morning as Patrick pulled the suit from its hanging bag. The overhead lights made the stars on the shoulders and the wings on the left breast pocket sparkle. 'Woo-oo,' Brad said. 'You got a nice suit there, Daddy.'

'Thanks, big guy,' Patrick said.

He pointed at the command navigator wings, a pair of Air Force silver eagle's wings with the rampart crest in the center shield and a wreathed star on top. 'You going fly-ning?' Bradley asked.

'They're going to fly me to Washington.'

'You going to meetings? You going to give a

496

bree-fling?' Bradley didn't wait for the answer, having decided that when Daddy brought the blue suit instead of the green, that it was going to be meetings and briefings. He grabbed one of Patrick's Corfram shoes and pretended it was an airplane, zooming it up and down the uniform and across the Rollaboard suitcase Patrick was packing. 'Time to give a bree-fling again!'

'What are you going to do while I'm in Washington?' Patrick asked. 'What are your standing orders while I'm gone?'

'Take care of Mommy, do as Mommy says, be a good boy, and ... and...'

'One more. And think–'

'And think about Daddy!' Bradley said triumphantly.

'Very good, big guy,' Patrick said. 'High five.' Patrick held up a hand, and Bradley slapped it.

The little boy dropped the shoe he had been playing with onto his father's left foot and wrapped his arms around Patrick's leg. 'I love you, Daddy,' he said, except it sounded more like, 'I wuv you, Daddy.'

Patrick picked up his son and hugged him tightly – he knew exactly what he had said. 'And Daddy loves you, son,' he replied.

'You do good in Wash-ton,' Bradley said, punctuating his suggestion with an upraised index finger.

Patrick tried to sound upbeat. He smiled and said, 'I'll do good, big guy.'

Bradley wriggled out of his dad's arms, picked up the shoe, then rubbed his eye with his free hand and gave the shoe to Patrick. 'I'm *really* tired,' he said, leading the way to his bedroom. 'Maybe it's time for bed.'

'Good idea, tiger.' Patrick followed his son into his bedroom and watched as his son lowered his pull-up diapers so he could check to see if they were wet, climbed up on the stool next to the sink for a drink of water, then carried his stool over to the bed so he could climb in. Patrick tried to put him under the covers without his tattered old blanket, but his son automatically curled up atop the covers with his blanket underneath him and his butt in the air.

He pushed away from the bed long enough to give his father a kiss good-night, then plopped back down. 'You do good tomorrow, Daddy,' Bradley said. 'And turn out the light, please.'

'Good night, big guy.' Bradley peeked at his father over the safety rail to his bed, then smiled and giggled as his father turned back and gave his son a thumbs-up just before he shut off the lights.

Do good tomorrow, Daddy, he said. Yeah, right, Patrick thought.

Patrick joined Wendy in the living room of their high-rise condo overlooking the city of San Diego. Wendy Tork McLanahan had dimmed the lights so that the only illumination in the room was from the city lights filtering through a thin marine layer that had crept over San Diego Bay. She had poured two glasses of Silver Oak Cabernet Sauvignon and had loosened her wavy brunette hair and let it cascade over one of his Sacramento Kings basketball team jerseys – Patrick noticed with a grin that the jersey and a smile was all she wore. He went to her, handed her a glass, and sat beside her. Their glasses touched, and then their lips.

'Bradley blows me away with how much he seems to know and realize,' Patrick said. 'I think he's psychic sometimes.'

'He's our son – what did you expect?' Wendy said with a warm smile. She had been a civilian electronic warfare engineer when she'd met Patrick McLanahan at Dreamland, and since that day their lives had been tightly intertwined – with each other, and with the top-secret research facility in the Nevada desert. If predicted that Bradley would someday be the next Edison or Bill Gates, most folks who knew Bradley's parents would not disagree. 'The little monster actually sent an e-mail to your mother the other day.'

'He what?'

'He sent an e-mail,' Wendy said. 'No kidding. I know he's watched me send messages and reports to Jon on the computer a thousand times, but I thought he was only waiting until he could play "Freddie Fish" or "Pajama Sam" or some other game. He absorbed all he needed to know and sent your mother a page of gibberish – with a "Classified" cover page on it.'

'That's my boy,' Patrick said proudly. He took a sip of wine and tried to relax.

'Did you talk with Dr Canfield today?' she asked.

'Yes – twice,' Patrick said. Colonel Bruce Canfield was the Director of Aviation Neuropsychology at Brooks Air Force Base near San Antonio, Texas, the center in charge of evaluating David Luger following his incident at Dreamland.

'David is still undergoing tests, but he thinks it's a case of something called delayed adjustment disorder. David's memory of past incidents while in the Soviet Union – probably first activated by the Ukrainian crews we've been working with, then cued up again by Samson telling him he might be unbalanced and needing psychological help – activated a stress defense mechanism in his mind. He was able to shut off all external sensory inputs to free him from physical, emotional, and psychological damage.'

'My God, it sounds horrible. Does he think he'll be all right?'

'Too early to say,' Patrick said. 'Adjustment disorder is usually treated by medication at first, which disqualifies Dave from flying and laboratory work. But he also said that adjustment disorders are one of the few conditions that don't automatically keep a person from resuming his duties once the treatment has concluded, and that includes flying. It's a relatively common condition, especially among the military, and Canfield says counseling and treatment are usually very successful. Patients have an excellent chance of recovery.'

'That's good news.' Wendy kept silent for a few long moments, then leaned back against him and wrapped his arm around her body. 'I did some checking – there's room on that flight for me and Brad,' Wendy said.

'I just put him to bed, sweetheart.'

'Bradley would be overjoyed to fly along with you no matter what time it was,' Wendy reminded him. 'The Sky Masters apartment in Crystal City is available, too. I'm ready to go. What do you say?'

'Sweetheart, this thing could either be over in a day, or it'll have just begun, in which case I'll be right back home,' Patrick said. 'There's no use dragging you away from work and Brad away from preschool to spend two entire days on a plane. Let me meet with the Area Defense Counsel, do the preliminaries, and find out where I stand.'

'Jon called again and offered his entire legal staff to help you,' Wendy added. 'I'm sure the chief Area Defense Counsel of the Air Force is good, but Jon can have a dozen of the best litigators and legal researchers at your side with one phone call. Why not at least talk to them?'

Patrick shook his head. 'You know I'm not allowed to talk with contractors about Air Force matters outside of their contracts, or accept any gifts or favors,' he said. 'Staying in the Sky Masters condo, even if you accompanied me there, would look pretty suspicious. Our relationship with Jon and Sky Masters is too cozy already, without him sending in his legal sharks to help me work over the Air Force.'

'That is not what would happen, and that's not what Jon's offering.'

'I know, I know. But still ... I don't know, Wendy. Something's happening here. Things are changing.'

'What do you mean, Patrick?'

He searched his feelings for several long moments, then took another sip of wine and shrugged. 'Wendy, I did what I always do – I'm faced with a problem, a crisis, and I did something about it the best way I knew how with the re-sources I had. Ten years ago, that was okay. Today,

501

I'm being court-martialed for it. Things have changed. I have a feeling that either I need to change with it, or I'll ... cease to exist.' He put on his faraway look, his 'thousand-yard stare,' as if silently querying the faces of his dead friends for help in finding answers. 'I'm not sure if I want to fight the court-martial and retire, or fight it and win, or fight it and go to prison.'

Wendy looked truly surprised. 'Why in hell not?'

'Because it feels to me like there's an alternative life out there, a path opening up for me, and I'll miss it if I do what everyone expects and fight it. If I allow whatever happens to happen, I think I'll be happier.'

'This doesn't sound like the Patrick McLanahan I know.'

'It doesn't sound like him to me either,' Patrick said honestly. 'I know I have friends, and I think I have friends I don't know, enough to take on even the Pentagon. But if I can't see the path I'm meant to take, I don't think starting a brushfire will help me find it.' He held Wendy tighter. 'I know I'm supposed to be talking to you about what I'll say once I get to Washington, that we should discuss and decide this as a family. I also know that I'm supposed to have a plan, an idea of what I want out of my own career and my own life. But truthfully, I have no idea what I'll do. All I'm sure about is that I don't want to march into the Pentagon with a bunch of civilian lawyers and try to engage the brass in combat. I'm not afraid of losing – I'm afraid of creating so much smoke and confusion that I won't see the path I want.' Wendy's body appeared tense, and the fingers stroking his thighs seemed stiff and aimless. 'What is it, sweetie?'

'I have a feeling you're ... tired, that's all,' Wendy said. 'You're tired of the bureaucracy, tired of the fighting, tired of jeopardizing your life over and over again in secret. I wish you could rest, but I know you're not ready to rest. All I see is the good you've done and the contribution to national security you could make, a contribution that doesn't include having your friends turn on you.' She turned to face him. 'Terrill offered you a chance to retire, an honorable discharge with your current rank and time in service, and have your record expunged. I know he gave you a deadline, but I think with your record of achievements and service to the country, that the offer will stand a while longer. I think you should take it.'

'And come to work for you, Jon, and Helen?'

'You'd be a vice president of a major high-tech firm again, getting paid twice what you earn as a one-star general, with better benefits, and with stock options that would double in value every two years,' Wendy said. 'Jon tells me six times a day he wants you back – he's got an office, a car, a plane, your e-mail mailbox, and a locker in the gym ready for you. He's even given you a staff and projects to get started on, in anticipation. Yes, I'd say he wants you back in the worst way.' Wendy lowered her eyes, as if considering her words carefully, then looked at her husband again. 'I know you're not a prideful man, Patrick, but I can't help feeling that part of this has to do with you feeling you were *right* to turn around and fly back to Russia to protect Annie and Dev, that you shouldn't be getting punished for doing what you did. I think you're fighting this to protect your principles.'

'Do you think I was wrong?'

'Don't you see, Patrick?' Wendy asked, almost pleading. 'It doesn't matter. You did it and saved your friends. That's all that matters. You tell me a dozen times a year that Congress or the Air Force could close down Dreamland at any time and give all of you involuntary retirements. You tell me one slip-up, one crash, one more security breach, and you'd all be gone. Half of our salary goes into mutual funds and money market accounts every month because you anticipate everything ending suddenly. When Thomas Thorn got into the White House, you thought your dismissal was imminent.'

'So?'

'So all that time, you were emotionally and mentally prepared for a sudden, perhaps unhappy end. Now, all of a sudden, you're not ready. You're fighting it. Why? It's not your family – you've prepared us well for the day you'd leave the service, or the day you would never come home from a mission. Now, you're not ready. What changed?' Patrick took another sip of wine, then angrily drained the glass and got to his feet. Wendy saw the stern look in his face, and knew she had hit on the source of his anger. 'Terrill Samson, right? You feel betrayed by him. He was a student of Brad Elliott, just like you, and he's in charge of HAWC, and you thought you'd be more ideologically in sync. That's it, isn't it?'

'Maybe a little,' Patrick said. 'I knew from the beginning Terrill didn't have the fire in his gut

504

that Brad did – hell, who does?'

'You do.'

'But they didn't make me commander of HAWC – they made *him* commander,' Patrick said bitterly. 'But that's not who betrayed me.'

'Who is it, then?'

'Thorn – Thomas Nathaniel Thorn, the damned President of the United States,' Patrick replied angrily. 'TNT, the Young Turk, the New Age president, the assassin from Desert Storm turned peacenik isolationist. He doesn't bother to show himself to the American people. Doesn't show up for his inauguration, doesn't show for the State of the Union speech. All this crap about doing away with the Army, with not having any troops stationed overseas, with not guaranteeing the security of any foreign nation – it's driving me crazy. I feel like my country's going down the toilet and I can't do a thing about it. Thorn is the one who encourages commanders like Terrill Samson to turn their backs on their friends and get rid of their warriors, just like he's turning his back on our allies and kicking our soldiers out onto the street.'

'So you think you're going to Washington to fight the President of the United States?' Wendy asked incredulously. 'Patrick, you have got to think a little clearer right now. You can't go to Washington with a chip on your shoulder. There are too many folks there, wearing too many stars, ready – some eager – to knock that chip off for you, long before you ever reach Sixteen Hundred Pennsylvania Avenue. Even Brad Elliott never had the nerve to take on the White House.'

She stood with him, took his hands, and looked deeply into his eyes. 'I'm being selfish now, Patrick, but I think I've earned the right to say this: think about your family before you say one word there tomorrow. Whatever the reasons you feel right now, I'm telling you, forget your feelings and your anger and think about your son and me. If you lose, you'll go to prison. Your son will visit you in Leavenworth, along with all the other wrecked military lives, and he'll see you like he'll see them. How will you explain that what you were fighting for was right? How long will it take even our intelligent son to understand? You may be justified and you may even truly be right, but you'll be in prison as surely as if you were wrong. *Julius Caesar* is a fine heroic play, but it's still a tragedy, because the hero is destroyed at the end.'

Patrick could not look at her, but he didn't have to. She embraced him tightly, warmly, then kissed his lips. 'You'd better get going,' she said simply, and turned and left for the bedroom.

Nellis AFB, near Las Vegas, Nevada
that same time

'*Shto bi khaoteeteye?* What in hell do you want?' David Luger exclaimed over the phone. 'I can't believe you called me here. Are you trying to make me jump in front of a train or something?'

'Calm yourself, Colonel,' Colonel-General Roman Smoliy, chief of the Ukrainian Air Force, said from his Distinguished Visitors suite at Nellis Air Force Base. 'This is important and has

506

nothing to do with you.' He was calling on a secure line set up in his room – if it was tapped by the Americans, it was tapped, and there was nothing he could do about it.

'So what is it?' Luger asked. He plopped down on his bed, almost unable to move but not daring to miss a word either. Luger was in a visiting officers' room at Brooks Air Force Base near San Antonio, Texas, undergoing a three-day series of tests by the Aeromedical Consultation Services, as a prelude to a full workup by the Aviation Neuropsychiatry Department of the Air Force Hospital, to discover exactly what had caused his sudden paralysis episode. *Shto eta znachyeet?*'

'Stop talking Russian to me, damn you, Colonel,' Smoliy snapped. 'You are no longer a Soviet prisoner, and I am no longer working for a Soviet research laboratory. I am Ukrainian, and you are American.'

Luger took a deep breath, silently chastising himself for his strange and unexplainable confusion in time and space. 'What do you want?'

'I need information,' Smoliy said. 'The Turks are hurrying out of here as fast as they can pack up, but I cannot find out a thing. General McLanahan is gone, home I think, and General Samson is not saying a word. This whole place is going upside-down. You are the only high-ranking person I could find.'

'I'm not exactly in the loop right now either, General,' Luger admitted.

'Where are you? Why are you not here?'

Luger was about to tell Smoliy to stuff his questions and his fake concern up his ass, but he was too busy thinking about the situation he had left at Dreamland: Samson on the warpath, Patrick and Rebecca probably on their way to be court-martialed – things were going to hell in a hand-basket.

To his own surprise, Luger began running it all down to the Ukrainian general: the spy in Russia, the stealth warplane shed uncovered, the rescue missions, the charges leveled against them, the court-martial, and Luger's psychoparalytic reaction. 'It's this stealth fighter, General, I know it,' Luger concluded. 'Someone is directing these attacks against Albania and Macedonia. The NATO AWACS plane just got in the way. The question is, why?'

To Luger's double shock, the first thing Smoliy asked was 'And how are you doing, Colonel?'

Luger was thunderstruck. Out of all the questions a Ukrainian general could have asked about possible Russian stealth air strikes in Europe, Smoliy asked about *him*. 'I ... I'm doing okay,' Luger heard himself say.

'What do the doctors say? What are they doing?'

'Just a bunch of tests,' Luger replied. 'It's a standard battery, and a physical exam to start the medical exploratory process. All the usual stuff, along with a shitload of psychiatric tests.'

'Ah. Psychiatric tests. When I saw you the other night, I thought I noticed a sort of dissociation. I never truly believed you might be suffering from a psychotic condition. Could it be related to what happened at Fisikous and then seeing me again?'

'Possibly.' A strange sensation began to creep into Luger's brain, starting in a spot in the back of his head. What Smoliy said made more sense than anything else he had heard in years of therapy or hours of tests and questioning here at Brooks. But it made sense – because no one at Brooks knew, or ever would know, of the Fisikous episode, because that might reveal details about the Kavaznya mission, which in turn would reveal details about Dreamland. Smoliy did not know a lot about Dreamland, but he knew everything about Fisikous, and he could certainly make the connection now. The key to whatever was going on inside Luger's head would be locked away forever. The government would rather have him locked away in a loony bin for the rest of his life than reveal anything about Dreamland.

'Could it be,' Smoliy's voice caught, cracked, then went on, 'that it was what I *did* to you that has caused this to happen?'

Luger instantly felt sorrow for him – and it was a strange feeling, because it seemed like an eternity since David Luger had felt *anything* for *anyone* else. In fact, not since being rescued from Fisikous had David Luger been able to connect on an emotional level with another human being. He had tried to do so with Annie Dewey – but then he had to remind himself that it was Annie who had been trying to connect with *him*. He had never really contributed much to the relationship.

Annie.

It was as if a thick fog had just lifted from inside his brain. All this time, Annie had been trying to get closer to him – holding his hand, inviting him to meals, spending time with him while he worked on the flight line or in the labs. It was as if he was watching himself on television. He had been ignoring her all this time. Had he ever tried to return her kindness, her warmth? Did he even know *how* to do it? All this time, he'd been pushing her away with his emotionless attitude. Now Deverill wanted her, and David was watching her depart his life. Why? Did he think that's what he deserved? Did he want to be alone because he thought he only deserved to be alone, that being alone was the only way he could hide the pain and humiliation of being tortured at Fisikous?

Funny – it finally took one of his chief tormentors talking about his internal pain to show him the source of his own loneliness. Someone else was experiencing the same detachment.

'I ... I don't ... no, I don't think so,' David said. When moments before he had hated this man, wanted to kill him with his bare hands – now he found himself not only feeling sorry for him, but actually apologizing to him! 'That was too long ago, General. I've been through a lot of stuff since then. Don't blame yourself.'

'I could not bear to think I have hurt another human being on that level,' Smoliy said. 'I am trained to kill the enemy with speed and efficiency, but I would never have thought I could ever mentally hurt someone, cause them mental pain. It is too horrible to comprehend, like trying to think what it was like for a prison guard to exterminate a Jewish prisoner during the Holocaust.'

'Forget it, General ... Roman,' Luger said. 'I'm the wacko in this group, remember.'

He heard the Ukrainian chuckle, then he had to move the receiver away from his ear to avoid the general's big, booming laugh. 'You Americans, you surprise me,' he said. 'You are in a mental hospital, and you make jokes.'

'General, you've got to find out what happened out there, find out why the Turks are leaving,' Luger said.

'Things are exploding in the Balkans...'

'I heard that,' Luger said. 'Albania declared war on Macedonia. Some kind of border skirmish set them off.'

'But there's more than that. Russian and German peacekeepers are swarming into Kosovo, Macedonia, and Albania. KFOR has all but disbanded. The British and French are still in Kosovo, but the other major powers are sweeping south. NATO seems to be handing the fate of the Balkans over to Russia and Germany.'

'All this sounds too staged,' Luger said. 'Just like that attack on Kukes. A small hot spot that quickly spreads into a major wildfire, and the Russians and the Germans ready and eager on such short notice to push right in.'

'You think there is a puppetmaster at work here? A Russian puppetmaster, to be exact?'

'A Russian puppetmaster with a stealth fighter-bomber,' Luger said. 'I'll lay odds that the Russian stealth fighter has struck again. The Russian—' Luger froze, his words jamming in his throat until all he could exclaim was 'Oh, my God...'

'What is it, David?'

'Roman, the spy that was rescued in Russia was working at a facility at Zhukovsky Air Base run by the Metyor Aerospace firm.'

'So you said.'

'Don't you get it, Roman? Don't you remember what Metyor used to be?'

'I do not know this. Who–?' Then he stopped, and Luger heard a sharp intake of air even over the scrambled line. 'Good God ... you mean, *Fisikous? Metyor* is *Fisikous?* Are you telling me...?'

'The stealth fighter that launched from Zhukovsky, the one suspected of attacking Kukes – it's the Fisikous-179,' Luger shouted. 'It has to be! There's no other stealth fighter-bomber that can fly those missions in all of Europe!'

'But the stealth aircraft were destroyed in that attack on Fisikous.'

'They weren't destroyed, Roman. I took the Fi-170 *Tuman!* Me and General McLanahan.'

'Neprada!'

'It's true. He was leading a rescue mission, him and Colonel Briggs, when the CIA discovered I was at Fisikous. But Russia was on its way to destroying Lithuania and rebuilding the Soviet Union, and we had to act. We took the Fisikous-170 and flew it out of there. We flew it to Scotland and dismantled it. But the United States never set out to destroy the facility – they were looking for *me*. The facility itself was almost untouched.'

'Incredible ... unbelievable!' Smoliy breathed. 'So it must be the second model, the Fisikous-179.'

'We took the curled-wing flying prototype model, so it must be the forward-swept-wing model,' Luger said. 'We started working on an aircraft that had just as great an air-to-air capability as it did an air-to-ground bombing capability. We hadn't even rolled it out yet – it was still years from its first flight.'

'Maybe whoever bought Fisikous finished the Fi-179 and is now flying it,' Smoliy surmised.

'Fursenko,' Luger said. 'Pyotr Fursenko. He was the director of the facility. I think the spy had him on tape, along with Pavel Kazakov.'

'Kazakov? The drug dealer? That scum runs Fisikous?'

'He runs Metyor Aerospace,' Luger said. 'And he runs several other companies, too.'

'*Tak*. He runs construction companies, shipping, banking, petroleum, exporting, mining–'

'Petroleum? I remember something about him building a pipeline from the Caspian Sea to the Black Sea.'

'Yes. That was completed a year or so ago. He pumps almost a million barrels a day from the Caspian and ships it through Azerbaijan and Georgia. Ukraine buys much of it. He–' And then Smoliy stopped and gasped again. 'And I heard he wanted to build another pipeline, a huge one, from the Black Sea to Western Europe, to bypass the bottlenecks in the Bosporus Straits and Turkey's high transit tariffs.'

'Western Europe from the Black Sea,' Luger mused. 'That means through Bulgaria–'

'And Macedonia and Albania,' Smoliy said incredulously.

'It can't be,' Luger said. 'It can't be that simple.'

'The word was that Kazakov did not build the pipeline because of the war in Kosovo, the unstable relations between Albania and the West, and the West's increasing intervention in Macedonia – perhaps even Macedonia to join NATO,'

513

Smoliy said. 'But with Thorn wishing to disengage from NATO, and Russia wanting to secure its positions in the Balkans, the opportunity presents itself to get the pipeline built...'

'With the help of the Russian army,' Luger said. 'Russian "peacekeepers" swarm into the Balkans and secure the region, and Kazakov is free to build the pipeline. And if any governments balk, they find a city or maybe even their national capital under attack.'

'Under attack by a stealth aircraft – unseen, silent, and untraceable,' Smoliy said. 'Russia can claim complete ignorance of the attacks, and Western spy satellites have no idea where to look for the stealth aircraft or have any idea where it will strike again.'

'It must have struck in Turkey,' Luger said. 'That's why the Turks are packing up and going home – their country is under attack.'

'There was nothing in the news about an attack on Turkey,' Smoliy said. 'But I cannot find out anymore.'

'I think I can,' Luger said. 'It might be a problem getting out of here, but I'll try.'

'Are you a prisoner there?'

'No,' Luger said, 'but I'm not free to go, either.'

'Says who, David?' Smoliy asked. 'The same people who want to court-martial you? They send you to a hospital because you might be going insane? If you are, they will confine you for the rest of your life, but if you are not, they will court-martial you? What loyalty do you have for these men?'

'Good point,' David said. 'But I'll need to get

plugged back into the information network at Dreamland.'

'And I know just the person to set that up for you,' Smoliy said. 'Be patient. We will be in touch shortly.'

Dozens of trucks rolled up onto Nellis Air Force Base's main parking ramp, and crews from many nations were helping load pallets of supplies into two Turkish C-135 military cargo planes. At the same time, crews were busily preflighting the Turkish F-16 fighters, preparing them for immediate takeoff. Crews were also loading weapons aboard the F-16s – all of the Turkish fighters that were fully capable of carrying air-to-air weapons were armed with AIM-9 Sidewinder missiles plus ammunition for the internal guns. The cargo planes were going to have fighter escorts all the way home. All the men and women worked quickly, purposefully, some even feverishly...

...as if they were preparing for war.

Inside, the mass departure briefing had just concluded, and the crews were splitting up into individual flights. The Turks worked swiftly, speaking only Turkish, not willing even to attempt to slow their pace long enough to translate their thoughts into English. American crews simply helped out where they could and stayed out of the way. This time, it was not their fight. Their commander-in-chief said so. Their allies, their fellow air warriors, were going home to prepare to fight the unseen, invisible enemy on their own.

Colonel-General Roman Smoliy, commander of the Ukrainian Air Force, stepped to the door of one of the briefing rooms as the flight briefing finished. Major-General Erdal Sivarek, chief of staff of the Turkish Air Force, was packing up his papers, preparing to depart. 'I need to speak with you, sir,' Smoliy said in English.

Sivarek looked at the big Ukrainian. 'I am sorry, Colonel-General, but I do not have time.'

'I received a briefing about the incident over the Black Sea,' Smoliy said. 'I have information you must hear, and I have a proposal–'

'What incident over the Black Sea?' Sivarek asked. 'I know of no such incident. I must go.'

'General, I know you lost an F-16 fighter earlier today while it was on a training exercise over the Black Sea,' Smoliy said. 'I know your pilots and your ground radar controllers never saw whatever downed your plane. But because you have some of your country's best fighter pilots here, your government has ordered all of your forces returned to Turkey immediately and to make preparations for war, although you do not know against whom yet – Kurds, Russians, Greeks, Iranians, Iraqis, Syrians, Martians.'

Sivarek's eyes were wide with disbelief – he knew there was no use in denying it any longer. 'How do you know all this, General?'

'Because I briefed him, sir,' Major Nancy Cheshire said. She stepped into the briefing room and closed the door behind her. 'I intercepted the satellite feeds and radar data, and combined them with CIA listening post intercepts to piece the incident together. I don't know why you chose not to brief NATO on what happened–'

'NATO? Why bother with NATO?' Sivarek

snorted, scowling at the lady test pilot. 'NATO has all but ignored Turkey ever since we were inducted into the organization. We were allowed to be the only non-Christian members of your exclusive European club only because you did not want us falling into the Russian sphere of influence, perhaps even turning communist ourselves. My government appears to have had enough of your weak leadership in NATO, first with your aimless and politically motivated interventions in the Balkans, and now by your insistence in not getting directly involved in affairs that concern your European allies. Turkey will take care of itself, with no help from America.'

'General, I'm not going to say our relations with Turkey have been exemplary,' Cheshire said. 'I'm not going to apologize or offer any explanations. But I'm telling you now – we think we know who attacked your F-16 tonight, and we think we have a way to help defend against future attacks.'

'Who was it?'

'We believe it was a stealth fighter-bomber,' Smoliy said. 'A Soviet fighter-bomber, built years ago but only recently activated. It is a combination fighter and bomber, with an equally effective air-to-air as well as air-to-ground attack capability. Its stealth technology is second-generation at best, but it is extremely effective against standard air defense systems – including those deployed in my country, and yours.'

'How could you know so much?'

'Because I helped build it,' Smoliy said. 'Years ago, in a Soviet research and development facility in Lithuania.' And he quickly, breathlessly ex-

517

plained everything. Sivarek's eyes were soon wide in complete and utter shock. 'We believe this aircraft is responsible for the attacks against Albania, the downing of the NATO AWACS aircraft, and your F-16. We can help you find him.'

'But how? If it is a stealth aircraft, how can such a plane be found, unless you simply stumble over it?'

'Because we know everything involved in its design, construction, testing, and capabilities,' Cheshire replied.

'The general was just a test pilot – he said himself he did not even fly it. How could he possibly know all these things?'

'Because we also have the aircraft's chief design engineer, sir,' Cheshire replied. 'Colonel Luger.'

'*Luger?* Luger is really a Russian aerospace engineer? I always thought the man was odd.'

'Luger's an American who was ... involuntarily a guest of the Soviet Union,' Cheshire explained. 'He was forced to apply his knowledge and expertise into building Soviet warplanes, including the one we believe is flying right now.'

'This ... this is extraordinary,' Sivarek breathed. 'All this, just so a money-hungry gangster can build a *pipeline* through the Balkans?'

'What would you do for a hundred million dollars a day, sir?' Cheshire asked. 'That's how much Kazakov can earn if he builds his pipeline. But more important, Russia occupies the Balkans again.'

'And if this plan works, what will stop Russia from moving against other countries so they can build more pipelines and occupy more territory?'

Smoliy asked. 'You know as well as I that there are two nations in the region that will certainly be prime targets for both this stealth warplane and the Russian army...'

'Turkey and Ukraine,' Sivarek responded. 'Neutralize both nations, and the Black Sea belongs to Russia, just as it did in the Soviet era.' Sivarek grew silent, his mind racing.

'You are thinking of your homeland, General, no?' Smoliy asked. 'You are thinking, who stands with Turkey? Believe me, sir, I have thought of little else regarding my homeland as well. No one stands with Ukraine at all. We are already dependent on the Russian Federation for so much of our raw materials, trade, foreign debt, and political influence. But if we opposed Russian interference in the region, to whom can we turn? We have already been battered to near obliteration by Russian bombs, and we are not yet full members of NATO.'

'Why is your president doing this to us?' Sivarek snapped at Cheshire again, running his fingers through his hair in confusion and frustration. 'Why has America become so weak? Do you enjoy your prosperity so much that you are willing to see madmen destroy the rest of the world so you will have no more competition?'

'You know that's not the situation, sir,' Cheshire explained. 'I believe our president wants to show the world how strong our country is, not by stationing tens of thousands of troops on foreign soil like the world's only supreme superpower, but by letting our friends, allies, and adversaries have their own identity, free of American influence and interference.'

Sivarek snorted. 'Pretty words ... to describe isolationism. Or cowardice.'

'I would call President Thorn a lot of things, but not a coward,' Cheshire said. 'He's the first American president in the last hundred years not to rely on American military power to back up our foreign policy interests. Think about it, General – you're arguing that America is withdrawing back inside its own borders, while at the same time you're fearful that another country will march across yours. Do you want foreigners on Turkish soil or not?'

'You understand so little about life in my country, Major,' Sivarek said. 'Turkey is surrounded by enemies. We chose to look to the West for the strength to survive. We feel the West has turned its back on us. It appears Germany has joined Russia in spreading its influence through Europe – who will join with the Republic of Turkey?'

'Ukraine will, General,' Smoliy said. 'I think you are wrong about Thorn. If he wants to bring his troops home, so be it – I would not want Ukrainian troops stationed in any foreign country for any reason. But if you want an ally to stand squarely against the Russian Federation in the Black Sea region, Ukraine will stand with you.'

Sivarek looked at Smoliy with a shocked expression. 'An alliance ... between Turkey and Ukraine?' he asked. 'Is it possible? Can we stand against the might of the Russian army?'

'I have served in the Soviet army and I have seen the Russian army at work, and they are not as imposing as they seem,' Smoliy said confidently.

'Do not pay attention to all their propaganda. Besides, we do not think of it as having to take on the entire Russian army – we just need to exert our own influence in the Black Sea region. This gangster Kazakov wants to ship oil across the Black Sea to fill his trans-Balkan pipeline – he will have to do it with our blessing. Any problems from Russia or from this stealth warplane, and those Metyor oil terminals in Bulgaria and Georgia are smoking holes in the ground!'

'What will keep Russia from decimating both our countries if we dare oppose them?'

'Let Russia worry about what they will do first,' Smoliy said. 'They are acting very bold and think they are clever because they think no union of nations will oppose them. The only way we can hope to survive a confrontation is to stay together. One nation, even one as large as Ukraine or Turkey, can be swept aside with ease by Russia. But two such nations – that is an entirely different situation.'

Sivarek nodded, looking at Smoliy with a growing realization in his eyes. He suddenly did not feel quite as alone as he had just moments before. He turned to Cheshire and asked, 'And what of you, Major? What of the United States?'

'I'm not ready to completely count America out yet, sir,' Nancy replied. 'President Thorn is a man of deep personal beliefs and convictions, he's intelligent, and he has the power of law on his side – he doesn't play politics. But he's a young president, too, and perhaps he can be convinced that not all foreign alliances are bad for the United States. Plus, he's a military man. He understands military threats and military geopolitics.'

'Your confidence and loyalty to your hippie president does not inspire me in the least bit, young pilot,' Sivarek said, with a dark smile. 'But he has left my country with very few alternatives.' He turned to Smoliy, straightened his shoulders, crisply bowed his head once, then extended a hand to the big Ukrainian general. 'I will be pleased to convey your thoughts and wishes to my government, General. I pledge to you that I will do everything in my power to see to it that both our countries act in complete friendship and mutual security interests. It would be my pleasure and honor to see an alliance between our countries become a reality.'

Smoliy took the Turkish general's hand in his, then gave him a big bear hug and kissed him on both cheeks. *'Z velikim zadovolennyam!* This gives me much hope and pleasure, sir! And if we are both wiped off the face of the earth, it is good to know we will burn together!' He turned to Nancy Cheshire. 'I will notify the base commander that my forces will be departing soon. But I have a few requests of General Samson before we leave.'

'May I make a suggestion, sir?' Cheshire asked. 'Let me give General McLanahan a call first.'

'Oh? A little dissension in the ranks, I see?' Smoliy chuckled. 'Or is General McLanahan the real person in charge?'

'No, General Samson is *definitely* the man in charge,' Nancy said. 'But for what you two are cooking up right now, I think Patrick will be the one to help you – as long as he survives his ordeal in Washington first.'

Chapter Eight

The Pentagon, Washington, DC
the next morning

He felt stupid at first, with everyone watching. The place was packed, and most of the people looked as if they had nothing better to do than to watch him. Or was it just because he was here to face the music, and he thought everyone here knew it?

The nearly six-hundred-acre Pentagon Reservation was like a little city unto itself, so it was generally easy to hide among the over twenty-six thousand military and civilian Department of Defense employees and three thousand staff persons there. You automatically felt anonymous when you walked into the place. The Pentagon building itself was an impressive, imposing structure encompassing thirty-four acres and almost four million square feet of office space, making it one of the largest office buildings in the world. Built in just sixteen months at the beginning of World War II over a former garbage dump and swamp, it was said that the building was designed so efficiently that anyone could walk from one end of it to the other in less than ten minutes (although it could take as long as thirty minutes just to walk in from the parking lot). If you were one of the thousands of persons walking into the North Parking entrance, you could easily feel insignificant indeed, like a tiny ant climbing into a huge anthill.

Even at six A.M., the Pentagon Officers

Athletic Club at the end of Corridor Eight was nearly full. Patrick McLanahan would have liked to use a treadmill or a recumbent bicycle – since there were so many of them, lined up three deep practically the entire width of the complex, he would have felt a lot less conspicuous. But every one of the dozens of machines was already taken, so he had to go with his trusty weight machines. Besides, some of the soldiers on the treadmills, even the older ones, were jogging or running on them at a pace that made Patrick cringe. The POAC did not have the newer weight machines, the ones that electronically set and varied the resistance, so Patrick did it the old-fashioned way – set a weight, tried it, adjusted it, then did three sets of ten reps with heavy weights. Once he got into the rhythm, he forgot about being the only guy in the entire facility lifting weights.

His body quickly shifted to automatic workout mode, freeing his mind to work on other problems – like what was going to happen to his career and his life now.

He was gone from the High-Technology Weapons Center, dismissed for security reasons pending court-martial, after twelve occasionally turbulent, oftentimes dangerous, most times thrilling off-and-on years. When he'd arrived there in 1988, HAWC – known then simply as Groom Lake Test Range – had been little more than a collection of old weather-beaten Atomic Energy Commission wooden shacks and bird's-nest-infested hangars surrounding an old World War II runway built on, then hidden on, the dry lake bed, with a few high-tech security updates added by

Lieutenant-General Brad Elliott, its first full-time commander, in order to attract the attention of military scientists and Pentagon program managers. Over the years, under Brad Elliott, Dreamland had grown, expanded, modernized, and then finally taken the lead in futuristic weapons and aircraft research and development. Patrick had been there to see most of it.

With Brad gone, Patrick had hoped that he might someday take over the reins at Dreamland and take it to the next level of innovation and leadership. A command assignment at Dreamland was considered a sure ticket to a four-star billet. That was almost certainly true – if you could adapt to the strict security and compartmentalization and ignore the fact that for the entire time you were there and for some time after you departed, you became virtually invisible, even dead to the rest of the world. You quickly had to learn to live with the fact that being part of the future of the US military would forever alter your life.

Patrick had accepted that fact, and even learned to enjoy it. Having a wife who used to work there helped considerably. But it took a special mind-set to work at Dreamland, just as it surely took a special mind-set to work at the Five-Sided Potomac Puzzle Palace. Patrick preferred the hot, dry, wide-open skies of Groom Lake to the stifling, confining, prisonlike feel of this place.

In between sets, he was able to peek at the televisions throughout the POAC. They were filled with news stories about the recently declared war between Albania and Macedonia, the unraveling of the Dayton Peace Accords and the cease-fire in

Kosovo, and the expansion of German and Russian peacekeeping forces in the Balkans to try to maintain order, on the heels of a rapid American withdrawal from the region. But mostly, the stories were about the dismantling of the American military and the American loss of prestige as the protector of world democracy.

Maybe it was good that I'm getting out now, Patrick thought grimly, as he started working on lat pull-downs. The US military looked as if it was in the midst of a complete cultural and ideological meltdown – thanks to the new hippie president and his eighteenth-century ideas. They just had no place in the twenty-first century. Unfortunately, the United States was about to find this out the hard way.

More folks were looking at him again, and Patrick realized he was pumping away at the weight machines like a maniac. The more he watched the rapid, shocking dismantling and denigration of the military in which he had spent most of his adult life, the angrier he became. The workout was supposed to relax him before he went on to his Pentagon appointments, but they were unfortunately having the opposite effect. It was time to go and face his future.

Screw 'em, Patrick told himself. If they want to take my stars or courtmartial me, let them try. I'll fight them every last step of the way. The military is worth a fight ... at least, the *old* military, the one Patrick thought he knew, was worth it.

He showered, then dressed in his Class A uniform. For the first time in many years, he studied himself in a full-length mirror. It wasn't often he wore Class A's, and the blue cotton-polyester outfit was shiny and oddly creased from disuse and improper storage. The single silver stars, given to him by the former president of the United States Kevin Martindale, and the shiny command navigator wings given to him by Brad Elliott, looked awfully good, but everything else seemed extraordinarily plain. Only two rows of ribbons, the same as he'd had as a junior captain – Brad Elliott didn't believe in awards and decorations and prohibited the release of any information whatsoever from Dreamland that might reveal something about its activities.

A rather plain uniform, he thought. Like his uniform, maybe his career in the Air Force really didn't amount to anything after all. Even though he had done a lot of very cool, very exciting things, in the end maybe it didn't matter, any more than he did among all the superstar military men and women in the Pentagon.

As he put the uniform on and prepared for his meetings, Patrick realized with surprise that it would possibly be the last time he would ever wear this uniform – except perhaps at his court-martial.

After dressing, Patrick went right to the H.H. 'Hap' Arnold Executive Corridor and the Secretary of the Air Force's and Air Staff offices. Although HAWC was 'overtly' run by Headquarters Air Force Research Laboratory, Air Force Materiel Command, at Wright-Patterson Air Force Base near Dayton, Ohio (the actual chain of command was classified, but if anyone did any checking that's what they would find), the work at HAWC was so classified that the Secretary of the

Air Force himself, Steven C. Bryant, oversaw most matters dealing with HAWC.

Patrick's appointments stemmed from his court-martial – as Terrill Samson promised, formal charges against him and David Luger had been preferred at the close of business the day of their meeting – so his first stop was the offices of the Air Staff. At first the chief Area Defense Counsel from Air Force Materiel Command headquarters, a full colonel, had been assigned to his case, and he had been given all the preliminary briefings and paperwork. That was all window dressing, of course, because none of this would ever go through the normal legal channels. The matter stayed at Wright-Pat for less than twenty-four hours before being referred directly to the two-star Air Force Judge Advocate General (TJAG) at the Pentagon.

His 0730 appointment with TJAG lasted five minutes. The two-star's recommendation: request early retirement at current rank and time in service and end this thing with an honorable discharge and an unblemished record. All the paperwork was ready, the chief Air Force Area Defense Counsel, a one-star general, standing by to answer any questions. The Area Defense Counsels were the Air Force's 'defense attorneys,' answerable to no one but the chief of staff of the Air Force, General Victor Hayes. He, too, recommended he request early retirement; he had reviewed the memoranda from the Secretary of Defense and found the offer of a clear record, full time in grade and service, and an honorable discharge complete and acceptable, even generous considering the seriousness of the charges.

Patrick's simple answer: 'No, sir.'

Patrick's next stop was the office of the three-star Deputy Chief of Staff for Personnel. Again behind closed doors, he was notified that his security clearance had been taken away, he no longer had a nuclear weapons security or surety authorization, was no longer authorized to fly as a crew member in military aircraft, and could not handle or employ any kinds of weapons, from an airborne laser all the way down to a handgun. Patrick was also notified that his Air Force Specialty Code had been changed from an XO, Commander and Director, to OX, or 'Other' – 'other' in this case meaning a defendant in a court-martial case, an officer with no specialty, no responsibilities, no unit, no team. The change in AFSC would be entered into his official personnel records for everyone to see, virtually guaranteeing that he would never be selected for another assignment, never selected for promotion, and never be given any awards or decorations. That record could also be made public, so any future employers would see it, too, guaranteeing that he would never be chosen to sit on a board of directors or be hired for any position, either home or abroad, that required a security clearance.

Each time Patrick was told of some new surprise, he was required to sign a form notifying him that he understood everything that had been said and all of the possible consequences of what was happening. At the same time, each time he was warned of some dire consequence or advised about some new potentially embarrassing or stressful step in the courtmartial process, he was

531

offered another chance to voluntarily retire with full rank, time in service, his records expunged, and a completely honorable discharge – definitely 'carrot and stick' tactics. Each time, his answer was the same: 'No, sir.'

By the time he'd finished, Patrick felt like a gang of thugs had beaten him. His briefcase was stuffed with dozens of copies of all of the forms, letters, memos, and directives outlining the beginning of the end of his seventeen-year Air Force career.

When Patrick emerged from the meeting with the DCS/Personnel office, a lieutenant colonel with gold piping on his shoulder was waiting just outside the door: 'Sir, General Hayes would like to have a word with you,' he said simply, and led the way out. Well, Patrick thought, he couldn't get it any worse from the Chief of Staff than from all the other Air Staff officers he had already encountered. Might as well get it over with.

General Victor 'Jester' Hayes's office was large, with a twelve-person triangular videoconference table setup and a comfortable casual conversation pit in front of his desk, but it was simply decorated, with pictures and items celebrating the history and advancements of the US Air Force rather than celebrating his own career. Although Jester's undergraduate degree had been in engineering from the Air Force Academy, his first love was twentieth-century American history, especially as it related to aviation. His office was like a small aviation museum: a copy of the Wright brothers' patent for the first powered airplane; a machine gun from a Curtis-Jenny biplane flown during World War I; a Norden bomb sight; a control stick from his beloved F-15 Eagle; and photographs galore of aviation pioneers, aces, and Air Force Medal of Honor recipients.

The history buff was right now seated at the base of the triangular conference table, facing the triangle's apex and a bank of large video monitors along the wall. Seated beside him, Patrick recognized, was the deputy chief of staff, General Tom 'Turbo' Muskoka, and the deputy chief of staff for operations, Lieutenant-General Wayne 'Wombat' Falke. They were all three seated before computer terminals, making notes and reading e-mail messages and computer reports. Muskoka and Falke looked angrily at McLanahan as he was led over to them; Hayes did not look at him, but was studying the monitors and talking on the telephone.

As were most televisions in every military installation Patrick had ever visited in the last ten years, one of the large monitors on the wall was tuned to CNN. The 'Breaking News' logo was all over the screen. It looked like a videotape archive of wreckage from a plane crash; then he gulped as he saw the caption 'Near Moscow, Russian Federation.' Patrick McLanahan had to struggle not to look at the big screen as he stood at attention before the conference table and the three Air Staff generals.

Hayes barked something into the phone, practically threw the receiver on its cradle, took a gulp of coffee, and then glanced at Patrick. 'We found your Vampire, General,' he growled. He hit the ENTER button on his computer terminal with an angry stab to issue his directives, then motioned toward the screen. 'Stand at ease. Take a look. Recognize anything?'

'Yes, sir. That's Vampire One.'

'How do you know for sure?'

Patrick went over to the large-screen monitor and hit the digital replay button – most televisions now had the capability of digitally recording the last two hours of a broadcast – until he came to the shot he'd seen when he'd first come in. 'I saw the shot of the tail section. Our planes don't have a very tall vertical stabilizer, and Vampire One didn't have a horizontal stabilizer – it used adaptive wing technology for pitch control.'

'What's that?' General Falke asked.

'We found that we don't need to use conventional flight control surfaces on planes anymore, sir – all we need to do is change the nature of the air flowing over any surface of an aircraft,' Patrick explained. 'We use tiny hydraulic devices to bend the aircraft skin, all controlled by air data computers. A change too small to be seen by the naked eye can make any surface create lift or drag. We're experimenting with the possibility of building a B-1 bomber with twice the speed and efficiency with wings half the normal size – we can turn the entire fuselage into a wing. We can make a brick fly like a paper airplane with this technology.' The three generals looked apprehensively at McLanahan.

'The Russians could've sawed off sections of the tail to make it look like one of yours,' General Muskoka mumbled.

'How would they know what it looked like, sir – and why would they bother?' Patrick asked. He scrolled through the images. 'Here's definite proof, sir: a LADAR array. The Vampire used six of these laser radars for targeting, terrain following, aircraft warning, missile tracking, intercepts, station keeping, surveillance, everything. It could see fifty miles in any direction, even into space. The design of that array was one of our most closely guarded secrets.'

'And now the Russians have it – and they're trotting out their prize for everyone to see,' Muskoka said acidly. 'If your Captain Dewey had followed orders, McLanahan, this never would've happened.'

'If given the opportunity to do so, sir, I'd authorize her to do it again,' Patrick said.

'That attitude, mister, is why you're here today!' Muskoka snapped. 'That's how come *you* almost got shot down, why your friend Terrill Samson entered charges against you, and that's why your career is going to come to an abrupt, unfortunate end. You don't seem to grasp what's going on here.'

'Permission to speak freely, sir?'

'I advise you to keep your mouth shut, General,' Muskoka said.

'Same here,' General Hayes said. 'But speak your mind if you want.'

'Major Deverill and Captain Dewey did an outstanding job rescuing Madcap Magician and Siren,' Patrick said. 'Siren had valuable information on Russian activities that are right now threatening to disrupt all of Europe. We got definite proof that the experimental Russian fighter-bomber from the Metyor Aerospace plant at Zhukovsky bombed that Albanian village–'

'The ends do not justify the means, Patrick,' Hayes said. 'I would've thought after seventeen years in the Air Force and twelve years watching Brad Elliott get slapped down by Washington, you'd understand that. Unfortunately, you're going to find out the hard way.'

'My God, look at that,' Falke breathed. Patrick looked. CNN was now showing actual civilian satellite photos of Elliott Air Force Base. The resolution showed a lot of detail – he could easily count the aboveground hangars and buildings, and he could see the mobile control tower that was out only for a launch, which meant the photo had been taken just before or just after a rare daytime flight test. The captions identified the image as the top-secret Air Force research base north of Las Vegas that was the home base of the B-1 bomber that the Russians had shot down. Other amateur photos taken by 'UFO-hunters' that sneaked out to Dreamland – some several years old – showed ground-level details of some of the larger buildings; superimposed graphics showed where the runway in Groom Lake was located. They were pretty darn accurate, Patrick thought, except the real runway was much longer and wider.

'How in hell did they know the plane came from Dreamland?' Falke asked.

'Because the President told them, sir,' Patrick replied.

'*What?*'

'He's right,' General Hayes said. 'The President told Russian president Sen'kov everything when he called them asking that our guys not get shot down.' He looked at his staff officers, then at Patrick, and added, 'But it was supposed to be kept secret. That was the deal – we don't tell what we knew about the Metyor-179, and they don't tell about our Vampires overflying Russia.'

'That's what the CIC gets for making a deal like that with the Russians,' Muskoka said bitterly. 'So what do we recommend to the JCS and SecDef?'

'First, we'll need a list of all the classified subsystems on that plane,' Hayes said. 'What else will the Russians find out about along with LADAR?'

'I can brief you on all the subsystems of the Vampire – I've worked on it for several years,' Patrick said. Hayes just glared at him. He knew he was the best choice to get the information for them quickly, but he also did not want to have to rely on a man they were possibly about to courtmartial.

'What about destroying the wreckage?' Falke suggested. 'Have a special ops team go in and destroy the classified gear?'

'It may not be necessary, sir,' Patrick said. 'The best the Russians or anyone else will be able to do is reverse-engineer the basic design. If the Russians tried to put a current through any component after a crash, the firmware is designed to dump fake computer code and viruses into the detection-and-analysis machines they use. If the computers they use are networked – and the systems are designed to wait until they encounter a networked computer – the viruses will spread through the entire network in milliseconds. We may want to consider sending in a team to make the Russians *think* we want to destroy the equipment – have the team get intercepted just before they go in and pull them out, make the Russians think they stopped us. But it may not be worth risking a team penetrating a Russian intelligence laboratory for real.'

Hayes looked at McLanahan closely, studying him. He appeared as if he was impressed and disappointed all at the same time. 'Good point – and good planning on your part, General,' he said.

'The question remains, sir – what about the Russian stealth bomber?' McLanahan asked.

'What about it?' Muskoka asked.

'It's still out there, and it's a major threat,' McLanahan maintained. 'We've proven that it committed that attack on that factory in Albania, we've put it in the exact vicinity of the NATO AWACS plane that was shot down over Macedonia, and we have credible evidence that it was involved in the raid on Albanian and Macedonian border forces that started the war. If the President made a deal not to reveal the existence of the stealth bomber, the Russians broke that agreement. We should not only spill the beans about the Russian stealth bomber, but we should be going after it.'

'"Go after it,"' Muskoka breathed. 'That seems to be your answer for everything, McLanahan – just "go after it." Bomb the crap out of everything in sight.'

'How do you propose we "go after it"?' Hayes asked.

'We have to find a way to draw it into a fight.'

'How do we do that? Bomb a Russian air base

538

hoping to hit it? Bomb Moscow until Sen'kov coughs it up to us?'

'President Sen'kov may not know anything about the plane,' Patrick said. 'We know the plane was activated shortly after the death of Colonel Kazakov in Kosovo. We know that Kazakov's son Pavel owns the factory that makes the plane. The stealth fighter was in storage until Kazakov came to see Fursenko at Zhukovsky. After that, the plane was launched and hasn't been seen since – and at the same time, all these attacks in the Balkans have taken place.'

'I'm not following you, McLanahan,' Hayes said. 'What makes you think the Russian government doesn't know about the stealth fighter?'

'They could know about it, but not be in control of it,' Patrick said. 'The stealth fighter at Metyor was never delivered to the Russian or Soviet air force. The only pilots ever to fly it worked for Metyor, not the air force.'

'Or this could be some elaborate fantasy of yours,' Muskoka said. 'I don't believe anyone – not the Russian, not Kazakov, no one – would be crazy enough to fly a stealth bomber all over eastern Europe and attack military and civilian targets without proper authorization from the highest levels in government. The political and military consequences would be enormous. He'd be playing with fire.'

Patrick looked directly at General Muskoka and said with a slight – Hayes would have said 'evil' – grin: 'I did it, sir.'

Muskoka looked angry enough to bite through the conference table. 'And look what's happening to you, McLanahan – you're about to be shit-canned.'

'Sir, do you think a gangster like Pavel Kazakov is worried about being "shit-canned"?'

'I think you'd better worry about *yourself*, McLanahan,' Muskoka said.

'That's enough,' General Hayes said, after seeing that neither Muskoka nor McLanahan were going to back down from this argument. He stood and stepped away from the conference table toward the door to his office, motioning for Patrick to follow him. He then stepped toward him and in a low voice said, 'You and your teams have done some good work, McLanahan, good stuff.'

'Sir, someone has got to do something about that stealth fighter,' Patrick maintained. 'I know it's the key to everything that's happening in the Balkans right now.'

'We'll deal with that when the time comes, Patrick,' Hayes said. 'We're dealing with you now.' Patrick looked deflated, disappointed that his efforts were all in vain. 'I'm told you didn't agree to put in your papers and punch out. Why?'

'Because I've still got a lot of work to do, sir,' Patrick said. 'I've got a unit to train and a center to run, and there's a Russian warplane out there trying to set Europe on fire while we twiddle our thumbs and toes and pretend it doesn't matter to us anymore. I'm ready to get back to work.'

'That's not going to happen, McLanahan,' Hayes said seriously. 'SecDef and the JCS left the question about what to do with you up to the Air Force, and SecAF left it up to me. I've thought about it long and hard. You've done a lot of extraordinary things for the United States and the Air Force, McLanahan. You deserve a whole lot better.

'But Terrill Samson is one of our finest officers as well. If I thought there was one milligram of malice in these charges, I'd dismiss them in the blink of an eye. I've spoken with Terrill a half-dozen times in the past two days, and so has most of my staff, and we all agree: the charges are real, and so are the crimes. I'm sorry, McLanahan.

'I'm going to repeat what you've heard today a dozen times at least: request early retirement and you'll get it, with full rank and time in service, an honorable discharge, and all traces of these charges completely expunged. Fight it, talk to the press, or file a countersuit, and you'll end up in Leavenworth for seven years, a Big Chicken Dinner, reduction in grade, and fines.' The 'Big Chicken Dinner,' as Patrick knew too well now, meant a Bad Conduct Discharge – the kiss of death for any ex-military officer seeking a civilian job much above short-order cook. Jester could see the hesitation in McLanahan's face. 'You don't think you did anything wrong, do you, McLanahan?'

'No, I don't, sir,' Patrick replied.

'Then I'm sure you've been in Dreamland too long,' the chief of staff said. 'Because if any other crewdog did this to his wing commander, he'd be court-martialed within twenty-four hours, and you know it. If one of your officers did it to you, you'd see to it that they were grounded perm-anently. Am I wrong?'

'Yes, sir,' Patrick said. Hayes's eyes were wide

541

with surprise, then narrowed in anger and suspicion. 'Sir, in my world, we reward airmen that show creativity, initiative, and courage. In the flight test world, we build a game plan, and we go out and fly the plan – but we leave it up to the crew to decide whether or not it's time to push the envelope a little. All of our crews are tough, smart, and highly skilled operators. If we tell them to try a launch at Mach one point two and they get there and they think the plane and the weapon can handle one point five, they'll take it to one point five. We don't punish them for breaking with the program.'

'But you weren't flying a test mission, McLanahan...'

'Sir, every mission for us is the same – our job is to get the mission done, no matter what it takes. We at Dreamland are not just program managers or engineers. Our job is to test the new generation of aircraft and weapons in every conceivable way. If we do our job, some crewdog in a line unit may not get his ass shot down because he thought he had to slow down or climb to employ his weapons or get out of a hostile situation.'

'I say again, McLanahan – you weren't in a flight test situation,' Hayes emphasized. 'You were on a support mission that depended on stealth and strict adherence to the rules at all times.'

'Sir, if you wanted strict rule-following, you shouldn't have asked us to do the job,' Patrick said.

'That's bullshit, McLanahan,' Hayes retorted. 'I expect discipline and professionalism in all of my combat-coded units, or they are *history!* You

542

play by the rules, or you're out.'

'HAWC doesn't play by the rules, sir,' Patrick argued. 'We never have. The brass hated General Elliott – they cringed whenever his name was brought up. But I also realized that his name kept on coming up for one good reason – he was effective. He did the job he was asked to do, no matter how impossible it was. He wasn't perfect, he wasn't a team player – but he was the best. Men like Terrill Samson play by the rules.'

'I'm sorry you feel that way, Patrick,' Hayes said, the disappointment and frustration evident in his face and voice. 'I like you. You speak your mind, you stick to your beliefs, and you get the job done. You have a lot of potential. But your loyalty to Brad Elliott and his twisted brand of warfighting is turning you into a loose cannon. Terrill Samson was right: you are dangerous, and you don't fit in.

'I've taken the matter out of your hands and out of the UCMJ, Patrick.' The UCMJ, or Uniform Code of Military Justice, was the separate set of federal laws governing conduct and responsibilities of military men and women. 'I've recommended that you be involuntarily retired if you didn't agree to request early retirement, the Secretary of Defense agreed, and it was done. SecDef doesn't want a court-martial, and personally I don't want to see you hauled up in front of one. You were retired as of oh eight hundred hours this morning. Your service is at an end.' He extended his hand. 'Sorry to see you go, General.'

Patrick was about to shake his hand when a very distinctive phone rang in the outer office.

'Batphone,' someone called out, but it was picked up before the second ring. At the same instant, Hayes's pager went off – he acknowledged it, but didn't need to read the message. Moments later, an aide came to the door: 'Meeting in the Gold Room in fifteen minutes, sir.' The Gold Room was the Joint Chiefs of Staff conference room. This was an unscheduled meeting – Patrick knew something was happening.

Hayes knew it, too. 'Thank you.' He turned to General Falke: 'Wombat, I need an intel dump right now.'

Falke had already been on the phone as soon as he heard the 'Batphone,' the direct line between the Chairman of the Joint Chiefs of Staff's office and the chief of staff of the Air Force. 'It's on its way, sir,' he said. 'I'll have an aide drop it off for you ASAP.' A few moments later, an aide stepped into Hayes's office with a folder marked 'Top Secret' – the 'intel dump,' the latest intelligence summaries for the entire world updated minute-by-minute, and the 'force dump,' the latest force status reports from the eight Air Force major commands. A moment later, another aide came rushing in with the latest force status reports for the Single Integrated Operations Plan (SIOP) and non-SIOP nuclear forces. Although, technically, the American nuclear forces were under the combat command of the US Strategic Command, a unified military command, in day-to-day operations the nuclear-capable bombers, land-launched intercontinental ballistic missiles, and their warheads were under Air Force control until gained by Strategic Command.

Hayes was putting on his Class A blouse and getting ready to hurry off to the 'Tank,' what most everyone in the Pentagon called the Gold Room. He nodded to Patrick as he hurried to the door. 'I'll be seeing you, McLanahan. Good luck.' An aide rushed into the Chief's office to hand him another folder, and then he hurried off, followed by his deputy and his chief of operations.

'I have a message for you, sir,' the aide said to Patrick. 'Your civilian attorney is waiting for you at the Mall Entrance right now.'

'My civilian attorney?' Patrick asked. 'I don't have a civilian attorney.' The aide shrugged his shoulders and departed, leaving him alone in the big office. It was a long, lonely walk to the Mall Entrance, and an even longer walk outdoors into the hazy sunshine. Patrick felt as if he should take off his hat, remove his jacket with his stars and ribbons on it. He felt strange, having junior officers salute him, like he was some sort of spy in a military costume trying to infiltrate the place. He had been kicked out of the Air Force almost the entire time he'd been in that building, and he hadn't even known it. The Pentagon now seemed alien to him. A few hours earlier, he'd walked into this place apprehensively, but feeling very much a part of what this place was all about. Now all that had been taken away from him.

Patrick didn't see anyone at the entrance who looked like he was looking for him. But he didn't need to talk with an attorney anyway: there was going to be no court-martial, no appearance in court, no opportunity to fight the charges brought against him. He was out, just like that.

There was a big stretch limousine parked right in front of the Mall Entrance in a 'No Parking' zone, with a Secret Service-looking agent, a female, in a long dark coat and sunglasses standing beside it, and he thought that had to be for the Chairman of the Joint Chiefs of Staff or the Secretary of Defense so they could be whisked off to the White House.

This was indeed a very exciting place to be, Patrick thought. He certainly had had a very exciting, very unusual career. He thought back about all the missions and all the situations he had found himself involved in over the past twelve years: thought about how many times he had made that 'Batphone' ring, how many times the chief of staff of the Air Force had stood before the Chairman of the Joint Chiefs or the Secretary of Defense or even the President and had been unable to explain what was going on because Brad Elliott hadn't informed him or anyone else what he was going to do before he did it. How many frantic limo rides had he been responsible for? How many sleepless nights, tirades, memos, confused phone calls, and lost careers had he and HAWC caused because of their own brand of warfighting?

No matter – it was all over now.

But as Patrick approached the limousine on his way to the taxi stand that would take him to his hotel, the Secret Service-looking agent approached him. 'Excuse me. General McLanahan?'

'Yes?'

She removed her dark glasses and smiled at him. 'I'm not wearing a disguise this time, Patrick.'

He stared at her harder, his mind finally returning to the here and now. 'Marcia? Marcia Preston?' He shook her hand warmly, then gave her a hug. 'You have this thing for always popping up unexpectedly, Marcia.' Marcia Preston had been one of the first US Marine Corps combat fighter pilots, but she'd seen only limited duty in that capacity. Her knowledge and expertise in military affairs, foreign military capabilities, tactics, and both land and aerial combat had led her to be chosen as an advisor and aide to two successive National Security Advisors to the President. Patrick glanced into the limo's windows, but of course could not see anything. 'Who are you working for now, Colonel? Last I knew, you were working for General Freeman in the National Security Advisor's office.'

'It's not Colonel anymore, Patrick,' Marcia said. 'And my new boss wants to speak with you. He's waiting for you.'

'He's waiting for me? In there?'

'Hey, General!' Patrick turned toward the familiar voice and was surprised to see none other than Hal Briggs emerging from the limousine.

'*Hal?* What are *you* doing here?'

Hal Briggs waved him over to the car so they could talk discreetly. 'I got a deal I couldn't refuse, sir.'

'I'm not a "sir" anymore, Hal. Just Patrick.'

'That's okay, because I'm just "Hal" now, too,' he said with a smile. 'Early retirement, same as you.'

'How did you know that?' Patrick asked. 'And why in hell did you accept early retirement? You haven't done anything wrong – in fact, after that rescue in Russia, you're a genuine hero. I'm the one who screwed the pooch. You didn't punch out because of me, did you?'

'With all due respect, old buddy,' Hal said, with a broad smile, 'I don't do shit for no one unless they give me some serious money or some serious humma-humma, if you catch my drift. But if I was going to trash my career for anyone, it would be for you. How's that?'

'Sounds like bullshit to me. What is going on, Hal? How did you know where I was? How did you know what happened to me? *I* just found out ten minutes ago.'

'My new employer knows everything, Patrick,' Hal said. 'He wants to talk with you, too.'

Patrick's warning antennae were tingling like crazy. Having trusted friends like Marcia and Hal together helped, but this strong feeling of caution couldn't be ignored. 'You know this guy, Hal?' he asked. 'Did you check him out first?'

'No.'

'*No?* You stepped into a car with a guy you don't know and you didn't check him out first?'

'I said I didn't check him out, and I've never met him – I know *of* him. But you *definitely* know him.'

Patrick looked at Hal suspiciously, but with a gleam of interest in his eyes now. Hal noticed it, stepped aside, and let him peek inside. He saw Chris Wohl inside, also in civilian clothes, looking moody and inconvenienced as always, and he wondered if the Marine Corps veteran had retired also. Then he looked in the very front of the passenger compartment – and his chin dropped open in sheer surprise.

'C'mon in, General McLanahan,' the man said, with a broad smile. 'We need to talk.'

The Oval Office, The White House, Washington, DC
several minutes later

'The Joint Chiefs are meeting right now at the Pentagon,' Secretary of Defense Robert Goff said, as he was ushered into the Oval Office. 'They'll be ready with some recommendations for you shortly. It's pretty clear what happened: someone in Russia leaked the information about the downed bomber to the world press. The State Department tells me several world leaders have already called our embassies asking for an explanation. The press is going nuts. Every bit of information they've ever had about Dreamland is being trotted out and fitted together with the information the Russians are publicizing, and it's all coming together. Dreamland has been blown wide open.'

President Thomas Thorn put down the papers he was looking at, motioned to the sofa, and nodded. Goff took his usual place on the sofa; the President continued to pace the floor, looking thoughtful if not concerned. 'It'll still be a classified installation,' the President said. 'Only now, everyone will know it's classified.'

'If I didn't know you better, Thomas, I'd say you were just trying to make a funny,' Goff said.

He knew, of course, that he wasn't. 'Thomas?' Goff prompted, the concern evident in his voice. 'What are we going to do?'

'Admit to it, of course,' Thorn replied. 'Admit that it was our bomber, our aircraft, on a spy mission inside Russia. We were trying to rescue a spy that had valuable information for us. We're going to do exactly what I told Sen'kov I'd do – go in front of the American people, in front of the world, and admit everything.'

'I disagree. I think we shouldn't say anything,' Goff said. 'The Russians trumped us. Anything we say now will sound like we're making excuses.'

'We're not making excuses – we're offering explanations,' the President said. 'We can't deny any of it, Bob. We knew we were working off borrowed time anyway. Expecting the Russians to sit on the intelligence bonanza of the decade was too much to hope for. We had to face the music eventually. I'm surprised the Russians waited this long.'

'Then why in hell didn't we do something more?' Goff snapped.

'Because our objective always was to get our men and women back home,' the President said. 'The Russians had their hands on two American aviators from a top-secret weapons research facility. They could have had the other bomber, too – they almost did. They could have sent a hundred planes after them. We made them hesitate with a half-baked threat that shouldn't have worked but did. All we needed was enough hesitation to get our people clear. I expected Sen'kov to renege on the deal the next morning. Nobody won, but the important thing was, *we didn't lose.*'

He punctuated the last sentence with an angry glare.

'Congress is going to roast us,' Goff said. 'The media is going to chew on us for weeks, maybe months.'

'It doesn't matter.'

'Doesn't matter?' Goff asked incredulously. 'Don't you get it, Thomas? Don't you understand? Congress, the American people, the world will think we are completely inept. They'll think we don't care about our allies, that we're afraid, that we can't protect ourselves. If we can't protect our own people, how can we protect our friends and allies?'

'Our job is not to protect the rest of the world, Bob,' Thorn said. 'We are not the defenders of freedom. We are one nation among hundreds of other nations around the planet.'

'Are you joking, Thomas?' Goff asked. 'You are the president of the United States. You *are* the leader of the free world. This office is the center of hope, freedom, and democracy for billions of people around the globe–'

'I don't buy any of that, Robert – I never did, and you know it,' the President said. 'This office stands for one thing and one thing only: the executive branch of the United States, one of three branches of the American government. The Constitution specifies exactly what this office is and what my responsibilities are, and I'm quite certain the Constitution does not authorize me to be the leader of the free world, defender of liberty, truth, justice, or of anything else except to faithfully uphold and defend the Constitution. I am the president, that's it.'

'It's not a Constitutional thing, Thomas. It's ... it's symbolic,' Goff said uncomfortably, irritated that he had to explain this concept to his friend. 'The president of the United States is a symbol of democracy and freedom. It's not legislated or conferred upon you – you've got it because people have come to believe it.'

'So I don't have a choice? That's nonsense. I have a choice, and I choose not to be a symbol of something like that.' But it was obvious he wanted to change the subject – and besides, he didn't like arguing with his friend.

Thorn motioned to the reports on the EB-1C aircraft coming in from intelligence analysts and experts. 'All this stuff about how our country has been compromised by the Russians revealing information on the bomber? It's all nonsense. These analysts put all that gloom-and-doom stuff in their report simply because if they underestimated the impact of the news, they'd be judged unreliable in their estimates. They'd rather be known for predicting the worst and hoping for the best than the other way around. The information reveals *nothing*, Robert. It's a sensational episode that in the end affects nothing.'

Robert Goff stared disbelievingly at his old friend, then shook his head. 'What's happened to you, Thomas?' he breathed.

'I was wondering the same about you, Robert,' Thorn said, angry that he had decided not to engage his friend in a half-philosophical, half-personal argument, but that Goff had come back wanting more anyway. 'I thought we both believed in the same things – smaller government, fewer foreign entanglements, less reliance on military power. America first, foremost, and always – that was our vision. The office – yours and mine – seems to have diverted your attention.'

Goff ignored Thorn's observations. He chuckled and gave him a wry smile. 'I remember when you got back from Desert Storm, when I brought Amelia to Dover to be there when you got off that plane with your unit. There you were, with your "chocolate chip" battle-dress uniform, beret, desert combat boots, still with your web gear on like you were getting ready to go into battle again. You looked like John Wayne and Superman rolled into one. You had several dozen confirmed kills to your credit, and regular folks treated you like the second coming of Elvis – twenty years earlier, they would have spit on you if they even *thought* you were military. You cried when those people cheered for you. You cried when the band started playing "Yankee Doodle Dandy" and the crowds broke through the barricades and surrounded you.' Thorn had stopped his pacing and was staring off into space as if reliving that moment.

'You were proud of your men and the Army,' Goff went on. 'You went back and thanked every one of your men for their service. You got down on your knees on the tarmac and thanked the ones who didn't come back. You were a proud man, Thomas.'

'I'm still proud of our soldiers,' he shot back, almost defensively. 'I'm proud enough of them that I refuse to send them away from home just so they can be "trip wires" or so we can maintain a "presence" in some foreign country. Soldiers are meant to fight and kill to defend their country, not to fight and die for someone else's country, or for the latest slogan or jingle or buzzword, or so we can police a country whose people want nothing more than to kill one another, or because the media saturates our senses with scenes of downtrodden people supposedly in need of liberation. I won't follow the pattern of past leaders and send troops overseas just because we *can*, or because someone believes we should because we're the leaders of the free world.'

Goff's half-smile was vanishing rapidly. 'Now you've turned into a cynical reactionary. It's like you hate everything you were back then, and you're driven to see it all destroyed.'

'Not destroyed – changed,' Thorn said. 'Changed into what it was meant to be. Changed into what the Founding Fathers wanted it to be.'

'That was then, Thomas,' Goff argued. 'That was the eighteenth-century world, where time was as much a barrier as a mountain range or an ocean. Now information travels at the speed of light into almost every home on the planet. The world is a far more dangerous place than ever before, and we need every advantage we can take.'

'You can't convince me, Robert,' Thorn said. 'I'm not going to change my philosophy of how to run this government simply because a military plane gets shot down, an espionage operation is uncovered and exposed, or some country thinks they can get away with invading and occupying a smaller, weaker nation.'

'"Think they can get away with it," Thomas?' Goff asked. 'Thomas, they've *already* "gotten away with it." It's a done deal. Russia has sent over twenty thousand troops into the Balkans in the past two weeks alone. None of those nations can do or say anything against them. How are we going to deal with Russia now? They've taken over Macedonia, they are staging massive resupply missions and setting up huge hardware and ammunition depots in Bulgaria and Serbia, and they're conducting crossborder raids into Albania that look suspiciously like another invasion operation – the Germans are virtually stepping aside, letting them cruise anywhere in the Balkans. We've implicated them in mass murder, surprise attacks, and even genocide. Someone has to stop them.'

'We're not going to deal militarily with Russia,' the President said.

'*What?*'

'If the Balkan countries want Russia to occupy them, let them go ahead and do so,' Thorn said.

'What do you mean, "if they *want* them to occupy them"?' Goff asked. 'Why would any country *want* Russia to occupy them?'

'Robert, have you heard of any opposition to Russia's new peace-keeping role in Macedonia?'

'We get briefings and see video of anti-Russian protests every day.'

'But there's no opposition from the government, the Macedonian parliament is still in session, there's no government in exile, and the Macedonian army is still intact,' the President observed. 'Yes, we've heard from opposition leaders in their government asking for American troops to counterbalance the Russian troops, and we've heard dire predictions of a Russian invasion of Greece and Turkey. But it's all background noise, Robert.'

'"Background noise."' Goff's voice was intentionally monotone, as if he was too stunned to even react.

'It's all rumor and possibility and threats and panic,' the President said. 'It's opposition groups in every country in Europe vying for position. It's ethnic and religious groups in *this* country vying for press and donations and influence. It's congressional representatives vying for votes and donations. Everyone's got an agenda, Robert, including you and me. But their agendas don't have to influence my thinking.

'That goes double when it comes to deploying the armed forces of the United States,' the President went on. 'I refuse to use the military as a hammer against anyone who happens to have thoughts, actions, or policies contrary to ours, no matter how horrific or dangerous they seem to be.'

'Then you're willing to sacrifice the peace, security, and freedom of every one of the democratic nations in Europe, just like *that*, in order to preserve your way of thinking?' Goff asked incredulously. 'Even if Russia takes the Balkans, breaks up NATO, reoccupies the Baltic States, and re-erects the Iron Curtain, you're still willing to stand aside and watch it all happen?'

'You are living in a fantasy world of someone

else's making, Robert,' the President retorted. 'You're starting to believe all the hype in the press. Yes, I believe Russia has hostile intentions toward the Balkans, and possibly elsewhere in Europe. But what's the solution, Robert? Send troops to Macedonia or Albania or Bulgaria? Send in the Sixth Fleet? Then *we'd* be the invaders. We'd turn the Balkans into a battleground, just like before the start of World War One–'

'To preserve freedom and democracy in Europe, I damn well think it's worth our sacrifice!' Goff retorted. 'Would you have stood aside and let Hitler take Europe or the British Isles, or let Mussolini take Greece? Would you have let the Japanese island-hop their way to California without opposing them? Would you have let Israel defend itself against Egypt and Syria? Would you have allowed Saddam Hussein to keep Kuwait and then take Saudi Arabia?'

'I'm not going there, Robert,' Thorn snapped. 'I'm not going to rewrite history, for you or for anyone else. I'm only concerned about what I'm going to do here and now–'

'Which is *nothing?* Turn your back on our friends and allies?'

'I'm not going to engage Russia or China or any other nation unless the very existence of the United States of America is at stake. And I don't mean losing a few markets for wheat or soybeans or soda pop – I mean threaten our shores, threaten our national security.'

'You're going to unravel decades of alliances, friendship, and trust between the free nations of the world, Thomas.'

'Am I? Do you think the German chancellor had this discussion when he decided to divide the Balkans between themselves and Russia? Did the Germans care about NATO? Did Russia care about maintaining years of mutual trust and friendship between us and them? Or do you think they were motivated by self-interest to do what they felt was right for their countries?'

'Or maybe they're just in it for the money.'

'So what if they are?' the President argued. 'What if Sen'kov is really getting billions of dollars from that Russian gangster Kazakov to invade the Balkans just so he can put up his pipeline? Do you think the Russian people will stand idly by and watch him do this? Do you think the Russian military will happily march into Albania and risk another Afghanistan or Chechnya debacle just so Sen'kov can get rich and retire wealthy to the Caribbean?'

'Maybe they can't do anything about it.'

'Boris Yeltsin proved that even a nobody can stand up to the power of the Red Army if he has the strength of his convictions,' Thorn said. 'History is full of stories of successful visionaries.'

'And dead martyrs,' Goff added.

'I don't intend on becoming a martyr, Bob,' the President said. 'But I am going to fight for my beliefs. The American people elected me for one simple reason: to form a government with my vision, my ideals. They wanted less interference in foreign affairs, to bring our troops home from endless, pointless peacekeeping missions, to downsize government, improve our quality of life without raising taxes or polarizing our people, and to make America strong by putting America first. If they don't like what I'm doing, there's a way to get rid of me without my becoming a martyr too – impeach me. But it won't happen, and for one simple reason – because I follow the rulebook: the Constitution of the United States.'

Secretary of Defense Goff shook his head, not knowing exactly how to respond to his friend. He was either a true visionary, he thought, or he was going insane. 'So you're going to let Russia and Germany march into the Balkans unopposed,' he said after a long, frustrating pause. 'You're going to let them carve up the Balkans, followed shortly by Eastern Europe, then perhaps by Western Europe. We lose all our trading partners and allies in Europe. Then a spark ignites a third world war, and we either sit on the sidelines and watch Europe go up in flames, or we have to send another thirty-five million men and women into combat to restore the peace, like we did in World War Two.'

'When the combined Russian and German tanks roll through Buckingham Palace, Robert, you can tell me you told me so,' the President said. 'I don't think it's going to happen, at least not on my watch.'

'You're betting the peace and security of the entire world on this, Thomas.'

'If the world wants peace or the world wants war, Robert, they'll get whichever they choose,' Thorn said. 'My job is to protect and defend the United States. I'm going to make America the shining example of a strong, peaceful, democratic nation, and invite others to join *us*. I'm not going to send our armies out to enforce our ideas

559

of what kind of society or government they should live under.'

Robert Goff shook his head and looked down, and looked at his hands, then at papers on the President's desk – anywhere but into his friend's eyes. He was not convinced one bit that the President was right, but he knew that arguing with him was not going to help or change his mind. That's why he was surprised when the President clasped him on the shoulder. 'You okay, Bob?' he asked softly.

Only then did Goff looked into the President's eyes. He responded, 'Yes, Mr President.'

Thorn's face clouded a bit in disappointment when he heard those words – Goff did not use them very often when they were alone – but he still smiled warmly. 'You still with me?' he asked.

'I'm with you, Thomas,' Goff responded. 'Even if it's there to help pick up the pieces.' And he turned and departed the Oval Office without saying another word.

Thomas Thorn returned to his desk and shuffled some paperwork around without really noticing what they were, then retreated to his study. He fielded several phone calls and visits from his secretary, then hit the DND (Do Not Disturb) button on his phone, settled into his chair, closed his eyes, and began his deep-breathing exercises, commanding his muscles one by one to relax, and then letting his mantra echo quietly through his head until, gradually, all conscious thoughts raced away over the horizon.

Many casual practitioners called it a very intense 'nap,' but meditation was much more than just a period of relaxation. The transcendental state was a span of time, in which the subconscious mind was exposed, and at the same time the conscious mind was free to expand – to roam the vast areas that were generally closed to it. It was far different from a nap – in fact, meditation was never meant to be a substitute for sleep. Quite the opposite: the transcendental process was an energizing, invigorating process, because letting the conscious mind race about in the wide-open energy field of the subconscious mind filled both the mind and the body with incredible power. It was akin to a racehorse, tied to an exercise trundle: it was fine going around in a twenty-foot circle. It was even better when allowed to run on a mile-and-a-quarter racetrack during practice or on race day. But let it out into an open field, and the horse becomes a different animal, random and tireless and almost wild. The human mind worked the very same way.

It was also a two-way exchange. Many thoughts, experiences, even realities existed in the subconscious mind, and the transcendental state allowed those waves of energy to emerge. In that sense, meditation was an educational experience, a way of reliving, preliving, or even creating a whole new lifetime in just an instant.

But like any exercise, the human mind can grow weary if left to roam too long, and through years of training and discipline, Thorn called his mind back to the conscious world and let the doorway to his subconscious mind close. It was not a sad or reluctant event at all. He knew the doorway was always there, to summon when needed, and he knew that the potential energy available to him there was limitless.

But the subconscious realm was an alternate reality he had created to explore the universe that was himself – the person, the being, the energy that was all of his pasts and all of his futures right there, in one instant, available for him to see and study and experience. He had created other realities – this one, of him as president of the United States, in the beginning of the twenty-first century, on the planet called Earth. It was time to play that role, immerse himself in that universe, and act out his part in that performance. But he could do so armed with the knowledge and experience that he had gained from his other realities, because to him they were all *his* realities, all pertinent, all interconnected.

He picked up his phone and punched a button. 'Yes, Mr President?' his vice president, Les Busick, responded.

'Your friend, the one you mentioned the other day? Is he in town?'

'Yes.'

'I'd like to talk with him. Today. Right now.'

Busick hesitated for a moment. Ever since he had learned his 'friend' was coming to town with a radical, dangerous proposal, he knew the President should meet with him. Every time he had brought it up, the President had turned him down. He might have been tempted to give him an 'I told you so,' but Busick knew that things had to be pretty serious for the President to want to talk with him now. 'Where?'

'In the residence.' Every place in the entire

building – in the entire District, for that matter – was open to dozens of prying eyes, except for the residence itself; and as many presidents soon learned, there were many very discreet ways of getting inside the President's private residence without half of Washington finding out. 'As soon as possible.'

'Would you like me there, too?'

'It might be better if you weren't.'

'I see.' English translation: I might be doing something you might have to deny. Finally, Busick thought, Thomas Thorn is doing something like a real president. 'I'll buzz you when they arrive.'

'This place is so neat and organized,' the visitor said, with a smile. 'Was I that big of a slob?'

President Thomas Thorn watched his visitor with a mixture of apprehension and irritation. They were seated in the President's study in the private residence in the White House, far from the prying eyes of the media, Congress – and, he hated to admit, some members of his own Cabinet. But now he had this gentleman to contend with. Somehow he had the feeling he was in the process of making a deal with the devil, and he hated the prospect of doing so. 'Let's get down to business, shall we?' President Thorn prompted.

'Whatever you say, Tom,' former president Kevin Martindale responded, casually concluding his distracted little tour of the residence and returning to the seat offered him. Since losing the White House to Thomas Thorn in the last election, Martindale seemed much thinner and had let his hair grow longer. It was just as wavy as before, with the 'photographer's dream' – the two long curly silver locks that seemed to drop down across his forehead whenever he got mad or excited – still present, but now the rest of his mane was very nearly the same shade of silver. He wore a short, thin, partially gray beard, too.

'This is a different look for you, isn't it?' Thorn asked.

'I'm not in front of the public every day,' Martindale replied. He regarded the President with a half-amused, half-accusing expression. 'But then, neither are you.'

'Maybe that's how you always wanted to look,' Thorn offered.

'We're both kids of the sixties, Tom,' Martindale said. 'We learned it was okay to be different, to follow whatever our hearts told us instead of what others were telling us.'

'True.' It was still a damned unusual look for Kevin Martindale, Thorn thought, and it didn't fit his image at all. Martindale was a career politician, and ever since he'd burst on the national political stage almost twenty years before, he'd always looked and acted the part of a savvy, smooth, well-spoken, intelligent insider. 'Especially an ex-Marine – four years in the Corps, including two tours in Vietnam. State attorney-general, US senator, secretary of defense briefly, then vice president, private citizen, then president.'

'Then private citizen again,' Martindale added. It didn't impress him at all that Thorn knew details about his background – he had been in Washington a long time, and the things he'd done had definitely set a place for him in the history books. 'But I guess after all those years of being straightlaced and buttoned-down, it was time for a change.' Thorn didn't say anything right away, so Martindale went on: 'Talk about your big-time changes – Rambo to Mr Rogers, warrior to wallflower? Will the real Thomas Nathaniel Thorn please stand up?' His eyes narrowed, and his casual smile vanished. 'Why'd you call me here, Thorn?'

'I heard you've been doing some recruiting.'

'Oh?'

'Present, former, and retired military guys, especially special ops and aviators.'

'That's interesting,' Martindale commented. His sources would have advised him if any US or foreign intelligence agencies were checking up on him, and none were. Thorn might be guessing – and then again, he might not be. 'What else have you heard?'

'That guys are joining up.' Martindale shrugged and said nothing. 'I just wanted to touch base, find out what you're up to.'

'Since when, Thorn?' Martindale retorted. 'Since when did you care about me? Since when did you care about anything or anyone?'

'Excuse me?' Was he trying to goad him into reacting? Thorn thought. How childish can a grown man be?

'Tradition, respect, legacy, honor – none of that stuff means anything to you,' Martindale went on, 'or else you would have attended the inauguration, and you would have stepped up in front of Congress and the American people and talked about your vision of the future of our nation in your first State of the Union.' Thorn looked like he was going to say something, but Martindale interrupted him with an upraised hand. 'Hey, I've heard your reasons before. "It's not in the Constitution." Well, the United States and the American people are much more than the Constitution.'

'I know exactly what our country is, Mr President,' Thorn said. 'I know the United States is embodied in the Constitution and our laws. I was elected because I believe that, and the American people believe it, too.'

'You got elected because me and the Democrats were too busy hammering away at each other to notice you slipping up behind us.'

'That's one good reason,' Thorn said. 'The military questions, especially the attacks on Taiwan, Guam, and the *Independence*, killed it for you.' Martindale scowled. 'Tell me, Mr President – why didn't you retaliate?'

'Against whom?' Martindale asked, perhaps a bit more sharply than he wanted. 'China? Everyone said China was the "obvious" attacker. But we *still* don't know exactly who planted the nuke on the *Indy* to this day, only that there were no nuclear weapons on the ship. I had no authority to attack China in retaliation for attacking Taiwan. As far as the attack on Guam – well, I had other players waiting to go to work. They did the job, and I didn't have to be the first American president since Truman to use nuclear weapons in anger.'

'"Other players,"' Thorn repeated. 'You mean

HAWC and Madcap Magician.'

'I see you're familiar with them,' Martindale said. 'They're good troops – at least, they were until you sold them out. Now they're useless. What was the purpose of telling Sen'kov who they were?'

'It put Sen'kov off guard, it bought us time, and it allowed our troops to get out safely,' Thorn replied.

'And it shot to hell almost twenty years of weapons development and all future covert-action capability from Dreamland,' Martindale pointed out. 'Why? So you can soothe your conscience? So you didn't have to get into a fight with the Russians? I think you've heard this before, Thorn, but let me tell you again in case you've forgotten: the Russians *like* to fight. They like to argue, they like to deceive, they like to confront and challenge. And they don't respect anyone who doesn't argue, fight, deceive, confront, or challenge in return. I'm sure your national security advisor briefed you on basic historical tactics for dealing with the Russians.' But before Thorn could answer, Martindale snapped his fingers and added, 'Oh yeah, that's right – *you don't have a national security advisor!* What in hell is up with that? You're surrendering a valuable advisor and critical White House staff organization just to save a few bucks?'

'Robert Goff is a good man.'

'He's the best,' Martindale said. 'But his job is to run the Department of Defense, to keep the American military, such as it is, running smoothly. His job is not to help you formulate policy – his job is to carry out your orders. He's overworked and understaffed, and it'll hurt your military effectiveness.'

'My military force structure and my staff of advisors is exactly what I'm supposed to have – no more, no less.'

'That's true – if you were living in the eighteenth century,' Martindale said. 'But you're actually in the twenty-first century – maybe not mentally, but physically. You understaff the White House and force the Pentagon to do more work, which understaffs them, and all the shit rolls downhill – it screws everybody up. Just because Thomas Jefferson didn't have a national security advisor. Well, I'm sure if he had thought of it, he would've gotten one. Wise up, Thorn.'

'Fortunately, I don't have to justify or explain my budget or staffing strategies to you.'

'I'm a citizen of the United States, a taxpayer, and a voter, not just your predecessor,' Martindale reminded him sternly. 'You sure as hell *do* have to explain that stuff to me.'

'Maybe later, then,' Thorn said irritably. 'Right now, what I want to know is: why?'

'Why what?'

'Why were you so afraid of using the military?'

'I wasn't afraid of jackshit, Thorn.'

'Then why didn't you use the military more often? Conflicts all over the world, nuclear weapons flying, threats to peace and security almost every year – and yet you never once started any massive deployments, never called up the Reserves or Guard. You massed a few carriers, put a few bombers back on nuclear alert, but never made any real attempt to prepare the nation for the possibility of a general war, even though you were clearly authorized and expected to do so. Why?'

'Read it in my memoirs,' Martindale snapped.

Thomas Thorn spread his hands in a symbol of surrender. 'Mr President ... Kevin,' he said. 'I really want to know.'

'Why? Because you're scared that your precious, righteous philosophy of disengagement and isolationism from world affairs isn't working?' Martindale shot back, angrier than ever. 'That after a year of slamming me during the campaign about my ineptitude over how I handled crises around the world, you're discovering that maybe it's not so easy to do nothing?'

Thorn couldn't be goaded into firing back. 'Because I need to know, Kevin,' he said softly. 'I know you didn't do *nothing*. But why did you do what you did? Why didn't you just use the immense power we have to solve these crises?'

Martindale fell silent, then shrugged his shoulders, as if not caring if Thorn knew his reasoning or not. 'Plain and simple: I hate the idea of losing,' Martindale finally replied. 'Spending weeks or even months mobilizing an army, then sending them across the globe to fight and die in a war, just doesn't sound *right* to me. It sounds like a wasteful, inefficient, risky thing.'

'So if you send in HAWC or Madcap Magician,' Thorn summarized, 'and they get beat, you think you haven't lost?'

'No, I've lost, all right – but I've lost a scrimmage, not the real game,' Martindale explained. 'And both those units have been pretty darn good in their scrimmages – sometimes they beat the bad guys so badly that there is no game afterward. In any case, the secret units were fast, efficient, highly motivated, they reported directly to me, and their funding and support were buried in black programs with minimal congressional oversight. That is, until now.'

'I see,' Thorn said. He looked at Martindale carefully – then, to Martindale's surprise, he smiled and nodded. 'Very well. Thank you for your time, Mr President.'

'That's it? That's all?' Martindale asked incredulously. 'No threats, no warnings, no condemnation?'

'Of what?'

'Of–' Then Martindale stopped. He smiled, wagged a finger at Thorn, then stood up to leave. 'I see. Very clever. You shove me around a bit so I'll reveal some information, then simply leave me to fend for myself.'

'I don't know what you're talking about, Kevin,' Thorn said. 'I just wanted to ask you about some of the aspects of your tenure as president. I think I have a pretty good idea now.'

'Let's stop playing games, Thorn,' Martindale said angrily. 'You called me in here for a reason. Spit it out.'

'Very well, Mr President–'

'And stop with the "Mr President" shit,' Martindale interjected. 'I'm not the president – you are. You have about as much respect for me as I have for you.'

'All I have to say is this, Kevin: what you're planning to do is dangerous – maybe not to you, but to the men and women you're recruiting to work with you,' Thorn said. 'Executive privilege won't protect you, and the Geneva Conventions won't protect them. No matter what you do, no matter whom or how it benefits, the United States won't come to your rescue. As they said in the old TV shows, we'll disavow any knowledge of your actions. You'll be nothing more than high-tech vigilantes.'

'Then do something yourself,' Martindale said, all traces of bravado gone for now. 'Sponsor us. Underwrite us. We'll take the risk, but we'll do it under your direction. We'll keep ourselves out of the spotlight, follow the spirit of the law, cooperate as much as possible with domestic and foreign governments. But this isolationist, laissez-faire policy of yours will drag this country down, and someone has to act to protect our vital interests.'

'You want to follow the law, Kevin? Drop this crazy scheme,' the President said. 'You've done enough damage as it is already.'

'We haven't even begun to fight, Tom,' Martindale said. 'You are not going to be able to stop us. You might as well work with us.'

'Who else is involved in this, Kevin?' Thorn asked. 'Who in my administration? Which active-duty officers? Which retired officers?'

'You expect me just to give you a roster?'

'Don't you trust me?'

'Not as far as I can throw you,' Martindale replied. 'Of course, if you'd agree to join us, or even not to interfere and to pass us some intelligence information every now and then, perhaps

'I'd be convinced that you could be trusted.'

'I'm not going to spar with you, Kevin,' Thorn said. 'I'll assume you have some sort of ultra-miniature recording device on you. It doesn't matter. I'll say this plainly: I'll oppose anyone who wants to conduct their own foreign or military policy. I don't know if what you're doing is illegal or not – that's a question for the Justice Department. But if you give me the names of all your members, and if Justice deems your operation illegal, which I think they will–'

'Of course they will. The Attorney General works for the President,' Martindale interjected. 'I know how that works, Thorn, remember? I played that game. The Justice Department doesn't stand for "justice" – it stands for whatever the White House stands for. Justice's job is to make the laws fit the wishes of the White House.'

'–then I'll give the participants you list one free pass. No judicial punishment. They'll be allowed to go free if they keep their noses clean.'

'I'll give you an offer in return,' Martindale said. 'You continue to do whatever the hell it is you do in this place, whatever your pointed little head tells you is the will of the people. When Russia invades Turkey or Ukraine or Georgia, when China tries to invade Taiwan or take over the South China Sea again, if Iran tries to take over the Persian Gulf or Red Sea, and suddenly the bad guys mysteriously start losing ships and planes and bases, you just keep swearing that the United States isn't doing anything. You promise to investigate the matter, then simply drop it.

'Every now and then, your folks pick up the

phone and toss us some information or a few old satellite photos or EM intercepts. Nothing direct – a file carelessly left on a desk, a fax or e-mail to a wrong address, an intel package or classified situation report mysteriously delayed a few minutes on its way from the Pentagon to the White House. You continue to deny everything, chastise the press for spreading accusations and being alarmist, and continue on your merry mission of burying your head in the sand. Someone else will take care of all the messes in the world.'

'You think this is a big joke, eh, Martindale?' Thorn responded. 'I assure you, this is a very serious situation. I can pick up the phone and have you arrested right now. The FBI will eventually find the rest of the members of your little gun club. You'll be disgraced and vilified for the rest of your life. Your participants' lives and careers will be ruined.'

'Thorn, don't be an ass,' Martindale admonished him. 'You know as well as I do that nothing will be proven. You will have arrested, harassed, and slandered a former president of the United States, and none of the accusations will be found to be true. Congress will completely abandon you – you'll have zero chance of getting one piece of legislation passed. You'll be even more of a laughingstock than you are now.'

'I'm giving you one last chance, Kevin,' Thorn said. 'Abandon this crazy scheme. Tell me who your main officers are, and they'll be exempt from prosecution one time only, after we sit down with them and advise them of the trouble they're in and the punishment awaiting them if they're found guilty.'

Martindale looked at Thorn for what seemed like a long time, then shrugged his shoulders. 'It was nice talking with you, Thorn,' he said, as he extended his hand to the President. 'Your naïveté is exceeded only by your dedication to your convictions. Maybe you really are the reincarnation of Thomas Jefferson, like all the weirdos claim you are.'

Thorn looked disappointed, but he shook hands with Martindale nonetheless. 'It was nice talking to you, too, sir,' he said. 'I don't envy the path you've chosen for yourself and your misguided followers. I predict it will be long and difficult.'

'Sure,' Martindale said, as he headed for the door. 'Burn some incense for me when you're done communing with nature. Meanwhile, I've got work to do.'

North Las Vegas, Nevada
that evening

Duane Deverill popped open the bottle of Duckhorn Merlot and poured, finishing with a flourish. 'There you go,' he said proudly. 'A pretty good '95. Should go well with dinner tonight.'

Annie Dewey had arrived a few minutes earlier, still in her flight suit. She plopped her briefcase down on the sofa table. 'Sounds great,' she said distractedly, unzipping the flight suit to her waist. 'What are you fixing?'

'Fixing? Me? Sorry, babe, but I called Pizza Hut. Hope you don't mind.'

'Heck no,' she said. 'Red wine and pizza are my favorites.'

He came over to her with a glass of wine, touched rims, then gave her a kiss before they drank. 'Here's to you,' he said. After he took a sip, he added rakishly, 'Hey, that was nice.'

She smiled enticingly, but pushed him away. 'Sorry. I need a shower first. I smell like I just got done with a week in the cockpit instead of just three hours.'

'Allow me.' He sat her down on the couch, removed her flying boots and socks, then helped her slip out of the flight suit. She wore a white T-shirt atop an athletic bra, and cotton panties. Smiling mischievously, he then started at her toes, kissing and sucking them, then moved up her leg to her waist, then her belly, then back down to her waist.

She gently but firmly lifted his head. 'Shower first, okay?'

He smiled back at her, but his eyes registered his concern. 'Sure.' He let her up off the couch, then watched as she collected her flying gear. 'Everything okay?'

She half turned toward him and nodded. 'Everything's fine. I guess I'm just tired. Long day today.' She turned to face him and smiled wearily. 'You're wonderful, you know that?'

'*That's* what I've been *saying!*' Dev said happily. He took a sip of wine and watched Annie as she headed off toward his bathroom, shedding the rest of her underwear. 'Well, wine can *definitely* wait.' He kicked off his sandals and pulled his T-shirt off with one hand. 'I'll join you.' But at that exact moment, the doorbell rang. Dev made a big, demonstrative pantomime of disappointment, punching and kicking the air in mock animal frustration. 'We'll reheat it. Don't worry. You go ahead and start, and I'll be right there.' He collected cash from his wallet and went to the door, mentally calculating the amount and the tip and getting the cash ready in his hand to hurry things up as he opened the door...

...and saw Colonel David Luger standing there. He shook off the confusion and embarrassment quickly. 'Hello, sir.'

'Dev.' Luger noticed that Deverill was definitely blocking not just his way but his view of his apartment, so he didn't try to look around him. 'Could you ask Annie to come out to the patio and have a few words with me?'

'Maybe,' Dev said.

'Maybe?'

Dev eyed Luger suspiciously. 'We heard that you were decertified, sir,' he said. 'The last we heard, you were being evaluated at Brooks for delayed stress syndrome.'

'Something like that.'

'You on medication?'

'None of your business.'

'That's where you're wrong, sir,' Deverill said. 'You're at my house, we're not in uniform, and Annie's a friend and my aircraft commander. It *is* my business.' He looked carefully into Luger's eyes. He couldn't tell if Luger was on antidepressants or sedatives – he looked perfectly normal – but he knew he was no expert. 'Were you discharged from Brooks? Are you coming back to the Lake?'

'Ask her to come out here, please,' Luger said.

'When were you released from Brooks, Colonel?' Dev asked. 'Or ... *were* you released from Brooks?'

'None of your *fucking* business.'

'Hostile, Colonel, very hostile,' Deverill said. 'Could it be possible you broke out of the hospital? Maybe I should call the sky cops and ask them.'

'Do what you want. Just ask Annie to come out here.'

'I don't think so,' Deverill said. 'If you're okay and you've been released from Brooks, you can see Annie at the Lake tomorrow. But if not ... you might be dangerous.'

'Dangerous? What the hell do you mean? What do you think you're doing?' He saw Luger's face and neck muscles tense up.

He went on full alert, eyes narrowed, measuring Luger up. They were of equal height; Luger was younger, but Dev had at least forty pounds on him. 'I don't think I like your tone of voice, sir. I'm asking you to leave.'

'I asked you to ask Annie to come out and talk with me,' David said evenly, controlling his temper. Dev stood his ground. He knew he had absolutely nothing to stand on – if Dev said no, that was it, unless Annie herself knew he was here. He raised his voice and peered over Dev's left shoulder, 'Annie, it's David. Would you come talk to me?'

Dev put his hands on Luger's chest and tried to push him away from the door. 'I asked you to leave, Luger. Now I'm telling you – *get out.*'

Luger swept Deverill's hands away from his chest with a speed that surprised him. 'Don't push me, Deverill.'

'Don't raise your voice at me in my own house, Luger,' Deverill snapped.

'David?' Annie was standing behind Dev in the doorway, wearing one of Dev's tank tops, which barely covered her bikini bathing suit bottoms. 'What are you doing here?'

'Annie, I want to—'

'I told you to leave, sir,' Deverill said, quickly restoring his polite but firm, protective voice. It was too late to try to keep them apart. He turned to Annie. 'The colonel is being loud and rude, and he's not being very straightforward about his mental condition.'

'His *mental condition?*' Annie charged to the front door and tried to push Dev away. 'Dev, move aside...'

'This is not a good idea, Heels,' Dev said. He had one more chance to break the bond that still existed between these two, and he decided in that instant to go for it. 'I think he broke out of whatever medical mental exam program he was going through. I think he's AWOL. Look at his eyes – I think he's on drugs. He came up here looking for you and itching for a fight.'

'Screw you, Deverill.'

'Tell her, Colonel,' Deverill goaded him. 'Tell her. Are you supposed to be here? Or are you AWOL?'

'Fuck you, Deverill!'

Deverill couldn't believe it – maybe he had happened on the *real* reason for how Luger was here. Could it be that Luger really had escaped from Brooks? Had they had him in the loony bin, or almost there, and he'd escaped? 'Which is it, sir? Are you on drugs? Did you break out of custody somewhere?'

'Dev, stop it!' Annie shouted. 'What are you doing?'

'You want to take me out now, don't you, Colonel?' Dev shouted. 'You gonna take a shot at me?'

He did. It came out of nowhere, with a snap that surprised Deverill again, even though he was on full alert and he had already seen Luger move once tonight. The blow landed on the left side of Dev's face, staggering him.

'David!' Annie cried. She helped Dev into the living room, holding his face. There was a drop of blood coming out of the corner of his left eye. 'David, are you *crazy?*' David Luger's face went blank, and his mouth dropped open in surprise. Her face registered surprise when she realized what she'd said. 'I ... I didn't mean that...' she stammered. 'David...'

'I'm leaving, Annie,' he said in a low, solemn voice. The sight of her in his shirt, fresh out of the shower, from *his* shower, holding *his* face, was almost too much for him to bear. 'I won't be back.'

'D-David? Where are you going?'

'Away.'

'Where? I don't understand.'

'There's nothing to understand, Annie,' Luger said. 'I just came here to say good-bye.'

'What's going on?'

'I can't tell you, Annie,' he replied, the hurt obvious in his eyes. 'But I'll be okay. Everything's going to be okay.'

'David, you're scaring me. Tell me what's going on. Please.'

'Good-bye, Annie,' he said. Annie wanted to get up and follow him, but Dev grasped her wrist, and it froze her. Luger didn't seem like he was on any kind of drugs, not agitated or wild at all – in fact, he seemed very calm. Too calm. What in *hell* was going on?

'Will I ever see you again, David?' she asked. But he said nothing, only turned and walked down the stairs and out to the parking lot until he was out of sight.

Sky Masters Inc. Corporate Headquarters, Arkansas International Jetport, Blytheville, Arkansas several days later

Little Bradley J. McLanahan couldn't take his eyes off the big Sky Masters Inc. DC-10, brightly illuminated by banks of ballpark lights, as the last forklifts moved away and the big port-side cargo doors motored closed. He pulled on his mother's blue jeans. 'Are we going flying, Mommy?'

'Not tonight, honey,' Wendy replied. 'Daddy's going flying tonight.'

'I need to go flying,' he protested. The big cargo plane/tanker/command aircraft started up its fuselage engine. He turned to Patrick, realized he had not made his request politely, and pleaded, 'Please, can I go flying with you, Daddy?'

'Not tonight, big guy,' Patrick replied. 'When I get home, we'll go fly the 210, okay?' But his son's attention was fully riveted on the DC-10, saving Patrick's heartstrings from his son's earnest pleading.

'Stealing away in the middle of the night,' Wendy said to Patrick. 'This can't be right if we have to sneak away like this.'

'President Martindale said go, so we're going,' Patrick said. 'I just wish you were coming along.'

'Jon's still got a business to run,' Wendy said. 'Helen and I are it.'

'Just until things cool down.'

'Then I think you'll be gone an awful long time,' Wendy said, 'because I think things have barely begun to warm up.' She sighed, then asked, 'Any idea where you'll be?'

'Turkey or Ukraine,' Patrick replied. 'We won't make the final decision until we depart our refueling stop, either in Spain or Belgium.'

'I feel like we're being pursued harder than the guy we're trying to stop.'

'We are – for now,' Patrick said. 'Something will happen soon. My guess is that we'll get a sanction from the White House. Kevin will eventually make President Thorn realize we're not a threat to him or his administration.' They heard the port engine on the DC-10 spool up, which was a signal to board. 'I'd better go.' He kissed his son on the cheek, then gave Wendy a hug and a kiss.

'I wish I was coming along,' Wendy said. 'No, actually, I wish we weren't doing this. For some reason, it seems wrong.'

'I don't know if it's wrong or not,' Patrick said as he hugged her tightly. 'I wish I knew.'

'Just be safe, then.'

'I will.' He kissed her one last time, then pulled away and headed for the airstairs. He took a seat near David Luger, Jon Masters, Hal Briggs, Chris Wohl, and Marcia Preston. Moments later, the starboard engine fired up, and they began taxiing for takeoff.

Patrick was just settling into his palletized passenger seat when he heard via his subcutaneous transceiver: 'Patrick, this is Wendy. I see three helicopters in formation coming in low over the airport. No marking that we can see.'

At that same moment, Patrick heard on the cabin intercom: 'General McLanahan, you'd better get up here.'

Patrick raced for the cockpit. Through the windscreen he saw the helicopters as they raced in at treetop level from the southwest. They broke formation, so Patrick could see only one of them.

'Who are they?' the DC-10's copilot asked – then blanched as he heard an announcement on the emergency UHF frequency. 'Oh, shit...'

The flight engineer handed Patrick a headset. 'You'd better listen to this, sir,' he said.

'Attention Sky Masters DC-10 taxiing for takeoff, this is the FBI,' Patrick heard. 'You are hereby ordered to stop immediately and shut down your engines. Repeat, stop and shut down immediately.'

'What do we do, sir?' the pilot asked.

'Keep going,' Patrick replied. 'Take the next

taxiway onto the runway, get airborne as soon as you can.'

'We're pretty close to gross weight, sir,' the engineer said. 'An intersection takeoff won't give us enough accelerate-stop distance.'

'Just do it,' Patrick said. 'If those choppers get any closer and block our path, we'll all be in jail before you know it.' The pilot made a sudden turn onto the intersecting taxiway, and while the copilot and flight engineer frantically completed the pretakeoff checks, the pilot swung right on the runway, lining up for takeoff.

'General McLanahan, this is Earthmover.' Patrick heard Lieutenant-General Terrill Samson's voice in his head through the implanted transceiver. 'Better shut it down. The FBI is going to block the runway.'

'Terrill, what did you do?' Patrick asked.

'Yes, I told them you might be here – hard to believe, but the FBI didn't know about Sky Masters or this facility,' Samson said.

'So you told them.'

'I cooperated with a federal investigation,' Samson retorted. 'They have a warrant to search the facility and all the aircraft. You need to cooperate with them. Shut it down. Don't continue the takeoff. You'll kill everyone on board that plane.'

'Then I wish you were on board with me, Samson,' Patrick said bitterly. He shouted to the pilots, 'Get this thing in the air!' The last thing he saw over on the parking ramp was a large group of armed FBI agents surrounding Wendy, his son Bradley, and the others. One FBI agent had an M-16 pointed at his wife and son, the muzzle just inches away. Wendy was clutching their son tightly, afraid to move.

The FBI's Jet Ranger helicopter had just set down about three-quarters of the way down the runway. The pilot immediately realized the DC-10 wasn't going to stop, and yanked the helicopter off the run-way and quick-taxied clear. The DC-10 had started to rotate to takeoff attitude at that spot, and the wingtip vortices sent the chopper spinning and flipped it on its side.

'McLanahan,' Terrill Samson's disembodied voice said, 'what has gotten into you? You may have killed that helicopter crew! Are you crazy?'

'If any harm comes to my family, I'll be looking for *you*, Samson,' Patrick vowed.

'They're taking Wendy and your son into custody,' Samson said. 'She won't be placed under arrest unless she fails to cooperate. I advise you to orbit the field and burn down fuel until you can land right back here.'

'Not one hair disturbed on either of their heads,' Patrick warned. 'I hold you responsible.'

'*I am not your enemy, Patrick!*' Samson thundered. 'Dammit, don't you understand? The ghost of Brad Elliott has got you completely screwed up. Don't let it affect your family as well. If you don't give yourself up, Patrick, I can't be responsible for what happens to them.'

It was the hardest thing Patrick ever had to do – *not* to give the order to turn around.

Terrill Samson walked over to check out a noise far louder than the roar of the Sky Masters DC-10 taking off or the sirens on the police and FBI cars

584

still streaming onto the tarmac – the noise of a screaming child. An FBI SWAT officer dressed in full black combat gear and carrying an MP-5K submachine gun was trying to take Bradley James McLanahan out of Wendy McLanahan's arms.

'Stop resisting!' the officer was shouting. Wendy was now fighting off three FBI agents. 'Let the kid go!'

Samson stepped in and pulled the FBI agents away from Wendy and the boy. 'Back off, Officer, back off.'

'They're suspects, General,' one of the hooded officers said. 'They need to be handcuffed until we can search the area.'

'I said, back off,' Samson said. The big three-star general put his arms around Wendy McLanahan and eased her away from the armored officer. 'I'll take responsibility for these two.'

But Wendy shrugged away from him. 'You get away from me, too, Samson,' she cried. 'I'd rather be in an isolation cell than be near you.' But Samson continued to escort her away, the FBI agents did not protest, and Wendy turned her attention to Bradley's screaming and did not resist further.

'Where is Patrick going, Wendy?'

'Go to hell, Samson.'

'This is an investigation only, Wendy – we have no arrest warrants,' Samson said. 'But if Patrick disappears with that aircraft, he'll be charged with interfering with a federal investigation, evidence tampering, and withholding evidence. He'll be a fugitive. If we find evidence that any-one here conspired with McLanahan to take that plane, this whole place will be shut down and locked up and everyone will go to jail. This is serious, Wendy. You've got to tell me where he's going, and tell me fast.'

'Samson, I'm not going to tell you a thing,' Wendy said, turning Bradley's eyes away from the red flashing lights to try to soothe him. 'But I will ask you one question.'

'I know, I know – you think I'm the bad guy because I won't go along with McLanahan and help him fight his little personal war,' Samson interjected. 'You're going to ask: Where's my loyalty? Where's my integrity? Don't I care about what's going on? Why don't I do something about it?'

'No,' Wendy McLanahan asked. 'My question is: are you having fun?'

'Fun?' Samson was incredulous. The place was sheer bedlam, police were leading technicians and engineers away in handcuffs, and her son was screaming in holy terror. 'Fun? Are you trying to be funny, Doctor? I see nothing fun going on here.'

'Then you're just doing your job, is that right, General?'

Samson could not reply. Helping the FBI track down his friend and ex-deputy commander, raiding a private company, and handcuffing men and women he knew and trusted because Patrick McLanahan *might* be planning to stage an attack on another country was certainly not in his job description. So why was he doing this? Just because he was ordered to do it? 'No, I'm not having fun, Wendy. I'm having a really terrible time.'

'I just wanted to check,' Wendy said bitterly.

'Because I'm sure you're not doing this to learn how to be a better person or help contribute to your world. Since the only other reason to do something is to have fun, and you're obviously not having fun, I'm confused. Why are you doing this?' And Wendy took her screaming son and walked toward the police vans, where she submitted to having a police woman take Bradley out of her arms. She was handcuffed behind her back, searched from head to foot, and seated in the front seat of the van beside the police woman and her son.

Terrill Samson wanted to go after her, steer her and Bradley away from the confusion and lights and noise, but he could not make his feet move. His world was unraveling. First the President of the United States, then the Russians, and now the press blows the doors off his command; his deputy commander engineers a one-man war against the Russians and against a powerful Russian mafioso; now he helps the government bust a private company accused of attacking the Russians. He had no idea what was going to happen next.

But one thing was certain: Patrick McLanahan was a fighter, a warrior, and he was continuing to fight. And so far, he was winning. Maybe not every battle, maybe not even most of them – but he was winning. Terrill Samson sure as heck couldn't call himself a winner right now.

Somehow, he had to find a way to make himself a winner.

Chapter Nine

Over the Black Sea
several months later

'There they are, sir,' one of the lookouts radioed. 'They look like Russian helicopters. Mil Mi-14s, long-range land-based helicopters. No markings on them.'

'What in hell do they want?' the ship's captain, Sergei Trevnikov, muttered nervously, restlessly peering at the helicopters through his binoculars. He hoped they were just joyriding or patrolling, since there was no place for helicopters that big to set down on his ship. 'Still no response on hailing frequencies or aviation emergency channels?'

'No, sir.'

'*Pasasi zalupu!*' Trevnikov swore. Trevnikov was the skipper of the Russian oil tanker *Ustinov*, a privately owned tanker based out of Novorossijsk carrying almost a million barrels of crude oil bound for the big new oil terminal at Burgas, Bulgaria. He was accustomed to supply, medical, and VIP helicopters coming out to the ship all the time, but these three helicopters were unidentified, unannounced, and definitely unwanted.

'Quickly, have the quartermaster break out rifles and side arms,' Trevnikov ordered. He switched channels on his radio to the Black Sea emergency distress frequency. 'Russian Federation Navy, Russian Federation Navy, Russian Federation Navy, this is the Russian flag tanker vessel *Ustinov* on emergency channel, under way ninety-eight kilometers north of Zonguldak, Turkey, heading west on transit approach to the Metyorgaz terminal at Burgas. Three military helicopters are approaching us from the north. They appear to be Russian-made military Mi-14 helicopters. They are unidentified and are not responding to our hails. We request immediate assistance. Over.'

It took several calls, but moments later a Russian Federation Navy radio operator sent the captain over to another channel. 'Tanker *Ustinov*, we read you loud and clear,' the radioman said. 'Are you in danger at this time?'

'Danger? *Da, byt v glubokay zhopi!* Yes, I'm in deep shit! I think these bastards mean to board us! They are maneuvering in on our bow right now.'

'We acknowledge, Ustinov,' the Russian radio operator said. 'We are passing along your request for assistance at this time. Maintain a watch on this channel and advise of any hostile action. Over.'

'What should we do in the meantime? Suck our thumbs? Should we stop?'

'Command suggests you comply with their instructions to avoid any damage to your vessel that will render you dead in the water or unable to maintain steerageway,' the radio operator replied. 'Are you laden at this time?'

'Hell, yes, we're laden – we have a *million barrels* of crude oil on board!' Trevnikov shouted. He paused, decided, and then added, 'We are a Metyorgaz vessel. Do you understand? *Metyorgaz.*

Check our records – you'll learn who owns this vessel and all the oil in it. I suggest you tell that to your superiors, and you had better do it quick.'

It was indeed quick. Only a few minutes later, a different voice came on the radio. 'Tanker *Ustinov*, this is Commander Boriskov, commander of the destroyer *Besstrashny*, Seventy-ninth Destroyer Group, Novorossijsk,' came the announcement. 'We copy you are being interdicted by unidentified military helicopters in treaty waters. Describe any markings you see and any weapons visible.'

'They are big fucking transport helicopters,' Trevnikov replied. Now the Russian Navy was doing something. Mention 'Metyorgaz' to them, and they all start quaking in their boots. No one, not even the Russian Federation Navy, wants to fuck with Pavel Kazakov. 'I don't see any markings or weapons.'

'We acknowledge. Patrol and action aircraft and vessels are under way,' the commander said. 'We recommend you reverse course if able and do not give permission to be boarded.'

'Well, no shit,' Trevnikov said. 'But I will miss my off-load slot if I come about.' The new Metyorgaz terminal at Burgas, Bulgaria, which had just opened, was one of the largest and finest in all of Eastern Europe. The new Metyorgaz pipeline from Burgas to Vlore, Albania, was cutting the cost of transporting petroleum to markets in Western Europe by thirty percent at least, which meant huge profits for all users. As a result, the Burgas terminal was always booked, and reserved slots could be held open only for very short periods of time. A delay of even six or seven hours could mean sitting at anchor in the Black Sea for days waiting for another slot. 'Can't you send a fighter jet out here to scare these bastards away?'

'We are readying armed aircraft at this time,' the Navy commander said, 'but it will take them some time to reach your position. You will help us by reversing course. Acknowledge.'

'All right, all right,' Trevnikov said. To his helmsman, he ordered, 'Helm, hard about.' He liked giving that order, because it took big tankers like the *Ustinov*, over two hundred meters long and over one hundred and fifty thousand tons, almost an hour and about thirty kilometers to execute a course reversal. 'I am executing a heading change, coming to starboard to heading zero-six-zero,' Trevnikov radioed.

'Very well,' the Navy guy said. 'Where are these helicopters now?'

Trevnikov searched the horizon and followed his bridge crew's pointing fingers. 'About two hundred meters off my bow,' he replied on the radio. 'They are carrying fuel tanks. They look like torpedoes, but they are fuel tanks. My men tell me they are Mi-14 transport helicopters. They are approaching amidships ... wait! I see ropes! They are throwing ropes down from the helicopters ... they are rappelling down from the helicopters! Soldiers! Commandos! They are invading my ship with commandos! About eight from each helicopter! They are on my deck, moving toward the wheelhouse! *There are commandos on my ship!*'

'Remain calm, Captain,' the Russian navy

commander said. 'Our patrol aircraft is less than ten minutes out, we are dispatching jet aircraft, and we have a warship about two hours away. Can you secure the bridge?'

'Against commandos? For two hours? Are you insane?' Trevnikov ordered the doors shut and barred. He had no illusions that he could put up any kind of defense against them, but he was determined to try. He had his crew members take cover in front of the helmsman's console, where they had good cover and could see both bridge wing doors, and he secured and locked the two weather doors and the inside passageway door. Four of his crew members were armed, two with automatic rifles and the other two with automatic pistols.

Ten minutes later, the steel weather door on the port side of the bridge blew open. To the captain's surprise, a lone, unarmed figure stepped into the doorway. 'Open fire!' the captain shouted. All four men began firing as fast as they could. The figure simply stood there ... and stood there. He never went down. They must have emptied eighty rounds on him – he was less than ten meters away – but he did not go down.

'*Astanavleevat'sya!*' the officer shouted in very poor Russian, with a definite Western accent. '*Gyde deerektaram?*'

'Who are you?' the captain shouted in Russian. The air was thick and hazy with the smell of burnt gunpowder. Did they have blanks or noise-makers in their guns? Why didn't he go down...? 'What do you want?' To his men, he said in a low but urgent voice, 'Reload quickly, dammit!'

'*Gyde deerektaram?*' the figure repeated.

'Speak English – your Russian is giving me a headache,' Trevnikov shouted, now in English. 'I am the captain. What in hell do you want on my ship?' At that moment, the starboard-side weather door blew open too, and just like the first, another figure stood, unarmed, in the doorway. One crew member with a rifle opened fire, emptying a thirty-round magazine on him in five seconds – but like the first, he did not go down. The first armored terrorist just stood there, calmly observing while his partner was shot at with a rifle. '*Who are you?*' the captain repeated, his eyes bugging out in sheer terror now. 'What do you want?'

'I want you to shut up and do as you are told,' the first commando replied. 'Drop your weapons and no one will get hurt, I promise.'

'*Ssat ya na nivo hat'el!*' the executive officer shouted, and he raised his reloaded pistol at the first man, who had taken several steps toward the Russians. But before the XO could fire, they heard and felt a snap of electricity emanating from somewhere on the figure's body, and the XO flew backward, crumpled against the forward bulkhead, and lay jerking and twitching in muscle spasms on the deck.

'Drop your weapons *now!*' the second figure ordered. They did, and they all stood up from behind the console with their hands raised in surrender. More commandos ran in and quickly began to search the bridge crew. They quickly bound the bridge officers' hands behind their backs with nylon handcuffs, all but the captain, and led them away.

'Your ship is now under my command,' the first figure said in an electronically synthesized voice, like a robot's. The captain stared in disbelief at him. He was dressed head to toe in what appeared to be a thin gray outfit, with a full-face helmet and a thin molded backpack. There was not a mark on him from bullets or from anything else. The captain noticed small protrusions from his shoulders that looked like electrodes – probably the source of the shock beam that had disabled his executive officer.

'You are hijacking an *oil tanker?* In the middle of the fucking Black Sea? Do you have any idea of what the hell you are doing?'

'We'll see,' the strange commando said. He began issuing orders to his men as they herded the bridge crew out. The second commando, dressed in the strange but obviously very effective body armor as well, departed the bridge.

Trevnikov stepped closer to the masked commando. 'Do you know who owns this vessel, asshole?'

'Metyorgaz,' the commando replied.

'And do you know who owns Metyorgaz?'

'Metyor IIG.'

'And do you know–?'

'I know perfectly well that Pavel Kazakov, the Russian gangster and drug lord, owns this vessel and all the oil in it,' the commando said, with a hint of triumph in his voice. 'But you won't be making any deliveries for him anymore.'

'That is not your first mistake today, *aslayop,*' Trevnikov said. This time it was his turn to give

597

the terrorist an evil smile. 'But it could very well be your last. When Comrade Kazakov finds out some American commandos in silly dance costumes hijacked his tanker, he'll take great pleasure in roasting you all alive.'

'Don't count on it, *sraka*,' the commando said. He took a plastic handcuff from a belt pouch behind his back and bound Trevnikov's hands behind his back himself, and he was led out of the bridge.

Twenty minutes later, the terrorists had rounded up the entire crew and had them assembled on the bow with their hands on their heads. Two more helicopters soon arrived, carrying two dozen masked men, armed only with side arms, who took over the controls of the ship, plus several long crates and other supplies brought in slung under the helicopters. Soon the tanker *Ustinov* was heading south, toward Turkey.

But they were not alone for long. Several minutes later, several more helicopters arrived: one belonging to a state-controlled Turkish Radio and Television Corporation TV crew from Ankara, plus two Mil Mi-14 Haze land-based marine assault helicopters belonging to the Russian Federation Naval Infantry.

'Attention, commandos aboard the *Ustinov*, this is the Russian Federation Naval Infantry,' the radio call came. 'You have illegally commandeered a Russian Federation flag vessel on the high seas. We have orders to take control of the vessel. We order you to immediately surrender control of the vessel and all of you come out on deck in plain sight and with weapons on the deck.' No reply. 'Do not be a fool,' the Russian commander went on. 'We have a Russian Navy destroyer less than two hours away. You will not reach any shore before our destroyer reaches you.' Still no reply. 'Very well. Prepare to die.'

The Russian transport helicopters kept coming. They were within a mile of the *Ustinov* when suddenly a bright line of fire arced across the darkening evening sky from the mid-deck of the tanker. A missile struck one of the Russian Federation Navy helicopters, its engine exploded into a thousand pieces, and it plunged into the Black Sea. The other helicopter immediately reversed course and headed back to Russia. A Turkish Coast Guard helicopter, on the scene monitoring the tanker as it headed toward the Turkish coast, was on the crash scene immediately to help rescue survivors.

Darkness had fallen by the time the second wave arrived: a Russian Federation Navy Sukhoi-24 'Fencer' attack plane from Novorossijsk. The Su-24 carried two Kh-29 'Kedge' imaging-infrared guided air-to-surface missiles. It remained above fifteen thousand feet and kept its speed up to avoid being a target for shoulder-fired missiles from the hijackers on the ship. At a range of ten miles, the pilot was able to lock the stern of the *Ustinov* in his imaging-infrared telescopic sensor. His orders: shoot out the *Ustinov's* rudder and propeller and disable it. At a range of five miles, the Kh-29 was within range. The pilot unsafed his firing button...

...and at that exact moment, the Su-24's right engine exploded in a ball of fire, and the crew

599

ejected seconds before the whole plane exploded.

It took another hour for a second Sukhoi-24 attack jet to reach the tanker, but it, too, disappeared from radar shortly before launching an attack on the tanker – and it, too, was well out of range of a man-portable antiaircraft missile. Several minutes later, one of the engines on a Russian Federation Navy Tupolev-95 maritime patrol and attack plane inbound toward the tanker was hit and destroyed by another missile, and was forced to turn back.

By then, the Russian Federation Navy destroyer *Besstrashny*, originally based in Ukraine but moved to Novorossijsk when the ship was transferred back to Russia after the breakup of the Soviet Union, was close on the scene. The tactical action officers aboard the Russian destroyer had warned all air and surface traffic away from the area, and its Kamov Ka-27 helicopter had already been datalinking the tanker's exact position to the ship. There were several Turkish Coast Guard vessels in the vicinity, all coastal patrol vessels carrying light weapons – no threat to the *Besstrashny*, one of the largest warships in the Black Sea.

The skipper met with the weapons officers and tactical action officer in the Combat Information Center. 'When will we be within range of the *Ustinov?*' Captain Boriskov asked.

'We are well within range of the 3M-82 *Moskit*, sir,' the weapons officer responded. The *Moskit* was a large supersonic, radar-guided antiship missile.

'I don't want to sink the damn ship, just disable it,' the captain said.

'Then all we have is the forward AK-130 until we're within helicopter range,' the TAO cut in.

'What do we target? The rudder area? The props? Engineering?'

'I suggest we hit the superstructure, sir,' the TAO said. 'Create some confusion, maybe kill a bunch of the terrorists, and send the naval infantry aboard to try to take control of the ship again. If we disable the ship's steering and propulsion systems, we could create an even larger disaster if we can't stop the ship and it runs aground in Turkey.'

'Ask me if I care if it runs aground in Turkey,' the captain sneered.

'But if it did, it would be partially our fault – and that might be the terrorists' ultimate objective,' one of the intelligence officers said. He lowered his voice, then added, 'Remember who owns that ship and its cargo, sir.'

The skipper's face blanched. Pavel Kazakov.

In the last several months, Pavel Kazakov had become one of the wealthiest, most well-known, and most talked-about men in the entire world. He'd already had an evil reputation that had made him simply dangerous. Now he had real, legitimate power behind him. His oil empire stretched from the Caspian to the Adriatic Sea. He was shipping more oil than half the members of OPEC, and he was doing it more cheaply and more efficiently than anyone could believe. Nations and corporations were becoming rich from him, which meant more and more nations were protecting and underwriting his ventures.

His chief underwriter seemed to be the Russian

Army itself. From Georgia in the east to Albania in the west, the Russian army maintained a continuous, ominous presence. Although Russian troops were not in Georgia itself, the Republic of Georgia knew that thousands of Russian troops were massed on its northern border, ready to invade if the government was unwilling or unable to control rival factional fighting in the Nagorno–Karabakh region that might affect Metyorgaz oil-transport operations. The Russian army was already cracking down on the cross-border movement of Muslim rebels between the province of Chechnya and Georgia, and they were not shy about crossing the border on occasion to pursue Muslim guerrillas. The Russian navy had also increased patrols on the Black Sea to protect increased tanker traffic.

Most significantly, the Russian army was back in the Balkans with a force and presence unseen since World War II. Fifty thousand troops were stationed in eleven key bases in Bulgaria, Macedonia, Serbia, Bosnia-Herzegovina, Croatia, Montenegro, the Serbian provinces of Vojvodina and Kosovo, and Albania, ostensibly as 'peacekeepers' enforcing United Nations resolutions. Their presence was centered around the new Metyorgaz pipeline route, so there was very little doubt about their real mission, but they also enforced United Nations resolutions and even abided by most NATO rules of engagement and operations orders, operating almost at will throughout the Balkans, from Slovenia to the Black Sea, from Hungary to the Greek border.

But rather than feel threatened, the countries

saw this as an advantage. Fighting between the government and gunrunners or drug dealers had all but vanished – the Russian army was ruthless in pursuing anyone even suspected of illegally crossing the borders, selling drugs, or trying to rearm rebel forces anywhere in the Balkans. Incidents of clashes between Serbs and other ethnic groups in the Balkans, and between the various religious factions, had all but ceased as well. The Balkans were actually enjoying the first real semblance of peace since the bad old days of Marshal Tito.

True, there were always large numbers of Russian or German transport planes on almost every large airport in several major cities in the Balkans, or a Russian or German attack helicopter flying overhead all the time. This made many folks nervous, especially the older generations, who could still remember World War II. Whereas a few months earlier Pavel Kazakov had been reviled and pursued throughout Europe – he was still under indictment for narcotics trafficking and other violent crimes in twenty-three countries around the world – today he was being lauded as some sort of savior, a dashing entrepreneur rescuing the poorest nations in Europe from abject poverty. He was sponsoring drug-eradication programs in several dozen nations around the world – this from the man who had perfected the art of drug smuggling in Europe to a fine art, whom some had once accused of pumping heroin through his pipelines instead of oil.

But no one could doubt that their presence was benefiting everyone. The bottom line: everyone seemed to be getting rich from the oil. What was there not to like?

'A sort of eco-terrorist thing?' the skipper asked, immediately aware that it was his responsibility – not to mention in his, and his family's, best interest – not to screw this up. He shook his head when the intel officer nodded. *'Ni kruti mn'e yaytsa,'* he said with disgust.

'The tanker has an alternate control center on the second floor of the superstructure,' the chief engineer's mate said, producing a faxed sketch of the tanker. 'If we shell the bridge, even destroy it, we can still control the ship from there. The terrorists are very likely up on the bridge – we're bound to nail a few of them there.'

'All right,' the captain decided. 'We close the distance until we can get within pinpoint firing range of the tanker, then shell the superstructure only, staying away from the alternate control center, the rudder, and the propulsion system. Weapons, what range would that be?'

'We should use the optronic sights and laser rangefinder,' he suggested. 'In this weather, in these conditions, we should close to at least fifteen kilometers.'

'Very well,' Boriskov said. 'Just before we start shelling the superstructure, we'll launch the air and surface assault craft. Coordinate your shelling with the assault.' The officers nodded their heads in agreement. *'Loshka gavna v bochki m'oda.* There's still a spoonful of shit in the honey barrel. What about the Sukhoi-24 and Tupolev-95 attacks? What hit them? Any ideas?'

'No idea, sir,' the TAO replied. 'We're just now

within radar range of the area where they were hit. We've been monitoring Turkey's air traffic control network, and there's no sign of any attack aircraft launching from there.'

'I don't think Turkey would be stupid enough to interfere with this incident,' the captain said. 'It doesn't make sense – Turkey helping a bunch of idiotic terrorists trying to hijack an oil tanker. Where do they think they are going to go? We'll put a stop to this in no time.'

Codlea, Bulgaria
that same time

'Wake up!' Fursenko shouted wildly. 'Wake up, damn you, or he'll kill us all!' He could smell alcohol, and beads of sweat popped on the back of his neck.

Ion Stoica's head felt as if it was going to explode, and his mouth and tongue felt as dry and as rough as sandpaper. He rolled wearily onto his side. 'What in hell do you want, Fursenko?'

'One of Metyor's oil tankers in the Black Sea is under attack,' Fursenko exclaimed. That got Stoica's attention. 'Someone has hijacked it! Comrade Kazakov wants you to launch immediately!'

Stoica struggled to his feet, put on his flight suit over a pair of light-weight cotton underwear, stumbled into his boots, and headed out of his room in a small building adjacent to the main hangar. That little wooden building had been his home now for over eight months. Up until three months before, he had had to share it with

Gennadi Yegorov, his weapons officer aboard the Metyor Mt-179 stealth fighter, but he'd finally convinced him to get his own place. Yegorov had made up a place over the main hangar – the noise from the aircraft maintenance crews below didn't bother him.

They made their way across the dark dirt streets toward the security checkpoint to the main hangar where the Mt-179 Tyenee had been stored. Except for just a few test flights, they hadn't flown the bird too often. NATO and Romanian air patrols had come fairly close to the base, but the Mt-179 had been able to dispatch them quickly and easily.

'You've been drinking!' Fursenko said, horrified, as they passed through the outer security post.

'Screw you, Doctor,' Stoica said. 'I've been holed up in this place for over half a year with no leave and no time off. The food is lousy and I haven't seen a woman worth fucking in three months. I bought some homemade wine from one of the locals, and if I'd had a chance to drink some then, I probably would've fucked the old hag. Now shut up. You're making my head hurt.'

Yegorov was already inside, drawing on a chart of the Black Sea and northern Turkey. The guy was unreal, Stoica thought – noise, loneliness, quiet, and deprivation didn't bother Yegorov one bit. He didn't smoke, drink, play cards, or party like the others assigned here. He had a lot of male friends in the maintenance department – maybe Gennadi was curing his loneliness with some late-night visits to the maintenance group's barracks. Maybe that's why he'd agreed to relocate to over the maintenance hangar.

'Ion's here, sir,' Yegorov said to a speakerphone.

'Nice of you to join us, Stoica,' the sneering voice of Pavel Kazakov came over the speaker.

'Sorry, sir. I came as soon as I heard.' He stopped himself from making an obscene gesture to the speakerphone, motioned to a maintenance officer for coffee, and pulled out a cigarette from a flight suit pocket. 'Some retards are attacking one of your tankers?'

'A group of terrorists – the exact number is unknown, but around eight to twelve – fast-roped onto the tanker *Ustinov* a couple hours ago,' Yegorov summarized. 'They have shoulder-fired antiaircraft missiles and have shot down a Navy helicopter. The tanker is heading south into Turkish waters, destination unknown.'

Stoica shook his head, totally confused. He took a big sip of coffee. 'So what are we supposed to do?'

'Two Russian maritime patrol aircraft, a Sukhoi-24 and Tupolev-95, were attacked by an undetected aircraft en route to the tanker,' Yegorov explained. 'Mr Kazakov believes someone – NATO, the Americans, or perhaps the Turks – have sent stealth aircraft into the area to keep the Russian aircraft away. He wants us to investigate. Tonight.'

'Yes, sir,' Stoica said, trying to sound enthusiastic. 'If someone's up there, we'll nail his ass to the wall.' He turned to the maintenance officer. 'How long before we are ready to fly?'

'About twenty minutes, sir,' the officer said. Stoica nodded, inwardly groaning. It was going to take him a lot longer than that to sober up. Maybe coffee and some one-hundred-percent oxygen would help.

'There is a Russian destroyer pursuing the tanker, getting ready to land some naval infantry on the tanker to recapture it,' Kazakov said. 'If there's another aircraft out there, I want you to get it. Don't let anyone get a shot off at either the tanker or the destroyer. I want that tanker recovered intact and the oil safe. Do you understand?' The line went dead before anyone could respond.

Stoica finished the coffee with a gulp. 'Good luck to you, too, sir,' he muttered sarcastically.

Aboard the Russian Federation Navy destroyer *Besstrashny* a short time later

With the captain back on the bridge monitoring the attack, their plan got under way. The tactical action officer (TAO) fed in information from his India-band surface-search radar when it came within range, followed by more precise targeting information from its optronic telescopic night sight and laser rangefinder. The tanker was on a constant heading and speed, so targeting was easy. 'Bridge, combat,' the TAO radioed, 'we've got a clear sight of the target, Captain.'

The captain got up, went to the aft part of the bridge, and checked the repeaters of the targeting screens from the Combat Information Center. The sights were clearly locked on the upper.

portion of the large white superstructure. 'Very well. Range?'

'Twenty-one kilometers, sir.'

'Any change in target heading or speed?'

'No, sir.'

'Any other aircraft or vessels nearby?'

'No vessels within ten kilometers of the tanker, sir. All of the vessels nearby have been accounted for. No threat to us.'

'Very well. Launch the surface and air attack teams.' A small team of six Russian Federation Naval Infantry commandos were launched aboard the *Besstrashny*'s Ka-27 helicopter and sent to try to secretly board the tanker; at the same time, they loaded a launch with two dozen Naval Infantry commandos to attempt a raid from the sea.

When fifteen kilometers out, the stern section of the tanker was in clear sight on the optronic monitors. 'Still no change in target heading or speed,' the TAO reported. 'It looks like it's simply going to ground itself on the northern Turkish coast, about halfway between the Turkish naval base at Eregli and the coastal resort city of Zonguldak.'

'Any oil facilities there?' the skipper asked his intelligence officer. 'Any way the Turks can off-load the oil?'

'You mean, *steal* it?' the intel officer asked incredulously.

'Just answer the damned question.'

'Zonguldak is a coastal residential, resort, and university town,' the intel officer said. 'Large desalinization plant, large nuclear-power-generating facility there, but no oil refineries or oil off-loading or transshipment facilities.'

'A nuclear power plant, eh?' the captain mused. 'Is it on the coast?'

'It's about twenty kilometers south of the projected impact area and about two kilometers inland, closer to the naval base.'

The captain was still considering the eco-terrorist angle, but it was starting to distract him, and he didn't need that right now. 'Comm, Bridge, send one last message to fleet headquarters, requesting permission to begin our operation.'

A few moments later: 'Bridge, Comm, message from Fleet, operation approved, commence when ready.'

'Very well.' He picked up the ship's intercom. 'All hands, this is the captain. We will commence attack operations immediately.' To the officer of the deck, he ordered, 'Sound general quarters.' The alarms and announcements began, and the captain was handed his helmet, headphones, and life jacket. 'Release batteries. Commence...'

'Bridge, Combat, high-speed air bandit, bearing zero-five-zero, range three-two kilometers, low, heading southwest at nine-two-zero kilometers per hour!'

'*Byt v glubokay zhopi*, there's our mystery attacker,' the captain swore.

'Recommend heading two-three-zero, flank speed, and canceling the attack on the tanker, sir,' the executive officer said.

'My orders are to stop those terrorists from taking that tanker into Turkish waters,' the captain said. 'Maintain course and speed, stand by to open fire.'

'He's not turning,' the satellite surveillance officer reported. 'Increasing speed to twenty knots.'

'Looks like he's not going to break off his attack on the tanker,' Jon Masters said. 'We might be too late.'

'Not yet,' David Luger said. 'I'll push AALF up and take it down, and let's see what he does.'

Masters and Luger, along with a team of technicians, were aboard Sky Masters Inc.'s DC-10 carrier aircraft, orbiting sixty miles north near Ukrainian airspace. The satellite images they were viewing came from a string of six small imaging reconnaissance satellites called NIRTSats (Need It Right This Second satellites), launched earlier by Masters specifically for this operation. The satellites, beaming their signals to a geosynchronous relay satellite that then sent the images to the DC-10 launch aircraft, would provide continuous images of the entire Black Sea region for the next week.

Luger happily entered commands into a keyboard. Fifty miles to the south, a small aircraft began a steep dive and accelerated to almost the speed of sound. The small aircraft was called 'AALF,' an acronym that stood for Autonomous Air Launched Fighter. Launched from the DC-10, AALF was a sophisticated, high-speed, highly maneuverable cruise missile with a brain. AALF was not steered like other unmanned aerial vehicles. It was simply given a task to do, and AALF would use its neural computer logic functions, combined with sensor and preprogrammed threat data, to determine its own way to accomplish the mission. David Luger simply acted as the coach, telling AALF what they wanted it to do. After it had been first launched from the DC-10, AALF had been ordered to be an interceptor, and it had sneaked up on the Sukhoi-24 and Tupolev-95 aircraft and attacked them with internal Sidewinder air-to-air missiles.

Right now, Luger wanted AALF to pretend it was a sea-skimming antiship missile. AALF descended until it was less than two hundred feet above the Black Sea, then accelerated to six hundred miles an hour and headed for the destroyer *Besstrashny*, making an occasional zigzag pattern as a sophisticated antiship missile would do. The *Besstrashny* responded as expected, turning hard to starboard to present as small a target to the incoming missile as possible and also to bring its aft 130-millimeter dual-purpose guns and aft SA-N-7 antiaircraft missiles to bear.

Then, just before AALF flew within gun range, it turned away, staying outside maximum gun range. The crew of the Russian destroyer couldn't ignore the threat, so they kept on maneuvering to keep its stern to the missile in case it started another attack. As it did, the tanker *Ustinov* sailed farther and farther away, well out of gun range now. The KA-27 helicopter with its commandos on board had no choice but to turn around – they could not risk facing more shoulder-fired anti-aircraft missiles without some sort of covering fire to help screen their approach. The launch carrying two dozen naval infantry commandos continued their approach, easily overtaking the much slower tanker.

'See 'em yet, guys?' Luger radioed. He was watching the launch's approach on the satellite surveillance video. 'About four miles dead astern, heading toward you at forty knots.'

Patrick McLanahan deactivated his helmet's electronic visor. He and Hal Briggs were wearing the electronic body armor and had led the assault on the tanker. The armor had originally been developed by Sky Masters Inc. as a lightweight protective anti-explosive sheathing inside airliner's cargo compartments. But the material, nicknamed BERP (Ballistic Electro-Reactive Process), had been adapted for many other uses, including strong, lightweight protection for special operations commandos. Patrick picked up the electro-magnetic rail gun rifle and steadied it on the safety rail of the starboard pilot's wing. He searched, using his helmet-mounted imaging infrared sensor, positioned the rifle, then activated the rifle's electronic sight. 'Contact,' he radioed back to Luger. 'Brave boys. They keep on coming, even though their cover is completely gone.'

'Don't let them get within mortar or antitank range, Muck.'

'Don't worry, Dave,' Patrick said. He aimed his rifle and fired. A streak of blue-yellow vapor ripped through the night sky, followed by a supersonic *CCRRAACCKK!* as loud as a thunderclap. The sausage-size hypersonic projectile pierced the front of the launch, passing between the launch captain and helmsman and barely missing one commando, before passing through the deck, right through the diesel engine, out the bottom near the stern, and through one hundred and fifty feet of seawater before burying itself seventy-five feet in the bottom of the Black Sea. The launch's engine sputtered, coughed, and died within seconds. The automatic bilge pumps activated as the water in the bilges started to get deeper. Soon, the commandos and the crew were scurrying for life preservers. 'Target neutralized,' Luger radioed. 'He's dead in the water. Good shooting, Muck. I'm going to recall AALF for refueling. That destroyer won't be back in gun range before AALF gets refueled.'

'Roger,' Patrick responded. 'We're working on rigging auxiliary control for remote operation. Stay in touch. You should be expecting company any minute.'

'We're ready for them. Texas out.' Luger entered commands into the computer. AALF stopped making false attacks on the Russian destroyer *Besstrashny* and headed back to the DC-10. It automatically began an approach behind the launch aircraft. Luger extended a refueling probe, much like a US Air Force KC-10 Extender tanker, and, using its onboard radar as well as following laser steering signals from the DC-10, AALF flew itself toward the refueling probe. A small receptacle popped open on the upper portion of its fuselage, it guided itself into position, and the drone flew itself into contact with the probe. Mechanical clamps secured the drone onto the probe, and it began taking on jet fuel directly from the DC-10's fuel tanks.

But while AALF was attached to the DC-10's refueling probe, the crew was in its most vulnerable position – and AALF's approach had been watched and plotted by Russian ground-based and airborne radars. Minutes after AALF attached itself to the probe, threat-warning receivers on board the DC-10 bleeped to life. 'Russian MiG-27s, bearing zero-seven-zero, forty-seven miles, coming in fast!' the sensor technician shouted. 'We've got company!'

'I'm detaching AALF and sending it after them,' Luger said. 'Jon, tell the flight crew to get us out of here ASAP.' Luger entered instructions into AALF's computerized brain, and the little craft detached itself from the refueling probe, drifted behind and away from the DC-10, then turned and flew toward the oncoming MiGs. The DC-10 turned north-west and headed for the Ukrainian coast.

AALF was a small aircraft, much smaller than a MiG-27, but it had been built for speed and maneuverability, not stealth. It detected the MiG's radar-guided missile attacks, evaded the first salvo, and flew close enough to the pack to cause them to break formation and scatter. But there were too many Russians versus one unarmed aircraft, and no matter how smart, fast, and maneuverable it was, it couldn't evade its attackers and protect the DC-10 at the same time. When it turned to pursue two MiGs that had pressed their attack westward toward the DC-10, two more MiGs managed to bracket it from behind and kill it with a heat-seeking-missile shot.

'Those MiGs got past AALF,' the sensor operator said. 'They're on our six, thirty-nine miles and closing fast.'

The two MiG-27s in the lead had shot their two long-range radar-guided missiles at the drone already, so they had to continue to close in on the DC-10 for a heat-seeking-missile shot. But they had orders to get a visual ID on the aircraft first, so they continued inside missile range. They closed the distance quickly – their quarry was obviously very large and not very maneuverable, with three big engines glowing bright enough to be seen ten kilometers away on the IRSTS infrared sensor. The pilot of the lead MiG could feel buffeting and hear the engine roar from five kilometers away. This aircraft *had* to be big to create turbulence like that! He flew a bit farther to one side, out of the turbulent air, and continued. Just a few more seconds and he'd–

Suddenly the Russian MiG pilot's threat warning indicators lit up like a holiday centerpiece. They were surrounded by fighters! Where did they come from? Who...?

'Attention, attention, unidentified MIG-27 aircraft at our twelve o'clock position,' the MiG pilots heard in fluent Russian, 'this is *Eskadril* Twenty-seven, Six-twenty-six *Polk*, Odessa, *Viyskovo-Povitryani Syly*, Air Force of Ukraine. You are in violation of Ukrainian airspace. You will turn right immediately to head south, decelerate, and lower your landing gear, or you will be attacked without further warning.'

'Twenty-seventh Squadron, this is the Ninety-first Squadron, Novorossiysk, Air Force of the Russian Federation,' the lead MiG-27 pilot replied. 'We are in pursuit of unidentified hostile combat aircraft that attacked a Russian tanker and a Russian Federation Navy destroyer. The unidentified hostile is at our twelve o'clock position. We request your help to pursue and identify this hostile. Over.'

In response, the MiG-27 on the leader's right wing exploded in a ball of fire.

The Russian pilot couldn't believe what he'd just seen. 'You ... you shot down my wingman!' he cried on the radio. 'You *bastards!* How could you do this? We are allies! We are neighbors!'

'Negative, Russian MiG, negative!' the Ukrainian pilot responded. 'Turn starboard right *now* or you will be destroyed!'

'You cannot do this! This is not permitted!'

'You will be fish food if you do not comply immediately!' the Ukrainian pilot responded. 'Turn *now!*'

He had no other choice. The MiG-27 pilot pushed his control stick right and pulled his throttle back a few notches. The large unidentified aircraft quickly disappeared from his IRSTS sensor. He thought about turning and trying a missile snap-shot at the aircraft – but at that exact moment, he saw a burst of cannon fire shoot from a fighter just a few meters off his left side. The damned Ukrainian fighter was *right there!* The threat warning receiver counted six more aircraft in the vicinity. 'Flaps and gear, or you will be shot down!' the Ukrainian warned him. He had no choice but to comply. With his flaps and landing gear down, his fire control system automatically shut itself down.

'Bastards!' the Russian pilot shouted. 'What do you think you're doing? We have permission to overfly Ukrainian airspace when necessary for defense purposes! Aren't you familiar with our memorandum of understanding? We are allies!'

'Not anymore, we're not,' the Ukrainian responded. 'The Russian Federation is no longer welcome over Ukrainian airspace.'

'What in hell are you talking about? Russia has the right to fly over the Black Sea or anywhere else we choose.'

'This airspace belongs to the Black Sea Alliance,' the Ukrainian pilot said. 'Russian warplanes are not welcome over Alliance airspace.'

'The what? What Black Sea Alliance?'

'This,' came a different voice. The Russian pilot looked. The aircraft off his left wing turned its identification lights on...

...and revealed itself not as a Ukrainian fighter, but as a Turkish F-16 fighter! It still wore the star and crescent of Turkey, but it wore the blue and gold of the Republic of Ukraine on its tail as well!

'Left turn smartly heading one-eight-zero, then flank speed to intercept that tanker!' Captain Boriskov of the Russian navy destroyer *Besstrashny* ordered. 'I want all the patrol and smaller combatants available to rendezvous with us as soon as possible. We need help to stop that tanker before it reaches Turkish territorial waters.'

'Our fighters report downing one unidentified aircraft,' the tactical action officer reported. 'But now our fighters are surrounded by Turkish and Ukrainian interceptors, and one of our fighters had been shot down. Our fighters are greatly outnumbered.'

'*Turkish* interceptors?' the captain retorted. 'What are Turkish interceptors doing flying over Ukraine?'

'They call themselves the Black Sea Alliance,' the executive officer replied. 'The aircraft are flying both flags. They prohibited Russian aircraft from entering their airspace, and they shot down one of our planes.'

'My God, are they insane? What is this Black Sea Alliance? What in hell is going on here? How many fighters are up there?'

'There are at least six up there, outnumbering them two to one – MiG-29s and F-16s. They have forced our fighters to withdraw.'

'Is Novorossiysk sending more fighters?' the captain asked.

'Negative,' the TAO replied. 'They were pursuing an unidentified aircraft when they entered Ukrainian airspace, but that aircraft has disappeared over Ukraine. There is no longer any justification for overlying Ukrainian airspace, so no more aircraft will be launched.'

'What about helping us?' the captain shouted. 'We need helicopter-capable warships out here to launch an assault on the terrorists holding that tanker.'

'The frigate *Ladny* is two and a half hours out,' the executive officer said. 'They are switching their ASW helicopter with an armed attack helicopter to assist in an armed assault on the tanker. Three Border Patrol Type 206MP missile hydrofoil patrol boats are also en route, about seventy minutes out.'

'Barely enough time,' the captain muttered.

'How long until the tanker crosses into Turkish waters?'

'Should be within Turkish treaty waters in ten minutes on present course and speed.'

The captain shrugged. 'No matter. We won't let a little thing like lines on a map stop us. Notify me when the hydrofoils come into range and the Ka-27 is refueled, and we'll try another assault on the tanker. How long until we get back within gun range?'

'Fifteen minutes.'

'We'll try a couple shots on the superstructure and perhaps convince them to give themselves up,' the captain said. 'Notify me when we get within extreme gun range.'

It was the weirdest chase anyone had ever seen – two massive ships, separated by just a few miles, with one pursuing the other at barely the speed of a brisk bicycle ride. With aircraft, Captain Boriskov thought, everything happens so fast; with maritime warfare, everything happens so slow. But soon they were within maximum range of the forward AK-130, and the big twin-barreled gun opened fire. Two 70-pound high-explosive shells impacted the superstructure just a few seconds apart, ripping huge holes in the living spaces. A second two-round volley hit the bridge itself. A small fire started in the living and engineering spaces from the first blast.

'This is the *Ustinov*,' a voice came on the radio. 'Congratulations on your shooting – you have managed to destroy the bridge. I don't think we can control the ship well enough from the auxiliary control station. But I wouldn't fire any more rounds at the superstructure. We have sent the *Ustinov*'s crew into those spaces. Hit us again, and you'll be killing your fellow Russians.'

'Cease fire, cease fire,' the captain said, looking on with his repeater of the telescopic low-light optronic gun sight. 'This is Captain Boriskov of the Russian Federation Navy destroyer *Besstrashny*,' the skipper responded on the radio in English. 'What kind of cowards put hostages in harm's way? You should release the crew into lifeboats. This is between you and me.'

'I think we will leave the crew where they are for now – they're safe as long as you stop firing into our superstructure.'

'Who are you? What do you want?'

'Never mind who I am,' Patrick McLanahan responded. 'We wish to send Comrade Pavel Kazakov a little message: if he flies his little stealth toy any more, he and all of his partners and business associates will suffer.'

'What stealth toy? What are you talking about?'

'Pavel Kazakov has been involved in a campaign of terror and mayhem throughout Europe,' Patrick went on. 'He has been responsible for creating enough fear and destruction within the Balkans that the international community was forced to respond by sending Russian peace-keepers into otherwise peaceful countries. But all this has been created specifically so the Russian army can protect Kazakov's new pipeline.'

'You claim the Russian Army is in league with Pavel Kazakov? Ridiculous.'

'President Sen'kov, Colonel-General Zhurbenko, and many others in the Russian military high command are on Kazakov's payroll,' Patrick replied. 'If they weren't enticed by Kazakov's money, Kazakov sent his Metyor-179 stealth fighter-bomber in to attack. Kazakov has killed thousands in order to create enough fear to convince others to go along.'

'What proof do you have of all this?'

'We have sent a tape recording of conversations between Kazakov, Metyor Aerospace Director Fursenko, Chief of the General Staff Zhurbenko, and Russian National Security Advisor Yejsk, to the world's major media outlets, discussing this plan,' Patrick said. 'Zhurbenko and Yejsk agree to mobilize the Russian army in response to the terror created by Kazakov and his stealth warplane, specifically so Russian troops could occupy and control foreign territory that Kazakov needed to build his pipeline across the Balkans from the Black Sea to the Adriatic Sea. By tonight, the whole world will have heard this tape.'

'How do we know this tape is authentic? How do we know any of this is real?'

'Because we have also included a tape recording of President Sen'kov of Russia discussing the matter with President Thorn of the United States,' Patrick radioed. 'Sen'kov agreed to let two captured American pilots free in exchange for Thorn agreeing not to reveal the contents of the tape. The Russian government eventually leaked the information on the two captured Americans and their aircraft shot down over Russia.'

'So President Thomas Thorn was involved in this as well?'

'President Thorn's goal was the release of his captured fliers,' McLanahan replied. 'Sen'kov's goal was not to have embarrassing intelligence information leak out on how he was going to go along with crime boss and drug dealer Kazakov in taking over the Balkans in order to share in the profits of a one-hundred-million-dollar-per-day oil venture. If Thorn is guilty of anything, it is of trusting Sen'kov. Sen'kov is guilty of collusion with Pavel Kazakov.'

'Well, this is a very interesting fairy tale,' Boriskov said. But he was worried. For the past several months, this is exactly what most of the Russian military forces had been doing: protecting Pavel Kazakov's business interests. He and many of his fellow officers had been wondering about the grand scheme, although it seemed to be a lucrative deal for everyone. Perhaps that was the reason: Sen'kov, Zhurbenko, and others in Moscow were getting kickbacks from Kazakov, in exchange for providing protection for his oil enterprise. Now the Russian Navy had become his unwitting bodyguards, too. 'What do you intend to do with the tanker?'

'We intend this to be a down payment on the very large bill Kazakov owes to the people of the Balkans,' Patrick replied, 'especially the people of Kukes, Struga, Ohrid, Resen, and those who died in the NATO E-3 AWACS radar plane and the Turkish F-16 shot down over the Black Sea by his marauding stealth fighter. This tanker and its cargo represent a half-billion-dollar investment for Pavel Kazakov. We are going to send it to the bottom of the Black Sea.'

623

'*Shto?*' Boriskov shouted. 'You cannot do that! It would be a monumental ecological disaster! That spill would pollute a large portion of the Black Sea for years!'

'Let it be on Pavel Kazakov's hands,' Patrick said. 'Maybe by sinking this ship, the world will soon learn everything about Kazakov and his bloody greed.'

'What are we going to do, Captain?' the *Besstrashny*'s executive officer asked. 'We won't be able to reach it in time.'

'We are going to have to disable it,' Boriskov said. 'Combat, this is the captain. Target the rudder and propulsion area of the stern on the tanker. I want it stopped dead in the water. Once we catch up to it, we'll board it and hold it until help comes from Russia.'

'We are inside Turkish treaty waters, Captain,' the navigator warned. 'We are prohibited from discharging weapons.'

'This is an emergency situation,' the captain said. 'Combat, carry out my last—'

'Bridge, Combat, high-speed aircraft inbound, low altitude, bearing zero-two-zero, range eight-seven kilometers, speed ... speed thirteen hundred kilometers per hour!' the radar operators in the Combat Information Center called out. 'Multiple contacts.'

'Attention, attention, destroyer *Besstrashny*, this is the Black Sea Alliance bomber north of you,' the bridge crew heard moments later. 'You have entered Alliance treaty waters and are hereby ordered to reverse course immediately or you will be fired upon.'

624

'There's that Alliance bullshit again,' Boriskov exclaimed. 'Number One, battle stations.' The battle stations alarm range once again. 'Combat, release batteries on the forward 130 only and open fire. Disable the tanker before it gets too far into Turkish treaty waters.' The AK-130 cannon opened fire on the tanker, one two-round volley every four seconds. The stern of the tanker *Ustinov* exploded in a burst of flames.

'Bridge, Combat, *inbound antiship missiles*, bearing zero-two-zero, eighty kilometers and closing, speed nine hundred kilometers per hour and accelerating, sea-skimmer! Additional radar contact aircraft, bearing three-four-zero, multiple contacts, low altitude and high speed, possible antiship missile attack profile as well.'

'Helm, hard to port heading zero-two-zero,' Boriskov ordered. 'Combat, Bridge, cease fire on the tanker. Stand by to defend against high-speed sea-skimmer. All defensive batteries released.'

'Sir! Look! The tanker!' Boriskov turned and saw a massive ball and column of fire, like a small nuclear explosion, erupt on the forward portion of the tanker. The fire was so bright that it cast shadows on the deck of the *Besstrashny* over twenty kilometers away. Seconds later, the shock wave from the blast rolled over them, rattling windows and sending a vibration through the deck.

'The tanker is gone,' Boriskov said. 'It'll be on the bottom in minutes, and they'll be cleaning up that oil slick for the next ten years.'

'Bridge, Combat, numerous small vessels approaching the tanker from the south,' the radar operator reported. 'Possibly Turkish naval patrol boats or fire boats.'

'Never mind the damned tanker – it's gone,' Boriskov shouted. 'Time to impact on that sea-skimmer?'

'Sea-skimmer passing twelve hundred kilometers per hour,' the radar operator reported. 'Time to impact, three point four minutes.'

'Count down every fifteen seconds.'

'Destroyer *Besstrashny*, this is the Black Sea Alliance Air Command. You will reverse course immediately or we will continue our attack,' the radio message said.

'How dare you attack a flagship of the Russian Federation Navy!' Boriskov retorted. 'I warn you, abort this attack or consider it an act of war!'

'You have committed an act of war by opening fire in Turkish waters without authorization,' the bomber crew responded. 'We have begun the countdown on five more antiship missiles, Captain, and we will launch them if you do not cease fire and reverse course immediately. It may be an act of war, but the *Besstrashny* will be the first casualty if you do not head out of Alliance waters immediately.'

'Time to impact, three minutes.'

The bridge crew looked over at their captain in horror. They were positioned correctly to defend against the first missile, but not against more fired from a different angle. If the other bombers launched, the *Besstrashny*'s defenses could be quickly overwhelmed.

'Black Sea Alliance, or whoever you are,' Boriskov radioed, 'this is the *Besstrashny*. We will exit your waters without further incident. Abort your attack.' Seconds later, they saw a flash of light in the sky, and the CIC reported they had lost contact with the first sea-skimmer.

'*Yibis ana v rot!*' Boriskov swore loudly. 'Comm, Bridge, notify Destroyer Group in Novorossiysk – tell them we came under attack by some group calling itself the Black Sea Alliance. Give position, include details of the weapon they fired at us, notify them that we are being directed on where to go from here under threat of massive aerial attack, and ask for instructions.'

Rather than make it better, the oxygen just seemed to be making Stoica's headache worse. He tried to gulp down some water to keep his mouth and throat moistened, but his liver was sucking all the moisture out of his body to try to digest all that rotgut wine, and he was losing that battle.

Yegorov wasn't making it any better. He was continuing a steady stream of chatter on the intercom, repeating every message over and over. 'Six bombers! Did you hear that? This Black Sea Alliance has surrounded the *Besstrashny* with six bombers! This Black Sea Alliance has got balls, I'll admit that.'

'Can you please shut up and just find the one closest to the destroyer, Gennadi?' Stoica asked.

'I'm not sure which one without activating the radar.'

'Then just pick one, and let's let him lead us to the others,' Stoica said impatiently. 'This is not rocket science.'

'The nearest one is at our eleven o'clock, range approximately fifty kilometers,' Yegorov said.

'Just outside maximum missile range.'

'I know what the maximum range of our missiles are, damn you, I know,' Stoica moaned. Along with the four emergency R-60 missiles in their wing launchers, the Mt-179 Tyenee carried an AKU-58 external weapon pylon on each wing with one radar-guided R-27P missile on the bottom of the pylon and one R-60 heat-seeking missile on each side of the pylon, plus two Kh-29TF TV-guided missiles in the bomb bay, with its receiver pod bolted onto the aft external centerline weapon station behind the bomb bay. The R-27P was one of Russia's newest air-to-air missiles, developed by Metyor Aerospace, that was designed to home in on enemy radar signals – it did not need any guidance signals from its launch aircraft.

'You're lucky if that old hag didn't mix some kerosene in with that wine, Ion,' Yegorov said, and chuckled.

'*Idi na-huy*, Gennadi.'

'Forty kilometers. Coming within R-27 range. Ready to commit weapons.'

'Where are the other bombers?'

'I'm detecting two more aircraft at our two and three o'clock positions, range unknown, so they must be farther than fifty kilometers away. Surface search radar only – no fire control or uplink signals. I think they're the bombers that are covering the *Besstrashny*.'

'Any sign of those fighters?'

'None.'

Stoica ripped off his oxygen mask in frustration. The one-hundred percent oxygen he was breathing to try to recover from his hangover was drying out his mouth and throat even faster. He knew, but didn't want to concede, that pure oxygen really did nothing: only time was effective in recovering from the effects of too much alcohol. He had already drained both of his canteens of water on this flight, and they had been airborne less than an hour. His skin was starting to crawl, his hands were shaking, and if he moved his eyes too fast, all the gauges would start to pinwheel around the cockpit on him. He would never make it through an entire four-hour patrol. If he didn't get down out of this plane and into bed in the next hour, he was going to pass out.

'Warm up the R-27s and give me a hot button,' Stoica ordered.

'Roger,' Yegorov said. A moment later: 'R-27s ready. What's your plan, Ion?'

'Simple – take them all out,' Stoica said. He got a lock-on tone in his headset and pressed the launch button. The first R-27 leapt off the starboard rail and disappeared into the night sky on a yellow line of fire. The sudden burst of light sent slivers of pain shooting through Stoica's head. Seconds later, they saw a large, bright explosion off in the distance – the missile had found its target. 'Splash one bomber. Line up the next one, Gennadi.'

'Radars are down, Ion,' Yegorov said. 'All the other bombers shut down their search radars.' Without an enemy radar indication, the bombers assumed that their attacker had a home-on-radar guided missile – all they had to do was turn off their radars to take that capability away. That meant that the Tyenee had to turn on its radar to lock on to the bombers.

'Then fire up ours,' Stoica ordered. He turned slightly to the right. 'We know he's off our nose right now – radiate for five seconds and let's go get him.'

'It's too dangerous, Ion,' Yegorov said. 'There's still at least five enemy aircraft out there, and we don't know where the fighters are. Let them reveal themselves. Don't worry – we've got lots of fuel.'

Stoica bent his head down so his mouth was pointing directly down on the floor and so nothing in his stomach would hit his instruments, but it was only dry heaves. Those were definitely the worst. 'I said, go to radiate on the radar and let's nail those bombers,' Stoica ordered again. 'We don't have time to waste. They can begin their attack on the destroyer at any second.'

'But they're not–'

'I said, *turn the damned radar on*, and do it *now!*' Stoica shouted, tasting and nearly retching again on bile in his throat.

'Radar on,' Yegorov finally reported. 'Bandits at twelve and one o'clock, forty-five and sixty kilometers.'

'Got him,' Stoica said. 'Keep the radar on.' He locked up the first bomber and shot their second R-27 missile.

'Enemy aircraft inbound!' Yegorov shouted. 'Five o'clock, fifty kilometers and closing fast! Enemy fighters, probably F-16s!' Stoica started hard S turns around the axis of attack on his quarry, not willing to break radar lock and trying to confuse the inbound fighters. 'Still closing, forty kilometers, intermediate lock growing to a solid lock. Ion, let's get out of here!'

The two Metyor pilots could see beads of decoy flares ejecting into the night sky, their bright magnesium spheres bright enough to be seen for a hundred kilometers. They knew that the second bomber had detected the missile-steering uplink signal, which meant a missile was in the air, and it began ejecting chaff bundles to decoy the radar. Sure enough, Stoica could see his radar lock-on box remaining stationary, not following the string of decoy flares, then suddenly following, only to be decoyed off its target again.

'It missed, Ion!' Yegorov shouted. He realized they had stayed on virtually the same heading for too long, allowing the pursuing fighters to deploy in a wide spread-out pattern – no matter which way they turned, one of the fighters could begin a high-speed tail-chase on them. 'Bandits at thirty kilometers! Let's get out of here! Radar down!' The lock-on box disappeared, meaning Yegorov had shut off the attack radar. 'Solid lock on us, Ion! They've got us!'

'Then we fight our way out,' Stoica said. 'Radar to transmit. Warm up the R-60s.' Just then, they heard a *DEEDLEDEEDLEDEEDLE!* warning tone in their helmet headsets. 'Missile launch radar! *Chaff! Flares!*' Yegorov ejected decoys while Stoica threw the Mt-179 into a hard right turn. 'I said, radar to transmit!' he shouted.

Yegorov had to fight through the rapidly building g forces to turn on the attack radar and pre-arm all of the remaining R-60 missiles. 'Your button is hot, Ion, R-60s external and internal in sequence are ready.'

The nearest enemy fighter was just starting a hard climbing right turn, apparently after firing a radar-guided missile. Stoica quickly reversed directions, shoved in full afterburner power, and climbed after him. He saw and then felt a hard *SLAM!* underneath and just behind him – one of the enemy missiles had just missed by less than fifty meters. Seconds later, he got a 'Lock' indication on his heads-up display and fired one R-60 heat-seeker. He knew he shouldn't turn away from an enemy fighter above him – he had plenty of energy to turn back and pursue – but he was one versus at least four, and he had to keep moving. Besides, the guy above him was either defensive now, or he was dead.

Stoica immediately executed a hard-right diving turn to aim his radar back to where he thought the enemy fighters were. The fighter farthest to the west was turning after him, but another was still flying straight, crossing under and behind to cover his leader's tail. Stoica tightened his turn even more to go after the wingman – but he received a stall warning buffet and felt his wings rumble in protest. 'Airspeed!' Yegorov warned.

'Screw airspeed – this bastard's mine!' Stoica growled. He kept the turn in. The turn bled off lots of speed, but the dive helped, and he was able to keep it just above stall speed. When he rolled out, the enemy fighter was almost in front of him, starting a turn to the east to cover, and Stoica fired an R-60 at him.

Another warning warble. 'Missile launch!' Yegorov cried out. *'Break left!'*

632

Stoica threw the stealth fighter into a tight left turn. But that was a mistake. They had been just above stall speed for the past several moments, and the level break he had just made pushed him into a full stall – and with one wing down, the Mt-179 entered a snapping left spin. Stoica heard a loud *WHACK!* and a yelp, then a moan, then silence. 'You all right, Gennadi?' No response, just another moan. What in hell happened? But Stoica had no time to check him out further – if he didn't stop this spin quickly, they'd both be hurting.

Because of its forward swept-wing technology, the aerodynamic characteristics of the Metyor-179 stealth fighter were unlike those of any other aircraft. A stall-spin in an aircraft designed to be super-maneuverable was usually fatal, and stall recovery was not like any other aircraft. Rather than trying to counteract the spin with rudder, lower the nose, and level the wings as in a normal airplane, Stoica had to pull power, use flaps, the speed brake, and ailerons to slow down as much as possible, turn off the automatic flight-controls, match the control stick and rudder controls to the aircraft attitude, then reset the automatic flight control system. He had to do that as fast and as many times as necessary until the plane recovered itself. Sometimes it happened on the first try and the stall-spin lasted one or two turns; other times it lasted longer and he could lose a frightening amount of altitude in a hurry.

It took four complete turns and almost a thousand meters' altitude before Stoica could regain control. The threat scope still showed three enemy fighters out there – he had tagged only one. The spin recovery routine had sapped almost all his airspeed, so he had no choice but to stay straight and level until airspeed built back up.

The enemy fighters didn't waste time – they started in after him again, rolling in behind him in the blink of an eye. Stoica immediately turned left, staying level until his airspeed built up enough, then raised his nose and aimed for the first fighter, waiting until it presented itself. He knew he couldn't stay like this long, so he fired one missile, acquired a second fighter, fired another missile nose-to-nose, then veered right and dove before he stalled out again.

Stoica knew he had used all of his pylon-mounted missiles, so it was time to jettison the empty pylons. Just in time – once they were gone, they'd regain their stealth profile, and it sure would help his chances of survival if the enemy couldn't see him. He leveled off. The three enemy fighters were still up there, but they had dodged away and were defensive. 'Okay, Gennadi,' he said to his backseater as he leveled off. 'Jettison the pylons and let's take those *zas'er'as* on a trip to the bottom of the Black Sea.' No response. 'Gennadi? What in hell are you doing back there?' He adjusted his mirror to inside the rear cockpit – and saw Yegorov's head lolling down from side to side. One of the sharp turns must've caught him unawares and knocked him unconscious against the canopy.

There were only a few things the pilot of the Mt-179 could *not* do from the front seat – unfortunately, jettisoning pylons was one of them. Stoica was stuck with them until Yegorov woke up. 'Gennadi!' he shouted. 'Gennadi! Wake up!' Yegorov did not appear to be fully unconscious, just stunned, but he was definitely not responding.

Definitely time to get the hell away from here. Stoica turned westbound and started a rapid descent, trying to get to a lower altitude quickly while the F-16 fighters were regrouping. The Tyenee wasn't totally stealthy anymore with the pylons on, even though they were empty, but the farther he could fly away from the F-16s, the harder he would be to detect – and if there were any seas below, he might be able to hide in the radar reflections from the–

DEEDLE DEEDLE DEEDLE! Not so fast, Stoica thought – one of the F-16s had locked on to him already, about forty kilometers behind him. He increased his descent rate to six thousand meters per minute and reached one hundred meters above the Black Sea in less than a minute. Now it was a foot race. The Romanian coastline was four hundred kilometers ahead. It was very flat until about one hundred and fifty kilometers in, but then the Transylvanian Alps rose quickly across the interior, and he could hide. It would be a long flight, almost twenty minutes at this speed, but maybe the Turkish F-16s were already low on fuel and wouldn't be able to give chase.

The threat warning receiver was blaring constantly. The F-16s were still behind him about thirty kilometers away. Any second now, if they still had any radar-guided missiles, they would–

DEEDLEDEEDLEDEEDLE! came the missile launch warning. Stoica pulled his throttles to idle, popped chaff, and started a tight right break. He could hear Yegorov's head slam against the left side of the cockpit, and he wondered how much brain damage the guy had suffered...

'Where am I?' Yegorov moaned.

'Gennadi! Wake up!' Stoica shouted. 'Don't touch any controls! Do you hear me? Don't touch anything!' Stoica knew that a crew member awakening suddenly while sleeping in a cockpit or after passing out from lack of oxygen or g forces will sometimes grab something, responding to a dream or a sensation – they'll punch themselves out, drop weapons, or even shut down engines.

'I ... I can't breathe...'

'We're defensive, Gennadi, trying to get away from a gaggle of Turkish fighters,' Stoica said, grunting through the g forces. 'I need you to jettison the pylons–'

'Fighters!' Yegorov suddenly shouted. He'd obviously just got a look at the threat receiver, which depicted three enemy fighters and at least one enemy missile bearing down on him. 'Break! Break! I'm ejecting chaff–!'

'I'm rolled out,' Stoica said. 'No chaff.' The jammers had taken care of the uplink signal, and clouds of radar-reflecting chaff strewn behind them had drawn the Turkish missile away. 'Are you all right, Gennadi?'

'I think so.'

'Slowly, carefully, jettison the pylons,' Stoica said. 'They're empty. Don't jettison any other weapons, just the pylons.' Stoica rolled straight and level. 'I'm wings-level, Gennadi. Punch 'em off.'

'What...?'

'I said, punch the goddamned pylons...!' But Stoica heard yet another *DEEDLE DEEDLE DEEDLE!* radar lock-on warning. He had no choice. He banked steeply right and climbed into the enemy fighter. Seconds later, he got another lock-on tone, and he fired one R-60 missile at him from an internal wing launcher. Stoica immediately faked left, dropped chaff and flares, and then rolled right and descended back to less than a hundred meters above the sea. He saw a bright flash off his left side – he hoped that was another Turkish fighter on his way to taking a swim. 'Gennadi, punch the pylons off, *now!*'

'Ack ... acknowledged,' Yegorov said weakly. Stoica rolled wings-level just as he felt a rumble through the aircraft as the weapon pylons popped off.

'Fault indication,' Yegorov said weakly. Stoica glanced at the MASTER CAUTION light, then at the caution panel. No problem – a fault in an empty launcher – and he punched the caution light off and ignored it. There were only two F-16s behind him now – he'd got another one! – and the last two had their radars on but could not lock on to him. He was stealthy again!

Stoica jammed in full military power and started a gentle climb back toward the east. Now he had the advantage. He lined up on the nearest F-16, using his radar threat receiver until the infrared search-and-track system locked on, then fired another missile from an internal launcher from less than six kilometers away. That missile tracked dead-on and hit seconds later. Another kill!

Stoica considered going back after the remaining bombers. Now that he was stealthy again, the bombers were his to plink apart as he chose, and killing F-16 fighters was not much of a challenge right now for him. But as he scanned the warning and caution panel again, he knew he was done for the day – and maybe for a long time. Sure enough, the internal missile launchers had a fault – no, not just a fault this time, a major failure, a LAUNCHER HOT message, meaning there was an electrical fire in the wing. 'Gennadi, launcher hot, cut off weapons power now!' Fortunately, Yegorov was alert enough to do it, and the LAUNCHER HOT warning light went off a few seconds after he isolated power. There were still a few yellow advisory lights on, including the launcher shutter door jam, the same problem that had been dogging them for months now, but there were no red warning lights, and for now they were okay.

It didn't mean they were out of danger, only that they probably weren't going to fly apart in the next few minutes. Good time to get out of here. The remaining bombers were indeed tempting, and he still had his internal cannon to use instead of the internal R-60 missiles, but that would be pushing his luck. He had already scored kills against two Ukrainian Backfire bombers and two Turkish F-16 Falcon fighters. That was a pretty good night's work. Plus, his head was still ready to split open, and Yegorov was certainly in no shape to fly the plane. Stoica turned the plane westbound again toward Codlea, again thanking the stars he was alive and victorious.

'Stand by, *Besstrashny*,' they heard a few moments later. He read off a series of geographical coordinates. 'That is your exit point from Alliance waters, *Besstrashny*. Steer directly for that point. We will be monitoring your departure with patrol aircraft. Any deviation will result in an immediate attack, and this time we will not abort the missiles.'

'Acknowledged,' Bonskov spat. 'Combat, Bridge, what's happening up there? There is a Russian fighter up there?'

'We don't know if it's Russian or not,' the tactical action officer responded. 'All we know is that one Ukrainian bomber and two Turkish fighters were suddenly shot down. The unidentified aircraft may have been shot down, too – the Turkish fighters seemed to have lost contact.'

Captain Boriskov smiled and nodded enthusiastically – whoever it was, he should be given a medal, even if he got shot himself. 'Did the bombers depart? Where are they?'

'They just shut down radars, but they are still up there, just outside our antiaircraft missile range.'

Too bad – Boriskov would've liked one more chance to get that tanker. 'What's the situation around the tanker?'

'Surrounded by numerous vessels and aircraft now, sir,' the radar operator replied. Boriskov went out to the port wing and scanned the horizon aft. There was still a very bright glow where the *Ustinov* was – it was going to burn for a very, very long time.

He hated to leave a fight like this, Boriskov thought. Another nation had actually shot a supersonic antiship missile at a Russian warship, in the Black Sea – once considered a Russian lake – and he could do nothing but turn tail. It was humiliating.

But as bad as running was to him, the idea of being a part of defending scum like Pavel Kazakov was even worse. If the story that terrorist had told was true, that Russian president Valentin Sen'kov was part of a deal with Kazakov to use the Russian military to help secure land to build an oil pipeline just to fill their own pockets, that was truly humiliating.

Boriskov didn't like being pushed around by anyone – not someone calling themselves the Black Sea Alliance, not by a worthless politician, and especially not by a thug like Pavel Kazakov.

Chapter Ten

Codlea, Romania
the next morning

'He let them go?' Pavel Kazakov shouted into the secure satellite telephone. He was in his office at his secret base in central Romania, in the foothills of the Carpathian Mountains. 'That damned destroyer captain was just a few miles away from my tanker, and he let them go?'

'He did not "let them go," Pavel,' Colonel-General Valeriy Zhurbenko, Chief of Staff of the Armed Forces of the Russian Federation, retorted angrily, speaking from a secure communications room in the Kremlin. 'He had six large aircraft with antiship cruise missiles bearing down on him. He had two choices – turn around as ordered, or get blasted out of the water. Besides, he thought there was nothing he could do – the terrorists set off an explosive on the tanker, and he thought it was on its way to the bottom of the Black Sea anyway.'

Kazakov turned angrily at his satellite television set, turned to CNN. 'Oh really? Then why am I watching the damned Turks off-loading *my* oil onto *their* tankers in *their* harbor?' It was true: there was no fire or explosion on the tanker, at least not one set by the terrorists. Shortly after the Turkish Navy and Coast Guard had arrived on the scene, the tremendous fire in the forward hold had mysteriously disappeared; it had turned out it was in no danger of sinking after all. The tanker had continued under its own power, and pulled into the Turkish Navy base at Eregli. As if by magic, another tanker happened to be at anchor in the vicinity, empty of course, and it was pressed into service transferring oil to it from the *Ustinov*.

The terrorists were nowhere to be seen.

The stories of the *Ustinov's* crew were even more fantastic. There were only two terrorists, they claimed. They were invincible. Bullets bounced off them like spitballs. They carried no weapons. They shot lightning bolts from their eyes and carried rifles taller than a man that fired bullets as big as a sausage that could stop a ship many kilometers away.

'What in hell is going on here?' Kazakov fumed. 'I'm surrounded by cowards and incompetents. What is the government doing to get my tanker and my oil back? This amounts to an act of piracy on the high seas! That tanker was flying a Russian flag. What are you doing about it?'

'The Supreme Tribunal is appealing to the World Court on your behalf, as a Russian citizen,' Zhurbenko replied. 'Unfortunately, your ship was struck and damaged by illegal activity – namely, the unauthorized discharge of a weapon – in Turkish treaty waters. That brought the matter up before the Turkish military. The vessel was clearly in danger of sinking, both by the terrorists' acts and the Russian Navy's actions, so the matter was again transferred to the Turkish Coast Guard, Minister of Commerce, and Director of Environmental Protection. There will certainly be a criminal and a military investigation.'

'This all sounds like bureaucratic mumbo-jumbo, General,' Kazakov retorted. 'When do I get my ship back? When do I get my oil back? That product is worth twenty-five million dollars!'

'There is another matter, Pavel,' Zhurbenko said.

'And that is?'

'You happen to be under indictment in Turkey for narcotics smuggling, murder, robbery, securities fraud, tax evasion, and a half-dozen other felony crimes,' Zhurbenko said. 'It is no secret that you own both the ship and the oil, so both have been seized by the Turkish courts because of your failure to appear in a Turkish court to answer charges against you.'

'*What?*' Kazakov shouted. 'They can't do that!'

'They can and they have,' Zhurbenko said. 'Your bond in all of your indictments equaled precisely five hundred million dollars, which is how much the ship and the oil are worth, so both have been seized by the Turkish courts.'

'I want you to get that ship and that oil back,' Kazakov snapped. 'I don't care what you have to do. Send in the military, send in Spetsnaz, kidnap the Turkish president – I don't care! Just get them back! I will not be thumb-tied by a bunch of Turkish lawyers and bureaucrats!'

'The government has its own problems right now,' Zhurbenko said. 'In case you haven't noticed, the lid is exploding off our little deal. The taped conversations between Thorn and Sen'kov and between us at Metyor have been broadcast in a hundred countries and twenty languages around the world. When I ... when *we* leaked the details of the deal between Sen'kov and Thorn, we sealed our fate and Sen'kov's as well. No one is even paying any attention to the American president – the spineless popinjay has admitted everything, and the world loves him for sacrificing so much to rescue his men and women from the evil clutches of the Russians, or some such nonsense. All eyes are on *us*. And I think Sen'kov may have found a way to insulate himself from this whole mess – after all, he never gave any orders and never authorized any of this.'

'I have plenty to implicate Sen'kov,' Kazakov said angrily. 'I have bank records, wire transfers, and account numbers in seven banks around the world. I've paid him millions to get him to issue orders and deploy the army in my favor.'

'All his bank accounts are numbered, all anonymous,' Zhurbenko said. 'Not one of them points to Sen'kov. Besides, the Russian constitution prohibits Sen'kov from prosecution for anything he does while in office, and if the Duma tries to impeach him – which they will not do, he is too powerful for that – he can simply dissolve it. The worst that will happen to him is he'll be accused of being a dupe. It is I and the others in his cabinet and security council that will go to prison.'

As if to punctuate Zhurbenko's words, the images on CNN shifted to demonstrators outside German and Russian embassies around the world, from Albania to Moscow, from Norway to South Africa, protesting the actions of the German and Russian armies in the Balkans. The entire world now feared a Russo-German Axis alliance, another attempt to occupy all of Europe, and perhaps even a third world war – but this time, with no help from the United States expected, a successful one.

All this, CNN said, because of Pavel Kazakov and his bloodthirsty greed. Kazakov had once been feared for his reputation. Fear had been replaced by grudging respect for his entrepreneurial audacity and success. Now he was hated. He was the world's Public Enemy Number One. He could never walk anywhere in the real world, even with an army of bodyguards. Even without a reward on his head – and Pavel had no doubt one was soon going to be announced – he was not safe from anyone. Who wouldn't want to be known as the one who'd rid the world of such a monster?

Kazakov's eyes grew narrow with anger, but slowly his logical mind took over from his emotions, and he started to devise a plan. 'Then I assume,' he asked sarcastically, 'you are speaking to me from a private chartered aircraft taking you over the Mediterranean to some nameless African republic with no extradition treaty with the Russian Federation?'

'I am not a rich drug-dealing bastard like you, Kazakov,' Zhurbenko said. 'I did all this for Russia. Yes, I took your money, and I hope I can get my wife and sons out of the country so they can enjoy it before the Interior Ministry takes away everything I own. But I did all this for mother Russia, to regain some of our lost power and influence around the world. I will not abandon my post or my country.'

'Then I suppose you have to live with your

decision, General,' Kazakov said casually.

'Oh, I can live with myself just fine, Pavel,' Zhurbenko said. 'Russia again has troops in the Balkans and throughout Western Europe – all legal, all sanctioned by the United Nations – the NATO alliance has been fractured, we have a powerful new ally in Germany, and Caspian oil is making my country rich. I am proud of what I've done for my country, Kazakov, even if I end up going to prison for it. The loss of your tanker and your million barrels of oil is of no consequence to me.'

'Then I think our business is at an end,' Kazakov said. 'You enjoy being a good little soldier in Lefortovo Prison. Remember, if you drop the bar of soap in the shower, don't bend over to pick it up.'

Kazakov slammed the phone down so hard, he nearly broke the receiver on his three-thousand-dollar satellite phone. He had tried to sound casual and flippant on the phone with Zhurbenko, as if the loss of half a billion dollars was no big deal for him, but in actuality it was a huge blow. Since he owned the oil from the well to the refinery, including the terminals all along the way, and since he had numerous 'side deals' with the individual countries to transport the oil, none of his product or the ships that carried it across the Black Sea was insured – not that many companies around the world would sell insurance to a drug smuggler and gangster. In addition, his investors expected to be paid whether or not the oil made it to the pipeline, and that was seven and a half million dollars that had to come out of his own pocket. There was no interest on this money, no grace period, and no declaring bankruptcy – it was either pay up or be hunted for the rest of his life.

Further, the loss of one tanker by some shadowy, obviously powerful terrorist outfit – probably some CIA or SAS strike team – put the brakes on any more shipments on tankers bearing his name. That meant leasing other tankers, and that didn't come cheap. In any case, his oil was as much of a target as his tankers were, and shipping companies would either simply refuse to transport any Metyorgaz crude, or charge a hefty premium to do so, to compensate for the possibility of another terrorist attack.

There was only one answer: divert the world's attention away from him and onto another topic.

He left his private office and stormed out to the aircraft hangar. Although they continued to move the Metyor-179 Tyenee from place to place on a regular basis, most of Metyor's known or suspected bases in Georgia, Kazakhstan, Russia, and Bulgaria were under heavy surveillance, so the base in Romania seemed to be the safest. He marched past the security guards and found Pyotr Fursenko standing in front of the Mt-179 stealth aircraft, worriedly discussing the streaks of black and gray on the leading edge – the internal missile launchers. 'Doctor, get the aircraft ready to go tonight,' he ordered.

The technician Fursenko was talking to stepped away, thankful to get away from Pavel Kazakov. 'We have some problems, sir,' Fursenko said.

'I'm not interested in problems right now, Fursenko, only action and results.' Fursenko said nothing, only looked at the hangar floor. 'Well? What is wrong now?'

'There was more damage to the wing structure after the last missile launches–'

'I thought you had that problem solved.'

'We could not reengineer the internal launcher system and still keep the plane operational and on around-the-clock alert as you wanted,' Fursenko explained. 'We could do nothing else but make minor repairs and impose operational limitations. The crew was restricted to firing internal missiles only in an emergency, after all other missiles were expended, only if the aircraft was in danger, and with a zero-point-eight Mach speed restriction, two-g acceleration, and five point zero angle-of-attack limits.' Fursenko could tell that this flurry of aeronautical technospeak was giving his young boss a headache, so he quickly decided to conclude with more or less happy news: 'But we have repaired the damage, and I think we can be ready to fly.'

'So if you had operational limitations, why was there damage to the wing?' Fursenko hesitated, and Kazakov guessed the reason. 'Obviously, because Stoica and Yegorov violated the restrictions, is that correct?'

'Their orders were to shoot down the patrol planes,' Fursenko argued. 'They did a very good job–'

'They only got one bomber!'

'Which is very good, considering the odds they were up against,' Fursenko pointed out. 'They faced four well-trained Turkish adversaries and managed to get two of them, maybe three.'

Kazakov looked up at the cockpit. Gennadi Yegorov was up there in the forward cockpit, making notes on a clipboard as the technicians tested electrical circuits, his head in a bandage. 'What happened to Yegorov?'

'A slight concussion during some of their evasive maneuvers. The corpsman thinks he'll be fine.'

'And Stoica?'

'Over there.' Fursenko looked apprehensive. Kazakov saw Stoica nursing a cup of coffee, one hand covering his eyes. 'I think he has a touch of flu. When will you give us a list of new targets, sir?'

'Right away,' Kazakov said. He stared angrily at Stoica and realized the bastard did not have the flu. 'There will be two of them, both to be hit on the same night.'

'That is risky, sir,' Fursenko said. 'A heavy weapons load will mean using external weapon pylons—'

'Why? You have the internal weapons bay. Two air-to-ground weapons, two targets.'

'That's risky, sir,' Fursenko explained. 'We typically plan on twice the number of weapons than necessary to ensure success of the mission – two targets, *four* weapons, in case of a miss or a weapons malfunction.'

'So then use the external pylons.'

'If we put air-to-ground missiles on an external pylon, it means we cannot put air-to-air missiles on a pylon because of weight restrictions. The air-to-ground weapons are much heavier than air-to-air weapons, and they have a narrower carriage envelope.'

'So? Use the pylons and the weapons bay for

offensive weapons, and the internal missiles for defense.'

'But we cannot use internal defensive missiles, sir,' Fursenko said. 'The damage—'

'I thought you said you repaired the damage.'

'We have repaired the damage caused by launching missiles from the last mission, but we have not solved the underlying problem yet,' Fursenko said. 'And there is certainly much more damage to the wing that we can't see. I would caution against using any internal missiles at all except in an emergency, and to be extra safe I would advise not even to load missiles into the launchers.'

'I pay those men a lot of money to take certain risks, Doctor,' Kazakov said flatly. 'Besides, if it might help bring them and the aircraft back in one piece, I want it used. The missiles go on, but they are not to be used except in absolute emergencies – no chasing after targets of opportunity. Issue the order.'

'But that leaves us with no defensive weapons to counter known threats,' Fursenko argued. 'We will need the external pylons both for defensive and for offensive weapons.'

'Fursenko, you are beginning to talk in circles,' Kazakov said irritably. 'First you say we cannot use internal missiles, and then you say we cannot do the mission *unless* we use internals. What are you really saying, Doctor? Are you saying we cannot fly the aircraft?'

'I ... I guess that's what I'm saying,' Fursenko said finally. 'It cannot be safely used without extensive inspection and repair.'

Pavel Kazakov seemed to accept this bit of news. He nodded, then seemed to shrug his shoulders. 'Then perhaps we will strike just one target,' he said. 'Will that satisfy you, Doctor? You can use the internal weapons bay for offensive weapons, and the pylons for defensive weapons.'

'Our other problem came with using external pylons, because using them greatly increases our radar cross-section and destroys our stealthiness,' Fursenko explained. 'If we only strike one target, we can still use the other two internal launchers for emergency use, and then use the internal bay for offensive weapons.'

Kazakov nodded again. 'And what of Gennadi and Ion?' he asked. 'Will they be all right?'

'Gennadi seems to be well. He has been under close supervision, and seems to be suffering no effects of his concussion.' Fursenko frowned at Stoica. 'Ion ... we'll have to see how well he can recover. From the flu.'

Kazakov nodded. He looked at Yegorov, who was flipping switches and speaking on a headset to the technicians. 'If we need to do a test flight, Gennadi can do it?'

'Of course. Gennadi is a trained pilot and is almost as familiar with the Tyenee as Ion. We would substitute myself or one of the other technicians in the weapons officer's position for the test flight.'

'Excellent.' Kazakov strolled over toward Stoica. The pilot did not stand or even acknowledge Kazakov's presence, just sat with his hand covering his eyes. 'Ion? I hope you are feeling better. Is there anything I can do?'

653

'I've done everything I can think of, Pavel,' Stoica moaned. A faint whiff of fortified wine caught Kazakov's nostrils. 'I just need a little time so I can get my head together.'

'It'll take more than time to get your head together, Ion,' Kazakov said. Stoica raised his head and looked at Kazakov through bloodshot eyes and was about to ask his boss what he meant when Kazakov pulled a SIG-Sauer P226 nine-millimeter pistol from a shoulder holster, held it to Stoica's forehead, and pulled the trigger. Half the contents of Stoica's skull splattered out onto the table, and his limp, lifeless body collapsed on top of the mess of brains, blood, and bone. Kazakov fired three more rounds into Stoica's eyes and mouth until his head was nothing more than a lump of gore.

He turned back toward Fursenko, still holding the smoking pistol clenched in his fist, and wiped blobs of blood and bits of brain matter across his face until he wore a macabre death mask. 'No more excuses from any of you!' he screamed. 'No more excuses! When I say I want a job done, you will do it! When I say I want a target destroyed, all the targets, you had better destroy them, or don't bother returning to my base! I don't care about safety, or malfunctions, or caution lights, or excuses, or danger. You do a job or you will *die*. Is that clear?

'Fursenko, I want that aircraft airborne with as many weapons as you need to do the job, and I want it airborne *tonight*, or I will slaughter each and every one of you! And you will destroy *both* targets I give you, both of them, or don't bother coming back – in fact, don't even bother living anymore! Do I make myself clear? Now, get busy, all of you!'

The White House Oval Office
that same time

The three Air Force general officers entered the Oval Office and stood quietly and unobtrusively along the wall, not daring to say a word or even make any sudden moves. They all expected the same thing: a major-league ass-chewing, thanks to Patrick McLanahan and his high-tech toys.

The President finished reading the report that Director of Central Intelligence Douglas Morgan had given him moments earlier. After the President read the report, he gave it to Vice President Les Busick, then stared off into space, thinking. Busick glanced at the report, then passed it along to Secretary of State Kercheval. Robert Goff had already briefed both men; Kercheval seemed even more upset than the President. After a few moments, President Thorn shook his head in exasperation, then glanced at Secretary of Defense Goff. 'Take a seat, gentlemen,' he said.

After several long, silent, awkward moments, the President stood, crossed in front of his desk, then sat down on its edge. The seething anger on his face was painfully obvious to all. Thorn stared at each of the generals in turn, then asked slowly and measurably, 'General Venti, how do I stop McLanahan?'

The Chairman of the Joint Chiefs of Staff

thought for a moment, then replied, 'We believe McLanahan's raid started off from a small Ukrainian base near Nikolayev. Special Operations Command is ready to dispatch several teams into the area to hunt them down. Meanwhile, we retask reconnaissance satellites to scan every possible base for their presence.'

'If we get lucky, we'll find them in a couple days – if they haven't packed up and moved to a different location,' Morgan interjected.

'If they modified other Ukrainian helicopters to act as aerial refueling tankers,' Air Force Chief of Staff General Victor Hayes pointed out, 'that could double the size of the area we'd need to search. It'd be a needle in a haystack.'

'Not necessarily,' Morgan said. 'If we knew what their next move was, we might be able to set up a picket and nab them.'

'And if we got a little more cooperation from the Ukrainians or the Turks, we'd find them easier, too,' Kercheval added. 'But this Black Sea Alliance is refusing to give us any information, although we're certain they've been tracking and perhaps even assisting McLanahan in his raids.'

'They stole a damned supertanker loaded with a million barrels of oil in the middle of the Black Sea,' Vice President Busick retorted. 'Who would've guessed they'd try something like that? Are we supposed to set up surveillance on every tanker in the area? What are they up to? What do they hope to accomplish?'

'McLanahan told me exactly what he hopes to accomplish, sir,' General Hayes said.

'Draw the Russians out into the open,' the

President said. 'Attack Kazakov's center – his oil empire – and force him to retaliate.'

'Exactly, sir.'

'Oil tankers first, then oil terminals next?'

'They're fairly easy targets for the weapons McLanahan has at his disposal, sir,' Lieutenant-General Terrill Samson added.

'We can set up round-the-clock AWACS patrols and nab him as soon as he appears,' Hayes said. 'We interdict every noncorrelated flight in the area. A few fighters and tankers on patrol should take care of it. We can set that up immediately.'

'Find him,' the President ordered bitterly. 'I don't care if you have to send every fighter in the force to do it. Find him. No more sneak attacks.' The President glanced again at Goff, then at Terrill Samson. 'General, you can help me get in contact with McLanahan.'

'Sir?'

'That subcutaneous transceiver system you use at Dreamland,' the President said, pointing to his left shoulder with a jabbing motion. 'That works almost anywhere in the world, doesn't it?'

'Yes, sir. But I've attempted to contact General McLanahan and other members of his team several times. No response.'

'He thinks you betrayed him.'

Samson looked frozen for a moment, then shrugged. 'I don't know what he–' He stopped when he saw Thorn's knowing glance, then nodded. 'Yes, he does, sir.'

'He thinks I betrayed him, too,' the President said. 'He thinks I'm selling the United States down the river.'

657

'Sir, it shouldn't matter what McLanahan thinks,' Samson said emphatically. 'He's a soldier. He was ... I mean, he *is* supposed to follow orders.'

'You know where he is, don't you, General?'

Samson swallowed hard. 'Sir?'

'McLanahan may not be answering you, but those implants allow you to track and monitor anyone wearing them,' the President said. 'You said so yourself. You know exactly where he is, but you haven't told General Venti or Secretary Goff. Why?'

'What in hell is this, Samson?' Joint Chiefs Chairman Venti exclaimed. 'You've been keeping this information from us the whole time?'

'No one ever ordered me to locate McLanahan, sir,' Samson said.

'You're busted, General,' Venti thundered. 'That kind of insubordinate bullshit just landed you in hock.'

'Permission to speak freely, sir?'

'*Denied!*' Venti shouted.

'Hold on, General,' the President interrupted. 'Go ahead, General Samson.'

Samson paused, but only for a moment. He gave the President a firm look. 'Sir, I don't like what McLanahan's doing – but only because he's doing *my* job.'

'Your job?'

'My job is to track down wack-jobs like Kazakov and his stealth fighter-bomber and knock it out of the sky, not try to knock down one of our own,' Samson said. 'Sir, you're not prepared or not willing to get involved in this matter, that's fine.

You're the President and my commander-in-chief, and your decision is the final word. But when honest fighting men like Patrick McLanahan do decide to act, they shouldn't be persecuted by their own government.'

Samson looked at Venti, then General Hayes, the others in the Oval Office, and then President Thorn. 'If you order me to find McLanahan and bring him in, sir, I'll do it. I'll use every means at my disposal to do it.'

'Fine. I'll give you a direct order, General Samson,' the President said. He paused for a moment, then said: 'General, I want you to install one of those subcutaneous transceivers in me. Today. Right now.'

'*Sir?*'

'You heard me. Make the call, get one out here immediately.'

'But ... but what about McLanahan?' Busick retorted. 'How is that going to stop him?'

'I'm going to talk with him. I want to hear his voice,' Thorn said. 'If he's turning into some kind of high-tech terrorist or supervigilante, I need to find out for myself. If I determine he or the ones that fly with him are unstable, I'll send every last jet and every last infantryman out to nail his ass.'

Tirane, Republic of Albania
two nights later

For the second night in a row, the crowds had gathered in front of the four-story office building across from the German embassy in the Albanian capital of Tirane, the headquarters of the United Nations Protection Force, composed mostly of Russian and German troops, assigned to patrol the southern Albania–Macedonia border. Since the stories had broken in the world media about the deal between Pavel Kazakov and members of the Russian government, massive protests had broken out all over the Balkans, but none larger or louder than in Tirane. The German government, considered Russian collaborators, became equal targets for the protesters.

Tonight's protests were the worst. Albanian troops were called in early, which only angered the protesters even more. Albanian labor unions, upset because Kazakov had not used union labor to build his pipeline, led the protests, and the army and police were not anxious to confront the unions. The crowd was unruly, surging back and forth between the United Nations headquarters and the German embassy. Shouting quickly turned to pushing, and the police and army had trouble controlling the massive crowds. Pushing turned to fighting, fighting turned to rock and bottle throwing, and rocks and bottles turned into Molotov cocktails.

Virtually unheard and unnoticed in all the confusion and growing panic in the streets was the wail of an extraordinarily loud siren, but not a police or fire siren – it was an air raid warning siren. Moments later, the lights on all Albanian government buildings automatically started to extinguish – another automatic response to an attack warning dating back to the German blitzkriegs of World War II. The sudden darkness, combined with the lights of emergency vehicles and fires on the streets, sent some protesters into flights of sheer panic.

The police had just started to deploy riot-control vehicles with water and tear gas cannons when hell broke loose. There was an impossibly bright flash of light, a huge ball of fire, and a deafening explosion that engulfed an entire city block, centered precisely on the German embassy. When the smoke and fire cleared, the Germany embassy was nothing more than a smoking hole and a pile of rubble. Everyone within a block of the embassy – protesters, police, army, embassy workers, and curious onlookers – were either dead or dying, and fires had broken out for several blocks around the blast.

The President's study, The White House, Washington, DC
a short time later

'The devastation is enormous, sir,' Director of Central Intelligence Douglas Morgan reported, reading from the initial reports on the incident. 'The entire Germany embassy is gone – nothing but a pile of concrete. Police and news media estimated a crowd of perhaps five thousand was outside the embassy involved in the protest, with another five to ten thousand police, news media, and onlookers within the blast radius. The joint United Nations–NATO headquarters across the street was severely damaged – casualty estimates there could top three hundred dead or injured.'

President Thomas Thorn sat quietly in his study next to the Oval Office. He was dressed in a casual shirt and slacks and wearing only a pair of sandals, having been awakened shortly after going to bed with news of the terrible blast in Tirane. His bank of television monitors were tuned to various world news channels, but he had the sound muted on all of them and was listening to his Cabinet officials feeding him reports as they came in, staring not at the televisions but at a spot on the wall, staring intently as if he could see for himself the horror unfolding thousands of miles away.

'Sir, the situation is getting worse by the minute,' Morgan said urgently. 'The German government has ordered troops bivouacked in three Albanian port cities to move eastward, toward the capital – the number of troops deploying into the capital Tirane is estimated so far to top three thousand. An estimated five thousand Russian troops are moving from outlying camps in Serbia and Macedonia into the cities and are setting up so-called security checkpoints – it looks like an occupation.'

'They're overreacting,' Thorn said in a low voice. Secretary of Defense Robert Goff looked at the President with a surprised look on his face, as if Thorn had just grown donkey's ears. Was that a trace of hesitation, maybe even *doubt*, in Thorn's voice? 'I need facts, Doug, not speculation or newspaper hyperbole. If it's an invasion force, tell me so. If it's a redeployment of troops in response to a major terrorist incident, tell me that.'

'It's a major redeployment of troops, obviously in a defensive response to the explosion in Tirane, that can easily escalate into an invasion force.' Morgan narrowed his eyes to emphasize his last point: 'And that's not some newspaper's assessment, sir, that's *mine.*'

'Thank you, Doug,' the President said, not seeming to notice Morgan's emphatic response but with a touch of apology in his voice nonetheless. 'Any more details about this air raid warning that was issued moments before the blast?'

'No information about that, sir,' Morgan said. 'The Albanian Ministry of Defense claims the Interior Ministry ordered them to blow the horn to try to disperse the protesters. There is no word from the Transportation Ministry on whether or not there was an unidentified aircraft over the capital. Russian or German radar stations claim they were not tracking any unidentified aircraft.'

'So there could have been an unidentified aircraft – only no one is admitting that one got by them,' Secretary of Defense Robert Goff observed.

'What other forces are mobilizing?' the President asked. 'German forces in Albania; Russian forces in Serbia and Macedonia. Any troops on the move in Russia? In the Commonwealth states? Any Russian naval forces moving? Any Russian or German tactical air forces?'

Morgan shook his head, glanced quickly at his briefing notes to double-check, then shook his head. 'No, sir. Only tactical airlift and sealift units, and they look like routine support missions.'

'I would think that an 'occupation' force would

need a lot of support units set in motion fairly quickly for an occupation of an entire capital city to be successful,' the President observed. 'And few successful occupation forces leap into action from a standing start. I don't see an invasion happening yet.'

'Not that we could do anything about it if it *was* happening!' Goff commented.

'Perhaps not,' the President said, with only a hint of annoyance in his voice.

'I can't believe we are going to sit here and do nothing!' Goff said. 'Shouldn't we be calling the German chancellor and the Russian president, warning them that their actions resemble an occupation force and that we object to such a move? Shouldn't we be calling the Italians or the Bosnians or our NATO allies, reassuring them that we're at least monitoring the situation and perhaps discussing some options?'

'I'm sure they know that we are doing and thinking all those things,' the President said easily. 'Besides, actions speak louder than words. Even watching and waiting is doing something.'

'Not in my book, it isn't,' Goff said under his breath.

'What would you have me do, Robert?' the President snapped. 'Tell me right now: what forces would you like to commit? We have two Marine Expeditionary Units nearby in the Med and in the Adriatic Sea, plus one aircraft carrier battle group in the Aegean Sea. We have two B-1B bomber squadrons on alert in Georgia and two B-2A stealth bomber squadrons ready to go with conventional bombs and cruise missiles in Missouri, plus one air expeditionary wing in South Carolina ready to deploy if needed. That's about twenty-five thousand men and women, fourteen warships, and perhaps one hundred combat aircraft we can have over the Balkans in eight hours, and perhaps double that number in twelve hours. Do you have a target for me, Robert? What's the mission? What do you want to blow up now?'

'I don't want to blow up anything, sir – I just want to make it clear to Sen'kov, Keisinger, Zhurbenko, and all those other nutcases that we don't like what they're doing and we are ready to act if they persist!' Goff replied. 'In case they interpret our silence as disinterest or even as tacit acceptance or permission, I want it clearly and emphatically known that we will tolerate no offensive moves in Europe, no matter what the provocation.'

'I think it's *you* that needs to be told,' the President said. 'Robert, I'm telling you now – don't *you* interpret my so-called inaction as tacit permission or disinterest. But I am not going to respond to the threat of war with a threat of my own.' He went over and clasped Goff on the shoulder. 'Robert, you seem to think there's someone out there that needs to get slapped down. I'm here to tell you: there isn't. Let it go.' He could tell that there was a lot that his friend still needed to say, so he took away the reassuring tone in his voice and said, 'Go home, Robert,' and it was an order, not a suggestion.

Goff took a step closer to the President and asked, 'Is that what you told President Martindale during your little meeting with him? "Just go home"? Or did you tell him or help him do something else?'

If Goff expected the President to be surprised that he knew about the private meeting, he didn't show it. 'That's exactly what I told him, Robert – whatever he wants to do, whatever ideas he has, forget about them,' the President replied. 'He is not the president any longer. He does not run US foreign or military policy – I do. He's a private citizen now, subject to all laws, with no special protections or considerations because of his previous position.'

'Then why did you keep the meeting secret from me?'

'Because it was between him and me,' Thorn said. 'It was one president talking with another. If I couldn't convince him to stay out of it, without the rest of my Cabinet behind me, it was my failure.' Goff looked skeptical. The President gave his friend a slight, knowing smile, then said, 'Maybe the same reason you didn't tell me *you* met with him.' Goff's mouth dropped open in complete surprise, then bobbed up and down like a freshly caught trout. 'How did I know? You told me – not in words, but in your eyes, your mannerisms. I know you, Robert, just like you know me. The problem is, you know me so well you think you can reason with me, change my mind. You can't. I know you so well, I know Martindale approached you – and I know you turned him down.'

Goff couldn't hide his amazement, but he couldn't help toying with Thorn anyway – he was so infuriatingly confident, Goff actually wanted to try to get his friend mad at him any way he could, just to get a rise out of him. 'You're sure of that? You're sure I turned him down, Thomas?'

'Fairly sure,' the President said. 'What Martindale wants to do is bold and exciting and challenging and risky, and it's what you want to do. Problem is, it's also illegal, and you know it, and you will *not* break the law. That's why you're trying so hard to convince me to do something – because if I don't do it, Martindale might, and if he does, he will probably fail, and then the United States looks even more like an inept failure. Whatever's going to happen, Robert, will happen. I'm not going to add to the confusion and fear. We let it play out. So go home, my friend. I'll call you if I need you.'

Both Morgan and Goff exited the study, leaving the President alone with his thoughts – and his secret fears.

Over the Black Sea
that same time

The attack on the German embassy in Tirane went off with surprising precision and flawless execution – even Pyotr Fursenko, who had enormous trust in his constructs, was as pleased as he was surprised. It went off so well and so quickly that he had little time to prepare for the second part of their dangerous mission.

Gennadi Yegorov was the quiet, unexcitable captain of their pickup strike team. Even with the constant threat of Pavel Kazakov and his demonic

667

anger hovering around them, Yegorov took his time, refamiliarizing himself with the forward cockpit and explaining several key pieces of information to Fursenko – he was mindful of the fact that although Fursenko had designed and built the plane, he had never flown in it or any other aircraft before. Yegorov got Kazakov to agree to an extra day to prepare, and it was time well spent. By the time they were ready to launch, Fursenko felt confident he could play the role of Yegorov's assistant and flip the right switches at the proper time.

If not, and their mission ended in failure, he felt *very* confident he could punch them both out of the aircraft.

It was without a doubt the biggest warload the Metyor-179 had ever carried: a pylon with one R-60 air-to-air missile and one Kh-73 laser-guided one-thousand-kilogram bomb under each wing, two Kh-73 bombs in the internal weapons bay, and four R-60 missiles in the internal wing launchers for emergency use only. The R-60s on the wing pylons were a last-minute suggestion from Yegorov. His logic was simple: the Tyenee was most vulnerable with the two big bombs on those pylons, so why not carry some extra insurance? When the external bombs were expended or if they got jumped before the target area, they could use the two extra missiles to fight their way out, jettison the bombs and pylons, and use their stealthiness to get away. It turns out they were not needed, but Yegorov proved he was definitely in charge of this mission and this aircraft.

The navigation system was as tight and as

accurate as could be during the short flight from Codlea to Tirane. The radar warning receiver bleeped during most of the flight, especially near the Macedonian and Albanian capitals, but no fighters or antiaircraft weapon systems ever appeared to challenge them. Yegorov had made Fursenko some drawings of what the German embassy might look like in the targeting display, in case he had to refine the aim, but the targeting box was right on the correct building all the way, so Fursenko didn't have to touch a thing except to be sure the weapon arming and release switches were in the proper setting for the bomb run, which of course he could do with his eyes closed – after all, he'd designed and positioned each and every one of them, and he knew to the smallest detail exactly what had to happen to get a successful weapon release.

But Fursenko did not have his eyes closed – and he saw everything, including the thousands of persons filling the streets near the German embassy. One one-thousand-kilo bomb was certainly enough to destroy the small embassy building. The second weapon was targeted on the very same point, but actually impacted several meters short – right into the crowded street in the midst of the protesters. When the first bomb hit the German embassy, and as the impossibly bright cloud of fire blossomed across the screen, Fursenko thought he could see the people as individuals, could see the shock wave hit them first, knocking down their signs, blowing tons of debris toward them in the blink of an eye, and whisking their heads back just milliseconds before the wall of heat and concrete washed over them. Then the laser targeting system automatically flipped to a wide bomb damage assessment shot of the target area, so Fursenko could not see any more details except for the second bomb falling short and adding its fury to the first.

But he knew there was going to be death down there. They had only targeted buildings, sure – but Kazakov must've known that those protesters were going to be there. He could've waited a few hours until the streets were clear, but he didn't. He could've targeted another building, or picked some other target to make his point and cause a distraction, but he hadn't. He'd deliberately chosen this target because of the number of people that would be in the path of that blast.

It was true: Pavel Kazakov was a murderous monster. He would order the deaths of thousands just to cover his tracks as easily and as casually as he'd order Cornish game hen from a restaurant menu.

'How are you doing back there, Doctor?' Gennadi Yegorov asked.

'All right,' Fursenko asked. 'And call me Pyotr, please.'

'I will. And call me Gennadi.'

They fell silent for a few moments; then: 'I was thinking...'

'Yes, Pyotr?'

'I was thinking about how coldly Comrade Kazakov can kill a person,' Fursenko said. 'Human life means absolutely nothing to him.'

'It certainly adds a new dynamic to our business, doesn't it?' Yegorov said with casual, dark humor. 'Just too many ways to die.'

Fursenko dropped his mask, afraid he might hyperventilate. He looked at Yegorov's eyes in the rearview mirror, then raised his oxygen mask and spoke into its microphone: 'He will not let us live if we return. You know that, don't you?'

'Ion was falling apart, Pyotr,' Yegorov said. 'He couldn't handle the task. He was getting bored and making mistakes.'

'But Kazakov shot him four times in the head, as easily as ... as cutting open a melon for breakfast,' Fursenko pointed out.

'Pyotr, forget about Stoica. He was a drunk and an idiot.'

'As soon as he's done with us, he'll discard us, the Metyor-179, and everyone working out there in Codlea. He'll kill us all, just as easily as he killed Stoica and those soldiers in Bulgaria.'

'Pyotr, you agreed to work for the man,' Yegorov pointed out. 'You did it voluntarily, same as I. We both knew who he was and what he wanted long before we agreed to work for him. After we shot down that unarmed AWACS plane, we took his money. After we killed those people in Kukes, we took his money. After he killed those soldiers in Bulgaria, we took his money. We're heartless butchers, just like he is. What do you want to do now? Fly away? Try to run and hide?'

'How about we save ourselves?'

'Then you had better find a way to make sure he's dead,' Yegorov said. 'Because if he's alive and you cross him, he'll find you and devise some ugly, horrible way to kill you. He did Stoica a favor by killing him quickly.'

'Should we ask the West for protection?'

'The West would want us to testify as witnesses against Kazakov, and then our lives would be worthless,' Yegorov said. 'We're co-conspirators with him now, Pyotr, can't you understand that? We're his hired killers. Just because you're a scientist and not a pilot or gunman doesn't absolve you from guilt. If we testify against Kazakov, we'd be put in prison ourselves, and then we'd be targets for his worldwide network of assassins. If we're put into a witness protection program, our lives would be at the mercy of some government bureaucrat – no guarantee we'd be safe from Pavel Kazakov. No. We have a job to do, you and I. Let's do it.'

'Are you crazy, or just blind?' Fursenko asked incredulously.' 'Can't you see what's happening? Kazakov is a killer. Once he's done with us, we're dead. He'll have his billions, and we'll be dead.'

'Doctor, to my knowledge, no one in Kazakov's employ has ever been killed without good reason – they were killed either for disloyalty or incompetence,' Yegorov said. 'Kazakov is generous and loyal to those who are loyal to him. I told you before, Ion was unstable, unreliable, and taking unnecessary risks. He was a danger to Kazakov's organization, and he had to be eliminated. Ion was my friend and longtime colleague, but under the circumstances, I agree with Comrade Kazakov – he had to be eliminated. And if there was any other way Ion could have been retired without blabbing his drunken mouth off to the world about what we'd done, I'd be angry about how he died. But he brought it on himself.

'I will not let that happen to us,' Yegorov said, impaling Fursenko with a stern gaze through the rearview mirror. 'We are going to accomplish this mission successfully, and then return home, and get ready to fly and fight again. If we did any less, we'd deserve to die ourselves.'

There was simply no arguing with Gennadi Yegorov. Fursenko was stunned. This intelligent, soft-spoken pilot and engineer had turned into some kind of mindless killing machine. Was it the money? The power? The thrill of the hunt and the kill? Whatever it was, Yegorov was not going to be deterred.

There was no more time to think about it, because the last target complex was coming up. Yegorov had Fursenko configure the release switches and pre-arm the last two remaining Kh-73 laser-guided bombs several minutes before the bomb-run initial point. His trigger was hot. Once IP inbound, Fursenko extended the imaging infrared scanner and laser designator and began searching for the last set of targets.

It was easy to find – because the Metyorgaz oil tanker *Ustinov* was one of the world's largest vessels. Surrounded by Turkish military vessels and a second tanker, to which the last five hundred thousand barrels of oil left in its holds was being transferred, the cluster of ships made a very inviting target.

'There's the *Ustinov*,' Yegorov said, as he looked carefully into his targeting monitor. 'The navigation system is dead on, just like over Tirane. Remember, we release on the *Ustinov* first. We'll probably lose it in the fireball, but we have to keep aiming as long as we can. If we miss the *Ustinov*, we'll drop the second Kh-73 on it. If we hit the first time, we'll shift aim to either the Turkish tanker or that big Turkish frigate nearby.' He actually laughed. 'This'll teach the Turks to take something that doesn't belong to them! Get ready, Doctor.'

The bomb run was short and quick. There were enemy aircraft nearby, but they were patrolling farther north and east, probably to protect against any attack aircraft coming from Russia. The Turkish frigate was scanning the skies with its air search radar, but with the external pylons jettisoned long ago, the Mt-179 was too stealthy to be picked up by it. By the time it flew close enough to be detected, the bombs would already be in the air. One bomb would certainly be enough to send the *Ustinov* to the bottom, and the explosion would probably destroy the Turkish tanker and severely damage any nearby vessels too – the second bomb would ensure complete and total devastation. Half the oil from the *Ustinov* was already off-loaded, but spilling half a million barrels of crude oil into the Black Sea would certainly qualify as the world's biggest oil spill, more than double the size of the enormous *Exxon Valdez* oil spill in Prince William Sound, Alaska.

The white computer targeting square was dead on the tanker. Yegorov had Fursenko move the pipper slightly so it centered on the very center of the middle hold, the structurally weakest point on the upper deck and also one of the empty holds. The bomb detonating inside an empty hold would ignite the petroleum vapors and quadruple the size of the blast, which would certainly rip the tanker into pieces and create the enormous spill they wanted. Yegorov had already had Fursenko set up the secondary target pipper on the Turkish frigate, although he wouldn't switch targeting away from the *Ustinov* until they were sure it was holed.

Switches configured, final release checks accomplished, Fursenko opened the inwardly-opening bomb doors, and the first Kh-73 bomb dropped into space. 'Bomb doors closed! Laser on!' Yegorov commanded. Fursenko activated the laser designator and received a good steering signal from the weapon. 'Data good, laser off.' They only needed to turn the laser on for a few seconds after release to give the bomb its initial course, then for ten seconds before impact to give it its terminal steering. The pipper stayed locked on target. Everything was going perfectly, just like Tirane. Everything was–

DEEDLE DEEDLE DEEDLE! they heard from the threat warning receiver – an enemy radar had just locked on to them. It was the Turkish frigate's air search radar. Yegorov started a shallow turn away from the ship, careful not to turn too suddenly so as to break the laser's aim. Yegorov wondered about the warning, but soon dismissed it. The frigate might be trying to lock on to the bomb, he thought – the Kh-73 one-thousand-kilogram bomb probably had ten times the radar cross-section of the Metyor-179 stealth fighter right now. No problem. The bomb was tracking perfectly.

Ten seconds to impact. 'Laser on!' Yegorov shouted. He immediately received another 'data good' signal from the bomb. Nothing could stop it now...

'Contact!' Duane Deverill shouted. 'Annie, come thirty left *now!*' He keyed the voice command button on his target tracking joystick and ordered, 'Attack target two with two Anacondas!'

'Attack command two Anacondas, stop attack ... bomb doors open, missile one away ... launcher rotating, stop attack ... missile two away ... doors closed, launcher rotating,' the computer replied, and it fired two AIM-152 Anaconda long-range air-to-air missiles from twenty-three miles away. The missile's first-stage motors accelerated the big weapon to twice the speed of sound, and then the missile's scramjet engine kicked in, accelerating it well past five times the speed of sound in seconds. Traveling at a speed of over a mile per second, the Anaconda missile closed the gap in moments.

Steered by its own onboard radar, the missile arrived at a point in space just two hundred feet above the tanker *Ustinov*, then detonated – at the exact moment the Kh-73 laser-guided bomb arrived at the exact spot. There was a massive fireball above the tanker, like a gigantic flashbulb popping in the night, that froze everything within a mile in the strobelike glare. The Anaconda missile's sixty-three-pound warhead split the big Kh-73 into several pieces before it exploded, so the size of the fireball wasn't enough to do much damage to the tanker except cook some paint and blow out every window not already destroyed on

676

its superstructure.

'Any aircraft on this frequency, any aircraft on this frequency, this is Aces One-Niner,' Deverill radioed on 243.0 megahertz, the international UHF emergency frequency, as he studied his supercockpit display, 'I have an unidentified aircraft one-seven miles northwest of Eregli at thirty-one thousand feet, heading south in a slow right turn.' He was aboard an EB-1C Megafortress Two bomber, flying high over the Black Sea about thirty miles north of the Turkish naval base at Eregli. He had been scanning the area with the Megafortress's laser radar all evening, but had detected nothing until seconds before the bomb came hurtling down from the sky toward the Russian tanker. 'Just a friendly advisory. Thought someone would like to know.'

'Aces One-Niner, this is Stalker One-Zero, we read you loud and clear,' David Luger replied. Luger was aboard the Sky Masters Inc.'s DC-10 launch-and-control aircraft, orbiting not far from the EB-1C Megafortress at a different altitude. He, too, had been scanning the skies with a laser radar mounted aboard the DC-10, and he had detected the unidentified aircraft and the falling bomb at the same instant. 'You might want to contact Eregli approach on two-seven-five-point-three. Thanks, guys.'

'You're welcome – whoever you are,' the Megafortress's aircraft commander, Annie Dewey, replied. She found it impossible to hold back a tear and keep her voice from cracking. 'Have a nice flight.'

'You too, Aces One-Niner,' David said. Annie

677

heard his voice soften for the first time, and it was a voice filled with promise, and good wishes, and peace. 'Have a nice life, you guys.'

Dev reached over and touched Annie's gloved hand resting on the throttles. She looked over at him and smiled, and he smiled back. 'We will,' Annie replied. 'Thanks. Be careful out there.'

David Luger switched over from the emergency frequency with a touch of sadness, but no regrets. He knew it would probably be the last time he'd ever talk to Annie. But she had made a life with Duane Deverill, and it was hers to hold on to and build if she wanted it. His destiny lay elsewhere.

On the new secure interplane frequency, he radioed, 'Stalkers, Stalkers, this is Stalker One, your bandit is now two-two-one degrees bull's-eye, range three-one miles, level at angels three-one, turning right, possibly racetracking around for another pass.'

'Stalker Two-Two flight of three, roger,' the Turkish F-16 flight leader responded. 'Converging on bandit at angels three-four.'

'Stalker Three-One flight of two, acknowledged,' the Ukrainian MiG-29 flight leader responded. 'We will converge on target at angels two-niner.'

'Stalkers, datalink on blue seven.'

'Two-Two flight, push blue seven.'

'Two.'

'Three.'

'Three-One flight, push blue seven.'

'Two.' Each fighter pilot set the same laser

frequency channel into their receivers, cor-
responding with the frequency that Luger, in the
DC-10, was using to track the unidentified aircraft with the laser radar. Since none of their air-
to-air radars could pinpoint a stealth aircraft, the
laser radar on the DC-10, tuned to the only
frequency that could track the aircraft – a fact
known by the Metyor-179's first chief designer,
David Luger – was the only way to do it.

'Two-Two flight, tally-ho!' the Turkish flight
lead called out.

'Three-One flight has contact,' the Ukrainians
called a few moments later. 'Three-One has the
lead.'

'*What happened?*' Yegorov shouted. 'We lost
contact with the weapon! What is going on?'

'The weapon exploded before it hit the tanker,'
Fursenko said. The infrared scanner was still
locked on to the tanker *Ustinov*. Except for some
minor damage, the tanker was still very much
intact.

The attack had looked perfect until one or two
seconds before impact – what could have happened? Yegorov wondered. Now the threat warning receiver was blaring constantly, with multiple
lock-on signals – and there was no longer a bomb
in the air, meaning the enemy radars were definitely locked on *them*. Yegorov furiously scanned
his instruments. Everything looked perfectly
normal – no speed brakes or flaps deployed, no
engine malfunctions that might be highlighting
their position, no warning or caution lights, no–

Wait, there was one caution light, but not on

the 'Warning and Caution' panel, but on the 'Weapons' panel on the lower right side – the bomb doors were still open. 'Fursenko, damn you!' Yegorov shouted, staring wide-eyed at the engineer in his rearview mirror. 'The bomb doors are still open! Close them immediately!'

Fursenko looked down at his instrument panel, then up at Yegorov almost immediately. 'I can't,' he said in a calm, even voice. 'The hydraulic system B circuit breaker has popped, and it will not reset. I have no control over the doors.'

If Yegorov thought the scrawny pencil-necked scientist had it in him, he would've thought the old man was lying to him! 'Disengage the hydraulic system B and motor the doors closed with the electric motor.'

'I tried that,' Fursenko said, still in that calm, even voice – the voice of someone who was resigned to his fate. 'The door mechanism must be jammed – I cannot motor the doors closed. Maybe the Kh-73 dropping on partially opened doors caused it to malfunction and detonate early.'

The bastard, he *was* doing this on purpose! He didn't believe for a second it was a malfunction! 'Damn you, Fursenko, do you realize what you're doing?' Yegorov shouted in utter fury. Whatever Fursenko had done to the bomb doors, Yegorov couldn't undo them from the front seat. 'You are signing our death warrants!'

'Why, Yegorov?' Fursenko asked. 'Don't you think your buddy Pavel Kazakov will understand when you tell him your bomb doors were jammed open?'

'Fuck you!' Yegorov shouted. He immediately started a turn back toward the tanker, then hit a switch on his weapons panel to override the backseater's laser aiming control. 'I advise you not to touch another switch or circuit breaker back there, Fursenko,' he warned. 'If we strike our intended target, Kazakov may let you live, even if he does discover it was sabotage.'

'You fool, look at that threat scope,' Fursenko shouted. Yegorov had indeed been looking – it appeared as if the entire Turkish Air Force were after them. 'Forget this bomb run – the Turks will be all over you in one minute, long before you can line up for another bomb run. Get us out of here while you still can!'

'*No!*' Yegorov shouted wildly. 'This is my mission! Comrade Kazakov ordered me to take command and complete this mission, and that's what I'll do! No one is going to stop me!'

The threat warning receiver now showed two sets of enemy fighters – one set Turkish, the other Russian-made fighters, probably Ukrainians – bearing down on them. 'We're not going to make it!' Fursenko shouted. 'Turn away! Turn back before they shoot us down!'

'No!' Yegorov shouted again. He armed his internal R-60 missiles. 'No one is going to get me! *No one!*' He flicked on the Metyor-179's infrared scanner, lined up on the closest set of fighters coming in from the north, waited until he got a lock-on indication, opened fire with one missile per fighter, then turned back toward the tanker *Ustinov*. The aiming pipper had drifted off the tanker slightly, and he–

The MASTER CAUTION light snapped on. Yegorov checked the warning panel and saw two LAUNCHER HOT lights on. Both internal launchers that he had just used were on fire. 'I'm going to cut off power to the stores panel!' Fursenko shouted.

'No!' Yegorov shouted. 'Keep power on until after bomb release.'

'We can't!' Fursenko shot back. 'There's a serious short or fire in the wing launcher, and there's no way to stop it unless we cut off all power to the weapons panel. If you allow that fire to continue, it could completely burn through the wing. I'm going to turn off weapons power before that wing fails and we are both killed!'

'I said, leave it on, you traitorous bastard!' Fursenko was reaching for the master weapons power switch when he heard a tremendous *BANG!* and felt a sharp stinging sensation in his left shoulder. To his amazement, he realized that Yegorov had pulled out his survival pistol, reached back between the seats, and shot him! The bullet tore through his shoulder, bounced off the metal ejection-seat back, and lodged deep in his left lung. Fursenko tasted blood, and soon blood was pouring from his mouth and nostrils.

Fursenko's head was spinning, and he tried to keep himself upright and find the weapons power switch. He felt as if he was only moments away from passing out when he looked out the left side of the cockpit canopy and saw a flash of fire burst from just aft of the leading edge of the wing beside the fuselage. He knew precisely what it was. At that same moment, he felt a jolt and a

682

rumble as the last Kh-73 laser-guided bomb fell free from the bomb bay.

He reached between his legs just as the burst of fire became an explosion, and the entire left wing separated from the fuselage. With his last ounce of strength, Fursenko pulled the ejection handle between his legs and fired himself out of the Metyor-179. The spinning, flaming remnants of his longtime pride and joy narrowly missed him as he plummeted toward the Black Sea. His man-seat separator snapped him free from his ejection seat, and his body began a ballistic arch through the air, decelerating as he fell. At exactly fourteen thousand feet above the water, his baro initiator shot his pilot chute out of his backpack, which pulled his main chute safely out of its pack. He was thankfully unconscious through the entire ride.

Once he hit the water, his life vest automatically inflated and infrared seawater-activated rescue lights illuminated, and he lay halftangled in the parachute riser cords, half-submerged as his parachute began to sink. Luckily, a Turkish Coast Guard patrol boat was just a few miles away, and he was picked up just moments before the parachute dragged his head below the surface.

The Metyor-179 splashed down about ten miles away, with Gennadi Yegorov still in the front pilot's seat, trying to fly his bird down to a safe ditching in the Black Sea. The impact broke the stealth warplane – and Yegorov – into a thousand pieces and scattered them across the ocean.

Unguided, without even an initial beam to get

it moving in the right direction, the second Kh-73 one-thousand-kilo bomb missed the tanker *Ustinov* by two hundred and fifty yards and exploded harmlessly in the sea.

Epilogue

The White House, Washington, DC
the next day

'The Russian and German governments vehemently demand an answer, sir,' Secretary of State Edward Kercheval said. 'They keep on insisting we have information on this so-called Black Sea Alliance, and they claim we are secretly supporting them.'

President Thomas Thorn sat with his fingers folded on his chest, staring as usual into space, leaning back in his seat behind his desk in the Oval Office. 'They have any proof of this?' the President asked absently.

'Several radio transmissions between Turkish and Ukrainian aircraft and an unidentified aircraft flying over the Black Sea in Turkish airspace, protected by aircraft that are part of this Black Sea Alliance,' Secretary Goff replied. 'The transmissions were picked up by a Russian intelligence-gathering ship operating in the free navigation lane created by this Black Sea Alliance for international ships. The Russians claim the broadcasts were directing Alliance aircraft to an intercept with another unidentified aircraft.'

'This second unidentified aircraft being the Russian stealth fighter that was about to attack the tanker in the Turkish port,' President Thorn added.

'Yes, sir,' Goff said. 'Of course, the Russians

and the Germans claim they know nothing of this stealth fighter.'

'So no one is offering any ideas as to the identity of any of these unidentified aircraft,' Thorn went on, 'except we had something to do with them?' Kercheval nodded. 'Tell the German and Russian governments that we will cooperate in any way possible to help identify these aircraft and to find out exactly what happened last night near Eregli, but we maintain we have nothing to do with this incident or with the Black Sea Alliance.

'Furthermore, the United States does not recognize or oppose this Black Sea Alliance,' the President went on. 'The United States remains an interested but completely neutral third-party observer in all foreign military alliances and treaties. We urge all governments and all alliances to come to peaceful settlements of arguments and conflicts, but the United States will not interfere with any nation's foreign or domestic activities unless, in my opinion, it directly affects the peace and security of the United States of America. Deliver that message right away to the Russian and German governments and to the world media. I'll make myself available for a press conference to discuss the statement later today. Have the Vice President's office set it up for me.'

Kercheval departed, leaving the President alone with Robert Goff. The Secretary of Defense had a big, childlike grin on his face. Thorn pretended not to notice and went back to making notes and sending e-mail messages from his computer; but finally he said without looking up, 'What are you grinning at, Robert?'

'Okay, spill it, Thomas,' Goff said. 'What did you do?'

'Do?'

'That incident over the Black Sea? It's got HAWC written all over it. That Turkish frigate said they detected a bomb dropped from what was apparently a stealth bomber – but it was shot out of the sky by a missile fired from another aircraft that never appeared on radar. Did you authorize HAWC to send in one of their Megafortress ABM bombers to patrol that area?'

'Directing military aircraft on combat operations, secret or otherwise, is your job, Robert. If you didn't direct such a mission, it never happened.'

'Spoken like a real twenty-first-century president, Mr President,' Goff said, beaming. 'I'm proud of you.'

'I still don't know what you're talking about.'

'So you actually assisted Martindale's Night Stalkers?'

'Martindale's who?'

'Stalkers – the call sign he used during that mission, the call sign the Black Sea Alliance aircraft used, and the call sign he once mentioned to me that he was going to use,' Goff said. 'Was it just a coincidence that there happened to be a bunch of folks using "Stalkers" call signs flying around last night?'

'Robert, I'm not in the mood for word games and puzzles right now,' the President said. 'I've never heard the name "Night Stalkers" before, and if there is such an organization, it was probably just a coincidence. But that's not what's important here.

'In case you haven't noticed, nothing has really changed in that region, even after all this fuss about phantom bombs and missiles and strange call signs and radio messages. Russia and Germany still occupy most of the Balkan states, and they're sending in a thousand troops a day as reinforcements against any more so-called terrorist actions against their peacekeeping forces. The rest of NATO has all but left the Balkans. This Black Sea Alliance is threatening to start a naval war in the Black Sea. World oil prices are skyrocketing in response to what's happened with that tanker – the media thinks this Black Sea Alliance is really out to torpedo all Russian oil shipments. Russia may start escorting tankers across the Black Sea with warships, and then what's this Black Sea Alliance going to do? And do we want American warships in the area?'

Goff looked on the young president as a proud father looks on his son who has just won a science fair ribbon. 'Press conferences? Statements to the world media? Concern over what the media thinks? Analysis of world military events? Even considering sending American warships into harm's way?' Goff asked with feigned surprise, beaming happily. 'Why, if I didn't know better, I'd say you were giving a damn about foreign affairs, President Thomas Nathaniel Thorn.'

Thorn glanced at Goff, then gave him a barely perceptible smile. 'Have you been keeping up with your meditation exercises, Robert?' he asked seriously.

'No – but I think I will,' Goff said as he headed for the door to the Oval Office. He stopped before he opened the door, turned to the President, and asked, 'I wonder if that wristband you're wearing right now would help my meditation exercises?'

The President smiled contentedly as he absently fingered the strange new electronic wristband on his right wrist, and suddenly he became acutely aware of the spot on his right shoulder recently irritated by the subcutaneous miniature transceiver and what it meant to him now. But he just replied, 'Talk to you later, Mr Secretary,' he said.

'Yes, Mr President,' Robert Goff replied. I'm sure I won't be the only one you'll be talking with, my friend, Goff said to himself as he departed the Oval Office.

Codlea, Romania
a short time later

When the Metyor-179 aircraft did not report in before its scheduled landing time, Pavel Kazakov's security forces were put on immediate alert and reviewed their preplanned escape procedures. When the aircraft became overdue, one hour past its maximum possible fuel endurance time, Pavel Kazakov's security forces went immediately to work. They worked quickly and with grim efficiency. Explosives were set in a pile in the main hangar, classified records and documents having anything to do with the Metyor-179 were set atop them...

...and then the bodies of the Metyor Aerospace engineers, technicians, and workers at Codlea were stacked atop those.

Pavel Kazakov was notified a few hours later when the grim work was done, and he went out to inspect their work. The whole gory pile had been covered with tarps and then weighed down with tires to contain the blast. More explosives had been set up on the hangar's roof, designed to blow downward to simulate a gravity bomb dropped through the roof. 'Good work,' Kazakov said. 'We wait until we are clear of the area, and then–'

'Aircraft inbound!' one of the security men shouted. 'Unidentified aircraft inbound!' Security men with machine guns and assault rifles ready rushed outside. Other security men pushed Kazakov's helicopter back inside the main hangar to keep it out of sight.

'It's a tilt-rotor aircraft!' someone shouted. 'Still in full airplane mode! I do not see any markings or insignia. Probably American or NATO Marines or special forces commandos. We've been discovered.'

Kazakov looked through a set of binoculars and saw the big aircraft bearing down on them. 'Don't worry,' Kazakov said. 'It will still need to slow down to drop off its soldiers. When it does, blast it with everything you have.' But the aircraft did not slow down. It was traveling well over three hundred nautical miles per hour when it passed directly overhead. 'It may try to drop para- troopers, or land and off-load its commandos away from the compound,' Kazakov said. 'That'll

692

give us time to escape and time for you to hunt them down. Pull my helicopter out and get it–'

'Look!' someone shouted. Kazakov looked. They saw three soldiers leap off the tilt-rotor's open rear cargo ramp. Each soldier was carrying a very large rifle and appeared to be jumping directly into the center of the compound between the hangar door parking apron and the runway ... *but none of the three was wearing a parachute!* 'What in hell are they doing? Are they insane?' As a stunned Pavel Kazakov and his security men watched, the three crazy soldiers hurtled earthward, still in a standing position, still with the rifles at port arms. They were sure they were going to see three broken bodies bounce off the concrete aircraft parking apron in just half a second.

But at the very last moment, a loud *WHOOOSH!* of high-pressure air erupted from each of the strangers' boots – and all three soldiers touched down gently on the concrete apron with about as much force as if they had jumped off a chair after changing a lightbulb, still standing upright, still with their large rifles at port arms, as if they had just materialized there. Each soldier was wearing a dark gray combat bodysuit, a thick utility belt, thick boots, some sort of harness or device on his shoulders, a full-face helmet, and a thin backpack. The rifles were of completely unknown origin, resembling fifty-caliber sniper rifles but with a complex firing mechanism unlike any other firearm they'd ever seen.

'I don't know who they are,' Kazakov said, 'but if they are not all dead in the next sixty seconds, we *will* be.' Kazakov bolted and ran for cover around the back of the main hangar, followed by three of his bodyguards, while the other security officers spread out and opened fire on the strangers. Kazakov saw at least three lines of bullets fired on full automatic walk across the ramp and intersect right on the strangers – but they did not go down.

He then remembered the stories from frantic crewmen aboard his oil tanker *Ustinov* about invincible commandos who shot lightning from their eyes, and he ran faster than he ever ran in his life. They were real, and they were here.

The security officers got only one burst off at the strangers before all three of them disappeared – only to reappear moments later several dozen yards away, leaping into the air by using jets of compressed air from their boots. One by one, the commandos shot a round from their weird rifles into any available target – the helicopters, vehicles, communications rooms, power-generating facilities, any valuable target. They appeared only slightly staggered if hit by a bullet, then resumed their methodical attack on the compound. If they got close enough to a security officer, he was immediately put down either by a short blast of electrical energy, like a massive Taser blast from as far as twenty feet away, or by a fist or knife-edge hand that landed as hard as a chunk of steel.

In moments all of the security officers had been dispatched, and the entire area was a smoking ruin. 'All clear,' Hal Briggs reported, after carefully scanning the area with his helmet's sensors for any signs of survivors or escapees.

'Clear,' Chris Wohl responded.

'Clear,' the electronically synthesized voice of Paul McLanahan replied. Paul, Patrick's younger brother, was a California attorney and former police officer, who'd been horribly wounded on his first night on duty. He'd survived the attack but remained dead inside – until an incredible new technology had given him a renewed will to live. The electronic battle armor had enabled Paul to play an active role in defending peace even with his debilitating injuries; and as one of the first to wear the armor and its associated weapon systems, Paul had become an instructor in how to use the system, as well as a fighter himself. 'Patrick? How copy?'

'Loud and clear.'

Hal Briggs took another fix on Kazakov and his bodyguards, then on Patrick, using his electronic locating device. 'He's headed your way, Muck.'

'I'm ready for him.'

'Security Three? Security Four?' Kazakov shouted into his walkie-talkie. 'Answer, dammit! Someone answer!'

'No response from any of the security or transportation units,' one of the bodyguards confirmed. 'They knocked out our entire force.'

'They'll be looking for us next,' Kazakov said. 'We split up. You two, separate directions. You, with me. Their armor may make them bulletproof, but try anything you can think of to slow them down – trip them, dunk them in water, decoy them, make them fall off a cliff, anything. Now move!' As his men bolted in opposite

695

directions, Kazakov and his one remaining bodyguard turned...

...right into the path of another armored commando.

Gunfire erupted on both sides. Kazakov hit the ground, closed his eyes, and covered his ears as heavy-caliber bullets and even a forty-millimeter grenade shell burst around him. He lay as flat on the ground as he could, screaming and crying as the bullets and bombs flew and wave after wave of gunshots, explosion concussions, and earsplitting noise roiled over him. But it did not last long. When he opened his eyes and ears again, everything was still. When he got to his feet...

...only the commando stood before him. His men were all lying on the ground, jerking and flinching as the last watts of electrical energy dissipated through their unconscious bodies.

Pavel Kazakov smiled, then raised his hands in surrender. 'Well, well, so you really do exist,' the gangster said in English. 'And there is a little army of you people, I see. Very impressive, although you appear to be the shortest in stature of the group. Americans, I assume. Special operations? Delta Force? Navy SEALs?' No response. 'How did you find me?'

'Fursenko,' the commando said.

'Indeed? The good doctor is still alive? Good for him. I'll take great pleasure in plucking off his gonads myself and stuffing them into his empty eye sockets. So. Are you going to shock me into oblivion, too?' No response. 'Well, it was certainly nice chatting with you.' But as he turned to leave, Kazakov felt sharp snaps and pings of electricity all around him, like an invisible electrical fence, hemming him in.

'Damn you, what do you want?' Kazakov screamed. 'Take off that armor and tell me to my face, you cowardly bastard!' No response. 'What is it? Money? Do you want money?'

'Yes,' the figure said.

'Aha. Now we are getting somewhere,' Kazakov said, an evil smile creeping across his face. 'Money in exchange for my freedom.'

'Money ... in exchange for your life,' the commando said.

'That is hardly fair. I'm sure we can ... *ouch!*' Another crackle of electricity jolted his head and made it feel as if a million ants were crawling all over his body. 'You son of a diseased whore! You are *robbing* me? Is this a stickup? You are *actually* robbing me? My money or my life? How dare you?' He was answered by another crack of electricity that this time sent him to his knees. 'All right, all right, you win!' He got to his feet, then made a pantomime of searching his pockets. 'Oh, sorry, I seem to have forgotten my wallet. Maybe you'll take my, how do you say, IOU?'

The commando reached into his utility belt, withdrew a handheld satellite telephone, and tossed it to the Russian gangster. When Kazakov opened it, he found a card with account numbers and Interbank address codes on it. As he dialed a number, he said, 'I suppose we should agree on an amount, no?'

'One-half billion dollars,' the commando said.

Kazakov laughed. 'Whatever you have heard about me, my friend, it is obviously wrong. I do

697

not have–' He was cut off by another bolt of energy that knocked him backward onto his ass. 'Hey! I am telling you the truth, bastard boy! I do not have a half a billion dollars!'

'Then you will die,' the electronic voice said.

'I mean to say, I have it, but I cannot get it with just a phone call–' He was silenced by another bolt of energy, this one deep enough to cause substantially more pain, but not enough to render him unconscious. 'You scum-sucking bastard! I will kill you for this, I promise! You and your friends are *dead!* You understand me? Dead!'

'One-half billion dollars, confirmed in five minutes, or you die,' the futuristic commando said.

Kazakov redialed the telephone. To come up with the money, his comptroller at Metyorgaz had to liquidate all of his boss's personal holdings in the company, along with several other asset accounts under his direct control – including the loans from his international 'investors,' the crime bosses and drug lords trying to launder money through Metyorgaz from all over the world – but in just a few minutes, the money was transferred. The commando pocketed the phone. Kazakov could hear him talking inside his helmet, apparently on a helmet-mounted communications network.

'Now you let me go, eh?' Kazakov asked.

'Now you come with me,' the commando said.

'A deal is a deal! You said you would let me go!'

'I said I would let you live,' the figure said. Three more armored commandos appeared, along with a man in a green battle-dress uniform and helmet – wearing the insignia of the Turkish Jandarma, the Turkish National Police. 'But there are warrants for your arrest issued by nine different nations, and as a member of Interpol, this man is authorized by the Romanian government to make an arrest here.' The Jandarma agent snapped handcuffs on Kazakov, then searched him carefully, blindfolded him, and led him away to a nearby waiting helicopter. Kazakov was screaming his innocence, screaming about the money he just paid, screaming about revenge, all the way until the door was closed on the helicopter that had come to take him away.

After the police helicopter was gone, Patrick McLanahan collapsed to one knee on the ground and removed his helmet. His head was sweaty and his hair matted, despite the suit's excellent air-conditioning system. The other armored commandos surrounded him, wordlessly waiting to lend any support they could. After several long moments, Patrick's brother Paul finally asked, 'You okay, Patrick?'

'Sure.'

'Good work, Patrick,' they all heard former President Kevin Martindale say via their subcutaneous satellite transceivers. 'The funds are already being redistributed out of the phantom holding account. International and private relief agencies based in Albania, Macedonia, Bulgaria, and Turkey will get most of it to pay reparations for what Kazakov has done to their people. Some of the rest will go to pay for a private security force to make sure Kazakov stands trial – I hate to say it, but even Turkey's government police agencies probably have some of Kazakov's men working deep in them.'

'But we keep the rest of the money, right, Mr President?' Patrick asked angrily.

'What we do, what we're *going* to do, isn't cheap,' Martindale said.

'Then what makes us so different from bastards like Kazakov?' Patrick asked bitterly. 'We steal, we attack, we raid for money.'

'The difference? The difference is *you*, Patrick, you and everyone who wears that Tin Man battle armor, flies the robot planes, launches the missiles, and everyone who decides to join us,' Martindale replied. 'Yes, we are going to help ourselves to blood money. We are going to distribute it to those we feel will benefit from it the most, especially the victims of the criminals we hunt down, but we are going to help ourselves to it as well.'

'We're criminals!' Patrick shouted. 'Stealing money, even from human crap like Kazakov, is still a crime!'

'No, it isn't, sir,' Wohl said. 'It's justice.'

'Whose justice?' Patrick grabbed Wohl's gauntlets. 'The justice of the most powerful? Whoever has the strongest armor or the biggest gun?'

'It's not how justice is dispensed, Patrick, but how justice benefits society,' Paul said. 'The money you got from Kazakov will help a lot of lives. That's justice.'

'Then let's take off this armor and stand up in front of the same judges that Kazakov will face and tell them that,' Patrick retorted. 'Will they tell us it's all right to invent our own definition of justice? Will they allow us to do whatever we like, attack whoever we wish, in the name of our own brand of so-called justice? Let's see what their answer will be!'

'We are not lawmen, Patrick,' Kevin Martindale said, through their ethereal electronic bond. 'I didn't make you swear an oath to uphold or defend anything when you agreed to join me. We don't serve any government, any court, or any set of laws. We are not soldiers, lawyers, or politicians. We are *warriors*.'

'What in hell does that mean, sir?'

'It means we fight not for country, not for law, not for money, but for *right*,' Martindale replied. 'I believe we know what is right, what is *just*. Your brother Paul knows the law. You, Hal, and Chris are soldiers. We all came from different backgrounds, different perspectives, and different experiences. But we're all standing here, together, right now. There's a reason for that. Whatever shaped us, whatever we were, and whatever we *are*, I believe we are warriors. Members of the warrior class. No rank, no flag, no master. We fight for what is right.'

'And sometimes you have to fight on their level, Muck,' Paul McLanahan added. 'You taught me that when you first put on this armor back in Sacramento. It wasn't pretty, it wasn't nice, but it worked. You taught me we *can* do some good with it.'

'And you know something else? I didn't *force* you to make Kazakov pay you,' Martindale added. 'I *suggested* you squeeze him so we could help some of his victims, but I didn't come up with this numbered bank account or satellite phone idea – *you* did. You could have turned him

701

over to the Jandarma without making him do anything. But you did it because you don't think Kazakov will ever stand trial, and even if he does go to prison, he won't suffer and he won't be in long. You believe the only way to hurt him is to take what he loves, and that's money. I agree.'

'We all agree, Muck,' Hal Briggs said.

'Affirmative,' Chris Wohl agreed.

'So stand tall and be proud of what you did, and don't concern yourself about squeezing a bug like Pavel Kazakov,' Martindale said. 'But if it bothers you so much, if you think what you did and what I suggest we all do together is wrong or illegal or immoral, you can take off that armor and go home and live peacefully in retirement. You've earned it. Those of us who want to stay will continue the fight, however we decide to do it, for as long as we want to do it. Either way, you have the thanks and best wishes of us all, General McLanahan.'

Patrick said nothing. He stood, handed his helmet to his brother with his head bowed, and walked slowly toward the tilt-rotor aircraft that would take him home.

This Large Print Book for the partially sighted, who cannot read normal print, is published under the auspices of

THE ULVERSCROFT FOUNDATION